D1141360

Alicia's Gift

Also by Jessica Duchen

Rites of Spring

JESSICA DUCHEN

Alicia's Gift

HODDER &
STOUGHTON

Copyright © 2007 by Jessica Duchen

First published in Great Britain in 2007 by Hodder & Stoughton
A division of Hodder Headline

The right of Jessica Duchen to be identified as the Author of the Work has been
asserted by her in accordance with the Copyright, Designs and Patents Act 1988.

A Hodder & Stoughton Book

I

A CIP catalogue record for this title is available from the British Library

ISBN 978 0 340 83932 4

Typeset in Plantin Light by Palimpsest Book Production Limited,
Grangemouth, Stirlingshire

Printed and bound by
Clays Ltd, St Ives plc

Hodder Headline's policy is to use papers that are natural, renewable and
recyclable products and made from wood grown in sustainable forests.
The logging and manufacturing processes are expected to conform to the
environmental regulations of the country of origin.

Hodder & Stoughton Ltd
A division of Hodder Headline
338 Euston Road
London NW1 3BH

For Tom

Acknowledgements

Thanking everyone who has helped this book into existence would take up most of the next 400 pages if I gave them all the credit they deserve. I've always loved the way that composers like Mozart, Schubert or Chopin could use minimum notes to convey maximum emotion, so here are a few select thank-yous, which, though too brief, are delivered with all my heart.

First, this book would never have come into being without the encouragement of my marvellous agent, Sara Menguc, and my equally marvellous editor at Hodder & Stoughton, Carolyn Mays. Thanks to them and their devoted teams.

Next, thank you to the many teachers, friends, colleagues and musicians through whom, over many long years, I've learned the agony and ecstasy of life at the piano. You know who you are, and I love you all. But special thanks must go to the fabulous pianist Leon McCawley for his expert advice; to Steve Cass, who helped me understand a little about how motorbikes work; to Allison Sharpe and Stuart Band for insights into Chatsworth; and Herbert and Gisela Eisner, long-time Buxtonians, for double-checking the local Derbyshire detail.

Alicia's favourite French poems are 'En sourdine' by Paul Verlaine and 'Le poison' from *Fleurs du mal* by Charles Baudelaire. I have deliberately left these extracts in French only, but translations may easily be found online.

Synaesthesia, a 'union of the senses', is a condition experienced by numerous musicians; further information about it can be found at the UK Synaesthesia Association's website, www.uksynaesthesia.com.

Finally, boundless thanks to Tom for introducing me to both Derbyshire and Denmark; for putting up with me so patiently; and for hiding the chocolate on top of the kitchen cupboard.

Alicia used to imagine living inside a perfect raindrop. Her father would hold her up to the window and she'd watch them in the dusk, trapping white-gold lamplight in a shimmering kaleidoscope. They streamed down, merging, gathering pace towards the edge of the pane. Each was a tiny globe of possibility trembling on the glass in front of her when she raised her fingers to press against them from the safe, dry inside.

Her tears and the autumn rain distort the moorland night into a morass of water, wobbling around her like a hall of mirrors. Nothing seems firm, not the Tarmac under the wheels, or the sheep that glare towards her out of the darkness, not even her body or mind. Part of her seems detached, watching while she drives as fast as the spray on the dark road will allow, watching while she tries to catch her breath and stop crying, but fails.

An isolated structure looms ahead – the pub that tops the moor close to home. Her headlamps catch its name: the Cat and Fiddle. She wonders how she's managed to travel so far west. Mirror, signal, manoeuvre, said her driving instructor, but Alicia has neither checked nor signalled during her headlong plunge out of Yorkshire. Nor has she looked back.

A few cars and motorbikes are parked behind the pub and Alicia, numb with exhaustion, pulls in alongside them. In the neighbouring field blank-eyed sheep form a glowering, unwanted audience. She switches off the engine. Rain drums random music on the roof. The drops slide down the windows, glinting in the dim light from the pub, which feels a hundred miles away. Alicia raises a hand to the windscreen – her fingers strong and slender, nails cropped short, as a pianist's must be – and presses on the raindrops from inside.

She sees what she's looking for in the shadows near the pub's outbuildings: an incongruous hosepipe, redundant in this damp, moortop desolation. Her mobile phone churns out a Tchaikovsky melody that she's begun to loathe. Her detached self says she should silence it: either answer or turn it off, never to be switched on again. The rest of her has thrown open the car door and is running through the rain towards the hose, which beckons to her, a coiled smile that promises salvation.

I

BUXTON
IN THE PEAK DISTRICT

The green notice marks the Roman road's final approach from moor to town: Buxton, a grey stone fan spreading across the Derbyshire hills, which undulate like the phrases of an English folk song. Buxton is one of the highest towns in England, proud of its water, proud of its once-flourishing spa; sometimes it imitates Bath, complete with eighteenth-century crescent (a low-calorie version). Hikers gather at the pubs, knocking mud from their boots outside, comparing notes on the day's adventures around the Peak District's moors and villages. In the well-tended Pavilion Gardens, children feed the ducks and their mothers and grandmothers gather in the tea room to eat Bakewell tart and sip a good, warming brew to keep out the bitter north wind. By the bridge over the stream stands the Bradley family's favourite road sign: a red triangle bearing the immortal words DUCKS CROSSING. How, Alicia asks herself, are the ducks supposed to know?

One side of the Bradleys' house begins higher up than the other. It and its semi-detached partner stand well back from the road, which curls up a hill in Buxton's Park area, protected by a spruce hedge and a row of sycamores that, as Guy was quick to point out when they first saw it, is just far enough away not to threaten the foundations. Tall rather than wide, the house is Victorian, made of the goldish-grey local stone that gives so much of Buxton its reassuring solidity, as if it had grown organically out of the hillside without a vestige of human help. The slope cuts through the base of the building, which has been levelled so that the inhabitants can imagine they are living on a safe, steady surface, not perching precariously on top of a remote and soulless mound of limestone.

To visit the Bradleys, you'd turn into the gravel driveway beside the hedge and pass the small oval lawn that Guy tends on Saturday afternoons. You'd walk up three stone stairs to the blue door and press the bell, which plays an imitation of Big Ben, and you'd hear Cassie the collie barking in ecstasy at the prospect of visitors. The big front window would show you an oblique view of the lounge; you'd glimpse the shiny curve of the piano and Alicia's fair hair gleaming as she curls over the keyboard, concentrating. And you'd hear her playing, perhaps a Chopin study or a carefully extracted line of Bach. You might catch a whiff of roasting chicken from Kate's dinner preparations, or smell simply the sweet, fresh country air, the light, watery scent of moorland wind through the trees.

On the day when everything will change, though nobody knows this yet, Kate opens her eyes to find Guy leaning over her, his face full of tenderness and worry. Her pillow is damp and her pyjamas soaked with sweat. Her eyes feel sore.

'It's OK, darling,' he whispers.

'I had the dream again.' Unwept tears clog her throat.

'I know. You're fine now. It's morning.'

Kate sits up and reaches for a tissue. Downstairs the dog barks and from the second floor, where the children's rooms are, comes the sound of Adrian flushing the loo. Kate moves her feet around, looking for her slippers, while Guy kisses her cheek and vanishes into the bathroom. Her mind is still half closed in the after-effects of her dream. Somehow she pulls herself upright and makes her way down to fix breakfast for her family and the overjoyed collie, who is five months old, with flailing paws that are too big for her.

Kate switches on the radio and hears that three hundred thousand people in Strathclyde have defaulted on the poll tax; terrible clashes have taken place around elections in South Africa; and a demonstration in East Germany has been brutally dispersed. It all seems a very long way from the Peak District – except, of course, for the poll tax. Guy spends his days focusing on local news for northern England; sometimes Kate wonders whether they're in the same galaxy as the world that's portrayed on the radio and television. It's easy to forget about the Berlin Wall when the biggest event of your day tends to be your son grazing his knee or your husband losing his shoes.

'Katie,' Guy calls from upstairs, 'do you know where my brown shoes are?'

'Probably where they were yesterday and the day before.'

'They're not. I can't find them.'

'Why can't you keep them in the same place every day? Then you'd know where they are, instead of always having to ask me.' Kate pulls the coffee canister out of the freezer and thumps the door closed.

Just as exasperation is setting in, she glances round and sees Alicia's shiny pale hair and round face, her small arms encircling the puppy's neck, her cheek pressed to its brown and white hair as if both their lives depend on it. Cassie turns her long collie snout to lick the nose of the little girl who loves her. They'd stumbled on the name Cassie by accident, during a scrambled attempt not to call the puppy Lassie. Kate finds herself smiling. Ali is only three, but her love shines through the kitchen as brightly as the sun. How can a three-year-old have such an instinct for love?

Ali, says the nursery-school teacher, is a sweet, affectionate child. Kate knows she's more than that. She can see a radiance in Ali that she can't see in any of the other tinies there, let alone Adrian's primary-school classmates. Sometimes she wonders if she's kidding herself, whether she sees in her daughter what she wants to see, because she happens to be her mother. Or because she needs a daughter with such capacity for love to help blot out the memory that sparks her recurring nightmare.

Guy has wolfed down cornflakes, toast and coffee and is whirling about in his usual morning chaos, looking for things. His glasses. ("They're on your face," Kate says.) His notes for the editorial meeting, which he'd worked on the previous night. His briefcase. His diary. His wallet. His keys. And, of course, his brown shoes. How such an absent-minded, disorganised man manages to edit anything, let alone a section of a newspaper, is a perpetual mystery.

"Wear the black ones."

"I can't, not with brown trousers."

"Wear different trousers, then."

Guy whistles the tune he always whistles when he can't find things – a twiddly, satirical theme from Walton's *Façade* that Kate is extremely tired of hearing.

Ali, cuddling her dog at the end of the kitchen, begins to sing it too. While Kate juggles her morning preparations – getting Guy out of the house and Adrian into school uniform, preparing Ali for nursery and herself for work – it occurs dimly to her that three-year-old children generally can't repeat a tricky melody so well.

Guy pulls on his coat and rattles the keys that he's located, at last, in its pocket. 'I'm off,' he says. 'You OK, love?'

'Fine,' Kate says, kissing him. He squeezes her waist. They're the same height, but for half an inch in Guy's favour: he is five foot ten, she is five foot nine and a half. He's considered slightly too short; she's considered a little too tall. 'Go carefully,' she says, as she usually does. Guy has to drive for an hour and ten minutes every morning and evening, to Manchester and back.

'Will do. Love you,' he replies, as he usually does. 'Be good at school, Adie. Bye-bye, Ali, be a good girl.'

'Bye-bye, Daddy,' Ali pipes from behind the dog. Guy swoops across the room and sweeps her into his arms, where she squeals with joy. Then he ruffles Adrian's hair, grabs his brief-case, says yet again, 'I'm off,' and is gone. Kate hears the car pulling out into the road.

For a few seconds she feels alone. Then it's action stations, getting the children's shoes and coats on and loading up her briefcase with notepad, sandwiches and some chocolate. She's been fighting a half-hearted battle against chocolate addiction for years.

Ali doesn't want to wear her coat, although there's a bracing wind.

'Cassie's wearing her coat,' Kate encourages.

'Cassie's a *dog*,' the rational Ali says.

'Dogs always have their coats on. They're born with them, so they're always warm.'

'I wasn't born with my coat on. Why wasn't I, Mummy?'

'Mum, I want to get to school and play,' Adrian butts in, glaring at his little sister.

'Coat on, Ali, *now*. We're making Adie late.'

Ali begins to whine as Kate shoves her arm into the pink woollen sleeve, then holds her firmly with one hand, fastening the buttons with the other. They set off down the hill at as brisk a pace as Kate can make the children walk. Adrian loves school; he strides tall and proud for his five years, his brown head bobbing along by her waist. But when they reach the busy street that leads uphill to school, their progress slows again because everybody in Buxton simply has to stop and say hello to the puppy.

Kate tells herself three times a day how lucky she is to have her job. Her office looks out towards the green hill beneath the Palace Hotel, close to the spreading dome of the Royal Devonshire Hospital. She is a solicitor with a local law firm that deals mainly with conveyancing, divorces and small financial disputes. There's always something to do, but never too much for comfort, at least where Kate is concerned. Her boss, Mike, is happy for her to work until three every afternoon, then leave to collect the children; she's willing to take work home, but mostly she doesn't have to. Now, to cap it all, he's letting her bring her dog to the office. Cassie is already well trained enough to curl up and snooze the morning away, giving an occasional canine snore while Kate sips coffee and makes her first phone calls.

Kate has never quite stopped thinking of her job as occupational therapy. Their fresh start in Buxton was an escape from the stresses of London, which Guy partly blamed for what had happened – probably, Kate thinks, because he had to blame something. Kate, if she blamed anything, blamed herself. Guy, though, had always hoped to move out of the capital. Perhaps it was his excuse to do what he wanted; a suitable time to convince her, while she was at emotional rock bottom, that it would be good for both of them.

Guy's job had appeared at exactly the right moment. She couldn't have denied it to him: becoming an assistant editor at the *Manchester Chronicle* in his twenties was an exceptional opportunity, especially as his dream was to live in the Peak District, where his great-grandfather had been born. Family legend had it that this historical Bradley used to walk across the moor from Buxton to Macclesfield to court his sweetheart. Infused with that fairytale from childhood, Guy had always sensed his roots in the bleak, heather-strewn landscapes, nourished by mysterious waters bubbling through the caverns beneath.

More practically, he'd argued that in Buxton they could have a house three times the size of their London flat and, someday, a dog to share it with them; his parents' place in Cheshire would be only an hour and a half away; best of all, every weekend they could drive for a few minutes and find themselves bang in the middle of what he considered the best hill-walking in Britain.

Kate met Guy on a University Walkers' Club ramble in the Cheviots. She can still picture him pacing along, leading twelve bedraggled students in rain trousers and cagoules, his hair blowing around in at least three directions. Undaunted by the driving Northumbrian rain, the mud, the bitter wind, he was making a joke about needing windscreen wipers on his glasses. Kate had been wondering what could have possessed her to join this walk, other than that she could think of nothing more different from her weekend activities back in north London. Talking to Guy had warmed her, despite the chill. His broad smile, his bright eyes, his gameness for whatever the day threw at them made her trust him. He was positive, active and extremely bright. And although he was studying English and history and said he wanted to be a journalist, he was also physical, strong, oriented to the outdoors. She found the combination compelling.

Looking for him later, she found a note on his door saying that he was – to her surprise – practising. She found him in the small music room, sitting at the piano, improvising. Kate played the viola and faithfully joined every orchestra in the university, all of which clamoured for her services; good violists were few and far between. But even with her comparatively substantial musical experience, she had never before met anyone who could improvise on the piano.

He greeted her with a generous smile, and while they talked he kept playing, picking out intriguing chords, delicate patterns, startling combinations of sounds. After ten minutes they'd agreed to meet for supper in the refectory – and Kate had lost her heart to him somewhere in the airborne spaces between the notes.

They were soon inseparable. Even in the peculiar music-and-hill-walking clique that gathered around them, they were no longer two individuals, Kate Davis and Guy Bradley, but just

Kate-and-Guy. Perhaps they seemed an odd couple: he was dark and alert, active as a busy bird in spring; she was fair, big-boned, inclined to dreaminess.

Law wasn't her decision. Her parents would not allow her to study music. Guy empathised with this more than anybody she'd ever met.

'You could have been a pianist if you'd wanted,' Kate pointed out one night, while they lounged companionably together in Guy's bed, sipping cocoa. 'If I'd had your talent, maybe I'd have had more ammunition to throw at them.'

'Oh, Katie, it's not fair.' Guy was running his fingers through Kate's long hair in the same absent-minded way he'd run them over the keyboard. 'You wanted to be a musician, you play beautifully, you could have had a life in it, and your parents won't let you. My parents would have let me do anything I want, but I don't fancy being shut in a practice room for eight hours a day. I love playing, but I don't want to end up hating it because I have nothing else in my life. I like being in the middle of things.'

'What "things"?'

'Well, if Ted Heath comes to give a talk, I want to be there asking him questions, preferably doing an interview. If the president of the United States resigns, I want to find out the truth and tell people why. Katie, there are thousands of pianists who play a million times better than I do. I'd be much happier being a journalist.'

'At least you had the choice.' Kate felt a familiar surge of resentment. What she couldn't understand, couldn't begin to imagine, was how her parents could have encouraged her to practise her viola, love it and long to perfect it for so many years – yet as soon as she'd wanted to pursue it seriously, they'd snatched away her dream. They'd threatened to cut her out of their wills if she were to study music instead of something sensible with proper employment possibilities, such as law.

'I can't believe it,' Guy said. 'Katie, it's so bourgeois. It's so bloody middle-class. You push your child into learning a musical instrument, you force her to take exams, you put up her certificates, and when your friends come to dinner you make her play to show off your marvellous, talented family. But if she's really good, in kicks the old British instinct – a daughter on the stage? Heaven forfend!'

'Hmph,' Kate grumbled, into her cocoa.

'But how can they? How can they have a daughter like you and behave like that? How can they have a daughter like you *at all*?'

Moving to Buxton, of course, meant that they were a long way from Harrow. There, the Davises' house was spotless, gleaming with magnolia paint, a brass carriage clock on the mantelpiece and never a vestige of clutter, let alone anything as messy as a book or a record in the living room. Any they possessed lived in Kate's bedroom. The first time Kate brought Guy home to meet her parents, William and Margaret Davis offered him vol-au-vents and sherry and asked why he wanted to go into journalism. Wasn't it dangerous? Wasn't there a risk of injury in cars that travelled too fast, chasing a story, or being caught in the crossfire of a war zone? Guy tried to reassure them that he had no thought of becoming either a *paparazzo* photographer or a war reporter, although he wasn't averse to politics. Meanwhile, Kate had taken an instant liking to Guy's parents, Didie and George, and to the florid, open-hearted Cheshire countryside around their house. The decision to go north was much eased by their closeness.

Kate's phone rings; the dog's ears prick up. Kate answers and speaks to a client who's buying a farm outside the town.

She has not touched her viola for eight years.

At three she leaves the office, Cassie trotting at her heels, and goes to pick up Ali from nursery school. She ties the dog's leash to the railings outside and wanders in, sniffing the aroma of Plasticine and milk, biscuits and finger paints and looking at the bright pictures pinned to the wall – each page of splodges a source of immense pride to its creator's parents.

The children are clustering round a cassette player; Lucy, their teacher, is putting a tape into the slot. As Kate listens in the doorway, out comes the sound of a piano playing something strongly rhythmical. Kate recognises it: it's the 'Ritual Fire Dance' by Manuel de Falla. Lucy has given each child an instrument: one a drum, another a triangle, a third a tambourine. She encourages them to make a noise with the instruments on the beats. One small girl begins to jump up and down. A little boy puts his hands over his ears.

Ali stands slightly apart, staring at the cassette, ignoring the drum in her hand. At home, Kate and Guy keep their still-new CD-player and burgeoning CD collection on a high shelf, well out of harm's, or at least Adrian's, way. Ali is apparently hypnotised by the spinning tape. Lucy glances at her, but as Ali is listening, even if she's not participating, she doesn't interfere.

Afterwards, Ali, Kate and Cassie fetch Adrian, then head home for tea. Kate gives the children toast and Marmite. While they're eating, she hangs up a load of laundry, puts in another and runs the vacuum-cleaner across the lounge. She'd stopped to buy fresh flowers on the way back and puts them in a white vase: her favourite anemones, a vibrant mix of crimson, carmine and imperial purple, with black stamens standing to attention.

Adrian wants to play in the garden, so she goes with him, listening while he rattles on about school. Watching him and trying to calm the barking Cassie, who wants Adrian to throw his ball for her to retrieve, she's also attempting to keep an eye on Ali, who's jumping about on the patio in some unfathomable game of her own.

Kate is filled with dread if she takes her attention away from Ali for longer than four seconds. For a child of Ali's age, every household object threatens disaster. She's curious enough to pick up a bottle of detergent to see what it is, but not aware enough to know she mustn't drink it. She can open doors, go up and down stairs or in and out of the house, but Kate can't be certain that she won't run into the road. Kate panics too easily over Ali. Somehow she's never worried about Adrian in the same way. She knows her feelings are conditioned by the trauma eight years ago – but she still can't stop them taking her over, sometimes bringing on trembling, sweating and even nausea at the slightest hint of danger.

The sound of small, skipping feet has gone.

'Ali! Where are you?' she shouts, diving into the house.

She hears a note sound, then another. The piano?

Guy's old upright stands against the lounge wall. Ali has managed to lift the lid and is prodding gingerly at the keys. Kate is about to demand whether her hands are clean after the Marmite, when she notices that Ali is using more than one finger on the keyboard. As Kate watches, Ali lifts her left hand and begins to press the bass notes too.

When he has a spare moment, Guy still loves to plough through some of his favourite pieces, Beethoven sonatas or bits of Chopin. Ali often stands next to him, watching, her mouth slightly open. Kate has never thought anything of it. All children are fascinated by musical instruments and love to see the peculiar antics of adults coaxing out the noises; or, even better, to try it themselves. Ali always begs Guy to play; and she always wants to have a bash at it herself, though Kate worries about sticky paws on the keys. But now—

Ali has got her bearings. Her chin level with the keyboard, she has somehow worked out which sound comes from which note. She looks up at Kate with huge blue eyes and says, 'Mummy, I can play it.'

'What, lovie?'

'The music. On the tape.'

'Can you, darling?' Kate smiles, tolerant. But Ali is bouncing impatiently and Kate understands and winds the piano stool higher for her.

Ali beams a thank-you, gives her hair a proud shake and shunts her small behind to the dead centre of the piano stool's edge, as if to say, 'There we are, at last.' She sits up straight, lifts her right hand and begins to pick out a tune. It isn't perfect, as she hasn't found out what the black notes are for, but the complicated rhythm is unmistakable. Ali pouts. 'That's not quite right.'

'It's nearly right, though, darling,' Kate says, astounded. 'Try again.'

'I'm going to,' Ali declares, clearly outraged at the notion that she might do anything else. 'Mummy, what are these?' She points at the black notes.

'Try them and see.'

Ali's forefinger moves from F to F sharp. Her eyes widen. A few minutes later, she has learned to play what is essentially a chromatic scale.

Kate, dazed, picks up the phone. 'Any chance you could come home a little early?' she asks Guy. 'Ali has something to show you.'

Guy, delayed by antisocial newspaper hours and a long drive, usually arrives home after Ali is in bed. Her routine with Kate is always the same. There's bathtime, where Ali plays with a white plastic swan and a yellow plastic boat. Then the pantomime: 'I don't want to go to bed'; 'Oh, yes, you do'; 'Oh, no, I don't.' One way or another, Ali ends up in her pyjamas, and in her bed. Her room and Adrian's are oppo-site each other on the second floor; Ali's overlooks the garden. African animals parade across the curtains; the walls are prim-rose yellow. Kate puts on the nightlight; in its soft glow, she sits on a bean-bag by Ali's bed and plays a cassette of soothing songs. It has never occurred to her that there's anything unusual about Ali singing along, even though Adrian used to listen to the same tape and had never learned the words, let alone the notes.

Then Ali always asks the same question. 'Where's Daddy?'

'Daddy's coming back from work,' Kate whispers, reassuring. Ali's little face looks worried, her eyes entreating, her forehead creasing into a childish frown. Kate puts her arms round her baby daughter and kisses her. 'He'll be home very soon and he'll come and kiss you goodnight when you're asleep. Daddy loves you very much.' Ali is a real Daddy's girl. A child psychologist whom Kate had met at a talk in a bookshop had assured her that this was quite normal for a three-year-old, along with the requisite pink dresses, fairy wings and princess tiaras.

'I love you, Mummy.' Ali's eyes are closing and she wriggles down under her covers, putting her thumb in her mouth.

'I love you too, baby. Sweet dreams.' Kate gently extracts the thumb. Ali, asleep, doesn't stir.

Today, when Guy walks in, Ali hasn't even had her bath. She flings herself across the hall, yelling, 'Daddydaddydaddy!'

No homecoming could be happier for Guy. He's had a tough day, dealing with late copy and last-minute information, and he's had to think of a lame excuse to get away. Telling Martin, the editor, that his three-year-old daughter wants to show him something is not calculated to inspire confidence, so he'd invented a bad throat and temperature for Ali, plus difficulties looking after Adrian, then made a dash for the car. As soon as Ali appears and he gathers her up, every moment of the day becomes worthwhile.

'How's my lovely girl?' He looks at her shining face and then at Kate's. 'OK, what's happening?'

'Come on, Daddy – come *on*!' Ali, on her feet, tugs at his hand.

'It's a surprise,' Kate says.

Guy dumps his coat on the banister. Kate picks it up and hangs it on a hook.

'It's stupid,' says Adrian, stumped by his sister's absorption in the piano, though glad it kept her out of his way while he repulsed some intergalactic invaders from the back garden.

'It's not, so.' Ali sticks out her lower lip and pulls on Guy's hand.

'It's certainly not stupid, Adie.' Kate tries not to snap at her son.

Ali climbs on to the piano stool – where she's spent the better part of the last two hours – and plays the tune she's worked out, with a basic but deft accompaniment. It doesn't have the twirls, snaps and intricacy of the 'Ritual Fire Dance', but the outline is definite. Guy's mouth falls open.

'Ali, where did you learn that?'

Ali, absorbed, doesn't look round.

'Lucy played it to them,' Kate says.

'What? And she remembered it? And worked out how to play it all by herself?'

'Well, I helped her a little, but mostly she did it on her own.'

'Gordon Bennett!' Guy takes off his glasses and rubs his eyes. 'Ali, do it again.'

He stands beside her, watching her fingers on the keys. When she's finished, he dashes to a shelf and pulls out a CD of the piece, played by Arthur Rubinstein. A few seconds later the disc has told him what he wants to know.

'There we are.' Guy stops the record. 'You again, Ali.'

Now Kate understands: Ali begins the tune unerringly on the right note, the same as the recording. She is three years old and she has perfect pitch. What's more, she knows how to find the notes on the keyboard.

Kate and Guy stare at each other over Ali's head. Perhaps Guy can see, in Kate's wide blue eyes – the adult replica of their daughter's – an inkling of what lies ahead; perhaps she can glimpse in his bird-like gaze the revelation that they've given life to an energy more powerful than themselves.

Perhaps it's premonition, or merely imagination, but a ray of understanding passes between them: they, and their children, may be embarking upon a profound, irrevocable journey.

For now, only one thing is obvious: they need to find Ali a piano teacher.

2

In the first version of her dream, Kate relives everything as it was. She's gazing into an aquarium-like tank in which her daughter, weighing one and a half pounds, is a helpless minnow wired up to a Pompidou Centre of tubing, oxygen, monitors and drips. She can detect her minuscule breaths, but she can't lift and cuddle her because taking her out might kill her. In a fit of optimism, she and Guy had named her Victoria.

In the second version, Kate is at home, with Victoria strapped to her body in a baby sling. Life carries on. She can be cleaning the kitchen, hoovering the stairs, getting ready for work, but Victoria is there, silent, motionless. Probably dead, though in the dream Kate never remembers this. The baby hangs on her, growing heavier and heavier until Kate feels that the weight will break her neck, and just as it becomes too much to bear, she wakes up.

The third version shows her and Guy at the kitchen table, feeding their children. Ali is eating. Adrian is being naughty. Victoria is eight years old and is helping Kate, fetching fruit juice from the fridge, scolding her brother, laughing at her sister's crumb-coated face. It's a normal family scene, but with three children instead of two. And this is the version that leaves Kate, when she wakes, feeling that a medieval torture rack has pulled her to shreds.

Kate and Guy married young, some thought too young; they'd never had any doubt that they'd spend the rest of their lives together. First they'd sailed through three carefree student years. Guy became editor of the university newspaper and secretary of the students' union, booking cutting-edge politicians, writers and broadcasters to speak there – including Margaret Thatcher, who had just become the first woman leader of any British political party. He played his piano, attended all Kate's performances with her string quartet, and dragged her out for walks in the Cheviots. Often they'd go to concerts in the cathedral and sit deep inside its ancient darkness, drinking in the sounds they loved – Schubert, Sibelius or Guy's favourite Beethoven. Surely life would always be as beautiful as this. Strolling by the river not long before their final exams, while the leaves were young and tender on the trees, Guy said, 'Let's get married when we move to London?' Kate said, 'Yes, let's.' And that was that.

After graduating they had engineered a year together in Guildford. Kate, her engagement ring the envy of her fellow students, tackled her obligatory stint at law school and Guy took a junior editorial job on a local paper. But only when they'd found work placements in London did they take the plunge and tell Kate's parents that they'd like to get married in a register office with nobody there except family and a few close friends.

As they'd expected, William and Margaret took it as a personal affront that their daughter was refusing the big church wedding they'd saved towards for years. But Kate and Guy didn't want fuss. They were together; that was all; that was how it would stay. The best things, they insisted, were the simplest.

Margaret took Guy aside over sherry one evening and explained that, in her day, it was accepted that a church wedding blessed the couple in the sight of God; marriage without this was not a real marriage. Guy heard her out. Then, quietly, he told her that to him and Kate, their love was already so sacred that no outward demonstration could make it more so. Kate, more practically, pointed out that they'd prefer to use the money to set up home while they started their new jobs. Guy, with his impressive track record in student and local journalism, had been accepted on to a graduate-trainee scheme at a national newspaper; Kate was to do her articles with a firm of lawyers on Gray's Inn Road. A chorus of approval went up from George and Didie, who provided funds for them to have a honeymoon in Paris.

At the wedding party at a small hotel in Harrow, William and Margaret shook hands with George and Didie; and if dark, sparkling Didie in her tailored purple suit, Chinese jade necklace and high heels was remotely fazed by the hard stare of Margaret in her beige blouse, flat shoes and pearls, she did not show it once as she enfolded her son's new wife in her welcoming arms.

Kate had rarely been out of Britain. Davis family holidays had mostly consisted of annual fortnights on the Devon coast, during which she, her older brother, Anthony, and their younger sister, Joanna, had squabbled all day every day. In Paris, twenty-three and newly married, she walked on air. She filed away under 'daft' the protests of her best friend, Rebecca, the cellist in her string quartet. She and Guy were ready to tell the rest of the world to leave them alone for ever. 'If people say we're doing the wrong thing, they're obviously not our real friends,' Guy pointed out.

'But, Katie, you've never slept with anybody else,' Rebecca said, when Kate glanced round her door in college, sporting her brand new solitaire diamond. 'How will you ever know if what you've got is the right thing?'

'I do know.' Kate beamed. 'I'm happy with Guy. Why should I want anyone else?'

'But don't you want to live a little? Don't you want to explore, find out what you like, meet more people or see the world before you settle down?'

Rebecca's room was opposite Kate's in the hall of residence. Her eyes were chocolate-brown and her hair sleek and
midnight-dark. She wore translucent Indian-cotton skirts over
her long legs, usually with sandals. She came round to Kate's
almost every day, often with stories of her latest meditation
class, consciousness-raising group or all-night party. She'd
been through a number of boyfriends – college rumour had
it that she'd tried a girlfriend or two as well – and she was
planning to travel round India for a year before looking for
a job.

'Are you happier than me?' Kate challenged her.

'I hope not,' Rebecca riposted.

Kate and Rebecca had met on the landing on the first day
of their first term. Kate wasn't sure quite how they'd become
such good friends. She suspected that it had been Rebecca's
decision and that she had found it easier to comply than reject
her, especially when they started the string quartet, which was
also Rebecca's idea. Rebecca's risqué private life and upmarket,
progressive-boarding-school education sometimes made Kate
feel strait-laced, conventional, suburban and deeply inadequate.
Yet best friends they remained.

'Maybe she gives me adventure and I give her stability,' Kate
told Guy, after he had met Rebecca for the first time.

'Sounds like you're married,' he teased her.

But, back in bed after a late Parisian breakfast of café au lait
and croissants, Kate reluctantly agreed with Guy that she could
scarcely maintain a friendship with someone who thought she
knew what was good for Kate better than she did herself –
and whose nose had been put ridiculously out of joint when
Kate started going out with Guy. Kate remembers that only
too well.

She'd come back to her room after a concert – it was the
Sibelius Violin Concerto in the cathedral, it had been pouring
with rain and her umbrella had flipped inside out on the front

steps. After bidding a lingering goodnight to Guy, who wasn't yet staying, she'd knocked on Rebecca's door across the hall. It was unlocked, so Kate went in. Rebecca was sitting in her threadbare armchair in front of the electric bar heater, staring into space. She gazed up at Kate and said nothing. Just looked at her with those big, reproachful eyes. Kate wondered what she'd done wrong. Rebecca couldn't possibly have taken it personally that she'd gone to a concert with Guy, not her? She didn't know what to say, except 'Tea?' It wasn't a comfortable moment. Kate spent too much time silently puzzling over her friend's reaction, but never dared to raise the matter with her, or anyone else.

After graduation Rebecca took off for India – something Kate couldn't have afforded even if she'd wanted to. By the time she returned, Kate and Guy were so busy with their new jobs, not to mention gutting, rebuilding and decorating their flat in Stoke Newington, that they had neither time nor patience for travellers' tales of far-off lands. Rebecca and her cello disappeared into the past. Gradually Kate began to forget about her. Life as an articled clerk ensured that.

It didn't take her long to work out that the senior partner had employed her not because she was bright but because she was a tall, long-legged blonde. She spent her days preparing bills, photocopying and running bizarre errands for the partner including several to Marks & Spencer lingerie department. Guy bounced out every morning, eager to get to his office; by contrast, she was bound to a vile company merely because her parents wanted her to be a lawyer. On the rare days when she didn't work late, she practised her viola, trying to keep her technique up to scratch – though 'scratch' often seemed an appropriate word. She joined an amateur orchestra, which sounded appalling but was enjoyable as long as she concentrated on playing rather than listening.

'I dread every day,' Kate admitted to Didie, visiting Cheshire.

'Try not to let that beastly man demoralise you,' Didie comforted her. 'He's the problem, not you, because he has the power.'

'You're so sensible, Didie. But I don't know how I can stick it out.'

'Eventually you'll have a proper job. It's a matter of doing your time to qualify.'

'I wish I'd never got into this. I wish I could just stop and have kids.'

Didie pressed Kate's hand. 'Give yourself time, darling.'

Kate felt relieved. If she'd confided these thoughts to her own mother, Margaret would have told her to stop complaining: 'Stiff upper lip, dear.' No matter whose choice her profession really was, her feelings would have been judged entirely her own fault.

It should have been so simple. It seemed to work for everyone else. All around her, young professional women were getting married, setting up their first homes, blossoming into pregnancy. An unsettling pang would sweep through her when she passed pushchairs in the supermarket. One day an ex-colleague came into the office to show everyone her eight-month-old son. Kate picked him up and loved holding the warm, laughing child so much that she almost couldn't bear to put him down.

It was 1980. Guy's newspaper declared that half of Britain's married women were now going out to work, the highest proportion for any country in the EEC. A career was essential. Broodiness wasn't top of the agenda in women's groups, as Kate discovered when she tried one. Listening to the others' stories over tea and Bourbon creams, she wondered if she was a freak. Several women had toddlers and had come to the group to express, in a supportive environment, resentment against the ties that bound them. Others were fighting for promotion at work. One was suffering with a violent husband. Kate's husband was supremely unproblematic, beyond his preoccupation with the British Olympic Association's refusal to boycott the Moscow Olympic Games after the USSR invaded Afghanistan. Her issue was the only thing that seemed, to her, impossible to talk about: the gnawing, aching, physical longing to hold in her arms a baby of her own.

It should have been so simple. She'd stopped taking the pill when they got married. But nothing had happened.

They went for tests. Guy was fine. So was she. Nobody could say why this young, healthy, loving couple were unable to conceive a child. The doctor started Kate on a regime of hormones that soon made her fractious and sore; and she had to keep a diary of data, taking her temperature several times a day. When the correct signs were there, she was supposed to call her husband, drag him home and get him on the job immediately. This was easier said than done; but after the fifth month of hormones, thermometer, diary and shoulder-stands after sex, she missed her period and began to experience nausea in the mornings and hypersensitivity to the smell of coffee.

Their first child was due in mid-March 1981. Kate and Guy phoned every family member to break the news. Kate's colleagues gave her a bouquet; Guy's boss provided a bottle of champagne, which Kate, laughing, declared was unfair because she shouldn't drink any. They painted their second bedroom a bright, baby-friendly yellow and bought a cot and a pushchair; on the bus going to work, Kate taught herself to knit. Inside, she felt small fluttery motions; gradually they strengthened into kicks. She lay in bed at night with her hands pressed to her bump, loving the child within her.

Driving home after Christmas Day at her parents' house, Kate remarked, 'My back is really aching. I must have lifted something heavy. Maybe the turkey.' It was an innocent enough observation.

By noon on Boxing Day, her backache was worse; and discomfort between her legs signalled a discharge streaked with blood. 'Don't panic. Give it another day,' Guy said.

The next morning, while Guy was at the office, Kate went to the GP, who sent her straight to hospital.

Kate stayed there, with constant checks kept on the baby, around which there was apparently less amniotic fluid than there should have been. Everyone told her not to worry. Guy played cheerful, though she knew he wasn't: 'Don't worry, darling, I'll look after everything at home.' Her mother told her not to worry: the family history was one of strong and plentiful children. Didie sent flowers and volunteered to come down the moment they wanted her; they mustn't worry about asking. Kate's boss told her not to worry about being off work. Kate spent her days telling her concerned callers not to worry, and her evenings lying flat, trying to read, trying to knit, repeating silent prayers.

One day just into the new year, she walked to the ward door to see Guy off. As she raised her arm to wave to him, something gave way deep within her and a rush of warm liquid cascaded down her legs.

After a short, terrifying labour, Victoria appeared, only to disappear. Kate, weeping in the delivery room, her nails leaving crimson incisions in Guy's hand, thought she heard the faintest of cries as the minute baby was whisked away to the incubator. When Kate was finally allowed to see her, Victoria was swamped by tubing, wiring and monitors, her tiny face so wrinkled and skeletal that she looked a century old. It wasn't even safe for Kate to pick her up.

During the worst weeks of her life, each day lasted a year. She existed in a state of heightened awareness in which every glimpse of a doctor heading her way induced blind terror or irrational hope. She'd had no idea that so much could go wrong with a premature baby. Twice Victoria stopped breathing and turned blue, only to rally as Kate was giving way to despair. The doctors warned that some of her organs might not be properly formed. Her hearing or vision might be impaired. Her brain might be damaged. She might not survive. Equally, she might grow up well, normal and happy.

Hope, then hopelessness. One moment, certainty that Victoria would live; the next, no doubt that she would die. Panic, elation, panic again. The formerly self-assured, self-contained Kate felt that she was drowning in seas of emotion with fluxes and tides all their own.

Guy brought her some tapes, music that he thought might calm her. In a quiet room in the unit, her head on his shoulder, listening to the slow movement of Ravel's G major Piano Concerto and watching Victoria living from second to second, she reflected that she'd never known such extremes were latent inside her, never suspected how suffering can mangle time and leave it distorted and misshapen. Victoria was inches long and weighed less than a bag of sugar. Yet everything had to carry on, regardless. Guy was dealing with the inauguration of a US president called Ronald Reagan, the charging of a serial killer known as the Yorkshire Ripper and the rumoured imminent takeover of his newspaper. Whole worlds were exploding, compared to one tiny creature fighting for her life. But this helpless baby was Kate's universe.

Kate stayed in hospital with Victoria. Guy visited early each morning and late each evening. In between, he had to keep going, maintaining a semblance of normality for all their sakes. Kate could see the strain round his eyes, the shadows deepening by his nose. He seemed to have aged ten years in two weeks.

He'd sit by Victoria's incubator, holding Kate's hand, talking about goings-on at work. One editorial assistant had broken her wrist. His boss was getting married for the third time and threatening to leave if the takeover went ahead. If it did, there could be multiple redundancies. In his view, Thatcher's ruthless administration was destroying the moral fibre of—

'Guy,' Kate cut in, 'I really don't care.'

There was a short silence, but for the slow tenderness of Ravel.

'No,' Guy said. 'Neither do I.'

Guy grew quieter during his visits. They'd sit together waiting, wondering, not talking. Now and then a doctor would bring them good news. Sometimes it was less good. Then good again.

Alone in the flat, Guy sometimes let himself cry. He stayed busy, working, keeping their families informed, fielding phone calls and trying to talk himself into a positive frame of mind. But some solitary nights, he began to wonder whether this would go on for ever, whether he and Kate must spend the rest of their years waiting for Victoria to live or die. In his worst moments, to his horror, he almost wished that none of it had begun, that they had neither conceived the child, nor got married, nor even met each other. If he'd taken up the place he'd won at Oxford, not decided to rebel and study in the north, Kate would have lived in blissful ignorance of him and Victoria would never have existed. Fate, he decided, is character plus timing plus a large dose of luck, good or bad.

He detached himself by deciding to approach the incident as he would a journalistic assignment. He would experience it for the sake of documenting it. Then, perhaps, once Victoria was safely home, he could write an article, maybe a book, to help other families encountering the same trauma.

He started to keep a diary, writing down everything that had happened since Christmas. Back from the hospital around midnight, he'd sit at the kitchen table covering page after page of a spiral-bound notebook with scrawls in black biro. On the seventeenth day of Victoria's life, he drafted a pitch to show the editor of the newspaper's health section.

On the eighteenth day, he arrived at the hospital to find a doctor, grey-faced, saying, 'Guy, Victoria isn't doing quite so well today.'

Guy began to run. He came to a halt in the doorway. Kate was standing by the incubator, her gaze fixed on the tiny bundle she was cradling.

She handed him Victoria without a word. The baby's eyes were closed. Although she was warm under her white woollen blanket, he could scarcely sense her breath. Her skin had the bluish tint of a northern winter sky.

'We can hold her now. There's no hope,' Kate said, taking her back from Guy although he had barely grown used to the sensation of having his child in his arms.

They sat together all morning, holding Victoria. At two o'clock in the afternoon, she died.

In the weeks and months that followed, Kate cried every day. The office gave her compassionate leave; she stayed home and let the tears flow. She had had no idea that her mind could leach such leaden despair, or that her eyes would not become exhausted from crying but would go on until there seemed to be nothing left in the world except grief.

Guy held her, comforted her, but said little. No soft words could make her feel better – or him. Margaret suggested that Kate should stay in Harrow for a while, to escape the room that should have been Victoria's, but Kate preferred to be at home. At least the nursery meant that Victoria had once been real.

Kate's siblings rallied round as best they could. Joanna was still at university, though, and when she came to visit, Kate could see how frightened she was at the sight of her level-headed sister falling to pieces. William and Anthony, emulating him, soon found that their instinctive 'Come on, old girl, pull yourself together, things to be done, chop chop,' got them, and Kate, nowhere.

Margaret's next idea was more productive. She took Kate out to lunch in town, then steered her towards the haberdashery in John Lewis, where she bought her a present of some wool, some patterns, a range of knitting needles and a wicker basket to hold the lot, plus a book of challenging Kaffe Fassett designs. Kate, attracted by the warm, bright colours, the varying softnesses of mohair, lamb's wool and merino, and the patterns that showed happy families wearing fabulously patterned sweaters, accepted her mother's gift and carried the bulky packages home on the seventy-three bus.

When Guy had gone to work the next morning and the tears had temporarily worn themselves out, Kate blew her nose, sat on the floor with a cup of tea and unpacked her parcels. Margaret had suggested a simple jersey to start her off. Kate knew the basic stitches; a half-finished yellow blanket, intended for the baby, had vanished when Guy decided to clear out every disposable reminder. But knitting a full-sized sweater felt way beyond her.

The thread under her fingers required control. She needed to find the correct tension and keep it constant. She had to concentrate; if unsteadiness set in, the knitting began to sag, scrunch or stretch. She made herself persevere by leafing through the Kaffe Fassett book. Once she'd mastered the technique, then she, too, would be able to create fantastical patterns in flame-hued diagonals, blue, green and white snowflakes, or gorgeous mottled designs that looked as if they had been plucked whole from the contours of a coral reef.

Her jersey was far from perfect. It fitted Guy – she'd measured it against him so many times that it could scarcely not – but in the cream-coloured fabric lurked tremulous kinks where the tension was inconsistent. It was evidently home-knitted by a beginner, but Guy insisted on wearing it to work. Kate knew that that was just to make her happy. But it did make her happy. It showed she'd produced something useful; and that Guy cared.

She seemed to need reassurance of that now. Curled in her armchair, feet tucked under her, a needle in each hand and a ball of wool in her lap, she wondered whether they had talked to each other more often, more freely, before all this had happened.

Long silences dominated their evenings. She couldn't remember those happening at university. Perhaps as you get older, as you spend more time together, there's less to say; companionable quiet becomes an end in itself. These silences, though, didn't always feel companionable. They isolated her from Guy, as if they each retreated alone to worry at their wounds without troubling the other. Victoria and the grief that went with her were being driven underground.

Kate, clicking away, felt a twinge of sympathy for Guy. It couldn't be easy, living with a woman whose heart had been ripped out. But Victoria had been his daughter as well, even if he had not carried her inside him, feeling her fluttery kicks through the days and nights. He had lost a child too, but he was trying to live. He didn't cry for hours on end. He'd try to avoid waking her and go off to work without breakfast – he'd have a croissant and coffee later in the canteen. In the evening, he'd come crashing back in, telling her about the features he was fitting to the page, the admin that drove him bananas and the office gossip that bored her rigid when he repeated it to her, but at least kept him in touch with the world outside their claustrophobic flat. While he was out during the day, she barely noticed that she didn't miss him.

Men, Didie reminded her on the phone, aren't good at expressing their feelings.

'If keeping going helps him,' Kate said, 'then he's lucky. I wish I could.'

'You will, darling. Take all the time for yourself that you need,' Didie encouraged. It was good to hear that. Kate's mother was growing restive, prodding her gently but insistently to go back to work. And of course, Guy reminded her, they could try for another baby as soon as she felt ready.

Kate returned to Gray's Inn Road after six months – not least because she couldn't stand the flat any more. Even walks to the café at Clissold Park were wearing thin, thanks to the endless stream of mothers and babies she'd see there. Besides, she didn't want to forget her training and render herself an unemployable lawyer as well as a useless mother. The office wasn't so bad – better than eyeing other people's pushchairs and imagining what Victoria would have looked like now, sitting up, smiling, laughing.

She brought her knitting with her for bus journeys and lunchtime. Her colleagues came in to admire her latest effort: a Fair Isle scarf, although it was midsummer. The first weeks dragged, leaving her exhausted, but the routine propped her up; soon she could pass whole half-days without descending into her private pit of grief. Periods of twenty-four hours could go by without her shedding a tear. Work was the best therapy.

Going home was more difficult. Every time she passed the closed door of the nursery, it seemed to accuse her of failing its intended occupant. She suggested to Guy that they should think about moving. She offered to visit an estate agent and get a valuation.

'It's a good idea,' he said at once. 'But could we hang on here for a tiny bit longer? Just a few months? Would you be OK with that?'

Kate didn't ask why. Presumably he had his reasons. Her bus ride home had taken twice as long as usual, she felt exhausted and she didn't fancy sparking another flood of Guy's newspaper gossip. It was easiest to agree.

Two weeks later, Guy whirled into the flat carrying a bottle of wine and a bunch of roses. 'Sit down, Katie,' he demanded, pushing the bouquet into her hands. 'I'll pour you a glass of this and then there's a lot to tell you and a lot to ask you.' He grabbed two wine glasses from the cupboard, opened the bottle with a flourish of corkscrew and sat down next to her. She wondered when she'd last seen him smile like that.

A job had come up at the *Manchester Chronicle*: assistant editor of the weekly news-review section. His boss had recommended him, so he'd been up for an interview—

'You went to Manchester for an interview?' Kate exclaimed. 'When?'

'Last week. I didn't want to tell anyone in case I didn't get it.'

'You went to Manchester for the day and I didn't know?'

'You weren't supposed to, love. They might have hated me, I might have hated them, it mightn't have worked out, so there'd have been no point in you worrying about it.'

Kate took a moment to digest this. Then she reached for her knitting.

The environment was a little less stressful than his present one, he went on, and the pay a little better – if modestly so, because the site was out of London – but, still, it was a dream job, an extraordinary opportunity for a journalist still in his twenties.

'It would be a fresh start,' he said, holding her wrist. 'Just stop knitting a second and tell me what you think.'

'I don't know what to think. It's wonderful for you. But I can't believe you didn't tell me sooner. I had no idea that you were up to anything – and suddenly you're talking about moving two hundred miles?'

'Darling, I thought you'd be happy. You seemed keen to move. And you're finishing your articles, so the timing is . . .'

'Yes.' Kate's needles clicked.

'Katie, put down the knitting. *Please*.' Guy put both his hands over hers to still them. 'What do you want? Tell me. I need to know.'

'I want—' Kate looked into his anxious eyes. She couldn't tell him that she wanted him not to grow more and more distant from her just when she needed him to come closer. 'I only want a home and family like everyone else. A normal home with normal, happy children,' she said eventually. Though true, it sounded lame.

'So do I,' Guy said. 'And we could enjoy having all of that near Manchester, couldn't we? There'd be so many advantages, Katie. We could live in Cheshire, or Buxton, or a village in the Peak District.'

'I'd prefer to be somewhere with trains and shops.' Kate imagined a scenario – irrational but vivid – in which every person in a small, nosy village would know that she had failed her first baby.

'Buxton, then. We could have a wonderful house there. Look at these.' Guy pounced on his desk and extracted a sheaf of folded pages from a drawer.

'You sent off for a property paper and I never noticed?'

'At the office. Look.' He pointed at a row of adverts for beautiful stone cottages in Derbyshire that cost roughly the same as their Stoke Newington flat. Startled to discover her basic indifference to her own fate, Kate looked, listened, nodded and forced a smile.

Guy's traineeship at the newspaper and Kate's articles in Gray's Inn Road came to an end at the same time. They put the flat on the market. They took to driving north late on Fridays, staying overnight with Didie and George and setting out to house-hunt in Derbyshire first thing on Saturday morning. Kate saw the world through a glass thicker and darker than the windscreen of their old Beetle. From its wrong side she watched herself going through the motions: telling estate agents what they needed and could afford, enthusing to Didie about how happy she was that they'd live closer to her, explaining to her own shell-shocked parents that this was an opportunity Guy could not possibly miss. She'd look for a job once they'd made the move.

Buxton pleased her when they wandered about, 'casing the joint', as Didie put it. The air's freshness made her feel cleansed inside (how different from Stoke Newington) and the properties they viewed were roomy and light. They investigated a detached 1920s house on a busy road, a brand new town-house on a cul-de-sac, an older, sandstone villa on a quiet side-street; but on their third visit, the agent took them up a curving hill past the house where Vera Brittain had spent part of her girlhood, as a blue plaque told them, and thence to a tall, semi-detached Victorian pile in a state of considerable disrepair. It needed total modernisation – it had no central heating in a town where it was too cold to grow apples. 'But there's your chance to make it your own,' the agent pointed out, 'and, of course, the price is much lower than you'd normally see for a house of this quality.'

'How can anyone live in a house like this and let it get into such a terrible state?' Kate wondered aloud. 'It seems so uncared-for.'

'It's too easy to stop noticing things when you've been among them for a long time,' Guy suggested. 'Katie, look at these windows. Look at all this light.'

Kate, gazing out at the back garden's neglected lawn, felt a prickle on the back of the neck: the intuition that told her she was looking at her new home.

They sloped off to a pub to confer over a ploughman's lunch. Afterwards, they strolled back to the house and stood under the sycamores, looking up at it, picturing themselves living inside. A normal home with normal, happy children. Hill-walks close by, Didie and George an easy drive away and no memories clinging to the stones around them.

Kate's sole condition was dramatic: she wanted to move Victoria's grave to Buxton. Guy balked at the idea of digging up the coffin, reburying it, going through the whole trauma again; but when Kate made it clear that if Victoria didn't go, neither would she, he nodded assent. They could manage. They'd managed worse things before.

The day before the move, while Guy was wrapping the wedding crockery in newspaper and piling it into cardboard boxes, Kate went to his desk to pack his files. She lifted too many at once and the top wallet fell, spilling its contents at her feet. She bent to gather up the papers. Words caught her eye at random. 'Statistics' . . . 'greatest pain' . . . 'Victoria' . . .

'Guy? What's this?'

Her husband looked at her and she thought for a second that he had turned pale. 'Oh, Katie,' he said, 'I've been meaning to run this by you. The thing is, I didn't want to upset you, I didn't want to bring it all flooding back.'

'You're writing about Victoria.' Kate sat down at the kitchen table, one hand pressing her forehead under her untidy, moving-house hair.

'Darling.' Guy swooped in beside her. She felt him gazing into her face, but she wouldn't look up. 'I wanted to write something that might help people going through what we went through. The health editor thought it was a marvellous idea.'

'And the health editor has let you write *twenty pages*?'

'The thing is – well, I want to do an article, but that would be a kind of pilot for this publisher I've been talking to. It'll help to prove that I can write something that will really compel people, something they identify with that mirrors how they feel . . .'

'You want to write a *book* about Victoria?' Kate seemed to be sinking into a swamp that waited below the kitchen to swallow her. 'You don't just want to write it. You're writing it already.'

'It's valuable, Katie. It means so much to me. Can't we find a way to bring some good out of what happened to us? If we can help other people, give them something to make them feel they're not so alone . . .'

'*We?* I don't recall hearing I'm part of this. You never even asked how I felt!'

'I was waiting for the right moment.'

'Christ, Guy. How could you?' Kate pulled away her hand and stood up. Guy shrank back in his chair. 'Did it occur to you to wonder how I feel? No, of course it didn't! You're only thinking of yourself, your brilliant career, your marvellous move to Manchester. You wouldn't care if I said I'd kill myself!'

'Katie! Calm down. You know that's not true.'

'From where I am, Guy Bradley, it looks true. How can you do this to me?'

'Darling, can't you see? It's not only for other people, it's for us, so we won't have suffered and Victoria won't have died in vain.'

'But it's my grief! It's private. It's not for everybody to read and pry and say, "Ooh, look at them, look how miserable they are, they couldn't keep their baby alive." What made you think that I'd ever, in a million years, consider making that public?'

'Sweetheart. Please don't cry.'

'Leave me alone. You're a bloody journalist. You don't give a damn.'

'Katie—'

'Just leave me alone.'

The van arrived at eight o'clock the next morning. Kate, standing on the front step, her hair blowing about her shoulders, let the movers in. She made them some tea and packed the valuables into the back of the Beetle. Guy, who hadn't slept all night, swallowed two cups of coffee and a caffeine pill in preparation for the long drive north. That morning when they locked the flat for the last time, climbed into the car and started the engine, they had spoken three words to each other that were not directly connected with moving house.

Through the car window on the M1, Kate watched her old life receding into the distance, imagined the new house lying ahead, needing to be rethought, remodelled, rewired, replastered and repainted, and wondered what was to become of them now.

3

'I don't really know what to do with her,' Glenda Fairburn says, after Alicia has had two piano lessons. 'I've never seen anything like it. She just – knows.'

'She does, doesn't she?' Kate says.

'She doesn't have any trouble co-ordinating. She doesn't see why she should play with one hand at a time. The most incredible thing is that she concentrates. How do you do it? Do you not let them watch TV?'

'We're a completely normal family,' Kate says, smiling. 'They're the same as any other kids.'

'Well, this one's special.' Glenda's face is full of tenderness. She's a young Scottish musician who's recently moved to Buxton with her husband, a scientist at the Safety in Mines Research Establishment. 'I'll do my best for her, Kate, but I need you to know I'm feeling my way. With most of the little ones you just do the animal songs and the first exercise books and hope they take some interest. You don't generally find a child picking out pieces by ear.'

Alicia reaches out her hands to the keys. They loom huge in front of her like a row of pale ice lollies. She touches and sounds C, then D, then E. Deep red, royal blue, lemon yellow. The piano is better than a paintbox, for colours blend, flicker and dance through her mind when she hears music and the world seems delicious for it. Each note has its own colour in her head. The colours of the white notes are easy to identify, solid and bright. The black ones are more difficult: peculiar, in-between purples, greens and pinks. Except for B flat, which mysteriously looks like chocolate.

Alicia hasn't told her parents that she sees colours in music. Once she began to explain it to Mum at bedtime, but Mum looked so indulgent and said, 'Yes, darling, go to sleep now,' so many times that Alicia knew she hadn't grasped any of it. As for her beastly brother, there's no point trying. Adie, who is enormous, a whole two years older than her, does nothing but tease her. Once he caught a frog in the garden and put it in her shoe, where she nearly trod on it; worse, when she shook it out, it started leaping around the kitchen in slimy green arcs and Mum screamed. She wonders what it would have been like not to have a brother. Or to have a sister instead, a sister who was like her, understood her and was her friend, not her enemy.

Cassie is her best friend. Alicia, looking into the big canine eyes that gaze back at her with such love, wonders what Cassie would say if she could talk. Sometimes the dog jumps on to her bed to wake her up, cold nose and rasping tongue prodding her face in the hope of games ahead. 'We shouldn't let her go on Ali's bed,' Mum protests, but Dad insists there's no problem – 'Oh, come on, love, a dog like Cassie would never hurt a child, especially not Ali.' Alicia loves Cassie so much that if she cries when Mum leaves her at nursery school it's not because she misses Mum – it's because she won't see her dog for hours.

Alicia wants to tell Dad about the colours in the music, but he's usually gone too early in the morning for her to talk to him; and by the time he gets home, she's asleep. Sometimes, when he tiptoes into the enfolding darkness of her room to kiss her goodnight, she pretends that she's sleeping even when she isn't, because Mum will be upset if she thinks he's woken her. Later she opens her eyes in the traces of downstairs lamplight and hears him playing the piano before she drifts back into her dreams. She feels she's falling asleep on a boat, floating on a lake of music.

At weekends, she asks him to play to her. She stands close, watching, transfixed by his fingers, so certain, so strong, so fast. Hers won't move like that. When she grumbles to Glenda about it in her piano lesson, Glenda, who is her favourite person apart from Grandma Didie, laughs her lovely Scottish laugh and assures her that by the time she's thirteen, her fingers will be able to do anything she wants. That makes it worse. Alicia can't believe she'll ever be as old as that.

She can never remember the name of the composer who wrote her favourite piece. A short, funny name, like Shopping. 'Please, Dad, play the riding-over-the-moors piece,' she'd beg. At first Dad didn't know what she meant. Now he knows exactly and begins it at once. He says it's called a Ballade, which means a song telling a story. Alicia has made up her own story for the music. 'Four friends are talking to each other. Then they go on horseback across the moors. There's a witch or wizard, something evil, that tries to stop them and scary things happen. But in the end they find each other again and they're so pleased that they forget all about going out riding.'

Dad is surprised and stays silent for a minute. Eventually he asks her, 'Why do you think that, Ali? Why do you think they've forgotten?'

'Because their talking tune comes back, but the riding-over-the-moors one doesn't.'

'Gordon Bennett,' Dad says. 'You're full of surprises, Ali. Shall I play it again?'

'Yes, please!' Alicia bounces. Dad's face melts into his sweetest smile and he turns back to the keyboard. Alicia sits cross-legged on the floor and lets her favourite tunes dance behind her eyes in deep golds, burnished reds and emerald green.

At the end, Dad says, 'You know, Ali, one day you'll be able to play this yourself.'

'It's too hard,' Alicia protests. 'I'm too small.'

'Darling, you'll be much bigger very soon.' Dad beams.

'Come on, give us a hug.' She jumps on to his lap and hugs him, his woolly jersey warm and scratchy against her cheek.

Adrian has been given a camera for his birthday. After Dad has left the piano to mow the front lawn, Alicia pulls at her brother's sleeve and begs him to show her how it works.

Adrian adopts his most bossy older-brother voice. 'You look through here, Ali – that's it. Don't drop it. What can you see?'

'It's all blurry.'

'You twist the lens. Like this. That's right.'

'Everything's sharp now.'

'Yes. It's called focusing. You're bringing the picture into focus. That's what Dad says.'

Alicia nods. She understands exactly what he means, because that's what music does to her world. In nursery school she sits daydreaming and never knows the answers to the questions, until Lucy puts on the music – then everything sharpens and brightens, coming into focus. Dad brings home into focus when he plays.

Sometimes, though, she thinks he focuses things just by being *there*. At weekends, when he takes his place for breakfast and tucks his napkin into his shirt to protect it from spilled marmalade or egg, the wooden table edge seems firmer to her; when the scent of fresh-cut grass drifts through the window and she sees his curving shoulders as he pushes the mower along the lawn, each leaf in the garden seems brilliant and sure of itself; and she always wants more of Mum's sponge cake at teatime, because it tastes extra good when Dad's there. She sometimes doesn't realise how much she misses him when he's at work until he comes back, making her world clear, bringing it into focus. She thinks she'll never forget the day he came home early specially to see her play the piano.

Nobody understands her the way Dad does. At nursery school, everyone seems to think she's strange when she talks about music. She'll say, 'You know that bit in the Ballade that sounds like a witch?' and her friends, Sarah and Matthew, look at her as if there's something wrong.

'Let's play the piano,' Alicia says, at Sarah's house one Saturday.

'We don't have one,' Sarah says.

Worse, when Matthew, his brother Tim and their mother come round, Alicia pulls Matthew over to the piano and starts to play, while Tim runs off to the garden with Adrian. Matthew sits awkwardly beside Alicia and prods at the keys with one finger, too loudly and on completely the wrong notes.

'Yuck!' Alicia puts her fingers in her ears. Matthew starts to cry.

'I think we'd better go home,' Matthew's mum says, gathering up the bawling child. Alicia begins to cry too, because she likes Matthew so much and doesn't understand why he's upset. He has sweet eyes and he's quiet, not preoccupied with making noise, playing football and hitting people like most boys. The other children tease her and say she fancies Matthew, but she doesn't. She just likes him. What's wrong with that? The next day he doesn't want to talk to her. Alicia has to gather every bit of courage she can find in order to go up to him and say, 'Matthew, I'm sorry, will you be my friend again?'

Matthew looks at his feet and mumbles something that sounds like 'All right.'

'Ali,' Mum says later, giving her and Adrian their fish-fingers, 'you've got to understand that not everybody has a piano and not everybody who does have one can play it.'

'Why?' Alicia demands. 'It's so easy.'

'Darling, it's not that easy for everybody. Piano lessons cost money and not all people are as keen to learn as you are.'

Alicia says nothing. She wonders why on earth they wouldn't be. Nothing else is so much fun. It's like walking inside a map. When she's playing, she knows exactly where she is.

★   ★   ★

'I don't really know what to do with her,' says Jonathan Bowen, two years later.

'I'm not sure anybody does,' Kate replies.

Jonathan is Parkhill Comprehensive's head of music – or, rather, what's left of music, post-Thatcher. He's also organist at St Edmund's, the church to which Ali and Adrian's primary school is attached. Glenda, abdicating reluctantly, had told Kate he's the best piano teacher in Buxton; Ali should have the best. Glenda is afraid of not giving her the right guidance; besides which, she's expecting a baby.

'How are you getting on at school, Ali?' Jonathan asks her.

Aged five and a half, Ali is holding on to Kate's hand, swinging herself back and forth as if dancing, anchored, to some unheard melody. 'It's OK. I don't really like school, though,' she says, looking up at Jonathan with her huge blue eyes. 'I wouldn't really like any school.'

'No, Ali, I expect you wouldn't. Kate, do you play yourself? What would really benefit Ali is if you or your husband were to practise with her. Not just supervise, but work with her – show her the movements and stop her getting into bad habits. Would either of you be willing to watch her lessons and put some serious time into this? Your daughter has exceptional talent, Kate. She's not just good. She's something special.'

'I'm special,' Ali sings. Kate senses that she's singing out the words without taking in the meaning. Ali hears the musical contours of sentences more than their content.

'It's a hundred years since I last played, but as of next time, I'll join in,' Kate assents. 'OK, Ali?'

'I'm special, I'm special,' Ali sings. 'Where's Cassie?'

Kate's boss, Mike, has been to the house and watched Guy playing the Note Game with Ali. She turns her back to the piano; Guy plays a note and asks her what it is. 'F,' declares the gleeful Ali. He plays another. 'A flat.'

She's always right; that's nothing new, but Guy never fails to give her a hug and say, 'Well done, you clever old thing!'

So, when Kate asks Mike for extra time away from the office – as Jonathan points out, it makes no sense to teach a small child in the evening when she's tired and fractious – Mike suggests that she might consider a four-day week. Guy has been promoted to assistant editor of the newspaper, with an associated salary rise, so Kate's day off is financially viable; and she's relieved to have Thursdays free, with time to get to grips with everything that she and Ali have, together, to learn. She's grateful for Guy's extra income – although, as she tells her mother, she hadn't expected to spend it on high-class piano lessons and multiplying stacks of CDs. Luckily Adrian is happy with football boots.

Watching Jonathan moulding Ali's little hands to the keyboard, seeing the games he plays with her to strengthen her ear, Kate becomes absorbed in something more significant than herself. Jonathan knows how to tap into the mystery that is Ali's music, how to stimulate her mind and how, Kate thinks, to inspire her. At the end of each lesson, he plays to her for a few minutes. Sometimes he improvises – being an organist, he's good at this – but sometimes he plays a whole piece and asks her if she likes it and whether she knows the composer's name. Ali says she likes Mr Shopping best.

Free Thursdays also give Kate the chance to begin redecorating. The house is a gift for anyone with a feel for interior design, which Kate, loving wool, fabric and colour, has aplenty. Its initial decorative makeover had had to be cheap and functional – new wiring and central heating had eaten up swathes of cash. Nine years on, it's time for an upgrade.

New carpets; new paint. Paint first. What's the point of beautiful new carpet if you spill paint on it afterwards? For the lounge, a creamy, eggy yellow that makes the most of the sunshine and will keep the house looking warm during the cruel Derbyshire winters. The stairs will be two lighter shades, one below the dado rail and the other, paler, above it. The carpet will be a burnished ochre that doesn't show the dog hairs too much.

Kate decides to make the lounge curtains herself: white damask patterned with roses. She buys a sewing-machine – something for which she's hankered for years (she isn't good at buying herself presents) – and sets it up on a table in the first-floor guest room, which also serves as her space, accommodating her store of leftover wool. Guy's study, beside the children's bedrooms in what had once been a loft, is a no-go area. Even she can't enter it without knocking. She suspects that he doesn't want anyone to see what a mess it is.

Their bedroom needs decorating too.

'You choose, darling,' Guy says at breakfast, when she suggests it. 'You always choose wonderfully. Have you seen my keys anywhere?'

'Why can't you keep them in the same place every day?' As always, it's a rhetorical question.

When he's gone, she wanders up to the bedroom, imagining. Though airy and large, overlooking the front lawn, it feels neglected. The walls are a dull white and, by the windows, diagonal cracks plough through the plaster. The carpet by the bed is wearing thin. On Guy's bedside table stands a tower of books that could topple with one false move of a feather duster. A biography of Margaret Thatcher perches on top, Guy's place kept by a pencil with which he's been underscoring the passages that make him most angry. Kate's bedside table houses a volume of Kaffe Fassett patterns, a childproof bottle of painkillers and a box of wax earplugs.

The chintz has to go; better curtains will help to keep out the cold in winter and the early light in summer. She'll put in the same gold-coloured carpet and the walls will be rich cream instead of flat white. And they need a new bedspread, maybe an ethnic pattern. Indonesian batik is very *in*, according to the magazines she dips into at the doctor's surgery, to which she takes the children constantly with sore throats, stomach upsets and, alarmingly in Ali's case, earache.

Why do her kids get sick so often? Each time, worst-case scenarios shoot through her mind: a headache could be meningitis, a sore throat may be tonsillitis requiring an operation, a tummyache might signal a burst appendix. The doctor always says something soothing. 'With most of these viruses, Mrs Bradley, you really just have to keep them warm and let nature take its course. Kids haven't been around long enough to meet all the germs and build up their resistance. It's quite normal.' Kate is reassured; still, deep down, she expects the worst.

The magazines make her taste look impersonal. Liven up your bedroom, they shout, by using sensual props. Put a deep, warm colour on the walls. Put up a shelf and stand vases of contrasting flowers on it; burn incense sticks or use scented candles to create a sexy mood. Put attractive, silk-covered cushions on the bed to evoke eastern exoticism, like a harem. In Derbyshire?

Kate experiments. While the children are at school, she drives to Manchester – she has a car of her own now – and goes to her favourite department store. There she runs her fingers across rolls of watered silk and deep-piled velvet in rich blues, greens and purples, and bright cushions edged with beads. She can't picture them in her bedroom, which presumably will emerge from its refit looking as functional as it had when she began. At home, she puts on her dressing-table a vase of her favourite black-centred anemones. It doesn't help. Harem, indeed. The bedroom has become nothing more than a domestic commuter-belt, with the lounge as the capital city in which the family energy is spent and the piano the seat of government at its epicentre.

The bedroom, in short, depresses her. So she starts with the lounge – and when Ali sees the piano covered with a

dustsheet, her howl is so loud that Kate is afraid the neighbours will hear.

Coming out of the department store in Manchester on a damp
winter Thursday at lunchtime, Kate pauses, her hands full of
plastic carrier-bags. Instead of decorating equipment, she's
bought a sports shirt for Adrian, some dog treats for Cassie
and some white wool to knit a jumper for Ali. The *Manchester
Chronicle* offices are a ten-minute stroll away. Perhaps she
could drop in to see Guy. Her drive had been worse than
usual. There'd been road closures and jams; eventually she'd
parked over a mile from the centre and trudged the rest of
the way. Even then she'd been surprised to see some streets
entirely shut off, pavements included; she'd had to take a long
way round. It has left her reluctant to go back to the car too
soon.

How funny, she thinks, that she should hesitate to arrive
unannounced to see her husband. Newspaper headquarters,
though, are frenetic places.

'Is Guy Bradley available?' she asks the receptionist.

'I'll try him for you. What name shall I say?'

'I'm his wife.'

It's years since Kate last visited Guy at work. The people
he talks about are nothing to her but names; and now that
he's been promoted, he has a new office and she can't even
picture him going about his day's work.

'Darling!' Guy bursts into the lobby from a side door.

'I was passing so I thought I'd drop in,' Kate says, feeling
awkward.

'Come up. I've got a meeting in a minute, things are
completely manic today, as you can imagine, but Diane's made
some coffee . . .'

Kate hurries after him through long, modern corridors of
grey paint and greyer carpet. An air of intense concentration hangs over the open-plan offices. Through glass insets

she can spot people typing on computers and talking on phones.

'I'm in the nerve centre now,' Guy tells her, opening doors, bounding up stairs. 'Diane,' he calls to a dark-haired secretary, 'this is Kate. Any chance of a coffee?'

'Hi, Kate!' Diane jumps to attention.

A door opens and someone shouts from inside: 'Guy! Dave needs you to call him urgently about the bombing. The photographer's biked round some shots.'

'OK, Mart,' Guy shouts back.

'Mrs Powers called about the complaint she wants to make,' Diane tells him, from the percolator. 'I said you'd be in touch, but she was a bit upset, so can you call her?'

'Di, please, next time, can you ask her to write to the readers' editor?' Guy begs. 'I keep telling her. She's got to take it on board some time.' He ushers Kate into the rare private office that is his. 'Darling, I won't be a mo,' he says, and dashes away.

Kate, sniffing the synthetic scent of industrial carpet and sipping impossibly stewed coffee, watches her husband through the doorway as he darts around like a beagle responding to a hunting horn. He hurries into another, empty, room and she sees him barking into a phone. There's little to look at outside except the block opposite, where plants on the window-ledges have begun to wilt. Guy's office contains no plants. A picture of the two of them with the children sits beside his computer. His desk is invisible under piles of paper and his shelves are crammed with overflowing box files, reference books and telephone directories.

A plump, balding man in a shirt and tie half strides into the room, then pulls up short on seeing Kate. 'Where's Guy?' he demands.

'Over there.' Kate points. The door shuts as fast as it had opened. Kate feels redundant. The coffee, cooling in the chipped mug, tastes more bitter and poisonous by the moment.

'Guy,' she hears the intruder yell, 'editorial meeting, we need you *now*.'

Guy waves from the phone, finishes his conversation, scoots back to Kate like an actor on speeded-up film. 'Darling, I have to run. The bombing this morning has thrown everything completely. Don't worry, enjoy your coffee, and I'll see you tonight, OK?'

'Bombing?' Kate echoes, but he's vanished before the word is out.

She leaves the mug on the desk and makes her way downstairs. In any case, it's time to head back to collect the children.

No wonder Guy is so tired when he gets home, if he spends his days functioning at such intensity. She feels guilty – she'd intruded on him when a visitor was the last thing he needed. She decides to make amends by cooking him a special dinner.

Kate drags the kids round the supermarket, fielding their demands for crisps and chocolate. She buys chicken, fresh tarragon, a lemon and vegetables, plus a bottle of Australian wine, which the food and drink section of Guy's paper says has recently become more popular than French.

Once the children are in bed, she sets about transforming the kitchen into a more romantic environment, if not quite a Derbyshire harem. She prepares the chicken in a casserole, lights several candles, dims the overhead spotlights, tidies away the toys, then goes upstairs and digs out of a bedroom drawer a low-cut, mid-blue sweater that Guy used to say matched her eyes. She expects him home by eight.

By nine, the candles are burning low and the chicken is more than well cooked. Her stomach is rumbling. Kate opens a packet of Adrian's crisps and pours herself a glass of wine. Her mind delivers disasters. Overturned lorries on the motorway, a mudslide in the hills, a sheep in the road. Sheep are the most dangerous creatures in Derbyshire. She wishes her parents wouldn't laugh at this, because it's true. There are no fences on the moors; sheep can wander freely about. If a sheep goes into the road in the dark and you don't see it in time . . .

Her mother has been telling her about mobile telephones, brick-like gadgets prized as status symbols in London by estate agents and young stockbrokers. Damn the status symbol, Kate thinks, the wine releasing the fury she won't usually let herself feel. It shouldn't be a status symbol but a convenience tool so that people can let each other know when they're going to be late home. Cassie leans her snout on Kate's knee, gazing up at her with deep collie eyes. Kate pets the dog's ears and tries not to let a stubbornly forming tear escape on to the makeup over which she's taken so much trouble.

She drifts upstairs, past the test patches of paint on the walls, and peers into the children's rooms. Adrian is flat on his back with his mouth open, sleeping as only a tired-out small boy can sleep after an afternoon on a cold, muddy sports field. Ali is curled under her blankets clutching a toy penguin, a present from Didie. The sight of them, so small and vulnerable, deepens Kate's maudlin mood. She shouldn't have had so much wine on an empty stomach. She can't help picturing another, imaginary door off the landing; behind it, a small desk bearing a schoolbook covered in childish handwriting, and in the bed Victoria asleep, ten years old, with blonde hair like her little sister's.

At nine forty-five, the dinner has dried up and Guy is still not home. Kate removes her blue jersey and cleanses away her makeup. In her old towelling dressing-gown, which used to be white, she makes herself a sandwich and a mug of cocoa, then heads for bed.

She is semi-conscious when a warm presence creeps round her in the dark and kisses her forehead.

'Darling. I'm so sorry. These IRA bombs – we had to rejig the front page a hundred times, and then the reports kept coming and—'

'Where were they?'

'In Manchester! You didn't hear? Two IRA bombs went off this morning, one in Parsonage Gardens and another near the Anglican cathedral. How did you manage to be in Manchester and not hear about it?'

Kate, half asleep, can't think straight. Her head hurts – she'll have a hangover tomorrow – and her eyes are sore from crying. So that was why her journey had been difficult. Her mind had been so full of carpets, colours and Ali that she hadn't registered the closures were more than mere roadworks. In the house the radio is tuned permanently to BBC Radio 3, for Ali's sake. She hadn't bothered listening to the news. She remembered hearing someone in the office mention a bombing, but she hadn't imagined that such a thing could have happened right there.

'Darling, you've been crying.'

'I'm sorry,' says Kate. 'I had the dream again.'

4

Guy and Kate, with the children strapped into the back seat and Cassie confined to the luggage area, drive west across the windswept moor. As they descend past brown-red Victorian Macclesfield, the countryside softens. At this lower altitude, the trees seem happier to grow, crops push up green and hopeful in the spring fields and the children shout at the sight of lambs tottering about on unsteady legs.

'Mint sauce!' Guy says.

'Don't be horrid, Daddy,' Alicia chimes.

'I know these lanes so well, children, that I could do the whole drive in reverse gear,' Guy declares over his shoulder.

'You say that every time we come here,' Kate reminds him.

'Will you do it, Daddy? Just once?' Adrian begs. 'It'd be so cool.'

'I don't think Grandma would see it that way,' Kate says.

'*Please*, Dad?'

'Nearly there,' Guy announces. Alicia is singing to herself. Cassie shunts about, making the pleading noises that dogs make when they long to bound unleashed through open, green nature.

The house where Guy grew up stands in a tiny complex at the end of a tree-lined lane. He manoeuvres the car in a flamboyant semi-circle and reverses through the gate, which makes Adrian bounce with excitement. Alicia shouts, 'Grandma!'

Didie is in the drive to welcome them, wearing an apron emblazoned with a cartoon of a woman snoring happily on a

sofa while a frazzled man does the washing-up. Alicia charges
into her arms. 'What an affectionate child Ali is,' Didie often
says. Kate reflects quietly that a child's affection doesn't always
direct itself to the mother.

George is in the greenhouse, feeding his plants – he's growing
tomatoes, gooseberries, raspberries and a delicate, tangled
complex of sweet-peas. He loves retirement with a passion;
Didie insists he's busier now than he ever was in accountancy.
He wanders out, waving, then ushers them into the house for
a glass of refreshing sparkling wine.

Alicia doesn't follow them. A brook crosses the end of the
garden; she runs as fast as she can down the sloping lawn to
watch the ducks. Grandma Didie, knowing Alicia's Cheshire
routine, goes after her.

'These are mallards,' Grandma tells her, taking her hand to
stop her getting too close to the water's edge. She's brought
out some bread so that Alicia can feed them. 'The ducks with
green heads are the males and the brown, speckled ones are
the females.'

'They look like different kinds of duck,' Alicia remarks.

'Yes, but they're the same species. And they always know
that they belong together.'

Alicia tosses out a handful of bread and the ducks stream
towards it, ruffling the water, pecking at each other in their
haste. Then her eyes widen. 'Here they come!'

With a smooth motion at the bend in the brook, a line of
stately visitors glides into view. A large white swan sails ahead,
leading the procession; behind it swim three fluffy, grey cygnets;
another adult brings up the rear.

Alicia holds out her hands. Grandma fetches, from beside
the garden wall, two plastic bowls, which she fills with loose
stuff that reminds Alicia of Mum's breakfast cereal. Grandma
hands one bowl to her; she places it ceremoniously, in a familiar
ritual, on the grass by the stream.

One by one, the swans drift across and lumber out of the water towards the bowls, abruptly clumsy on their huge black feet. Alicia holds her breath. However often she's seen the swan family come to lunch, she can never quite believe it's real. 'Now will you do the other birds?' she asks.

Grandma winks. She takes two handfuls of seeds, goes to the middle of the lawn and whistles. A moment later the air is shivering with wings. Dark, speckled wings, rustling, swishing, diving. Alicia shrieks, then stops, trying not to scare them off: the starlings soar down from nowhere, some to peck the food from the grass, some to alight on Grandma's hand and grab a seed from her palm. A squirrel loops out of a bush; when Grandma bends and reaches out to it, it makes a lightning motion towards her, then bounces away, a hazelnut in its mouth.

'You can learn a lot from animals, Ali,' Grandma tells her softly. 'What do they say to you?'

'Dunno,' Alicia says. 'But I love them.'

'Why do you love them?'

'Because . . .' Alicia knows what she wants to say, but has trouble finding the words. Animals are easy. You know what they want; you know what they do. Sometimes, with people, you can't tell what they're going to do or say next.

'They're natural,' Grandma prompts her. 'It's lovely to be natural. Sometimes nature can be cruel, but mostly it's beautiful and good.'

Alicia drinks in the horizon of grassy hills and turquoise sky, and nods.

A volley of barks from Cassie, furious to have been shut inside while this goes on, sends the birds wheeling into the air. Alicia dances back to her dog. Adrian trails out of the house. 'Adie, we saw the swans and the ducks!' Alicia cries.

'I hate ducks,' says Adrian. 'They give me the creeps. Quack, quack, quack. They sound like Mum fussing over you.'

★   ★   ★

Didie has been busy in the kitchen, making a pot of vegetable soup, baking olive bread and setting out delicious bits and pieces from the village delicatessen. Guy and Kate prefer Didie's unpredictable feasts to the overcooked beef and soggy Yorkshire pudding that always greets them at Sunday lunches in Harrow (luckily, comparatively rare events). Didie displays roasted Italian peppers, sun-dried tomatoes and some Parma ham as if exhibiting them at the Chelsea Flower Show; in the centre a blue and white tiled platter, a souvenir from Amsterdam, is set with a selection of intriguingly patterned cheeses.

'"Cheese, please, Louise,"' Guy quotes.

'You always have to say that,' Kate growls.

'I remember,' says George. 'That advert, back in the sixties.'

'I don't remember the ad,' Guy says, 'but *you* always said, "Cheese, please, Louise", so it stuck.'

Kate finds that it's hard to laugh at a joke when you have heard it more than four thousand times.

'Then there's the baked beans one . . .' Guy begins to sing a decades-old jingle.

'Fresh out of baked beans, dears.' Didie notices Kate fidgeting. 'Adie, darling, have some more bread.'

'Don't like olive bread.'

'Where's Ali?' George asks.

'I know exactly where she is.' Didie smiles.

A thread of music reaches them from the lounge. Nobody thinks of confining Alicia to lunch when there's a piano around. She's had some food – and gone. The others fall silent, listening despite themselves.

'Did she bring her music?' George asks.

'No,' Kate says. 'She plays from memory.'

'Katie,' Didie says, 'I know I say this every time, but she's *musical*. She makes you listen to her, God knows how. She doesn't sound like a child who's only six years old. She plays like a real musician. How—?'

'Does she know?' Guy finishes the sentence. 'We don't understand either.'

'Didie . . .' Kate has been trying to pluck up the courage to face an issue that she doesn't want to face; if the answer is what she expects, her little girl is no longer a baby, but something much more complicated.

Didie's wise, dark eyes are all attention.

'Do you really think Ali has something extra? Some kind of natural gift? A vocation?'

'Anyone with half a brain can see that,' George declares. 'Katie, that granddaughter of mine is a flipping child prodigy.'

Kate looks at Didie, who nods.

There's a sound of heavy, childish footsteps and Alicia appears in the doorway. 'Come on, everyone!' she announces. 'I'm ready now.'

'She always has to do this.' Adrian kicks the table leg. 'It's boring! She always has to play. She always has to make everyone stop what they're doing and listen. I hate the piano.' He kicks harder.

'Adrian! Stop it!' Kate snaps.

'All right, Ali, let's be having you, then, lass.' George leads the way to the lounge. Cassie has already taken up her vantage-point beside the piano.

Her audience in place, Alicia goes out and conceals herself behind a wall. Then she marches in to obliging applause. She's big for her age, as Kate had been as a child; her feet and hands resemble the large paws that betray the size to which a lion cub will grow. She walks with the determination of a shot-putter and the pride of an Olympic champion, then bows as if she has never seen her family before.

She plays, in succession, all the pieces she has already run through in a rehearsal that she doesn't know is called a rehearsal. Her memory never falters. The piano hasn't been tuned for a year and some of the notes stick; Alicia pulls a face when she can't induce the exact sound she wants.

'Show-off,' Adrian grumbles.

Kate knows she isn't showing off. She is doing what an Alicia does. A swan knows that it must live upon water. Alicia, too, is a child of nature. She doesn't question why she is who she is, but she knows she must play a piano and she wants, instinctively, to play to people. There's no reason for it. It's just how Alicias are made.

Taking the baby Adrian in her arms for the first time, Kate's initial sensation was relief. The next was dismay. She'd expected something else. She wanted the feeling she'd experienced before: the sense that that helpless, microscopic creature needed her so much. The new infant was all he ought to have been. He weighed eight and a half pounds, yelled with well-formed lungs and wriggled and kicked with a vigour that told her he wanted to get away from her and head out to the football field, fast. She wasn't sure how to hold him, how to soothe him, how to breastfeed him. His greed left her nipples raw and painful. His restless nights meant that she had to walk him up and down the lounge for hours, jigging and humming, which seemed to make no difference.

She had what she'd wanted: a healthy baby. Yet now that she had one, she didn't know what to do with him.

'I can't help it,' she admitted to Guy one weekend, when Adrian was seven months old and they were all confined to the house with raging colds. 'I still keep looking at him and expecting to see Victoria.'

'Katie.' Guy's head was under a towel, where he was inhaling eucalyptus. 'Different baby. He's strong. He's normal. He laughs and cries and has a healthy appetite, and if you dropped him, he'd bounce. What more do you want?'

Kate could hardly disagree, but neither could she understand why she didn't love Adrian enough. Perhaps because he was a boy; his experience would never match hers. Or perhaps because he had committed the innocent yet cardinal sin of not being Victoria. When he eventually took the bottle instead of the breast, she felt guilty and relieved in almost equal measures – the balance favouring the relief.

Alicia arrived two years later, surrounded by magic numbers. She was Kate's third-born, thrice blessed. Her birthday was the third day of the seventh month and Kate laboured for seven hours to give birth to her. The sun was shining and Alicia's eyes were as blue as the sky when she first gazed upon it. And why Kate connected at once with this infant the way she could not with her sulky, whiny two-year-old – perhaps even more than with their sister, lying in the cemetery on the outskirts of Buxton – was something as mysterious to her as the birth of a child is in itself.

'Aren't there any of those little competitive music festivals in Derbyshire?'

Margaret, during one of the Davises' rare visits to Buxton, is pondering Alicia's future.

'She's too little.' Kate is terse, annoyed. Having her parents to stay, with their judgemental views on child-rearing, isn't her favourite way to spend a weekend.

'But these events are so good for children, dear. We put you in for your first one on that little three-quarter-sized violin when you were nine.'

'Ali is only seven. And you weren't too pleased when I started taking the viola seriously.'

'I'm not suggesting for a moment that Ali should follow this as a profession. Merely that you give her a chance to be motivated. Winning a prize . . .'

'In case you hadn't noticed, Mother, Ali *is* motivated. I can't keep her away from the thing. But she's too little to go on stage.'

'Maybe after another year, then. Depending on how she develops.'

'We'll see, Mother.'

Kate finds it difficult to keep the anger out of her voice. She's not sure which is worse: her mother advising her to follow the same course of action that had caused Kate herself so much pain, or the idea of Ali being turned into a performing monkey, to be gawped at by the good people of Derbyshire. A premonition slews through her mind: she'll have enough of this later.

From the *Buxton Advertiser*, 18 May 1995
ALICIA IN WONDERLAND

Little Alicia Bradley (left), 8, wields her trophy proudly after winning the Under-11s Piano Class in the Ashton Music Festival last week. 'I'm really happy,' the Buxton schoolgirl said. 'And my dad's pleased too.' Alicia Bradley's father, Guy, 39, is deputy editor of the *Manchester Chronicle*.

Alicia, with her long fair hair and blue dress, looked as if she had stepped from the pages of *Alice in Wonderland*. She played a movement from a Bach French Suite and the Waltz in D flat major by Chopin to gain her prize.

From the *Derbyshire Herald*, 10 July 1996
ALICIA PULLS IT OFF

Alicia Bradley (10) is the winner of this year's Under-12s piano class in the Derbyshire Festival. Alicia, described by her teacher Jonathan Bowen as 'the most talented pupil I've ever had', played alongside 15 other competitors to carry off the prize.

'I wasn't nervous,' Alicia said, backstage after performing a Mozart sonata and a Chopin mazurka, which drew gasps of delight from the audience. 'I never get nervous. I just enjoy playing. I love being on stage.'

Alicia's mother, Kate Bradley (40), says that Alicia gets up at six every morning to practise before school. 'It's part of her daily routine,' said Mrs Bradley.

What of Alicia's future? Could this Derbyshire lass one day

grace the platforms of the country's finest concert halls? 'Alicia has the natural gift to go anywhere she wants,' said Mr Bowen. 'But becoming a professional pianist takes a great deal of hard work and nothing in the musical world is ever certain, even for those who have such talent. I hope she has the chance to fulfil her potential in every way.'

From the *Sheffield Gazette*, 12 September 1998
PEAK DISTRICT PRODIGY

The North of England Festival yesterday made an unprecedented award to a 12-year-old girl from Buxton, Derbyshire. Instead of entering the Under-13s piano class, Alicia Bradley followed the suggestion of her Manchester-based teacher, the eminent professor Deirdre Butterworth, and performed in the Under-16s section. She faced stiff competition from students several years her senior.

Young Alicia wore a plain blue dress and flat shoes. She played a movement from Beethoven's 'Pathétique' Sonata, Mendelssohn's 'Spring Song' and a challenging piece by Debussy entitled 'Gardens in the Rain'. 'I live in Buxton, so I know a bit about rain,' Alicia joked afterwards, preparing to pin up her certificate on a bedroom wall that, according to her mother, Kate Bradley, is crowded with similar success stories.

Mrs Bradley, 42, has recently resigned from her job as a solicitor in Buxton to concentrate on taking care of her exceptional daughter. 'Alicia's talent demands complete commitment from us as her parents,' she explains. She ferries Alicia weekly to Manchester for lessons with Mrs Butterworth, who was recommended to the family by Alicia's former teacher, Jonathan Bowen, until last term head of music at Parkhill School where Alicia is now a pupil. This month he takes up a post as head of music at Elthingbourne College, Dorset.

'We couldn't be happier,' said her proud mother. 'I can imagine no better vocation than giving Alicia the attention, help and support that she needs.'

'Are you sure?' says Guy.

'One good reason why not?' asks Kate.

'You're good at your job. Your clients like you. Mike values you.'

'What you mean is, because you're at work the whole time, I should be as well. Because otherwise I'll just be at home wondering where you are.'

'Katie, for heaven's sake—'

'Well? Isn't that so?'

'I worry that you're going to be lonely.'

'I want to be there for Ali. If I can help her with her practising and drive her to her lessons and yell at the school when they try to make her play dangerous ball games, then my time will be well spent.' She doesn't meet his gaze.

Every Wednesday Kate bundles Alicia into the car with her books of music, which now include the second volume of Beethoven's piano sonatas, as well as Chopin's Études and Rachmaninov's Preludes. Alicia finishes school early on Wednesdays. The other kids have sport, drama and occasional outings to local stately homes or walks on the moors; Alicia goes to her piano lesson in Manchester.

Mrs Butterworth teaches at her home, a double-fronted Edwardian house in Withington, its front garden florid with lilacs. She lives alone; Mr Butterworth, an architect, has been dead for years. Kate's tentative enquiries about what had happened to him produce a stony response.

Jonathan's recommendation hadn't been without sub-clauses and small print: 'She's tough but very effective, and she'll equip Ali with a sound technique for life,' he'd said. 'She's controversial in some circles, she's not for everyone, but I have great respect for her. Why not just see how you get along?'

'When I met my husband in 1965 and set up my teaching practice,' Mrs Butterworth tells Kate, at Alicia's initial consultation, 'I had to contend with the fact that there is no *system* in this country. Children do well at school, they go to good universities, they do sport, sport and more sport. But music? Forget it. There's no system.'

'What about the Associated Board exams?' Kate asks.

'Oh, yes. Music exams.' Mrs Butterworth stifles a yawn.

Kate stares at Mrs Butterworth's hair, mid-brown and bundled into a chignon above the tiny, light-boned figure that she makes up for with force of presence. She wonders whether the chignon is a wig.

'Everything here,' the sharp-eyed teacher carries on, 'is built around helping amateur children to impress amateur parents. They play nicely to the dinner guests and sometimes they play for school assembly and everybody claps. They're nice, middle-class children showing off, by implication, what nice, middle-class parents they have. Isn't that *nice*? That, Mrs Bradley, Alicia, is not what my teaching is about.'

Kate nods. She's starting, unaccountably, to like Mrs Butterworth. She may seem a tad scary, with her uncompromising manner and fierce gaze, but she knows all about the social scene that had damaged Kate so much.

'No!' Mrs Butterworth slaps a hand against the arm of her chair. Kate jumps. 'The British view music as a diversion, an amusement, something that it's not quite cricket to be too good at. If you're talented, people think you must be a snobby little élitist. But in Paris, where I studied first, young pianists were properly equipped with technique from the start, both pianistic and musical. They learned *solfège*. They could play anything in any key. And in Russia, where I studied for years, great art was almost a matter of life and death. I have a talented student. He's twenty-one, he's going to play in America for the first time. And his visa says 'Entertainer'. At the Moscow Conservatoire we were taught to be *artists*. Not clowns. Not acrobats. Not fire-eaters. Those are entertainers. We have something profound to say about life, why we're alive, what it means to be human. We don't jump through hoops to show our parents' friends how talented our parents' offspring are. Now, *do you understand?*'

Kate flinches, but declares, with feeling, 'I certainly do.'

'And you?' Mrs Butterworth's piercing gaze falls on Alicia, who has been sitting, silent, in the corner of a large leather sofa, one hand on Cassie's head (fortunately Mrs Butterworth likes dogs). 'Are you ready? Because this isn't going to be fun and games. This is not an afternoon out, enjoying yourself. You've been playing at playing. You have talent, young lady, but you've barely scratched the surface of the technique you need if you're going to make music your life. If you come to me, Alicia, you will be working harder than you've ever imagined. But remember this: what you sow, you reap. And when you come out, you won't be an English amateur. You'll be ready to become an artist. Is that what you want?'

Kate watches Alicia raise her chin, look Mrs Butterworth in the eye, and say, 'Yes.'

The reality is less easy to accept.

Mrs Butterworth sets her three times as much work as Jonathan had. The studies by Pischna and Moszkowski are supposed to stretch her – but it takes three hours at the piano every day to get through them and all the new pieces, without the frequent playing-through that is, naturally, what Alicia likes best. That's forbidden, and would be even if she could already play, fluently, every note on the pages. As for the scales—

'I can't,' says Alicia, at six thirty one freezing January morning.

'You can. You always have,' Kate reminds her.

'Not Russian scales. Not now.'

Russian scales involve processes that Kate suspects Jonathan Bowen has never heard of. Alicia starts at the bottom of the keyboard and goes up the scale for two octaves. Then her right hand continues up for another two octaves while her left hand goes back down in 'contrary motion'. Both hands return to where they left off; in 'similar motion' they continue up another two octaves then down the same two octaves; then part company for two octaves, back and forth, in contrary motion; finally they run back to the starting point at the bottom. She has to play this pattern fluently and fast in every key. Next she has to do the same, but with her hands a third apart and then a sixth apart; with different kinds of touch – legato, non-legato, staccato; and in rhythms that Kate hadn't realised scales could have.

As for the technical studies, each has to be played accurately in its original key – then transposed into any key that Mrs Butterworth happens to name. A piece in E major must suddenly be played in B flat major. Alicia's unerring ear is an advantage. But for every triumph, there is a stiff price (apart from Mrs Butterworth's fee, which, compared to Jonathan's, is from another planet). One task successfully accomplished means another for next week commensurately more demanding – set not with praise for Alicia's achievement but with a brusque, wordless nod. It reminds Kate, applying ash-blonde colourant in the bathroom, of the rumour that if you pull out one grey hair, two, twice as strong, will grow in its place.

'I can't,' says Alicia.

'You must,' says Kate.

'I can't,' Alicia says, in the car, a year later, outside Mrs Butterworth's house in Withington. 'I can't go in.'

'Ali, we've been here for fifteen minutes and it's not going to get any easier. The longer you leave it, the harder it will be. So go in. *Now.*'

Alicia gets out and walks slowly up to Mrs Butterworth's house. There she slumps on to the step with her back to the door, head in her hands. Cassie, confined to the car, watches, whines and barks.

Kate follows Alicia and sits down next to her. A film of sweat laces Alicia's forehead, and she is breathing too hard.

'Ali, are you all right?'

'No! I'm bloody petrified!'

'Language. Please. Darling.'

'You try, then! You don't know what it's like because she won't let you in the room while it's going on!'

'Ali. Sssh. It's going to be fine. You've made so much progress—'

'I can't go in.'

Kate puts an arm round her shoulders and holds her. 'Got the envelope?' she asks. Mrs Butterworth likes to be paid her substantial fee in cash, in a white envelope that must be handed over upon the student's arrival. Her eyes gleam when her fingers close round it, Alicia reports. Kate, listening to her description, tries not to imagine an iguana curling its tongue over a fly. 'In you go. OK?'

Alicia rises on shaky feet and presses the bell.

The latest festival, delivering Alicia's biggest trophy to date, declared her its most gifted winner ever. Alicia had accepted with the requisite modesty. It's not really *done* to admit the hours of slog involved – somehow the public expects music to be as natural as breathing – so Alicia says little about how hard she works. Kate says nothing to her interested neighbours or her book club (discussing *Captain Corelli's Mandolin* over coffee at the Pavilion Gardens) of the way she too gets up at six and stands directing Alicia like a conductor. 'Again! And again! Once more for luck . . . Now try it in D minor . . . and F minor . . .' She doesn't even tell Glenda, whom she sees frequently and who always wants to hear about Alicia's progress. Some instinct tells her that Glenda might respond in the wrong way.

'Katie,' Guy says wearily, searching for his keys one morning, 'Ali's only thirteen. This is ridiculous.'

'I didn't ask her to be talented,' Kate retorts. 'I didn't ask her to want to be a pianist. But she can't have it both ways. She can't expect to be what she wants to be without hard work.'

'On Sunday afternoon, why don't we go out, like a normal family? We'll go for a walk at Dovedale, or we could take the kids to Alton Towers . . .'

'Ali can't go to Alton Towers. The rides are too dangerous.'

'No, they're not. Thousands of kids do those rides every day.'

'Thousands of kids don't depend on their hands for their career.'

'Oh, it's a career now, is it?'

'To me, this hardly looks like a hobby.'

'I've got to go. I'll be late for the editorial meeting. Have you seen my keys?'

'Just keep track of your own damn keys for once!' Kate slams the lounge door.

'Oh, Mum,' comes Alicia's muffled, tearful voice from the direction of the piano, 'please don't yell at Dad. It's not his fault.'

5

They go to Dovedale, not Alton, for a January Sunday of fresh air, exercise and countryside. In summer, they avoid this walk – it's one of the Peak District's top tourist favourites, thanks to its deep-sliced, relatively sheltered valley and a set of wide stepping-stones upon which everyone loves to leap across the fast-flowing River Dove. But today only hardened locals are about, greeting each other when they pass on the pathway; the sole tourists are a distressed-looking Spanish couple who aren't used to the cold.

Walking is good for us, Kate reminds herself, tucking her scarf into her padded jacket. Walking is when talking can take place, assuming it ever will.

It's freezing, but unusually bright; the air feels as if it's been poured out of a mountain glacier; the river, swollen with winter rain and melted ice, dances along its pebble-strewn bed more excitably than usual. Alicia, high on freedom, taps her brother's shoulder. 'Race you!' she shouts – and they're off, running, yelling and pushing each other like any teenage brother and sister in the sunlight. Cassie bounds along beside them. Guy and Kate, watching, join hands.

'Let's stop at the Hartington cheese shop on the way back and get some Stilton,' Kate suggests.

'"Cheese, please, Louise."' Guy looks at her from the corner of his eye. 'We could try their Wensleydale with cranberries for a change.'

Kate smiles. She's enjoying this. It's a long time since the Bradleys last had an afternoon out. With the demands of Guy's office, never mind the Derbyshire weather, they're lucky if they have even one Sunday each month on which they could, potentially, go for a walk. But Guy is still a hiker, the way Ali is a pianist, a swan is a waterbird and Adrian is – whatever Adrian really is, which so far hasn't become apparent.

They cross the arching wooden footbridge and Guy sets a brisk pace along the riverside path, his boots laced up to his ankles, a stick in one hand and one of Kate's home-knitted scarves round his neck.

'Adie, don't!' Kate hears Alicia say.

There's a plop and an angry rustle of wings and webbed feet on water: Adrian is throwing stones at ducks from the riverbank.

'Adrian! Stop it!' Kate runs towards him. 'What do you think you're doing?'

'I hate ducks. They're disgusting. I hate the noise they make.'

Kate senses the eyes of at least five other huddles of walkers burning into her and her peculiar son. The poor ducks: helpless scapegoats for a lot else that Adrian hates. 'I don't care whether you like them or not,' she snaps. 'You're not going to throw stones at them.'

'You're talking to me like I'm a kid.'

Adrian's dark eyes are so resentful that an image of a changeling with horns skids across Kate's retinas.

'If you behave like one, what do you expect?'

Guy is keeping a safe distance; she wonders vaguely why he doesn't come to help her with a little discipline. He looks oddly distant; as if only half of him is standing in Dovedale waiting for his family to get its act together. Exasperated, Kate turns her attention back to her teenagers. Someone has to.

Alicia and Adrian barely seem like siblings, though physically they are almost replicas of their parents. Adrian could have been made to a template of Guy aged fifteen and Alicia to one of Kate at thirteen – but for the addition, in Adrian's case, of rapidly increasing height, complicated by a taut, sizzling frustration that resembles a furious wasp; and, in Alicia's case, an inbuilt candle flame that reignites no matter how hard anyone tries to extinguish it. Ali, Kate fancies, represents day and Adrian night. She and Guy are the opposite. Guy is the warm, active sun and she – even if she wasn't always – has become the moon, filled with inexpressible shadows in shades of deepening grey.

'What do you think?' Guy is asking her.

'Sorry, I missed that. I was miles away.'

'About Adrian and school. Mr Browning didn't mince his words.'

The parents' evening two days earlier hadn't been the best of occasions. First, the PE teacher had had views on Alicia's music. 'Such a pity she can't enjoy the piano as part of a broad spectrum of interests,' she'd remarked. 'It seems rather sad and a little precious that she must miss out on hockey to protect her hands. It's not like she's going to be Daniel Barenboim.' Kate, furious, had demanded, 'Have you *heard* her play?' and the woman had admitted she hadn't. As for Adrian's Mr Browning—

'He doesn't mix easily with the others, though, goodness knows, fifteen is a tricky age,' he'd remarked. 'He's a good lad, though. He's good at French.'

'French? Adrian?' Kate was incredulous.

'And art. He's a creative boy, but complicated. Angry, I'd say.'

'I'd had the impression he wasn't much good at anything,' Kate admitted. 'Getting him to do his homework is a daily battle. He only wants to watch television.'

'Like every other lad his age. Perhaps a little more encouragement?'

'It's not like we don't try.'

'He's capable of doing well. He's bright,' Mr Browning

affirmed, shaking their hands. Just as they began to move away, he cleared his throat. 'Um, Mrs Bradley. Are you aware that Adrian didn't come in on Wednesday?'

'Wednesday? This last Wednesday?' A brake screeched in Kate's brain. 'I was out all day after twelve – it's Ali's piano lesson on Wednesday – but as far as I know Adrian went to school in the morning.'

'I'd like you to keep half an eye on him. Make sure he's where he should be when he should be. All right?'

Now, in the ravine beneath the steep hills and bare trees, Kate looks at Adrian's back a little way ahead: dark hair, fleecy jacket, a determined walk, as if he's been watching gangster movies and is bent on emulating them. He's growing fast; perhaps his build is following her father's. William had been a keen rugby player and still looked the part, tall, broad and hulking. He'd been a Boy Scout and a prefect at public school; he'd done a stint in the army. He and Margaret go to church every Sunday. He'd had a calling, Kate thinks, to be *good*. Adrian, though, moves between shadows and light without noticing the difference.

Kate can hear a thread of music through the soft rush of the river. Alicia is singing to herself.

'I guess it's not easy to be her brother,' Guy remarks quietly.

'Do you think it's true about him not going to school last Wednesday?'

'Wednesday?' Guy echoes.

Suddenly he isn't with her any more. He's – somewhere else. What had happened on Wednesday? Kate remembers the day she'd failed to hear about the IRA bombings and wonders what she's missed this time.

They turn back after an hour, the children and dog well exercised, Kate chilly, tired and aware of something uncomfortable in her husband's state of being. All of them are looking forward to a good hot drink from the wooden coffee and ice-cream stall beside the car park. On the final stretch, Kate and

Alicia hurry ahead for the loos; Guy goes to buy some tea. Adrian waits with Cassie on the riverside path, upstream from the weir.

When Kate and Alicia return, the spot that had held boy and dog is empty.

'Adrian!' shouts Kate.

Guy comes up the path, two cups of tea and two of hot chocolate balanced between his hands.

'Where's Adrian? Where's the dog?' Kate demands.

'Probably throwing stones at ducks again,' Alicia grumbles. As she speaks, there's a splash and a shout, and before she knows what she's doing, Kate is running, terror-stricken, across the muddy stretch of grass and bracken towards the riverbank, her walking-boots too heavy on her feet.

'Adrian!'

The boy, who'd been hidden by a clump of bushes, comes out into the open and Kate gasps with relief – until she sees that his eyes are fixed on the water, a pair of pointed ears and a set of frantic, scrabbling paws. Cassie loves to splash about in shallow rivers, but she's not used to this powerful winter current. Somehow she's paddled further in than she should have and the water has grabbed her, threatening to sweep her away towards the narrow yet treacherous stone weir.

'Cassie!' yells Alicia. Before Kate can grab hold of her, she's off.

Everything happens so fast that Kate barely has time to take it in. Yet those twenty seconds also move in slow motion, opaque beads of spray springing around Alicia as she charges into the water. Kate hears herself scream, 'Ali, *no!*'

'Ali, come back!' Guy rushes after her.

A crowd of fellow walkers assembles to try to help. 'Call the warden!' someone shouts. 'The poor things, they'll freeze!'

Alicia is reaching towards the struggling Cassie, wading forward through the surging current. Guy stumbles towards her and grabs her waist. Alicia gives a shout of protest, turns and, as Kate watches, misses her footing, felling them both. Alicia is briefly submerged; Guy, picking himself up and trying to pull her out, twists, then yelps as if in pain. At the same moment, someone bumps into Kate and the jolt sets off tears of fright that she doesn't want to shed in front of her son. Why can't she turn the clock back just ten minutes? How could she have been stupid enough to leave Adrian to his own devices? This is his fault, which means it's hers.

'There, there, love, they'll be all right.' A stranger's arm is round her shoulders. 'The river's not deep. Don't you worry, we'll have them out in no time.'

'My little girl,' Kate chokes out. She feels faint; black dots fizz behind her eyes. It's the shock, the anger and, of course, the alarm that assails her as it always has when Alicia is in danger.

A big, sopping, brown and white shape is loping towards her; stopping nearby, it shakes a fountain of river water out of its long-haired coat before leaping up to lick her face. Cassie is fine. Just a dog going for a swim, her big, innocent eyes tell Kate. Dogs like swimming. What's wrong with that?

Kate rubs tears and wet dog out of her face and sees Guy and Alicia, supporting each other, hobbling along the riverbank. Guy releases his drenched daughter, then flops on to the grass, clutching his foot.

'Mum, is Cassie OK?' pleads the saturated Alicia. Water is streaming from her clothes and hair.

'You *stupid* girl! What the hell did you think you were doing?' Kate explodes.

'Katie.' Guy, on the ground, is ashen. 'I think I've broken something. I bashed my ankle and it's bloody excruciating.'

Alicia, hugging her sodden dog, is shivering.

'Guy, we've got to get Ali home, she'll catch her death. Can you walk to the car?'

Guy, who's shivering too, tries to stand up, but can't.

'Ali, are your hands OK?' Kate demands.

Alicia nods, big-eyed and shame-faced.

Adrian is hanging his head in a way that Kate recognises. 'Adrian, why did you let Cassie go into the water?'

'But, Mum, she just, like, went off and—'

'And what were *you* doing? Can't I trust you to be on your own without causing trouble for even two minutes?'

Guy has been helped up and is now supported by the girl from the coffee stall on one side and Alicia on the other. Together they manage to manoeuvre him across the last hundred yards to the car. Kate takes the driving seat and rifles through the road atlas to locate the nearest hospital with an A and E department. Guy, beside her, props up his injured foot on his backpack; he breathes deeply, trying to bear the pain. Kate pulls off her own jersey and insists Alicia wears it instead of her wet clothes. Alicia huddles in the back seat, sipping hot chocolate. Cassie, in the rear, and Adrian, beside Alicia, are in disgrace.

Kate stews together relief, fury and a perplexed sensation that she can't identify. *What kind of a child rushes into a winter river to save her dog?* It's unthinking instinct. The urge to rescue something she loves.

Alicia grins at her mother in the mirror. 'Dad saved me,' she declares.

'Just don't ever make me do it again,' Guy groans.

Guy is trying to hide extra distress that he's afraid Kate will notice: there's more on his mind than a broken ankle.

'Bosnia?' said Martin.

'Sarajevo,' said Emily Andersen.

Guy and Martin, as deputy editor and editor, were spending Wednesday afternoon interviewing candidates for the post of staff reporter.

'This is what I wrote. And here are the photos.' Emily handed

Martin a plastic folder. Guy took in the headline, the pock-marked walls, the dark-eyed children.

'It was an incredible project.' Emily's voice cracked a little as the memory moved her. 'The way music helped those children was one of the most extraordinary things I've ever seen. It taps into emotions they can't express any other way.'

Guy glanced at Martin's notepad, where the editor had written:

BAGS OF INITIATIVE

BAGS OF COMMITMENT

NICE TITS

'I know certain parts of the north-west can resemble a war zone at times,' Martin was saying, 'but your work here would be a little more mundane. You'd be reporting on issues like cleanliness in hospitals, talking to people having diffi-culty paying their council tax or, if you're lucky, rooting out corruption in the running of a posh golf club. How are you going to feel about that after your freelance adven-tures?'

'Fine,' Emily said. 'That's what I need at the moment.'

'So, basically, you'd like a salary because you want to settle down?'

'I want a place of my own, I want to live near my mother, because she's alone now, and I'd like a little more security in my life.'

Emily looked each of them in the eye. She had a strong, direct gaze, neither aggressive nor defensive. Her eyes were a peculiar silvery grey. Her father, who had died a year ago, had been Danish and she'd spent her early years in Aarhus. Her hair was brown, but shone gold when sunlight struck it. Her skin was fair, her mouth wide and full-lipped. She had shortish legs, a deeply curved lower back and a generous, spreading behind. Her CV told Guy that she was thirty.

'Any special enthusiasms – other than war zones – that you'd like to be writing about?' Martin asked her.

'I love walking, which is another reason I want to live here. I love music, and I'd like to write about that more than I do. But I like talking to people about what's important to them. I like being in the middle of things.'

'Pressure? Deadlines?'

'No problem. I work well under pressure.'

'Which are your favourite walks?' Guy asked her. He didn't know why. The words slipped out before he could stop them.

'The Peak District,' Emily replied, unhesitating. 'I love it. One day I'd like to live in one of those wonderful villages in Derbyshire, like Castleton.'

'Castleton!' Guy echoed. 'I go there whenever I can! And do you know the cheese factory at Hartington?'

'Best Stilton in the country!' Emily's face lit up.

Perhaps at this moment, or perhaps earlier – he would never be certain of anything except that it had happened – a synapse in Guy's mind flipped silently inside out. 'Did you ever try their Wensleydale with cranberries?' he was saying, semi-conscious yet super-conscious.

Martin cleared his throat softly, with a pointed glance at the office clock.

'Anything else we can tell you about, Emily?' he said. 'Apart from Wensleydale with cranberries?'

Guy sat alone in his office with his face in his hands. He pressed his eyelids with his fingers until he saw rippling patterns in red and orange rolling from left to right.

This, he reminded himself, is one of the greatest mysteries known to mankind. One moment you're having a normal day; the next, you look into a stranger's face and recognise it, as if you and she have known one another for longer than both of you have been alive. You love your job. You meet fascinating situations, interesting people and beautiful women all the time. But this experience is beyond you. There's no obvious reason for it. Of course there's beauty in the soul of someone who's moved by music therapy for children in Sarajevo and who's brave enough to go there to write about it; and there's beauty in grey eyes and soft, shining hair. But why she should give him the jolt of recognition that changes the structure of the world in one stroke – that nobody can explain; and nothing can change it now that it's happened.

He wasn't sure which would be worse: Emily getting the job, or Emily not getting the job. If she did, he'd have to see her around the office, make chit-chat with her in the canteen, sit across the table from her at meetings, have her presence constantly, excruciatingly close. A small, quiet pressure, like water-torture. Perhaps he should insist that they don't accept her; he should say she was too ambitious and internationally minded for a provincial paper. She'd use them as a stepping-stone and move on.

The alternative, though, was never to see her again. And that he couldn't stand. His world was half the world it had been two hours earlier.

'So, Guy, what do you make of our candidates?' Martin wandered into Guy's office and sat down.

'Thinking it over. What about you?'

'Emily Andersen is head and shoulders above the others.'

Guy thought of the scribbled notes on Martin's pad. Emily did have nice tits, it was undeniable, but that, oddly, didn't matter to him. It wasn't what he saw when he looked at her. *O she doth teach the torches to burn bright.* Nice tits you can deal with. Shakespearean *coups-de-foudre* you can't. 'I wonder whether she'll stay, given that she's so talented,' he said. Perhaps it would be better to prise her out of the picture before she'd entered it.

'Yes, she may not be a staff reporter for long,' Martin assents. 'But there's plenty of room for someone so bright to climb the ladder. I think we should grab her. I'll draft the letter right away. OK?'

So Emily Andersen is about to join the *Manchester Chronicle* and not only Guy's ankle, but also his mind is in splinters.

Guy makes his way to his desk under the eaves; the sound of Alicia's piano drifts from the lounge. Going upstairs takes a long time with his injury. Now that he's there, he may as well stay. He pushes aside a pile of papers on the floor, unlocks the desk's bottom drawer and takes out a yellow note-book he hasn't looked at for years. This was the book in which he used to attempt to write poetry. It's been a decade or more since he last tried, but he still keeps it near him, just in case. He leafs through the pages, noticing the long-term evolution of his own handwriting. These days, it's no longer the impulsive scrawl of an ambitious youngster; it's smaller, marginally neater, but the pressure is stronger, the lines fuller and more sensual.

He reads words he barely remembers writing, phrases about the mystery of balance between life and death, as fine as a skein of silk; about painful inability to get through to the person you love, however much you adore them; about the way a landscape can be part of you and you a part of it, as if you are made of earth, stone and water. Some of the poems, he acknowledges, are appalling. Others aren't as bad as he'd expected. He opens a fresh page and makes a mark on it with a ballpoint pen. The words won't come. He may be a writer, but even he can't find the language to express the cataclysmic shock of looking into Emily Andersen's face.

There's a knock on the door. Guy shoves the notebook under a heap of paid bills awaiting filing (as they have been for several months).

Kate looks round the door, her gaze taking in Guy Bradley in his natural habitat: papery chaos. 'Coffee?' she says.

'Darling, you're a mind-reader.' Guy pushes his chair back

and pats his knee. Kate comes over, casting around for spare desk space on which to balance the coffee cup. She perches briefly on his lap and kisses his nose.

'It's wonderful being home,' Guy says. 'Can't we go to bed while the kids are at school?'

'It's Wednesday,' Kate points out. 'It's Ali's lesson.'

'Tomorrow, then.'

'What about your foot?'

'I don't need my foot in bed.' Wednesday again, thinks Guy. It's a whole week ago; yet only a week. He's acting out the self he had been then. He's speaking on automatic pilot words he'd have spoken genuinely just eight days ago.

'When did you last tidy up in here?' his wife asks.

'I can't find anything if I tidy up.'

'But all these filing cabinets—'

'When I file things, I can't remember what I filed them under. This way I know where things are. There's method to my madness, Katie.'

'Glad to hear it.' Kate makes for the door. 'I have to get Ali ready to go.'

Kate. The same Kate he'd always loved, but remoulded by life like a pebble watered and whittled under the stream. The same, yet not the same. In the woman he can still see the girl, the golden-haired student with her extraordinary smile in the Cheviot rain, but he can never grasp the essence of what makes her herself. How can he imagine that he understands Emily Andersen, after a single meeting, as securely as if she were his twin? Is he going crazy?

With a pounding noise on the stairs, Alicia is there, a bolt of electricity bowling towards him. Her arms fly round his neck and her warm cheek presses against his.

'Darling,' he says. 'Have a good lesson.'

'Dad, I wish you were home all the time!' She kisses him noisily beside one ear. 'Gotta run, see you later.' And she's gone.

Stranded at home, he's been listening to her practising, with incomprehension, delight and deep-seated fear. Hearing her soar through Beethoven's 'Les Adieux' Sonata, he can't help wondering what her gift means for her future; all their futures. 'A good servant but a bad master,' was how Margaret had once described Kate's passion for the viola. The piano was neither servant nor master to Alicia: she simply couldn't do without it. He thought of her running through Dovedale, her fair hair flying, before she went charging into the river after her dog. One moment she was a normal child. The next, she was not.

Now, from the low-set loft window, Guy can see her climbing into the car beside Kate, cradling a bulging music case. Guy has never met Mrs Butterworth. He doesn't like the sound of her and he doesn't like the way she makes Alicia spend her time. When he hears the finger exercises, the studies, the transpositions, the Russian scales, he can't help wishing that his daughter had been good at netball or gymnastics instead.

He rubs his eyes. He's not sleeping. He's told Kate it's because of the pain in his ankle. When he goes back to work, Emily Andersen will be at her new desk, waiting to greet him with her eyes like pewter planets and her wide smile and her skin that he wants to touch so badly that he doesn't know how he can look at her again without doing so. He'd forgotten what it's like to want anything so much.

And what would happen? Supposing his feelings aren't one-sided? There'd be no stopping it. If he had an affair with one of his journalists and the company found out, he'd have to resign. If Kate found out, he'd have to leave home. How would he feel now, if the door were to open – a different door in a different home – and his wife said, 'Coffee, darling?' yet the wife was not Kate, but Emily?

And Alicia wouldn't dash in and embrace him; he would no longer hear her practising; he wouldn't be there to give her the support she needed as she followed her gift. How could he bear that? His mind is running away with him. He knows he's thinking nonsense, but he thinks it all the same.

His foot aches in its plaster cast, helpless, hurting and immobilised.

6

Mrs Butterworth sends Alicia into her studio and gives Kate a conspiratorial wink. The sound of warm-up exercises reaches the front room. Kate smiles automatically. She has a wary respect for her daughter's teacher and her perfectly placed wig (it has *got* to be a wig).

'Katherine, I would like a quick word if you have time,' Mrs Butterworth says. She is the only person who insists on calling Kate Katherine. It's disconcerting, especially as Kate dares not call Mrs Butterworth by her first name, Deirdre. Mrs Butterworth pats a cushion on the sofa and Kate sits down, obedient as any pupil.

'Your daughter,' Mrs Butterworth begins, 'is a talented girl. Are you serious about her career?'

'Do you think she can have a career?'

'Katherine, I believe that Alicia is not only a good pianist but potentially a great one. She has something exceptional. She has charisma.'

'I always feel there's something radiant in her,' Kate says, nodding. 'But it's difficult for me to judge.'

'Of course. I know how this feels.' Mrs Butterworth's eyes seem to cloud for a moment.

Kate glances round the room for signs of grown-up children – postcards, photographs, mementoes. There are none. 'So you think . . .' she prompts.

'Yes. But there is something she needs. I know it's asking a lot. Grand pianos are not cheap, but without one she's handicapped. Working on an upright is fine for most schoolgirls.

But to develop as an artist, to form a sense of colour, nuance, a full range of dynamics, Alicia must have a grand piano, and a good one. Otherwise when she gives a concert, she will play a grand piano and not know how to handle it.'

Kate moistens her lips and her fingers twitch a little. She wishes she had her knitting. 'How much *do* grand pianos cost, Mrs Butterworth?'

Kate drives into the centre of Manchester and makes for the city's largest music shop. The ground floor is occupied by racks of sheet music and CDs. There Kate notices a section marked SOLO PIANO and browses through the discs. Each bears a picture of a beaming or brooding virtuoso, or a painting to match the character of the music. The pianists, scores of them, some alive, some long dead, are in alphabetical order from Martha Argerich to Krystian Zimerman. Only a few are women; very few are British. Alicia is up against long odds.

A CD under NEW RELEASES catches her eye: the Chopin Études. Alicia struggles daily with these. The pianist is French. Kate doesn't recognise his name, Lucien Delamain. The front cover shows a personable man, about her own age: dark, smiling, clad in polo-necked jersey and tweed jacket, against a blurry background of winter trees and pale sky. On the back, press quotes declare Delamain 'inspired', 'exciting' and 'a poet of the piano'. That sounds good, so Kate buys the disc. Then she goes down to the basement, which houses the piano department.

Kate had never realised how many different permutations of wood, strings, felt, imitation ivory and gleaming pedals pass by the name of PIANO. To one side masses an array of electronic instruments, from basic keyboards played through earphones – like heads that have lost their bodies – to sophisticated creations that appear to be normal pianos, but can be transformed into electronic ones at the flick of a switch. Next, she spots a group of new, clean, unbattered uprights, which show how well-worn their own has become. And at the far end, the grands stretch out like a pride of lions, black and white teeth bared, proud of their glowing cases. Some are french-polished in matt black, others coated with veneers of mahogany, rosewood or richly gnarled walnut.

Among them stands a black, nine-foot concert grand, its lid raised, its trademark in gold letters reading STEINWAY. Kate runs her fingers softly over the keyboard and the piano purrs in fine, sensual response. How extraordinary that human beings could invent such a bizarre contraption to make music; how strange that a child could be born with a natural affinity for something so contrived.

Then she sees the price tag.

Outside, Kate turns away and plods through the dank afternoon. There's a possible alternative, though she doesn't much like it. At Alicia's music festivals, talking to other competitors' parents, she's been garnering information about different options for educating musical children. In an ancient building, one of Manchester's oldest – complete with baronial hall and historic library – there is a specialist music school. Its gifted pupils study music alongside normal lessons. Most of them are boarders.

Before long Kate finds it. It's built of dark brick, encompassing gloomy archways and a Gothic courtyard; only a modern wing beyond the entrance gate betrays the fact that it's a functioning, contemporary school. From the windows drift the clank of pianos, a glimmer of a flute, the deep song of a cello. If Ali were to join this school, she'd be among children and teachers who understood her. Kate can't deny that Ali's school, so far, has been remarkably accommodating to her needs and proud of her achievements. But the thinning-out of birthday-party invitations from classmates, a running battle with one PE teacher and two exam papers – physics and chemistry – that had appeared almost unmarkable are proof that normal school and Ali aren't particularly compatible.

But Ali would have to go, physically *go*, to Manchester. The whole family could move there, of course, but that would also mean uprooting the already troublesome Adrian and sending him to an inner-city comprehensive, which Kate doesn't fancy. Assuming that isn't an option, Ali would have to board or, alternatively, commute. Theoretically she could travel with Guy; but then she'd spend more than two hours a day in a car, time in which she could neither practise nor do homework; and there'd be late evenings, because Guy often works until eight and sometimes ten. Ali would be sitting in school, practising there, waiting – then she'd come home, exhausted. But if she were to board, she wouldn't be home at all.

Without Ali, Kate would be alone. Guy's working hours are utterly antisocial. Adrian isn't interested in keeping his mother company; he's either out with his friends, mooching about the Pavilion Gardens, or in his room watching TV (she hadn't wanted him to have a TV, but since Ali practises ever longer in the lounge, it seemed only fair). And though Kate goes to her book club and meets fellow reading enthusiasts, neighbours or mothers for occasional lunches, there's nobody in Buxton to whom she feels genuinely close. Glenda Fairburn is the only other music-oriented woman she knows there, and Glenda has her hands full these days with her own children.

Kate can hardly remember what it's like to have a close friend. She'd lost touch with her old university companions after Victoria – how unfair it would be, she'd felt, to unload her grief upon them. With the move to Buxton, the uprooting had been complete. She, or maybe Guy, had imagined that a good-sized guest room would be ample temptation for visitors; but those visitors tend to be William and Margaret, who leave Guy fuming, or, rarely, Joanna, or Anthony and his family, who are worse.

Joanna, still single, works for a merchant bank and enjoys a lavish lifestyle with frequent postings abroad – most recently to San Francisco, where she hopes to stay. Anthony, who'd set up home in Harrow near their parents, has a wife named Fiona whom Kate and Guy describe to each other as '*so* nice, *but* –'; and their three children don't make life easy for Alicia and Adrian when they visit. They shiver in the icy Buxton wind, grumble when it rains – as it frequently does – and want to know where the *real* shops are. In the last year or two, the three 'Horribles' (as, to Kate's chagrin, her son and daughter call them in private) have become wary of their country cousins. They court Alicia at her piano as if trying to tempt a beautiful Persian cat into a garden – she seems exotic to them, which is fair enough since none of the three, at ten, eight and six, appears to have a morsel of talent for anything. And they shrink from Adrian, who at fifteen seems immeasurably old, has an aura of faint, threatening remoteness and hates them coming into his room to watch TV.

Kate's days pass: collecting Alicia from school, taking her to her piano lessons, trying to keep a futile eye on Adrian and making small-talk with women among whom she still feels an outsider because of her stubborn home-counties accent and her talented child. When they ask about Alicia's progress, she tells them of the latest festival or a photo in a newspaper – then feels embarrassed when they return quietly to discussing the merits of removing tonsils or what to do about appalling school dinners.

When Alicia comes home, Kate's life begins. She'll have tea and cake ready to boost her energy, and she'll often try to find some novelty to interest her: a tape of a concert from the radio, a book about a composer from the library, or a CD – like Lucien Delamain's Chopin disc. She will give Adrian tea and cake too, then persuade him to do his homework. Soon she'll be ensconced with Alicia at the piano, ready to spur her on if she feels disheartened, or to point out when she's straying from Mrs Butterworth's copious demands ('Darling, you're strumming now, do that page again, slowly . . .'). If there are tears, she'll be there to dry them. Alicia feels her music very deeply and any hint of failure can send her spinning into excessive emotion, which the onset of puberty doesn't help.

Supposing Alicia went to boarding-school? How would she manage? She's so young, so raw, so instinctive. She hasn't learned to hide behind the masks that her schoolmates are already forging for themselves. What Alicia feels, she shows. What she wants, she declares; what she doesn't want, she will never accept. If she loves someone, she hugs them. If she hates someone, she ignores them. If she respects someone, she obeys them, and if she doesn't respect them – well, the PE teacher was a case in point.

Most young girls love to wear makeup, but Alicia has never experimented beyond a smudge or two for the stage. Most other teenagers want to be cool, but she appears not to care about the style of her clothes, though she likes blue, which suits her, and is unaccountably fussy about the colours she wears for performing. Adrian, in a rare bout of Making an Effort with Little Sister, gave her a khaki T-shirt that he'd outgrown, emblazoned with the logo of a chart-topping band; Alicia thanked him, but hasn't worn it once. And this is a girl with a capacity for devotion that can induce her to plunge into a winter river after her dog. How would such a self-willed, innocent child survive in a boarding-school? It's unthinkable. So, if Alicia is not going to the music school, she must stay where she is and practise at home. That means she must have a grand piano.

'Well, why do you think we never had one?' Guy is lying on his back, staring at the bedroom ceiling, which still needs replastering. His foot, he's been joking, should change places with it.

'But it's madness. How can we spend eighty thousand pounds on a piano?'

'We can get a good one second-hand for a lot less, you know. It's a question of finding one she likes.'

'Are they really that different?'

'You bet. I'll keep a look-out in the small ads.'

It's half past eleven at night. Guy reaches towards his bedside drawer.

'What's that?'

'Sleeping pills. The foot's been hurting.'

During his first days back at work, Guy has been keeping the lowest profile that a deputy editor reasonably can. The sandwich man appears with a tray at lunchtime, so he can avoid the canteen; Diane brings him as many cups of coffee as he can drink; and if Martin needs him, he knows where he is. At editorial meetings, Guy makes sure he's half concealed by a door or a potted plant.

It is therefore from behind the conference room's *Ficus benjamina* that Guy catches his next glimpse of Emily Andersen's left profile: the concave tilt of her nose, the breadth of her forehead, the slant of the grey eyes that have been haunting him. She's wearing jeans, a black sweater and the merest touch of makeup. Her pen and notebook are poised, ready to snap into action. She's still the new girl, but looks as if she's worked at the *Chronicle* for ever. He watches her; she hasn't noticed him. She's talking to her colleagues, joking around as if they're old friends. He keeps watching, but soon stops observing: all he can think is: 'God, she's lovely.'

Emily turns her head. Her gaze lands on him and he feels the jolt of contact: recognition, a question-mark, pleasure. She raises a hand and waves.

After the meeting, he doesn't go to her; instead, she comes to him. Around them the others disperse to their desks.

'Guy, how are you? How's the foot?'

'It's seen better days, but it's mending, thanks.'

'I'd been looking forward to talking to you about all those local walks,' Emily sparkles, 'but on my first day they said you'd jumped into a river to save your dog!'

'Actually, it was my daughter. She thought *she* was saving the dog.'

'But she's OK?'

'Very much so. Thanks.'

They hover outside Guy's office. He wonders whether he'd seen a flicker of doubt in Emily's bright smile when he said 'my daughter'.

'What are you doing for lunch?' she asks.

Guy tries to say that he's busy, but instead says that he's free.

Alicia isn't afraid to go out alone with Cassie, and Mum isn't afraid to let her, especially when Mrs Butterworth has wound her into a state of tension that can't be soothed by a cup of hot chocolate. Mum imposes a half-hour time-limit, but it's long enough for Alicia to centre herself as well as walking – or, rather, running – the dog. Alicia can't see why she has to have a time limit while Adrian doesn't; but she makes the most of her brief freedom.

She grabs Cassie's leash and they head for the fresh air and wide, peaceful space of the golf course down the road. They're allowed to run there as long as they don't bother any golfers. Alicia keeps half an eye on Cassie to make certain she doesn't go after the balls, but Mum has trained her to leave them alone. Dad – whose attempts at exercise are sparse but enthusiastic – has advised Alicia that real jogging is slow, steady and sensible. But she prefers to sprint as hard and fast as she can, with Cassie galloping alongside, all four paws outstretched in the welcome air.

Here, you can see for miles, up into the empty moors. She feels she could run for ever; that if she could reach the grey horizon at the top of the farthest hill, she could puncture it where the earth and sky meet, and break through it, like a silk screen, to the other side. There she'd find rainbows and shooting stars; she and Cassie could fly out, defying gravity, with no need for wings to rise and soar.

Alicia feels as if she's a piece of jewellery that her mother keeps in a box, wrapped in cotton wool. Mum takes her out and polishes her, then wears her round her neck like a pendant of Blue John, Derbyshire's answer to amethyst, which glistens raw in the caverns under the hills. Even if Alicia's arms are aching, her shoulders are stiff, her fingertips are sore and her head is humming, she mustn't stop practising. Mum will say, 'Have a little break and a Panadol, darling, and then get back to it, because if you don't you won't be able to play for that music club,' or 'We'll have to cancel your Buxton Festival recital because you won't be ready,' or simply 'Mrs Butterworth will be able to tell straight away.'

She barely stops practising even at school. Lessons in maths, IT, physics and biology flow past without touching her; her fingers tap on her legs under the desk while her mind plays her the notes. Sometimes the teachers scold her, though that's becoming half-hearted.

The other kids taunt her. 'Freak,' spits Kelly, who chews gum with her mouth open. 'Icky-sicky classical music! Ali pally, silly cow! Ali pally, silly cow!' Alicia's latest newspaper report from a competition in Sheffield has been pinned to the school noticeboard, beside clippings about pupils' successes in the pony club, and the football team's triumph against a snotty private school in Yorkshire. But Kelly, or somebody like her, has defaced Alicia's picture by drawing a moustache and beard on it.

Adrian swoops to her defence from two classes higher. Finding his sister crying at lunch break, he pulls down the paper and says, 'When I catch them, I'll break their legs.' Silently Alicia hopes he doesn't catch them, because she fears he really might do it – Adrian is huge these days. It was nice, though, to feel he'd protect her.

Alicia does have a friend. A new friend whom she can't see easily because she lives in Birmingham and goes to school in Surrey. At the competition in Sheffield she had wandered over and started talking to Alicia: an Indian girl named Anjali Sharma, a year older than herself, shepherded by a tall, fierce-looking father who never took his eyes off her. While Mum talked to Dr Sharma, who seemed keen to tell her about his daughter's concerts and competitive successes, Alicia and Anjali shyly exchanged stories. Anjali attends a specialist music boarding-school for exceptionally talented children.

'It's very small and everyone is really into music,' Anjali said. She had a wonderful accent that combined a twang of Birmingham, a twist of Indian subcontinent – her family came originally from Madras – and a slight resonance of posh Surrey exclusivity. Alicia listened to the intriguing sound of her voice almost more than to the words she spoke. 'You'd get in easily, I'm sure,' said Anjali, whose fine-featured, modest face could break abruptly into the loveliest of smiles.

The school's pupils are supported by scholarships, Dr Sharma told Mum, so paying fees isn't an issue. The real trouble is that Surrey is at the other end of the country.

When Alicia hints at home that she likes the sound of a school where everyone is musical, Mum and Dad look so upset that she's filled with appalling guilt. She acknowledges that she'd have to board, like Anjali.

'But, darling, I hate the idea of you not being at home, having a normal family life,' Mum explains. 'Those schools are such hot-houses. I can't imagine you being happy in a place like that.' Alicia doesn't know what she means, but suspects that Buxton would be too cold to possess a hot-house of its own.

Alicia had given Anjali her address and it's not long before a parcel with a Surrey postmark arrives, containing a glossy prospectus. In the privacy of her bedroom, Alicia turns the pages: extensive green lawns, a long programme of school concerts, a piano on every page. She shows it to Adrian, who thinks it looks brilliant. 'There's a school a bit like that in Manchester,' he tells her, 'but I guess you'd have to be a boarder there too.'

'Why?'

'Because Mum would say you're wasting two hours a day travelling when you could be practising.'

Adrian is right: as soon as Alicia raises the possibility, Mum homes in on exactly that. 'A normal family life is so important,' she adds.

'Bollocks,' Adrian interjects.

'What do you mean, Adrian?' Mum says, icy.

'We don't have a normal family life, do we? Call this *normal?*'

'Oh, and isn't that your doing? You never want to join in anything we do any more.'

'I never *did* want to. This family gives me an effing headache. Can't you see Ali doesn't have any friends?'

'But she's got her family round her. That's much more important.'

Alicia looks on, mute. It's not only that Mum isn't listening to Adrian; it's as if she can't even hear him. Alicia doesn't bother trying to get a word in edgeways. She wonders silently whether she'll ever have any say in her own life.

Admittedly, if she went to music school as a boarder, she'd have to leave Cassie at home and she'd hardly ever see Grandma Didie. Also, the teachers might be less good than Mrs Butterworth. Alicia loathes Mrs Butterworth, but she can't deny that she gets results: Alicia's technique is racing ahead and she can't remember the last time she'd failed to win a competition. Mum says that the reason Mrs Butterworth doesn't teach at any of the music schools or colleges is that she's too good for them, too demanding, too individual. She must be fantastic, because she charges a vast sum for Alicia's lessons.

The information has finally reached them on the grapevine – Glenda, via the friend of a friend – that Mrs Butterworth had had a daughter who died when she was twenty, from a rare form of bone cancer. She had been a very promising pianist; and although it had happened decades ago, Mrs Butterworth has never got over it. Alicia feels sorry for her. But when she goes out running with Cassie, for that half-hour she can let herself think things that she's not allowed to think inside the house – and then, occasionally, she wonders what it would have been like to be Mrs Butterworth's daughter. And she feels almost more sorry for the girl before she became ill.

Kate looks up from a recipe book when a rush of chilly air, a slam and a volley of barks signal that Alicia and Cassie are back. The kitchen clock shows that they've been out for precisely thirty minutes.

'Hi, Mum.' Alicia bounds over and gives her a big, damp hug. Her clothes are coated with gossamer drizzle: for some perverse reason, she hates umbrellas. She dashes upstairs to change into something dry.

'An hour till supper,' Kate says, when she returns in clean jeans and sheepskin slippers. 'Are you going to practise?'

'Can't I help you cook?' Alicia adores food in all its forms, and Kate worries that what is currently puppy fat may grow worse if she carries on.

She lets Alicia off the hour's practice: she has already survived Mrs Butterworth's onslaught today. Mother and daughter stand side by side at the worktop; Alicia puts leaves, olives and cherry tomatoes into a salad bowl and Kate chops onions and cucumber. They switch on Radio 4 and listen to a comedy programme that soon has both of them in stitches. Adrian is out with his mates. Guy has phoned to say he has to work late and won't be home for another two hours.

'I thought it went really well today,' Alicia remarks, once the broadcast is over. 'Mrs Butterworth actually said, "Good."'

'Would you like to ask her,' Kate says carefully, 'what she thinks about the idea of you going in for the BBC Young Musician of the Year competition?'

Alicia freezes, tomato in hand. 'Do you think I could?'

'Of course you could. But you'd need your teacher's consent.'

'Oh, she'll be fine. If you want Mrs Butterworth to be happy, enter me for a competition!' Alicia rolls her eyes heavenwards. She catches Kate's eye; they laugh. They both know what makes Mrs Butterworth tick. 'I think Anjali's entering it,' Alicia adds. 'I might ask her how it works.'

After supper, while Alicia is in the bath, Kate tiptoes into her room. The yellow paint and African animals are long gone; now it's lavender and white, a calm, pretty space to soothe a busy young girl to rest. Guy sometimes remarks that it looks more like a unit in a bed-and-breakfast than a child's room. On the bookshelves stand competition trophies: silver cups bearing inscribed plaques that could have been for tennis or swimming, but happen to be for playing the piano. Framed certificates garnish the wall, prizes from the competitions that don't give trophies.

Alicia has a desk at which she's supposed to do her home-work. Not much of it gets done, but Kate is impressed by how tidy the surface is. Alicia is chaotic in certain ways: no worldly ploys or manipulative tricks, no sense of 'cool'. But she's punc-tual, polite and – at the piano, where she always seems older and more sophisticated than she is – extremely confident. Strange girl. Strange and marvellous, Kate smiles to herself.

She spots on the desk, the latest letter from Anjali, whom Kate thinks Ali is in love with, in the way that young girls sometimes are with slightly older girls.

Last weekend Lucien Delamain came and did masterclasses with some of the sixth-formers. He was AMAZING. He showed us all kinds of things about the way the melodies relate to each other. I came away feeling like I'd heard the pieces for the first time, although I thought I knew them very well. Ali, I wish you'd persuade your parents to let you audition. You'd love it here. It would be so great to have you.

From the bathroom comes the sound of water gurgling down the plughole. Kate puts the letter back in exactly the position she'd found it and makes her way downstairs, troubled. When Guy comes home, she'll discuss with him the issues of boarding-school, the competition and excessive affection for other girls. But he's working late.

Guy, as it happens, is not working late. He's in the pub with Emily Andersen. The paper's local is typical – he would have written – of gloomy, industrial Manchester's transformation into a modern metropolis, full of go-ahead people and newly fashioned media companies. Once a cavernous Victorian monstrosity, its interior has been remodelled with chandeliers of opaque glass globes casting luminous reflections into big mirrors. Moreover, Guy tells Emily, it offers one of the best selections of draught beer in the city.

'You should come to Denmark one day,' she says, with a smile, leaning on the counter while he waves a ten-pound note towards the barman. 'We have great beer.'

Guy orders two pints, two packets of crisps and a platter of cheese and biscuits. Emily tries to pay for her share, but he refuses. 'My treat.'

They settle at the quietest table they can find.

'So, tell me about Denmark,' Guy says. 'I've never been.'

Emily, hands cupped round her glass, begins to describe her home town, Aarhus. There, they had lived on a long hill overlooking the harbour; on Saturdays her mother would nip down to the fish market and bring back a bucket of fresh prawns for lunch. Nearby, the old town's low, historic buildings, pink, yellow and white, would be abuzz with cafés, bars and students on bicycles. It was easy to get out into the countryside, which looks, she says, a little like Suffolk, only prettier. Lots of sky;

lots of sea; forests of beech trees that burst into leaf over a few days in early May.

Guy, listening, pictures Emily walking through a Danish beech forest. 'So why did you move to England?'

'My mum never quite got the hang of the language, so Dad finally caved in and looked for a teaching post here instead. I don't think Danish is so hard, really. It's like Geordie English, only a thousand years out of date.'

'I bet that helped,' Guy teases her. 'Give us a demo?'

'*Rød grød med fløde.*'

'What?'

'That's what we teach foreigners to say first, because they usually can't! It means stewed red berries with cream.'

'I can't hear any consonants.'

'Oh, there are consonants. It's just that we don't pronounce them.'

'I feel for your mother,' Guy says. 'So you're bilingual?'

'Kind of.'

'Homesick?'

'Sometimes. I like it here, though. How's life in Buxton?'

'Much as ever. You must come over one day and we'll go for a good walk.'

'Are you from Derbyshire?'

'I grew up in Cheshire, but Buxton's home. My great-grand-father lived there. He used to walk all the way to Macclesfield across the moor to court my great-grandmother.'

'Wow, that's romantic!'

'What's a few hours on a moor to true love?' Guy says – then wishes, peculiarly, that he hadn't. To distract her, he leans back and puts on his best Derbyshire voice: 'Ye knaw what they say, eh, lass? "Derbyshire born and Derbyshire bred, strong in arm but weak in 'ead!"'

Emily laughs. Her face lights up as it had during her inter-view. Arrows pierce Guy's brain. He beams back at her. 'Derbyshire equivalent of your red berries,' he remarks.

'Try some of this. It's good.' Emily motions to the cheese platter.

'"Cheese, please, Louise."'

'Sorry?'

'TV ad from the sixties. I always find myself saying that. It drives my family bananas.'

'Oh, but it's *cute*! Anyway, I don't remember TV ads from the sixties. I wasn't conscious until about 1975.'

Guy takes a long swig of beer. Emily is more than a decade younger than him. She is gorgeous, fun and straightforward, he's completely in love with her, and he is middle-aged and married and has to see her every day at the office. What is he doing?

But sitting in the pub with her, laughing, listening and talking as if he's known her all his life, he knows exactly what he's doing: he's flying.

7

Things happen, life-changing things, with the simplest of signals: the ring of a telephone or the plop of a letter on to the doormat. The latest plop involves a large brown envelope, which heaves in one morning to Cassie's noisy welcome. Kate slices it open. Inside is the information pack she'd requested from the BBC.

Kate fills in the application form and buys a large Jiffy-bag. Into it, with the form, go a CV as long as the dog's tail, a reference from Mrs Butterworth that would make Apollo himself blush, a copy of Alicia's birth certificate, a photo, an audiotape and a video-cassette. She seals it with packing tape and strolls down to the post office. Some weeks later, there comes the inevitable news that Alicia has been accepted.

The wheels grind into action. The competition is spread out over more than a year from application to final. First there are regional heats – for Alicia, in Manchester. She's pleased to find she has to play for only fifteen minutes. Mrs Butterworth plans her programme: a Chopin study, a short but deliciously showy Mozart Gigue, and Ravel's *Jeux d'eau*. Pianos, Alicia tells the BBC people afterwards, are good at evoking water. The chains of notes are like rivers, rain and fountains because they're both fluid and defined, or should be.

'It's your fourteenth birthday tomorrow?' asks the regional administrator, double-checking her form. 'Do you know what presents you're getting?'

'Probably some books of Chopin that I don't have already,' Alicia says eagerly.

'What about going out to celebrate? A movie? A party?'

'The thing is, there's no cinema where we live and my friends are – well, music's what I love best.'

The administrator and her assistant exchange a glance.

Three months later the regional finals take place: back to Manchester, fifteen more minutes of music and, this time, TV cameras. Everyone's performances are recorded now, just in case.

> *Dear Alicia,*
>
> *I heard you got to the quarter-finals – so did I! I'm so glad you'll be there too. Which concerto are you learning? I wanted to do Saint-Saëns Two, but Dad says I should do something with a little more 'depth'. He only likes German music. So I'll probably learn some Mozart, not that I'll be performing it in any case. We must get together in Birmingham and go out somewhere afterwards. Here's a picture of school. See you in December!*
>
> *Love,*
> *Anjali*
>
> *Dearest Anjali,*
>
> *Thanks for your postcard!!! Yes I'm in the quarter-finals and it will be great to see you again. I'm learning the Ravel G major Concerto, I know it isn't 'deep', but its SO beautiful and Mrs Butterworth says I should go for it cos I love it. I hope I'll have a chance to play it, but who knows. Mum is coming with me to Birmingam and we'll all go out definatly afterwards. Do people keep asking you if you're nervous? I'm not and everyone keeps saying 'she's not nervous, why isn't she nervous?' which nearly makes me scared, only not quite. See you very soon!!!!!*
>
> *Luv,*
> *Alicia*

While the cogs turn and Alicia plugs away at her next programme, the phone rings. Guy's voice says, from the office, 'Katie, I've got an idea. Why don't we have a dinner party for some of my colleagues?'

Dinner parties at the Bradleys' are rare events. Most guests have been family, Kate's former employers, or neighbours who chat about the weather while Kate fusses over chicken and salad. At least the newspaper people, if they can be persuaded to make the journey over the moor, should bring with them some livelier conversation. Guy wants to invite the editor, Martin, with his wife, Liz, and two of the best young journalists: a girl named Emily Andersen and a boy named Robert Wilder. Emily, he says, reports on the arts, education and community issues, and Rob specialises in politics. Kate agrees, but stresses that they must avoid Tuesdays and Wednesdays because of Alicia's piano lesson.

Kate's latest acquisition for the house is a larger dining-table, made of reclaimed oak floorboards; it sits at the garden end of their sizeable kitchen-diner and opens up to seat ten. It strikes Kate that since the children won't be taking part and the evening risks being dominated by newspaper talk, perhaps they could ask someone else as well.

Mrs Butterworth has never been to Buxton.

'That,' Guy says, 'would be extremely interesting!'

Sometimes you don't know a life-changing moment – that ring of the phone, rustle of paper or, in this case, chime of the bell – until years afterwards. When the doorbell sounds Big Ben at seven thirty on the last Saturday of October, nobody suspects that it will presage anything but an informal meal with friends.

Alicia and Adrian are deemed, respectively, too young and too unsuitable for a dinner party. Adrian has gone to see his friend Sam. Alicia, having feasted on breadcrumbed fish and oven chips, is using the last of the visitor-free early evening to practise. The window is slightly open; Ravel, all glitter and poise, floats into the drive and greets the guests as they gaze up at the house on the slope. They arrive together. Martin and Liz, who live near Withington, have agreed to bring and return Mrs Butterworth; and Rob Wilder has brought Emily Andersen.

Emily pauses at the bottom of the steps and takes in the wide bay window, the sound of music through the chestnut-dark autumn evening and the gleaming hair of the girl at the piano, whose face is hidden.

'All right, Em?' asks Rob, who fancies her.

'Sure. Just got to fix my shoe,' she says, bending so that he can't see her eyes.

Mrs Butterworth looks in at the upright piano – no second-hand grand in good enough condition has yet presented itself – and shakes her hand.

Kate has spent the afternoon preparing her house and herself. The ground floor, the bathroom and the stairs have been scrubbed and vacuumed within a millimetre of their lives. The books are ranged in ruler-straight rows on the shelves; Alicia's music, normally piled beside the piano, has been concealed in the cupboard where it ought to live, and even the kitchen shows little sign of the frantic chopping, stirring, roasting and garnishing that has been taking place. The wine glasses gleam on the table, each with an expertly folded red napkin tucked into its bowl; a vase of lilies adorns the side-board; and at perfect intervals along the table stand three slender red candles. Kate's hair is freshly coloured, a slightly more golden shade than usual, and she's wearing a long, sleek, flowered skirt and a loose, oatmeal-coloured jacket. Round her neck is a string of chunky mock-ivory beads. The aroma of rosemary, garlic and lamb melds into the scent of fallen leaves and the sound of Ravel.

Alicia's choice of the Ravel G major Concerto is

unfortunate. Kate can't hear the slow movement without thinking of the dying Victoria; they'd listened to it constantly in the hospital. But it's Alicia's favourite and unless Kate is willing to explain why – which she isn't – she's in no position to convince her to choose something else. Gradually, painfully, she's getting used to it.

She steps forward to welcome her guests. 'Martin! Liz! How wonderful to see you, it's been far too long. Do come in . . . And Mrs Butterworth!'

'Deirdre. Please, Katherine. Tonight I am Deirdre.' The matchstick figure of Alicia's piano teacher glides into the house, incongruous out of her normal context.

'Deirdre's been telling us all about her studies in Soviet Russia. It's quite hair-raising. I think we should do a feature,' Martin tells Kate, giving her a kiss.

'Darling,' Guy says, 'I'd like you to meet our two bright young things. This is Rob. And this is Emily.'

'Welcome to Buxton.' Kate smiles, shaking their hands. She's struck by the openness of Emily's face, the clarity of her complexion and the unusual hue of her eyes. Unaccountably, this girl makes her feel her age more than she normally does.

Rob is much taller than Kate, and as fresh-faced in his own way as Emily, who, Kate thinks, inspecting the vibes, may be his girlfriend; or perhaps he merely wants her to be. His features are even, his curly brown hair plentiful (unlike that of the older men) and his smile is wide and friendly. Mrs Butterworth gazes up at him, pressing his hand as warmly as if she herself were the hostess.

The front-room door opens. Alicia looks out, her face tired and hopeful. She's wearing faded jeans and a Minnie Mouse T-shirt. Emily swings round from talking to Guy and meets the young girl's gaze. For a moment their eyes lock. Then Alicia's swerve to her teacher. 'Hello, Mrs Butterworth,' she says quietly.

'Hello, Alicia dear.' Mrs Butterworth sounds unusually benevolent.

'Ali,' Kate exclaims, 'you don't need to stop. Go and finish the last movement.'

'Oh, Mum.' Alicia looks at the guests.

'Everyone knows you're in the competition and we all love to hear you playing, so it's no problem. Go and finish your practising.'

'Yes, Mum.' Alicia slides back behind the door. A moment later there comes the clack of a metronome and the careful rattling of Ravel passagework at half speed.

Emily and Rob exchange a glance. Emily does not look at Guy.

'Let's sit in the kitchen,' Kate suggests – Alicia occupies what used to be the lounge. Guy makes for the fridge where two bottles of champagne lie chilling.

Soon the glassy edges of formality have dissolved amid the bubbles. Alicia is finally permitted to stop her metronome and go to her room; for background music, Kate puts on an Ella Fitzgerald album. Guy taps his fingers in time and Emily's feet dance under the table despite themselves. Kate brings out the starter – smoked salmon and cucumber mousse with dill sauce and triangles of crustless toast. Guy refills the glasses. In the golden light from the red candles, Mrs Butterworth bats her eyelids at Rob, who appears transfixed by her stream of horrific stories from the world of international piano competitions.

'. . . And then you know what the competition director, this great, legendary pianist, says? He declares, "Well, I'm deaf. Let's give the prize to the prettiest girl!"'

Emily, Rob, Martin, Liz and Guy laugh. Kate doesn't. Convinced that Mrs Butterworth isn't making this up, she's wondering how often such incidents affect the fortunes of young women in supposedly musical contests.

'But surely they're looking for the best pianists?' Emily protests.

'Darling, if only that were true. But I've seen decisions taken in competitions that would make your hair stand on end, if not fall out altogether!' Mrs Butterworth, beaming, reaches out a hand and ruffles Rob's light brown curls.

Kate, fork poised half-way to her mouth, can't believe her eyes. Especially when Rob – who has plenty of hair-raising stories of his own, when he's allowed to get a word in – doesn't object, but laughs. 'Deirdre, one word from you and all those corrupt jurors would run for their lives!' he declares.

'Deirdre', who eats so slowly that she finishes her mousse ten minutes after everyone else, is the only person who accepts more. Kate goes to the oven to remove the lamb, which would otherwise turn from suitable, moist French pink to very unsuitable, dry school-dinner brown. Mrs Butterworth, despite her delicate build, is evidently fond of her food, and her drink too. Kate wonders how she manages to stay so thin; she must burn up all her energy in teaching.

After another fifteen minutes, during which Mrs Butterworth works her way morsel by morsel through her second helping, Kate, her head spinning from slightly too much champagne, asks Guy to carve the lamb.

'This is such a lovely house,' Liz enthuses to her, while Guy turns his attention to the meat. 'Guy tells us you've designed everything yourself, Kate. You've got the most wonderful eye.'

'I'm glad you like it,' Kate says, 'but it's very simple . . .'

There's a clonk and an expletive. Guy's hand has slipped. 'Damn it!' He dashes to the sink to run the cut under the cold tap.

'Oh, God, are you all right?' Emily gasps.

Rob glances at her, surprised.

'You must never let Alicia handle a kitchen knife,' Mrs Butterworth advises Kate. 'Far too dangerous.'

'I know. It's a shame, because she loves cooking,' Kate says.

'Sacrifices must be made for such a talent.'

'You didn't go on holiday this year, did you?' Liz says.

'No – with Ali being in the quarter-finals, we didn't want to take her away from her piano for two weeks. It wouldn't have been fair. We can have wonderful days out locally in any case.' Not that they often do. Kate pushes, impatient, past her injured husband and takes over the carving.

'Wouldn't it do her good to have a break? To be a little refreshed?' Emily is watching Guy at the sink; he's wrapped his bleeding finger in kitchen towel and is rummaging in a drawer for a plaster.

'It's really up to her,' Kate explains, cutting lamb in neat slices beside Guy's irregular chunks. 'She's very happy this way.'

'I hope you don't mind me asking,' says Liz, fidgeting with a curl of her hair, 'but isn't she missing out on things that most children do? Going to the seaside, seeing her friends . . . ?'

'Alicia is not "most children".' Mrs Butterworth answers before Kate can. 'Alicia is unique. In all my years of teaching, I have never found a talent like hers. And here, in a little English town known only for its mineral water! It's quite incredible.'

'She does miss out,' Guy growls. 'Of course she does.'

'She doesn't have many close friends she wants to go out with,' Kate says. 'It's difficult, being the only exceptionally talented child in her school.'

'Katherine,' says Mrs Butterworth, 'she does still need a grand piano.'

'Fourteen is such a difficult age,' Liz says. 'Our Harry was in all kinds of trouble when he was fourteen.'

'Emily, I hope you're hungry?' Kate piles meat, gravy, potatoes and vegetables on to a plate. Emily's expression, sombre in the candlelight, suggests she's miles away. She starts visibly at the sound of her name, but gives Kate a quick smile and says, 'Yes, thank you.' Kate notices later, though, that Emily is eating almost, if not quite, as slowly as 'Deirdre'.

'Sorry about that.' Guy is back at his place. Emily asks him quietly if he's in pain. 'Just being stupid. Not concentrating,' he tells her. Kate plonks a plate in front of him.

'. . . So then he says, "And what might *your* business be?"' Rob is talking to Mrs Butterworth, imitating a broad Scottish accent. 'So I explain I'm a journalist out for a holiday ramble, and he says, "Not here, you're not. Not on *my* land. How'd you like it if fifty thousand people came *rambling* across your office in their mucky boots?" And I pointed out that my boots were quite clean, as boots go, to which he says, "Aye, there's muck and there's muck . . ." And this was a public right of way! But you can't tell a nutcase like that where to go, in case he's got a gun in the van . . .'

'How's your son doing?' Liz asks Kate.

'He's fine, thanks. He's at a friend's place tonight.' Kate hates to think of what Adrian and Sam might get up to together, but this is no place to say so.

Guy, at the head of the table with Emily at right angles on his left, reaches downwards, apparently looking for something. Emily pulls her chair closer in.

When the plates are (mostly) empty, the wine bottles depleted and the faces flushed and happy, Martin taps his glass for attention. His face is red and content and his eyes full of beneficence as he lumbers to his feet.

'Friends, Buxtonians, countrymen,' he begins. 'I want to say two things. First, a huge thank-you to Guy and especially to his wonderful wife, Kate, for this fabulous gourmet cuisine!' He waits for the noises of approval to die down. 'Next, I've got some news. I've decided, after much soul-searching, that it's time to cash in my chips. The newspaper needs a new look, a new approach. Not tired old me, ploughing on through the production line after twenty years.

So I'm going to take early retirement, join the golf club, if they'll have me, and see something more of my home and my long-suffering family.'

Kate takes a breath, guessing what comes next. Guy is serene, smiling up at Martin, showing no surprise – or, indeed, anything else. Fury flashes through her: has he known about this all along, without telling her? Was this the reason for his hare-brained dinner-party idea?

'The *Manchester Chronicle* has a distinguished background,' Martin goes on. 'It was founded, as you know, over a hundred and fifty years ago and has been through a chequered history, every time rising from the ashes like a phoenix – because the *Chronicle* needs Manchester and Manchester needs the *Chronicle*. Together they've gone from strength to strength, enriching each other like an old married couple. I'd like the finest possible person to carry on our tradition of fairness, justice and quality writing. Therefore I've recommended the perfect candidate to the top dogs on the top floor. Who better than my noble deputy – our host – the one and only Guy Bradley of Buxton?'

Emily, Rob, Liz and Mrs Butterworth cheer.

'Oh, my God,' says Kate.

Guy takes a deep breath and stands up. 'Martin, I can't thank you enough for your faith in me,' he says. 'It's not only a wonderful job. It's a huge responsibility, an honour and a privilege. And – if Kate and our kids will forgive me – nothing could make me happier than to accept.'

The scene swims in front of Kate's eyes and there's a peculiar buzz in her ears. Perhaps she shouldn't be surprised that she hadn't seen the news coming before; or that Guy has kept it a secret – he'd have had the best of intentions, as usual, wanting to surprise her; or that once again, he's made a decision that affects all of them without consulting her. On the other hand, he's acting to salve her anxieties: replacing the income that she hasn't earned since quitting her job and affording the expensive support – lessons, concert dresses, transport and the rest – that Ali needs, not to mention a new piano. Her husband is about to take the best editorial post in the north of England. She mustn't complain, even if she knows it means he will now never, ever be at home.

'Darling,' she announces, forcing herself to stand beside him, 'I couldn't be happier.' Guy turns and embraces her. Their guests give another cheer.

In the deep-blue darkness of her bedroom, Alicia lies still, eyes closed, listening. Her brain latches on to sound; her hearing dwarfs her other senses. Music echoes, magnified, inside her brain cells; it won't leave her alone. She follows every note of the Ella Fitzgerald CD being played downstairs. Cassie, in her basket by the foot of the bed, slumbers on regardless.

Alicia hears the faint thread of voices making speeches – the fat man, Dad's boss; then Dad; then, briefly, Mum. Cheering. Then Mrs Butterworth, rattling on and on, probably making everyone feel that everything she says is of the utmost importance.

Someone is coming upstairs: a light female step she doesn't know. It's certainly not her mother's brisk footfall and it's unlikely to be Mrs Butterworth, who'd be wearing fancier shoes with sharper heels. The guest – either Mrs Boss or Miss Journalist – goes into the bathroom. There's the sound of the loo flushing and the gurgle of water in the pipes. Whoever it is comes out on to the landing and pauses. Cassie shifts and gives a grunt. Alicia keeps quiet. The steps move closer. Instead of returning to the kitchen, they're continuing up the stairs towards the second floor.

Dad's study is directly beside her room. It's firmly out of bounds to her and Adrian; if Dad is in there, they have to knock, in case he's working. When he's out, he doesn't lock the door: he's always said that he trusts them not to go in, and they don't. Yet now the strange steps are creaking on the floor-boards next to Alicia's wall. She pictures the guest – probably the pretty young journalist, who doesn't know any better – standing in Dad's office, gazing aghast at the mess.

She's not sure how much time has passed when she hears another footstep, this time bounding and vigorous, unmistak-ably Dad's. He, too, pauses on the first floor landing; instead of making for the bathroom, he continues up, more quietly, past her room and into his study. She hears two voices, low, indistinct. She tries to make out their words, but she can't; she's too tired. Her arms are aching, there's a painful point between her shoulder blades and sleep is just too tempting for her to stay awake another moment.

'Sorry about the mess,' Guy says.

Emily is standing in the middle of the study under the eaves, looking at the stacks of paper that half bury his computer on the unvarnished wooden desk. 'The shelving's marvellous,' she says. 'Did you build all this?'

'With Ikea's help.'

'It's nice to be able to picture you here, writing. Will you still write when you take over as Big Boss?' Emily teases.

'God knows. God alone knows what's going to happen.'

Emily walks up to him. They stand face to face.

'Your wife is very striking,' Emily says. 'She's nothing like I'd expected.'

'What were you expecting? A dragon?'

'Not exactly . . . Just someone a little more – this sounds awful, but I thought she'd be more housewifey. More mumsy. She seems like a London businesswoman who's been trans-planted to Buxton.'

'Kate used to be a solicitor. Now I'm afraid her business is Ali.'

'Ali's lovely.'

'Yes. Ali is lovely.'

'And how does she – er – get along with Deirdre Butterworth?'.

'I do worry.' Guy sits down on his office chair. Emily presses his shoulder briefly. 'I worry,' he goes on, 'that everything we do for Ali might be wrong. There's an equal possibility, of course, that everything we do for her is right. It's so hard to know.'

'I can imagine. I love music, but I wouldn't know what to do with a talented kid.'

'It's so silly, Em. Every parent dreams about having a gifted child. But it's actually a big headache, because whatever you do is going to feel wrong in some way.'

'Is there anything I can do to help?'

'You do. You help just by being you.'

'I'm not always too happy being me. Not at the moment.'

'What is it, Em?' asks Guy, before he understands.

Emily moves away and stares into a bookshelf. Her back is to him. 'You know Hans Christian Andersen?' she says. 'My compatriot? My "distant relative possibly"? You know *The Little Mermaid*?'

'Sort of.'

'The Little Mermaid goes to the Sea Witch to have her tail turned into legs so that she can go on shore to win the man she loves. But when she has her feet, every step feels as if she's walking on knives.'

There's a short and dreadful silence.

'I don't know how I can go on like this,' Guy says at last.

'Guy, are you fighting what I'm fighting?'

'Oh, God. Em, if only you knew . . .'

She goes to him, takes his hand. 'Really?' she asks. Her eyes are bright with tears as their palms touch.

'I don't know what to do.' He can barely meet her gaze. 'Em, I want you, I want to sleep with you, I can't bear it. I think I'm falling in love with you. Do you mind me saying this?'

She looks away. 'You know . . . sometimes I wake up in the morning – and I wonder why you're not there with me.'

Guy stands and lifts Emily's chin towards him. As he bends his head to kiss her for the first time, his mind glazes over with the sweetness of red berries and cream.

Downstairs, Kate has opened another bottle of wine. Rob, clearly annoyed at being abandoned by Emily, who hasn't come back from the bathroom yet, has one arm round Mrs Butterworth and the other round Kate.

'I never thought I was going to be surrounded by so many lovely lasses on the same evening!' he declares.

'Tell us about you, Rob,' Kate says, moving closer. She's tipsy enough to find that the sensation of this much-younger man's arm across her shoulders makes her want to purr like a cat. 'Where do you come from? Where do you want to go?'

'I come from Worcester and I want to go everywhere,' Rob says, his hand moving up and down Kate's back. 'I want to see Machu Picchu. I'd like to cross America on a motorbike. I want to go across Asia overland.'

'Wouldn't you be worried?' Liz asks. 'About the wars? Bandits? Dysentery?'

'Oh, a nice strong boy like you,' says Mrs Butterworth, who's still working her way through the final quarter of her lamb, 'you wouldn't need to worry.'

'Martin wants to write his memoirs once he retires,' Liz says. 'He's seen a thing or two in the north of England that could make your blood curdle!'

Martin has quietly nodded off, his head bobbing down towards his substantial paunch.

Kate has been smiling at Rob and feeling her face flush. If Mrs Butterworth, who must be seventy if she's a day, can flirt so shamelessly, then so can she. She's glad to find she's not entirely forgotten how to feel the buzz in the blood that comes from an approving male eye trained on certain parts of her anatomy. Recently she's been too busy taking care of Ali to think about whether she's losing her looks or settling into middle-aged spread. Not that she'd dream of getting close to any man other than Guy. But since he's been so busy at work, and their sex life has dwindled to once every three weeks (maybe once a month – she dares not count), perhaps a little harmless flirtation after copious champagne isn't so dreadful.

'Where's Guy?' Liz asks.

Just as Kate is about to wonder that herself, the telephone rings. She extricates herself from Rob's arm, leaving him to the tender mercies of Mrs Butterworth, and picks up the receiver.

'Mrs Bradley?' The voice is unfamiliar; local and male.

'Speaking?'

'I'm calling about your son.'

'Sorry?' Kate puts a hand over her other ear. 'Did you say my *son*?'

'Adrian Bradley is your son, I believe?'

'Yes, he is.'

'I'm calling from Buxton police station. My name is Sergeant Walker. Adrian is with us. We'd like someone to come and get him.'

'What's he doing there?' Kate feels abruptly sober.

'He's been in some trouble. Suspected arson, since you ask. Now, if you or your husband could oblige us . . .'

'We'll be right there,' Kate says. She rings off and wonders, in a blinding, horrible second, how she will explain this to her guests.

Guy appears on the stairs. One look tells him what's wrong.

'I've had too much to drink,' Kate says. 'I can't drive.'

'Me too. We'll have to ask Liz. Or Rob.'

'We can't tell them what's happened. Your promotion—'

'What's he done?'

'Arson. They think.'

'Shit.'

'We'll have to go and get him.'

'I'll go. You stay and look after everyone. Don't let them know. I'll drive very slowly. It's not far.'

'Be careful.'

'Don't worry.'

Guy takes a long drink of water – which he needs badly – then makes his way to the door alone. Starting the car, he sees in the mirror a smudge of pale pink on the side of his face. Kate, thank heavens, had been too preoccupied to notice it.

The sight that greets him in the police station is not pleasant. Under the glaring fluorescent light three drunken louts are spitting abuse at an officer. A distraught woman with a black and purple bruise across one cheek is being led into a side room by a WPC. And, on a bench in the corner, two teenaged boys slouch together over the baseball caps in their hands. Adrian looks up and his brown eyes burn reproach into Guy before anyone has said a word.

Guy can imagine that he looks reproachable. There he is in dinner-party garb, the worse for a few glasses of wine, and though he's done his best to wipe away the traces of Emily's lipstick, some may have lingered.

'What on earth—?' he says.

'So, now you're interested, are you?' his son grunts.

'Adrian, there's no need for that. What's going on?'

'You're this young man's father, are you?' Sergeant Walker is beside them, surveying Guy in a way he doesn't like.

He looks him in the eye and says, 'I am.'

'Found these two legging it from the allotments. Good blaze they'd got going in that shed. Nice surprise for the geezer who grows them tomatoes.'

'Weren't us,' mumbles Sam – who, since Guy last saw him, has shaved his head and acquired a ripe crop of zits.

'"Weren't us",' the sergeant whines in imitation. 'Course not. Never is, is it? Little shits, both of you. If I had my way, you'd be locked up. Better still, deported to Australia.'

'Yes, please,' Adrian ripostes.

'How old would they be, sir?'

Guy has never heard such a sarcastic 'sir'. Restraining himself from slugging Sergeant Walker for calling his son a little shit, he gives him the details he needs. How fortunate for the Bradley family's reputation, he reflects, that a gutted shed is not earth-shattering news in the north-west, in parts of which people shoot each other comparatively often. Besides, the law, not tallying remotely with the teenage brain, stipulates that Adrian is too young to be publicly named. Even if he has to appear in court, nobody need know that the son of the editor-designate is, in present-day terminology, a yob.

'Ought to breathalyse you while I'm about it,' Sergeant Walker mutters after Guy. 'Try teaching your kid some respect for authority, rather than sitting about sipping your bloody champagne.'

'Authority?' Adrian snipes. 'What's that?'

'Shut it, Adrian. *Now.*' Guy marches him out.

Guy and Adrian drive home in silence. When they reach the house it's one a.m. and the guests' cars have gone. Guy's heart, which he'd assumed couldn't sink any lower, falls an extra metre through the Derbyshire limestone.

He switches off the engine and sits beside his son in the dark. 'Did you do it?' he asks.

'Do you care? No, you effing don't.'

'I effing do. Because you should know better.'

'Why should I? I can do what I like. Cos you're not going to stop me, and nor's Mum and nor's school and nor's anybody. Not that shitty policeman either.'

'I am going to stop you,' Guy says. 'Adrian, you're grounded.

From now on your mother is going to walk you to the school gate and collect you in the afternoon—'

'I'm not a kid!'

'You are a kid. You're a stupid, irresponsible, idiot kid and you're not going out on your own again until you learn to grow up.'

'So I have to sit in the effing house and listen to my sister play her effing piano all day? You've got to be fucking joking.'

'In Victorian times, if children used language like that, their parents would wash their mouths out with soap.'

'You can't,' Adrian snarls. 'You'd get done for cruelty.'

'You just *won't be told*, will you? Listen, you're grounded and that's that. Curfew is end of school day. Every evening I'm going to look at your homework, and if it's not done you shall stay up and work until it's finished. OK. In we go.'

Adrian half opens his door, then turns back, staring at Guy under his cap. 'What would they say,' he grunts, 'if they knew I have to set fire to some sad bastard's garden shed before you know I exist?'

One week later, Guy and Emily slope out of the office in succession and go, separately, to Emily's flat nearby in central Manchester. After two hours Guy, shattered, exhilarated and almost tearful with the relief of opening the floodgates, leaves to drive home, wondering how he can tell Kate that he is in love with another woman and wants to live with her.

When he pulls into his drive, he sees that something in the house has changed. The shape in the front window is not squat, but long, black and elegant. Alicia is sitting by it, darting about its keyboard, conjuring a shining, magical sound out of its sensuous belly that in no way resembles the clattery noises that used to emanate from the upright piano.

'She has to have the best,' says Kate, standing in the lounge doorway, watching her.

The bill and the paperwork are on the kitchen table. Guy picks them up and discovers that his mortgage has increased by £80,000. And Alicia has the face of a brand new angel freshly initiated into heaven.

8

In May, a week before Alicia is to play in the BBC competition final, Kate goes to Manchester on Saturday afternoon to buy herself a new suit for the occasion. Guy is at the office. Adrian is out with Sam. His grounding had lasted barely two weeks: Kate had been too busy with Alicia to walk him home from school every day and, as Guy always said, he 'would not be told'.

Alicia is alone, sitting at her beautiful grand piano, working on the Ravel Concerto. She knows it backwards. She could play it in all twelve major keys if she needed to. But although she's given recitals all over Derbyshire, Yorkshire and Staffordshire, as well as the Buxton Festival, she's never played a concerto with an orchestra before. At the semi-finals she'd found the TV cameras alarming while they swooped about her like small prehistoric carnivores. It wouldn't be so bad if they'd keep still. On the day, she knows, she'll be surrounded by distracting things in motion: the musicians playing, the conductor waving his arms, the cameras curious and prying, and she'll have to fight to keep her concentration. If her fingers know the notes so thoroughly that they'll play accurately even when her brain is in meltdown, all will be well.

'Ali,' Mum said, driving home from Withington a few days earlier, when Alicia had voiced one frustration too many, 'do you realise what a responsibility you have? A lot of people have invested a great deal in you. Think of your father. He nearly collapsed when he saw the cost of your piano. Think of Mrs Butterworth. She says you're the most talented pupil she's ever had. I gave up my job so that I could help you. When you win this competition, we'll all win with you. We'll be there with you, going through every moment of it. You won't be on your own.'

Alicia almost said, 'And if I don't win?' but decided against it. Reading between the lines, she deduced that if she didn't win, she'd be letting them all down.

How can they place such a load on her? Why can't Mrs Butterworth give her own concerts instead of obsessing about her pupils? Why can't her mother go to work, like normal mothers? Why does she *have* to win this competition or face hellfire and damnation?

It hadn't felt so bad up to the quarter-finals. That was easy. Fifteen minutes of music (again), this time in Birmingham, with Anjali backstage in her gorgeous orange Indian trouser suit waiting, laughing and joking with her, until Mum sent her off to warm up. Which was sensible. She'd needed to warm up, but she'd enjoyed being with Anjali so much that she'd forgotten to give herself enough time. Alicia has to admit that sometimes she needs Mum to help her keep her head.

Afterwards they went out with Anjali, her parents and her little sister to an Indian vegetarian restaurant, where Alicia munched through a massive rolled-up pancake called a dhosa, unlike anything she'd eaten before. Dr Sharma told her about the medicinal properties of cardamom and ginger, new to her since her mother never cooks with them. Later, the girls were still so excited that, instead of going straight home, the Bradleys went back to the Sharmas' house, a little way out of Birmingham city centre.

Here, while their parents talked about Having Talented Children, Anjali spirited Alicia upstairs and helped her try on a sari (it belonged to her mother) made of glorious, deep blue silk. Anjali wound the material round and round Alicia's torso, tucking and pinning; eventually, staring into the mirror, Alicia thought she looked like a fairytale princess. She'd never seen a blue to match this, and the draped silk struck her as infinitely more beautiful than the frilly, little-girl dresses that her mother bought her for her concerts. She's always disliked frills. She gazed at the kaleidoscope of colours in the cupboard – Anjali's mum had quite a range – and each sang a different key, a distinct and seductive sound to her. Anjali put one on too, in emerald green. They couldn't have looked more different – Alicia tall and fair, Anjali tiny and dark with enormous eyes, like a night creature from a tropical forest; but wearing similar clothes, Alicia declared, they could pretend to be sisters. 'You're like the sister I never had,' she told her friend.

Later, on the way home, Alicia suggested that she'd like a sari as a concert dress.

'Darling,' said Mum, 'it's totally inappropriate.'

'Anji sometimes wears them.'

'Anji's Indian.'

'So what?' Alicia protested. 'She wears Western concert dresses too, so why shouldn't I wear Indian ones?'

'Don't be silly, darling,' said Mum, who evidently didn't know how to answer this.

After that, the competition's pressures had started to mount. Next came the semi-finals, which involved a twenty-five minute recital, plus an interview with a BBC presenter and a camera crew filming her at home. They nosed round the piano room looking for good angles and remarking on how pretty Buxton was – and she'd been wearing the wrong colour for the piece they wanted her to play and had had to persuade Mum to distract them while she ran to her room to change. Playing wasn't a problem; and of course she's used to being watched. Now, though, she senses invisible eyes all around, thousands of them, trained on her every move.

Since she's won the entire piano section, Alicia will play her Ravel Concerto, pitted against the winners of the strings, percussion, brass and woodwind sections, live on national TV. She feels as if she's in a tunnel, pulled from one end and pushed from the other; she's trapped with nowhere to go except forward, hurled inexorably on with no power to turn back or stop time in its tracks.

'Ali?'

Alicia pauses in mid-melody. Dad is in the room, smiling at her.

'When did you last go for a walk?' he asks.

'A *walk*?'

'Come on, love. It'll do you more good than hammering away all afternoon. It's not like you're unprepared.'

'Mum'll kill me.'

'No, she won't. She needn't even know we've been out. And if she gets wind of it, I'll take the flak. Promise.'

'Can we go to Mam Tor?'

'We'll go wherever you like.'

Alicia dashes upstairs. Guy watches her: away from the piano, she's a normal girl again, a blonde teenager bounding around like any other – as she ought, perhaps, to be.

She comes down in a blue and white Kate sweater; it's May now, but although London is reportedly enjoying twenty degrees, in Buxton the temperature has only reached twelve. Driving away, they feel like a pair of children playing truant.

About twenty minutes outside Buxton, in the Peak District National Park, Mam Tor rises out of the landscape like a capsized ship buried under the rocks since time began. It's an Iron Age fort and the beginning of the Pennine Way, where the earth presents two hundred and seventy hilly miles that you can, if you wish, walk in their entirety. This, Guy has often told Alicia, is the backbone of England.

At the top, a look-out point with a telescope gives Alicia a full circle of wonder. On every side, the view offers her colours as elusive and mutable as those she pictures in her music. In late summer the moors are flecked with purple heather and the ground hums with the bumbling of a million bees. In January the world transmutes into black and white; and when the frost strikes, the rugged, hilly outlines are rapt with shades of silver. April brings emerald edges to the valleys and October and November turn them to bronze; July is dusty, warm and peculiarly artificial, for this almost treeless landscape is most natural in winter, sluiced with slanting rain, low clouds impaled on outcrops of rock, the wind tearing at Alicia as if determined to lift her off her feet and over the edge. That's when she loves it most. She can stand with an ecstasy of rain drenching her, letting the elements pour out the feelings she can't pour out herself except in music.

Today, though, it's spring. It's remarkably quiet for a Saturday; the Easter tourists have gone home, the summer ones haven't arrived and day-trippers, fearing showers, have stayed away. A few hang-gliders haven't been deterred: they sail in soundless flight over the wide, wild space, tiny amid its treachery. Alicia and her father watch white puffballs of mist swirling in the valleys. The only interruptions to the silence are the whispering wind and the high chatter of a skylark.

'You might see into the future on a day like this,' Alicia says, her gaze scanning the horizon.

'You spend a lot of time thinking about the future, don't you?'

'I guess I haven't much choice.'

'Ali, you're fourteen. Try living in the present a bit. It's good, sometimes, the present. Practising isn't everything. You need to do some living too.'

'That might be easier after next week.'

'It might. But what worries me is that it might not.'

Alicia turns. 'What do you mean?'

'You're thinking of the concerto final as the end. But it might be the beginning. It doesn't matter whether you win or not because everyone will see you on TV and if people like your playing, they'll want you to give concerts. There might be agents watching. Anything's possible.'

'Dad, do you *want* me to win?'

'Oh, Ali, of course I do! I just want you to know that it's not the most important thing on earth.'

Alicia leans against the telescope and looks at her feet. She's growing, fast; each weekend, when Guy has a moment to catch his breath between crises of one kind or another, he notices a change in her. Soon her height will match Kate's; she's already among the tallest in her class at school. The puppy fat is giving way to long, lean legs and a healthy, developing figure.

'What do *you* want, Ali?'

Her back is to him, her golden hair hanging in loose trails. She says nothing.

She wants to say too much, but she doesn't know how. She can't find a way to tell him that she wants him to be proud of her; that one word of approval from him would be worth ten of Mum's and twenty of Mrs Butterworth's; that it's his approval she craves because it's the rarest. Without it, she's just a lump of growing cells and young, hopeful energy that has landed in the middle of Derbyshire and learned how to play the piano. An image lingers from her childhood, of her father lifting her to the window to watch the raindrops slide down the panes; and of how, when there was music, he would come into focus. Perhaps the music was conjuring him for her, like magic.

Even before the final begins, Kate, sitting beside Guy in Symphony Hall, Birmingham, seems to be looking back on this day from a moment far in the future.

The competition buzz is centred on Alicia. She's the youngest of the five finalists. She's up against a violinist two years older than herself, a clarinettist who is nearly eighteen, and two contestants who, in Kate's opinion, are a waste of space: a trumpeter and a percussionist.

'What's the use of making brass and percussion players do concertos?' she remarks. 'They'll only end up in orchestras, wondering why they're not famous soloists.'

'Most pianists end up bashing out exercises for ballet classes,' Guy reminds her.

'Not Ali.'

'I didn't mean Ali.'

'Steady on, you two,' says George, a couple of seats away on the other side of Adrian. 'No fights, please. This is Ali's big night.'

A bright, dark figure turns round from the row in front and waves to Kate.

'Hello, Anjali,' Kate says. 'How lovely that you could come.'

'How's she feeling?' Anjali asks. Kate assesses her deep eyes, sleek hair, slender, self-possessed face. There's not an ounce of malice in her. Just as well, since Ali has beaten her.

'She's fine. A little nervous, perhaps, but very excited.'

'She's got to win. Everyone's saying they've never seen anything like her. My piano teacher watched the semi-finals and went into ecstasies. I'm so happy for her.'

Kate is surprised at Anjali's lack of competitiveness. Watching her and Ali taking their turns in the quarter-finals, Kate had been so impressed with Anjali's playing that she'd found herself half hoping that some disaster would befall either the piano (a broken string, an insecure lid, a sticky key) or maybe Anjali herself (a gently sprained finger or brief dose of flu). Such emotions weren't pleasant; but on the other hand, this was Ali's big chance and it was essential that nothing should get in her way. What's the point of devoting such swathes of time and energy to music if somebody else does better?

'Anji,' Kate says, 'this is Adrian. You haven't met before, have you?'

'Hi, Anji,' Adrian mutters. He's not generally shy around girls, Kate has noticed, unless he likes them.

'Lovely to meet you.' Anjali, her head turned over one

graceful shoulder, smiles at him. He smiles back for a split second, then stares down at his hands. Anjali's father, beside her, gives her a brief, sharp glance.

Backstage, Alicia had locked herself inside her dressing room, telling Kate that she wasn't nervous, but wanted to be alone. Kate had trusted her and left. She's so nervous that she couldn't feel worse if she had to play the concerto herself. Her stomach ties itself into reef-knots, her palms are sweaty and freezing – she's dreading having to shake anybody's hand – and there's a humming in her ears, maybe the hall's air-conditioning, maybe a creation of her stressed-out mind. How does anybody achieve the remotest degree of accuracy on a musical instrument if this is what nerves do to their bodies?

Mrs Butterworth, her small, bony figure encased in dappled blue and violet silk, turns from three rows in front to nod to them. Kate nods back, noticing with satisfaction that some of the people around them comment quietly to one another, 'That's Alicia Bradley's mother; that's her teacher, Deirdre Butterworth . . .' Her stomach jolts again.

The clarinettist plays first. She's a large, smily girl who gives what the television commentators will describe as an incredibly musical performance of the Mozart Clarinet Concerto. Alicia is to play last. They wait amid the audience on red seats, surrounded by pale wood and brilliant TV lights, through the percussion concerto, the violin concerto and the interval; then they'll have to endure the trumpet concerto before Alicia's turn.

'And here we have Alicia Bradley's family.'

Kate glances round, startled; she had barely glimpsed the television presenter, a cheerful young woman named Isabel, heading their way with a cameraman in tow. The lights make her blink as Isabel bounces up to them, microphone at the ready. 'Mrs Bradley, how are all of you feeling tonight?'

'It's very exciting for everyone, but especially Alicia.' Kate gives her widest smile.

'Of course the competition's very stiff and she's the youngest by several years. How does she feel about that?'

'Absolutely fine,' Kate says. 'She's here to make music. We're all here to celebrate music-making, first and foremost. And whoever wins the prize, I'm sure he or she will be a very deserving performer.'

'Well, best of luck to Alicia Bradley, who's been the hot favourite in a very special year for this competition,' Isabel says, into the camera. 'The stage has been rearranged, the piano is in place and in a moment Alicia Bradley will be coming on to play Ravel's glorious Piano Concerto in G major.'

Kate's whole body is trembling as applause blazes round the hall – and Alicia is there, sailing across the platform in her turquoise dress (she'd insisted that was the only colour she could wear to play this concerto). She strides to the piano as confidently as a woman of thirty. Rustles, whispers and thrills go through the audience. Kate reaches for Guy's hand, almost as clammy as her own.

Alicia, her back tree-trunk straight, her hands poised to begin, fixes her gaze on the conductor. He smiles at her – a famous maestro with a rack of awards and titles, grinning at Kate's fourteen-year-old daughter as if she's a colleague, an equal. He raises his arms. A snap like a whipcrack, the first note of Ravel's score, and they're off, Alicia's fingers glittering, flickering, coaxing, the orchestra sitting forward to listen during her solos.

It's not Kate's intense slow-motion experience; it's not her imagination; it's not just because Alicia is her daughter. Something extraordinary is happening. An enchantment is settling over the hall that defies breath. The audience is motionless. Nobody coughs. Nobody wriggles, not even Adrian. The sounds reaching their ears are not like the sound of Alicia practising. The figure on stage is not that of a schoolgirl ploughing through her first concerto.

Alicia is making the piano sing in a way that pianos usually don't. She turns Ravel's jazzy phrases almost like Edith Piaf or Ella Fitzgerald. The glint in her eye as she toys with the music, the glances she exchanges with the orchestra members who duet with her, the shared confidences with the conductor, the sophistication in the sounds – none of these match the unsophistication of the Alicia who bounds about at home and goes running in the rain with no umbrella, her dog trotting beside her. She is the music and the music is her. The piano is an extension of her. As she plays the sustained, unaccompanied start of the slow movement, the mesmerised atmosphere deepens. Silent ecstasy emanates from a thousand people towards the Birmingham night sky. Kate's cheeks are wet with tears; she has no idea how they've got there, whether they're for Ali or for the ghost of Victoria, haunting the music to which she had so briefly lived, then died.

At the end, the hall explodes. Kate's head spins. Anjali and her family leap to their feet. Didie on the other side of George is wiping her eyes, Adrian is whooping and whistling and the cheers and stamps around them won't stop. The place is in a frenzy, shouting for Alicia Bradley.

Alicia has retreated off the platform with the conductor, but he sends her back alone and she's greeted by a roar like a storm at sea. Tall and radiant in her turquoise silk dress, she extends both arms in a gesture of thanks, as graceful as a ballerina, to Kate's astonishment – she thinks of her daughter as gawky. What seems too loud and too large close to is transformed, on stage, into a personality that projects to perfection.

Guy is motionless beside Kate. 'So it's true, then,' he says. 'This isn't the end. It's only the beginning.'

With Mrs Butterworth strutting behind them like a small hawk that's fallen into a pot of purple paint, and Anjali alongside laughing with joy, Guy, Kate and Adrian struggle upstream to get backstage. Kate can see Alicia's bright hair and blue dress; she's surrounded by well-wishers, the BBC team, members of the orchestra, some contestants who've been eliminated, people in suits or expensive dresses who have a vague air of importance . . .

Then Alicia spots them. Kate holds out her arms.

'Dad!' Alicia cries, flinging herself on to Guy's neck.

Kate is poised between breaths, lowering her hands, wondering how to laugh this off, when someone brushes her elbow.

Life-changing events can be crowned with TV cameras; they can start with the ring of a bell on door or phone; and, sometimes, they're heralded by the soft touch of a finger upon an arm.

'Kate?'

The voice is oddly familiar. Kate turns and looks into the face of a slender, sinewy woman with short-cropped hair and deep brown eyes, wearing an elegant linen trouser suit and an exotically fashioned gold necklace.

'You don't remember me, do you?'

Kate's brain dredges images long forgotten, traumatised by time. She knows these eyes. *'Heavens!'*

'Rebecca – Rebecca Young, from university. And quartet. Don't say you've forgotten me, Kate?'

'Oh, my God,' Kate says.

'You must be a very proud mum.' Rebecca presses her arm harder.

'Yes! My God – Rebecca . . . Just a moment – *Ali*!'

'Mum!' Alicia reaches out and hugs her. Kate can feel her exhaustion – the dress is soaked with sweat and the muscles are trembling slightly – but her face is alight with triumph.

'Ali, this is Rebecca. I haven't seen her since university,' Kate says.

'Congratulations, Alicia,' Rebecca says. 'You were outstanding.'

'I haven't won yet,' Alicia reminds her. The jury is absent, considering its verdict.

'I'll be amazed if you haven't,' Rebecca declares. 'They're mad if they don't give you the prize. Kate, it's so fantastic to be here and to see you and meet your family. We must get together and talk properly. But I can tell tonight's going to be difficult.'

'It's fantastic to see you too. Call me?' Kate grabs a pen from her handbag and writes the phone number on the front of Rebecca's programme.

'Here's my card.' Rebecca presses a small red rectangle into Kate's hand. It reads:

EDEN CLASSICS
Rebecca Harris
Director, A&R

Before she can ask what A&R means, or why Rebecca was backstage trying to meet Alicia, there's a peal of electronic bells and a flurry of anticipation as the jury troops by, heading for the stage.

'See you later, darling. Fingers crossed,' Kate whispers to Alicia.

Adrian hasn't had a chance to talk to his sister, beyond a peck on the cheek; neither has Anjali; but, Kate notes, they seem quite happy talking to each other.

Ten minutes later, Alicia Bradley has been named BBC Young Musician of the Year. Some while after that – nobody is counting now – Guy and Adrian hoist her on to their shoulders and carry her out of the hall into the crowd that has amassed outside the stage door to cheer her. The next morning, the front page of *The Times* displays a huge photograph of Alicia aloft, smiling and shining across a forest of wild, clapping hands.

Two days later, they're at home, trying to rekindle normality. Kate, shadows under her eyes, sips a third, much-needed cup of morning coffee, wondering whether she was dreaming and what her next step should be, assuming she wasn't. As if in response, the telephone rings.

'Is that Kate?'

'Speaking.'

'Kate. It's Rebecca.'

9

Alicia wakes late, when Cassie jumps on to the bed and licks her face. She's sweating. She hadn't been able to sleep for hours, feeling too churned up; she'd finally drifted off at four o'clock, when dawn was breaking. The dog has woken her from a nightmare.

It was about Cassie – Alicia's worst nightmares always are, usually about the day she was nearly swept away in the River Dove. This time Cassie was in the water, trying to paddle upstream, but great lumps of ice were cascading from the hills, intent on carrying her with them. Alicia leaped in after her, only to find herself submerged beneath an ice floe.

She'll never forget how the water felt. She'd only been in it for a few moments, but the cold had been more bitter than she could imagine, and the current stronger. The fright of falling and feeling it had nearly winded her. The most terrifying thing, she thinks, is the power of natural elements – water and earth, fire and air – because each is filled with energy greater than that of anything alive. That energy can crush a human being whenever it likes.

As the dream went on, she and Cassie were trapped by a freezing, solid mass that scarcely let them breathe, and Alicia was more worried about Cassie than about herself, yet at the same time confused over which of them was which. She couldn't move her legs; she tried to scream, but no sound came out. Mercifully, at that point the real Cassie arrived and woke her. Alicia found that her legs were entangled in the duvet, which was why she couldn't move them. Now it's nearly half past eleven, but luckily this is half-term and she doesn't have to go to school for a week.

The competition is over; she's won it; the future stretches ahead, paved with teeth. What will happen to her now? The final had had a momentum of its own. They had stayed in a wonderful modern hotel; she had spent the next day giving interviews, and in the evening the Sharmas met them and took them to their favourite Indian restaurant. They drove home so late that Cassie barely looked up when they arrived. Alicia is grateful that their neighbours don't mind looking after the dog now and then; otherwise she'd have spent the whole time wondering whether Cassie was all right without her.

She couldn't stop remembering, though, that she had 'beaten' Anjali, among all the others. There should be nothing to 'beat'. They'd played different pieces of music in their own ways. Who was to say that hers was better? Maybe she'd played faster, maybe she's a little more confident, but that's no reason for her to become famous overnight while Anjali goes straight back to being a schoolgirl.

Anjali's father, who'd showered Alicia with praise and insisted on paying for dinner for everyone, had taken some photos of them in the restaurant, promising to send them to her. He kept telling Anjali that she must try to work as hard as Alicia does; advice that made Alicia uncomfortable. Dr Sharma is a GP and Anjali says that his patients adore him. Alicia advises him too, because he's so interested, so proud of Anjali, so much there for her – unlike Alicia's dad. But Anjali looks positively scared of him.

It's time for her to face her own family. Dressed, she takes a deep breath and opens her bedroom door to go downstairs and see what's waiting for her there today.

The phone calls and letters haven't stopped. Mum puts on the answering-machine, then shows the letters to Alicia: from agents, record companies, PR companies, fans ('Dear Alicia, I am six years old and I loved seeing you play on the TV, now I am going to have piano lessons too . . .'), music festivals, music clubs, concert promoters, dress designers and charities ('Of course we can't pay you, but we hope that you will find the concert a worthwhile experience . . .'). The BBC has an association with a young musicians' advisory scheme, which offers guidance to all the finalists for the two years until the next competition; even so, Alicia wonders how she's supposed to make head or tail of her new situation.

'What are we going to do?' she asks, eating Weetabix. She's itching to learn some new pieces. Mrs Butterworth has told her to choose anything she likes and she's picked the most difficult things she can find: a Prokofiev sonata, more Ravel, lots of Chopin and the famous Piano Concerto No. 1 by Tchaikovsky.

'I had a call from a very old friend,' Mum says. 'You met her backstage – her name is Rebecca Harris. She works for a record company and she thinks she can help us, so I've suggested she comes to stay for a weekend and we can talk it through. She knows the music business. Of course, the advisory scheme will be useful, but it might be nice to have another viewpoint as well. Don't you think it's a good idea?'

There's a clomp on the stairs and Adrian, his face pale and his eyes full of sleep, peers round the kitchen door. 'Is there coffee?'

'"Good morning, Mum, good morning, Ali, is there any coffee?"' Mum prompts.

Adrian grunts, 'Whatever,' and pads across to the percolator. 'Hey, Ali,' he says, without looking at her. 'I'm proud of you.'

'Really?'

'Sure. You were *cool*. All those cameras and crowds and you just went on and did it. The lads said they saw you on TV and they were dead impressed.'

Alicia jumps up and hugs her brother.

'OK, OK, cool it,' he says, turning red. A moment later he's vanished, taking the rest of the coffee with him.

Kate surveys the empty pot with some anger, wondering why such small matters annoy her so intensely. After she's loaded the percolator with more ground coffee and water, she succumbs to something she's desperate to do. She's been keeping one eye on the clock, waiting until a suitable hour, not wanting to appear too eager. It isn't her normal attitude towards making phone calls. Her pulse, irrationally, seems to have increased. She dials the number on Rebecca's card.

'How about this weekend?' Kate suggests.

'I shall drop everything and run,' declares Rebecca.

By the end of the afternoon, juggling practice, phone calls and discussions with Mum, Alicia feels that her head will burst like a balloon if she doesn't get some air. The weather is clear, the clouds puffy and sparse. She pleads, 'Half an hour, Mum?'

'OK, half an hour. Mind how you go darling.'

Running down the hill towards the golf course, Alicia looks at Cassie and wonders why, in her dreams, she muddles herself up with her dog. Perhaps it's because they need the same things: fresh air, exercise and, now and then, the blessed freedom of being let off the leash.

It's an amazing time of year: everything is bright and sprouting. The posters for the Buxton Festival in July are in place outside the little opera house and the flowerbeds in the Pavilion Gardens have become rich blocks of colour that dazzle Alicia like the sun. Cygnets swim on the pond and the hills are teeming with lambs – lovely as long as you don't think too hard about what will happen to them later.

Alicia and Cassie haven't been out for five minutes when a bicycle whirs down the hill towards them, wobbles, then stops. Someone calls her name. Alicia, Mum says, must get used to people recognising her in the street (something Mum seems to like more than she does herself). But this is only Matthew Littlemore, who's in her class at school and had been at her nursery school too. Alicia has known him all her life, though never sees him much beyond the school gates.

'Hey, Ali, I saw you on TV,' Matthew says. His eyes are sweet. They always were.

'Yeah?' Alicia beams. 'Thanks.'

'Me and my brother Tim, we're having a party tomorrow. Want to come?'

'A party? I'd love to. But I don't know if Mum'll let me. It's my piano lesson the next day and I've got all this new stuff to learn.'

Matthew's face falls. Probably his mum lets him do whatever he likes, as most mums seem to, other than hers.

'It'd be so cool,' he urges. 'There'd be all uz crowd and then in walks the Young Musician of the Year. You'd be guest of honour. Please come, Ali. Have you got our address?'

'Write it down?'

Matthew has a pen, but there's nothing to write on except the back of Alicia's hand. When he touches it, he does so as carefully as if it were made of icing sugar. People are funny about Alicia's hands. She nearly tells Matthew that just because they play the piano it doesn't mean they don't do normal things too, like scrunching the loo roll. But her half-hour is running by.

'I'll try to get there,' she says. 'See you later.'

'See you, Ali.' Matthew swings one long leg back over the bike and sails away downhill. Cassie is jumping and whimpering, impatient to get moving, so they spend the rest of their time sprinting for all they're worth.

They arrive home sweaty (Alicia) and panting (both of them). Mum looks surprised. 'What's that on your hand?' she asks.

'Oh, that. It's Matthew Littlemore's address. He asked me to a party tomorrow. I can go, can't I, Mum?'

'Oh, Ali. It's the night before your lesson.'

'So?' Alicia gives her best Adrian-like pout, but Mum isn't amused.

'So, you have to prioritise. What's more important? Piano lessons or parties?'

'I have a piano lesson every week. I hardly ever go to a party.' Alicia feels tight anger pressing out from her solar plexus – why does she has to fight for every little thing she wants to do away from the piano? 'I don't see why everything has to revolve around Mrs bloody Butterworth!'

'Ali, don't use language like that about your teacher.' Mum, of course, overreacts. She reminds Alicia of Grandma Margaret. 'She's just helped you win the biggest prize in the country. Ali, don't you see? You've got to put your playing first, because now there will be concerts for you to do in some very, very important places and . . .'

'Does that mean I can't go to one party at the house of a friend I've known my whole life, who lives round the corner?'

'Yes, Ali, that is precisely what it means. Now, feed that poor dog, will you? And then go and practise.'

'But, Mum—'

'*Now*, Ali.'

Cassie is whining for her food; probably whining because Alicia is unhappy, too. At least, Alicia thinks, somebody is on her side. She gives Cassie a bowl of her favourite meat; after gobbling it down, the dog follows her to the piano. Some dogs howl when musical instruments are being played, but luckily Cassie can't be bothered. Instead, she lies under the Steinway and goes to sleep.

On the piano sits the plump volume that is Tchaikovsky's Piano Concerto No. 1, waiting for Alicia to learn it. It's extremely difficult, but working out how to get round that is half the fun. After two and a half hours, Alicia feels as if she's only been there for ten minutes, making the music that she adores come alive in her hands, discovering how to shape it as she wants to. It will be hers and she will belong to it. There's no feeling in the world as astonishing as this.

Eventually Mum calls her for supper. Alicia washes her hands and Matthew Littlemore's address rubs off in the soap, but it doesn't seem to matter any more.

Adrian, though, has other ideas. He knows all about the Littlemores' party through Matthew's brother, Tim. 'You've got to go, Ali,' he says later on.

'How can I?' Alicia is lying on her bed, reading. 'Mum's right. It's Mrs B the next day.'

'Mummy doesn't always know best.' Adrian slinks in and closes the door. His eyes are permanently angry these days – maybe because he has GCSE exams soon. But sometimes she thinks he's cleverer than the rest of them put together. Adrian sees things as they are, more clearly than she does; his head isn't filled with Tchaikovsky and Ravel.

'You're nearly fifteen, but Mum's treating you like you're nine,' he insists. 'You've got a life of your own and you look fit – all my friends think so. You should have more fun. You can't play music well if you don't have fun.'

'How do you mean?'

'Music says something, right? It's not just a load of notes designed to keep you plugging away until you can play them?'

'Yes. No. I mean, yes, it means something, and no, it's not just there to keep you working.'

'So if you never do any living, how are you ever going to feel anything that you can put into the music?'

'But—?'

'I like that thing you were playing earlier. What is it?'

'The Tchaikovsky Concerto.'

'It's – what? Half an hour long, or more? And it's full of all kinds of different feelings. So if you never have a chance to feel those feelings for yourself . . .'

'It's not that I don't feel them. I do. I just haven't done anything about them.'

Adrian obviously hasn't thought of this any more than Alicia has until now. 'Well,' he says eventually, 'if you want to go to that party, you tell me and I'll help you.'

'Aren't you coming too? Mum wouldn't say no if she knew you'd be looking after me.'

'The whole point is you don't get looked after, for once. Anyway, that wouldn't make a blind bit of difference with Mum. She doesn't trust me, she never has. And she doesn't *mother* you, she *smothers* you. She's like a mother elephant that goes completely fucking nuts if anything threatening goes near her baby, and when the stampede happens, I don't want to be in the way.'

At the thought of Mum as a stampeding elephant, trumpeting and charging in Alicia's defence, Alicia and Adrian both crack up laughing so hard that Alicia falls right off the bed.

If Mum is an elephant, Alicia is a baby elephant and Adrian is a lion cub – a wicked one, but a lion cub all the same – she wonders where that leaves Dad in their Buxtonian family jungle. She pictures him as a marmoset, shimmying to safety up a tree where he can swing from branch to branch and watch everything beneath, without getting too involved.

'I love you,' says Guy.

Emily is lying in his arms, her hair soft against his chest. He's moving his hands against the nubbly curve of her spine, the shadowed hollows of her neck, the fine, sweet skin on her inner thigh. He can't stop touching her, now that he's started. She turns her face to him and, in the glow from a single lamp on the floor, he sees tears in her eyes. He kisses them away, tasting salt.

'I love you too,' she says. 'Stay with me.'

'I have to go. It's half past nine.'

In the street a siren wails. Blue lights shimmer against the curtains.

'Don't worry,' she jokes, 'they're not after you.'

'Perhaps they ought to be.'

'Nonsense. I'm guilty too. I don't have to do this, you know. You're here because I want you to be. I know you have to go home, even if I wish you didn't.'

'I worry about you living here. It's not the safest area.' Every time Guy is round, a hundred police cars and fire engines seem to career past the block.

'I'm a big girl. I can look after myself.'

'You should have someone to look after you.'

'I don't want anyone to look after me but you, and you can't. That's nobody's fault.' Emily pushes back the covers and crosses to the window to peer out, concealing her nakedness with the long curtains.

'God, you're beautiful.' They've made love twice in two hours, but Guy, looking at her, is still faint with longing. He reaches out his arms and she comes back to him and wraps the essence of all that she is, her musky skin, her clear grey-eyed gaze, her open soul, round his aching body. In a few minutes he'll have to leave her bed, shower away every trace of her and drive out of Manchester across the moor to Buxton, which to him is no longer one of the highest, coldest towns in England for no reason.

'Couldn't you stay?' Emily coaxes. 'Can't you tell her something came up, you're too tired to drive and you're going to stay in a hotel?'

It sounds so easy that Guy hesitates before shaking his head. If he does it once, he'll do it again. Before he knows what's happened, he'll be spending several nights a week in a fictional hotel and then Kate will find out.

'She's already angry because I refused to put Ali's picture on the front page,' he says.

His own staff had been surprised. Local girl wins national

competition? Of course she should be on the front page. But she happened to be the editor's daughter. He would, he'd explained to one perplexed young journalist, be in deep ethical shit if he put a picture of Alicia on the front of his newspaper. It wasn't a sackable offence, but he'd lose his credibility at the office.

Instead, he'd lost his credibility at home. Kate couldn't understand it. The point was Ali, not him. What was the use of his powerful position if he couldn't help his daughter? Guy was so startled by her attitude that he fell over his words trying to explain simultaneously that that wasn't why he'd taken the job, that that kind of action was precisely what it was his duty to avoid and that in any case it wouldn't make the slightest difference since Ali had already snaffled the prize live on TV and had had her picture on the front of *The Times*, compared to which the *Manchester Chronicle* was small fry. Kate hadn't seen it that way. She couldn't see it any way but her own – just as her parents couldn't see any possibility for Sunday lunch other than overcooked roast beef.

'You did the right thing,' Emily says, 'and you know it.'

'Thanks, love. Glad someone believes in me.'

'Guy, come to Denmark with me?'

'*What?*'

'Please. I'm dying to take you there. There's so much I want to show you.'

'Sweetheart, there's nothing I'd like better, but how am I supposed to get away? What am I supposed to tell them?'

'Tell them – as so many men do when they're having affairs – that you're away at a conference. Just be consistent. Yes, I know, I'm shameless. But I want to take you to Denmark and I know that other people do this kind of thing, and if they can, then we can too.'

'Em, I'm not proud of this, you know. I don't *want* to have "an affair". I don't *want* to cheat on my wife.'

'But you are. So either do it, or don't do it. But for heaven's sake, *don't* lie in my bed and make love to me saying you don't want to!'

Guy closes his eyes in despair.

'Hey.' Emily taps his chest with one finger. Through half-raised eyelids he sees her face close to his, shining with help-less affection. 'You're not the first man to have an affair and you won't be the last,' she says. 'Other people manage to go away on trips with their "mistresses". So you can manage to go away with me if you want to. You just have to decide whether you want to. If you do, we'll find a way. I never set out to do this either. I don't want to have an affair with a married man. But I can't pretend I don't love you. I can't go against the feelings we have for each other. If this is the only way we can have them, then this is how it has to be.'

'It's not who we are, but it's what we're becoming. Is that dreadful?'

'Of course. And of course not. Come on, darling, it's nearly ten. You'd better get going.'

Guy takes the dreaded shower, then puts on his suit and prepares to leave. His feet feel like lead as he laces up his shoes.

'Briefcase,' says Emily, handing it to him. 'Glasses.' She retrieves them from the kitchen table, where they're lying beside her pasta bowl, which contains the tomatoey leftovers of their supper. 'Keys.' She fetches them from the floor where, earlier, they'd fallen out of Guy's pocket as he pulled off his jacket in a hurry.

'You're an angel,' Guy says. 'We'll find a way. I promise. See you tomorrow.'

Emily waves to him from her door as he dashes away down the stairs.

Alicia, preparing for bed, hears something light strike her window. At first she thinks it's rain. A louder tap convinces her that it isn't. She pulls back the curtain. Adrian is standing in the garden, throwing pebbles. 'Adrian, what the—'

'Come on, Ali!'

'Mum'll hear.'

'Just do it! Cos if you don't, you'll be sorry. Hurry up, and say goodnight to Mum first. She's doing letters, she won't even look up.'

'Where's the dog? She'll bark!'

'She won't. I gave her some extra grub and she's fast asleep in the kitchen. Useless watchdog, anyway.'

Alicia doesn't like the idea of her dog being manipulated, but she can't help smiling. Cassie would probably bound up to a burglar and lick his face. She goes to her door and calls, 'Night night, Mum.' A faint call comes back from the spare room, which is slowly being transformed into a study: the sewing-machine, knitting basket and guest bed now cohabit with a desk, two filing cabinets and a computer.

She picks up her trainers and inches on tiptoe towards the stairs. She can hear the faint patter of Mum typing. In the kitchen, the over-fed Cassie is sleeping off her feast, nose on paws. At last Alicia manages to edge through the front door and, to her astonishment, she and her brother are soon making their silent way up the hill towards Tim and Matthew Littlemore's home.

The Littlemores live on a cul-de-sac in a small, semi-detached brick house that matches all its neighbours. As Alicia and Adrian approach, they can hear a thumping beat and whoops from inside. Shadows dance on the curtains, silhouettes jumping around and drinking from plastic cups. Alicia stops. 'I can't go in there.'

'Yes, you can. Don't be silly.'

'Please stay. Don't just leave me there. Please, Adrian? Otherwise I'm going straight home and I'll tell Mum.'

'You little blackmailer! I'll stay but, remember, it was for your own good that I didn't want to. Now, ring that bell.'

Alicia steps forward and presses. The door swings open and Matthew is in the doorway, his face registering first surprise, then delight. 'Ali! You made it!'

Tim – a taller, even lankier edition of Matthew – waves a greeting to Adrian, who wanders past his sister into the kitchen.

'It's so great you could come,' Matthew enthuses, ushering in the hesitant Alicia. 'Let me get you a drink.'

'Orange juice, please.'

'Oh, come on, have something stronger. Your mum's not here. What do you like?'

'I don't know,' Alicia admits. 'I've never tried.'

In the hall, Tim is saying to Adrian, 'Your sister's cute, but she doesn't have a clue, does she?'

'Yuck.' Alicia, in the kitchen, is sampling a lurid alcopop.

'I'll have that,' says Kelly from school, whom Alicia hates. Her clothes tonight are so skimpy that Alicia – in a home-knitted yellow jersey and jeans – wonders why she bothers to wear any at all. Her face is caked with makeup. Alicia puts on a little basic makeup for concerts, but hates it: it makes people look like clowns. She hands Kelly the drink, wishing it were even nastier than it is.

'Try this one instead.' Matthew pours a mix from two different bottles, tops it with orange juice and gives it a stir. Alicia sips. Kelly and her group smirk, then snort with laughter as Alicia pulls a face. She decides to stick with the drink to spite them. So much for being Matthew's 'guest of honour': she's up against the resident nasties here too. Being Young Musician of the Year doesn't change that. Matthew's the only person who thinks it matters; as for the others, not only will her prize fail to stop the taunting, it may make things worse.

Tim, Adrian and Sam have sloped away to Tim's bedroom, from which sweetish smoke is now drifting down to the hall. When Alicia breathes it in, it makes her dizzy.

'Want to dance?' Matthew asks her, ignoring Kelly and her crowd.

'Will you teach me how? I never tried dancing before.'

Matthew looks confused, but nods. 'This is the Young Musician of the Year!' he announces, to his friends in the front room, but the music is so loud that nobody hears him. Alicia is glad.

She stands opposite Matthew and jigs around. It seems a slightly pointless exercise. The drink has left a vile taste in her mouth and she can't hear what anybody is saying through the noise. 'Don't the neighbours mind?' she shouts at Matthew.

'So what?' he shouts back.

Behind them, a group of lads from school – the ones who get up to no good in the Pavilion Gardens – are slumped on the sofa and armchairs, drinking beer from tins and pretending they're gangsta rappers.

'Yo, bitch,' says one of them – Alicia recognises him as the biggest troublemaker in Adrian's year, always being hauled to the headmaster for truancy, fighting and, once, carrying a knife. She hesitates. She can't always tell what's real and what's being put on to tease her. The troublemaker's name, she vaguely remembers – she never concentrates on who's who at school – is Garth.

'You's the cool bitch what won a TV prize,' says a boy with pop eyes like a fish, who comes from a farm at the edge of the moor and speaks, at school, with a plain Derbyshire accent. He's trying to be the coolest thing since ice-cubes, but this time Alicia isn't taken in: he sounds like a total plonker.

'You know Alicia,' Matthew says to them, an arm round her. 'She's famous now, but she's still one of us.'

'Hi,' she says. She's sweating desperately in her jersey.

'So where's your mum?' Garth asks Matthew. The Littlemores' father had left them years ago.

'Seeing my auntie in Wolverhampton for a few days. "Be good now, boys. Bed by half past ten."'

Alicia is beginning to wonder what time she's going to get home from this weird experience. Mum was right: she has her lesson tomorrow. Everyone else is on half-term, and although some of them should be revising for GCSEs, they obviously aren't. The clock on the mantelpiece – it reminds her incongruously of her grandparents in Harrow – tells her that it's nearly eleven thirty. In fifteen hours, she has to play her Tchaikovsky to Mrs Butterworth for the first time.

'Playing the piano?' says the fish-eyed boy in his normal voice. 'Why d'you do *that*?'

'Dunno, really,' Alicia says. 'I just do.'

'Is it hard?'

'Yeah, but it's fun.'

'Ali's dad is editor of a newspaper,' Matthew says, stroking her arm. Alicia wishes he wouldn't. The lads swig beer and look at her legs in their tight jeans. They don't care about what her dad does, what she does or, she thinks, anything much else.

'Where does your mum work?' she asks Matthew.

'She's a secretary at the quarry. It's OK. She's cool.'

'Won't she mind this when she comes back?'

'She won't know. We'll clear up. We always do.'

At the end of the room, Kelly is snogging her boyfriend. Garth, who gains street cred for always skipping school the day after he's sent to the headmaster, extends a lordly hand towards the thinnest, blondest girl from Kelly's group. She teeters towards him in her high heels and half collapses into his lap. Alicia feels as if the music's beat is hitting her repeatedly on the back of the head. The room spins round her. This is meant to be *fun*?

'Have another drink,' says Matthew. Alicia tries to refuse, but he gets her one anyway.

A muscular boy who plays in the school football team has wandered in and is watching the thin blonde girl kissing Garth, outraged.

'That's Flaps's boyfriend,' Kelly tells Alicia. 'Even he doesn't dare hit Garth!'

'I thought her name was Flora,' Alicia says.

'It is. We call her Flaps because – well, work it out.'

'Ali.' Garth, disgorging the leggy blonde from his lap, waves a regal summons to her. She walks towards him, but keeps a safe distance. 'Flora wants to make her boyfriend jealous,' he explains, 'so she kisses me, to make him keener. Who do you like, Ali?'

'Nobody, really,' says Alicia, glancing about to see if Matthew's listening.

'No boyfriend? Why not? You're fit, you know. You should come to Manchester with me. Come out shopping. We'll get you some proper gear.'

'I like what I'm wearing. I have to dress up for my concerts so I prefer not to the rest of the time.'

Garth recoils. Then – apparently remembering he's supposed to be cool – he gives a slow smile instead. 'So what you got under this?' he says, plucking at her knitted yellow sleeve. 'Hot in here, isn't it?'

'Yeah, a bit.'

She doesn't know how it's happened, but a minute later she's no longer wearing her jumper. Under it is a white camisole with a low, round neck. She knows it shows her bra a little, but it can't be helped. The gazes of the boys on the sofa seem to carry barbs as they turn towards her. Feeling self-conscious, she heads for the kitchen, where Matthew gives her another drink and strokes her arm again, this time on her skin.

'What're you doing Saturday?' he asks her. 'Fancy coming to Stockport with me and your brother and Tim and Tim's girlfriend? We're going to the Leonardo DiCaprio movie.'

Alicia has never been to the cinema with a group of friends. She has no group of friends; and the nearest cinema is in the next town.

'I'd love to,' she says, 'but Mum's got this friend coming to stay who has something to do with the competition and I think they're expecting me to be there.'

'It's all your family and your music and your career with you, isn't it?' Matthew looks not only sorry, but annoyed too. 'Why aren't you allowed to let your hair down?'

'That's what Adrian said. They don't bother keeping *him* in the house.'

'He wouldn't let them if they tried. You got to assert yourself, Ali. You're not there just to please them.'

Alicia, through the spinning room, the thumping beat and the smoke from the older boys' spliffs, dimly registers that the clock is showing midnight. She wonders where the time has gone. She's trying to find words to explain why she does what she does. Instead, she realises there's a tear on her cheek.

'Ali. Don't cry,' Matthew says softly. Before she can stop him, he has kissed her where the tear had been and his hands are stroking her long hair. Muddled, she hesitates a moment too long and then his mouth is on hers, pushing her lips apart, his tongue prodding at her teeth. Her nostrils are full of his scent – beer, crisps and something very boylike, plus some aftershave – and she finds that her left arm is round his neck. Waves of sensation wash through her stomach and weaken her legs, her neck is tingling and her skin, under his hand, feels warm and alive.

'Ali,' he whispers. 'Mmm.'

'Mmm,' she echoes. She feels so muzzy-headed and wobbly that she lets him manoeuvre her into another room, she's not sure what it is, but there's nobody else there and it's dark. He kisses her harder and his hands move under her camisole and over her breasts and it feels absolutely wonderful.

'I thought you'd be scared,' he says.

'No,' says Alicia, whose heart is pounding, but not from fear.

'You haven't done this before, have you?'

'No.' Alicia giggles. 'Have you?'

'Once or twice. I prefer doing it with you, though.'

Alicia leans her back against the wall while Matthew leans

his front against her and snogs her. Her lips feel swollen and sensitive and her joints are hot. He's breathing fast and pressing her rhythmically with something hard inside his trousers.

'What's *that*?' she asks.

The door bursts open and a hand grabs her elbow. 'What the hell's going on?' Adrian, in his best big-brother mode, has inadvertently saved Alicia from more embarrassment than she had imagined possible. 'Get off my sister!' he barks at Matthew. 'She's only young. Ali, you're drunk and really stupid and I'm taking you home.'

'You stink,' Alicia says. He reeks of smoke, herbs and beer.

'Where's your jumper?'

'In the lounge. You sound like Mum.' She realises her words are slurring into each other and, after her protracted snogging session, she's having trouble standing up straight.

'Yo, Al.' Garth tosses her jumper towards her when she wobbles back, looking for it. 'Don't forget, you're coming shopping with me in Manchester.'

'Can't take you anywhere,' Adrian mutters, half shoving her out of the front door. She's giggling – somehow she can't stop – and, as the night air hits her, she finds she has hiccups as well. It's a difficult mixture to cope with and suddenly she discovers she's going to be sick.

Adrian stands by, hands in pockets and back turned, while she doubles up over a patch of wallflowers in a front garden. 'Good to get that out of the way,' he remarks.

'Oh, God.' Alicia is praying that she will never see an alcopop again. 'What's Dad going to say?'

'Dad mightn't even be in. Anyway, it's the mother elephant you've got to worry about.'

'She thinks I'm asleep.'

'Let's keep it that way. Think you can make it back?'

'I don't know. Oh, God . . .' and she doubles over the wallflowers again while her insides turn outside.

'Try to walk,' says Adrian. 'You're going to be fine. Drink

pints of water when we get in, and I mean *pints*, and you'll feel OK in the morning.'

Adrian marches and Alicia staggers, supported by him, down the road and into their street. The house is dark and silent: Mum and Dad have evidently gone to sleep unaware that their kids have so much as ventured outside. Adrian unlocks the door.

'Just go slowly,' he whispers.

The journey to the second floor seems insurmountable. She won't make it; she'll slip, fall down and break her hand or arm or finger. Or her back. Or she'll throw up again, on Mum's beautiful golden carpet.

What's Mum going to say? Even if she doesn't fall, tomorrow could be nastier than she can bear to think about right now. Sometimes she wishes she could be normal, like Kelly and the others. She inches upwards.

'Al, *hurry*. They'll wake up.'

Adrian and Alicia don't know that their mother can hear nothing, wearing earplugs against Guy's snoring; nor that their father is dead to the world, worn out by too much work, too much driving and too much sex with someone he's not meant to be having sex with. It's only when Cassie gives a quiet, relatively useless yap from her basket near Alicia's empty bed that the prospect of real danger makes Alicia accelerate. At last she finds herself, with immeasurable relief, inside her room.

She manages to calm Cassie, pull off her clothes and slide under her duvet. Before she's had time to wonder how she'll explain herself in the morning, she's sunk into irresistible sleep.

10

Rebecca arrives on Saturday afternoon, her black Golf GTi crunching into the drive while the Bradleys are finishing lunch. She steps out of the car, cool and relaxed: a helicopter might have transported her to Buxton in twenty minutes. Her hair glistens with highlights and her jeans, under a Burberry summer raincoat, look more expensive than a fur wrap. Gone are her Indian skirts, open sandals and flowery necklaces of the seventies. Rebecca's eyes, though, have not changed, despite the crow's feet at their corners. Kate, through the window, glimpses the chocolate brown she used to know so well and finds she's running down the front steps towards her.

'Katie!' Rebecca cries. Nobody but Guy and Didie has called Kate 'Katie' for twenty-five years.

'You're really here!' Kate hugs her. 'Come in. Let me take your bag.'

'It's fine, don't worry.' Rebecca picks up her Louis Vuitton case and follows Kate inside; her gaze rests briefly on the curve of the piano in the window.

'This,' says Guy in the hall, 'is incredible.'

Rebecca – who'd been no great fan of Guy's at university – kisses him on both cheeks. Adrian steps forward, slightly pink round the ears, and shakes her hand brusquely before sloping away, claiming revision. Alicia hovers nearby and allows herself to be embraced and congratulated. The Bradley family is presenting a united front. There's no point in discussing with a newcomer, who is there to help them, the ongoing nuclear fallout from the Littlemores' party.

The years concertina upon Kate. But for the competition final, she hasn't seen Rebecca since before Buxton, before Stoke Newington, before Victoria – yet those long years of despair and relocation and the discovery of Ali's talent have compressed to the size of a pinhead. 'Milk and two sugars?' she says in the kitchen, making coffee.

'Black, please,' Rebecca says. 'And I gave up sugar. It's extraordinary, isn't it? At eighteen you can have as much sugar as you like, but after forty, one spoon and you're up a size.'

'Oh, come on, Becs, you haven't changed a bit.'

'Older. Much older. And, hopefully, wiser.'

The piano starts up in the front room: Alicia is practising Tchaikovsky. Rebecca blinks.

'Five days,' Kate says. 'She's only been playing it for five days, and listen.'

'You're joking.'

'I wish I was. Becs, my daughter is a prodigy and I don't know what to do!'

'That, darling, is why I'm here.' Rebecca reaches over and presses her wrist.

'I thought,' Kate says, a lump in her throat, 'that this afternoon I could show you Buxton, and tonight I'll cook dinner at home. And tomorrow we could go to Chatsworth House, if you like.'

'You're so lucky, living in the middle of this marvellous countryside.'

'And you're so lucky living in the middle of all that marvellous culture. I worry about Ali not having access to it. There's plenty going on here, but not often on the level she needs now. The best we can do is a touring opera or two per year at Buxton Opera House and sometimes a concert in Manchester.'

'You must bring her to stay with us whenever you like. My two boys are in their teens, I'm sure they'd get along.'

'Becs, you have to tell me *everything*. I didn't even know you had two boys.'

Rebecca laughs into Kate's smile, though her eyes look oddly moist. She sips her coffee and begins to talk. After university, she'd spent a year in India and Nepal, where she'd experienced spiritual revelations, Himalayan trekking, an encounter with a black rhino and amoebic dysentery. Eventually she'd come home – to find that her friends had moved away, she had no job and nowhere to live and her cello technique had sunk to an all-time low. She'd started temping and ended up working for a record company, where she'd answered phones and done the boss's typing before becoming an assistant press officer. The company was taken over; she'd been made redundant, moved on to another record company; and so it continued, a slow but steady climb until the news reached her that the A&R director of Eden Classics was emigrating to Australia. By then, she knew the classical CD market inside out; and A&R – Artists and Repertoire – was the field she loved. It involved selecting musicians and helping to choose what they should record. She'd applied, and here she is. Kate, listening, feels the hair prickle on her neck.

'Darling?' Guy looks in. 'I've got to go to the office for a few hours.'

'Must you? Will you be home for supper?'

'Yes. Absolutely. Home by seven.' He vanishes.

Rebecca looks at the empty doorway, then at Kate's expressionless face.

'It's the job. I shouldn't complain,' Kate declares. 'He loves the work and, goodness knows, we need the money, with that piano to pay off.'

'Ali will be paying off her own piano very soon. You'll see.'

'You think?'

'Come on, Kate. She's Young Musician of the Year. The whole country knows her. Even people who think they don't know anything about classical music know her. All we have to do is to make sure she's got the right support.'

Cassie trots up to Rebecca, wagging her substantial tail and sniffing at the visitor with her new scents (which, Kate notices, include more than a whiff of St Laurent's Paris). 'What a *wonderful* dog. *Aren't* you?' Rebecca rubs Cassie's back. The collie lowers her snout and lets her.

'How about a walk?' Kate suggests.

Leaving Alicia at the piano and Adrian 'revising' upstairs, Kate and Rebecca set off down the hill, falling naturally into step as they used to at university. Kate had forgotten this; it happens of its own accord. She points out the wide dome of what used to be the Royal Devonshire Hospital and is now being transformed into a new section of Derby University. Nearby lurks the ageing splendour of the Palace Hotel in its grounds, while round the corner, in the Pavilion Gardens, a craft fair is in full swing. Rebecca exclaims on the prettiness of the flowerbeds, the freshness of the air, the cuteness of the little Victorian opera house, which is advertising a show for children starring a former TV presenter. At the spring-water fountain on the Crescent, she insists on stopping to sip some from her cupped hands. Kate leads her up to the market square and down again past an olde-worlde pharmacy, an antiques arcade and, in due course, DUCKS CROSSING, which makes Rebecca crease up with laughter.

'Do you have many friends here?' Rebecca asks, as they amble along.

'Not that many,' Kate admits.

'No string quartet? No local orchestra?'

'I haven't played my viola since 1981.'

'Oh.' Kate registers that her friend has recognised problem territory. Rebecca changes tack: 'Don't you meet people through the children?'

'I know a lot of nice people. Ali's first teacher, Glenda, is a friend, and I used to go to a book club, but I'm afraid I've let that slip – I'm too busy with Ali. You know, having a musical child changes your life. People can find it intimidating, even

Glenda. I don't mean her to, or anyone else. We haven't changed. We're exactly the same. It's just that people expect us to be different, so they treat us differently.'

'You must be lonely, with Guy working so hard, Ali practising, Adrian busy being a teenager.'

'How do you *manage*, having two teenage boys?'

'We're lucky. They get along, they're at a good school and they're sporty. Their dad got them both season tickets to Arsenal. That keeps them happy.'

Rebecca's husband – ex-husband, rather – is finance director of a large electronics firm. The boys attend one of north London's most expensive private schools.

'I don't know what to do with Adrian,' Kate confesses. 'You wouldn't believe what happened the other day. He smuggled Ali out of the house . . .' The full story comes out: Alicia's first hangover had not been a pretty tale. Rebecca laughs, though, and Kate finds herself smiling, despite insisting that it wasn't funny at the time. That was a massive understatement – she'd been so alarmed that she'd not slept for two nights – but she doesn't tell Rebecca that.

'You know, it might be good to get Ali out a little more, have her meet boys who are more suitable,' Rebecca suggests. 'Just because she plays the piano, it doesn't mean she's not a normal teenager. Come to London. We'll go to a concert and she can meet James and Oscar. Who are her favourite musicians?'

'She's been smitten with that French pianist, Lucien Delamain, since his Chopin disc came out,' Kate tells her. 'I've bought her all his recordings and she adores them.'

'Lucien? Interesting. He's unusual. And very attractive. That curly hair. Those *eyes*.'

'Evidently.'

'But what I like is that he's such an individual. He's one of the few pianists you can recognise right away by his sound. You can switch on the radio and know it's him in a few seconds . . .'

By the time they're back at the house, it has been agreed

that when Lucien Delamain plays in London in July, Kate will bring Alicia to hear him, and they'll stay at Rebecca's place in Hampstead Garden Suburb. Perhaps Alicia will find a new interest there when she meets Rebecca's sons.

Meanwhile, Kate has learned a great deal about the music industry. Having explained which artists' management firms have contacted her via the BBC, she now knows which Rebecca thinks are a waste of time and which she likes – 'It's so important to have the right manager,' says Rebecca – and she has gathered that engaging a PR company might be no bad thing to manage all the press interest.

In Kate's study, where Rebecca will be sleeping, they sit on the floor together, sift through the letters and divide them into piles marked Good, OK and Fuck Off.

'Can't Guy help you organise this?' Rebecca asks, surveying the sea of paper.

'If you think this is bad, try *his* study.'

Rebecca encourages Kate to make a list of Alicia's repertoire – setting out, under Solo Works and Concertos, which pieces she can be engaged to play. She'll need a file of reviews, easily reproducible via computer – until now, Kate admits, colouring, she's been pasting them into a scrapbook – and some good photos. 'With professional hair and makeup,' Rebecca adds. 'Now, where do you buy her concert dresses?'

By six o'clock, Kate's study has morphed into a managerial office: everything has been reorganised, from filing system to letterhead, from calendar with sticky labels to positioning of desk (away from the window, to discourage daydreaming). The sewing-machine and knitting basket have been stowed away under the bed.

At ten past six, while Kate is pouring gin and tonic, the doorbell sounds Big Ben and Cassie barks. Adrian crashes down the stairs. On the doorstep are the two gangly Littlemore boys and a girl of about sixteen in a very short skirt.

'Is she coming?' Matthew says to Adrian.

The piano music breaks off and Alicia bursts into the hall, pushing her hair out of her eyes. 'Oh, please,' she says to her mother. 'We were going to go to Stockport to see the new Leonardo DiCaprio movie! Adrian, I can be ready in five minutes.'

'Ali, Rebecca's come all the way from London to talk to you,' Kate reminds her. 'It's really not a good day to go swanning off to the cinema.'

'Mum, *please*! I never, ever go to the cinema!'

'Please, Mrs Bradley?' Matthew echoes. 'We'll take good care of her.' His eyes are caressing Alicia's soft, bare arms.

'I'm afraid it's out of the question today,' Kate says, more firmly. 'It's a very important time for Ali and we need her here. Don't be back too late, Adrian.'

'Ali!' calls Matthew.

'I'm sorry.' Alicia reaches out a hand. 'I'd really like to go. See you at school.'

'*Al*—'

The door closes once again between Alicia and the rest of the universe.

Alicia deflates. She crouches to hug the dog, hiding her face in Cassie's coat.

Rebecca looks on. 'I'm sorry, Ali. I know you wanted to go out with your friends,' she says gently. 'But you'll be glad this time that you stayed with us. I promise.'

'That's kind of you. Thank you.' Alicia, head against Cassie's neck, doesn't turn round.

'Gin?' Kate says to Rebecca. They troop back to the kitchen, leaving the girl and the dog at the foot of the stairs. They're half afraid to look back.

Guy comes home an hour later, when Kate is basting the chicken. There are dark circles under his eyes and his step seems heavy and tired, but there's extra warmth in the way he embraces Alicia, who needs hugs tonight. Kate divines that he must be glad to get back; the office and the drive on a busy Saturday exhaust him excessively.

'Having fun, girls?' he says to Kate and Rebecca – and disappears into the bathroom without waiting for their gin-relaxed answer.

Alicia sits at her place at the dinner table. Mum has made roast chicken – as usual, slightly overcooked – and Dad has opened a good bottle of wine for Rebecca's benefit. Alicia chews a drumstick while the conversation jets over her head. Rebecca and Mum talk about artists' management firms, occasionally turning to her and saying, 'Don't you think so, Ali?' or 'You'd be so much better off with someone like that, wouldn't you?'

Alicia says, 'Yes,' because she doesn't know what else to say. From the way Rebecca is talking, you'd think that music was a business, not an art. Even Mum looks slightly shell-shocked.

Alicia imagines Matthew, Adrian, Tim and Tim's girlfriend in the cinema, eating popcorn and watching the lovely Leo. Why did Mum think she needed to be home for this conversation? She could have gone to Stockport, then come back and been told everything and it wouldn't have made any difference. Above all, it strikes her as peculiar that although Rebecca works for a record company she hasn't suggested that Alicia should make a CD. Why not? Alicia doesn't like to ask. Maybe Rebecca had hated her playing, but is embarrassed to say so. She half closes her eyes and imagines Matthew kissing her in the cinema.

This week seems to have lasted two years. During the day, she's been playing at being Young Musician of the Year, which involves hours on the phone talking to the BBC people, the conductor (he wants her to play with his orchestra as soon as possible), and journalists who want to interview her – why do they all ask the same questions and why are they fixated on whether she has a boyfriend? Any calls about potential management or concert bookings she delegates to Mum. The rest of the time, she's either dreaming about Matthew snogging her or remembering performing her Ravel concerto, when she'd reached the point where earth and sky touch and sailed through to the other side. Soaring. Adrian has told her he smokes weed because it makes him high, but she can't imagine feeling higher than she did that night.

And so she stays at the dinner table. She listens, she's polite, she takes notice as the adults talk about what she should wear, which pieces she should learn, where she should play. Because perhaps, if she does what they say, she can keep playing like that for ever.

'But it's *Derby*shire.' Rebecca is gazing up at the intricate bronze-brown turrets of Chatsworth House, serene in its parkland under a grey, blowsy sky.

'There's a legend that the king made a mistake,' Kate explains. 'The first thing I heard was that James I said "Devonshire" instead of "Derbyshire" by accident when he was bestowing the title and it was never put right. But that turned out to be complete nonsense. Actually, William Cavendish purchased his barony and the Devonshire title happened to be available. There never was a Derbyshire dukedom.'

'It's amazing how these legends go on and on. I once heard that "Thames" ought to be pronounced "Thaymes", but instead we all have to imitate George I's German accent!' Rebecca remarks. 'That's probably rubbish too. Honestly, the things people say. Rumours. And soon everyone thinks they're true.' She wraps her coat round her. 'God, it's cold here. It's meant to be summer. How do you survive?'

'We're used to it. Or, rather, Guy is,' Kate says pointedly. Guy doesn't feel the cold. But he, of course, isn't out in it today. He's at work – as is usual, now, on a Sunday afternoon. 'Are you warm enough, Ali?' she asks.

'Fine, thanks.' Alicia doesn't feel the cold either. She's striding ahead, enjoying the wind in her hair. She gives herself to the breeze, lifting her chin, radiating Alicianess.

'People notice her,' Rebecca remarks quietly, watching as passers-by glance at her despite themselves. 'Even if they've no idea who she is, they spot her and look twice. She's got charisma.'

'One review compared her to Jacqueline du Pré,' Kate says. 'It said she's the most important British talent since du Pré and that she has a similar quality, that incredible, natural, joyous gift for communicating, reaching people just by being there – but I don't want to sound conceited.'

'I saw that one. I think it should be the lead paragraph in her biography. It's about personal radiance. Jackie du Pré had it. So does Ali. I mean, look at her. She's amazing.'

'Becs, I so want to get this right for her.'

'We'll get it right together.'

They stroll through Chatsworth's Capability Brown gardens, past an elegant rectangular pond where a fountain blows rainbows of glittering drops into the breeze. Heading uphill, they skirt hedges of box and bay, explore concealed pathways and discover protected enclaves that entice the weary-footed with white wooden benches. They climb along leaf-shaded tracks and gaze down at the house in its splendour amid the greenery, shielded from the outside world and its dangers. Here there is nothing but elegance and peace, despite the number of noisy day-trippers.

'"*Luxe, calme et volupté*,"' quotes Rebecca. 'Take away all those people and Baudelaire could have been writing about this place. It creates an atmosphere of its own, just because of the way it's designed. Nobody could build it now.'

'You're into French poetry?' Kate says.

'Ah, I picked that up from someone who is. Someone I'd like Ali to meet. An agent.'

Alicia, strolling apart with Cassie on her leash, isn't listening. She's humming Chopin and moving her fingers.

While Alicia is out of earshot, Rebecca quietly changes the subject.

'Katie,' she says, 'can I ask you something? There's one thing I don't understand. Why did you leave your job and London? It seems so – *cataclysmic*. One minute you were setting up that flat in Stoke Newington, you worked for a good firm, Guy was on a national paper. The next minute you shift to Buxton. It doesn't add up. And you said you haven't played your viola for years. You know,' she adds, when Kate doesn't respond, 'when I was thirty, my mother and father died within eighteen months of each other. I haven't touched the cello since. It's as if something went out of me.'

'I'm sorry, Becs. That's awful.'

'I hope you don't mind me asking – but did something happen to you?'

Kate hesitates for a good ten seconds. She fights herself. She's not sure why she wants to confide in Rebecca, having confided in no one for so many years. Yet now she longs to let go, give herself up, tell her everything. Ali knows nothing of the history and this is not the time to reveal it; but as she's a safe distance away, Kate breathes in and turns to Rebecca. She won't indulge in an outpouring. She'll only give her the facts.

'Yes,' she says. 'Something did happen. We had our first baby. She was premature and she didn't survive.'

'Oh, my God. I'm so sorry. I had no idea.'

'No reason you should have. It's a long time ago. But—' Kate doesn't want to cry in front of someone she hasn't seen for decades. 'It was very difficult to get over it,' she says. 'We needed a change of scene and Guy's job came up.'

'So you left your whole world behind. Friends, family, job, all your support systems. You didn't even call me to let me know.'

'Becs, how could I? It had been such ages.' Kate blows her nose. 'I couldn't ring up out of the blue and say, "Oh, this awful thing happened . . ." Sorry . . . I'm not normally a running tap. But I haven't told anybody for years.'

Rebecca presses her arm. 'It's OK, Katie. You can tell me

anything. You always could. Your family's stiff upper lip can be destructive. It's good to let it out sometimes.'

'Oh, Becs. You don't know how much I missed you.'

'Probably not as much as I missed you,' Rebecca says quietly, putting an arm round Kate's shoulders. 'Do Ali and Adrian know what happened?'

'We never talk about it.'

'I guess you wouldn't.' Rebecca looks at the ground. 'What about Guy? Can you talk to him?'

'That,' says Kate, lips tightening, 'is a story all its own.'

'I see.' Rebecca reflects for a minute, in silence, watching Alicia running along the path with Cassie. 'Now, can I cheer you up?' she says, suddenly brisk. 'Might Ali like to make a CD?'

Kate brightens at once. She's been waiting for this for twenty-five hours.

'Ali,' she calls, 'come here a minute, darling.'

Alicia, the dog at her heels, bounds up to them, her hair blowing across her eyes and her flushed cheeks. Apart from that unthinking charisma, Kate reflects, Ali is becoming beautiful. No wonder Matthew Littlemore wanted her to go to the cinema. What appalling timing it would be if Ali started having boyfriends now.

'We were wondering, Ali,' Rebecca says, looking her straight in the eye, 'whether you'd be interested in making a recording for my company. It would be your debut disc, a musical portrait of you, with your picture on the front. You could play a selection of your favourite pieces. What do you think?'

Alicia clasps her hands together and stares at Rebecca, mute.

'I mean it. We all love your playing and we'd like you to have that opportunity, if you want it,' Rebecca encourages.

Alicia bursts out laughing, dives forward and hugs the astonished Rebecca.

'I think that's a yes,' says Kate.

★ ★ ★

They adjourn to the tea room to talk things over. By the time they've munched their way through chocolate cake, Bakewell tart (Kate insists that Rebecca tries the local speciality) and, for Alicia, a home-made scone laden with fresh cream and strawberry jam as white and pink as her skin, it's virtually settled. They'll start as soon as she's ready – the sooner the better, Rebecca adds, so that the competition is still fresh in the public's mind. Alicia can come to London and make the recording in the finest studio available – this CD will *sell*. After that, they can discuss what she should do next.

'Beethoven,' Alicia says, eyes shining. 'And lots of Chopin.'

'Concertos,' Kate prompts. 'How about the Tchaikovsky? With a good orchestra and a big-name conductor.'

'Expensive, but not out of the question.' Rebecca's smile gives nothing away. Kate remembers, from the distant past, that it never had. Rebecca had always been good at smiling her way through any public expression of opinion, then revealing later, in private, that her own views were a little different. For her, timing was everything.

'We must also talk about Mrs Butterworth at some point,' Rebecca says, through her smile. Alicia glances quizzically at her.

Guy, back from work at eight that evening, takes off his glasses and keeps quiet while Kate tells him the day's events. The monologue takes ten minutes.

'Well?' Kate finishes.

'Well, what?'

Kate thinks that while she's been talking, Guy seems to have aged several years. 'Isn't it fantastic?' she prods. 'Ali is going to be plastered all over every record shop in the country.'

'Katie,' Guy says, 'Ali isn't fifteen yet. Why so much, so fast?'

'What exactly is your objection?'

'She's a little girl! What are you trying to do to her?'

'She's not such a little girl any more.' An image flashes through Kate's mind of Ali standing in the wind at Chatsworth. 'Rebecca's right – one has to strike while the iron's hot. There's no point in Ali being Young Musician of the Year unless she uses it to her advantage. It's obvious she's never going to do anything except play the piano, and you have to seize the opportunities while they're there.'

Guy takes an open bottle of white wine out of the fridge and pours himself a large glass. 'Just because Rebecca, of all people, pitches up on our doorstep and starts taking over your life – which is what she always wanted to do – that doesn't mean she's right. It doesn't mean Ali shouldn't study longer, grow up a bit, save the recording for a couple of years' time when she'll be more developed as a musician and as a person. And it doesn't mean she shouldn't have the chance to live a normal life rather than being chained to that three-legged monstrosity!'

'I see,' Kate says, trying to replicate the inscrutability she has been learning from Rebecca. 'I didn't think you'd feel this way.'

'I object to you making decisions about Ali's future without running them by me.'

'You're never there to have anything run by you.'

'For Christ's sake, she's my daughter too.'

'Perhaps you should spend more time being a father to her, then.'

'So, Ali is going to have her childhood amputated by greedy music-business moguls, with your full co-operation, and it's all my fault for going to work.'

'Nobody is trying to amputate Ali's childhood.' Kate breathes deeply, keeps her hands folded, controls her need to move her fingers. 'I want her to make the most of her opportunities. She *wants* to be a pianist. She *wants* to be successful. She's never going to want to do anything else.'

'Has she been asked?'

'Of course. Rebecca asked her at Chatsworth.'

'But does she know what she's letting herself in for?'

'I want her to have the chances she deserves. Because I know what it's like to want those chances and to have them taken away from you. There's nothing crueller. I don't want Ali to have the experience I had.'

'Katie, it's not remotely comparable.'

'Well, how do you think she's going to feel if you suddenly tell her she can't do it because you don't want her to, now that she's got this far? If you stand in her way, Guy, do you think she will *ever* forgive you?'

Guy says nothing. He looks desperately tired. Kate watches him leave the kitchen. When he's gone, she reaches for her knitting.

Guy trudges up the stairs. On the landing, he pauses. A chink of light under Ali's door shows she's still awake. 'Ali?'

'Hi, Dad.'

Guy opens the door. Alicia is sitting up in bed, reading a book about Chopin. Cassie, in faithful attendance, is asleep in her basket, paws twitching as she dreams of long, cool walks through landscaped gardens.

'You OK, Dad?' Ali puts her head on one side and gazes at him with such affection that a lump rises to his throat.

'Yes, love. What about you? What's all this about making a CD?'

'It's funny, Dad – I know this'll sound weird, but something in me feels like I've done it all before.'

'What?'

'It just feels kind of familiar. Maybe I did it in a previous life. Anjali was talking about India the other day and she was saying how they believe that we don't just live once but we come back again and again and relive certain things until we work them out of our spirits. It's called *karma*. And I thought, Oh, that explains everything.'

'Gordon Bennett, Ali, you're full of surprises. Listen. Do you *want* to do this?'

'Sure.' She yawns, stretching her arms up towards the ceiling.

Guy looks at her hands and wrists. 'How would you feel,' he says carefully, 'if you didn't?'

'Dunno. Daft, I guess.'

'Ali, it's got to be your decision. You know that, don't you? And you know that whatever you decide, I'll stand by you?'

'Oh, Dad. I must go to sleep, we've got double chemistry first thing tomorrow.'

Guy closes the door quietly. Behind him, the light goes out.

Rebecca stays in Buxton an extra night so that she can be with Kate when the offices open. On Monday morning at nine thirty, she picks up the phone. By noon, Alicia's life has been reorganised as thoroughly as her mother's study.

She has an introduction to an upmarket artist's manager named Phyllida Brown, who works for a big firm in west London – the agent, Rebecca adds, who likes French poetry. A PR company is waiting in the wings ('Expensive but extremely effective,' Rebecca assures Kate, who gasps with shock at the fee). A recording studio in London has been booked for early September, so that Alicia can have the summer to practise, without missing school. Rebecca also has a long, flirtatious conversation with a gay photographer, whom she persuades to clear his diary the day after the final recording session. 'We'll find you a selection of wonderful dresses for the shoot,' Rebecca muses, looking Alicia up and down.

'Must I?' Alicia protests. 'I just want to be me.'

'That,' says Rebecca, 'is exactly the point. Being you is one thing; projecting that "you-ness" to the audience is quite another.'

When Rebecca arrived in Buxton on Saturday afternoon, Alicia was a talented teenager. By the time Rebecca leaves, Alicia is a concert pianist.

★   ★   ★

Kate calls the young musicians' advisory scheme to tell them what's happening. The director likes Phyllida Brown. She's not so sure about the CD. 'Are you quite certain Alicia feels ready?' she asks.

'Absolutely,' says Kate.

'Mrs Bradley, I know it's exciting, but do be careful. Try not to rush into the first opportunity that presents itself.'

'I'm not worried.' Kate scarcely takes the director's tone of voice on board. 'I've known Rebecca Harris for more than twenty years. She won't let us down.'

'Us?' says the director.

When Alicia steps off the train at Euston, the air assails her with unaccustomed warmth. It smells smoky and semi-chemical, with none of the fresh edginess she's used to in Derbyshire. Clutching her bag and staying close to her mother in the crowd surging down towards the Underground, she feels as if she's arrived in another country.

The tube, rattling up towards north London, is hot and fascinating. To one side, a couple talk in an extraordinary African language; opposite sit some young people not much older than herself, who Mum says are Polish. Mum, though, is thinking about other things.

'Shoes,' she says, somewhere near Camden Town.

'What shoes?'

'Did you bring any?'

'I'm wearing some.'

'No, something smart. We're meeting Phyllida Brown tonight, so you should try to look respectable.'

'These are fine.' Alicia's shoes are her favourites: pink, trainer-like walking-shoes that keep her as comfortable as the day is long.

Mum shuffles, tense, glancing at her watch. Alicia absorbs the adverts and the tube map above them, the grimy windows, the exotic array of fellow travellers, like a child at a theme park. She hasn't been on the tube for two years, not since they last stayed with Uncle Anthony, Auntie Fiona and the Horribles, and they'd dragged her round the London Dungeon.

The journey lasts twenty minutes. Outside East Finchley station a familiar black Golf is waiting. Mum's face lights up when Rebecca waves.

James and Oscar thunder into the kitchen while Rebecca is preparing much-needed mugs of tea for Alicia and her mother, who are perching on bar stools. The boys are rugby players by build, heavy-set for their age, and speak with posh public school voices. Alicia says, 'Hiya,' and they look at her as if she comes from Mars. James is seventeen and Oscar fourteen, so one, she decides, is too old for her and the other is too young. That's fine. She doesn't feel much like talking anyway because she's getting her period and her brain feels wrung out along with her body.

Mum and Rebecca are discussing business and university friends and recipes in an extraordinary muddled rush of enthusiasm, washing in waves over Alicia. 'Do you like Oasis?' James asks her and she replies, 'Not really.' Then Oscar wants to know which her favourite pop group is and she admits she doesn't have one. That stumps them – despite the expensive school, they're no different from the kids in her class in Buxton, who don't know anything about anything except pop music. Alicia asks Mum if she can go upstairs and take a pill for her stomach-ache.

She beats a retreat to the bathroom, which is white and modern with gilt-edged accessories, loo brush included. Beside the basin stand no fewer than three electric toothbrushes. Alicia pushes a button on one and watches it spin. She's never seen an electric toothbrush before and, meanwhile, she's almost afraid to tread on the bathroom floor for fear of contaminating it.

The minute she's back downstairs, Rebecca accosts her. 'Ali, darling, won't you play something for us? James and Oscar would love to hear you.'

Like hell they would, thinks Alicia, glancing at their impassive faces – Rebecca must have put them under orders. The piano is a small but pleasing upright; when Alicia tries it, the touch is even and the sound warm, so she pulls up the piano stool and begins the Ravel Sonatine. She can feel the boys' eyes on her back. What a country bumpkin they must think her. Just like the Horribles, who are sure they're *it* just because they live in London. In the slow movement she thinks she can hear them making bored noises, whispering. Probably poking fun at her accent. She'd like to see them last two minutes in her school with their voices. But their mother is effectively her employer now, so she has to be on best behaviour, even if they don't. It's not fair. She plays the last movement extra fast to make up for it. That impresses even them. Her playing is its own best defence.

The spare room is in the converted loft of Rebecca's small but perfect house, overlooking its cottage garden where white and pink roses are in bloom. Alicia and Mum will sleep on two futons, which feel like no bed Alicia has tried before. She wants to escape upstairs after she's finished playing, but Mum comes after her and begins to talk about something she thinks Alicia could play better in the Sonatine. Alicia is feeling so upset and shaky that she starts to cry. Mum looks awkward for a minute, but eventually obliges her with a reasonably comforting hug.

Then they have to shower, change and go out to dinner; there's no more time for crying. Part of performing successfully, Mum explains, is being able to do it at any time, no matter how awful you're feeling – and having dinner with a prospective agent is almost as much a matter of performing as playing the piano is.

Rebecca has booked a table in a smart restaurant near Notting Hill Gate, where they will meet Phyllida Brown. Alicia puts on a clean blue t-shirt, jeans and her pink shoes. Rebecca looks her up and down. 'What else did you bring, Ali?'

'Not a lot,' Alicia says.

Rebecca nods, inscrutable. 'Tomorrow we'll go shopping

before Lucien's concert, if you like,' she suggests. 'We could go round Covent Garden, or Selfridges, whatever you fancy.'

Alicia can feel her face flushing – not at the prospect of a London shopping trip, but at the way Rebecca had casually called Lucien Delamain by his first name.

Alicia hasn't told anybody how much she loves Lucien Delamain. She wants to marry him. She's taken the booklets out of all his CDs and pinned them up on her noticeboard – Mum won't let her put them on the wall because the sticky stuff would damage the paint. Lucien Delamain has the darkest of dark eyes, curly black hair and a snowy-toothed smile; when he plays, it sounds as if he's improvising poetry. His biography says he comes from Provence, which she imagines as a warm, sunny, French version of the Peak District, sprouting lavender instead of heather. And now she's not only going to see him play, but perhaps even meet him. She closes her eyes, feels that she's found a magical place where glimmering stars can spin and dance inside her.

Once they subside a little, though, she finds she's worried about how she looks. She doesn't care a jot what James and Oscar think of her, but Lucien Delamain is another matter. Alicia has never been into what she thinks of as 'girly stuff'. She doesn't want to be like Kelly and her crowd, who wear micro-skirts and push-up bras that show everything. Adrian calls them 'slappers'; they look as if they'd go with any boy in Derbyshire. She loathes the way the boys watch them – Adrian included, and Tim and even Matthew – like builders eyeing a breakfast fry-up. Alicia would love to have a boyfriend, but not one who looks at girls like that. She wants a kindred spirit. Someone who loves everything she loves: music, the country-side, dogs, not necessarily in that order. If Lucien were to be a kindred spirit . . .

While Alicia is in the shower, Oscar and James galumph out of the house – they're meeting friends in a local café, then going on to a party. Obviously they won't invite her. They live in a different world. Or she does. She has to spend her evening in a posh restaurant. She sits still and lets Mum put powder and blusher on her face, while Rebecca offers to lend her a necklace, a plain gold chain. Finally, Mum suggests she puts on some pink lipstick. Both women look at her shoes and sigh. Alicia decides she does look better wearing lipstick. Certainly a little older.

She sits in the back of the car on the way to Notting Hill, watching forests of unfamiliar streets go by. She imagines that she is as old as she's trying to look – perhaps twenty-one – and that she is a professional pianist and lives here on her own. She'd need to find her way round these convoluted one-way systems, deal with the noise, the traffic, the people . . . The thought is so alarming that she imagines, instead, staying in Buxton and marrying Matthew Littlemore. That doesn't appeal either.

Rebecca leads the way into the restaurant on Kensington Church Street. Alicia gazes. She's seen big, trendy places like this in Manchester, but the family never eats there. Mum has suggested once or twice that after Alicia's piano lesson they could meet Dad in town and have dinner – but Dad is either busy getting the paper 'to bed' or, Alicia senses, finds some excuse to say no. Strange. Normally he's keener than Mum on going out and having fun.

The ceiling's gaping height makes Alicia feel extremely small. The walls are black, the tables silver and the lights are tiny halogen bulbs suspended on fine wires. On each table stands a white vase containing one orange flower. A fair-haired woman in a dark suit catches Rebecca's eye from a round table by the window and raises a hand. This is Alicia's first sight of Phyllida Brown.

She'd imagined an 'artist's manager' as a larger-than-life individual – perhaps flamboyant, perhaps too thin or too fat.

Phyllida, however, is so normal that she could almost have been Alicia's aunt. Alicia decides at once that she prefers Phyllida to her aunts – she never sees Auntie Jo, who lives in San Francisco, and she can't stand Auntie Fiona. Phyllida, she reckons, must be about the same age as Mum, maybe a little younger. She wears slender rectangular glasses across her sharpish features. Her nose is long and fine, reminding Alicia of a rodent in a riverbank. Her eyes are close-set, perhaps a little too close, though they're a fascinating, unusual turquoise colour; and as she looks at Alicia, their edges soften. When they've shaken hands and ordered some drinks, she begins to talk to Alicia at once.

Phyllida tells her that she lives in south London, has no children and had trained as a pianist. In no time, they're chattering about the pieces Alicia is learning, some of which Phyllida has played too; they talk so much that Alicia forgets about her period pains and the waiter has to come back three times before they're ready to order their food.

Alicia samples the white wine – it tastes of vanilla and even the few sips she's allowed make the lights seem brighter and the voices louder. She chomps her way happily through a Caesar salad, then seared tuna with a pepper crust and sweet-potato mash – she's never met a sweet potato before – and rounds off with chocolate mousse flavoured with coffee and almond liqueur. If this is life as a concert pianist, she likes it.

Mum and Rebecca make good headway with the wine; especially Mum, since Rebecca is driving. Alicia has never seen her mother's cheeks so pink; talking about their days at university, she and Rebecca giggle as if they're younger than Alicia. Odd to think they've known each other longer than she's been alive.

She'd expected Phyllida to be serious and work-focused, wanting to discuss conductors and the concertos Alicia can play. But Phyllida is more interested in getting to know her. What's her teacher like? What does she do in her spare time?

Is her brother musical? Does she have a boyfriend? She side-steps the last question and tells Phyllida about Cassie. Phyllida says she adores dogs, but can't have one because she works such long hours. She's out at her artists' concerts almost every night. 'You're coming to hear Lucien tomorrow, aren't you?' she says. 'He's one of mine.'

Alicia gasps: she's going to have the same manager as Lucien Delamain. 'He's so incredible!'

If Phyllida notices her extra enthusiasm, she's tactful and says only 'He's wonderful, isn't he? You must come backstage and meet him. I'll introduce you.'

Alicia fumbles for words to tell her how thrilled she is, but she can't find them. Instead she reaches out and hugs Phyllida, who looks surprised but not displeased.

Mum and Rebecca, sitting next to each other across the table, have been so absorbed in their own conversation that Mum's salmon fillet is growing cold on her plate. Alicia, Lucien-powered stars circling in her brain, barely notices until the unfamiliar sound of her mother's voice singing reaches her ears. Mum and Rebecca are, unbelievably, singing together. Softly and in harmony. Two different lines of the same tune. Phyllida pulls up in the middle of a sentence. 'Schubert?' she asks, looking at the two women.

'We used to play it in our quartet,' Mum explains. 'A very long time ago.'

'Too long,' Rebecca adds, refilling Mum's glass.

Mum looks nothing like her normal self tonight: she's relaxed, glowing, *happy*. She has an amazing smile: it's rare, but when she uses it, it's brighter than any halogen bulb. Rebecca seems unable to stop watching her.

'Do you still play?' Phyllida asks.

'Sadly, no,' Mum and Rebecca reply in unison.

Alicia seems to be surrounded by women who used to play musical instruments, but no longer do. It's an alarming obser-vation. However much Mrs Butterworth scares her, however

upset she is by Mum breathing down her neck about practising, life without the piano would not be life. It's her real
world, the world she steps into when she's on stage or alone
in the house, free of people telling her what to do. That's where
she feels truly alive. She gathers some courage, turns to Phyllida
and tells her. She's never put it like that to anybody before.

'I understand perfectly,' Phyllida says. Alicia had known she
would. Still, she says nothing about the colours. Nobody knows
about Alicia's colours.

When coffee arrives, Phyllida begins to explain the business
arrangement, should they decide to go ahead. The company's
commission will be twenty per cent of Alicia's concert fees,
which sounds steep but is apparently standard.

'Phyllida knows everyone who is anyone,' Rebecca points
out, when Kate looks as if she's about to protest. 'Even the
Young Musician of the Year needs the right manager with
the right contacts, and the advisory scheme director will
agree.'

All Alicia knows is that if Phyllida manages Lucien, she'd
trust her with her life.

It is past eleven o'clock when they leave. Alicia is so tired
that her body is awake, walking about and talking, but her
brain has shut down, leaving her functioning on borrowed
time. All she can take in is the black night, the silvery street
lamps, the cloakroom attendant handing her back the Mum
jersey she'd brought but hadn't needed. Her eyes are dry and
sore, while her hands feel under-exercised. Then she hears
something that doesn't make perfect sense but alarms her all
the same.

'I think you should know,' Rebecca is saying to Mum and
Phyllida, 'that since Alicia won her prize, Deirdre Butterworth
has doubled her fees for her other students.'

Mum breathes in. Phyllida's eyebrows twitch upwards. Alicia
had told her everything she really feels about Mrs Butterworth
– once she'd started, she couldn't stop. Maybe that hadn't been

sensible, but it was a relief to find someone who understood and let her get it off her chest.

'We need to discuss Mrs Butterworth some time,' Rebecca says to Mum, as she had at Chatsworth. Nobody says anything to Alicia.

Although she's exhausted, Alicia can't sleep. She lies on her futon, listening to Mum snoring, new impressions shuttling through her brain and the prospect of meeting Lucien Delamain beckoning out of the night as if nothing could induce time to move fast enough to make it happen.

Outside Selfridges, an ornate clock guards heavy revolving doors; inside, Alicia gazes around at the shining railings, pale lights, elegant accessories and counters for more brands of makeup than she'd known existed. She's so boggled that she doesn't know where to start.

Rebecca takes charge, marching them to her own favourite and persuading the cheerful salesgirl to give Alicia a makeover. 'You've got to learn to do this properly,' Rebecca tells Alicia. She sits on a stool, a towel round her neck, and keeps her eyes closed until it's over.

Mum looks on. 'She's only fifteen, you know,' she says, when layers of dark mascara are being applied to Alicia's sandy lashes.

'It's a lovely age,' the girl replies, either missing or ignoring Mum's censorious tone. 'I've been wearing all this since I was thirteen. There you go, love, all done. How do you like it?'

Alicia, staring into the mirror, says, 'That's grand. Thank you.' She doesn't like to say that she'd much rather be out in the open countryside, mascaraless, walking her dog.

Mum decides which makeup Alicia should have and Alicia lets her. Next they go upstairs to look at concert dresses: Alicia picks the colours, but lets Mum choose the style. They buy two: one mid-blue, the other sophisticated, versatile black. Rebecca looks from her to Mum and back again, without commenting. Rebecca's silences, Alicia thinks, speak louder than her words.

The teenage section is more fun. Alicia bounces happily through the railings, emerging with a good selection of upmarket-fifteen-year-old gear. Later in Rebecca's house, after sleeping for half the afternoon, she puts on an entire new outfit to go to Lucien's concert. Rebecca looks efficient and expensive in a trouser suit, Mum wears her long linen jacket, beads and a frazzled expression, but Alicia glows in fresh eyeshadow, lip gloss and trousers in a shiny, greenish-beige fabric, with a light top that shows off her cleavage and, finally, deep-brown court shoes. James and Oscar, slumped in front of the TV, stare at her for the first time as if she is a girl, not a Martian.

'I think it's wonderful,' Alicia breathes, on the terrace outside the Royal Festival Hall, soaking in the atmosphere. The trees along the South Bank are rustling in the breeze, the Thames twinkles under the early-evening sun, and close to Hungerford Bridge someone is clinking out a Hebrew folk song on Jamaican steel drums.

'You're going to play here, you'll see,' Rebecca declares. Alicia looks up at the concrete and glass façade of the hall and its curving, copper-green roof. She says nothing; she simply radiates.

Phyllida is coming towards them, walking with a distinctive, brisk springiness and apologising for being slightly late. She's been backstage with Lucien and has told him all about them: he knows they'll be at the recital and is eager to meet Alicia.

'How old is Lucien?' Alicia asks.

'He's in his forties, though he doesn't look it,' Phyllida remarks. 'There's something youthful about him. He's still like a little boy in some ways.'

'That twinkle in the eye? That Gallic charm?' Rebecca's

tone is gently barbed. Phyllida's cheekbones and long nose redden.

'He's into French poetry, I take it?' Mum says, mysteriously.

Alicia, musing, follows them into the Queen Elizabeth Hall foyer, next door to the Royal Festival Hall. If Lucien were forty-five, like Mum, he would be exactly thirty years older than she is. The thought unsettles her. At fifteen, she may not feel like a little girl any more, but a man of forty-five would think her exactly that. She excuses herself, goes to the loo, then stands at the mirror to apply another layer of mascara and more of her new lip gloss.

It's soon obvious that in this piano-literate audience Alicia is being recognised. Walking towards the coffee bar, she spots several people following her with their eyes, others noticing her and whispering with their companions. Soon a smiling mother and a child of about ten come up and tell her how much they enjoyed watching her on TV. The child gazes up at her with huge, admiring eyes.

'What's your name?' Alicia asks her, bending. 'Do you play the piano?'

The girl lisps a reply and nods. She wants Alicia's autograph. Alicia signs her own name on Lucien's concert programme – it doesn't feel entirely right, but she does it anyway and gives her a kiss on the cheek. The child, pink and pleased, clutches her mother's hand as she walks away. Alicia watches them go, smiling, feeling warmed. She's surprised that Rebecca and Mum seem unmoved by the incident, though Phyllida says, 'That was nice, Ali.'

As they head into the auditorium, Alicia realises that her entourage of three adults has effectively formed a protective phalanx around her, ready to ward off intruders.

The hall is packed; the lights dim; and on to the platform strides Lucien Delamain, as dark and bright and shining as in the photographs on Alicia's noticeboard. There's a propulsive energy in his step when he comes forward to bow. Then he goes to the piano, and a second later the gloomy, concrete space is ablaze with Beethoven. Alicia notices the way he choreographs the music not only with his arms, shoulders and hands, but with his whole body. Soon she's lost in listening.

'What do you think?' Phyllida asks her, during the interval, while Rebecca and Mum go to the bar. Alicia has played both the Beethoven sonatas Lucien has just performed, knows their dangers from the inside and can dissect almost everything he had done with them. But while she's talking, people keep coming up to them and interrupting. Phyllida introduces her time and again. Alicia smiles and plays her new celebrity role as best she can; she can't remember all the names and the company titles mean nothing to her. She only wants to think about Lucien. She sips orange juice and gazes at the grey evening beyond the tall windows. Nothing has been the same since Matthew Littlemore snogged her. It's not that she'd like to kiss *him* again – rather the reverse – but the kiss itself was another matter. She wonders what it would be like to kiss Lucien.

The daydream stays with her through the second half. Lucien plays French music: Fauré, Debussy and Alicia's favourite Ravel. He plays 'Ondine' from the set *Gaspard de la nuit* more slowly than she does, and with a more beautiful tone, letting its pace ebb and flow as if he's telling a story. Mrs Butterworth has made Alicia concentrate more on the clarity of the notes than on telling stories. That kind of thing can come later, Mrs Butterworth says – for now, the stronger Alicia's grasp of the mechanism, the better. In general, Alicia has applied herself to exercises and études, learning to be as at home on the instrument as a dolphin in the sea. Magic, Lucien-magic, hasn't come into it much, except when she's on stage, free to play as she wishes, without interference.

'I'd like to play it like that,' she whispers to her mother, when the Ravel has drawn to its close. She's beginning to feel that she's been missing something.

The crowds backstage remind her of the competition; but now she's just a groupie. She feels very young, too young, and her new shoes pinch her toes. Her lip gloss helps her confidence, though; so does her height. She's beginning to enjoy being tall for her age.

Phyllida pays no attention to the green-room crush and the long line of people waiting to talk to Lucien. 'Come on, Ali,' she whispers, propelling her forward. For a moment there's annoyance at their queue-jumping; then, as Alicia is recognised, the crowds part like the Red Sea to make way for her. A second later she is face to face with Lucien. His eyes, alert and interested, sparkling despite post-concert tiredness, gaze straight into her own.

Phyllida kisses his cheek. He puts a hand briefly on her waist and says, 'Phyllie, *ça va?*'

'*Ça va.*' Phyllida looks at him, then away. She takes a breath. 'Lucien, this is Alicia Bradley, the young pianist I was telling you about.'

'Ah, the Young Musician of the Year! *Enchanté*, Alicia.'

To her astonishment, Lucien, who pronounces her name 'Alici-*a*', doesn't only shake her hand but lifts it to his lips. She flushes and tries not to laugh. 'I love your work,' she manages to say, trying to sound grown-up.

'And I am hearing great things about yours. It's true that you have learned all the Chopin études and all the Bach preludes and fugues?'

'Yes – yes, it is.'

'Amazing! And who are you studying with?'

'Deirdre Butterworth in Manchester.'

Lucien's smile doesn't change, but something in his face seems to freeze for a second, like a paralysed frame of film.

'We must talk some time,' he says, looking intently into her face. 'I would love to hear you, if you would like to play to me one day soon?'

Alicia, not having anticipated this, wonders what Mrs Butterworth would say if she were to consult another professional who might give her different advice. She finds a useful way out by grabbing her mother's arm. 'This is my mum, Kate Bradley.'

Lucien repeats the hand-kissing routine. Alicia notices that her mother is as fazed by it as she'd been.

'Alicia is a tremendous fan of yours,' Mum tells Lucien, after taking a fraction of a second to recover, the sort of fraction that only Alicia would have noticed. 'Whenever she stops practising, the house is full of the sound of your CDs. It feels like you're one of the family.'

'You have such a talented daughter!' Lucien is beaming at Mum. 'So young, such a gift!'

'She's just had her fifteenth birthday.'

'And she could not have a better manager than my lovely Phyllie.'

'Oh, honestly, Lucien,' Phyllida exclaims, glancing around. There are beads of sweat on her forehead.

'Phyllida will give you all my contact details,' Lucien assures Alicia. 'I hope to see you soon. Come and play for me, Alicia, any time. Promise?'

'Promise!' Alicia takes her last chance to experiment: she widens her smile to its most radiant, gazes at her hero and flutters her mascara-curled eyelashes. To her astonishment, Lucien's smile widens in return, his eyes gleam and his expression deepens for a second into something glowing; potentially, she senses, a little intimate. She's not sure which is more startling: the fact that he responds at all, or the understanding that she can make it happen so easily.

The trip back to Macclesfield, where Kate has left the car, feels very different from the journey to London.

'I can't believe we've only been away for two days,' Alicia remarks, sipping tea from a plastic mug as the train sails past Milton Keynes. In the luggage rack, their suitcase bulges with new acquisitions: not only Alicia's spoils from Selfridges, but also Lucien's latest CD, given to her by Phyllida, the concert programme which he'd signed ('*Pour Alicia, avec toutes mes félicitations, Lucien xx*'); and, most important of all, an official letter of agreement from Phyllida's firm. Mum has promised to look after the legal details of the recording contract when it arrives, and between them, the three women have assured Alicia that she need worry about nothing. All she has to do is play the piano.

Mum is quiet, watching the passing fields and towns, her fingers twisting her wool. Alicia closes her eyes and lets the train's motion and the click of Mum's knitting needles rock her to sleep.

12

Adrian, left in charge of Cassie, takes her for a walk out of Buxton towards the Cat and Fiddle. She pads to heel, head up, sniffing the air; the moor spreads, vast and empty, around them. He can't decide whether he loves the country-side or loathes it. Untamed, craggy, austere, it's definitely in tune, as Ali might put it, with something in himself. Even so, he wishes there were more interesting things to do here than walk and go to the pub. Ali loves the moors, but she, no doubt, will be moving to London before you can say Deirdre Butterworth. 'And I,' he mumbles to Cassie (he doesn't like to admit that he, too, talks to the dog), 'will be stuck in bloody Buxton. Might as well never have been born.'

He lets Cassie off her leash. He's not supposed to – the sheep farmers hate dogs with a virulence that has earned them the right to shoot a loose one on sight – but Guy had belted Cassie as a puppy the first time she tried to chase a sheep and she's never done it again. 'You're the best dog in Derbyshire,' Adrian tells her, because it's true.

A sound in the distance catches his attention and makes Cassie look round, ears twitching: a soft roar in the hills, increasing in volume at a tremendous rate. Round the bends of the road career seven or eight dark shapes on wheels. A group of bikers, leather-clad, immensely padded, assembles here, centring on the Cat and Fiddle. The road they love is the most dangerous in the country; they ride it for speed alone, without observing natural beauty, inclement weather or the speed limit.

Adrian stops walking, shielding his eyes from the sun. He's seen the bikers often enough. Now, though, he feels an unfamiliar pang of desire, recognition, something he could almost call destiny. He wants to be one of them. He wants to feel the road tearing away under him, to vanquish mankind and nature with the force of an engine, to be untouchable through speed to law and family alike.

He's been high many times – the novelty has, oddly, worn off. Dope makes him drowsy, which is nice but limiting, and an experiment with something stronger had upset him to the point that he didn't want to do it again – not that he'd tell Tim or Sam that. He reads Dad's newspaper enough to be aware of the dangers of getting hooked. Tim and Sam never read anything and never watch the news on TV, so they don't know and they don't care.

But riding through the Peak District at what looks like two hundred miles per hour would be a conscious high of a different kind: real, not chemically induced. That's what he wants: total aliveness. The same sensation, perhaps, that Ali sometimes tells him about after she's given a concert. He knows the bikers go to the Cat and Fiddle – he's seen them there, their motorbikes stationed in the car park. Somehow he must get to talk to them.

'It's booked,' says Emily. She's standing in Guy's office, her back against the door, silvery eyes shining.

'I only hope that the recording happens when it's supposed to,' Guy says. 'If it doesn't, I can't go.'

'You'd still have a conference to attend.' Emily seems unperturbed. 'It's not like you're saying to Kate, "I can only go away when you do because I'm off to Denmark with my mistress."'

'Em.' Guy takes off his glasses. 'I've got to tell her. I can't go on like this.'

'Don't do anything too fast.' Emily walks towards him with some caution; there are glass panels by the door and anyone astute, passing, could easily spot them.

'Fast? It's been over a year! I'm being torn in half.'

'All I ask is that you don't dump me.'

'How could I dump you? It'd be like cutting off my arm. But I can't go on putting all my energy into hiding my feelings. I'm going through the motions of being the person I used to be. It's not who I am any more.'

'Are you saying you want to leave your family and be with me? Don't say that unless you mean it.' Emily crouches beside him behind the desk, concealed from the door. She takes both his hands, then lifts one to her cheek. Guy's fingers grasp and twine in her hair. 'There's nothing I want more than that,' she says, 'but you've got to be five hundred per cent certain. We've never spent any length of time together. That's one reason I want to take you to Denmark. We'll see how we really get along.'

'I don't need to go to Denmark to know I get along with you.'

'But I do.'

Guy is constantly astonished by Emily: her self-knowledge, her self-sufficiency, her inner fibre. Most women in Emily's position would be the ones in tears. Not the men – thank goodness most of his staff don't know what a soppy old softie he is. Other women would be begging the indecisive bloke to leave home and move in with her. They would be desperate for attention too rationed from a heart too divided. Instead he's reached the point where he feels half dead from hiding the truth, but she is telling him to do nothing until she's certain she can stand spending several days on end in his company.

'The fourth of September,' she is saying. 'We'll fly to Copenhagen and take the train to Skagen. We'll stay in the hotel where everyone stayed in the nineteenth century, including Hans Christian Andersen. You'll love it – it's extraordinary.'

'Any place would be extraordinary if you and I get to spend three whole nights together in it.'

'You old cry-baby.' Emily squeezes his hand. 'I'm counting the days.'

'Me too.'

'And please don't do anything rash until we come back.'

'If that's what you really want,' Guy says, 'then I won't.'

'A portrait of me.' Alicia is lying on her bed, daydreaming. Her fingers feel warm and strong – she's had a good afternoon at the piano, playing her favourite pieces, trying to pick out the ones she wants to record. If the CD is to be a portrait of her, it needs music of the outdoors, the shifting subtle colours of the hills and sky. Beethoven, then – which Dad would love. She imagines the cover: herself in her jeans, windswept and happy, her dog at her side. The Beethoven D minor Sonata called 'The Tempest'; Chopin – the Third Ballade, which reminds her of riding over the moors; Ravel – the Sonatine that sparkles like the sea; and Debussy, so steeped in nature that once you walk into his landscape you'll never come out again.

The next morning she phones Rebecca to give her the programme.

'Oh, sweetheart,' says Rebecca. 'It's beautiful. I love it. Don't you think, though, that it might be a good idea to have something a little better-known, more obviously popular and virtuoso, just to start you off? We want people to know how amazing your fingers are.'

Alicia is taken aback. 'But there's nothing there I could play if my fingers weren't good,' she points out.

'Yes, of course. *We* know that. But do the punters, darling? How about some Chopin waltzes?'

'I've never learned them,' Alicia admits, biting her lip.

'I'm sure you could learn one or two very easily. How about the "Minute" Waltz? And what about some Rachmaninov? The C sharp minor Prelude – that's very popular. Or that incredible piece by Balakirev, "Islamey", so exotic and colourful. And if you want to do Debussy, why not "Clair de lune"?'

By the end of the conversation, Alicia feels wobbly. She goes to the kitchen and raids the chocolate that Mum keeps on top of the highest cupboard to stop herself eating it. Alicia stands on a chair.

The chocolate eases the physical wobble, but not the mental one. She's certain Rebecca had said she could choose her own programme. Yet Rebecca's ideas are so different from hers that there seems to be nothing of herself left.

'Mum?' she calls.

'Come up, darling.'

Mum is at her computer, typing. A huge calendar pinned to the noticeboard bears Alicia's concert schedule in coloured letters: red for solo recitals, orange for concerto performances with orchestras. The advisory service has instructed her not to do too many concerts, at least for now, because of school and, most of all, because she is only fifteen and needs to keep studying. But her earning power has shot up since she won her prize; now everybody wants her, and Phyllida, Rebecca and Mum don't always agree on how much work she should take on. Alicia finds it odd that Phyllida, whose company benefits financially from her work, wants her performances to be rationed to one per month, while Rebecca, whose company has no share in the proceeds, encourages her to do as many as she can handle because it's valuable experience. Mum, trapped in the middle, looks exhausted.

'Mum – this recording.'

'Mm-hm?' Mum keeps typing.

'I thought *I* was supposed to choose the pieces.'

'Of course, darling. But isn't it a good idea to take Rebecca's advice? She'll know much better than we do about what sells.'

'Has the repertoire got to "sell"? Even if people know who I am already?'

Mum pauses, apparently considering her words. 'I think it would be a good idea if it could. Then there's more chance that they'll follow it up with something even better. A concerto, perhaps, with a big orchestra and conductor. Think of it as an investment.'

'But, Mum, I'm not sure I want to play all these pieces.' Alicia tells Mum the details of her talk with Rebecca.

'I'm sure just one waltz would do,' Mum responds. 'And "Clair de lune" is beautiful. Then, if you play "Islamey", everyone will know that you can play absolutely anything.'

'But I don't know it!' Alicia wails.

'Just have a look at it, love. Take it slowly and see how you feel. It's a marvellous piece – I was listening to it yesterday.'

'Yesterday? Mum, was this your idea?'

'No, sweetheart, it was Rebecca's. I'm learning as we go along, as much as you are.'

Alicia is silent. It's obvious, from Mum's words, that she's already discussed everything with Rebecca, without Alicia's knowledge.

'Now, darling,' Mum says, 'why don't you go and practise and we can talk about the CD with Dad later? He might even be home for supper.'

Alicia wanders down to her piano. Dad will understand. He'll be her supporter; he'll help to talk them round. If he can't, then nobody can.

But seven o'clock arrives, then seven thirty, then eight. Adrian decamps to meet his friends. Alicia's stomach rumbles and the chicken begins to overcook. Eventually Mum looks at the clock, gives a sigh and says, 'OK, Ali, let's eat. I bet that once we've begun, he'll walk in.' This trick has worked before, though it's not infallible.

Mum seems, in a perverse way, to have given up on Dad. If he's there, he's there. If not, she doesn't seem bothered. She's occupied with writing letters, planning Alicia's schedule with Phyllida, and engaging in marathon phone conversations with Rebecca. Alicia doesn't want to seem ungrateful, because she knows that the detail would be beyond her. This way, she's free to practise and do what schoolwork she can

be bothered with. Mum's trying her best for her, Alicia knows
– even if sometimes it hurts. She should do her best in
return.

They eat in the kitchen with the clock ticking above them.
Dad doesn't arrive. With every mouthful Alicia feels her spirits
sinking lower. Mum has another card up her sleeve: 'I spoke
to Mrs Butterworth,' she says, 'and she thinks Rebecca's idea
for the programme is absolutely perfect for you.'

It's nine o'clock. Alicia clears away the dinner plates and
says, 'Mum, can I take Cassie out?'

'Not now, love. It's getting late.'

Alicia goes to her room, wonders whether to write to Anjali,
then picks up a book instead. At ten fifteen, she hears the front
door opening as Dad arrives.

She jumps off the bed and bounds down. Dad hugs her.
He smells of sandalwood soap, which they don't use at home.
She's noticed that before. Perhaps he's joined a gym and has
a shower there. He's certainly lost weight.

'Dad, you know this CD?' Alicia bursts out. 'Mum and
Rebecca and Mrs Butterworth want me to play totally different
stuff from what I want to play!'

'Darling, I'm sure they don't,' says Dad, whose eyes suggest
he's still not home although his body is standing in the entrance
hall. 'Let's talk about it tomorrow, OK? It's late and you should
be getting your beauty sleep.'

Adrian, Tim and Sam are in the pub, drinking lager. Nobody
has asked them how old they are, luckily – sometimes they are
interrogated, then banned. When the bikers come in, the boys
look on, half admiring, half afraid.

These are serious blokes, Adrian thinks, watching them
grouping round the bar. They're big men, even when the
helmets and jackets come off; a good bit older than him, some
in their twenties, others even older. They mean business.

'How old d'you have to be to ride a motorbike?' Sam asks.

'Seventeen, I think. We could do it,' Tim says, keeping his voice down. 'You have to take a test and get a licence.'

'Nah, you don't,' Adrian says.

'Course you do, and it costs money. And them bikes cost a fucking fortune.'

'Depends how you do it,' Adrian insists. 'I mean, nobody ever looks at licences, do they? Nobody can make you do anything you don't want to do if you don't let them.'

Sam and Tim stare at him. Sam has knuckled under and started to work harder at school, thanks to his father's horror stories of his likely future if he leaves with no qualifications. His dad's a farmer and times are hard, especially since the onset of the Foot and Mouth disaster. Tim, for his part, feels guilty and responsible for his mum, who's on her own; he has to be the man of the household, which means he needs to pass some A levels and not spend too much time messing about. Adrian knows they look up to him. He's the only one who's still a real rebel and he knows, though he'd never let anyone say so, that he's brighter than both of them put together. 'If I wanted to be a biker,' he declares, 'nobody could stop me. And I wouldn't do a stupid licence and I wouldn't buy a bike new.'

'What would you do, then?' Sam demands.

'Hang out with the right people,' Adrian says pointedly (Sam and Tim will know that they're not the right people). 'Go out, learn the tricks. I'd get a bike sooner or later. I'd save up and find someone who'd sell me one cheap.'

Coming in around midnight, Adrian creaks up the stairs. The house is dark and quiet. Mum has placed a mug and a tea-bag beside the kettle as a goodnight gesture to him. He leaves them untouched. He pauses outside his door. From Alicia's room, he can hear a noise. He goes closer. Her light is off.

'Ali? You awake?'

'Mmm.'

Adrian peers in. Alicia has pulled her pillow over her head to muffle the sound as she howls into her mattress.

'Hey,' Adrian says softly, uncomfortable in his big-brother shoes, switching on the lamp. 'What's going on?'

'The CD,' says Alicia, face down under the pillow. 'Nobody wants to listen to me!'

''Cos you're fifteen.'

'But it's *my* CD! What am I going to do? Even Dad won't listen. They all keep saying the record company knows best. But they *don't*. Rebecca talks to Mum all the time, but she doesn't know anything about me!'

'They can't force you, Ali. Don't let them. If you put your foot down strongly enough, nobody can force you to do anything. You remember that.'

'Do you think?'

'However much pressure anyone puts on you, it's still down to you to agree to be pressurised or not. If you say no, you say no. You have to keep on saying no, if that's what you believe. It's about willpower.'

Alicia casts around for a tissue. Adrian finds a box on her dressing-table and tosses it over. She catches it and flashes him a sudden smile, despite eyes that are so red and puffy that he realises she must have been crying for ages.

'Actually,' she says, 'I think I know what I'm going to do. And I'll do it in the morning.'

'Good,' says Adrian. 'You do that. Don't let them force you into anything. Promise?'

'Promise! Night-night, Adie.'

'Night, Ali.' Adrian gives Cassie a quick back-rub on his way out.

In the morning, as soon as Mum has gone to the supermarket, Alicia leaps up from the piano and grabs the phone. She dials Phyllida's mobile.

'Lucien's number?' Phyllida sounds caught off-guard. Her

voice alters when she talks about Lucien – it becomes strained, flattened out. She collects herself and says, 'OK, Ali, have you got a pen?'

'Ready.' Alicia listens and scribbles down two long French phone numbers and an email address. When she's rung off, she examines them. One chain of digits, after the French '33', begins with a seven; that must be the mobile. She presses its numbers.

'Alicia! *Chérie*! How lovely to hear your voice!' says Lucien Delamain.

Alicia sits down on the stairs, astonished at the simplicity of her success. 'Lucien, can you talk? Are you terribly busy?' she asks him politely.

'Darling, I am all yours. What is new?'

Alicia begins to tell Lucien everything that's been going on. He's a pianist. He understands. If she thinks about it logically, there's nobody else she could tell who *would* understand. People at school are either impressed or envious, but most of them have never heard of Chopin, let alone Balakirev. Adrian's done all he can, Dad's too stressed out, and Mum, Rebecca and Phyllida are stacked against her. Nor can she tell Anjali, because Anjali is a thousand miles away from any chance of a recording contract and it wouldn't be fair. As for the advisory scheme, if Mum doesn't like what the director says, she ignores it.

'Darling, what I would like is for you to play it all to me and together we choose the best,' Lucien says. 'Can you come to Paris?'

'I don't know,' Alicia says, 'but I'll try.'

'Have you been to Paris?'

'Never! I'd so love to.'

'We see what we can do. I will talk to Phyllie. She will help if I ask her, I promise.'

Alicia wonders what her agent would say if *she* tried to call her 'Phyllie'. 'Thank you, Lucien! Thank you so much!'

'We talk soon, OK?'

'Wonderful! I can't wait!'

'Me too. *Ciaociao*.'

Ciaociao? Alicia says it back – some kind of sophisticated Continental farewell? – and rings off. Feeling calmer than she's felt for days, she returns to Balakirev's 'Islamey', which is so ridiculously difficult that she's rather enjoying it.

If her teacher and her father are on the wrong side, she thinks, the fingers of her right hand picking out in slow motion a decorative flourish note by note, then maybe, just maybe, what she needs is an alternative teacher – and maybe an alternative kind of father. Not a fairy godmother, but a wizard godfather. A Lucien.

'You want to go to Paris to play to Lucien?' exclaims Kate, when her daughter, with eyes like stars, announces her plan.

'I want his advice about the recording. He said if I played him everything, then he'd help me decide.'

'But, darling, there isn't time for that!' Kate closes her eyes. She hasn't visited Paris in over twenty years. Images rattle through her brain of cramped hotel rooms, lack of pianos, Ali wanting to sightsee and go shopping. Worse, though, would be Rebecca's reaction: she has intimated gently but unmistakably that the company has to be happy with the promotability of Ali's repertoire. It has to be popular, accessible, virtuoso music, she says, otherwise it won't sell in the quantities they require.

Seeing Lucien Delamain would, of course, be exciting. Kate, who bolsters herself against the chilly temperature of her marriage with work for Ali, housekeeping and knitting, can't help responding to Lucien's testosterone-fuelled aura. But as for Paris . . . Could she handle the associations? Supposing she couldn't? She might find herself dropping apart, brain cell by brain cell, confronting the scene of so much happiness. If she fell to pieces, what would happen to Ali?

'Basically, darling,' she says, brisk, 'it's important that Eden should be happy, because this is going to launch you in the CD market. They know what they're doing. Maybe you can play to Lucien another time, but I don't think that going to him now would help as much as you think.'

'But, *Mum*—' Alicia's blue eyes fill with tears.

Kate looks away – she can't bear it when Ali cries. It makes her want to cry too. But the girl can't be permitted to scupper her own best chances.

Alicia walks quietly upstairs after dinner and a moment later calls down: 'Mum, can I send an email from your computer, please?'

'Of course, love.'

A long period of silence follows until there's another, rather small-voiced call – 'Mu-u-um . . .'

Kate finds Alicia fighting with Outlook Express. 'All you need to do,' she shows her, 'is click there to put in the address; then *there* to put in the subject; then write your message *there*. Easy.'

'Machines,' Alicia grumbles. She's trying to write to Lucien. 'I can't face phoning him to say I'm not going.'

Later, Adrian finds Alicia in her room, staring at a book without seeing it. Through the house, the air is frosty and miserable.

'Trouble?' he asks.

'A little.' She looks up. 'But it's OK.'

'Don't tell me. Mama knows best.'

Adrian notices his sister's shoulders – tense, too hunched for a girl of her age. That's what comes of hours and hours at the piano. And more hours. And then letting off steam in the only way you're permitted to: walking the dog.

'Don't let them push you around,' he says.

Everything in Skagen is golden. The houses along the old village's main street are painted a glowing shade of sandy ochre, contrasting with chunky dark beams and window-frames. The Nordic sky, pale, clear and brilliant, turns topaz at dawn, when Guy and Emily wake in each other's arms, and at dusk, when they relax over beer and crisps in the garden of a small bar.

They are staying in the hotel where Hans Christian Andersen had once stayed – wooden, rickety, lovingly restored – and nearby they find the museum that preserves the house where the artists Michael and Anna Ancher had lived, as well as the gallery that displays their works and those of their friends in the Skagen Group. Guy thinks they're the Danish equivalent of Renoir and his circle. There is art in the air here. He imagines that the painters only needed to reach out a metaphorical hand and allow a picture to drop into it, fully formed, out of the translucent heavens.

In the gallery, Guy and Emily immerse themselves in the soft colours, the generous outlines, the big, beautiful canvases – the scenes simple and everyday yet their poetry absolute. Two women walking by the sea with a dog can become an étude in sapphire, a plain yet perfect moment frozen under an ultramarine spell. Guy, arm round Emily, wishes that they, too, could preserve their moment of poetic everydayness. Normally they can't walk hand in hand for fear of being recognised. But in Skagen, they're anonymous and undisturbed: just an ordinary British couple on holiday.

'My father used to paint sometimes,' Emily tells him. 'He loved this place – we came here quite often when I was little.'

'You still are little,' Guy teases her. He's not had much chance, being married to a woman his own height, to feel big, strong and protective as he does now.

They walk the length of a straight, sandy, sea-bordered road to the far northern tip of Denmark, to see the point where the Skagerrak and the Kattegat meet. Emily smiles up at him. She's pale – perhaps because of the strain they're both under, beneath the surface of this brief, gold-frosted happiness – and he remembers that she hadn't eaten much lunch. He's concerned, but doesn't want to wreck the mood by needling her about whether she feels OK.

They drift along in silence. Finally they reach the end of the land. Before them, the blue-grey seas are leaping under the arching sky. To their left, the sun sinks towards the waves.

'There,' Emily says. 'Can you see it?'

Guy can make out a watery conflict in the distance. The two seas do not merge in a seamless, peaceful unity. Perhaps something invisible to the naked eye separates them – submerged sand, or rock – but it seems to him that each sea has its own habits of motion, which aren't necessarily compatible. Where they touch, there's a faintly discernible collision: a little extra foam, a dividing line that doesn't quite divide. Or is he imagining it?

'Amazing,' he says.

'Guy,' says Emily, 'I've got something to tell you.' Her hair is bright in the low sun, her eyes trained on the horizon. 'I'm pregnant.'

Guy tries to speak. Nothing comes out.

'I'm so happy,' Emily adds. 'I know I shouldn't be, but I can't help it. I want you to know that I'm not trying to trap you, but I so want to have this baby. I couldn't bear not to because it's yours. It's due in April.'

His eyes begin to water. He puts out an arm and draws her to him. She hides her face and he can feel, from the tremor in her shoulders, what courage she has needed to break this apocalyptic news. 'We'll work something out, Em,' he promises.

'I know,' Emily says. 'I trust you. More than I trust myself.'

There's little to say while they walk back. The seas have swallowed the sun, and in the deepening twilight Guy imagines that they are wandering into a Michael Ancher painting, that they could step through the canvas into another reality, lose themselves and never return. I'm forty-six years old, he reflects, I'm the editor of a newspaper and the father of two

– potentially three – children. How can it be that deep down I'm still a kid who wants to go through the looking-glass?

Four days after Guy comes home from his 'conference', a group of terrorists fly two planes into the World Trade Center in New York. Watching on TV, transfixed with horror as the flaming towers plunge to the ground, Guy senses the beginning of the end: their world, his world, a whole era crashing to smithereens in a smoking inferno.

13

The red light glares down at Alicia. She begins her Chopin Ballade for the fifth time. She's been allowed to keep it, and has learned some waltzes to follow. Then she'll play some popular Liszt, Rachmaninov and that crazy Balakirev (at least nobody can call that a soundbite). No Beethoven and no Ravel. The only Debussy is 'Clair de lune'.

She has been in the studio all day. She's recorded half the music for the CD, most of it at least ten times. In the listening breaks, she's been summoned to the control room where electronic numbers and level indicators flash, yellow, green and red, on equipment lathered with knobs and dials. She's impressed with the way her producer, Andy, has covered his copy of the music with red pencil, the way he can pinpoint every wrong note or distant passing aeroplane; they've even had disruption from two pigeons noisily trying to mate on the windowsill. But Andy's sharp ear means she has to play everything again and again and she's convinced that even if there are fewer mistakes, she's not playing the music, as music, as well as she had first thing in the morning. Andy's lovely, though, and they'd had a good laugh together, mainly because she'd told him how much she appreciated his efforts.

Amazing, she reflects, her fingers working almost of their own accord, what a difference it makes if you tell someone that you like what he does, and mean it. Most people don't bother.

On the other hand, when a project is supposed to be about

you, presenting you to the world, yet nobody wants to do it your way – what then?

Alicia's initial plan had been to invite the photographer to Buxton. They could go to Mam Tor, photograph her in walking-boots with her beloved view in the background, and Cassie could be in it. 'Don't be silly, darling,' Mum said. 'She's a collie. It'd look like a soundtrack for *Lassie Come Home!*'

The next best thing would have been Alicia with view, minus dog, but it transpired that the photographer, who is awfully expensive, would charge for spending two days away – he'd need two days, he insists, because it's such a long way to Buxton. The record company doesn't want to pay the extra, and as Alicia is in London to make the recording, she may as well stay longer and go to his studio – which had been Rebecca's initial plan.

Rebecca books a hair and makeup artist. Alicia's hair is long – she hasn't had time to have it cut – but after the girl has worked on it for two hours it's obedient, sleek and gorgeous. The makeup feels excessive, but the photographer, who's wearing black and has spiky, blond-dyed hair, assures her that it's necessary under his lights, otherwise she'll look like a ghost. Alicia is wearing jeans, but the photographer and Rebecca open an elaborate suitcase and suggest that she changes into one of the three concert gowns inside it. She chooses a dress that's blue and sparkly and matches her eyes. It shows rather too much cleavage, but she loves the blue – to her, the colour of A major. They drape her, in the dress, over a white sofa, surround her with huge vases of white and pink flowers and put up white umbrellas to control the light. Then the clicking begins.

'Oh, God,' Alicia says, when the contact sheets are spread out on the kitchen table in Buxton a couple of weeks later. 'I look like – like – I don't know what I look like. But it doesn't look like me.' She hates the picture: it's all hair, flowers and flesh.

But Rebecca says the CD, when it comes out, will be played on Classic FM five times a day. Mum insists it's a beautiful picture and is, in any case, just a means to an end. Dad looks at it with exhausted eyes, tells Alicia she's an angel and that it will probably be OK, then vanishes into his study.

Kate has been talking to her mother on the phone. Margaret has been encouraging her, not for the first time, to start going to church. 'Mother,' Kate protested, 'I'm not going to spend Sunday mornings doing something I don't even begin to believe in.'

'Contrary to popular opinion, it might earth you,' Margaret said. 'It gives you a structure, a system, something solid behind you. We all need solidity and consolation in these terrible times.'

'Well, church never felt solid to me.'

'It sounds, dear, as if you need something spiritual in your life. You don't seem happy.'

'I'm perfectly happy. Now that Ali's career is getting off the ground—'

'Kate, I'm not thinking about the children. I'm thinking of *you*.'

'Mother, *I'm fine*. I have to go, there's something in the oven . . .'

October leaves blow about the garden in whirlpools. Kate dishes out pasta at the table. Her kitchen is immaculate, its beechwood golden under the ceiling spotlights; her pasta sauce is home-made, a blend of tomatoes, garlic and marinated chicken; and her husband is, for once, home for dinner. The dog sits in attendance beside Alicia, gaze fixed hopefully upon her plate. Alicia slips Cassie bits of chicken when she thinks Kate's looking the other way.

There's nothing tangible about the tension tonight. You can't see it, touch it or knit with it, let alone keep it steady. Kate has no idea where it originates, no notion of how to wind it up and confine it to a safe wicker basket. It's run away with her and her family, like a ball of wool batted downstairs by a kitten.

Guy and the children are physically present, but mentally each is somewhere else. Alicia, her fingers tapping on the edge of the table, is still practising. Adrian is munching with his usual vigour and staying silent with his usual uncommunicativeness. And Guy—

Guy has dark shadows under his eyes and the grey hairs at his temples seem recently to have doubled in number. Kate can see that he is not just worried, but fearful. He has intimated that there are problems at the office – financial concerns to do with investment, advertising and ownership, far beyond the editorial issues he controls. Kate doesn't want to raise the possibility in front of the kids that the *Manchester Chronicle* could be in choppy waters. But trying to make lively conversation about school doesn't seem helpful either.

Alicia's career, amid this swamp of adolescent hormones and adult anxieties, is a beacon of light. Kate hands round the salad (Adrian takes a single leaf) and mentions that Rebecca is planning to book the same studio for the next recording, a Chopin album.

'Damn it!' Guy expostulates. 'How is she supposed to make another CD for these bloody cowboys when she's got wall-to-wall exams?'

Alicia looks up, distressed.

Kate glares. 'Cowboys? Eden is an excellent company and Rebecca's an experienced professional.'

'Rebecca is a menace second only to that wretched Butterfingers woman.'

In over twenty years, Kate has never seen Guy so angry.

'Dad,' Alicia pleads, 'don't.'

'Don't *what*, Ali? Don't sit by and watch a bunch of hysterical, frustrated women wreck your life?'

'Nice one, Dad,' Adrian grunts.

'Shut up, Adrian. Guy, how can you say that?' Kate protests, airbrushing herself out of the 'bunch'. 'Mrs Butterworth was recommended as the best teacher in Manchester. Rebecca has worked in the record industry for nearly twenty-five years. Phyllida—'

'Phyllida's a time-bomb on legs. Silly Phyllie, Posh Becs and Mrs Butterfingers! And you're putting Ali's future in *their* hands?'

'Just because they're single, older women, you're determined to pour scorn on them. All any of them has done is work for Ali's best interests.'

'If making Ali do another CD like that last one is in her best interests, then I'm the Dalai Lama. No good will come of that disc, you'll see. The "Minute" Waltz and "Clair de lune"? You think anyone's going to take her seriously if she records easy-listening favourite classical hits? Why don't you listen to the advisory service?'

'Why didn't you say any of this before?' Kate demands.

'Because, sometimes, I'm as much of an idiot as anyone.' Guy pushes back his chair with a dreadful scraping noise and thuds away up the stairs. Tears well out of Alicia's eyes. Adrian glowers at his mother. 'Now look what you've done. The first time Dad's been home for supper all week and you have to wreck it.'

'I'm not the one who started swearing at Ali's managers.' Kate's hands are shaking and when she realises she can sit down it comes as a relief. 'Ali,' she says, 'don't cry, darling.'

Alicia snuffles, hands moving through Cassie's long hair; the dog always seems to know when she's upset and comes to comfort her with the pressure of her warm snout on her knee. 'I feel so lost,' she mumbles. 'I don't know who to trust. And I thought Dad was pleased, and suddenly he isn't. I don't know what to do.'

And Kate, though she has no intention of going to church, whispers inside her own head, 'God help me.'

★   ★   ★

In his study, Guy shuts first the door, then his eyes, then his brain. What an idiot, he thinks. How could I be such an oaf? But that's how things happen: it's all in the timing.

He's been trying to decide how to tell Kate that he has a lover, a pregnant lover, and that he wants to move out and live with her. But here is Kate, wittering on about recording studios and the marvellous Rebecca – not even *noticing* that Rebecca is a dyke – while Ali sits in tears over her dinner. Kate has absconded from the family planet and is chasing some elusive star that has nothing to do with him and, possibly, not much to do with Ali.

How can he abandon Ali? Emily may be having his child, but Ali *is* his child, with all her talent and radiance, a precious gem that has plummeted into his hands for safekeeping until the world is ready to hold her – and she's surrounded by people who say that they know what's best for her although they only care about their own interests.

In this catalogue of incompetence, perhaps he's the worst. What could be more incompetent than committing adultery and fathering a child? Emily, at least, is blameless. He trusts Emily as he has never trusted anybody else. Well, perhaps he'd once trusted Kate that way – twenty-five years ago.

He won't be able to tell his wife about his mistress tonight, though it was with this intention that he'd come home early. It will have to wait, if not for the right moment – for there will never be a right moment – then at least for one that's slightly better.

A CD's gestation period turns out to be longer than Alicia had expected: months rather than weeks. When hers is finally released in April – spring, according to Rebecca, being an excellent time for launching new efforts, giving breath to new life – Eden Classics's PR department pulls out all its stops. A beautiful teenager, famous nationwide, reputedly more gifted than any British girl musician since Jacqueline du Pré, playing

popular pieces that show off her wonderful abilities. Twenty
CDs are stacked up at the end of the kitchen table, ready for
Kate to use as promotion.

'Sex,' Adrian says.

'What?' Alicia nearly chokes on her Weetabix.

'Look at it. What they're saying, underneath the crap, is
"This kid is sexy." That's why people will buy it.'

'That's horrible.'

'Why do you think they made you put on a dress that showed
your tits like that? Why do you think you had to lie down on
that sofa?'

'All I wanted on the front was a picture of me in my normal
clothes with Cassie!'

'Yeah. The girl-next-door look. That would have been great.'

'So why doesn't Mum see that? Why doesn't Rebecca?'

'Because you're fit.'

'I'm not! I just want to play the piano and walk my dog.'

'You look sexy, though. Of course, you're still too young,
but you won't be for long. Ali, don't go all shocked. Sex sells.
The company's not interested in *you*, only in making money
out of you.' He dumps his bowl in the sink. 'I'll take Cassie
out later,' he says, going upstairs.

Alicia sits at the table staring helplessly at the pile of CDs
from which her own manufactured image in its loathsome
setting stares back twenty times over.

Guy has been dealing with the shock waves at work caused
by Emily's maternity leave. Everyone is gossiping about who
the father can be – Emily is known to live by herself. He's had
to send off tomorrow's edition listening to his secretary rattling
on about whether it could be Rob Wilder, the office stud,
whether Emily will leave, how she'll make ends meet, how
she'd always seemed such an open person yet must be awfully
secretive . . .

Privately he has to deal with far worse than that. Emily went into labour at five o'clock one afternoon while he was at the office. He wanted to drop everything and go to her; between contractions, she'd mustered the self-possession to order him by text message to do no such thing. Someone would find out; there'd be a scandal; he'd lose his job and so might she. She was alone in the hospital for the birth, with no partner to stand by her and let her grip his hand when the pain became unbearable, or look on in terror and wonder as the baby slithered out into the world and was placed in her arms, or share the immortal moment when her moist silvery eyes filled with love at their first glimpse of the new little face.

He'd gone to her on her first day home and she'd filled him in on every detail. He'd imagined the scenes as she talked, a furious, pistol-whip resentment building in his chest, causing constriction in his breathing and a pain down his left arm. He should have been with her, but he had not dared break the rules. He should have broken them earlier. He should have told Kate when he'd meant to. But even if he had, how could he leave Ali? Holding his newborn daughter, whom Emily wants to name Ingrid after her Danish grandmother, he's so flummoxed by the quantity of different loves within him that he can't speak for nearly ten minutes.

The air on the moor is filled with the scents of spring: new grass, recent rain. Unleashed, Cassie trots beside Adrian, performing the nearest thing she can to a frolic. Though she's a dignified lady of advancing years, she's still charmed by April sunshine.

Adrian feels like whistling himself. He's thinking about a girl. Not something he'd like to reveal, or a situation that makes sense. He knows her only from one encounter in Birmingham, her photo on Alicia's desk and her voice on the phone. It's a quiet, modest voice, oddly blending the accents of Birmingham, Surrey and India. All he's heard it say recently is 'Hello, this is Anjali speaking. Is Alicia there, please?' Why that should seem so appealing is anybody's guess. Her image lingers in his mind, surrounded by the golden wood of Symphony Hall: a small, slender girl with huge eyes and an intelligent, serious face. Adrian can't imagine anybody more different from the slappers at school. There's no point in aspiring to an angel, of course, not for him, but his feelings aren't his choice. She's been in the back of his mind, lurking, for months on end. He's wondering, when the Land Rover approaches, whether he can persuade Alicia to invite her to Buxton.

The Land Rover slows as it comes up the hill behind him. Mud and sheep-shit congeal on its bumper; behind its wheel sits a red-faced farmer in a tweed jacket and cap, glaring at Adrian and Cassie as if they are emissaries of the devil.

'What do you think you're doing?' the farmer shouts through the window.

'Going for a walk,' Adrian says. Cassie sits obediently to his right, waiting.

'That dog's going to get shot.'

'My dog's none of your business.'

'How stupid are you, you bloody yob?' Adrian judges, from the hue of his nose, that the farmer has probably had a drink or two today and that he's most likely on his way to the Cat and Fiddle for another. 'I'll thank you to keep that dog on a leash around them sheep. Don't you know it's lambing season?'

'My dog doesn't chase sheep.'

'If I see her once more up here without a leash, I won't warn you again, I shall shoot her. Got my rifle in the back here, mind.'

'Fuck off,' Adrian says. But he fastens Cassie's leash – he believes the words about the gun. Belligerent farmers aren't his favourite people, any more than he and his friends are theirs. The Land Rover revs into indecent acceleration.

'Evenly balanced bloke,' Adrian mutters to Cassie, as they resume their walk, leash-bound. 'Chips on both shoulders.'

The encounter has left a nasty taste in his mouth, and by

the time they reach the Cat and Fiddle, he fancies a drink. Cassie is panting too, so he takes her into the car park where a stone trough is filled with water for thirsty animals. There, a sight meets him that restores his spirits on the spot.

The car park is full because the bikers are there. They've parked in spaces meant for cars and the latest arrival to find nowhere to stop on this sunny spring Sunday is the farmer in the Land Rover. He's leaning out of his window, screaming fit to bust at the biker who's grabbed the last place. 'I'll have you up in front of the magistrate by this time next week, see if I don't! Screeching over the moors and scaring my sheep in the lambing season. No respect, that's your trouble, no respect for decent, law-abiding citizens.'

'Wanker!' Adrian shouts, sticking a finger up at the farmer. 'Why don't you bugger off and mind your own business? He's got as much right to park there as you have. He got there first and there's nowt you can do about it.'

The biker, who's removed his helmet, turns and meets Adrian's gaze, looking surprised, even impressed. He has bright, piercing blue eyes and big shoulders. He's bigger, tougher and older (if not much) than Adrian and looks like the kind of bloke who wouldn't expect anyone to come to his defence.

'You again?' the farmer snarls at Adrian. 'I'll shoot that dog, see if I don't.'

'Piss off,' says the biker. 'You've no business shooting dogs when you can't even feed your livestock without making them into cannibals and spreading diseases they'd never have got otherwise. Your sort thinks the world owes you a living! Anyhow, I got that space first.'

'Move that bike. *Now.*'

'Bye-bye. Have a beautiful day.' The biker strides towards the pub; then turns and motions Adrian to follow him. Adrian, a spring in his step, needs no second bidding.

'Thanks, mate,' says the biker. 'The name's Josh. Pleased to meet you. What'll it be? Pint?'

'Yeah, thanks. I'm Adrian.'

'Great dog, that one. Pedigree rough collie, is she?'

'I think so.' Adrian watches Cassie jump up towards the biker's chest and try to lick his nose. Josh, to her delight and Adrian's, gives her a good back-rub.

'I had a dog. She was wonderful. Old English sheepdog, the kind that can't see out. Lovely creature. I miss her.'

'What happened to her?'

'She's with my family in Manchester. I don't go home much. Anyway, who do these blokes think they are, driving their fucking Land Rovers?'

In the pub, Josh leads Adrian and Cassie towards his fellow bikers. Adrian fidgets with Cassie's leash.

He once saw a documentary on TV about a pack of wolves. When a young male wolf from another valley wanted to join them, he had to approach the potentially hostile animals and let them surround him. While they growled, threatened and lunged, he had to stand firm and fearless, wagging his tail. Right now, Adrian feels that standing firm and wagging your tail takes more courage than fighting off a bunch of armed attackers single-handed.

'This is Adrian,' Josh says to the others. 'You into bikes, Adrian?'

'Well,' Adrian begins, 'funny you should say that . . .'

14

In her office – its wall laden with prints from Alicia's photo-shoot – Kate sifts through the sheaf of CD reviews, looking for quotable quotes. During the summer, quite a few have emerged; but however hard she stares at them, she can't make them any better. One praises Alicia's tone quality, fast fingers and range of colour, but disparages the presentation and populist programming. Another deems her too young and shallow. A third condemns the disc as a miserable attempt to exploit a young girl: this CD, the critic carps, is not a good idea. The advisory scheme, with a strongly worded letter, warns Kate of the same thing.

Yet when Rebecca calls her with the sales figures, the public seems to have thought the CD was a very good idea indeed.

'Becs, I don't know who to believe.'

'People are buying it, aren't they?' her friend replies. 'Critics hate anything that's popular and sells well. They always have. Just ignore them.'

'And her new album next spring? The Chopin? What will they say about that?'

'Katie, stop worrying! It'll sell. People love her.'

Kate hangs up and stares out of her window at the leaves turning from green to brown in the garden. Rebecca knows what she's doing. She must. She has to. And it's true: people are buying the CD, mean critics or no. All she can do is wait and see what next year holds.

Alicia makes a mistake at school. She lets Kelly know that she's going to London to be interviewed by national newspapers about her piano-playing. Preparing to go home at the end of a chilly afternoon, she reaches into her school bag for her gloves and feels something sharp on her skin. When she pulls out her right hand, it's streaked with red globules of blood.

Guy returns from a long, difficult day to find Alicia in tears, Kate pale and tight-lipped and Adrian in his room, pumping out the kind of music that doesn't do a stressed-out family any good.

'Adrian, turn that down!' he yells from the hall. His son can't hear him. 'Ali, what's going on?'

She doesn't reply. Instead she holds out her right hand. It's bandaged.

'Some of the kids at school thought it'd be fun to put a piece of broken bottle in Ali's bag,' Kate tells him. 'I've rung the headmaster.'

'I'm not going back,' Alicia says.

'Ali, you've got GCSEs . . .'

'I don't care.'

'It's lucky that she didn't actually take hold of it,' Kate adds. 'The cuts are nasty, but there's no damage to her tendons.'

'I'll go and see the headmaster,' Guy says. 'And I'm going to put something in the paper.'

'Thank you,' says Kate, icy. 'About time. Sad that it takes such an incident to get your daughter's name into your news-paper.'

A howl from Alicia brings them to their senses. Guy sits down on the stairs. He wants a drink, badly.

'Perhaps it's time for Ali to move on,' he says. 'How about calling the music school?'

A short conversation with the headmistress of the music school produces rapid results. The head of piano, who would be in charge of Alicia's studies, asks Kate to come and see him right away. He's younger than she is, a tall Scot with a youthful face, bright smile and a tweed jacket; his handshake is warm and firm. On his desk is a photo of his slender blonde wife and no fewer than five children. He couldn't be a greater contrast with Mrs Butterworth. He asks her to call him Ian.

'We've been following Alicia's progress with a great deal of interest,' he tells her. 'Now, tell me what happened.'

Kate explains. 'She says she won't go back to school. And when Alicia makes up her mind, she's very stubborn.'

'Was she stubborn over her CD?'

Kate tries, tactfully, to outline the difference between Alicia's hopes and the result.

'Did anyone notice that she might be right?' Ian says.

'Well . . .'

'Now, Kate, here's my view. Alicia has an extraordinary talent. But that talent has to be properly nurtured. She's been bounced, for lack of a better word, out of her depth. Everyone wants a piece of her, don't they? Her teacher. Her record company. Her agent.'

'She couldn't wish for nicer people around her than Rebecca Harris and Phyllida Brown.'

'I know Phyllida. She's great,' Ian agrees. 'It's a good agency. But they've got big plans, haven't they?'

'They're talking about a tour of Germany, and several European festivals want to book her.'

'Listen, Kate. I feel this very strongly: this isn't right. If Alicia is going to join us here, I have some very specific conditions that I need you to agree to. First, no more recordings until she's ready. And then only when she has total control of what goes on to the CD and its cover.'

'Rebecca thinks she *is* ready.'

'Rebecca would.' Ian fixes Kate with his straight, no-nonsense gaze. Kate puts a hand against the side of her neck.

'I've heard the recording,' Ian goes on. 'Yes, she's a lovely girl and her playing is often mature beyond her years. But in the bigger picture, that CD, even if it sells well, is not going to do her many favours. It's made the critics cynical about her, although they were on her side after the competition. The general consensus is that she's too young: she needs time to study and grow, but she's being coerced – by whoever – into doing too much work and the wrong kind. She's being launched on the wrong foot.'

Kate squeezes the edge of her chair.

'So: no tours of Germany – or anywhere else – until *we*'re convinced she's ready. Touring can be hell. It's tiring; it's tedious. Believe me, I've done it myself. Why put a kid through that at sixteen? These are years that Alicia needs, Kate, to consolidate her talent, to give herself something to build on for the future. It's as if you're asking her to spend her capital before it's had a fair chance to accrue.'

'I see.'

'If she's coming to us, the recording contract goes, ninety per cent of the concerts go and Deirdre Butterworth goes too.'

'Really?'

'It's nothing personal. I hardly know her, but I do know the playing of some of her pupils. Personally, I treat her teaching with caution. She has her admirers. She's good at drilling the fingers and developing technique. But a young musician needs to have her soul built too. Deirdre's methods can be effective, but her attitudes are extremely old-fashioned and a number of pianists feel they've had quite a destructive effect, long-term.'

'But the concerts . . . Alicia would have to let down halls, clubs and orchestras that have booked her to play. She'd have to break her contract with Eden.'

'Then so be it. If she has to let people down, that's a pity. But it's better than everyone else letting *her* down.'

'If we agree to all this, you'll take her?'

'We'll need to talk to her ourselves, of course, but I think there's a good chance.'

'And if not—'

'Then I'm afraid it's no.'

'I'll have to talk to my husband. And we'll both have to talk to Alicia.'

Later, Kate replays Ian's words in her mind. She'd tried to call Guy as soon as she came out of the school, but he was having a newspaper crisis; the aftermath of the events in New York on 11 September a year earlier is still sending extended jitters through every business in the country. Life is so short. Why waste the opportunities that come your way?

Her own life, as she sees it, is hopeless in all respects but one: Ali. Otherwise, what has she done that's been worth doing? She has three children; one dead, one uncontrollable and the last a child prodigy. Any one of them would have been enough to put her marriage under strain.

You have to make the most of every minute. She remembers the images of the twin towers collapsing. Who knows what will happen now? Perhaps Al Qaeda terrorists intend to bring not only America but Europe, too, tumbling into war, chaos and destruction. And they're supposed to worry about schooling, drop most of the concerts and all the recording plans, throw away every chance that Ali has now, in case something better lies in wait a few years down the line? By then none of them may be here.

Kate puts the matter to one side while they go to London; she says nothing to Alicia yet, because the girl must concentrate on her round of interviews, set up by a public-relations firm at a cost of several thousand pounds per month's work. Alicia charms all the journalists and claims that her hand is bandaged because she'd had a little accident in the kitchen. The PR company has rapidly muzzled Guy's plans to tell the truth in his newspaper. Rebecca embraces Kate and has the empathy to ask whether *she* is feeling all right.

Phyllida cooks dinner for them and Rebecca at her top-floor flat in Tulse Hill, an Italian meal that wouldn't look out of place in Rome. First, fresh mozzarella, tomato and basil, Italian cold meats and home-baked ciabatta; then pasta with pesto, and a main course of baked sea bass with fennel, lemon, capers and vegetables; and the most incredible tiramisu for dessert.

'Maybe it's because I don't have kids,' Phyllida declares, pouring prosecco, 'but I always end up mothering my clients.'

The light, bubbly wine makes them feel light and bubbly too.

'Phyllida,' Alicia asks, after her miniature ration, when her cheeks are flushed and her courage increased, 'why don't you have kids?'

'I keep falling in love with the wrong men,' Phyllida tells her.

'French pianists,' Rebecca needles.

'Not Lucien?' Alicia is horrified.

'But you still work for him,' Kate says.

'How could I not?' Phyllida's eyes, behind her small rectangular spectacles, turn towards the window and gaze over the rooftops of hilly south London as if seeking out any traces of the vanished presence for which she cared too much.

Alicia, exhausted after a long day, falls asleep in the car on the way back to Hampstead Garden Suburb. Kate and Rebecca talk quietly about Phyllida and Lucien. 'He trampled all over her,' Rebecca says. 'But she won't give him up as a client and she won't give up hope. If he had any sense of honour, he'd leave the agency – but he knows she'll do anything for him, so he stays and takes advantage of it.'

'She's crazy,' Kate says.

'Crazy about him. She says she'd rather have him somewhere in her life than nowhere, and that this way at least she can do something for him. She's still hoping she'll get him back if he thinks she's indispensable. She can't move on.'

'Does he have someone else?'

'Plenty of someone elses, besides the official one. He's living with a very beautiful girl in Paris – half Algerian, I believe. She designs jewellery. He's been with her for two years. I think she's the one he left Phyllida for, but it may have been another . . . He's got quite a network around the world.'

'Doesn't Phyllida *know*?'

'Of course she knows. But what can you do? He's a good-looking guy. He's charming, talented, charismatic, famous, and he has the cutest accent on earth. Women never could resist him. And there are always women who think it's noble to forgive.'

'You've resisted him,' Kate points out.

'That's different. I'm sorted. Since I broke up with David, I've found myself.'

'And where were you hiding all the time?' Kate teases her.

'Aha. Somewhere else.' Kate waits, but Rebecca smiles and says no more.

Kate privately adopts Guy's nickname for Phyllida: 'Silly Phyllie'. Poor girl – woman (she's forty) – slogging her guts out for a man who's ridden roughshod over her. At least if you devote yourself to working for your daughter, she's your own flesh and blood. Phyllida may never be Lucien's lover again. Kate will always be Ali's mum.

Back in Buxton, they find a letter from school on the doormat, declaring that the children responsible for putting glass in Alicia's bag have been caught and may be excluded. Alicia hovers, clutching her bandaged hand. Kate sits her down and gives her a somewhat postponed and selectively edited account of her conversation with Ian at the music school.

'What do you think?' she says at the end. 'Are you prepared to do what they want?'

'I don't think I want to keep going to any school anyway,' Alicia says. 'Maybe I could grit my teeth, go back to Parkhill and do the exams – and then just leave. I guess I can stand it for a while if they've got rid of . . . them. I don't need A levels to play the piano, do I?'

'We'll have to talk to your father,' Kate says, reeling.

But of course Alicia's father is home so late that Alicia is asleep and Kate is tired and fed up. Bundling laundry into the washing-machine the next morning, she's puzzled to spot what looks like a milk stain on the shoulder of the shirt he'd been wearing, and wonders why he sometimes comes home smelling of sandalwood soap.

'Alicia! *Bonjour, chérie, ça va?*'

'Oh, Lucien,' Alicia exclaims into the phone, 'I'm not very *bien* at all.'

She'd cried into her pillow half the night, not for the first time. Mum has often told her that everything feels worse at three o'clock in the morning, but this was the worst yet. With the bitter flavour of her home, with Mum and Dad fighting – it's grown unaccountably more extreme this year – and school, where she has to take horrible exams and has no friends, things couldn't seem much more miserable.

Mum and Dad's latest row is over school and her fervent desire not to be there any more. Mum is broadly in favour of her leaving to concentrate on music, but Dad is livid. She's caught, like Dorothy in *The Wizard of Oz*, in a tornado that's transforming people she'd loved and trusted into witches, scarecrows and Munchkins. Like Dorothy – her favourite movie character, because of the dog – she's miles from where she wants to be and she needs a wizard to help her.

Lucien the wizard listens to everything. Then he says, 'Darling, when do you next have a school holiday? Can you come to Zürich? I have started to teach at the Zürich Academy, and I will be there for two weeks. We could work together and talk this through.'

'Can I?' Alicia pleads. 'I'd so love to. I've got half-term soon.'

'Your mother didn't want you to come last time,' he reminds her. 'You must be strong, you must insist.'

'I'll try.' Alicia wants to tell Lucien about Dad's peculiar behaviour, his outbursts, his silences, his absences, but she doesn't know how to; and she doesn't know what she wants him to say anyway.

She's attempted time and again to persuade Mum that they should go to see Lucien in Paris, but so far to no avail. There's always a reason not to. Looming concerts, mainly; Alicia sometimes feels she's so busy performing that she doesn't have time to learn in any depth about the music she plays. She senses, too, that Mum and Paris are like oil and water, goodness knows why, though when she tries to bargain – couldn't Dad go with her, or Phyllida? Couldn't she go alone? – it only seems to make matters worse.

Today, when she tackles Mum in her office, gathering all her courage and saying 'Lucien' and 'Zürich' – not Paris – the response is different. Mum, at her computer, is pallid and tired. There's a deflated, defeated look about her. Alicia imagines their house rising up in the tornado, with all of them clinging on, whirling sleepless into the sky.

'If that's what you want to do, love,' Mum says, barely looking at her, 'then we'll do it.'

'Mum,' Alicia pushes, 'why do you hate Paris?'

'I don't,' says Mum.

Alicia gazes at Zürich and can hardly breathe for its beauty. When she and Mum have checked in to their guesthouse and set out to explore, she finds they're on the shore of a vast lake; across the water, dusky, smoky mountains are shrouded in a soft autumn haze. It's so lovely that it hurts. Everything is blue, bronze and purple. It's like walking through a Chopin nocturne in D flat major.

Alicia hasn't been abroad often. Lucien looks shocked when she explains her holiday routine. The family does take a break for a couple of weeks in summer – at least, they used to, before the competition – but it usually means going with Margaret and William to Sidmouth, Torbay, or sometimes Scotland, which is even colder than Buxton, but which Alicia loves for the scenery. A few times, when she was much smaller, they went to seriously hot places where Mum and Dad had crashed out on the beach – Mum still had her job in those days – and she and Adrian would mess around in the sea. But now, wherever they go, Alicia spends the first day hunting for a piano on which she can practise, and the rest of the holiday practising on it. 'Alicia,' says Lucien, 'you have to learn one thing: there's life away from the piano.'

Not that Lucien has much of a life. He travels all the time. After two weeks in Zürich, he'll be off for a recital tour in Germany and Holland, back to Zürich for more teaching, and eventually to America for three weeks. If he's lucky, he might be home for Christmas. He doesn't go home for more than a few days every month or two. He's constantly on his mobile phone – if he wants it to stop ringing, he has to switch it off – and he's the fastest texter Alicia has ever seen. It seems that he has a beautiful half-Algerian girlfriend waiting for him in Paris. She must miss him.

When Mum insists on sitting in on Alicia's lesson at the academy, Lucien tries a few charming discouragements, none of which work. Especially not when Mum turns on her own charm – something she does infrequently, but to startling effect. For Mum, to smile is to deploy a secret weapon that makes people do what she wants because they simply can't stop themselves. Lucien is no exception: when Mum beams at him, he dissolves into a hopeless grin and declares, 'You should be sisters, not mother and daughter!' Alicia wriggles inwardly: she tries, sometimes, to get him to look at her like that. Occasionally he obliges, but mostly he doesn't.

What does his girlfriend think when he looks at other women? Maybe she doesn't know that he does. Or maybe she doesn't mind. She must mind – but maybe she forgives him. Alicia hates being sixteen. There's too much that she doesn't understand and she's scared to ask because she's terrified of looking stupid.

In the studio, with Mum in the corner, notebook at the ready, and Lucien beside her at the piano, Alicia starts to play Chopin. Almost before she knows what's happened, two hours have passed. Mrs Butterfingers – as Alicia secretly calls Mrs Butterworth – usually scrawls instructions across her music with red pencil; when there's so much red that you can't read more, she switches to blue. She writes in the fingering for each note and tells Alicia exactly how to practise every passage: which to slow down in different rhythms, which to build up note by note, which metronome marks to use. Lucien does none of this. He asks Alicia what she thinks. What the music makes her feel. What she wants it to say. After they've worked through the Chopin, she plays some Schumann. It makes him think of another Schumann piece, he remarks, a song called 'Mondnacht'. He plays her the song, which she's never heard before; it's so magical that she nearly bursts into tears.

She doesn't know the other pieces he mentions – symphonies, a violin concerto, chamber music. She has no time to listen to recordings of pieces she's not learning to play, and she can't go to proper concerts unless she's in London or Manchester with no school the next day. Lucien turns to Mum and protests: 'A young musician has to have the background, the breadth of knowledge, the experience . . .'

Alicia knows that she's ignorant; filling in the gaps is a daunting task. It certainly isn't going to happen at school. Lucien, to her delight, agrees: Alicia won't glean the exceptional, specialised knowledge she needs from any A-level syllabus. At least this might help to sway Dad. Lucien says nothing on the subject that Alicia couldn't have said herself; the difference is that her parents will listen to him. Alicia decides that there's only one place to begin her real education: with

Lucien. She's a sponge and he's a great fountain, as full as the violet lake, with an endless pool of wisdom in which she can soak.

They go to Lucien's studio three times that week, once he's finished with his official students for the day. In between, he's arranged for Alicia to practise at the academy. After her lessons, the three of them go to a café for supper and Lucien talks for hours. He tells them about his studies at the Paris Conservatoire – he'd started there when he was only twelve; and about his year in Moscow (how funny, Alicia thinks, that he studied in the same places as Mrs Butterfingers, yet the two of them are light years apart). In the Russian winter, he says, he got frostbite. His ears swelled and turned purple. He'd looked like a donkey. Mum laughs, relaxed, enchanted.

Alicia is so busy watching Lucien's eyes that sometimes she doesn't hear what he's saying. Every shade of emotion shows in them: they are gleaming one moment, soulful the next, switching in a flash from inscrutable to teasing to tender. Mum is silent when he speaks; Alicia thinks her pupils become three times their usual size. She wonders whether she'll look like her mother when she's her age. She hopes so, though she'd dress differently. Mum prefers somewhat formal clothes, usually with a jacket and jewellery. She never wears jeans. Alicia likes to look natural.

After their last meal together, Lucien walks them back along the lake front to their guesthouse. The lights reflect in the water, silver on indigo, and the surface ripples in the breeze that drifts from the mountains. It's warm for October; people are out enjoying the evening air. 'You couldn't do this at home,' Alicia says. 'You'd freeze.' Here, colours seem brighter – there's something grey about England, as if the light has been rolled in dust. Mum tells her it's because she finds it exciting to be somewhere new, but Alicia is certain that there's more to it. She doesn't want to leave Switzerland.

Saying goodbye, Lucien kisses Mum three times and she

turns coy like a schoolgirl. Alicia hugs him and wants never to let go. The next morning, on the plane, she closes her eyes and daydreams about him. If only Phyllida wasn't his ex-girlfriend. She tries not to imagine them together; it makes her feel like a limp brown balloon that's been left outside for too long.

Lucien has told her that she must come to his masterclasses next year at the Moorside Summer School. It will be a popular event, so Mum will send in their booking form at once and Alicia plans to exhort Anjali to join them. In the meantime, she has to go back to Deirdre Butterworth who, she now understands, may have been teaching her how to play, but not why.

'It's great.' Emily is inspecting the new white paint, the stripped wooden floor and the relatively spacious second bedroom at the back. The flat is near Victoria Park on the ground level of a converted terraced house. It's less convenient for work than Emily's current home, but the area is quieter, more family-oriented, with a child-minder in the next street and a doctor's surgery less than five minutes' walk away. Emily's apartment in the centre of town has only one bedroom and is on the fourth floor, which is hopeless with a baby buggy.

While he holds Ingrid, Guy's mind flickers images at him of his other children. Adrian. Alicia. Victoria. Pain cuts through his chest, half real, half imagined, whether physical or emotional he couldn't say: the two are inseparable.

'One day,' Emily says, 'maybe we'll be looking at a cottage in a village.'

'There are some great places,' Guy says. 'Castleton. Or Hartington.'

'A little house with a garden and a local school and a real sense of community. We miss that here. In Denmark it's much stronger.'

'Maybe we should move to Denmark.'

There's a long silence then, because they know they're

fantasising. They keep doing it: building castles in the air, only to watch, helpless, as the walls disintegrate. Guy notices Emily turn away so that he can't see her face. The baby in his arms wriggles and whimpers. He gives her back to her mother, who caresses her back with one hand, infinitely gentle.

Guy has been to see the bank manager. He refuses to shirk his responsibilities: this child is his and he is determined to support her and Emily. The question is how to do so without Kate finding out. He has set up a direct debit to an account that will be Emily's but that will bear a different title. He hates to use Alicia as a pretext, but calling it Music Fund seems sensible: Kate, if she finds it, will assume he's started another savings account towards Alicia's studies. As he signs the form, he loathes himself for it – but whatever he does, caught in this impossible web, will be wrong.

It's not that he hasn't intended to tell Kate the truth – but Kate is so *busy*. Her existence centres on Alicia; if she's not occupied with trips to London to visit Phyllida and Rebecca or, now, to Switzerland to see Lucien (which has given him the leisure to house-hunt with Emily), then it's concert planning, letters, phone calls and, of course, escorting Alicia to her concerts, which can be anywhere in the country. Every time Guy steels himself, gearing up to an explanation with rehearsed speech and sinking stomach, she'll be so busy yakking with Rebecca that he can't get her attention; or Alicia needs ferrying to a far-flung venue, or there's hassle with Adrian – there's more and more hassle, these days, with Adrian, who seems never to go to school and vanishes like clockwork every weekend. So nothing happens and time runs on.

Guy's back has been hurting, he has a permanent headache and he's afraid he's getting a stomach ulcer.

Adrian takes a bus to Macclesfield one Saturday afternoon and wanders towards a shop that his new friend Josh has told him about. He wants to earn some money.

Standing outside it, he feels like a nineteenth-century orphan pressing his nose against a bakery window. Inside are ranged the most enticing objects he's ever seen. They vary in size from largish to humungous. Their bodies are shiny – black, silver, purple, ivory or red – and their wheels sleek, made for racing. Most of the labels bear prices in four figures. Adrian has a savings account into which his parents and grandparents pay regularly, building funds to support him when he goes to university (as they assume he will). He knows he'll be slaughtered if he raids it. He also knows he's supposed to have a licence if he wants to drive a motorbike. On the other hand, he'd have to ride around with an L-plate, as well as undergoing time-consuming remedial instruction that he doesn't need, maybe for six months; the shame would be more than he could take.

During heady summer weekends on the moors, he's learned everything he needs to learn from Josh and the others. Josh lets him ride pillion, but has made it clear that he can't do this for ever. If he wants to join them properly, he has to have his own bike. He's going to have to pay the deposit and then monthly instalments, which means he needs an income and therefore a job, which has to be evenings, weekends or both, but not more, because of effing school.

It's all right for Ali: she's *talented*. Adrian sometimes wonders why one of them should have been born with a talent while the other wasn't, and why that other should have had to be him. Why couldn't he be on TV, have a posh London agent, charge through the nose for his services? Adrian vacillates between being proud and protective of his little sister, and half wanting to strangle her. He doesn't feel that way often: just often enough for it to hurt. He could murder the idiots at school who'd thought it funny to put glass in her bag; but, staring past his reflection at the array of bikes with names like Panorama, Seductor and Freedom, he admits reluctantly that he can understand why someone might. Poor Ali. It's not her fault. She hadn't asked for this any more than he had.

The shop door is open. Adrian draws himself up. Josh has given him the manager's name and tipped him off that they need Saturday help. He tries to broaden his shoulders and walks up to the counter, hoping he looks cool.

15

On Christmas Eve, while Guy is overseeing the last of the seasonal rush at the office, Kate drives Alicia back through a damp, dreary night from a recital in a music club in the West Midlands, where she has played for an audience of twenty-nine over-seventies. At home, at half past eleven, Alicia has a cup of hot chocolate and a bath, while Kate wanders into her study and switches on the computer. As the screen brightens, she finds herself face to face with a picture of a bomb.

Her hard drive has crashed. Just in time for Christmas. Luckily she's backed everything up – she's scrupulous about this, thanks to Rebecca's urgings – but it's too late at night to phone Rebecca for advice or ransack the *Yellow Pages* for a man who can help. None will be available now, she suspects, until the new year. There's no point in stewing over it; she has other things to worry about, notably cooking Christmas lunch the next day. But tonight she does need to send one short yet vital email.

She rings Guy's mobile, but it's off. He can't possibly mind, can he, if this once she goes into his study and uses his computer? She checks that Alicia is all right, then makes her way to the top of the house.

Guy's study is in its usual chaos. Kate shakes her head as she steps across the clutter to the desk and computer. She presses a switch and, as she waits for the computer to buzz into action, she glances through a sheaf of papers beside it.

Credit-card statements; drafts for leaders, which he sometimes writes himself; letters, including something from the bank about a largish direct debit to an account called Music Fund, which she doesn't recognise. Odd. Why would Guy create another Ali account without telling her? Of course, he's so absent-minded that he probably forgot.

Kate logs on to the email, guessing the password successfully (Cassie) and types out her message to the music-club director, thanking her for a wonderful evening (it's important that Ali should at least have the chance to be reinvited). When she's finished, Guy's inbox appears in front of her. She sees:

emily.andersen

emily.andersen

emily.andersen

emily.andersen

emily.andersen

The messages from emily.andersen, dated across the past few days, have no subject heading. Kate stares, disbelieving, hand poised over the mouse. She moves it gingerly and the cursor glides towards the first one. She can't bring herself to click.

This is crazy. She trusts Guy. He's too busy, too preoccupied, too hopeless to *do* anything with anybody, let alone a lovely young thing who could have had Rob Wilder with one click of her fingers. Whatever would a girl like Emily Andersen see in a scatterbrained workaholic like Guy Bradley?

With a momentum that doesn't seem to be hers, Kate's hand reaches for the pile of papers and extracts several credit-card statements. September's is among them, marked 'PAID' in Guy's messy blue capitals. On it is a list of transactions: Ikea (where they haven't shopped in years), Tesco (there's no Tesco in Buxton) and, most peculiar of all, Mothercare.

Three facts collide in Kate's fast-moving mind. Emily Andersen is half Danish. Guy once went to a conference in Denmark. Why Denmark, for God's sake? And these places and payments remind her, peculiarly, of those on her credit-card

statements when they were kitting out their home after the birth
of Adrian.

Kate clicks.

Darling – everything's OK, health visitor says just wrap her up
warm and keep an eye on the cough. So don't worry, we're
fine. Exxxx

She reads the message five times. The words don't want to
penetrate her skull. This can't be real. It makes no sense.
'Darling'? A health visitor? 'We' are fine?

She clicks again.

Darling – don't apologise. You know I love you. I know you
love me. That's all that matters. Exxxxx

'Mum,' Alicia calls, 'I'm turning in, OK?'

'OK, love. Sleep tight,' Kate calls back brightly. She sits in
Guy's chair and breathes, counting to five between in-breath
and out-breath and in-breath. Keeping it steady. Keeping the
tension regular. Once Alicia's door has closed, she goes down
to the bathroom and throws up.

Knowledge is power – as Kate reminds herself later, lying alone
in bed, fighting bile in her throat, cramps in her stomach and
the gates of hell splitting open in her brain. She hears Guy's
car in the drive. The front door opens and closes. He takes
off his shoes in the hall. There's the hiss of the kettle, his steps
padding about as he makes tea. Now she understands: late
nights, long absences, too many showers, stress symptoms that
leave him constantly medicated for a stomach ulcer and a
suspected slipped disc. And, of course, sandalwood soap. How
has she managed not to spot what these add up to? How could
she be so blind, so naïve, so trusting?

She's not as young as she once was. Her hair, if she didn't
keep it artificially golden and glossy, would be turning grey;
her skin is losing its elasticity, despite expensive face creams;

and the weight doesn't stay off as easily as it used to, though this is perhaps also attributable to eating out more when she's away with Ali. She hasn't yet struck the menopause, but it can't be many years off. Emily Andersen is in her early thirties; she has lovely skin, beautiful grey eyes, a shapely figure and, it seems, a fertile womb. Why such a girl should pick Kate's hopeless husband to fall in love with is rather beyond Kate. But that isn't the point.

The pillow is darkening with tears. She turns it over before Guy can come up.

Knowledge is power. She may be in pieces, but she has the upper hand. She only has to decide how best to use it. Agony and despair, knitted together, produce fury and a sickening desire for revenge. What can she do? There is, she decides, gathering her long-forgotten resources, plenty she can do.

When Guy opens the door, she lies with her back to him, letting him think she's asleep. Downstairs in the piano room, the Christmas-tree lights are dark.

During the night, while Kate and Guy lie awake, each feigning sleep for the other's benefit, the clouds drift lower and spew a malicious mix of rain and snow over the sloping streets. Then they tumble away towards the moors, and under the stars the frost sidles across to seal wetness into the town's bones. In its wake, a high covering of grey cloud sucks the colour from land and air. By the time Kate hears Alicia clumping downstairs with Cassie, the pavement outside is a sheet of mean, treacherous ice. In the distance there's a squeal of car brakes and a crunch of impacting metal.

Alicia presses a switch: the tree beside the piano flares into brilliance. 'I love Christmas!' she cries, to nobody in particular. Cassie, happy after her breakfast, lets out a volley of barks.

'Cut the racket, Al,' Adrian says, wandering by in his dressing-gown, his face stubbly and his eyes bleary.

'Merry Christmas to you too,' Guy remarks, in the kitchen.

Adrian doesn't answer. He pours himself a bowl of Shredded Wheat and abducts it.

'Adrian, it's Christmas Day,' Kate calls after him. 'I think we should all be together.'

'Later,' Adrian grunts, half-way up the stairs. 'Ali, you look like a sheep.' Alicia is wearing a thick white jumper over her jeans.

'Don't be horrible to your sister,' Kate snaps.

'It's going to be one of those days, is it?'

Kate can't say, 'You don't know the half of it,' so she keeps quiet as her son disappears to his room and her daughter through the front door with the dog, who needs walking, ice or no ice. 'Ali, mind how you go. Don't slip,' she calls after her. Then she has to start preparing Christmas lunch. There's no more time to think.

Today, of all days, both sets of parents are coming to them. Anthony, Fiona and the Horribles have gone to San Francisco to visit Joanna (something Kate and Guy have been saying for years that they really should do, too). Because of this, William and Margaret had expected Kate and her family in Harrow; but George and Didie had been intending for months that they'd go to Cheshire. It had seemed easiest to base the entire caboodle in Buxton, rather than zoom round the country trying to please everyone but themselves.

'Guy,' Kate says, chopping onion, which makes her eyes water, 'my computer crashed last night.'

'What's up with it?'

'Bomb icon. The hard drive's dead. Know anyone who can fix it?' It was a bomb icon for the entire household, but she won't inform him of this until later. She feels his gaze on her back. All he says is 'I'll ask the IT department to suggest someone.'

The turkey waits in its roasting pan, big and fat and stupid. She puts on the oven to heat. Alicia and Cassie blow in with a tidal wave of icy air from the front door; Alicia stamps her feet to warm them. She begs Kate to let her help with lunch, but Kate urges her to do some practising first.

'It's Christmas!' Alicia protests. 'And I had a concert last night. I'm not going to practise this morning.'

'You can if you want to,' Kate reassures her.

'She *doesn't* want to,' Guy points out, in front of the small, recently acquired kitchen TV where he's eating toast and staring at an inordinately jolly news programme. The presenters are wearing tinsel round their necks.

Kate rubs butter on to the turkey's skin and puts foil over its breast. Outside, snow is trying, half-heartedly, to fall. From the TV, Bing Crosby's voice intones nauseating lyrics about what Christmas ought to be like.

When the potatoes are parboiling, the Brussels sprouts have been stripped of their outer leaves and the chestnut stuffing has been thoroughly whizzed in the food-processor, Alicia wanders up to her brother's room. He's got his TV on, loud.

'Adrian,' she says, 'something weird's going on.'

'Come on, Ali, surprise me.'

'I mean, like, *really* weird. Worse than usual. They haven't said a single word to each other for an hour.' She sits down next to him. The TV patters out a tinkly carol between programmes, over a sequence showing happy children opening brightly coloured presents.

'I hate Christmas,' Adrian says.

'I *thought* I loved it,' Alicia says miserably.

'Everyone would hate Christmas, if they thought about it.'

'That's not true. It's wonderful! Everyone can stop working and be together.'

'Yeah. Look where that gets them.'

'Do you have to be so grumpy?'

'Pissed off that I can't go to work for two weeks. I'm saving up.'

'What for?'

'If you must know, one of the beauts in our shop.'

'Seriously? They must cost a fortune.'

'Worth it, though, if I can find a way. There's nothing like it, Ali.'

'How does it feel?'

'Wicked.' Adrian gives a deep sigh – the nearest thing Alicia has ever heard him express to longing. 'It's the best feeling in the whole world. I just want to get on and go.'

'Go where?'

'Anywhere. Just – away. Away from here.'

While Kate is fussing over salad, Guy creeps into the piano room, deserted but for the decked yet lonely tree, and sends Emily a text. She's going to her mother's for the day. Guy, pressing out the words 'Merry Xmas, I love you', remembers that his child by Emily has a grandmother whom he's never met – and who would probably kill him if he did. His parents have rung in cheery mode to say they're on their way. They have a granddaughter whom they'll never know; how they'd have loved Ingrid. Perhaps he's imagining it, but did Kate glare at him when she mentioned her crashed computer? There was no possibility that, in the middle of the night on Christmas Eve, she'd have been so desperate to get on to her email or the Internet that she'd have used his and seen the wrong thing – was there? His ulcer stabs like a nail in his chest.

The grandparents arrive at the same time from opposite directions, bearing gifts and having traversed afar, over motorway and moor. William and Margaret shiver on the front step; George and Didie shake their hands and smile fixedly. Alicia charges down the stairs and flings her arms round Didie; Adrian gives each grandparent a diffident peck. The presents are piled under the tree and Kate puts on a CD of a choirboy warbling, 'Peace on earth, goodwill to men . . .'

William and Margaret are staying the night, sleeping in Kate's study, and William goes upstairs slowly; he needs a hip replacement and is in constant pain, but the waiting list is eight months long. Margaret stares with disapproval at Alicia's clothes and asks Kate whether her daughter always wears jeans for Christmas. Kate says that she probably does. Guy offers them sherry or gin and tonic in the piano room to warm them up; the Harrow team chooses sherry, Didie the gin and George a strong coffee. The aroma of roasting poultry drifts into their nostrils as they sip.

'I hate turkey,' Adrian mutters to Alicia. 'It's disgusting.'

'Not the way Mum cooks it.'

'Mama knows best,' he taunts.

'So, Adrian, I hear you're going out to work,' Margaret prods, legs crossed, hands folded on her lap.

'Yeah, I got a weekend job in Macclesfield,' he mumbles.

'Speak up, lad!' William prompts, jovial.

'I'm working for this firm that sells motorbikes. It pays OK.'

'Good fellow,' says William. 'So you're saving up for your studies.'

'I don't want to go to university.'

'Don't be silly, Adrian, of course you do,' Kate says, dashing between piano room and kitchen, basting and tasting.

'What for?'

'Don't be rude to your grandparents.'

'I don't want to study nowt.'

'And, for God's sake, talk properly!'

'Leave me alone, Mum.' Adrian takes charge by changing the subject. 'You have to hear Ali play. She's got a new teacher. Everyone says he's ace.'

'Trouble is, he's in Switzerland!' Alicia laughs. She's wondering, behind her bright smile, whether she does look like a sheep in her favourite jumper. 'After my exams in summer I'm going to apply for a scholarship to study with him. He's wonderful! He's helped me so much with—'

'Just a moment, Alicia,' William interrupts. 'Do you mean you're planning to leave school without doing A levels?'

'I only want to play the piano.' Alicia shrugs.

'Honestly, Kate!' Margaret expostulates. 'We worked so hard to make sure the three of you were well educated. How can you let your children throw themselves away without decent qualifications? The piano is very nice, dear, but . . .'

Alicia is starting to lose her appetite. 'Shall I play you my Chopin?' she says, casting about for an easy escape route.

'After lunch, Ali,' Kate instructs. 'There's plenty of time.'

Kate lays the table as slowly and neatly as she can: red table-cloth, best crockery, gold napkins and a cracker at each place. Her hands are shaking.

'Hark the herald angels sing, glory to the newborn king,' sings the choir of King's College, Cambridge, on the piano room stereo. Guy winces and moves a hand involuntarily towards his stomach.

'Are you all right?' Didie exclaims.

'You know, this isn't my favourite record. Let's put on something else.'

'If we can break a rule,' says Didie, whose eyes sparkle after her gin and tonic, 'why don't you go ahead and open a present I brought for you?'

William and Margaret look briefly outraged, but Didie and Alicia egg Guy on and the CD, retrieved from under the tree, emerges from its silver wrapping. It's of Argentinian tangos. Guy puts it on and the draughty room, safe from the concrete sky, icy pavements and north wind, blazes with South American heat and light.

'I used to be a tango champion.' Didie twinkles. 'My fiancé before George was the most fantastic dancer.' Didie's first fiancé had been an RAF pilot, killed on the Battle of Britain's final day. It had been some years before she met George; Guy had arrived when she was in her late thirties. 'I used to go and see him every weekend at the air-force base,' she goes on, 'and there'd often be dances. When we did the tango, everyone else used to stand aside and watch us!' Her feet are tapping. 'Guy, how about a go?'

'I haven't done this for years,' Guy protests, but a moment later he and his mother are striding together across the floor. Alicia claps her hands in joy; George winks at her. Adrian watches in disbelief and William and Margaret in stupefaction.

'Come on! You're the man, you're supposed to lead,' Didie prompts her son. 'That's how tango works. *You* make the decisions. Put your hand on my back – that's it – and use it to show me what you want to do next.'

'You mean I'm in the driving seat for once?' Guy grins, gliding in step with her, their opposite legs moving together. Didie, for an octogenarian, is sprightly as can be.

Kate, in her apron, appears in the doorway; Alicia just has time to notice an expression of extraordinary pain flash across her face before she vanishes.

The tango has thawed the atmosphere a little; now the turkey is ready and the table is groaning with food. Alicia is the first to pick up her cracker. There's a series of small explosions; soon everyone is wearing paper crowns. With another explosion, Guy opens champagne and Kate is troubled by a memory of another dinner round this table, corks popping, laughter, flirtation, a light footstep going up the stairs. She swigs back the golden liquid in her glass. Mercifully, everyone is too busy enjoying their food and drink to raise any of the difficult subjects they'd been treading in all morning. The only disruption comes when Alicia excuses herself briefly: she tells Kate that she has to text happy Christmas to Lucien. While she's gone, Kate takes another bottle of champagne out of the fridge. She needs all the Dutch courage she can get.

Later they watch the Queen's speech (William and Margaret insist) and afterwards, with tea on the table and a Christmas cake complete with marzipan and royal icing for those who have room, they open the presents. Alicia has a necklace and earrings from George and Didie – silver with blue topaz the colour of her eyes; and from William and Margaret a new leather music case. From Adrian there's a sweatshirt emblazoned with a motorbike, which makes Alicia laugh – she's sure he must have filched it from the shop – and from Mum and Dad, the present she'd wanted most: a mobile phone. Mum has also knitted her a new blue jersey, which she puts on at once.

'Do I still look like a sheep?' she hisses at Adrian.

'Yeah. A blue sheep.'

Guy has bought Kate a gold necklace a little like Rebecca's. Kate forces herself to thank him. It's the kind of expensive gift that a husband would buy his wife when he's feeling bloody guilty. She bides her time.

The early midwinter dusk has darkened the windows. Alicia pulls a book of Christmas carols out of her music cabinet and the family gathers around the lamplit piano to sing. Alicia plays perfectly at sight. They start with 'Away in a Manger', Margaret, Didie and Kate raising their voices confidently, while the men grunt along in a trio of reluctant baritones (Adrian refuses to join in). Then they do 'O Little Town of Bethlehem', which prompts comments from the newspaper editor that there is nothing still or dreamless about Bethlehem these days; and next 'O Come All Ye Faithful' at the end of which Kate breaks into a peculiar fit of laughter.

'Mum?' Alicia says.

'Nothing, darling. The champagne was nice, wasn't it?' She longs to call Rebecca, who would appreciate the coming, in other ways, of the unfaithful.

Alicia turns the page to 'O Tannenbaum, O Tannenbaum'. Guy jokes that it's the same tune as 'The Red Flag'. Alicia says she likes the rhythms and begins to play.

'O Christmas tree, O Christmas tree,' sing Guy, George, Didie, Margaret and William.

'Hypocrisy, hypocrisy,' sings Kate. Nobody notices. When the carol is finished, she cuts the cake, pours the tea and offers a shot of whisky to anyone who wants it, including herself.

By the end of the afternoon, when George and Didie declare it's time to go home and hug them all, Kate's mind is a slurry of emotions, ranging from despair to an odd, alcohol-induced elation. Something in her consciousness has expanded, letting her step back and watch, seeing the bigger picture, sensing that probably in every household across the country pretending to love family Christmases there lurk tensions, lies, deceptions. It's taboo to hate Christmas, of course. It's inadmissible. To some, it's sacrilege. What total shit, Kate thinks.

Ali's view is the ideal: a chance for everyone to relax together. But does any family get along well enough to enjoy such an obligation? Nobody, after all, has a choice: Christmas is Christmas, whether you like it or not. The population of the UK is around sixty million, so that probably means, at a rough guess, about twenty-five million families – and that's in Britain alone – all undergoing trial by convention on the selfsame day, overspending, overeating and driving one another to distraction, year upon year.

She feels reckless, strong, amused, because if she didn't, she might throw herself out of the nearest window, which, with her children in their teens and Ali needing her help with her career, wouldn't be a good idea.

'Mother,' she says, 'why don't you and Father go and have a little rest? And later we could watch a film and have a late supper.'

'I won't need to eat again for a week,' Margaret assures her, kissing her cheek. 'Come along, William.'

'Yes, dear,' says Kate's father, following her with some difficulty up the stairs.

Kate watches them go. Alicia whistles to Cassie to come for her evening walk and Adrian volunteers to join them. Kate watches them go too, then begins clearing up. She blows out candles and sweeps up debris from wrapping-paper, crackers and napkins. An unnatural stillness frosts the house.

'Let me do that,' Guy says.

Kate straightens up from the table, plates in hand. 'Thank you,' she says.

'Kate? What—'

'We have to talk.' Kate stacks the plates by the sink, ready for the dishwasher, alongside several large kitchen knives. 'While my parents are resting and the children are out.'

'What's going on?'

'I could ask you the same thing. Why is Emily Andersen calling you "darling"?'

'Katie, listen. I can explain everything.'

'I'm sure you can. For instance, what is she doing with a health visitor? Who has got a cough?'

'You read my emails?'

'Yes, I read your emails. I had to send an urgent message last night when my computer crashed, and I thought it couldn't do any harm to use yours just this once. And, faced with a list of Emily dot Andersens as long as my arm, I couldn't help being a trifle curious.'

Guy sits down at the table and takes off his glasses.

'The ulcer. The backache. The headaches. The late evenings. The "conference" in bloody Denmark.'

'Katie—'

Guy's dark eyes turn to her and she sees pain and defeat in them and remembers how they used to twinkle at her, just like his mother's, during those walks in the Cheviots. She fights back an unexpected tear – sentimentality is the downside of Dutch courage – and steadies herself. 'What are you going to do?' she demands. She keeps her gaze on his face in the appalling silence that follows.

'I don't know,' Guy says at last.

It's his confession. At least she's wrong-footed him. At least she's in control. 'She's a lovely young thing and there's a baby. Isn't there? So I'd imagine you're going to say you want to move out and live with her.'

'I haven't made up my mind what's best. But, yes, she's had a baby and it's mine. It's a girl. Her name is Ingrid.'

'My God,' says Kate, without meaning to. It's not as if she hadn't guessed – but the confirmation still knocks her like a demolition ball. Battling waves of nausea, she forces herself to continue on her mentally mapped path. 'So you're weighing up the demands of one child against two others.'

'Katie, I do love you, I do, and I love Adrian and Ali and I don't want to lose any of you . . .'

'*But.* Don't tell me. It just happened. Didn't it? A pretty girl walked into your office and you couldn't keep your hands off her. You just couldn't help it.'

'It wasn't like that. It isn't. It's more.'

'You're in love with her.'

'I never intended it. It wasn't meant to happen. But, yes, I am in love with Emily.'

Kate snorts, trying to conceal from him that this is far worse than she'd expected. She consults her map for the next step. 'Maybe you can't help what you feel, but you can bloody well help what you *do*,' she says. 'You should be remembering your responsibilities and putting them first.'

'I tried. I tried for a long time. You've no idea how long.'

That was true. She had no idea. 'So it's all *her* fault?'

'No, Katie. It's mine. I don't deny it's my fault.'

'And our marriage, you'll say, is dead.'

'We both know it could be in better shape.'

'So? What are you going to do? I need to know, Guy. Ali is at a crucial stage of her career and her life. If you leave, you're going to ruin everything for her. She'll be knocked very hard – possibly for ever.'

'You're using Ali to blackmail me.'

'I'm telling you to remember that you have a special responsibility towards her because of who she is, what she does and
what she's going to do with her life.'

'And if I go?'

'If you leave,' Kate says, cool and firm as she has planned,
'you will damage Ali so much that it will mean the end of her
career.'

The front door bursts open and there's a rush of damp dog,
blue wool and golden hair as Alicia strides in and hangs up
her coat and Cassie's leash, Adrian trailing in her wake. Alicia
is singing to herself and Cassie makes hopeful noises at the
dog-food cupboard. Kate grabs Cassie's dish and piles into it
the accumulated leftovers of lunch.

'You lucky, lucky girl!' Alicia cries, as Cassie plunges her
enthusiastic snout into the turkey scraps. 'You never get
Christmas dinner normally, do you?'

Guy presses Alicia's shoulder, then walks up the stairs
towards his study.

It's not as bad as Victoria. Nothing, Kate tells herself, driving
to the cemetery at a speed well above thirty miles an hour,
will ever be as bad as Victoria. She hates herself for feeling
any other pain, for nothing can match the loss of her baby,
even if it was twenty years ago. Victoria might have been at
university now. Kate parks and tramps the grassy, sodden paths
to the once-white stone that marks Victoria's grave.

Although the grave was the product of considerable effort,
heartache and trauma when she insisted on relocating it from
north London, nowadays she doesn't visit it often enough.
That's because of Ali and Adrian. They don't know about
Victoria and she doesn't want to burden them with the tale.
At the graveside, she throws some dead flowers out of the
small vase she keeps there and replaces them with clean water
and some bright pink and red anemones that have been in a

vase in her bedroom for two days but can do their job better here. Then she scrubs down the stone, dark with accumulated lichen. VICTORIA BRADLEY: the lettering emerges from the greenish murk as she scours it. Her handiwork complete, Kate sits back on her heels and lets the tears come.

16

On a misty morning in late August, Kate and Alicia leave Buxton at six a.m. and drive south. They pick up the M5 outside Birmingham and travel through busy traffic past Cheltenham and Bristol; then south-west to Exeter and beyond, towards the sea. Alicia sits beside her mother, watching the landscape grow greener, the hills lusher, the sky brighter. At last the sun emerges, filtering shards of gold through the trees that overhang the country lanes, an enchantment left behind from pagan times.

Funny, thinks Alicia, to go all the way to Devon and find a summer school beside a moor. She's spent her whole life beside a moor.

She hopes her mother won't insist on showing everyone they meet the reviews of her new Chopin disc. Mum has brought a file of photocopies of the best ones: they declare Alicia a natural Chopin player, wittering on about her spontaneity and communicative immediacy. Yadda yadda yadda. Other reviews had continued the malicious carping – as Mum calls it – that had greeted her début disc, full of words like 'immature', 'oversell', 'burnout' and 'misguided'. At least this time she'd got the picture she wanted on the cover: herself (without Cassie) on top of Mam Tor – of course, one critic wanted to know what the Pennine landscape had to do with Chopin. But Lucien had made encouraging comments when she sent it to him: that was what counted.

Despite some disagreement among the judges on the panel – some appear to have thought Alicia too downmarket for them – she had won herself a good-sized grant from a famous musical trust, a pointer to which had been the parting shot of the advisory scheme, now transferring its attentions to a new set of BBC winners and, Alicia suspects, relieved to bid farewell to her mother. The grant, along with seven GCSE passes, two failures and some tears and tantrums that she was obliged to stage for his benefit, has convinced her father to agree that she can leave school; and it provides the funds for her to travel to Switzerland with her mother for lessons with Lucien every six weeks, having gently but firmly severed herself from the furious Mrs Butterworth.

'You are only what I have made you. Without me you'll be nothing. This Frenchman with his fine words . . .' Mrs Butterworth hissed, when Alicia went to see her to break the news of Lucien and the grant. How ironic, Alicia thought, that for years Mrs Butterworth had been extolling the wonders of French musical training, yet suddenly she was using the nationality as a term of abuse.

In between her Lucien trips, she practises alone at home. It's not ideal, but she feels as if she's found her way onto a mountain track that she'd been seeking for years. Now that she's free of school, she can devote her time to her real work, not be forced to write essays about the industrial revolution or explain the structure of the periodic table. She lives for her Swiss days, when Lucien spends hours with her delving into inner workings of music that she hadn't realised were there. Thinking it through later on her own helps her to grasp the aural colours that plough rainbow furrows in her mind, helps her understand why they move as they do. Key relationships, recurring motifs, sonata form, enharmonic changes. This last, clever invention she adores, for a single note can pivot you into a totally unexpected colour by simply changing its name. Beyond the piano, Lucien makes her read things she'd never heard of at school. She's recently disgraced herself by pronouncing a German poet 'Go-ee-thy'.

Goethe is fabulous, but she loves Lucien's favourite French nineteenth- and early twentieth-century poets even more. Dad had been impressed one day when he'd found her with her nose in an anthology of French love poetry. Verlaine, Baudelaire, Rimbaud. She's been learning pieces by Fauré and Debussy, and Lucien says she can't possibly understand them without reading the Symbolists. Alicia had never heard of Symbolism before, but now, at last, she has time to explore, lying on her bed with the poems, a French dictionary and a book called *501 French Verbs*.

> *Calmes dans le demi-jour*
> *Que les branches hautes font;*
> *Pénétrons bien notre amour*
> *De ce silence profond . . .*

Verlaine speaks of passion, ecstasy, veiled sensuality. For others, sensuality sometimes isn't so veiled. Baudelaire opens a trap-door on to a universe of unsuspected dangers.

> *Tout cela ne vaut pas le poison qui découle*
> *De tes yeux, de tes yeux verts,*
> *Lacs où mon âme tremble et se voit à l'envers . . .*

Alicia finds it difficult to eat when Lucien is around. Everything he says means so much to her that she tries to absorb it ten times over. He gives her lists of pieces she must hear and learn about: at home she spends long evenings in her room, listening to countless CDs, following symphonies with printed scores from the library in Manchester. She reads avidly too: biographies of Beethoven, Ravel, Tchaikovsky and Bartók, or novels from Russia, France and America that her school curriculum had never even mentioned. Adrian teases her: 'You *eat* books,' he exclaims.

She's allowed, at last, to take a train to London alone from time to time. There she stays with Rebecca or Phyllida and spends a day or two away from the piano, going to exhibitions recommended by Lucien or to permanent collections that she's never seen. The Turners in the Tate blew her mind and now she's covered her lavender walls with prints of them: the gold, cream and slate-grey swirling clouds, which remind her of Debussy's subtle translucence; the ships' masts emerging from the mist; the storms and snowscapes, and an angel suspended, sword aloft, in the heart of a sunburst.

At Easter, Phyllida had booked some time off and Alicia had spent nearly three days with her. Freed from her office persona, Phyllida reminded Alicia of Cassie let off the leash, full of sparkle and fun, and the pair of them went out on the town.

They had facials at the beauty salon in Selfridges. They went round the National Gallery to view Rubens and Rembrandt and the Van Gogh sunflowers; they ate Turkish food, which Alicia hadn't tried before; and finally they went to see the Cirque du Soleil at the Royal Albert Hall, where, Phyllida told Alicia, the Proms might soon engage her to play a concerto. Afterwards, Alicia's head was so full of astounding things, shining gold and white and pouring like Alpine waterfalls into her imagination, that back at Phyllida's flat she'd burst into tears and found it difficult to explain that she was weeping for happiness – and for the frustration of knowing that she'd waited nearly seventeen years to discover that such wonders existed. The more she learns, the more she understands how much there is to learn.

Since her lessons with Lucien, a skin has split away from her and a new one, a fresh colour, an intriguing texture, is forming in its place. She dreams as she plays, her soul filling with fantasy. She can tell that her audiences have noticed a change in her; she senses the extra stillness in the atmosphere. One local critic said that there was an incipient volcano inside her, which pleased her tremendously – but he went on to say that she had to find another way of expressing it, rather than playing too fast and too loud, as so many of Mrs Butterworth's students tended to. Alicia fumes at the idea that her name is being linked, yet again, with Mrs Butterfingers, but deep down she doesn't care. She is Lucien's disciple now and she can recapture something at the core of her music that had gone missing. She thinks it's called joy.

Kate glances at the mirror and moves into the fast lane of the M5 at ninety miles an hour. Nothing delights her more than getting away from home, these days, and the faster she goes, the better.

'You're punishing yourself as well as me,' Guy accused her on Alicia's birthday, after the party was over and reality slapped them in the face. 'Why do you want to suffer?'

'I don't,' she said. 'But I won't let Ali be damaged. If we break up, it'll wreck her life and her career. I won't let that happen.'

'What makes you so certain?' he demanded. 'She's seventeen. She's a young woman, not a baby. Other kids cope with far worse situations.'

'Other kids are not child prodigies.'

'I'm dying in this marriage.'

Yet Guy stays. Whenever he threatens to move out, Kate always says the same thing: 'It's a straightforward choice, Emily or Ali. It's up to you.' He gives in. He stays. What else can he do? If Kate had said nothing, would he have been able to leave Alicia if he tried to? He can't find the answer, and Kate knows he can't.

Hypocrisy? Perhaps. He has a second life with Emily – it's not as if Kate doesn't know. The crucial thing, for her, is that Alicia mustn't. Her fragile adolescent imagination, drenched with Lucien-inspired cultural cramming, wouldn't stand the shock, let alone the double standards.

When Kate sees the pain in Guy's face, the agony in his chest that makes him swallow ulcer pills, the pain in his back from the burden of too much baggage, she gloats quietly. It no longer occurs to her that she shouldn't.

She hates sharing her bed with him now, but does so to keep up appearances for Alicia, her parents, Guy's parents, the neighbours and, she supposes, Adrian. Guy lies, rigid and awkward, as far from her as he can. They talk when they must, in the bedroom, like work colleagues confined within a too-small open-plan office. She suggests they buy a larger bed, two mattresses that can be zipped together. They stay unzipped. The nights are brittle around them and Guy adds stronger sleeping pills to his list of medication.

Kate, meanwhile, is worried about her hormones. She visits the GP to let off steam. The GP doesn't suggest HRT – tests reveal that it is much too early for this – but recommends anti-depressants. Kate refuses them.

Going away is such a blessed relief that Kate feels twenty years younger.

'Let's open the sun-roof,' she says. Alicia winds open the panel and the light floods in; then she twiddles the radio knob until she finds some jazz. They turn up the volume and speed wildly to the strains of Louis Armstrong crooning about how wonderful the world is. Mother and daughter feel the sun on their faces and start to sing along together.

After winding for a while through the close-set hills, Kate spots a wooden signpost to Moorside College, half concealed amid deep green leaves. They drive up a gentle slope lined with fields of golden wheat and huge, ancient oak trees and turn into the estate. Kate sniffs the humid air and Alicia gazes, starry-eyed, at the young people they pass, walking in small groups, many carrying musical instruments in cases.

Alicia can't wait to find Lucien and Anjali – her two favourite people in the world – and once they've parked, registered and found their rooms, adjacent cubicles in one of the college's modern dormitory blocks, Kate and Alicia make their way towards the archway that leads to the summer school's heart: a fourteenth-century Great Hall. Other paths radiate into the rest of the complex: landscaped gardens, studio blocks, tennis court and swimming-pool. Kate notices people glancing at Alicia, recognising her.

'Wow!' Beyond the arch, Alicia stops in her tracks at the sight ahead. The Great Hall presides over a courtyard, its lawn dotted with generous trees. Around it lingers a bubble of stillness, despite the stream of arriving students, a haphazard group of people lounging on the grass outside the bar, the distant shouts of those who've found their way to the pool. Moorside Hall is a legend in its own right, Lucien has told them. It's supposed to have a unique atmosphere: a sacred space built on the mystical convergence, so the story goes, of ley lines, accumulating centuries of mystery. Alicia and Kate, absorbing the picture, both sense at once that it might be true.

'Imagine,' Kate says, 'everything these stones must have seen in their time.'

She watches Alicia gazing up at the Gothic, arched windows and doorway. The intuition that sometimes quivers on her neck is quivering now. She doesn't know why, but wonders whether, when they leave this place, they will be quite the same people they were when they arrived. The thought is nonsensical and she banishes it at once.

A couple of hours after Kate and Alicia's departure, Guy jumps into his car and drives off to Victoria Park, leaving Adrian asleep and Cassie dozing in her basket by Alicia's empty bed.

He lets himself into Emily's flat. A heady mixture of smells greets him: fresh coffee, heating croissants, sour milk, clean laundry. There's a wail from the back room and Emily's voice calls, 'We're in here!'

In the doorway, he surveys the scene. Emily, her hair in need of washing, her face tired, strained but calm, paces slowly up and down, jigging the restive Ingrid against her shoulder. 'Why don't you have a go at calming down your daughter?' she says, handing him the angry, pink-clad one-year-old.

Guy takes Ingrid and kisses her. A rush of anxiety and adoration springs into him, as always, when he feels the warmth of her little body. He's lucky if he sees her twice a week; he doesn't understand how she can possibly recognise him. But after he's been holding her for less than half a minute, she quietens, holding on to his shoulder and staring around the room with her wide eyes, silver-grey like her mother's.

'I knew it.' Emily laughs. 'She's a real Daddy's girl. Coffee, love?'

They sit at the pine table in the compact white kitchen, with Ingrid in her high chair bashing her beaker against her plastic tray and squealing for fun. This is how they should be: Daddy Bear, Mummy Bear, Baby Bear. Goldilocks would have some trouble working out how things function in this home, though.

'Penny for them?' Emily says.

'The usual.'

There's a limit, he thinks, to the number of times he can prostrate himself with regret. He's been a coward. He's feared so much: their job security; Kate's fury; above all, the effects of the revelation upon Alicia, absorbed in her own world, suspecting nothing. He loathes concealment. It can't be healthy for anyone to live in a house where the air is filled with icicles.

It's his own fault, too, for not taking the initiative. If he'd revealed the truth before Kate stumbled upon it, he'd have held the balance of power. He could have called the shots. But because it was underhand, because Kate's discovery was accidental, because he was – at least, from Kate's perspective – in the wrong, she had been the one to make the rules. Being Kate, she put Alicia first. In her place, he might well have done the same.

So he's a coward for not risking his job, not finding the right moment to confess, not standing up to his wife. He is, basically, pathetic. How is it possible, he wonders, that such a pathetic man can edit a newspaper? How is it possible that he's won the love of a beautiful, giving young woman – and become the father of this miracle child, who would grow up into the image of her mother mingled with himself? And she, a blameless, laughing baby, would probably have to be the one who paid the price, psychologically, for his failure.

'Raspberry jam with your croissant?' Emily says.

Guy sits Ingrid on his lap while Emily bustles round the oven and the fridge.

'Don't say it.' Her back is to him as she reaches for the jam. She can sense without looking when his apologies are coming.

'You're so strong.'

'I'm not.' Emily slices the croissants in half. 'But I haven't much choice, have I?'

'It's incredible that you even talk to me, let alone feed me croissants on Saturday morning.'

Emily puts a plate in front of him. She brushes Ingrid's head softly with one finger. 'Do you seriously think that I'd be without *her* for one moment? No, Guy. I wouldn't change places with anybody in this world.'

They spend a quiet morning talking about nothing much and playing 'Incy-Wincy Spider' and 'This Little Piggy' with Ingrid; then Guy goes to the supermarket and does a week's shopping for his Manchester family. He nips into the office a little later, makes sure everything is running smoothly, and comes back by teatime.

Ingrid is sleeping, so they go to bed. First they crash – Emily exhausted by baby-filled nights and Guy by anxiety over Emily's baby-filled nights. Later, they make love, Guy hoisting Emily upright over him, seeking, deep inside her, the annihilation of his hopeless self. 'I love you,' he whispers, as she curves downwards to kiss him. 'I love you so much.'

Afterwards, he phones Adrian at work on his mobile. 'You in this evening?'

'No.'

'Can you walk the dog?'

'Oh, bloody hell, Dad. I'm in the shop, then I'm going down the Cat and Fiddle.'

'Look, I can't come back till late. Just take her out for ten minutes, OK? I'll take her again when I get in.'

'Families,' Emily says from bed, winking at him. 'Who'd have them?'

A clang from his mobile makes him start with alarm, but the text is from Alicia, not Kate. 'Having gr8 time,' it says. 'Beautiful place. Lucien 1derful. Wish u here2. xa'

Guy lies down beside the dozing Emily and breathes deeply. His chest hurts. He's not sure whether it's his ulcer or something worse. He's too young to have heart trouble. It must be the ulcer. Or stress, which can cause pains like these. One day, when he has time, he must have a check-up.

At nine thirty on Sunday morning, auditions are held for Lucien's masterclass in Moorside's largest studio. Kate and Alicia take their places side by side, close to the table from which Lucien is to officiate. It's soon evident that Kate is the only chaperoning mother; the other students are on their own.

Lucien paces in, as relaxed as if he were on holiday, wearing an orange linen shirt and barley-coloured trousers, dark hair shining in the sunlight, and his neck giving off a whiff of lemony aftershave, which, Kate decides, is rather more classy than she'd given it credit for. She thinks of Guy at home, his exhausted eyes, his bottles of medication: ulcer pills, sleeping pills, painkillers – not the kind that exacerbate ulcers – for his back. Perhaps the strain of screwing his employee is too much for him, she'd suggested. The acid of this remark was probably enough to increase the dose of ulcer medicine overnight. And there's Lucien, casually in charge, smiling, joking, basking in the adoration that wafts towards him from the would-be students and curious onlookers assembling in the studio. As Kate stares, he turns and winks at her. The floor dips under her feet.

After Lucien's recital in the Great Hall the night before,

they'd gone backstage to find him. Alicia cast herself, as she tends to, into his arms; Lucien embraced them both and said, 'You are not really mother and daughter, you are sisters!' and he held Kate as long as Alicia, long enough for her to feel the energy in his arms and his breath against her hair. Lucien is taller than Guy and this, to Kate, was a new sensation. She'd had trouble getting to sleep later. Away from home and routine, with the summer night pressing on the thin windows, she'd dreamed, only half dozing, of certain things, missing from her life, that she won't normally let herself remember.

She glances round the studio, forcing her attention back to the present and her daughter. Some of the onlookers are glancing at her and Alicia, talking under their breath. The former Young Musician of the Year and Her Mother. Yes, Ali will be stiff competition for everybody else; her audition, since she's Lucien's permanent student, is only a formality.

Alicia, who's wearing white, lifts a hand and gestures at a petite, dark figure slipping through the studio door: Anjali, who's wearing black. Anjali waves, her face lighting up. The girls embrace, the bright and the dark together. There's been no sign of Anjali until now; she hadn't appeared in the canteen for supper or at Lucien's recital, and Alicia, unable to get through to her mobile, had been anxious.

'Where were you, Anji?' she asks now, pressing her friend's arm.

'Oh,' says Anjali, 'I was tired. I went to sleep.'

Anjali is no longer a schoolgirl, but a young woman. She's eighteen, about to go to music college, and her face is thinner, her eyes more serious and her figure skinnier than Kate remembers. She hasn't seen Anjali for some time; Alicia's schedule hasn't left much room for asking friends to stay.

'Hello, Kate. Lovely to see you.' Anjali gives her a kiss and sits down beside Alicia, a book of Schubert sonatas in her lap. She holds the edges so tightly that Alicia, noticing, glances at her in concern.

'Don't worry, Anji, you'll be fine,' she says.

'I keep having memory lapses,' Anjali tells her. 'I don't know what's going on. I never had this sort of trouble before, but since I started doing competitions . . .'

'Are you the Bradleys?' someone asks Kate: a petite, auburn-haired woman around her own age with a bright, interested face and a strong Liverpool accent. 'I loved your CD, Alicia. I've just ordered the new one, too.'

'Thanks! I'm so glad.' Alicia replies. The woman smiles and Kate notices, pleased, that she looks genuinely moved.

'So talented and so young,' she remarks. 'It's wonderful. How old are you, d'you mind me asking?'

'She's just had her seventeenth birthday,' Kate says.

'I'm looking forward to hearing you play, Alicia. My name's Mary. I don't play anything, but I listen, and I sing in the choir. I'm a Moorside addict – I come here to recharge my batteries every year. There are lots of us. Glad you're on board!' She shakes Kate's hand, and Alicia's; Kate introduces Anjali. At summer school, she's starting to understand, it's mysteriously easy to make friends.

More students are gathering on the other side of the room; several are Japanese, one is German. Another sounds American: a dark, thick-set lad of about twenty, Kate thinks, wearing a navy blue T-shirt emblazoned with the words UNIVERSITY OF INDIANA. Across the studio, his brown eyes meet Alicia's blue ones. Unlike the others, he doesn't recognise her. Unlike the others, he doesn't look away. Alicia beams, radiant, towards him. For a second he's motionless, as if entranced; then he sits down and gazes at her, firm and definite. His eyes say: *You are the most beautiful girl in the world.*

Life-changing moments aren't always heralded by a door-bell, a ringing phone or even a touch on the arm. Sometimes they just happen.

'Somebody likes you.' Anjali nudges Alicia – smiling properly for the first time.

'But he's lovely!' Alicia breathes. Subterfuge, Kate under-stands, isn't her daughter's style any more than it's the American youth's.

'OK, everyone.' Lucien stands up and claps his hands. 'Let's begin. Who's going first?'

A Japanese girl volunteers; she tinkles through a Mozart sonata movement. Lucien catches Kate's eye. Kate feels sweat on her shoulders.

'All right,' he says, after he's stopped the girl at an appro-priate chord. 'Alicia, let's have your Chopin.'

Alicia strides to the piano and begins the B minor Sonata. A shock wave wobbles through the room as the piano rings out, abruptly massive-toned. The American boy sits forward, chin on hands, watching her every move. Beside Kate, Anjali stirs. Kate glances round – does Anjali have hiccups?

'This is Alicia Bradley,' Lucien says to the room at large, stopping her at the end of the exposition. 'I'm sure you know her already. Now, who's brought some Schubert?'

Anjali puts up a hand. The American boy raises his hand too; it is to him that Lucien beckons.

'Dan *what?*' Lucien exclaims, when the boy gives his name.

'Rubinstein,' Dan says. 'No relation!'

'You're a brave man. So, Mr Rubinstein, you've brought the big C minor Sonata. *Voilà, c'est à vous . . .*'

When Dan begins, it's Alicia's turn to sit forward. 'I like this,' she whispers to her mother, who agrees: Dan Rubinstein (poor bloke, sharing a surname with one of the greatest dead pianists on the CD rack) is extremely good. Kate notices that his phrasing sings naturally and the sound is full and round, not too hard and loud, unlike – well, Ali does sometimes *bash*. Lucien is combating this, but it's a bad habit she'd developed with Mrs Butterworth and it's proving difficult to eradicate. But Dan Rubinstein plays with the assurance and poetry of one who can see the beauty that eats at the core of pain, and the pain that eats at the core of beauty – just as Schubert could. He might be only nineteen or twenty, but he plays like a man, not a boy.

Anjali's body contracts and she doubles over, pressing her hands to her mouth. Alicia grabs her arm. 'Come and get some air,' she says.

'I'll be fine.' But a second later the spasm seizes her again and she leaps to her feet and dashes for the door. Kate tries to keep her daughter where she is, but Alicia shakes her off and runs after her friend.

Alicia waits by the basins while Anjali flings herself into a cubicle and is violently sick.

'Shall I get you some water?' Alicia asks.

'I'll be fine,' Anjali insists fruitlessly.

'Are you feeling better? Shall we go for a walk?'

Anjali emerges, her shoulders drooping, her face agonised. This isn't the Anjali Alicia remembers from the BBC competition days, positive, healthy and generous-spirited, helping her wind the luxuriant silk sari round her in front of her mother's mirror. This Anjali has been laid waste by nerves. Something everyone expects Alicia to have, but she doesn't. Alicia holds out her arms and gives Anjali a hug. Anjali's breath is sour and she's battling tears.

'I have to go back in and do my audition,' she says. 'Otherwise I'll have to tell my father and he'll be livid. He has to know every detail of absolutely everything . . .'

'You'll feel better if you get it over and done with.'

'I can't. I'll screw up.'

'You won't.'

'I will. I know I will. Because I always do.'

'Come on. Let's walk in the garden, it'll do you good. We can go back later – there are loads of people waiting to play.'

The two girls set out into the grounds, Anjali doing her best to keep up with Alicia's powerful stride. They walk past a thatched gazebo, a landscaped lawn framed with trimmed evergreen bushes, and a herb garden heady with lavender, sage and rose-mary. Further away, up the hill, some long, mysterious flights of stone stairs lead into the shade of the biggest and most beauti-ful trees Alicia has ever seen. 'This is amazing,' she remarks. 'It's magic! Let's go up.'

They climb the stairs in silence. The sun through the leaves dapples their skin with brightness and shadow. The hills gleam in the distance, the view broadening and deepening every few steps.

'I wish I could enjoy it,' Anjali says.

'Anji, what's going on? What *happened*?'

'I don't know. If I knew that, there wouldn't be a problem, would there?'

'But you were so confident.'

'And now I have memory lapses.'

'You only have them because you think you're going to.'

'That's what a lot of people say. But if you know you're going to, how can you not?'

'Isn't there anything you can do? Deep breathing or some-thing?'

'Tried that. Tried everything. Except pills. I haven't tried pills.'

'What pills?'

'Beta-blockers. They're heart pills. They stop your heart running away with you. They stop you producing too much adrenaline, so you don't get the physical symptoms of being nervous.'

'I've never heard of that.'

Anjali stares sideways at Alicia. 'Lucky you,' she says, a sarcastic edge to her voice which makes Alicia jump.

'Would they help?' Alicia prods, trying to ignore it. 'Why don't you give them a go?'

'Because my dad says that if I start taking them I'll never feel able to go on stage without them again. And he's right – I know I won't.'

'But just to get you through this patch—'

'Oh, what would *you* know?' Anjali snaps. 'You've never had a day's nerves in your life.'

Alicia flinches.

'You can do anything. You swan off to Switzerland to play for Lucien, your Mum takes care of everything for you, Daddy bought you a Steinway and you were Young Musician of the Year. You've got two CDs out. And you've never even *heard* of beta-blockers!'

'Oh, Anji,' Alicia says, crumpling, 'I never asked for any of it to happen, you know. I hate seeing you like this. I'd change places with you if only I could.'

'Sorry, Ali. Really. I am sorry, I didn't mean it. I'm just – I'm in such a mess.'

'It's OK.'

'Don't cry.'

'Nor you. Look, you've got to come and stay with us. We never see you enough. Will you come? One weekend?'

'I'd love to, if you'll still have me after what I just said. It's coffee time – shall we go back?' They turn towards the hall, outside which morning coffee is served on the lawn.

'What about the academy?' Alicia asks, linking her arm through Anjali's. 'Maybe they'll be able to help you, give you the right advice or whatever.'

'I don't know. I don't even want to go there. I can't face it. But if I don't, I'll have to do something else, and I don't know what to do. I got three A levels and Mum says maybe I should go to university, but . . .'

Alicia is silent, horrified that Anjali might be beset by problems that make it impossible for her to continue with her studies, problems that might scupper her intention of being a pianist – when two years ago, she'd seemed almost as at home on stage as Alicia is. What's happened to her? Why? And when? What happened to one would-be pianist could easily happen to another. Alicia thinks the unthinkable. What if it happened to her? What will she do if, for some reason, she can't continue playing?

Her train of thought screeches to a halt as she finds herself face to face in the coffee queue with Dan Rubinstein. Blood rushes into her cheeks. 'You'll have to explain,' he says to her at once. 'Why does everyone know you except me?'

'Oh, I won a prize on TV,' Alicia says, crimson. 'Hey, I loved your playing.'

'And I love your accent. It's cute. Where do you come from?' Alicia tells him. 'What about you?'

'Let me get you a coffee, then we can talk.'

Alicia glances round for Anjali, who's vanished, probably trying to muster courage, alone, for her audition. She should look for her. She should look for Mum. But she'd rather talk to Dan than do either. She stays. With their coffee, they make for the shade of the tree in the middle of the lawn and sit cross-legged on the ground, their restless fingers pulling at the green spears of grass.

Dan is the most direct boy Alicia has ever met. She'd never imagined that getting along with anybody could be so easy. Maybe it's because he's American; or maybe it's because they're in tune, on a shared wavelength. There's no pretence in either of them. You take us as you find us, she could have said at once, for both of them. It's a relief, a release, a rush of energy. She feels as if she's not met him, but found him: someone she'd been looking for, without knowing it.

He tells her about his studies – he's at a university in the Midwest that has a massive music department, though he'd grown up in Boston – and soon they're talking about Chopin and Schubert, Lucien and Anjali, and before they know what's happened the break is almost over and Alicia's mother is striding towards them in her linen trousers, saying, 'Ali, *there* you are. I've been looking everywhere for you!' Dan gives Kate a brief, shrewd glance before turning on the charm and introducing himself.

★   ★   ★

Kate hasn't really been looking for Alicia; she's been talking to Lucien in the sunshine on the studio-block steps. She should have tried to find her daughter and the ailing Anjali; but she'd rather talk to Lucien. She'd stayed.

'You are looking extremely well,' he said to her, staring at her figure with approval.

'Thanks. So are you.'

'So, tell me, Kate, how is life?'

'Fine. Busy. Now that Ali has finished school, we're planning next season very carefully with Phyllida.'

'Lovely Phyllie. She is a gem.'

'She thinks you are too,' Kate pointed out, a little sharply.

Lucien regarded her with eyes slightly lowered, as bashful as a naughty schoolboy. 'It was so difficult,' he said. 'She would never have been happy with me. She needs someone who is there. Not travelling all the time. I was not right for her.'

'My husband doesn't travel so much,' Kate remarked, 'but he's never there either.'

Lucien's eyes glittered into hers. Kate blinked. This is crazy, she thought. My daughter's teacher is making eyes at *me*? If it wasn't her imagination, she'd be the envy of all the bright young things who adored the adorable Lucien.

Rebecca has regaled her with stories of professors taking their students to bed; some who will only give their pupils an exam pass at a certain price; tales of abuse of underage girls by teachers whose employers protect them for reasons of their own. This wouldn't be tolerated in any other profession, Rebecca opined. Masterclasses, she said, ought to be called mistressclasses. She's said nothing, though, about teachers taking a liking to their students' mothers.

'I love this place,' Lucien said, gazing at the gardens, the sunlight and the ancient hall across the lawn. 'There is magic in the air.'

'You've been before, obviously?'

'I used to come here as a student. I will show you some special places in the gardens. We have a whole week. Did you know there's supposed to be a ghost? I'm sure I saw it last night. My room is in the courtyard, on the ground floor, and around three in the morning it became extremely cold. I got up and looked out of the window and this grey shape went by. Very strange. It was transparent, but it was there. Kate, do you believe in ghosts?'

'No, Lucien, I *don't*. Not remotely. But please don't tell Ali, she might be afraid . . . I wonder where she is?'

'With her friends. That's good. I worry about Alicia not having friends.'

'She hasn't had much time to have friends.'

'Make sure she does. We all need friends.'

'Mm-hm,' said Kate, holding his comment at arm's length.

'I know it's difficult. When I was a kid, I had hardly any friends until I went to summer schools and met other kids who were musical too. I was so lonely. Now I know it's not necessary! We'll have some duet sessions in the evenings – it helps the students relax and get to know each other. They need to be friends, not enemies, not competitors. Kate, you'll come, won't you?'

'I can't play, Lucien.'

'You don't need to. You just need to be there and listen and look beautiful.'

'Oh Lucien, *honestly*.'

'Yes, Kate, honestly.' He winked at her. 'Sisters.'

Kate flushed; she couldn't help it. She forced herself to make an excuse about needing to phone home; and hurried away through the garden to find her daughter – who is not her sister and has been getting on far too well with the attentive American boy who says his name is Rubinstein.

Adrian, after making sure the windows and back door are locked, says goodbye to the lonely Cassie. She'll howl if left by herself too long, but what's he to do? His father is AWOL, his mother's fussing over his sister in some fancy course at the other end of the country and he's damned if he's going to let his life be wrecked by keeping house for them all. He slams the front door and heads up the hill and out of town.

The others are there already and Josh pats his shoulder in greeting. Over a pint, Adrian tells him something about what's happening at home, in as few words as he can, for the bikers don't talk on the whole – they just bike.

'Time to move out,' Josh says. 'I did that. Know what it's like.'

'Can't, really. Can't afford it till I get a job.'

'Sure you can. There'll be a way. I'll ask around.'

Today they're going to do speed tests. They'll pick two spots, a good distance apart, on the A537 between Buxton and Macclesfield, and they'll go one at a time and see who's the fastest. Adrian is bothered that, riding pillion with Josh, he'll slow him down and be a handicap. Last time, some of the others did wheelies through a busy Peak District car park and Adrian had to stand and watch, feeling half an inch high. He'd loved the sensation, all the same, of being part of something that stuck two fingers up at all those respectable, law-abiding, 'decent' families, who pulled faces and sometimes, when they dared, yelled abuse at them. His family, he told Josh once, rolling a spliff in Macclesfield, was supposed to be 'decent'.

'All right, Ade,' Josh says today. 'Use the bike on your own. You've got to try speed tests some time. I reckon you can do it.'

'Thanks, mate.' Adrian tries to keep cool, but his heart pounds so hard that he half fears the others can see it under his leathers (old ones of Josh's, out of fashion but good enough for starters). He takes a long breath and begins to prepare himself inwardly for his first solo speed test.

Half an hour later, he's alone astride Josh's bike, waiting his turn. The others set off, a safe distance apart – Charlie,

their unofficial leader (the gang prides itself on its democracy), is a stickler for safety, rather to Adrian's surprise and
vague disappointment. Charlie shoots away down the hill,
bending the bike to the curving slopes, tipping over so far
that he'll almost scrape the road with the Velcro slider pads
on his knee. His bike is a blur of blackness, noise and exhaust.
Dave, who's a plumber when he's not biking, goes next, his
red bike and helmet streaking along, sending up wafts of dust
or smoke, Adrian can't tell which. One by one the others
follow. Adrian is last.

He says the nearest thing he'll ever muster to a quick prayer,
though of course it's nothing of the kind. He revs his engine,
slips the clutch. The bike leaps under him like a racehorse and
he's in perfect control as he takes off, concentrating harder
than he'd imagined he could. He'd hate to let Josh know, but
he's scared witless. And he can't turn back. He must keep
going, clinging on and trusting in something, God or the bike,
that he'll make it. Before he knows what's happened, though,
he sees the group waiting at the finish and they're cheering as
he pulls in. When he dismounts his legs are watery under him
with the fright and the thrill and the power.

17

'Katie,' Rebecca says, 'be careful.'

'I don't know what you mean.' Kate is sitting on a bench under a beech tree. Rebecca is in her London office. She sounds tense and alarmed.

'He's charming. He's a great musician, I'm sure he's a good teacher. But be careful. I'm not having you go the same way as Phyllida.'

'Becs!'

'Sorry, darling, I have to go, I'm meant to be in a meeting. Call me later.' Rebecca rings off.

Kate stays in the shade, pondering. Why should Rebecca be so worked up about her relationship, such as it is, with Lucien? Guy in his worst moods, and there are plenty, has sometimes called Rebecca names that make Kate extremely angry and are, moreover, nonsense. Anyway, he's a fine one to object to someone else's sexual preferences. Familiar pain tunnels through Kate; she lowers her head, feels it, tries to let it pass.

Rebecca isn't butch. She wears expensive, stylish clothes and makeup. OK, she's divorced and hasn't shown any particular interest in men since she reappeared in Kate's life. But that may be no fault of hers, since men who'll look at women in their late forties, rather than twenty years younger, are in short supply. What's certain is that she doesn't fit any of the stereotypes that Kate associates with terms like 'dyke'.

She remembers the college rumours well enough. Rebecca liked experimentation, they said. She had countless boyfriends (this was the seventies, post-Pill, pre-AIDS) while Kate stuck doggedly to Guy. Rebecca slept with other women too, they said; but since nobody had been under the bed at the time, it couldn't be proved. Kate had dismissed it as malicious gossip. Nearly thirty years later, she still does. Ridiculous. Totally ridiculous. How could her one close friend, the only friend she really has, be a lesbian? It's outside her range. It's not a stitch in any pattern she's yet learned how to knit.

Perhaps she's winding herself up because she has too much time to think. While Alicia practises, Lucien teaches and students flock to choir practice, cello workshops, tango lessons or the Indonesian gamelan, Kate is at liberty to do nothing. She hasn't much to occupy her except watching Alicia, observing the masterclasses, chatting to her new Liverpudlian friend, Mary, enjoying the gardens and, between classes, talking to Lucien.

Perhaps it's the encroachment of nature in every corner, the overwhelming presence of music, or the headlong collision of like-minded souls with just one short week to spark off one another; but the summer-school air feels humid with the promise of sex. To Kate – who hasn't had sex in a very long time – it's profoundly disturbing.

Musicians are often passionate, highly sexed people. She's not a musician. She's a mother, a cool-headed former lawyer, a survivor of tragedy. Sex for its own sake has never been important to her. Except for those early years, especially the honeymoon in Paris, she's never even liked it much. But now her body is doing strange things to her mind. She's breathing in the scents of herbs, fresh-mown grass and ripening wheat as if her life depended on it; she's been enjoying post-concert drinks in the bar; she's been assessing the physical merits of the youngsters in the masterclass. As for Lucien, sometimes she doesn't listen to him at all: she only looks.

She'd mentioned it to Rebecca. Talking was a relief, thinking aloud, wondering whether she was under a spell, or whether

her hormones were playing tricks on her. She's neither an artist nor a sensualist; and she's never been closer to regarding herself as a mixed-up, middle-aged mum.

'Katie, of course you're a sensual person!' Rebecca exclaimed, derisory. 'Of course you're artistic. Look at your wonderful house. Look at your knitting. You could charge a fortune for those jerseys. You love texture, colour, design – there's nothing more sensual than soft fabrics.'

'Yes, but . . .' Kate didn't like to carry on this strand, especially in the light of Guy's opinions, which she was trying to banish from her thoughts. Now and then, when they meet in London, Rebecca looks into her face with some unfathomable *thing* in her gaze, something chemical that induces a direct, physical reaction in Kate over which she has no control and which, if she's honest, she can see is not so different from that induced by Lucien. Other women don't, in her experience, look at her like that. And she certainly doesn't look back, or doesn't mean to. Under her tree, she fights with herself, some idiotic craving for physical affection threatening mutiny of many horrific kinds.

That night, she dreams about Lucien. He's running to meet her by a lake; there he is with his long legs, bright shirt and deep eyes, smiling, greeting. Behind him hovers a grey ghost. She wakes to find herself alone on the thin mattress in her cubicle room. Outside, planets hang low over the wheatfield and the distant dark hills. She tries to go back to sleep – Tuesday will be a big day, with Alicia the first participant in the piano masterclass; and Lucien is planning to round everyone up to play duets later.

Sleep, though, is elusive. Kate's head is still spinning, as she had spent most of the evening after the daily concert drinking too much cider with Mary, who loves singing and has been trying to recruit her into the summer-school chorus. Mary is a nurse and has three children. Already they're discussing the best route from Buxton to Liverpool so that they can get together again when the week is out. Further along the wooden trestle table in the bar – a cavernous fourteenth-century room behind the hall, where golden lamplight shimmers on white-washed stone walls – Alicia had sat with Anjali and Dan. Alicia is developing a taste for chardonnay, which, Dan teases her, she wouldn't be allowed in the States, being too young (she's too young here as well, but nobody's batted an eyelid). Dan is doing his best to make Alicia inseparable from him; Kate supposes she should object. But she's intrigued by the impression that now it's almost as if Dan is Alicia's old friend, while Anjali is the stranger.

Kate lies awake in her uncomfortable bed and replays the day, its music and its relationships until the first streaks of dawn lighten the lilac night. She's beginning to feel that she's seventeen again herself.

'Stop.'

Alicia, at the piano in the packed studio, stops. Lucien stands beside her, looking over her shoulder at the first page of the Chopin B minor Sonata.

'What is Chopin's indication here?' He points.

'Allegro maestoso,' Alicia squeaks.

'Which means?'

'Fast and – magisterial.'

'And you are playing – fast. Allegro, yes. But not maestoso. More maestoso, Alicia, less allegro. And don't hit the piano, because it hits back! We want a beautiful tone, not only a loud one. Start again.'

She starts again.

'Alicia.'

Her hands freeze.

'What is this mark, here?' Lucien indicates a shape in the score.

'A crescendo.'

'And this?'

'An accent.'

'So what is the direction of this phrase? Try again. Shape the music. This is an opening allegro maestoso, but it also sings. Shape it as if you're a singer. Sing it to me.'

'Pardon?'

'Sing, please.'

Alicia sings the phrase; it comes out as a soft, unhappy chirrup. One of Kate's hands clutches at the other. This isn't like Lucien. Alicia is supposed to be his star pupil.

'Darling. Chopin loved singers. Chopin was in love with a singer when he was young. He went every night to the opera to see her sing and he heard Italian composers, whose influence infuses every part of his music. You know any music by Bellini?'

'I thought a Bellini was a kind of cocktail.' Alicia gets the laugh she wants – for a moment.

'Darling, you must hear Bellini if you want to understand Chopin. And you must hear Mozart's operas. You've seen *The Marriage of Figaro*?'

She shakes her head, mute.

'OK. What about Chopin's great friend, the painter Delacroix? You've seen his paintings?'

'Only a few.' Alicia's eyes are gleaming with tears.

'Because what you do is you sit at home, you practise and you perform. *Fin. Voilà.* OK. Once more, again, please, from the top. Phrase the melody the way you just sang it to me.'

Alicia plays. It sounds better, to Kate's ears, but that doesn't change the fact that her daughter is being humiliated precisely when she is supposed to shine.

'Stop,' says Lucien. Alicia pulls her hands from the piano as if she'd been whipped.

'You're trying to give us a finished performance. I don't want a finished performance. This is work in progress. I want you to adapt. Just try it my way. OK? *Think* about what you're doing. *Apply* the ideas. Remember what I've been telling you and apply it! Don't plough on, exactly like before. The phrasing is vocal all the way through – not just at the beginning. Keep thinking. Keep applying. No?'

'Yes,' Alicia says, half choked.

Kate closes her eyes. Why has Lucien chosen today to put Ali through this? She wonders, too, what's happened to Ali. In the Ravel concerto she'd played in the competition, she'd phrased so beautifully. That was only two years ago. What's gone wrong? Is Lucien right: too many concerts, too little thought?

After an hour and a half, Lucien has deconstructed the first movement of Alicia's Chopin sonata. Alicia is normally a statuesque, glowing seventeen, a seventeen that could pass for twenty-one, were it not for the wide-eyed aspect that betrays her innocence. Now she looks like a little girl of twelve.

'All right,' Lucien says, pressing her shoulder. 'Time for coffee. But I want to say one thing.' He turns – hand still on Alicia's shoulder – and addresses the listeners. 'I've been very hard on Alicia this morning. But only because she's worth it. She has a fantastic talent. If there's no talent, why work so hard, why suffer such pain? Alicia, you've done well, darling.' And Lucien starts the applause himself.

Alicia walks out of the room, head held high, without looking round. Kate leaps up and fights through the crowd milling towards the door, almost pushing Lucien aside in her haste. Her hands itch to hit him for treating her daughter so. She thinks of her dream and smarts with mortification.

'Kate,' Lucien calls after her. She doesn't turn.

In the courtyard, Alicia gives way to hysterics. Anjali and Dan flank her and as Kate hurries over she seems to see reproach in their eyes. Why should Anjali and Dan reproach *her*? This débâcle was Lucien's doing. As she nears them, she's certain she hears Dan say to Anjali, 'And now the mother has to join in . . .' Or is she imagining it?

'Darling!'

Kate holds out her arms to Alicia, who swings round and clings to her like a baby. The two of them, she thinks, holding her tightly, must seem as alike and interlinked as Russian dolls. Never in seventeen years has she seen Alicia as upset as this, not even when the school bullies put glass in her bag. How could Lucien do this to her? Doesn't he know what power he has over these young people? Doesn't he know what power he has generally, over everyone he meets? Even as she thinks this, Kate understands: the problem is that he *does* know.

'Come for a walk, darling,' she says.

'Oh, please, Kate,' Anjali cuts in, 'let her stay with us? We'll look after her.'

'You bet we will,' Dan adds. Kate gives him a hard stare over Alicia's shoulder, but he gazes back, unflinching. His expression holds an echo of her own anger. It strikes her that Dan could possibly be a man – a boy, anyway – of more substance than she'd assumed.

'Ali? What do you want to do?'

'I'll just stay here, Mum. If that's OK with you.'

'Of course, my love. Anything is OK.'

Later, when Anjali and Kate have gone back to the studio, Alicia and Dan bunk off the masterclass and walk into the gardens alone. Climbing the stone stairs, Alicia blows her nose. She can't help remembering that only the other day it had been her comforting Anjali in tears.

'The thing is,' she tells Dan, who seems to sense instinctively that she needs to talk, not be talked to, 'I know he's right! I know I don't know anything. But what can I do? I've got all these concerts, I *have* to learn new pieces, I *have* to be at home practising and there just isn't time. I want to learn about poetry and art and literature, but there's so much to do . . .'

'Your old teacher sounds like a head-case.'

'Oh, God. I *hated* her!' Alicia, letting the words out, finds she's laughing and crying at the same time. 'You wouldn't believe how I hated her. And nobody would listen. They thought she was so great because she taught me to play fast and win prizes.'

'Fast and loud. The hardest thing, my teacher says, is to play slow and soft.'

'I knew it was all wrong, and now I feel so – lost.'

'You won't be lost for long. You're too good.'

'I feel like everything went wrong because everyone thinks they know what's best for me better than I do – and of course they should, but they don't. I'm stuck. I don't know what's going to happen to me.'

'Hush, Al. Let's go and sit somewhere. There's a great spot over here.' Dan reaches for her hand. She lets him take it. Energy courses through his palm, across the intervening millimetre into her own. She curls her fingers around his and feels him squeeze back, natural, necessary.

They walk, hand in hand, under the trees along a small grass track to the edge of the hill. Here there's a landscaped circle, virtually a turret laid open to the elements: it's paved with slabs fanning out from a central round stone, and edged with benching curved against a low wall.

'They call this the Magic Spot,' Dan says. 'You stand here – on the spot in the middle – and you speak, and you get the weirdest sensation. Like you're in a tunnel. Try it.'

Alicia plants herself on the central spot and says, 'Hello, Dan!'

'Anything?'

'No.'

'Say something else.'

'OK – "something else"! No – wait. I can feel something. If I keep on talking – it's like I'm in a tube or a chimney. It's echoing round me!'

'The sound bounces back from the wall. Say something. What do you most want to say on earth?'

'I don't know.'

'Yes, you do. Say it.'

'Anything? Even if it's *horrible*?'

'Yes! Go for it, Al!'

'OK. What I want to say is – Dan, this doesn't mean you . . .' Alicia glances about; the gardens, mercifully, seem deserted. She closes her eyes, takes a deep breath, and falters.

'Just say it!'

'I want to tell everybody to fuck off!' Alicia cries. 'Everybody! Mrs Fucking Butterfingers! Rebecca Fucking Harris! Young Musician of the Fucking Year! Even Lucien Fucking Delamain! And my fucking mother who doesn't do anything except say "Go and practise"! *I can't stand it!*'

'Yay, Ali! You've done it.'

'I WANT TO SCREAM!'

'Go on, then. Scream. Nobody can hear you.'

Alicia turns a full circle on the spot. The place is empty. She opens her mouth and screams blue murder. The sound shoots up and down the invisible column of air that holds her transfixed on the Magic Spot. Dan, sitting on the wall with his feet on the bench, claps and cheers.

Her fury spent, Alicia flops on to the bench, shaky and exhausted. Dan slides down and slings an arm round her shoulders. She leans her head on his chest as if she's been doing it all her life.

'Al, you're great,' he says. 'Damn the piano-playing, I think you're wonderful. I'd still think you were wonderful if you worked in a burger bar.'

'I think you're wonderful too.'

'Feeling better?'

Alicia looks up at Dan and says nothing. Then she does what she wants to do: she reaches out and pulls his head down towards her. His lips feel hungry on her own and, kissing him, she does feel better. Much better.

In the evening Alicia sits in the Great Hall with her mother on one side, Dan on the other, Anjali on the far side of Dan,

Mary on the far side of Mum, and Lucien a little way off on a bench beneath a window. A string quartet is playing Schubert. Alicia feels the music's sombre colours dancing through her mind like dusky moths. She can't concentrate. She hardly knows Dan, yet he seems to know her so well; and somehow she knows him too, although logically she can't. It doesn't make sense. She'd thought she loved Lucien.

She hasn't seen Lucien since this morning. Now he's a short distance away, his face illuminated by the setting sun. There's something catlike about the way he curves his long limbs and casts shafts of dark light out of his eyes. Dan doesn't transfix her the way Lucien does. But Lucien, whom she reveres, had deliberately humiliated her in front of fifty people a few short hours ago. She knows him better than Dan – she knows his restlessness, his hunger for knowledge and adventure, his passion for poetry – yet Dan is part of her and Lucien isn't and she doesn't understand it. She shifts in her chair while the musicians pound through the finale of the 'Death and the Maiden' Quartet. Dan moves as if to take her hand, but Mum is watching, so he stops. Sensible, Alicia agrees silently, beaming the thought towards him. If Mum thinks he's getting too close, there's bound to be trouble.

Since her screaming episode, Alicia has been most horrified by just one of those pent-up emotions: the desire to tell her mother to fuck off. She'd be nowhere without Mum. She owes Mum everything (as Mum has told her often enough). There's nothing Mum wouldn't do for her. How ungrateful is she? What does she expect? What does she want? What on earth is happening to her in this bizarre place?

'You OK, Al?' Dan whispers, while the applause rings out. 'Kind of.'

A whisper is spreading along the row of piano students, a private message from Lucien: they're going to play duets in the studio later tonight.

★　★　★

Adrian and Josh are in the Buxton graveyard, smoking a spliff. Maybe it's a macabre place to hang out, but it's peaceful. Nobody bothers them. Nobody tells them not to smoke. People would think they're up to no good – but since he's graduated from hooded tops to biker leathers, Adrian's noticed that passers-by look at him with less suspicion and more respect. Anyway, hooded tops are stupid, unless you're trying to avoid the CCTV cameras that seem to be everywhere nowadays.

Walking by the forest of gravestones – some from the eighteenth century, some from last week – Josh and Adrian talk bikes, fuel prices, hire-purchase schemes. Adrian explains his own situation: no more school, no uni because he doesn't know what to do, angry parents the cumulative result. All he's got is his Saturday job in Macclesfield. Josh talks a little about his own job, but not much. Computers. Boring stuff, he shrugs, but it pays OK. It's a means to an end.

Adrian knows he can't go on using Josh's Suzuki much longer if he's going to stick with the gang. He needs a bike of his own.

'If that's what you want, there'll be a way to get it. Take any job that'll help you fund the things you want to do,' Josh suggests.

'My dad will kill me. He edits a fucking newspaper.'

'Then he ought to fucking help you,' Josh points out.

'They don't know I exist. Cos of my sister.'

'I like the look of your sister. It's great, what she's done. Because she's done it herself. It's *her* talent, nobody else's.'

'See? Can't get away from her, can I?'

'You've got to move out. There's a house of bedsits two doors down from my place. Interested?'

They're strolling along a track near the edge of the graveyard. Something catches Adrian's eye: a bright splash of colour in a small vase, balanced beside a whitish stone that appears recently scrubbed after long neglect. Green lichen splatters the edges, but the pale marble shines when the evening sun strikes it.

'Victoria Bradley,' Josh reads. 'Relation?'

'Shouldn't think so. Thousands of Bradleys all over Derbyshire.'

Josh reads the dates on the stone and draws in his breath. 'This was a baby,' he points out. 'Three weeks old. Poor buggers, that must be the worst thing. Losing a baby.'

'Yeah. Guess so.' Adrian is surprised – big, tough Josh, who's a computer genius and a top biker, seems to have a soft side.

'I had a friend in the gang. Killed on the A537. He hit a lorry, or it hit him. Would have thought, with him, the lorry would come off worst, but it didn't.'

'Long ago?'

'Couple of years. You've got to be careful on that road, it's one of the worst in the country. I'm not being a wuss. You can't mess with your life. OK?'

'You do,' Adrian points out, thinking of Josh's wheelies in the car park, the most extreme, daring and crazy of any of them.

'That's different,' Josh says. 'You're still a kid.'

Adrian, burned by this put-down, reads the date on the stone. This small Bradley would have been only three years older than him. The wilting flowers in the vase are red, pink and purple anemones. They're familiar. He sees them at home the whole time. 'My mum likes those,' he remarks, as they wander by.

When the caretaker, rattling his keys, throws the pianists out of the studio at eleven o'clock, Lucien waves a wide arm as if to embrace everybody and says, 'OK, we go to the hall.'

The students have been taking turns, side by side with each other or Lucien at the keyboard, one playing the top half, the other the bottom. With four hands playing instead of two, the piano sounds like a full orchestra.

To avoid feeling useless, Kate turns the pages, following the music over the pianists' shoulders. Lucien plays a great deal and she tries not to relish her closeness to him, standing behind his left arm, reaching across at intervals to swing over the page. She's transfixed by his grace at the piano: he reminds her of a cat toying, light and swift, with a ball of wool. She breathes in the scent of his aftershave, watching the way his hair dances above his ear, the twisting mazes of the ear itself, the Adam's apple in his throat. She'd arrived hating him for Ali's humiliation; yet the minute the music began, the tension vanished while nine students, one professor, a doting mother and one or two listeners together steeped themselves in Mozart. Maybe that accounts for Moorside's atmosphere. Here, people share too much: not their lives, but their dreams. Sometimes dreams are more powerful than life.

In the Great Hall, the students grab chairs from the empty rows and carry them on to the platform, grouping close round the piano. It's late, but everyone is wide awake. The huge medieval blocks of stone, the soft lighting and the towering, dark windows have seduced all of them; even Anjali has been taken out of herself and is gazing at her fellow students as if she loves them like siblings.

'Alicia,' Lucien says, 'you haven't played yet. Please, play with me.'

'I'm surprised you want me to,' Alicia says, but it comes out as a laugh, not an accusation. Dan, beside her, gives her a quick glance – they'd promised each other they'd play together – but Lucien's invitation can't be refused.

'I do,' Lucien says simply. 'Schubert. We read the Grand Duo if you like.' Lucien takes the bass position and motions Alicia to the treble.

'OK,' says Alicia, who's never heard of the Grand Duo and wonders why Dan has raised his eyebrows.

Soon she understands. The Grand Duo, as her fingers etch it out, is a symphony on a piano for four hands. She has to employ every sliver of her brain to get the notes right, but it's worth it: the melodies and textures are so rich and beautiful that they turn her knees weak. Lucien's arm brushes hers as they navigate the keyboard. His warmth, close beside her, enters the music like a dancer, his aura blends with hers and she forgets her confusion and anger and loses herself, becoming one with Schubert and Lucien and the instrument. Dan's kisses – there'd been lots – are fresh in her mind; she feels vivid, turned on, wanting more. And wanting, she realises, not only Dan but Lucien as well. A year ago, she'd have been overwhelmed by the idea of playing music with her hero. Now she's a different person. She lets sensuality direct her fingers and help her shape a particularly gorgeous passage, like a singer, just as Lucien had instructed her in her Chopin.

'Beautiful!' Lucien breathes, without stopping. Their little fingers collide. Alicia's innards give a deep, resonant twang.

Kate is transfixed. Her daughter, nearly grown-up, beautiful, gifted and famous, is playing music with the world's loveliest man (she's mysteriously forgiven Lucien everything) in a medieval hall spellbound in ebony and gold. Guy and his mistress are a world away. Adrian can look after himself. The dog will be happy as long as she's fed. Kate, for once, is living for the present. The music, the warm night air, the vaulting roof weave into one engulfing pattern, full of unfathomable, magical symbols. She's overwhelmed, tearful, her longing tougher than she is.

When Lucien and Alicia finish the last movement, nobody wants them to stop, so Lucien turns straight to the next piece. And after that, yet another.

'More!' beg the students. Lucien and Alicia oblige. Schubert wrote a great deal of music for piano duet and most of it is in Lucien's book. Kate wonders whether Ali is tired, but her face is transfigured by the music. She's filled with inner light, even if there are shadows below her eyes.

Her radiance is approaching full bloom. Dan, who's taken over the page turning, misses one because he's watching her, not the notes.

It is one o'clock when Alicia and Lucien finish the book. Lucien closes the back cover; then, reluctantly, the piano.

'We have to stop,' he says. 'The caretaker will have our skins. But more soon, yes?'

Everyone choruses assent; but outside, in the deep night on the lawn, nobody can quite let the evening end.

'Anyone want to go for a walk?' Lucien suggests.

A small group wanders out into the dark grounds: Lucien, Alicia, Kate, Dan, Mary, Anjali. What light there is comes from the moon, slightly egg-shaped yet vast, amber luminous in the harvest sky.

'Let's go up to the Magic Spot,' Dan suggests, positioning himself beside Alicia as they walk.

'What's that?' Kate says, trying to take a place next to Lucien.

'It sounds intriguing,' Mary says, on Kate's other side.

'I know it.' Lucien points. 'Up there, *non*?'

Climbing the stairs, nobody is quite where they want to be, yet everyone is together. Alicia wonders how to describe it to Grandma Didie. She's never experienced this kind of comradeship before, even though it's full of peculiar edges that don't seem as comradely as she'd like.

'Al,' Dan whispers, manoeuvring her aside, 'can't you get rid of your mother for even two minutes?'

'This morning was the longest ever.'

Alicia has been fighting her resentment of her mother for half the day. But whatever had lurked in her mind, half formed for months, maybe years, alarms and shames her now that she's expressed it. Letting it out was a massive relief, but that makes the shame worse.

The Magic Spot is in front of them. Dan strokes her arm

for a second, away from Mum's gaze. Mum seems to have eyes only for Lucien, who's explaining to her, Mary and Anjali how the spot's acoustic illusion works. They take it in turns to test the sensation. Alicia lets nobody know that she's tried it already.

'"To be or not to be, that is the question,"' Kate says, standing on the spot with her eyes closed. 'It's no good, I can't feel anything.'

Mary tries instead.

'"This above all: to thine own self be true,"' she quotes. '"And it must follow, as the night the day, thou canst not then be false to any man."'

Above the faraway hills, the moon has turned blood red.

'I like that. What is it?' Alicia asks.

'*Hamlet*,' says Mary. 'It's Polonius's advice to his son, Laertes. Before he's stabbed behind the arras.'

'You know some Shakespeare to say for us, Alicia?' Lucien asks.

Alicia – not certain whether he's taunting or encouraging her – rises to the occasion. 'Better than that,' she declares. 'I know some Verlaine.'

She moves to the central stone, while the others form an audience of dark outlines on the bench around her. She recites 'En sourdine'. Nothing could be more appropriate, she feels, letting words and air, black trees and red moon blend into a spell she's ready to claim for her own.

> '*Calmes dans le demi-jour*
> *Que les branches hautes font . . .*'

Kate can't ignore the sensual promise in her daughter's voice, reciting French with a bizarrely good accent, magnetising Lucien and Dan to her rapt, moonlit face, her long legs, the golden hair that showers down her back.

A new fear is assailing Kate. Ali is a virgin, of course she is, Kate would know about it if not. But something in her is

opening out and there's nothing Kate can do to stop it. Today
has been one mad, emotional bungee jump; it's not healthy;
maybe they should go home. But she can't, at this moment,
march Ali away, pack the suitcases and drive back to Buxton.
In any case, she doesn't want to. If they left, they'd go to
London, to Rebecca's. Not home.

Alicia finishes her poem; the others applaud. Kate, mind
divorced from body, applauds too. Then, led by Lucien, they
leave the Magic Spot and amble towards the long, sloping path
that finishes at the furthest of the three residential blocks near
the back gate.

'Kate,' says Lucien's voice in her ear, his breath hot on her
skin. She jumps.

'Lucien,' she says brightly.

'I must talk to Alicia. May I?'

'Anything I can help with?'

'No, Kate, I need to talk to her on her own this time. It's
OK with you?' Lucien touches her forearm and Kate melts
instantly and says, 'Of course.'

What else can she say? She can't tell Lucien not to speak
to his student; she can't lose dignity by pleading harder, trying
to persuade him to talk to her instead. But as Lucien puts one
arm gently round Alicia and slows so that they fall behind,
Kate wrestles with jealousy. She'd have let Lucien seduce her
if he wanted to, despite everything. For a few, fleeting minutes
she'd thought that he might. She must therefore be exceed-
ingly stupid.

She buries humiliation behind a raised chin, a defiant stride
and a bright smile to Mary, who, prompted by a couple of
suitable questions, begins to tell her about the difficulty of
combating the MRSA superbug in her hospital. 'People walk
in to visit or go to outpatients and they bring in all sorts of
muck from the street,' Mary says. 'You can't stop them moving
around . . .'

Nearby, Dan is saying to Anjali, 'So you'll have to have an

arranged marriage?' and Anjali is saying, 'Well, not exactly, but . . .'

And behind them, Lucien and Alicia are lingering further and further away.

'Don't worry, they'll be busy debriefing about this morning,' Mary says, when Kate glances round. 'As I was saying, the real problem with superbugs . . .'

'You've been learning Verlaine.' Lucien's arm is still round Alicia's shoulders. It feels oddly languid. Dan's – more muscular, because he goes to the gym – is all concentrated energy, heat and passion. Lucien's arm is relaxed, cool, assured. He has all the time in the world and he knows it.

'I've been reading that book you gave me,' Alicia tells him. 'With a dictionary. It's incredible.'

'I'm pleased that you love it,' Lucien tells her. 'Darling, I know I gave you a bad time this morning, but I think you learned something. Will you forgive me?'

Alicia beams up at her mentor, trying – without much success – to read the mix of feelings she sees in his face. Regret. Sweetness. Hunger, of a kind?

'So on Friday you play your Granados, yes? "The Maiden and the Nightingale".'

'It's so beautiful! I love it so much!'

'It's a very sexy piece,' Lucien says. 'The feeling, the atmosphere – this is difficult to capture. You're so innocent, Alicia. You don't even know how beautiful you are, do you?'

Alicia tries to laugh, but Lucien doesn't want her to. 'I mean it, Alicia. You are an astonishingly beautiful girl. You have a glow that I've never seen in anybody else. Men look at you and they love you instantly. You know?'

'No! I don't know!'

Alicia, Lucien's shoulder brushing close to her, sees Dan in the group ahead looking back at them. A bell shrills in her imagination.

'You must know. You must take notice. You can't ignore it, because as you grow up it will grow with you. You must use it for your own advantage, not other people's. You understand?'

'No! I don't.'

'Your mother – forgive me, because she's a wonderful person who cares very much about you – your mother has the same power that you have, but she buries it. She has put everything, her entire soul, into caring for you.'

'She thinks I'm still six.'

'Of course. To her, you'll always be her little girl. But, Alicia, you are a young woman and you mustn't deny your woman-hood the way your mother denies hers.'

'Does she?'

'Oh, yes. She doesn't mean to, but she does. It's not good. You are not going to repeat any of this to her.'

'No.' Alicia sees the red moon reflected in Lucien's dark eyes. The others are out of earshot, a cluster of trudging char-coal shapes far ahead. Lucien's feet, which had been crunching along on the track, come to a stop.

'Alicia, you cannot play this Granados if you haven't been in love,' he says. 'It won't work.'

'Oh, Lucien!'

'You laugh. So English.'

Alicia hesitates. She doesn't like to tell him that what he's just said seems – well, laughable. Not that she's seen many caricatures of suave French men trying to seduce young English girls, but she imagines that they'd look like this. Still – and here confusion kicks in – this is Lucien, her hero, her teacher. The person who has brought back her love of music, recon-nected her with everything she'd lost through Mrs Butterworth. 'Lucien,' she says, 'is it possible to love more than one person at a time?'

'Darling, of course it is. We're not supposed to. Society doesn't want to let us. But your capacity to love is your own and the most important thing is that you possess that capacity.

If you have it, you will find your own way of expressing it. Sometimes it is so great that you love not only one person, not even only two.'

'But to be – well – *in love* – I mean . . .'

'That too, *chérie*. Our rules say one thing, but our hearts always say another. It's one of the most important things, how to reconcile this conflict. Alicia, have you been in love?'

'I don't know.'

'Alicia, you are so innocent. That means no. Yet you have that capacity. Perhaps the capacity to love many, which must be why you ask me this strange question. You'll know, when it happens, and then you must decide what to do about it.'

'Lucien?'

'Darling?'

'I can still play my Granados on Friday, can't I?' Alicia has just remembered that Lucien had set her 'The Maiden and the Nightingale' in the first place. Although he must realise she's never had a love affair – it's obvious – *he* set her this piece that he describes as sexy, this piece he says she can't play unless she *has* been in love.

Lucien bursts out laughing. 'Of course, *chérie*,' he says. 'Of course you can.'

Kate, walking ahead with Mary and half listening to Dan and Anjali's conversation about self-hypnosis for countering nerves, battles fright, shame and feeling too old beneath her polished exterior in the red moonlight.

18

Emily's birthday falls two days after Kate and Alicia are due home from Moorside. To celebrate, Guy takes her and Ingrid out four days earlier. 'Your official birthday,' he suggests, filling her arms with sunflowers and a bulging plastic bag of parcels.

He loves to buy presents for Emily and the baby. Emily neither has nor desires much, but whatever he brings her seems to be right. They have the same taste. They like tall glass vases and earthenware mugs with daft writing on the side. They prefer light, bright, simple rooms, curtains no heavier than muslin, floors wooden rather than carpeted. Emily says that in Denmark people generally don't have curtains and carpets. She's convinced that they do nothing but collect dust, cause allergies and shut you off from everyone else.

They love the same things beyond the house, too. Walking in the Peaks. Unusual cheeses. Sunsets over lakes. Relaxing with coffee and a good book or intelligent journal. Best of all, lots of sex. Once they'd conquered their guilt in bed, they'd begun to come together and now they've turned it into a fine art. Emily, gasping and contracting, laughing and crying against him, sometimes whispers that she can't tell which of them is which.

Today he embraces her the moment he's inside the flat, then hoists Ingrid into the air where she shrieks with excitement. Most of the presents are for Ingrid: plastic ducks for her bath, a mobile of dolphins to hang over the cot, a cute pink hat to protect her delicate head for the rest of the summer. Finally

Guy says, 'I hope you like this,' and pushes a parcel wrapped with silver paper and pink, curled ribbon into Emily's hands. 'I can change it for you if not.'

Emily lifts out a creamy-white wrap made of fine, knitted silk. She's allergic to wool, she'd explained once, when he'd tried to buy her a jersey. It makes her skin turn red and lumpy. Silk, though, is perfect. Guy folds the soft garment round her shoulders and kisses her. Associating wool with his wife, he's glad Emily can't wear it.

He dreams of spiriting Emily to London, dressing her in grey satin and pearls and taking her to the Savoy or Claridges to shower her with the vintage champagne she deserves. Instead they head for Pizza Express on the local high street. It's the only restaurant that seems to welcome the baby in her buggy, though Ingrid is a good sleeper – no child could be less intrusive. Emily chooses a Fiorentina, Guy an American Hot, and they share a salad and a bottle of house wine. When they've finished, they go back to the flat, settle Ingrid in her cot and retreat to make love.

At the end, half asleep, Emily sighs. 'I wish you could stay tonight. Can't you? With them away?'

'I have to walk the dog.'

'Oh, God. The dog.'

'She's a great dog. You'd love her.'

'Sometimes I think I'm more jealous of her than of Kate.'

'Because I have to walk her?'

'No. Because I think you love her more than Kate.'

Guy holds her while she dozes, her hair drifting across his shoulder. He has never known such raw love, love that lifts his heart clean out of his body as a butcher would lift the heart of a slaughtered creature. He wonders if she knows how he feels, if she feels the same and, if so, how they can stand it much longer. Pain flickers in his chest and rebounds in his left elbow.

★   ★   ★

At Moorside, the summer school steams into its final day. The temperature is up, a layer of clingy cloud veils the sky and Alicia complains to her mother that the piano keys are laced with moisture. That evening she'll be a star turn in the student concert, performing her Granados. Lucien had been gentler with her in class that morning, going out of his way to praise her, and Anjali, who had played before her and acquitted herself excellently, had hugged her afterwards. Dan sat listening, a half-smile on his face as Lucien said, 'Come on, Alicia, don't be so innocent.'

Dad phones at lunchtime, while Anjali is telling Dan how wonderful Alicia had looked in a sari. Mum and Mary are sitting nearby, trying to pretend they aren't chaperones. Alicia hasn't stopped to think about why Dad calls her, but doesn't always speak to Mum as well. She senses dislocation under the surface, a shark within a sunlit sea, but she doesn't want to put herself in danger by venturing closer to it. She has too much to do.

'Play beautifully, darling,' Dad says in his office.

'I'll do my best,' she tells him. 'Give Cassie a hug.'

Alicia wanders on to the platform in the empty hall for her practice session. The hall glows, rafters rearing towards the sky, wood, stone and glass cradling her in a sound-enhancing cocoon as she begins to play. Caressing Granados's melody, hearing it sing, Alicia can't quite believe that this week – weird, painful, inspiring – is about to end. She hates the idea of saying goodbye to Lucien and her friends, Dan most of all. Yet she's been aware of certain uncomfortable elements, a rustle of cynicism when she stepped forward to play in the masterclass that morning (it had evaporated by the end) and the odd looks that some of the listeners cast at her and her mother, especially when Mum turns promotional and tells people, 'She's just had her seventeenth birthday.' What has she done wrong? Alicia pushes the thought aside. The important thing is to play well today. That's all that matters.

★   ★   ★

'Something's not right.'

Kate is on her favourite bench, looking down at the hall and the herb garden from the beech trees close to the Magic Spot. She's calling Rebecca. Again. Trying to articulate the sensations that have been crowding her all week.

'With Ali?' Rebecca prompts. 'With Lucien?'

'It's the way people view Ali. They're so cynical. It wasn't just that Lucien took her Chopin apart. It's how they look at her and talk about her. She's been having so much fun that I don't think she's noticed, but I'm worried.'

'Darling, people are always cynical about prodigies. Either they adore them or they shred them.'

'But it's like – they view her as a downmarket bimbo. It's horrible. And there've been comments. Not to my face, but Mary's told me about it. People think I'm a Piano Mum. One of those ghastly, pushy mothers who try to live through their child. It's the stupidest thing I ever heard! It's not like Ali is talented because I made her work when she didn't want to. Ali has an amazing gift. I'd much rather she didn't. All I ever wanted was a normal family.'

'Katie, calm down. Stop worrying. It's up to Ali to prove herself in the concert today. And she will. I know her. I know she can do it. And so do you.'

'She's wonderful.'

'So are you, Katie. And don't you forget it.'

'Rebecca?'

'Everything's going to be fine, you'll see. Love you. Gotta run.'

The line goes dead before Kate can give even the most unthinking reply to her friend's farewell message. 'Love you'? What do you mean, 'love you'?

Alicia looks up as if returning from time travel. Someone is leaning on the end of the piano, smiling. It takes her a moment to realise it's Dan.

'Hi, gorgeous,' he says. 'Gonna be long?'

'Does someone else need the piano?'

'No, but I need you. Come for a walk. It'll do you more good than sitting here slogging. You're on in a few hours.'

'You sound like my dad. He also thinks it's better to go for a good walk than practise too much.'

'What do you say?'

Alicia jumps up.

'You live in good walking country, don't you?' Dan says, while they cross the lawn towards the herb garden.

'It's wonderful, where we live. I wish you could come and visit. You'd love it. There are wonderful old stately homes and little villages and pubs. The moors are so beautiful that I could live up there and never be bored because the light changes all the time.'

Dan laughs. 'I grew up in Boston, which has a bit of history to it, but Indiana's serious Midwest. Not many historic palaces! What I love about the States is that we're a country of immigrants. Most people originated somewhere else, a few generations back, but everyone pulled together. They all wanted to be American. Did you know we're the only country in the world that has the pursuit of happiness written into our constitution as a right?'

'The pursuit of happiness?' Alicia says, thinking. It has never occurred to her that this could be one of life's aims. 'I like that.'

'*You* should come and visit. You've never been to the States.'

'I'd love to. I'd love to so much.'

'So come. When can you come?'

'I don't know. I've got concerts.'

'You have to have a holiday some time.'

Alicia rattles off her schedule for the year ahead – music-club recitals, festival recitals, concertos with orchestras both local and national, plans for another CD – and watches Dan's face as she speaks.

'Al, you're seventeen. This is crazy,' he says, when she's finished.

'But what can I do? I can't get out of it. I can't just let everyone down and say, "Sorry, I'm off to America for two weeks."'

'I wasn't thinking of two weeks. I was thinking of two months. Or two years.'

'Two *years*?'

'You need time. You need to study properly. There are worse places you could go than Indiana. And you'd love my teacher, Professor Feinstein. He's a kind of guru. He's eighty, but he's got more energy than most guys of twenty-one.'

'Eugene Feinstein?' Alicia asks. 'I've heard of him.'

'You should meet him. Play to him, get some advice. He's one of the last Golden Age teachers. He got out of Poland as a kid in the war, made it to Paris, studied with a pupil of Busoni's, got out of Paris just before the occupation and wound up in Los Angeles. He worked in Hollywood as a youngster, then started to concentrate on chamber music and teaching, and now he lives for his teaching. He's a hoot, too.'

'I can't even think about going to study in America. Mum'd kill me.'

'That,' says Dan, 'is exactly what I mean.'

They walk up the steps, arms brushing together. At the Magic Spot they sit on the wall side by side and gaze out at the wide, green and grey view.

Alicia takes a breath and moistens her lips. Then she says: 'To me, this view is in G flat.'

'What?'

'I've never told anyone about this before. But it's something I've always felt. I see different keys and individual notes in different colours. I always feel this kind of green is G flat major. C is scarlet, A is sky blue, E is yellow. Do you think I'm crazy?'

'But that's amazing!' Dan, Alicia sees, is not distressed but delighted. 'You've got synaesthesia.'

'I've got *what*?' Alicia had thought synaesthesia was a mental illness that made you hear voices.

'No, no,' Dan says, 'that's schizophrenia. Synaesthesia is exactly what you described. You experience impressions of one sense in another. Loads of composers had it. Rimsky-Korsakov, Scriabin and Messiaen. Especially Messiaen. When he wrote about his music, he often described it in terms of colours.'

'Seriously? There's nothing wrong with me?'

'Of course not! It's a wonderful gift. It adds all kinds of sensitivities to you that the rest of us don't have.'

'That's why I make such a fuss about my concert dresses,' Alicia confides. 'If I'm playing a concerto, I won't feel comfortable if I'm wearing the wrong colour for the key. Mum thinks I'm being stupid, but I'm not.'

'Why don't you tell her?'

'Because . . .' Alicia pauses. She hasn't thought about how to articulate this. 'I think,' she says, 'that if I tell her, she'd tell Phyllida – my agent – and Rebecca and there'd be all kinds of fuss. And I don't want more fuss than there is already.'

'You see?' Dan holds out his hands to her. 'You've got to get away.'

Alicia plays last in the concert. The Granados piece, she imagines, is about a girl standing by her window, longing for her lover and listening to the song of a nightingale in the woods. For Alicia, the music is a deep shade of lilac, the colour of half-hidden floral bushes in a midsummer night. She doesn't have a dress that colour, so she wears blue, as she often does – it suits her and doesn't clash with foreign keys as red, pink or green might. Her mind is full of her talk with Dan. It's all right, then, to see her colours? To relish their shifting, melding beauties and let them seep into her playing?

The humidity makes the keys slippery and she can feel her dress soaking with sweat; but she's in perfect control of the piano. She feels the chords ease from one colour to another as the harmonies change; she highlights them with a subtle spot of pedal. She softens the tone as the melody slips from pink to purple and deepens to indigo. She gives her colours their head – and senses, despite her absorption, the stilling of the audience. Everyone thinks she's the Poor Little Prodigy with the Terrible Mother. It's up to her to show them that she's not; that she's a musician with something to say that's worth hearing. And show them she will.

When the applause thunders out, she stands up and sees hands clapping everywhere, flickering like a flock of birds taking wing from Grandma Didie's garden, and the tension inside her flies away with them. Dan's eyes beam out of the crowd as if from her own mind, an idea that makes no sense. Anjali waves and smiles, happy now that she no longer has to worry about her own playing in the masterclass. Lucien's in the front row, cheering. And Mum—

Mum isn't there. At the end of the hall a door opens and closes – there's a swish of linen – and Alicia understands that her mother has fled. What on earth—

A minute later she's in the green-room, being mobbed. Dan lifts her clean off her feet and she hugs him, loving the soapy, suedey scent of his neck. It's so easy to love Dan. It's as if she's loved him all her life. Anjali too – her oldest, dearest friend, cheerful though inwardly preparing to give up her dream. And everyone else, crammed into the oven-like space, pressing her hand, kissing her cheek, patting her back, stroking her hair, treating her like a prize cat in a show, but approving of her in a way that they haven't until now. She wipes moisture from her forehead. Where is her mother?

★ ★ ★

'I don't know,' says Lucien, the last person in the room. Dan and Anjali have left her to get changed, saying they'll see her in the bar. Alicia lingers in her blue concert dress, looking up at Lucien.

'Did you see her? Did you talk to her?'

'No. *Chérie*, could you bear to come back to the piano with me for just a moment? I want to show you something. You did so well. Something changed inside you, no?'

'How amazing that you noticed!'

'Not so amazing. Because, since this morning, something is different. This morning you sounded like a talented kid. Tonight you sound like an artist. What happened?'

Alicia reflects. If Dan says it's OK, then it's OK. 'Apparently,' she begins, 'I've got this thing called synaesthesia, where . . .'

Ten minutes later she's still talking. About how she never believed it, she never trusted it, she was scared to let anybody know – until now. When it was for her, not against her, the whole time.

Lucien sits at the piano, his wide smile widening. 'Something is freed in you,' he says. 'Wonderful. Now, listen. You know this melody . . .'

He begins to play Alicia's piece. Alicia finds she's holding her breath. A disturbing depth, sinister and dangerous, shines out of the music in Lucien's hands, something she hadn't put in because she never knew it was there.

'You play it beautifully, Alicia. As a young artist, you play it like a beautiful dream. But what's behind the dream? Where does the dream lead? You are a wonderful girl, but you are too innocent. You play it singing. My professor at the Conservatoire showed me this. I, too, was playing it – singing. Then he played it – weeping.'

'Lucien,' Alicia says, stepping nearer to him, 'I don't *want* to be innocent.'

★   ★   ★

Kate, gulping down fresh air after escaping the hall's oppressive heat, flops on to a bench and fans herself with her scrunched-up concert programme. It is a mystery, the way revelations come to you when you are clearing your mind, concentrating on listening, quieting the constant brain-chatter, but there it is, staring at her bright and clear: if Ali hadn't made that first CD, people would now take her seriously. It's not her playing that lets her down; it's the CD's presentation. And whose idea was that? Not hers. Certainly not Ali's. It's not as if she hasn't known this all along. But now she feels she understands it for the first time – and its implications.

Why did Rebecca want to sign Ali? Is she so devoted to Eden Classics that she will manufacture the rekindling of a close friendship, cultivate a young talent and then turn it in the wrong direction solely to make the company a bit of money? Where does 'love you' fit into that? What does 'love you' mean, anyway? Most troubling of all, why had she been so desperate for Rebecca to be right? She'd listened to her, not Ali, not even the advisory scheme director, all the time. She'd been too dazzled by Rebecca to hear her own daughter's anxieties. Questions pound upon her. She'd have done anything to please Rebecca. Why? The potential answers that present themselves are so frightening that only two solutions are possible: fight or flight. Maybe both.

She has several options. She could pussyfoot about, waiting for the right moment, once they're home and the dust had settled. She could accost Rebecca face to face in London tomorrow and tear up Ali's contract under her nose. Or she can phone her now and get it over and done with.

She presses her lips together, breathes deeply, then dials 'BECS MOBL'.

'I've been thinking,' she says, calm and collected, when Rebecca answers with a happy 'Helloo!'

'Is everything OK?'

'Yes,' Kate says, 'and no. Ali has just played in the concert. She was wonderful. She's won everyone over.'

'As we knew she would.'

'I've realised what the problem is. Or was. The problem is not Ali. It's not me. It's Ali's CDs. The downmarket give-this-to-Granny-for-Christmas image. I never believed that before, because I didn't *want* to. I trusted you. I wanted you to be right. I was wrong. You were never interested in what was good for Ali, only in how much money Eden could squeeze out of her. Rebecca, I'm severing our contract. Ali won't be making any more recordings for you. When I get home, I am going to phone Deutsche Grammophon and EMI and Warner's and I am going to fight and fight until I find someone who will take my daughter as seriously as she deserves. You've done her a disservice. I think our friendship is over.'

She doesn't wait for Rebecca's reply, but presses the red button with one wobbling thumb. Then she puts her head on her knees and tries to get a grip. Beside her, the phone begins to ring, tootling Bach. She turns it off.

When Alicia still has not appeared in the bar after forty-five minutes, Dan tells Anjali he's going to look for her. Kate, wandering in, pale and tired, is alone. He tries Alicia's mobile, but it's off. He doesn't want Kate to worry, so he motions her towards the glass of wine waiting for her at their table with Anjali and Mary, then slips out.

In the courtyard, he notices a light in one of the staff bedroom windows on the ground floor. Several times he's seen Lucien heading towards the big oak door that fronts this staircase. It's Friday night, the last night, the party night. Nobody in Moorside is ever in their room this early on Friday night. The curtains are not fully closed. Acting on some unhappy intu-ition, Dan walks quietly across the grass and peers in. The sight that meets him is not what he'd wanted to find.

Furious, hurt, he retreats, thinking quickly. He can interrupt this himself. But he doesn't want Alicia to know that he's witnessed it, let alone for her to see how upset he is. If he doesn't interrupt, though, what will happen to her is potentially a lot worse. He dashes over the lawn, back to the bar.

'Kate,' he says, 'come quick.'

Lucien hasn't locked the door; he must have been in too much of a hurry. Alicia is on the bed, her concert dress ruffling round her hips, its shoulder straps slithering towards her elbows as Lucien's hands caress her hair and her thighs while his lips and the tip of his tongue travel across her face, her arms and her neck.

Kate doesn't recognise the sound that comes out of her mouth or the strength that annexes her hands. There's a shout as Lucien collides with the open door, a cry of protest from Alicia, a flurry of blue material and soft white flesh trying to put itself back together, and a yell that emerges unbidden as if from a creature trying to save its young.

Later, calming down over a brandy, Kate will cast her mind back to a day when she had stumbled across a ewe on the moor trying to protect a lamb that was being attacked by a hawk – remembering the fearsome, unsheeplike noises that the animal emitted against the swooping predator, incandescent with the rage of mother love.

Lucien, one hand pressed to his face, does all he can do: he fastens his trousers and runs for his life.

'Ali!' Kate reaches out her arms to her daughter. 'Oh, my darling, are you all right? What's he done to you?'

Alicia is sitting up, her flushed cheeks damp with tears. Kate can't help casting her gaze down the girl's exposed legs in case there's any streak of blood on the inner thigh.

'Mum,' Alicia sobs, 'why don't you just get the hell out of my business?'

Kate can't believe her ears.

'Your business? Lucien tries to rape you and it's *your busi-ness?*'

'He wasn't raping me. He was making love to me.'

'A man like that doesn't make love to a seventeen-year-old student.'

'Mum, I *wanted him to,*' Alicia shrieks. 'How am I supposed to understand music if I've never loved anyone?'

'You stupid child!' Kate screams back. 'He's filled your head with that crap just so that he can jump on you. Can't you see that?'

'Just because it wasn't you! Just because you're jealous! He was flirting with you and flattering you to get closer to me!'

'Alicia, how dare you talk to me like that?'

'You're jealous! You want to live my life because you've got none of your own!'

Kate lifts a hand and slaps her daughter across one cheek, just hard enough to silence her. Alicia stops, stricken.

'Supposing you'd got pregnant?' Kate says. She controls the desire to slap her again, a great deal harder. 'Did you ever stop to think about that?'

'I wouldn't have,' Alicia mumbles. 'It's the wrong part of my cycle.'

Kate hadn't guessed that Alicia knew about fertile times. It's a sobering thought. 'How far did he go?' she demands.

'I'm *intact,* if you must know.' Alicia gets to her feet and pulls her skirt over her knees. As she rises to her full height, they're nearly eye to eye. 'Mum, I think you should say sorry.'

Kate says nothing. Alicia, staring at her with utter contempt, gathers herself and marches, tall, blue and gold, out of Lucien's room.

The pain is predictable, but excessive. Across the court-yard the hall, floodlit, looms out of a gathering night mist.

Kate moans aloud. She shouldn't be surprised. To be half in love with Lucien, to imagine he'd been attracted to her, had been pure self-delusion. Of course he'd been flattering her to get to Ali – simple and, with hindsight, so obvious. But she'd fallen into the trap, because in this summer-seduced atmosphere one kept feeling that anything could happen and probably would.

A silhouette is moving towards her through the floodlights. It's Dan. He looks at her white face and her tears and says, 'Is Ali OK?'

'You haven't seen her?'

'No. I saw Lucien. He's gone to the kitchen to ask for a beefsteak to put on his black eye.'

Kate can't help laughing. Dan smiles, but she can see genuine sorrow in his eyes.

'Can I tell you something very personal, Kate?' he says. 'I love Alicia. I know we only just met, but I really love her.'

'Oh, Dan. I'm so sorry. I wish this hadn't happened.'

'So do I. I thought – we were – I thought she cared for me.'

'She's so young. She's very inexperienced. I don't believe that what happened this evening has anything to do with her feelings for you. I think she does care for you. Maybe she doesn't know how much.'

'It's Lucien's fault. Of course it is. She doesn't know any better. But . . .'

Dan and Kate stand in silence outside Moorside Hall, thinking about Alicia. The medieval stones, Kate feels certain, have seen this many times before, and will see it all again.

The next morning, Kate taps on Alicia's door before seven.

'Ali, come on. Let's get going.'

Alicia emerges, weary and sleepless. 'Ten minutes, Mum.'

They slope away with their suitcases across the hushed and

hung-over complex before anybody is about: not Dan, not Anjali, certainly not Lucien.

The drive home is not accompanied by Louis Armstrong, sunshine or singing. Kate drives up the fast lane, concentrating hard so that she doesn't have to talk. Alicia is fuming, grudging, miserable. A week ago she had a mentor and a recording contract. Now her playing may have broken through a spiritual barrier, but she's been forbidden to see Lucien again and the contract will be torn up as soon as they're home. At eight thirty, Kate's mobile phone begins to pipe its Bach tune – ceaseless and infuriating. Kate doesn't answer and neither does Alicia.

Near Malvern, Alicia fumbles for her own phone and begins to press buttons with her thumbs.

'What are you doing?'

'Texting Dan. We didn't say goodbye.'

Kate says nothing. A few days ago, if she'd caught Alicia *in flagrante* with Dan, she'd have been furious. Now she feels she'd give anything for that to have happened instead. After yesterday, she wants Dan's forgiveness for Alicia almost as badly as Alicia does.

Fifteen tense minutes pass before a reply bleeps in. From the corner of one eye, Kate sees something approximating happiness illuminate Alicia's tired face as she reads.

They turn into their driveway at two o'clock in the afternoon. Alicia sprints into the house; Cassie greets her with noisy delight.

'Dad!' she shouts, hugging her dog. 'We're back! Dad?'

There's no reply. Dad, as usual, isn't there.

'Adrian?' says Alicia, softly.

Adrian's bed is made, the desk is empty and the ghetto-blaster and TV have gone.

In the kitchen, Kate, her suitcase by her feet, is standing

with one hand on the back of a chair and the other holding a note on a torn envelope.

MOVED TO MACCLESFIELD. WILL RING. ADRIAN.

'Ali,' Kate says, without looking up, 'why don't you go and unpack and do some practising?'

19

FROM: Dan Rubinstein
TO: Alicia Bradley
DATE: 31 August 2003
SUBJECT: Miss you

Dearest Al,

Hi from Boston. I'm home with the folks for a week or two now. I got your card – it's cute. Thanks.

I KNOW what happened wasn't your fault. I just hope you're OK, because you matter to me so much that writing this doesn't say the half of it. You've got to take good care of yourself because it's a very, very long way from Bloomington or Boston to Buxton, and I can't cycle over and check up on you. Forgive you? What's to forgive? I want you in my life for keeps, even if you are 4000 miles away. Do you mind?

Not great to think of you with no teacher, no school, no recording deal and all those concerts. Here's an idea. I think the problem is that you're stuck at a level of perception that you need to break through – and, goodness knows, you deserve to. The Leeds International Piano Competition's accepting applications for next year. You're probably sick of competitions, but it's a good one and I'm planning to do it myself, if they'll have me. Why don't you go in for it too? If you win a prize, you'll be taken as seriously as you should be, and if you don't, then at least you and I will have had a chance to be in the same place at the same time. Good plan?

Think over what I said about Bloomington? I'm posting you some of the official info. Told Prof Feinstein about you and now he's dying to meet you. And . . . drumroll . . . he's going to be on the jury in Leeds! So come to Leeds, whatever happens, even if you only come to play to him. Seriously, Al, I think it might be a good idea. Go to one of those teachers who specialises in preparing students for competitions and then GO FOR IT.

Write soon. You're wonderful. Miss you.

Much love,

Dxxx

FROM: Rebecca Harris
TO: Kate Bradley
DATE: 5 September 2003
SUBJECT: (no subject)

Dearest Katie,

I've been ringing constantly, but you never answer. I'm devastated. I wish you'd tell me what happened, because I think I'm entitled to a little more explanation.

I've done everything I can to help you and Ali, from the beginning. I feel hurt that you'd suppose, even for a moment, that I'd set out to do anything else. Of course Eden has done well from Ali's success, but so, I think, have you.

Please talk to me. Let's try again, sort out the problems and put them right. We can't do this if you won't talk.

I miss your friendship. As it happens, I always have. I beg you, Kate, call me. There's so much good, creative energy between us. Why throw it away?

Yours ever,

Rebecca

FROM: Anjali Sharma
TO: Alicia Bradley
DATE: 30 October 2003
SUBJECT: Giving up piano dream

Hi Ali,

I've done it. I've applied to uni. It seems like the best thing and unbelievably my dad thinks so too. I've applied to Manchester, York, Birmingham, East Anglia, Warwick and Liverpool – I hope I get Manchester so I can be nearer to Buxton! I'll have a year out because I'd have been at the Academy by now. But that's fine. It gives me a chance to get my head together.

It feels odd – all I ever thought of doing was performing. But I have to face it: I don't have your kind of talent. I've been having some counselling and I can see now that it was my father who decided I should be a pianist. If he hadn't pushed me so hard, I might never have tried. It's not like I'm giving up music – maybe I can do something else with it. Goodness knows what. But uni should be fun and it'll be nice to meet people who do other things besides playing musical instruments.

So you're entering the Leeds? Good woman. Go for it! Have you started driving lessons yet? I'm having my first one tomorrow – I didn't get round to it last year. Wish me luck!

Love,

Anji

PS – Say hi to your brother from me. He was in Birmingham last week, I'm not sure why, and we met for a drink. Amazed he remembered me, but it was nice to see him.

FROM: Alicia Bradley
TO: Anjali Sharma
DATE: 31 October 2003
SUBJECT: Driving

Hi Anji,

How did you get on??????!?!?!?

I have GOT to learn to drive. Mum doesn't want me to (why are we not surprised?) but the idea of driving to my own concerts is bliss because every time she takes me there's so much fuss. She has to treble-check everything in the cases before we set out and there are always problems about who's going to walk the dog.

It's completely freezing here.

My new teacher, Ian, who's head of piano at the Manchester Music School, is fantastic. He's letting me learn the Rachmaninov Third Piano Concerto. Might do it for Leeds. Nobody can say I'm a bimbo if I turn up with *that* and play it well. Did you know I'm doing the Tchaikovsky Concerto at Symphony Hall, Birmingham, in a couple of weeks? Aak! I haven't been there since the final of the BBC competition. There was a cancellation, another pianist who's with Phyllida's company, and Phyllida persuaded them to have me replace him. I hope you can come – let me know and I'll get you a complimentary ticket. Mum says the hall feels like a conference centre, but I remember liking it because the acoustic is so good. You can play as softly as you like and still be heard. Ian loves soft playing with lots of colour – so did the Unmentionable Lucien, of course. I miss him, but Mum wants to shop him to every newspaper in the country.

Apropos de Lucien . . . I don't know what to do about Mum and the papers. She's obsessed. Apparently I'm not the first student Lucien's jumped on. Phyllida mentioned that he'd done it before, a while ago, and Mum yelled at her, wanting to know why she hadn't told us earlier. Poor Phyllida was very upset. Lucien must have been her boyfriend at the time, so I guess she couldn't quite cope with it. Dad says that of course none of the newspapers will run anything about it, because they could be sued for libel. Mum says why would they be, if it's true? But I'd have to testify against him in court and I won't do that. So Dad tells Mum not to be stupid and then they row about it. It's crazy – it's been months now and she's still hopping mad! Now she's threatening to take my management away from Phyllida. And she and Dad are at each other's throats the whole time. It's HORRIBLE. I'm practising extra hours because while I play I can't hear anything but the piano.

I guess you know all about Adrian moving out and working full time in that motorbike shop!! He's learning everything there is to learn about motorbikes. Dad is livid because he wanted Adrian to go to uni. I think he's ashamed to be the editor of the biggest newspaper in the north and find that his son's not interested in studying Greek literature or whatever.

I'm pleased for Adrian, because he's got his life together. He's turning into a real biker. He wears leathers and talks about all kinds of technical things that I don't understand. Did he show you his new bike? It's wonderful, really fast – and he wanted to take me out on the back of it, but Mum went ballistic and wouldn't let me go. I don't know how I'll ever leave home, because of the piano. I couldn't move my Steinway into a Macclesfield bedsit – it would drive everyone bananas.

I miss you, Anji! I miss Lucien, despite everything. And I miss Dan . . . He's coming over in summer before Leeds, but it's ages away – it'll be ten months since I last saw him. I wonder whether we'll get along. I still don't understand how I really feel about him and Lucien. It's confusing.

So, basically, all the news I have is that I practise, give concerts and try to stay on the right side of Mum and Dad, and I haven't got anyone to talk to but the dog, who's going deaf.

At least I've got my own computer now. Thank God for email!!!

Lots of love,

Axxxx

TO: Phyllida Brown
FROM: Alicia Bradley
DATE: 4 January 2004
SUBJECT: Leeds

Dearest Phyllida,

I hope you had a wonderful Christmas. I thought I should let you know that I've been accepted for Leeds. I'd like to do Rachmaninov No. 3 if I get to the final, so I'm working hard on that at the moment, but the Tchaikovsky, Chopin and Ravel are still in good shape so if any last-minute dates come in for those, that's fine with me. Sorry you couldn't make it to Birmingham – hope you saw the reviews!!!☺

Where were you for Christmas? Did you go to your mum's? Ours was awful – Mum and I were down in Harrow with the Horribles, sorry, Uncle Anthony and Auntie Fiona and their kids who think I'm off my head. Dad didn't come. He said he had to work.

See you soon, lots of love,

Axxxx

TO: Alicia Bradley
FROM: Phyllida Brown/MCAA
DATE: 4 January 2004
SUBJECT: Out of Office Autoreply: Re:Leeds

Phyllida Brown is on leave until further notice. Please forward any urgent message to Alison Harvey.

TO: Dan Rubinstein
FROM: Alicia Bradley
DATE: 21 January 2004
SUBJECT: Miss you

Hi Dan,

Isn't it amazing that we can write to each other and the message goes 4000 miles right away?!?

The Rachmaninov is going fine, thanks. I love it to pieces. I'll wear black to play it – red would suit it too, but I think black will look more serious. Assuming I get to play it at all, that is. There's such a lot of repertoire to learn for Leeds. I'm working about nine hours a day and seeing Ian twice a week. It's crazy and tiring, and sometimes at night my head is so full of notes and colours that I can't sleep. Anyway, you know all about it because you're doing it too. We could work like this all year and then be thrown out after the first round . . . but I'm trying not to think about that. Driving lessons are fun – they get me out of the house and if I pass my test, I'll be able to jump in the car and just GO.

I'm worried about Mum. I think she's depressed. And Rebecca

won't leave her alone. Adrian came over yesterday on his bike (I'm still not allowed on the back) and he tackled her outright. Of course she told him to shut up. But he's right. She doesn't have any life of her own. She hardly talks to Dad. She doesn't do anything except manage me, especially now that Rebecca's in the doghouse and Phyllida's in hospital. It's awful about Phyllida. She's had a kind of breakdown. I miss her so much. Nobody knows how long she'll be off.

Mum says that now my career's better established, it's easy for her to manage me herself. She used to be a lawyer, so she knows about contracts and she's very organised. The only trouble is that she's raised my fee and I feel embarrassed. Not that it puts people off, so I guess it's OK.

It's not like I get the money – she's investing it for me, and paying off the piano (a.k.a. the mortgage). She gives me an allowance, which Adrian keeps telling me is too small, since I'm the one doing the work. I don't like to complain, though. I spend most of it on concert dresses, music, books and getting my hair done at a really good salon when I go to London. I hope she'll let me put it towards buying a car when I pass my test.

Now that I'm with Ian I can see that he's a much better teacher than Lucien. Lucien was good at giving me reading and listening lists, poems, paintings, etc., but for preparing for Leeds, Ian's the right guy. I wish I'd gone to him years ago. He's good on poetry and painting too, as it happens.

Dan, I MISS YOU. I think a lot about last summer. Do you, too? Here's what I feel now:

1. I'm very, very sorry about what happened on the last night at Moorside.
2. I wasn't in love with Lucien at all. Even when I thought I was.
3. I wonder if love is maybe not what we think. I imagined it was about being starry-eyed, feeling fluttery when you're near someone. But now I think it's more in the mind than in the body. It's like being in tune. It's like singing in the same key, feeling things in the same colour (I know you understand this!), not having to guess or doubt or fight. Feeling like you've known

someone all your life. You can relax, be yourself and know that they appreciate you exactly as you are, at your best.

That's what I feel about you. I feel like you're part of me and I'm not scared to tell you that. I don't want to hide who I am or how I feel. I used to watch girls at school playing stupid games with the blokes they liked and I don't want to do that. Perhaps I show too much – but that's tough. That's me. That's how I am. Why should I be ashamed? It's only shameful if you direct it to the wrong person. Perhaps that's what happened with Lucien.

Tell me it's not only me? Tell me you feel the same?

Lots of love from a very wintry Buxton.

A xxxxxxx ooooooo xxxxxxxxx

FROM: Dan Rubinstein
TO: Alicia Bradley
DATE: 21 January 2004
SUBJECT: YES

YESYESYESYESYESYESYESYESYESYESYESYESYESYESYES.

I feel exactly the same.
Love you. Am with you every moment.
D xxxxxxxxxxxxxxx ooooooooooo xxxxxxxxxxxxx

'Let's go to the lounge,' Phyllida suggests. 'I need a change of scene.'

Alicia is in Phyllida's room in the hospital, which, she thinks, feels more like a prison than a place where people are supposed to be healed. It's a large, red-brick building hidden behind a wall on a busy road in south London; the soundproofing is so good that you can't hear the lorries going by, or any noise from patients in surrounding rooms. The atmosphere is heavy with accumulated misery. If so many suffering people are thrown in together, Alicia muses, how is anybody ever supposed to get better?

Phyllida blows her nose.

'I go home from time to time. But I have panic attacks when I walk into my own flat. God, I feel so stupid.'

'Phyl, you mustn't! You're fantastic.'

'You're a sweetiepie, Ali. Just make sure this never happens to you, yeah?'

'Phyl—'

'Let's get you a cup of tea. I can't believe you came all this way just to see me.'

'Of course I did!' Alicia protests, following Phyllida, whose walk no longer bounces. As she wanders down the green and pink corridor towards the patients' lounge, Phyllida seems to be moving in a dream, almost under water. It must be the pills.

'When are you going back to work?' Alicia asks, when they've helped themselves to tea from an urn and settled down on a relatively secluded pink sofa.

'No idea. I can't face the office. And the idea of getting my head round the paperwork . . . it's just . . .'

'You must take as much time as you need,' Alicia encourages. 'You've got to get better. That's the only thing that's important.'

'I'm so ashamed of myself.' Phyllida sits with one hand over her eyes. Alicia can hardly recognise the elegant, sharp-nosed, besuited executive she first met in a Kensington restaurant. In jeans and soft purple jersey, without glasses, without makeup, her hair growing longer, Phyllida's lines have crumbled to dust.

'You mustn't be. It could happen to anyone,' Alicia says. She wants to ask if it's about Lucien. But she dares not say his name, in case it is.

'When you fall in love, Ali,' Phyllida says, without being asked, 'make sure it's with someone who loves you too.'

'But surely . . .' Alicia bites her lip. She wants to be tactful, but she also wants to find out what happened, and why. 'If you know he doesn't feel the same,' she begins cautiously, 'and you know he's cheating on his girlfriend and jumping on his students – doesn't it stop you loving him? It would stop me.'

'That's the bloody awful thing. It should, but it doesn't. After we had our – our – OK, call it an affair if you like, I suppose that's what it was, I honestly thought I could turn him into a friend. And then I thought that if I did every-thing for him and built up a fabulous career for him, he wouldn't be able to do without me. Instead, what happens if you behave like that is that he takes you for granted, he uses you, he tramples you underfoot. It's almost as if I've been begging him to walk on me. I'd lay down my life for him – so that's what he wants me to do. He doesn't feel anything for me except power.'

'Lucien likes power,' Alicia remarks.

'It's so demoralising. I feel so awful. I feel old. Fat.'

'You're not fat!'

'I feel fat because I feel so unattractive. I'm hopeless. I'm past my sell-by date. I don't even feel I can be any good at my job because when I'm with Lucien I start feeling like a stupid, insecure kid.'

'Phyl, I think you're *wonderful*,' says Alicia, her lip wobbling. She's never seen anybody in such a ferment of honest, devas-tated emotion and she wants to howl in sympathy – though that wouldn't help Phyllida in the slightest.

'You're a darling. I hate to think of him using you.'

'I can forgive him for Moorside, but if he's done this to you, I never want to see him again.'

'It's not him, really. It's me.'

'I think it's him. Not you.'

Phyllida wanders over to the window and watches the clouds chasing each other across the sky. Alicia isn't used to seeing her without her glasses. Her turquoise eyes are clear, deep and full of sorrow.

'You know, we deny these things,' Phyllida says, without

looking at Alicia. 'In the nineteenth century, a lot of opera and ballet stories were about girls going mad when they're betrayed by their lovers. Today, no matter how awful we feel, we're meant to *get over it*. Well, supposing I don't *want* to get over it? Supposing, despite everything, Lucien is still the most beautiful thing that ever happened to me? But it's not romantic today. It's pathetic. Look at this poor old bat who can't get her life together because she's hung up on a man who doesn't love her and she's wasted her youth trying to win him and suddenly found she's past forty and it's too bloody late?'

'Oh, Phyl! None of that's true!' Alicia protests, trying to imagine how it must feel to be forty. 'You're beautiful, you've done everything to make Lucien who he is today – and if he doesn't love you, he's an idiot! He doesn't deserve you. Tell me what happened. Why did you come here?'

'It didn't exactly happen overnight, but I lost all my confidence. I started having panic attacks, especially on my own at home, and then at Christmas . . . I sort of lost it. All these images of happy families and smiling children and Christmas carols and presents and people 'being together' – and there's my mum on her own, she can't get around because of her bad knee and her operation had been cancelled again. My dad's out in Australia with his new wife, playing happy families with them instead of us, and there are all my friends with their kids – and then there's me . . .'

'Phyl, Christmas is terrible,' Alicia confirms. 'I heard that more people—' She's about to mention that more people attempt suicide at Christmas than at any other time of year but stops herself. She wonders whether Phyllida had made such an attempt. Something must have happened to land her in hospital.

'It's a vicious circle,' Phyllida explains. 'You get yourself into a state over something, and then you get into a state over the state you're in . . . and you just spiral down. I'm taking these antidepressants, I have other pills to help me sleep, I have psychotherapy, I'm supposed to do lots of exercise and stop drinking and smoking. But I feel so *stupid* for having let this happen. I don't know if I'll go back to work. I'm not sure I can face being a manager any more. I can't even manage my-self.'

'Listen,' Alicia says, 'you're going to get better. You are. Take the time you need. And when you're back at the office, I want to be back with you, because you're the only person who understood me. I hate Mum doing my management. You see, *I* need you, Phyl. You might have wanted Lucien to need you, but I really do.'

'Darling,' says Phyllida, 'you're an angel. You just take good care of yourself. OK?'

Back at Euston, Alicia has more than half an hour before her train, so she goes into an Internet café on the concourse and writes to Dan: 'We're so lucky to have found each other. I can't believe the things that happen to people because – they say – of love. To look at Phyllida, you'd think that falling in love is the worst thing that could happen to anyone.'

When she's finished, she sits over her coffee and thinks herself into her Rachmaninov concerto. The piano comes in at the start, in a simple tune that rises and falls, the hands playing in unison. Then, from this strand of sound, there unfolds a stream of emotion, counterpoint and figuration, unravelling under her fingers as if the opening melody were a plain box concealing every colour of the prism. You lift the lid and watch the ideas ripple towards the sky, bursting out beyond the confines of the human heart. Alicia remembers reading the Greek myth of Pandora's box: the girl, ordered not to look inside it, does so from curiosity and out fly all the most terrible things in the world. Death, disease, famine, hate, jealousy and evil take wing; Pandora can't put them back. At last, from the bottom of the box, a beautiful white bird emerges. Its name is Hope.

Does love live with hope or with horror? Must they all hide together, under that lid, deep inside the music?

'The train at platform six is the 17.05 to Manchester Piccadilly . . .' comes the announcement. Alicia pulls on her raincoat and wanders towards the train, camouflaged: just another young girl among the crowds, going home.

Kate, in her study, tries to work while waiting for Alicia to come back. The battle that morning had left her weak and drained once Alicia had marched out, vanishing down the road towards the bus stop. No argument had budged her from her purpose. Nothing on earth would stop her going to London, alone, to see Phyllida.

Kate had tried everything. You have to practise, it's your lesson tomorrow. You can't possibly find your way to Roehampton on your own. The weather is dreadful, the trains will probably be disrupted. Then, finally, I'll come with you (that had been the worst one). Ali's willpower reminded her fiercely of the day she'd tried to save her dog from the river. Cassie, who has cataracts and arthritis, would no longer dream of going for a swim; but Ali hasn't changed. When her mind is made up, nothing will hold her back.

Alicia has decided, similarly, that she must learn to drive. They've found a local teacher and she is applying herself with the same determination she lavishes on her Rachmaninov concerto. The idea of Ali out alone in a car makes Kate feel faint with terror, but as nothing will stop her, it seems better to help her than to try, Canute-like, to hold back the tide. Her test is in May and the indications are that she'll pass. Sooner or later they'll have to buy another car.

Kate spends half an hour searching on the Internet for good second-hand car outlets in Derbyshire. She'll need to find around five thousand pounds if Alicia is to have a reliable tin box to get her safely from A to B. On Guy's salary, it ought to be possible.

These days, Kate has few qualms about invading Guy's study. She strides across the mess of paper, books and old newspapers that furnishes the floor and tackles the filing cabinet where he keeps the bank statements.

She runs a quick, practised eye down the columns of figures. Then she does it again, double-checking. And a third time. The pattern is not difficult to spot. A direct debit to an account entitled Music Fund swallows around a third of Guy's salary per month. Where does Music Fund go?

Cross-referencing is equally easy. Another file contains Music Fund statements. Copies, it seems, are being sent to an address in Victoria Park, Manchester. Music Fund has nothing to do with Alicia. It's the money he gives Emily to support her child. The name, she understands, must have been coined specifically to dupe her.

Kate tells herself she shouldn't be surprised, but her stomach heaves. She closes her eyes and breathes, waiting for the attack to pass. Sometimes she keeps the thought of Guy's other life at bay for so long that she almost forgets it exists. Moments like this make her realise the extent to which she's capable, even now, of kidding herself.

Since the Lucien incident, Kate has snapped shut like an oyster. If barnacles were to grow on her shell, she wouldn't care. Nobody but her children will have a place inside her sealed heart. This began as a conscious decision, following Moorside, but it has moved from thought to feeling, from deliberation to reality. Guy is an irrelevance: nothing more than a facilitator for Alicia, someone to share the bills and present a united front when required. He dares not go against her conditions.

Alicia, in blissful innocence, throws herself into her music, her driving lessons and her determination to love with all her soul those whom she loves – Phyllida, Anjali and Dan, who phones frequently, sometimes for two hours at a time. Ali has a normal family behind her, a solid base for her music. That solidity, or the illusion of it, is the string that flies her like a kite. And so Kate closes herself to all else.

Despite everything, she misses Rebecca. She misses her warm eyes, her caring voice, her athleticism, poise and the soft scent of Yves Saint Laurent. Mary, her auburn-haired friend from Moorside, is no substitute. With her normal kids, her husband who spends weekends on DIY and gardening, her sensible job in the hospital, helping people who need help, well-meaning Mary tends to make Kate feel worse than ever when they meet for lunch half-way between Buxton and Liverpool. Anyway, she doesn't have much time for friendship, now that Ali's career is her sole responsibility.

Kate launches a new document and begins to type a letter to the director of the Proms.

Guy sits in the surgery in Manchester, shaking his head. 'I can't.'

'Mr Bradley, I know you're a busy man,' says Dr Simons, 'but if you don't slow down and reduce your stress levels, you might become very sick indeed. There isn't a kind way to tell you this. You've got the symptoms of heart disease and you're not yet fifty.'

'I can stop drinking. I can watch my diet. But work . . .'

'How are things at home?'

Dr Simons, Guy thinks, can see straight through him. 'Stressful,' he says.

When he goes back to the waiting room, Emily is there to take him home – her home. Because of a bout of pain that had left them both dreading the outcome of this consultation, she wouldn't let him drive. Guy pauses in the doorway, looking at the image ahead: Ingrid on Emily's lap, being read a baby book full of pop-up pictures. He crouches, holds out his arms to his daughter and watches her face – the image of her mother's – crease into a squeal of joy as she slides off Emily's knee and bounces towards him on small, heavy feet that remind him of Alicia at nearly two. Pain twinges in his arm.

'Did he refer you?' Emily demands, taking his hand.

'Yes. I have to wait for an appointment.'

'How long?'

'Not long,' says Guy, who has no idea how long 'not long' may be. Emily pulls a face and looks away. Her hand in his feels clammier than it had a moment ago.

In the car, Emily does something unusual: she talks about Alicia.

'I don't see how you've managed to keep everything from her,' she tells Guy, who's in the back with Ingrid. 'She's a bright girl. Can't she guess?'

'She's wrapped up in her music, and Kate keeps it that way.'

'The longer she doesn't know, the worse it's going to be when she finds out.'

'Christ. I know that. You know that. But try telling Kate. She's got me over a barrel and there's fuck-all I can do about it.'

'Forgive me, darling, because I know that – in a funny way – it's not really my business.' Emily pulls up at a red light and gazes at Guy over her shoulder. 'But I have to say, it doesn't make sense. What does Kate think she's going to gain from behaving like this?'

'Power,' Guy suggests, staring out at the bleak, late-afternoon twilight. 'Power to control me, I guess. Power to stop me being happier than she is. But it's more than that. She has this ingrained idea about families. That a 'normal family' is the only way to be. That if Ali doesn't have a normal family behind her, it's going to ruin her career. This kind of twaddle, I'm afraid.'

'That *is* 'twaddle' and you know it. Kate's an educated, intelligent woman. She doesn't need to think like that. There must be something deep-rooted in her that's making her behave in such a twisted way.'

'Perhaps.'

'Do you know what?'

'No. Do you?'

Emily gives a soft laugh, though her face reflected in the rear-view mirror seems sad.

'There are plenty of possible reasons,' Guy thinks aloud. 'The premature baby we lost. That's when everything began to go wrong. Or that cold, proper, pressurised background of hers. It's one of those families that just doesn't allow emotion – though Kate's had plenty of emotions in her time. But why these things add up to one kind of behaviour in one person and something different in another isn't my area of expertise.'

'Nor mine. I guess Kate's had a hard time and it's catching up with her. Maybe it's as simple as that.'

'Sweetie, don't do that,' Guy says softly to his daughter, who's finding it fun to pull off her shoe and sock, throw them on the car floor, then wait for him to retrieve them and tell her not to do it again. She grins at him and, while he straightens up, she pulls off her other shoe and sock.

20

Mum is too scared to take Alicia out to practise driving, so Adrian comes over from Macclesfield and takes her instead. He'd passed his driving test first go, though Alicia doesn't know why he'd bothered since he refuses to take the one for his motorbike, the vehicle he actually owns. Crazy brother, thinks Alicia, beside him in their mother's car, bowling across the moor and handling the wheel with the smoothness and panache she tries to give her piano-playing.

'Good girl,' Adrian says. 'Don't look at the lambs. Watch the road. Here comes the left turn. Mirror, signal, manoeuvre. That's it.'

Alicia swings the car down towards the valley and smiles sideways at Adrian.

'Staying for supper?' she asks him, pressing her foot down.

'If Mum's in a good mood.'

'How's Macclesfield?'

'Cool. It's great being near Josh.'

'I wish I could live with my friends.' Alicia sighs.

'Which friends, Al?'

'The ones nobody knows I have because I never see them.'

'The Indian girl? She's fit. I like her.'

'Anjali. She's going to stop doing concerts. She kind of can't deal with it. At Moorside she had to be sick before she played in the auditions. Did you know there are musicians who are sick with nerves every time they go on a stage?'

'Not you?'

'No. I love it. I wonder if there's something wrong with me.'

'Cripes, Ali, just enjoy it. You don't want to throw up.'

'It's like driving. I love it and I can't wait to pass my test. But Anjali says she's too scared to learn. She stopped her lessons.'

'Anjali's dad is a control freak.'

'And Mum isn't?'

'She is, and how! But it's worse if it's a dad.'

'At least I'm not scared of Mum. Anjali's scared of her father.'

'There we are, then. How's the Boy In Bloomington?'

'Blooming far away! But he's coming over. He's coming to stay.'

'Mum's letting him stay in the house? That'll be interesting.'

'Dan says he was lucky I got into trouble with Lucien last summer because it makes *him* look like an angel. Mum likes him because he's not Lucien!'

'Mum was in love with Lucien herself. She just couldn't admit it.'

'Everyone was in love with Lucien,' Alicia muses. 'But – *why*? I know he seemed wonderful. I thought so too, but when you see who he really is, how he really behaves – why do we all fall for it? And why does he do it? I don't understand.'

'That's what every guy wants – to have every woman on earth wanting to go to bed with him. Most of us can't have that. When someone can, because he's rich or famous or good-looking, then he does. That's all.'

'I don't think Dan wants that. I think he loves me.'

'So what's he like? All I know is you met this bloke who lives four thousand miles away and you're determined to wait for him.'

'He's . . . he's lovely. He's twenty-one. He's funny. He reads a lot and he's clued up on politics and languages and movies, much more than I am. He comes from Boston, his dad's a doctor, a psychosomething, his mum's a cellist and he's got a little sister who's six years younger. He likes dogs and walking.

He's a fantastic pianist, but he's not so ambitious. He says he'd like to be a top professor and have masses of good pupils.'

'How would it be, two pianists living together? Noisy? Competitive?'

'Bliss. Someone who understands from the inside what you're going through every day.'

'Ali . . . You haven't seen Dan since August. You've known him for one week, plus lots of emails and phone calls. But you don't really know each other. And you're so young. Are you sure you're not just seeing in him what you want to see?'

Alicia is silent for a long time. The speedometer rises from forty-five m.p.h. to fifty-five.

'Steady on the bends,' Adrian says.

'I believe in him,' Alicia says at last. 'I believe in us. If I don't, who will?'

Later, Adrian sits at the kitchen table and glares.

'Adrian, why don't you take off your jacket?' Kate says, fussing over the sink where she's preparing a chicken in a roasting pan. 'It's warm today.'

'Not in here, it isn't.'

'I've got a few things to do upstairs,' Alicia says. 'Will you excuse me, please?'

'Don't be long, Ali. It's not often we have your brother and your father home at the same time.'

'Are you surprised?' Adrian mutters.

Alicia flees. Her laptop computer offers her escape via cyber-space. She dives for relief into her email, where a long message from Bloomington is waiting. She reads it three times.

Her emotional life centres on her email. She's devised a password that she's sure her mother will never guess, but deletes messages once she's read them, just to make certain. She's taught herself how to touch-type via an Internet program and when she expresses her thoughts on the computer keyboard instead of her black-and-white musical one, she's thankful for the piano exercises that have honed her fingers' responsiveness. She can type almost as fast as she can play.

At seven o'clock the front door opens and closes. Cassie gives a half-hearted bark, then drags herself to the entrance hall to welcome Guy, who has arrived from his hospital appointment.

'Dad!' yells Alicia, and careers down the stairs.

'Hello, Ali.' Guy hugs her. He looks exhausted. 'Come and sit down. I need to talk to all of you.'

Alicia follows him into the kitchen where Mum, reproachful, turns round from the oven and Adrian waits, drumming his fingers on his leather-clad knee. Guy pats his shoulder as he goes past and sits down.

'Apparently I've got angina,' he says, 'so I have to change my diet, my lifestyle, basically everything.'

'That's ridiculous,' Mum protests. 'You're too young. Why don't you ask for a second opinion?'

'This *is* the second opinion, Kate.'

Alicia hasn't heard Dad call Mum 'Katie' for a long time. Mum is no longer a convincing Katie. Kate, yes: her manner clipped, professional and sharp-edged – not a blowsy, relaxed Katie, happy to laugh and chat.

'They've given me some pills and a diet plan,' Dad says. 'As low fat as humanly possible. And I'm supposed to join a gym and reduce the stress in my life.'

'I see,' Mum says.

'In this house,' Adrian butts in, 'that's going to be easy, isn't it?'

'Adrian, watch your mouth!' Mum snaps. 'Don't talk to your father like that.'

'It's true. Living here's enough to give anyone effing angina.' Adrian shoves back his chair and strides to the window. He towers over the rest of them.

'How dare you?' Kate says.

'I'll say what I like, because it's true. You're bloody hypocrites!'

'Adrian,' Alicia pleads.

'Not you, Al. You keep living in your own little world. It'll help you stay sane.'

'Alicia, go to your room. Now.'

'Mum!'

'Let her stay, Mum. She needs to hear this as much as you do.' Adrian swings round. His face has turned scarlet. 'Because if you don't stop pretending, if you don't stop making such an effing charade out of your perfect family and your perfect talented daughter and you don't stop taking over Ali's life, then you're going to wreck everything for her and Dad and yourself! The atmosphere in this house isn't fit for anything to live in that isn't born with a suit of armour. I'm not coming here again.'

In a rush of helmet, leather and keys, Adrian's hulking presence tears itself up by the roots, bulldozes across the hall and is gone. There's the thunder of powerful engine; Alicia, running after him, reaches the front steps in time to receive a blast of motorbike exhaust in her face. Half dazed, she trails back to the kitchen, where Dad is sitting at the table with his chin in his hands.

'Ali,' Mum says, 'go and practise, there's a good girl.'

FROM: Alicia Bradley
TO: Dan Rubinstein
DATE: 5 May 2004
SUBJECT: HELP!

Dan, please help me. I'm going out of my mind. I think Mum is going out of her mind too. Dad's got angina. My brother blames Mum and says he's never coming back. I don't know what to do. Mum doesn't do anything except tell me to go and practise. Please help me, because I'm stuck.

　　Axxx

FROM: Dan Rubinstein
TO: Alicia Bradley
DATE: 5 May 2004
SUBJECT: Re: HELP!

Hang in there, Al. I'm coming over soon. I'll change my ticket.

Just hold on for now, OK? Keep practising. That's the most important thing you can do, because that's your get-out route. And be nice to your dad. Sounds like he needs you.

Do you know anywhere other than your house where I could practise? I want to be with you, but I don't want to get in your way.

Good luck for your driving test! Will be holding thumbs for you.

I'll let you know as soon as I've booked the flight.

Dxxx

FROM: Alicia Bradley
TO: Rebecca Harris
DATE: 10 May 2004
SUBJECT: An idea

Dear Rebecca,

Mum doesn't know I'm writing to you, but I've got an idea I want to run by you.

I'd love to make another CD. I wouldn't want to do another super-popular compilation, but how about French music? Debussy and Ravel, with a cover that looks classy? I'd love to work with you again, and if I do well at Leeds, that would help sales, wouldn't it?

Please let me know what you think. Maybe we could get together to talk about it. I've just passed my driving test so I can drive myself to London any time. Theoretically.

I hope you and James and Oscar are all well. I hope we can meet again soon. I miss you.

I'm going to delete this message from my outbox because I

don't want Mum to see it, and will do the same with whatever you write back.
Love,
Alicia

FROM: Rebecca Harris
TO: Alicia Bradley
DATE: 10 May 2004
SUBJECT: Re: An idea

Dear Alicia,

It's good to hear from you. Very pleased to know that you'll be doing Leeds. You must be working extremely hard. Congratulations on passing your driving test.

As you know, I've been deeply distressed by the change in your mother. I can see why she's not happy with the perceived outcome of the first CD, but I can't understand why she won't talk to me about it. It's quite extraordinary.

I'd be delighted to meet you and discuss the possibility of a new recording. If you can persuade your mother to be a little more forgiving than she has found possible so far, that would be wonderful too. But I'd like to see you, no matter what. Please call me and we'll make plans. Don't forget to delete this message.

Yours ever,
Rebecca.

FROM: Adrian Bradley
TO: Anjali Sharma
DATE: 20 June 2004
SUBJECT: Visit

Hello Anjali,
Ali tells me you're coming to visit. I'd like to see you too, but I don't go to Buxton any more. Any chance you might come to

Macclesfield? I could take you out on the bike after work. Glad
you got into uni. Hope you're well.
Adrian

Dan is flying to Heathrow on 25 June. He's managed to get a
cheap flight earlier than he'd originally planned, but it arrives
in London rather than Manchester. Alicia decides she will drive
down to meet him in the second-hand Renault that is now 'hers'.

'You're not seriously going to drive to Heathrow on your
own?' Mum exclaims.

'I've got a driving licence. We've got a car. I've got a boyfriend
in America. So I am going to use my driving licence and our
car to go to the airport and fetch my boyfriend.'

'I'll come with you.'

'Mum, no, you won't.'

'But, Ali—'

'It's much easier to drive without you breathing down my
neck worrying that I'm going to do something wrong.'

'Supposing we ask Uncle Anthony if he—'

'No, Mum. *I'm* going.'

After ten minutes of this, Alicia is almost in tears with
frustration; Kate is white, with red patches across her cheeks.
The phone saves them. Kate answers, efficient and profes-
sional as she speaks to the manager of the Manchester
Philharmonic about Alicia's imminent concerto at the
Bridgewater Hall.

Kate had been keen to arrange a 'run-through' of Rachmaninov's Third Concerto for Alicia before the competition.
Playing it will be her biggest challenge to date; tackling it for
the first time in a televised international competition final
wouldn't be ideal. The Manchester Philharmonic is what Kate
terms a 'windfall'. She'd phoned the manager on the off-
chance that they'd have space for Alicia to do something –
anything – only to find that a pianist had pulled out of a

concerto date at the Bridgewater Proms on 3 July and they needed a replacement. 'That's Alicia's eighteenth birthday,' Kate pointed out.

The manager had been hesitant at first, having heard negative comments about Alicia's populist recordings. Kate grabbed the initiative. She insisted that he see her in person, the next day. She went to Manchester armed with reams of material: recordings of recent recitals, Lucien's reference (written before the trouble), a file of good reviews and a heap of invective directed jointly at Deirdre Butterworth and Rebecca Harris. First the manager sat and listened; then he paced about his office while Kate talked; eventually he suggested Kate put on the CD of Alicia performing the Rachmaninov G minor Prelude in last summer's Buxton Festival. While it played, he grew very still. He wanted to hear the next piece, and the one after that. At last, he said, 'I see,' pulled a calendar out of his top drawer, and wrote Alicia's name in one of its squares in blue biro.

That's what's so annoying, Kate reflected, driving home afterwards. All that needs to happen is that the right people must hear what Ali can do. When they hear it, it's total surrender. But they have to be bludgeoned into putting on a CD and actually *listening* to it. You can send a CD to anybody, but you can't make them play it unless you stand over them with a whip.

The upshot is that Alicia is to play at the Bridgewater Hall on her birthday. But what pleases her most is that Dan Rubinstein will be there to hear her.

'If you don't let me drive down to meet Dan,' Alicia tells her mother eventually, 'then I'll cancel the Bridgewater. I just won't show up. The rehearsal will start and I won't be there.'

'You will do no such thing. How dare you even think of it? Do you want to ruin your career?'

'Stuff my career,' Alicia virtually spits. 'I'm going to Heathrow and that's the end of it.'

★　　★　　★

Alicia sets off from Buxton well before rush-hour on the M1. These days, she always wakes early unless she's had a concert the night before. The prospect of Dan's arrival has changed the world's colours for her. She sometimes stands at her bedroom window and watches the sky lightening from indigo to lilac to bluebell; pale, crystalline sunlight reaches her through the fronds of midsummer leaves. She imagines Dan beside her, imagines what it would be like to wake up with him in a bed somewhat larger than her own. She scarcely remembers Lucien.

That in itself is odd, she muses, making her way over the hills to Ashbourne, then Derby, then the M1 south. How can your mind be full of one person for so long, then suddenly not be? Might the same thing happen again? After longing for Dan for months, almost a year since Moorside, might she wake one day to find that she no longer does? Maybe Adrian was right.

Not that he can talk. 'When are you next seeing your friend?' he kept asking, when she phoned him.

'Dan?'

'No. The girl. The Indian girl.'

'Anjali.'

'Yeah. Anjali.'

'She's coming to the Rachmaninov.'

'Cool.'

It isn't like Adrian to be unduly diffident, or absent-minded about names. Alicia sees the motorway spreading ahead of her and, jubilant, presses her foot on the accelerator.

The traffic builds as she circles London anticlockwise – the M25 at this hour is no fun – and by the time she turns on to the M4 and sees the planes lining up low in the sky, ready to land, she's certain Dan's must be among them and she'll be late. She doesn't become nervous for her concerts, but she's nervous now. Nervous about the traffic, nervous that she won't recognise Dan, nervous that they won't know what to say to one another. Nervous that she'll find she doesn't love him after

all. Or vice versa. And he's here for months, until the competition is over. What if they don't get along? What if the family
feuding sends him scuttling home?

Negotiating the concrete slopes in the car park, Alicia feels
her foot shaking on the clutch and wonders whether she should
leave now and go back to Buxton alone. The construct she's
built around Dan is imaginary. He's a boy. Just a boy – like
all the others she's sent packing on his behalf since last summer.
And there have been a few, even a conductor who tried to kiss
her in the lift at St David's Hall, Cardiff. Maybe she's missed
opportunities. Maybe she's put her eggs into a basket woven
of nothing but dream fibre. Maybe she's too young. Mum and
Dad met when they were eighteen and nineteen and married
when Mum was twenty-three. Maybe that's why they don't
get along any more.

She parks on the roof. When she climbs out of the car, her
legs feel weak. She follows the arrows to the terminal building,
joining the anonymous world with its suitcases, trolleys and
holiday garb trundling towards the escalators. And when she
spots the sliding doors through which weary travellers emerge,
gazing round for their family, friends or taxi drivers, she scours
the crowds for any indication of Chicago, where Dan boarded
his connecting plane after flying from Indianapolis. She finds
a spot to wait against a railing: she needs to prop herself up.
Her head is spinning. Performing a concerto is a piece of cake
compared to this.

The minutes drag; arrivals emerge from Calcutta, Thailand,
Rio, Johannesburg. Just as she's beginning to feel that the plane
is imaginary and Dan a mirage, her mobile beeps with a text:
'Landed ok, cases coming thru, c u any mo xxx.' The woman
standing beside her glances at her. 'All right, love?' she asks.

'Fine, thanks. Excited.' Alicia beams back and notices that
the smile makes the strange woman look a second time, as
people always do. She can't stop radiating just because people
tell her she's radiant.

The sliding doors disgorge a group of Americans. The men are nearly seven foot tall; the women, large all round, stride along in elasticated jeans, T-shirts and sneakers; their aspect is positive and their voices loud; they radiate, too, with sheer confidence.

Then, not far behind them, Alicia spots a curly-haired youth, dark and strong, pushing a laden trolley, a leather music case slung over one shoulder, and it doesn't seem to be her who calls out his name, ducks under the railing and cuts across the stream of incoming travellers. She flings her arms round his neck and feels the warmth of his flight-tired body as he grabs her and kisses her full on the lips. He tastes the same, he smells the same and it's as if they had last seen one another only hours ago, not ten months. They say nothing for several minutes because they're too busy kissing.

'God, Al. Let me look at you!' He stands back, while people push by, tut-tutting because they're blocking the exit, but soon translating frowns into helpless smiles at the look of absolute love on the two young faces. 'You look *fan*-tastic,' Dan says. 'What's happened to you?'

'How do you mean?'

'Last summer you looked like a teenager. Now you look like a woman.'

'I'm nearly a year older.'

'Jeez. A year. There's such a lot you've got to tell me. Come on, let's get out of here.'

'Dan, I hope it's OK with you – I need to go into London to see someone. Mum doesn't know about it, so it's kind of got to be today. I'm really sorry to drag you around. Do you mind?'

'Al, I'll go anywhere on earth with you, you know I will. You'll have to forgive me if I fall asleep, though! Who've you got to see?'

'The woman who runs my recordings, or used to. I'd love to know what you think of her.

*   *   *

On the outskirts of London Alicia has to stop the car, phone Rebecca and ask how to pay the congestion charge. 'Sorry, I've never driven into London before.'

'Ali,' says Rebecca's voice, 'don't worry. Get yourself here and we'll organise it for you. OK?'

'I need to know how to do it myself,' Alicia remarks to Dan, after thanking Rebecca and ringing off.

'I bet people always do things for you,' Dan teases, patting her knee.

Alicia laughs. 'Are you good at maps? We need to get to Kensington High Street.'

Dan, whose eyes are shadowed from plane travel and jet-lag but who still can't stop smiling, takes charge of the map and tells Alicia to head due east. While they crawl along the A4, he tells her his news. He passed his exams with top marks. He's just turned twenty-two, but he hadn't wanted to celebrate because she hadn't been there to celebrate with him. They could save that for later. His parents are dying to meet her. His little sister, who's doing violin quite seriously, is dying to meet her too. Professor Feinstein is impressed that she's going to play Rachmaninov Three at the competition.

'If I get through,' Alicia says.

'You will.'

'I hope you'll be able to stand our house. Mum's putting you in Adrian's old room.'

There's a brief, awkward moment while both of them consider sleeping arrangements.

'Fine,' Dan says. 'Look, we'll play it by ear: if it's difficult, with your parents, I'll go to a bed-and-breakfast or find something to rent until the competition.'

'Seriously?'

'Of course. The important thing is to be here. Whatever it takes.'

★   ★   ★

Off Kensington High Street, they find a parking meter and fill it with coins ('I knew London was expensive, but this is nuts!' Dan remarks). They stroll past what is, to Alicia, a dazzling array of shops, then down a side-street towards a converted nineteenth-century terrace that declares itself the home of Eden Classics.

Rebecca comes to meet them in the sleek, chrome-laced front hall. She's aged since they last met: her hair is greying at the temples and her face is lined with more frowns but, Alicia thinks, fewer smiles. She's wearing a dark silk top that shows off her sinewy, well-exercised arms, and light trousers that accentuate her long legs. Rebecca, Alicia reflects, looks elegant and beautiful, but oddly unfeminine. With her muscular, slender figure, she could almost have been a male ex-athlete.

'You must be Dan. Nice to meet you.' Rebecca turns her firm handshake on Dan, who greets her with polite words and perceptive eyes. Alicia scarcely hears what he says: she's too busy drinking in the fact that she is looking at his face, not just imagining it.

In her office, Rebecca gives them coffee, which is welcome indeed.

'Now, Ali, you're keen to do another disc. What's brought this on?'

'Becs,' says Alicia, who has never called Rebecca 'Becs' before, 'you know how my mum is.'

'The same?'

'Worse. The more I try to do things myself, the more wobblies she throws. You wouldn't believe the fight I had just to drive down to pick Dan up. You see, all I've got of my own is my piano-playing. If I can make another CD, by myself, rather than involving her – if you see what I mean – and if it sells well, that will give me something to start me off.'

'Are you saying that you want to move out?'

'I don't know how I can, but . . .'

'Ali, you know I can't promise anything yet, but I'm more

than happy to consider it, if we can get the whole package right.'

'There are a few things I'd want,' Alicia says, her tone staying firm, though she doesn't feel so firm inside. 'I'd want the final say on the cover. I'd want to play pieces *I* choose, though I accept that you'd want them to be well known. I'd want it to be a serious, upmarket CD, and there should be proper coverage in the music magazines.'

Rebecca sits back in her chair and stares at Alicia with her head to one side. Alicia pauses, wondering whether she's gone too far.

'Good for you, Ali,' Rebecca says. 'Debussy and Ravel, you said?'

'Yes, I'd love to do that. Nothing too obscure, I promise. Maybe *Images* and *Gaspard de la nuit.*'

'I like that. If you're serious, I can pitch the idea at our next planning meeting and we'll take it from there. What would you tell your mother?'

'I'll think of something.' Alicia breathes again. There are ways. There have to be ways. It's up to her to find them. 'I don't know what's got into Mum,' she says. 'It's always been difficult, but . . .'

'I know that she'd lay down her life for you. And she's a woman of integrity. That can mean, though, that she's almost too consistent for her own good. It's understandable, of course, if you think of what happened to her before.'

'Before what?'

Rebecca stares at her. Alicia stares back. Beside Alicia, Dan shifts in his chair.

'You don't know?' says Rebecca.

'Know what?'

'Oh, God.'

'What is it, Becs?'

'About Victoria.'

'Who's Victoria?'

'Oh, God,' Rebecca says again.

Alicia feels the blood draining away from her head. 'Whatever it is, please tell me,' she says. 'I think I need to know.'

'So she's never . . . Don't worry, Ali, it's nothing that affects you directly. It's all a long time ago. Are you OK?'

'Yes.' Alicia, pale, sits forward and waits. Dan reaches for her hand.

'Before Adrian, your parents had another baby. She was born very prematurely and she died when she was a few weeks old. Her name was Victoria. It was extremely hard for your mother to get over it, and if she's a little over-protective of you, you only have to remember this to realise why.'

Alicia stays silent. She stares at her hands, folded in her lap, one of them encircled by Dan's.

'Oh, my God,' she says eventually. 'Poor Mum. Why on earth didn't she tell us?'

'I expect she didn't want to upset you.'

'Was that when they were still in London?'

'Yes. It's partly why they moved to Derbyshire.'

Alicia's eyes fill with tears.

'It's so weird,' she says to Dan later, walking back to the high street. 'It happened before I was born, but it seems to have affected everything about the way she treats me.'

'Has it, though?' Dan says. 'Isn't it maybe what she was always like, potentially – except that it's been accentuated through losing the baby?'

'I don't know what to think.'

'Nor do I. I've only seen her at Moorside and I guess she was right to be keeping an eye on you then!'

'Dan . . .' Alicia unlocks the car. 'What *did* you make of my mum at Moorside?'

Dan is quiet for a minute. Then he says, 'I thought she was basically a very good person. Complicated. But good. Caring. Solid.'

'I think some people hate her.'

'Maybe that's why she likes me. Because she can see I respect her. People always think that music mums are pushy for the heck of it, but there's got to be a reason you've done so well. You can't succeed at anything unless you've got some kind of support pushing you along.'

'She certainly does that,' Alicia growls.

'But would you have done all you have without that? Think about it.'

Alicia thinks. 'I don't know,' she admits.

'So, Al. Let's go home.'

21

FROM: Dan Rubinstein
TO: Judy Rubinstein
DATE: 1 July 2004
SUBJECT: Hi from Derbyshire

Hi Mom,
I'm going to delete this message the moment I've sent it because
I'm using Ali's computer and I don't like the thought of her
reading it.

You wouldn't believe this place. It's a weird set-up. I'm trying
to stay sane – more important, I'm trying to keep Ali sane. I knew
she was over-protected and prodigy-mothered, but I hadn't
realised how much.

Ali turns eighteen the day after tomorrow. Her mom, Kate,
does all her career management now because the agent she was
with is on long-term sick leave. Kate books her masses of
concerts and Ali spends all her time working for them, because
although she's the biggest talent I've ever seen, she has a
conscience and she's afraid of not doing her best. She's also
preparing for Leeds.

It's not that I don't like Kate, because I do. She looks very
much like Ali; she has a lovely smile, when she remembers to use
it; and she'd do anything for that girl, and I mean *anything*. At
first I was amazed she let me stay in the house, but I think she
knows I really care for Ali. It's something we share and we respect
one another for that. She knows Ali could have gotten involved
with somebody far worse.

Ali's dad, Guy, is great. Warm, caring, extremely bright and he has a fantastic ear for music. He works round the clock and stays in Manchester several nights a week. He's supposed to take care of his heart, but I don't think he does. Ali worries; he always tells her not to. She says she hardly ever sees him. I guess Dad, if he psychoanalysed her, would say it's no wonder she's fallen for someone who lives 4000 miles away – she's used to never seeing the man in her life.

Her brother left home after a massive row with the parents. Ali sometimes sees Adrian on his own. I haven't met him yet, but on Thursday we're going for a curry with him in Macclesfield, and Ali's friend Anjali is coming too. Ali's been hinting that Anjali is sort of involved with Adrian, but I don't know how much, since she's from a strict Asian family and is meant to have an arranged marriage. Very complicated.

What bugs me is that these people never *talk* to each other. I know we joke about how English people drink tea and discuss the weather. Well, I come down in the morning and Kate says: 'Good morning, Dan, did you sleep well? It's going to be a beautiful day, I hope you and Ali will find time for a walk. Would you like some tea?' I'm not kidding.

The house is spotless. Everything is lined up straight and tidy and it smells of beeswax and pot-pourri. Every last inch is clean and tasteful. It feels like a showhouse for a real-estate firm, not a home. Ali's allowed to have mess in her room, but she has to keep the piano room tidy – she's in there practising most of the time. Kate isn't a bad cook, but she scrubs down the kitchen as she goes along. She'll chop an onion and while it's frying she'll clean the chopping board and rub down the work surface; then she'll slice some mushrooms and do the same thing all over again. And at the end of each day she takes everything, and I mean *everything*, off her desk. Apparently Guy's study is a disaster zone – at least that sounds human. Except for Ali playing the piano, there's a silence here that works its way into every corner of your brain. It's like a negative energy. A black hole. An absence of livingness.

Ali's incredible. I know you say I'm besotted and I'll come to my senses, but I swear to you, Mom, I'd rather die than come to my senses over her. I've never met such a good person. It's like she's from another era, another century, maybe another universe. She's pure gold and I'm almost scared to touch her in case I'd contaminate her with the outside world. I don't understand how her parents can live as they do and have a daughter like her. I don't see how they can have a daughter like her at all.

She's never had a boyfriend before – she said she 'nearly went out with someone at school once, but didn't'. She doesn't go to parties. Seems her brother took her to one and she was so sick afterwards that Kate hasn't allowed her to go to any more (not that she was meant to go to that one either; Adrian smuggled her out of the house! Can you believe it?!?). She never listens to pop music – she's not snobby, she's doesn't dislike it, she just isn't bothered about it. She doesn't even bother much with TV. She does her own thing and as she sees it, that's her business and no skin off anyone's nose. Anything else bounces off her. She must be incredibly strong and, inside, secure about who she is. I hope that's true – for her sake.

She loves movies and there's a video-rental place down the hill, so I've been showing her my favourites. Buxton doesn't have a cinema and although Ali could drive to Macclesfield or Stockport, she's got no one to go with. Sometimes she meets Anjali in Macclesfield, or Derby, which is about half-way between here and Birmingham, but they always eat Indian food rather than see a movie, so that they have a chance to talk.

Anyway, she practises such long hours that she doesn't want to sit still afterwards. When we go out, we go jogging together, or drive into the countryside and walk. The air is incredible, so fresh and clean. I always thought the UK was a polluted, over-crowded, grey island, but Derbyshire is unbelievably beautiful, although it's bleak and quite cold even now. The villages are cute and the hills are full of fluffy sheep. Everything seems tiny compared to home. It's like walking into a storybook. I keep expecting witches and hobgoblins to jump out and start doing little dances in the road.

People are friendlier here than in London. The day I arrived, Ali and I bumped into her first piano teacher from when she was three years old, and this lady said at once that I could go and practise at her house. Amazing – catch anyone saying that in London. Ali ought to move to London, but she says she'd miss the countryside. Now I can see why. At least she has that to keep her on an even keel, and her dog, Cassie – though the dog is ancient. She's like Ali's alter-ego – a sort of 'familiar'. I hope Ali will be able to handle it when Cassie goes to the great hunting-ground in the sky.

Of course Ali's naïve and not very well educated – she left school early – and in some ways she's young for her age. But she works so hard that she never stops to wonder why she's doing it, why she never has any fun, why she never goes out or meets other kids. It's not healthy for an eighteen-year-old girl. And yet she's perfect. She's a natural, loving, passionate, instinctive, strong-minded young woman – as well as an over-protected little girl and an extraordinary musician. I only hope I'll know her in ten years' time, and twenty, and thirty, so that I can watch her realising everything within her to the full, and help her. She's wonderful. All I can do, for now, is be there for her. I want to take care of her. I want to get her away from here.

Take good care, Mom. Give my love to Dad and Steph and write soon.

Love,

D x

Alicia believes that time doesn't exist, not in its expected form. It's infinitely malleable. Days shoot past when you have too much work, a deadline for a lesson, an impending international competition. When you're waiting for something, or someone, minutes drag like months. As for distance – if you love someone, distance becomes even less distinct than time.

It should be incredible that she and Dan get along so well. Technically, they have little in common except music. Dan grew up in a family that never fights, or so he says, in a country she's never visited, and he's Jewish, a race, religion or both of which Alicia knows nothing. But through their music, they share everything that's most important to them. They exist in harmony. They feel music the same way: when they listen to a recording or to each other playing, the expression on Dan's face mirrors exactly the emotion inside Alicia. Even their favourite composers are the same: Rachmaninov, Chopin, Debussy, Ravel and Beethoven.

They both like to get up early to go running. Mum's face, when she sees them heading out for a jog in the rain on Dan's first morning, jet-lag or no, is a sight to remember. Dan loves dogs, and Cassie is trying valiantly to adore him, though Alicia suspects she's jealous. And although Dan is cleverer than she is – he's feeding her countless books and films – being with him isn't like being with another person. It's so easy. As if someone's watching over them.

Backstage in Manchester, preparing for her Rachmaninov concerto, Alicia can't work out whether time goes too fast or too slowly. Before her first few concertos at major halls, she lay on the sofa in her dressing room, trying to imagine she was anywhere else but there; yet also she couldn't wait to go on stage and begin. The longer she has to hang around, the more drained she feels.

Today she lies on the floor instead, knees up and spine flat, head resting on a pile of programmes. Ian has told her that this position helps to straighten the back and let the tension sink out of the body into the ground. Mum, Dad, Dan, Adrian and Anjali all want to stay with her, but she won't let them. She delivers her best Greta Garbo impression: 'I want to be alo-o-ne!' That makes them laugh, which is important. They mustn't feel offended if she sends them away.

There's more tension than usual in her at the moment.

Whenever she closes her eyes, she starts thinking about Mum losing her first baby.

It's obvious that Mum didn't want her to know, so Alicia has kept quiet. She's told Adrian, whose expression showed little emotion, although he revealed that he'd unwittingly come across the grave, which bore signs of recent attention and a jar of faded anemones. She's talked to Dan at greater length; but, being an open, non-secretive American, he doesn't see why she won't talk to her mother. Alicia can't explain. The last thing she wants is to upset Mum – who is easily upset these days.

She wonders what her sister would have been like. She'd have been twenty-three now. Maybe she'd have been musical. She might have played an instrument, the violin or the cello. They could have been the Bradley Sisters Duo. She could have had a real friend – the sister she'd wanted so much – instead of feeling so alone. She and Adrian are close now, but they'd had to grow up first.

It's difficult to see how lonely you are if you're used to it. When you find you're not alone any more, that's when it hits you.

The first morning at six, before they went jogging, Dan slunk into her room and her bed. They lay still and held each other. Now every morning, before anyone else wakes up, he comes in and they have time in bed to be themselves together. They touch each other, but no more, because Dan says he doesn't want to rush her. Alicia doesn't think it would be rushing, given their year apart; it's not as if she doesn't want to make love with him. But if he prefers to wait, she'll wait. She closes her eyes: heaven. To love him and to be free to express that love is all she wants. Not the competition prize, not having her picture in the paper, not being asked for autographs. Stuff that. Being in love, being with the person you love, that's what life is for.

Her new-found love doesn't stop her going through the

routines required of her. Dan has remarked on how 'professional' she is, and it's true that aspects of performing have grown easier through habit. She knows that, on the morning of a concert, she must try everything through on the venue's piano and, if it's a concerto, rehearse with the orchestra as much as the conductor permits; after that, it's best to let well alone. If she works all afternoon, she'll end up exhausted and confused. She sleeps from about two o'clock for as long as possible; and however tempting it is to test the most difficult passages, she forces herself not to. If she doesn't know it by then, she never will. Warming up before the concert, she'll play anything except the piece she's about to perform.

The Tannoy alerts her with a call: 'Five minutes, please, Miss Bradley.' Alicia picks herself up and gives her hair a final shot of spray. Looking at herself in the dressing-room mirror under the rectangle of bare lightbulbs, she can hardly believe that this glamorous blonde woman is herself.

Dan has given her a wrap for her birthday – blue silk that he says is the colour of her eyes. It's not as warm as the woollen shawls Mum knits her, but it looks better and Alicia adores it. From now on, she will use nothing else. Tonight it's the last thing she puts down before striding on to the platform.

Leaving the stage with her arms full of bouquets as the applause subsides, Alicia knows she hasn't played her best. Her stomach is knotted with anxiety. The Bridgewater Hall is an important venue and she'd wanted it to go better. Her concentration isn't brilliant at the moment and she'd had some small memory lapses. Not many of the audience would notice – but a crucial few would.

Well-wishers surround her backstage, hugging and kissing her – she's convinced she doesn't deserve it. She puts on a stage smile, greets people, thanks them, trying to make them feel important. Inside, she's feeling slightly sick and faint, wanting to cry. Those months of work – and that was *it*?

Even Anjali, who knows this feeling better than anybody, scarcely notices her subterfuge – but that could be because Adrian has muscled through the crowd to monopolise her. Anjali looks stunning, slender and huge-eyed amid the throng. Perhaps, Alicia reflects, she's too delicate for a life as desta- bilised as a musician's. Her brother, tall and hunky and biker- rough at the edges, slides a protective arm round Anjali's waist. He glares sideways at Mum, but because it's Alicia's birthday, he's promised a cease-fire for the evening.

It's Mum who has to make a *thing* of the memory lapses.

'Ali, what happened?' she demands, as soon as Alicia has bundled everyone else out of the dressing room so that she can change.

'I slipped a bit.'

'You certainly did. Why?'

'Dunno. It happens.'

'Not to you it doesn't. What were you thinking about? Was it Dan? Because if it was, Ali, if he's distracting you from your work, we'll have to send him to stay somewhere else.'

'Mum, I'd be much more distracted if I was going some- where else to see him every day.'

'It's not good. It's ruining your concentration.'

'"It",' Alicia tells her, 'is the best thing that ever happened to me.'

'Not if you give a bad performance because of it.'

Alicia feels stuck. Dan hasn't been distracting her – anything but. He listens to her play and advises her. She does the same for him. They inspire each other, spur one another on. What's been distracting her is the thought of the unknown sister she'd lost; and the fact that Mum has never once mentioned her in all Alicia's eighteen years. If she's distracted, it's not Dan's fault. It's Mum's.

Anyway, she hadn't played that badly. It could have been a lot worse. She'd had to take six curtain calls.

'Mum, it's my birthday,' she declares. 'Can we save the recriminations for tomorrow, please? I'd like to be able to celebrate with my friends.'

'In other words, Dan.'

'Tonight was nothing to do with Dan!'

'Ali, don't shout at me.' Mum's eyes are wild with fury.

Dan must have been listening outside the door, because he comes striding in on cue and exclaims, 'Come along, ladies, break it up. Miss Bradley, your carriage awaits!'

They leave the hall by the artists' entrance at the back after the orchestra has started the second half. Didie and George hug Alicia, but then go home – Didie isn't in the best of health. Alicia doesn't know what's wrong: all they tell her is that Grandma is 'feeling frail', a term that could mean anything and fills her with fright. Nobody will say more, so she has, somehow, to live with the uncertainty.

Dad has decided to treat everyone to dinner at a busy, brand-new restaurant that offers a menu of English, Italian and Thai food rolled together into unpredictable delights. The party sits at a round table: Mum and Dad, Adrian and Anjali, Alicia and Dan, Ian and his wife Carole. Dad orders champagne.

'Daniel, why don't you make a toast for Ali's birthday?' he says gallantly. Thank God, Dad likes Dan. He won't hear a word against him. Alicia thinks she may have to leave it to him to make sure Mum doesn't throw Dan out.

Dan jumps up, tapping his glass. 'Ladies and gentlemen, I'll be brief,' he says, without a moment's hesitation. 'Here's wishing a very happy birthday to our wonderful Alicia! Al, you're a star. Tonight's your night. All together now!' He conducts 'Happy Birthday' and Alicia, embarrassed as the whole restaurant joins in, sits and radiates as best she can.

This should be the happiest day of her life: turning eighteen, having just played Rachmaninov's Third Concerto for the first time, surrounded by the people she loves most. But even now, she can't enjoy it as much as she wants to, because she knows she hasn't played well enough. While she kisses Dan and thanks everyone for their moral support, in the back of her mind she's wondering whether any of the critics noticed her duff up that bit in the last movement.

The restaurant door swings open and a youngish woman walks in. She looks familiar; Alicia can't place her at first, but it turns out she's one of Dad's journalists. She vaguely remembers that she'd come to dinner years ago, when Alicia was too young to join in. Alicia notices her eyes: huge and light, almost silver.

She's come to meet a friend, but spots them, as they are relatively hard to miss. Dad leaves the table and goes to talk to her; it looks like quite a deep discussion for a chance encounter, but oddly he doesn't invite her to join them. She leaves immediately; her friend, it seems, isn't there. Mum stares after her. Alicia thinks that Mum has started to dislike younger women, though the journalist had seemed so calm and self-possessed that Mum could have learned something from her.

In the car going home, Alicia leans on Dan's shoulder and pretends to be asleep. Between Kate and Guy hangs a silence the thickness of velvet curtains. Dan stares out of the window. The moor is bleak and empty, other-worldly under the glow of a full moon. He holds the not-asleep Alicia against him – he knows what she's up to, even though her parents don't – as if to protect her brightness from the encroaching night.

The silence goes into the house with them. It's one a.m.; they hadn't left Manchester until after eleven thirty. Adrian and Anjali, who'd lightened the atmosphere at dinner, had last been seen talking to one another across Adrian's motorbike – Alicia hoped he wasn't going to take her friend back to Birmingham on it – and Ian and Carole had embraced Alicia, then headed home to relieve their babysitter. Alicia knows that Ian will have heard every error in her performance; her next lesson will involve a detailed post-mortem.

'Something to drink?' says Kate, in the kitchen.

'Thanks, Mum, but I'm going to turn in.'

'Not even chocolate?' Chocolate is Alicia's usual wind-down drink after a concert.

'Thanks, Mum, no. It's too hot.'

'Dan?'

'I'm going to get some sleep too, thanks, Kate. Goodnight, and thank you for everything.'

They hurry upstairs before anybody can say more.

On the second floor landing outside their separate rooms, they stop and kiss for a long time.

'Goodnight, darling,' Dan says. 'You were wonderful. You played so beautifully. I'm proud of you.'

'Night,' says Alicia.

Now that she can throw aside her protective mask, a tide washes towards her: anxiety, terror, panic. Yes, she is distracted – haunted by her mother's silence and the image of a small girl who had never lived. In her bedroom, she pulls off her post-concert summer dress, plus her underwear, and tosses them on to a chair in the corner. She's too keyed up and too hot to sleep. She takes a book from her bedside table and tries to read, but she can't concentrate and she's sweating terribly. Nothing helps the pent-up howl in the pit of her stomach.

She puts down the book and lies flat, naked, on her bed, with her curtains open, letting in the moonlight. Eighteen, distracted and desperate. She turns on to her front, holds the pillow over the back of her head and screams into the mattress. It's a valuable release and she's certain nobody can hear her. She screams several times, then lets herself cry, sandwiched between mattress and pillow to muffle the sound. She wonders whether her mother had cried a great deal after her baby died. She doesn't know where the pain inside her has come from.

Because of the pillow, she doesn't hear Dan's tap at the door or his voice calling her. She doesn't know he's there until her bed depresses under his weight.

'I'm not decent,' she manages to sob into the mattress.

'You're extremely decent.' Dan is stroking her bare back with the tenderest touch she's ever felt. 'What's going on?'

'Oh, everything. Mum. Rachmaninov. Dad. Leeds.' Alicia turns her gaze, though not the rest of her, towards him. She sees his eyes, black in the silver moonlight, caressing her face.

'Is your mum right? Am I distracting you? Al, this is it, you know – Leeds is your big chance. You've got to give it everything.'

'Don't you start. You sound like Mum.'

'Something's not right. Is it me? Because if it is . . .'

'No!' Alicia wails. 'It's not you. It's all kinds of things. Mum, mainly, and what – what Rebecca told us in London. I was so upset. It's got under my skin.'

'That happened a long time ago. You must try to put it aside. Yeah?'

'Dan, what if I screw everything up? What am I going to do? You know what happened to Anji last year. If that's going to happen to me . . .'

'It won't. I promise.'

'But what if it *does*?'

'Ssh,' says Dan. 'You're going to be fine.' He runs his hand up and down the full length of her spine, comforting and calming her by the second. She's forgotten to be shy about wearing nothing. 'My God,' he whispers. 'You're lovely. You're so beautiful.'

'Dan,' she breathes, closing her eyes.

'Do you want me to go?'

'*No.*' She turns over at last, lifts an arm towards him. He swings his legs on to the bed and gathers her to him, his lips in her hair and under her ear. The kiss on her neck is like tiger balm. Now, finally, she thanks heaven, and her mother, for having stopped Lucien. She reaches for his belt and undoes the buckle, and the button and zip below, because they both know they can't wait for each other for one more second. And when he comes into her, he's so gentle that the taking of her is not his possession but her gift. The tenderness shocks her, submerges her. Tears spring to her eyes while she moves with him, in consonance. Such unimaginable beauty, then, does exist; it's not confined to music. It's real.

Later, they lie still, getting their breath, half dozing, holding each other. Outside, the full moon hangs over the hills – not blood red this time, but a rich, deep gold.

'You know?' Alicia says.

'What, love?'

'I wish we'd done this yesterday.'

'I wish we'd been doing it all year.' Dan flops on to his back and gives her the naughtiest grin she's ever seen. She giggles, trying to stay quiet. 'Why yesterday?' he asks, stroking her damp hair away from her forehead.

'Because I think I know what to do with the Rachmaninov now.'

'Oh, Ali,' Dan mumbles into her shoulder, eyes closed. 'I love you. This is the real thing. I'll never let you go.'

'I love you too, Dan. Much more than any piano concerto.'

Alicia folds herself round him and, in the soft light of the setting moon, they sleep together at last.

22

Now that it's late July, Kate thinks it's time Alicia pulled herself together. With less than six weeks to go until the competition, she's decided to learn to cook. It's the latest in a stream of activities that are not how a young pianist aspiring to Leeds should spend her time. All because of Dan, naturally. Kate watches Alicia perusing the latest Nigella Lawson recipe book, stripping skins off tomatoes, hunting hopelessly in the supermarket for watermelon, and despairs.

They both practise, of course. Dan is off to Glenda's house by nine o'clock most mornings – though it's been getting later recently – and after he's gone Alicia closets herself in the piano room and works all day, barely stopping even for lunch, unless she goes to Ian for a lesson. But when Dan returns, she starts behaving as if they're a newly married couple. Waiting on him. Touching him constantly. Making fancy dinners ('Mum, do they sell red mullet in Marks & Spencer?'). The sight puts Kate off Alicia's beautifully prepared offerings.

Ian, Kate thinks, is wonderful. She's kicking herself for not having taken his advice, for not sending Alicia to his music school, for not seeing sooner through Mrs Butterworth's dragonish smokescreen. Ian draws Alicia out, lets her be herself, helps her understand and solve her musical problems. He encourages rather than condemns, praises before dissecting, offers new thought processes leading to solutions she hadn't expected. Afterwards she's invigorated and inspired, not drained and tearful.

How could she have been so wrong about Mrs Butterworth?

It's not as if people – including Ali – hadn't tried to tell her. Was it that she knew Mrs Butterworth had lost a daughter? Did that give her some kind of idiotic, misplaced, kindred feeling for her?

No use crying over spilt milk, Kate thinks, knitting. Alicia is doing well with Ian. The immediate problem is how to keep the girl's mind on her work. Kate can hear, from office, kitchen and garden, that Alicia, practising, is repeating things automatically. She's not listening to herself with her usual acuity. She's drilling her muscles; but her imagination is in the stratospheres. She's in love.

Kate saw Dan's withering gaze when she encouraged Alicia not to go out for a day with him and Adrian and Anjali – and she can't deny that her daughter is old enough to drive to Macclesfield for a curry with her friend, brother and boyfriend. Still, a whole day at Chatsworth is too much, and finally Dan let Kate win – 'Actually, Al, your mother's got a point.' An unspoken bargain has materialised between Kate and Dan. He lets her win some battles on condition that, now and then, she concedes him a victory too.

Kate is under no illusions about what's going on upstairs. She hears footsteps at night, the loo flushing at odd hours, an occasional muffled laugh, the creak of a bedspring. Alicia is eighteen; Kate has no right to order her not to sleep with her boyfriend. If she has to have a boyfriend, thank God he's caring, intelligent, understanding and devoted to her. But the devil is in the detail, and the detail is in the timing. With six weeks until Leeds, Alicia is sleeping too little and daydreaming too much.

She takes Dan aside one morning while Alicia is in the shower, and explains rationally and reasonably, Alicia-lover to Alicia-lover.

Dan hears her out. 'I thought you might feel that way,' he admits, 'and I asked Glenda whether, if the need arose, I could rent a room from her for a few weeks. But I think it's a pity for Ali, because we'll have very little time together after Leeds – I have to go back to Indiana. I hear what you're saying, Kate, and I understand, but I'd ask you to think about it a little more, for that reason.'

'I've been watching Ali,' Kate says, 'and I've thought about it a great deal. I think you should give Glenda a call, then pack your things. I like having you here, Dan, but we can't take risks with the Leeds.'

'You know, of course, that it won't make much difference?'

'I think it will, Dan. Because at least Ali will get enough sleep if you're not here. She won't be staying at Glenda's with you.'

When Alicia bounds down, ready to begin her day's work, she finds Dan in the hall with his suitcases. 'What?'

'Your mom.'

Kate braces herself for the onslaught. It's bad: tears, shouts, accusations. Dan tries to calm Alicia, but she weeps as hysterically as if he'd announced he was going back to America, not just moving three streets away. Finally, screaming, 'You're not a mother, you're a *Kamp Kommandant*! Wait till I tell Dad,' Alicia grabs Dan's second suitcase and flies out of the front door. Dan apologises softly to Kate from the front steps, then hurries after her. They leap into Alicia's car and drive away.

Kate waits – picturing them crossing the moor, then crossing the country, putting the car on a boat and sailing to Norway or France or the Hook of Holland. But later there's the crunch of wheels on driveway and Alicia is back, alone, her face tear-streaked. Glenda had comforted them both with tea, and Dan gave her a deposit for the room.

'Wasn't that a little extreme?' Guy says, when he comes home at ten that evening to find Alicia and Kate sitting in silence in the kitchen, without Dan.

'Ali has got to get her focus back,' Kate says.

'Oh, Kate,' Guy says. '*Why?*'

★   ★   ★

Alicia picks up Dan at half past five the next day, once they've both put in enough hours at their pianos. They drive to Mam Tor and climb to the top.

'This is my favourite place in the world,' Alicia tells him. She watches as he absorbs for the first time the view she knows so well, drinking in the ancient hillscape and the spreading sky.

'I can picture you here as a little girl, in your wellington boots. And maybe a pink coat.'

'Yeah. I had a pink coat once.' Alicia leans her head on his shoulder.

'What are we going to do?' he says.

'I've got an idea. Somewhere we can go. I know all the back routes and the special spots that nobody else knows.' Dan's banishment means that now they have nowhere to make love, for Glenda's house is full of children and pupils and laundry, and Alicia has been issued with a curfew.

'It's left me even more sure than I was,' Dan tells her, while they walk back down the steps to the car. 'We gotta get you out of here. You have to have your own life – preferably with me – somewhere where people talk to each other.'

Alicia swerves off the main road on to a smaller one that skirts the hills with twists and deceptive turns; then a road that is smaller still, transforming itself into a muddy track beside a brook edged with long grass. They pass a group of stone cottages, a barking dog and a field in which some hot but contented sheep are grazing. She turns along another track and a bumpy minute later they reach its end. Here the brook widens into a natural pool beneath a hill; a clump of trees stands close and protective round it.

Alicia switches off the engine. Dan waits.

'What I don't understand is why you take Mum's part in this,' she says finally.

'What can I do, Al? It's her house. I'm a total stranger.'

'That's not the point. She's chucked you out because she doesn't want me to sleep with you.'

346

Jessica Duchen

'She never tried to stop us before.'

'Because she knew this was the only way.'

'Also, she's right. Leeds is important and you've got to get enough rest.'

'Not to the extent of being in bloody jail. And that's not the reason anyway.'

'What is the reason, then?'

'Don't you see, Dan? She's jealous.'

'What? Of us?'

'Well, of me. Having a gorgeous young lover. Maybe she even fancies you.'

'Ali!'

'I know Mum. I know her too well.'

Dan can't argue with that. Instead, he opens the car door and winks at Alicia.

In a clump of ferns, they throw on the ground the rug Alicia keeps in the boot (Adrian's advice is always to carry a rug, a torch, water and chocolate). Then they throw themselves after it. The landscape around them is deserted: they have no witnesses but a few coots on the water, some fat, late-summer bees and a buzzard gliding far overhead.

'I've always wanted to do this outdoors.' Alicia is kneeling upright on top, stretching out both arms to the sides and soaking up the dappled sunlight.

Her bare skin looks milky, translucent, as though she's never sunbathed in her life. Probably, Dan reflects, she hasn't. 'You only just learned how to do this at all,' he teases her.

'That doesn't mean I didn't want to!'

'Al, come with me to Bloomington.'

'*Dan.* How can I?'

'You talk to Feinstein. You apply. You send in a form and you do an audition so they can make sure you're sane. Then you look for a sponsor or a scholarship – or you get some prize money from the competition you *are* about to win – and, next thing you know, you're on the first plane west.'

'You think Mum will let me go? Do you know how many concerts she's got lined up for me next season?'

'She's nuts. If you win Leeds, you'll have so many concerts you won't know what's hit you. I hope she's left room for those.'

'Oh, God. It's going to be a mess.'

'No, it isn't. It's going to be wonderful.'

'I feel so lost. I don't know what to do.'

'May I make a suggestion?' Dan puts his hands on her waist and turns her over and down.

Walking into the house much later, Alicia confronts her mother's accusing gaze. She stops dead in the hallway. Dan's words about the way people in this house don't talk to each other ring in her mind. Strengthened by love, she no longer feels afraid.

'You've got something in your hair,' Mum says. 'It looks like a bit of fern.'

Alicia takes a deep breath and aims. 'Mum,' she says, 'if you think Dan is the distraction, you're wrong. It's something else.'

'What do you mean?'

'See if you can guess what I've learned.' Alicia makes sure that her tight lips rival her mother's.

'Alicia, what are you talking about?'

'I'm talking about Victoria.'

Mum's colour drains. She's struck silent.

'I need to know things, Mum.'

An avalanche is taking place behind Mum's inscrutable expression. 'Ali,' she says, 'let's sit down a minute.'

They go to the kitchen. Alicia sits at the table. Mum stands behind her so that Alicia can't see her face while she talks.

Alicia listens. She accepts that Mum is leaving nothing out: the difficulty of conceiving, the hated job, the hospital, the flat, the brief little life and its snuffed-out ending, the months of depression afterwards.

'And then,' she finishes, 'your father got a job at the *Manchester Chronicle,* so we moved here and I moved her grave with us.'

'Oh, Mum,' Alicia says, no longer angry but tearful, 'why didn't you tell me?'

'It's a long time ago, love. It's best put behind us.'

'I wish I'd known. All I've been able to think of these past weeks is that I might have had a sister, I mightn't have been so lonely. I've been maybe a substitute for her and no wonder you won't let me out, no wonder you worried whenever I had so much as a cold. It helps me understand. I wish you'd said something years ago.'

'Darling, I did what felt like the right thing at the time. And if I'd had my way, you certainly wouldn't have found out now. When did Dad tell you?'

'He didn't. It was Rebecca.'

'*Rebecca?*'

Alicia explains; as she speaks, a peculiar light of under-standing dawns in Mum's eyes. 'Mum?'

'Nothing. Nothing at all . . . Ali, do you think you can get through it now? Do you think you can stop feeling unsettled and get your mind back on to your work now we've had this talk?'

'I'll try,' Alicia promises.

Kate drags herself into her office. The summer evening is fading into night. She sits for a while without turning on the lamp. Finally she reaches for the phone.

'Rebecca? It's Kate . . . Yes, *that* Kate.'

She doesn't stop to think about what Ali is doing while she's gone. She hits the M1 at Derby and makes for the fast lane. Thanks to summer holidays, the London-bound carriageway isn't as clogged as it might have been. Kate has hardly slept. Probably Ali hasn't either, but Kate hadn't waited for her to wake up before she left. Guy has no idea what's happened as he's stayed in Manchester and hasn't called her. Nor is she about to call him at Emily's.

Her mind buzzes like a swarm of wasps while she walks up Kensington High Street. It seems like someone else's hand that presses the bell at the Eden Classics office; another woman, not Kate Bradley, who announces herself to the receptionist and waits, legs crossed, on the leather sofa; and herself merely acting herself when Rebecca appears on the stairs and says, acting too, 'Kate. Do come up.'

Kate thinks, following her, that Rebecca hasn't changed; but in her office, seeing her in the sharper light from the window, she realises that's not true. Rebecca's eyes have grown intent and troubled; she's also thinner. To judge from the ropes that have taken up residence in her arms, she must have been going to the gym even more than usual.

'Ellie will bring coffee,' Rebecca remarks, settling businesslike at her desk. Kate, opposite, sits up straight, puts both feet flat on the floor and stares between Rebecca's eyes.

'So, Kate.' Rebecca moistens her lips. 'I hear nothing from you for nearly a year. Now suddenly you need to see me within twenty-four hours. What's going on? Is this about Ali's new recording?'

'Ali isn't going to make a new recording,' Kate announces, 'but that's not the point. She's a naïve girl. She always thinks the best of people.'

'How nice that *somebody* does.'

'Rebecca, why the fuck did you tell Ali about Victoria? How dare you?'

'Calm down, Kate. Please. It was a mistake.'

'Mistake, my foot. You knew I'd never told them because you asked me, at Chatsworth, the day I made the mistake of telling *you*.'

'But you didn't say they didn't know. You only said, 'We never talk about it.' And I would have thought that since they're grown-up—'

'Oh, you would, would you? Do you have any idea what's been happening since Ali found out? She's not herself. She's distracted. She's having memory lapses. You read the reviews of the Rachmaninov the other week. Don't tell me you didn't.'

'Isn't she preoccupied with the lovely Dan?'

'She says something else is bothering her. The idea that she might have had a sister. Wondering why I never told her. It's affecting her seriously, Rebecca, and don't you tell me you didn't know exactly what you were doing. You can't have Ali, so you've sabotaged her.'

'Kate, hold on.'

'Don't tell me to hold on! You've got the opposite of the Midas touch, Rebecca. You turn everything that's good and beautiful into cheap, third-rate trash, including my daughter.'

'I didn't invite you here so I could listen to this.' Rebecca stands up and makes her way to the door.

'I haven't finished.' Kate seizes Rebecca's wrist, pulling her hand away from the knob.

Rebecca is shocked out of the remnants of her cool. 'I don't have to listen to your crap! You've ruined your family with your lies and your stiff upper lip and your pretending. No wonder your son won't talk to you. No wonder Ali's having problems. It's incredible that any of you manage to stay out of Phyllida's clinic. I'll ask her to put the lot of you on the waiting list.'

Kate hears a noise like a whiplash: her hand against Rebecca's face. Rebecca recoils, clutching her cheek, which bears a red blotch. Silent, she retreats to her chair and puts her head down on the desk.

Kate picks up her handbag.

'Katie. Please don't go.'

Kate stares, contemptuous, at the curve of Rebecca's back.

'You don't understand,' Rebecca says. 'Please don't go.'

'I understand perfectly. Goodbye.'

'No. Listen. You've *no idea*. And if I don't tell you now, I never will. I don't know if I have the courage, but it can't make things worse.' She looks up. Kate is so startled by her expression, not to mention her words, that she stops dead.

She feels peculiarly detached. What a mad, operatic situation – on what is otherwise a plain, sunny summer day off Kensington High Street, with the area's workers, shoppers and tourists going about their business untroubled. Everything is normal around her. Nice and normal.

'I don't know what you're blabbing on about,' she says, staying detached, 'but if you've got to tell me something, then do it, because I'm not coming back.'

'Katie, don't you know?' Rebecca says, her hands cupped over her face. 'Have you no notion of how I feel about you?'

'What?' Despite herself Kate sits down.

'Christ, Kate. Am I such a good actress? I don't think so. I've tried to hide it for a long time. But it's no good.'

'Rebecca, are you saying what I think you're saying?' Rebecca takes down her hands. Kate sees in her eyes a type of anguish that she's only seen once before: on her own face in the mirror after she'd discovered Emily Andersen's emails. 'Becs. No.'

'I think, though I didn't know it at the time, that it was from the first day at college.'

'Don't be silly.'

'No. I swear. I knew there was nothing I could do about it. I saw you and your strait-laced, conservative, churchy, terribly-terribly family. The way you were set on marrying Guy from the start. I knew it was impossible. But we were talking in your room the first day, and you were telling me about your viola and how much you'd loved playing in your youth orchestra, and I suddenly saw something. It wasn't just the physical you, it was something in your soul.'

'Insane gibberish.'

'I'll only say this once, Katie. I love you. I only want what's best for you. I thought that if I could help make Ali a success then the money would mean you could get away from Guy and then maybe you'd understand. It wasn't that I expected you to change . . .'

Kate walks over to the window and presses her forehead against it. This can't be real, she reflects. Things like this don't happen to me. I'm Katie Davis from Harrow. I'm Kate Bradley from Buxton. Other women do not fall in love with me. Other women do not destroy my daughter by accident or design in an attempt to get closer to me. She wonders frantically whether to call a doctor, who'd bring a tranquilliser – maybe two tranquillisers; alternatively, the police.

'Becs,' she says, 'what do you expect of me?'

'Nothing, I've never expected anything.'

'In an ideal world, what would you want of me?'

'An ideal world . . . Oh, Kate, it's not an ideal world. End of story. Satisfied?'

'You haven't felt this way since college. It's not possible.'

'I managed to forget about you. I kidded myself into getting married and having the boys. I can't tell you what a relief it was when I threw *him* out. It took me years, decades, to be comfortable with who I really am. There've been others. Plenty of others. Meeting you again, it was different – but also, it was the same. Katie, if I'd had a choice, I promise I'd have chosen otherwise. Just because you haven't experienced something, just because you close yourself to anything beyond what you think is *normal*, that doesn't mean it can't happen to other people.'

Kate holds on to the window-frame with one hand, watching the scene outside. By the end of the road, on the high street, a double-decker bus has half pulled in to a stop, blocking the traffic behind it. A stream of passengers waits at its door: black, white, Middle Eastern, Oriental, some wearing jeans and skimpy T-shirts, others swathed in *hijab* headscarves. You see everything and everyone in London. Around the obtruding bus, drivers are hooting.

'What are you thinking?' Rebecca asks.

Kate watches the bus close its doors and move on. Millions of people, billions in the world, each one living a drama unlike any other. Each a unique mix of world events and intimate psychology, the product of generation upon generation that has struggled or oppressed, survived or squandered, created or destroyed, no two exactly the same. I will soon be fifty, Kate thinks; the world is a different place from the world where my parents grew up. Why should it matter to anyone if my son won't speak to me, my daughter is a musical genius, my husband has a second family, and now my oldest friend tells me she's a lesbian and is in love with me? Why should that be any more extraordinary than the story of any one of those people boarding the number-ten bus on Kensington High Street on a summer afternoon?

'Katie,' Rebecca says, emboldened by Kate's silence and the way she's leaning against the window, 'have you ever stopped to think about who you are? Not who your parents want you to be. Not who you think you have to be for your husband and children. But who you are. Yourself in essence.'

'I've never had time,' Kate says, without turning. 'And, frankly, I've never seen the point.'

23

As Bradley and Rubinstein, alphabetically distant, Alicia and Dan have been housed at opposite ends of the university hall of residence in Headingley. After unpacking, they meet downstairs and set off to explore Leeds.

'It's so cute. I can't get over it,' Dan remarks, looking around as Alicia drives.

'Cute? *Leeds?*' Alicia exclaims.

'Compared to where I come from. It's like being in a box of those things my dad used to collect – Dinky Toys. He had an uncle in London who used to send them over for birthdays and Christmas.'

'You were Jewish and you had Christmas?'

'Sure. Why not?'

'I don't know, I just didn't think you would.'

They chatter their way round the town centre trying to avoid discussing the matters that preoccupy them: pianos, repertoire and the other competitors. Nobody would have guessed they were musicians – but for the way Alicia taps her fingers, as if still practising. For the moment, they've escaped Kate.

After the initial euphoria, though, the intensity of what they must now do begins to dawn on them. Until they are knocked out of the competition, they will work all day every day, occasionally meeting their rivals at breakfast in the student canteen, where the young pianists discuss aching shoulders, repetitive strain injury, likely factions in the jury and fearsome tales from other contests. There'll be no relief from the stress.

Kate is staying at a bed-and-breakfast nearby and drives

over to meet Alicia before the day begins. She fields the attentions of the press officer; Alicia is one of only three British candidates and, with her well-known name, she's number-one target for interested journalists – especially since she's insisted on roping her 'partner', as she now calls Dan, into everything she does. It makes a wonderful story: a British prodigy and her American boyfriend pitted against one another in the country's premier piano competition. Such attention could be detrimental to Ali's concentration.

Leeds's more genteel suburbs are ablaze with enthusiasm for the event, a fixture decades old. Volunteers flock in to drive the contestants around, feed them, let them practise in their houses: Adopt-a-Pianist, Dan jokes. They're like exotic animals, he remarks, lent for temporary pampering. 'Afterwards,' he adds, 'we'll be released back into the wild.'

For daily practising, Alicia has been placed in the care of a retired couple, Leslie and Marina, who have both her CDs and are overjoyed to see her. Dan is down the road with a psychotherapist who owns a Bechstein grand; when she learns that Dan's father is also a psychotherapist, Dan is magically transformed into a member of the family. Glenda, meanwhile, phones him every day to see how he's getting on. Kate has been wondering, troublingly, whether she has ever been truly close to anyone except Rebecca, who fills her thoughts now. She's astounded at the way Dan can make friends so quickly, the way Alicia basks in his warmth, the way he seems so relaxed, practising as hard as anyone else but showing no sign of nerves, let alone competition with Alicia.

'She will,' he tells the journalist from the *Independent*, when she asks who he and Alicia think will win.

'Doesn't it put strain between you?'

'No, it's something we can experience together, something we can share,' Alicia declares. 'We share our dreams.'

'And if he gets through and you don't?'

'That won't happen,' Dan insists. 'Have you heard her play? She's incredible. She lights up the hall.'

Three days later the headline reads LIGHTING UP LEEDS: MUSIC'S NEW GOLDEN COUPLE.

Kate drifts on a lake of helplessness. She has never felt so spare. She takes Alicia and Dan out to dinner on the first evening, but the next day Leslie and Marina invite them for a meal, so she's redundant. The press officer quietly suggests that it might be best if she did not sit in on the interview for the *Independent*. When Alicia walks through the university campus on her own or with Dan, people bound up to her – other competitors, local fans, even one or two of the jurors. When Kate is with her, they don't. Kate can't even serve as chauffeur, since Alicia had insisted on bringing her own car, which, Kate senses, has come to symbolise freedom for her. Sometimes she wishes they'd never bought it.

To pass the time, she goes to listen to the other pianists in the first round, performing one after another in the university's Great Hall. It's not human, she reflects, watching a Russian girl strut to the piano at nine a.m. and play Chopin's Barcarolle. This music wasn't designed to be performed and appreciated in a draughty Victorian cavern at an unearthly hour, with a smattering of audience and a row of beady-eyed jurors listening for every fault. Surely this has nothing to do with music, its meaning, its communication? Whatever the critics thought about Ali's CDs, those discs existed to bring pleasure and insight to their listeners. They weren't part of any stressful, artificial Olympiad. But this is the nature of piano competitions, here and everywhere.

The pianists are good. Very good. Every one is a fully fledged musician, finely trained, determined and driven by vocation. But after the first round, just thirty-three will be left. Fifty-six will have to go home. By the concerto final, only six will remain.

Kate tries to concentrate, but it's not easy. Before long the pianists begin to merge in her mind. The perpetual onslaught of the piano sets up a ringing inside her ears. She starts to take longer coffee breaks – perhaps it doesn't matter if she doesn't hear every last performer. Sipping coffee in the competition tea room, she tries to shake off the strain. She wonders how the jury must feel if that's how she reacts, simply as someone's mother. And how frightening to think that at almost every piano competition in every corner of the globe young musicians are facing this same situation again and again, fighting simply for the chance to be heard, while the outside world shows ever fewer signs of caring twopence for their hard-won art.

The competition's octogenarian founder, Fanny Waterman, is chairman of the jury, a fierce, intently focused figure; beside her sits Dan's professor, Eugene Feinstein from Bloomington. Feinstein, his face remarkably youthful despite his age, has bright blue eyes and a ready smile. Now and then, when they encounter a moment of boredom or depression, he leans across to his fellow jurors and makes them laugh.

Guy phones Alicia every evening, but he's not coming to the competition. He doesn't have time. Alicia's face had shown pain as clear as Buxton water when she discovered he wouldn't be there. Of course, Kate thinks bitterly, if she gets to the final, he'll come to that. When it's important enough.

Alicia is to take her turn shortly before dinner on the third day. Kate feels someone sit down next to her after the tea break. She turns: it's Anjali.

'Darling!' she exclaims. Anjali hugs her. She's looking thinner than ever, Kate notices, and her eyes are bright, though not with happiness.

'I haven't missed her, have I?' Anjali asks. 'The bus was late.'

'No, she's on third.'

Dan clatters across the chairs to join them. 'How're you doing?' he asks Anjali, hugging her.

'OK. Good to see you.'

Kate sees Dan glance at Anjali with the shrewd look that she, for one, has learned to respect. Dan sees things as they are; you ignore that gaze at your peril.

'I can't tell you how glad I am not to be doing this,' Anjali whispers.

'I wish I weren't,' Dan grunts good-naturedly. 'Anji, how's your dad?'

Kate has become used to seeing pain on Alicia's face at the mention of her father, but that pain is only a fraction of what she sees on Anjali's now. All Anjali says, though, is, 'Oh, I'll tell you later.'

Alicia sails across the platform as naturally as a dolphin amid phosphorescent waves. Thanks to her substantial performing experience, she looks more at home on stage than off it, unlike some of the others. She launches straight into Beethoven's Sonata Op.90. Kate relaxes. Alicia's playing at her best, bringing the mood, the tension and the layers of melodic lines into vivid relief, the tone rich and the phrasing, in Kate's opinion, perfect. Kate notices Fanny Waterman sitting forward, her laser-beam gaze on Alicia's every move. Eugene Feinstein folds his arms behind his head, a broad smile on his face.

Kate smiles too. What audience there is has come to be supportive; Ali's host couple, Leslie and Marina, are watching her as if she's the Angel Gabriel. She senses Dan sending energy to Ali, experiencing every note with her, and she feels a rush of gratitude towards him. Everyone there, apart from the jury, is on Ali's side. At least Mrs Butterworth has not staged an invasion, something Kate had dreaded. She is rumoured to hate Leeds with a passion – the result, according to Ian, of never having been invited to sit on its jury.

Kate had also half dreaded – irrationally – that Rebecca would turn up, because she can't cope with the thought of what might happen if she did. Rebecca's image flickers in her mind when she wakes up in the morning and when she attempts to sleep at night. She tries to concentrate on Ali playing Chopin's A flat major Étude. A simple, tender melody sails over an inner waterfall of sound, a countermelody flickering like a broken reflection in the tenor register beneath the surface. She remembers Ali listening, entranced, as Guy played Chopin all those years ago; she'd called the composer Mr Shopping. Little Ali with her golden hair, her dog, her instinct for love.

Alicia walks off stage. The next contestant walks on. Kate, Anjali and Dan slink out of the hall.

'Thank God that's over,' says Alicia, when they find each other. 'Anyone want to go and eat?'

On the way out, they bump into two Russian contestants with whom Dan has struck up a friendship, and invite them to come out for curry. Anjali knows the best Indian restaurants in Leeds, so she goes with Kate to direct her; Alicia drives behind them, with a carload of pianists.

The restaurant's red walls are decorated with paintings, for sale, by a local artist. Dan and the Russian girl, Natasha, enthuse about them. Alicia stares at Natasha – tiny and fair, with a charming Russian accent. Natasha clearly likes the look of Dan, which in turn doesn't much please the Russian boy, Sergei. Who'd be their age again, thinks Kate.

Not that things change that much, deep down. She may be forty-eight, but since her encounter with Rebecca in London, the heart that she'd thought sclerotic has been showing her that it's still capable of the flaying emotion, comprised of pain, wonder and confusion, that seems so terrifying when you're young, despite its beauty. The only difference, being older, is that you should know what to expect next, more or less. She is on such new emotional territory, though, that ideas about the next step elude her. She doesn't believe in half of the shadows her mind is casting across her. It's not possible to feel such things for a former friend, another woman. Not for her. So she reminds herself countless times each day; but again and again, her dreams tell her different stories, leaving her frightened, mystified and wakeful.

Sergei is saying that he isn't Russian at all. 'I'm a Tatar,' he declares, 'like Rudolf Nureyev.'

'So your ancestors have probably killed mine,' Natasha points out, fending off his attentions. 'I am ethnic Russian,' she explains to the others. 'Is not as common as people think.'

'Come on, your people oppressed mine for centuries!' Sergei protests. 'We Tatars endured so much abuse, we were the poor servants, the bloody foreigners, the outsiders.'

'I thought the Tatars were warriors.' Alicia beams at him. Sergei is extremely good-looking: his eyes are as black as night. 'Didn't they have a reputation for marauding?'

'That's us. Marauding Tatars! Yes, we were horsemen and warriors.'

'And Muslims.' Natasha wears a large jewelled cross round her neck.

'Muslim Schmuslim.' Sergei winks at Dan, who's been having fun teaching him a little rudimentary Yiddish. 'I don't believe in any religion crap. Look what religion's done to our world.'

'I am devout Orthodox Christian.' Natasha has a limited sense of humour.

'Hey,' Dan interrupts, 'you guys think you oppressed each other? What about what all you lot did to my ancestors in the Ukrainian *shtetls*? When you weren't busy killing each other, you were raping and murdering my great-great-grandparents.'

'And what about the British Empire, oppressing everyone else?' Sergei takes over. 'You, ladies,' to Kate and Alicia, 'are from a background that made a big, big mess out of America and the Middle East and India! So anyone here who wasn't oppressed by you –' pointing at Natasha '– was oppressed by *you*!' indicating them.

'Even we're not that English,' Kate interjects. 'My grand-parents had blood that was Celtic, French and Scandinavian.

If you go far enough back, there's no such thing as "English". We're a great big mix of the different cultures that have settled here over the centuries.'

'Just think where we all come from,' Anjali says, declining Natasha's offer of a poppadom. 'Look at this table. We're a British Indian, a Tatar, an ethnic Russian, an American Jew and two English-ish women, sitting in an Indian restaurant run by Pakistanis in Yorkshire, arguing about who oppressed whom the most! Do you realise this is probably the only time in history when tonight would have been possible?'

'And we're all united by one thing,' Sergei adds. 'We're only here because we love music.'

'If you think about it,' Alicia says, 'music is one of the greatest forces for good in the world. It brings people together, like us, when we'd have nothing in common otherwise. And I remember Dad talking about a journalist who'd been to Sarajevo to watch a music-therapy project for children traumatised in the war – she said music helped them in a way that nothing else could. Music does so many positive things, but it gets bad publicity because there's this daft idea that it isn't "cool". What's "cool" anyway? It's so stupid. It doesn't mean anything. It just comes from people who started out as bullies in the school playground. People who didn't like anyone who was a little different.'

'Is it true that someone at your school put glass in your handbag, Ali?' Sergei asks.

'Yes. I've still got a bit of a scar. Look.' Alicia holds her hand out towards him and points.

He draws in his breath. 'This is crazy. In Russia we have special music schools. People love music and respect musicians. It's a great tradition, a big talent and a lot of work.'

'Oh, people love and respect music and musicians here too,' Alicia says, 'but only as long as you're not too good at it.'

The food arrives, a selection of steaming wonders: chicken in a sauce rich with coconut and almonds, lamb amid onions and tomatoes, a tandoori dish, trays of golden pilau rice, spiced spinach and potato, a vegetable biryani for Anjali, who doesn't eat meat, and several broad, bumpy naan breads. The pianists fall upon the feast in delight. Kate and Anjali smile at each other.

'What's going on with your dad?' Kate asks her.

'It's bad.' Anjali stares into her plate as if she isn't seeing it. 'It's very bad. Has Adrian said anything to you?'

'Adrian doesn't talk to me.'

'Silly boy,' Anjali sighs. 'Well, my dad doesn't want me to talk to Adrian. He doesn't want me to go out with English boys. What am I supposed to do? I live in Britain. I grew up in Britain. We left India when I was two years old and I went to a British primary school and a British boarding-school, and this is my country. Now he wants me not to be part of it, not to behave like other girls. I asked him, "Daddy, if you want me only to be Indian, why didn't we stay in India? Why do we live in Birmingham? And why do you want me to be a pianist, to have a career playing Western music, if I can't have a Western life too?" But he's so angry. I'm afraid every time I go out anywhere. I'm afraid whenever my mobile-phone bill arrives that he'll grab it and see how many times I've called Adrian.'

'You have to move out, Anji,' Alicia says.

'At least I'm going to uni next month but he expects me to go home every weekend. Because it's only Manchester, you see, he thinks that nothing will change. He'll still be in charge of me.'

'And your mom?' Dan asks.

'There's nothing she can do. She's under his thumb. If things are bad she'll hug me and comfort me, as long as he doesn't tell her not to. If he does, she'll listen to him.'

There's a moment of shocked, depressed silence.

'But he was always so kind to me,' Alicia says. 'He was so friendly when we came to visit. I thought you were the perfect family. I was envious that your father was so much with you and so interested in what you did.'

'Yes, and he loved it when I was best friends with the Young Musician of the Year. Now I'm friendly with her brother, he doesn't like it so much.'

'So he has this idea of what your life should be, and all of a sudden you're not complying with it any more,' says Dan.

'Exactly. And he can't talk about it with me. All he can do is be angry.'

'Children never *do* do what parents think they should,' Kate points out.

'Not even me?' Alicia ripostes. Kate winces at the sarcastic edge in her voice.

Just then the waiter comes over, carrying two bottles of red wine. 'Excuse me, madam,' he says to Alicia, 'the two gentlemen at the table in the window have asked me to bring these to you and your friends.'

Dan jumps to his feet and goes over to the two men: they turn out to be retired locals who adore the competition and attend every round. They've been listening since the start, and correctly identify all four pianists, remembering exactly which pieces each has played. There's much pouring of wine, glass-raising and toasting and, in the general geniality, the moments of darkness slide away, at least temporarily forgotten.

Three days later the pianists accepted for the second round are announced. Alicia, Dan and Sergei are through. Natasha is not, although she'd reached the semi-finals at a Russian competition, one of the biggest in the world, where Sergei had been eliminated in round one.

'Her teacher is like the Mafia there.' He shrugs when Alicia expresses astonishment. 'Of course she got through and I didn't. In Russia it's impossible to get anywhere in a competition unless you have the right teacher.'

'Seriously?'

'Of course. Didn't you *know?*' Sergei gives Alicia a withering look.

'I don't really know anything,' she says, making herself smile. 'I just play the piano.'

'You'd better learn something, my girl. It's a tough, nasty world.' Sergei shakes his head. Alicia watches him walk away and bites her lip.

'Do you think that sort of thing goes on here?' she asks Dan, squeezing into her hall-of-residence bed with him that night.

'I bet there are people who think I got through because Feinstein is on the jury.'

'Oh, Dan, you didn't, did you?'

'What do you think? You heard me.'

'I thought you played *wonderfully.*'

'Not that you're biased.' Dan presses his nose to her neck. 'Tomorrow I'm going to introduce you to him properly. Now so many people are going home, it'll be a little easier to catch him with some time.'

'Dan? I played OK, didn't I?'

'You played like an angel.'

'I didn't have any of the problems I thought I'd have. And you know why? I think being away helps. Not being stuck at home in that – that *house.*'

'Being able to spend the nights with me?'

'I like that too.'

'Come on, love, it's nearly two o'clock. We'd better get some sleep.'

Alicia turns off the light. 'Trouble is, Dan, right now I prefer being awake to being asleep.'

Kate, lying under a thin green sheet in the bed-and-breakfast, is having the opposite problem. She longs to sleep, but can't. When she dozes, she dreams: she, not Alicia, is on the platform, playing in the competition, and the jury consists

of her parents, her children, Guy, Lucien, Rebecca and
Victoria. She hasn't learned the music they expect her to
play, and she knows she will lose her way and make mistake
after mistake.

She'd felt like a spare part at dinner and hasn't felt much
better since. Everyone else is looking after Alicia: her boyfriend,
Leslie and Marina, the new friends with whom, despite the
competitive situation, she's enjoying a social scene she's rarely
encountered before. Kate has work to do – organisation for
the season ahead – and Cassie has to go to the vet for a check-
up on her arthritis. Alicia doesn't need her. Perhaps she should
go home.

She's trying harder than ever not to think about Rebecca.
Let that particular cat out of its bag and it will grow into a
tiger; nobody will ever be safe again. Perhaps I'm going crazy,
Kate thinks, falling asleep at last.

'Gene,' says Dan, standing in a splash of sunshine outside the
hall, 'this is Alicia.'

Eugene Feinstein smiles down at her – he is extremely tall.
She has never seen such an intent face or such bright, *seeing*
eyes. It's as if he's trying to assess the complete span of her
mind in a single glance. 'How nice to meet you,' he says. 'Dan
has been telling me about you. I understand you may want
to come to Bloomington.'

'Well, yes, if my mum'll let me,' Alicia says. She can't be
less than frank with this man. If she tries, his gaze will x-ray
through her.

'I hope you'll consider it,' he says. 'After hearing you play
the other day, I can tell you that I would be only too happy
to have you in my class.'

The class, he explains, is more than a lesson for each
student. It's a community under his guidance. Everybody
listens to every lesson; and beyond the studio they become
close friends, encouraging each other without any sense of

competition. If she were to go there, she'd be a 'freshman' while Dan, who's just graduated, is to start a masters' programme that will begin to qualify him to teach. But for Eugene, learning about music is learning about music: they work as a group, almost a team, benefiting from one another no matter their official placement.

'It sounds like *paradise*,' Alicia says.

Eugene Feinstein laughs. 'Well, maybe not,' he remarks, 'but I think, Alicia, that you'd like being with us in our little world; and you would get along easily with the others. We're all like-minded musicians. Your Beethoven told me everything I needed to know: you understand what it means to be in a state of grace – even if you don't realise that you understand.'

'How do you mean?' Alicia says, bemused, eyes shining.

'Come and join us, and you'll see. There'll be a place for you, if you want it. Good luck with round two.' He stoops and kisses her on both cheeks.

'Thank you, Professor Feinstein,' Alicia breathes, watching the lanky figure of Dan's teacher striding away.

'You see?' Dan says. 'He's a guru.'

'He's got an aura, hasn't he?'

'Exactly. And what we do in class is absorb it. It almost doesn't matter what he says. We learn from him just because he's him. He can spend two hours talking about the first line of a piece from every angle. Spirit, technique, sound, philosophy, history, literature. You name it, he does it.'

Alicia wonders how on earth she will get the words 'Mum, I want to study in the States,' past her lips. But she soon finds she doesn't have to – not yet. She waits for Mum. When she doesn't arrive, Alicia calls her mobile.

Kate has checked out of her bed-and-breakfast and gone home to Buxton. She says she'll come back for the semi-finals if Alicia gets through. Alicia is so startled that she almost cries. Five minutes later, though, she feels liberated; she wants to run headlong across the campus, throw herself into the air and fly, the way she used to dream of flying with Cassie towards the horizon.

'I've found a room with two pianos,' Dan tells her. 'Let's go and bash through some Rachmaninov.'

24

Alicia can't sleep. Her head is being assaulted by a muddle of music and new impressions that feels bigger than she is.

She's through to the semi-final. Dan isn't. Although he insists he's not disappointed, she's sure he must be. She declares that his elimination isn't fair; he insists she mustn't think about it, but simply concentrate on her own performance. At least, since he had been in the second round, he's allowed to stay and listen to the rest of the competition. But meanwhile pictures of the pair of them are everywhere. The newspapers love them, especially since Alicia is the only British pianist left in the contest, and a northerner to boot: a local heroine. Even Dad has swallowed his pride and run a story about them. They'd arrived virtually anonymous; now the whole of Leeds recognises them. The roller-coaster feels extreme even to Alicia.

When she does sleep, she dreams. About losing Dan in the current of a fast-flowing river. About Dad – that she's looking for him, can't find him and never will. About Mum – which is the worst because she's always doing something she would never do, such as trying to put a plastic carrier-bag over Cassie's head. She dreams about Cassie, dreading that she'll die soon. And she worries about Grandma Didie, whose health is deteriorating for reasons nobody will tell her outright, though Alicia has heard the word 'cancer' whispered when Mum, on the phone, thought she wasn't listening. Alicia can't imagine a life without Grandma or Cassie, but there will be one, and she can do nothing to

change that. She can scarcely bear her burgeoning consciousness of life's fragility.

She worries about Adrian and Anjali, because they're going
out together behind Anjali's parents' back. And more often
than not, they go out on the motorbike. Alicia knows that
Adrian doesn't have a licence. Everyone must assume that
he does – how else could he work in the shop, advise the
customers and hang out with Josh and his gang? With no
licence, Dan has pointed out, he probably has no insurance
either. Alicia once told Adrian he's crazy, but he shot back
that if she dares not get on the back of the bike for even a
short ride, she shouldn't order him about. She told him that
no way would she get on the back of a motorbike with
someone who has no licence and no insurance, even if he is
her brother. She'd warned Anjali, too, but to no avail. Adrian,
Anjali insisted, rides as if he's been doing it all his life; she
has absolute confidence in him.

It's nearly three a.m. Dan is asleep; Alicia watches him.
His breathing is quiet now that he's turned on to his side –
he only snores on his back. Fragility rips at the palms of
her hands; her eyes twinge with unshed tears. It's almost as
if the point of the world's existence and of the universe spinning through space is that he can be here and she can watch
him, love him, knowing that they belong together. She'd
never have believed she could love someone so much.

Mum, phoning her, had asked after Dan. Alicia told her how
supportive he is, how uncompetitive, how loving; and that even
if she gets nowhere in the competition, her weeks here with
him have been the happiest she can remember. She'd expected
a piano-focused tirade in response – but instead Mum just
sighed and said, 'Enjoy, darling,' her voice full of edgy longing
and regret.

Alicia understands. Such a love is something they may never
find again. Whether in the end they stay together or not, this
is an experience that she must treasure like sacred fire while

it lasts. She puts an arm over Dan's chest and closes her eyes.
She wonders, falling asleep, why Mum is changing.

On a cream-coloured sofa in Hampstead Garden Suburb, Kate
sits next to Rebecca. Table lamps cast bronze glints across
their nearly-empty wineglasses. The boys are spending the
weekend with their father; the two women are alone at home
for the first time. Now and then the blue eyes fix upon the
brown, wondering, frightened.

Kate's hands are twisted so tightly together that she's hurting
her wrists. She's not sure how she got there, how her resistance ran out, how Rebecca has coaxed her to London, what
may happen later, or how she will get through it, or, alternatively, escape, if it does. But there is another choice besides
fight or flight: acceptance. Acceptance with, possibly, joy –
assuming she can remember how to feel it.

'Have a little more wine.' Rebecca pours. 'I've got news for
you,' she adds. 'About Lucien. He's been a very naughty boy.'

'What? More than usual?' The distraction, for Kate, is
welcome.

'Oh, yes. He got a girl pregnant. A student.'

'Jesus.'

'She won't terminate. Lucien had to tell his girlfriend and,
of course, she left him right away. He's devastated.'

'That's his own fault, *n'est-ce pas?*'

'*Bien sûr*. Katie, I know Guy is a paragon in comparison,
but . . .'

'There's something you don't know.' Kate takes a long sip
of wine.

'What?'

'I shouldn't tell you this.'

'Oh, Katie. Out with it.'

Kate can't help herself any longer: she reaches out a hand.
Rebecca takes it. Their palms press together and Kate senses
a strength, a confidence, an honesty that reminds her of her

far-off early days with Guy. She begins to tell Rebecca about Emily Andersen.

'My God,' Rebecca says, at the end. 'Why didn't you kick him out?'

'I couldn't let him leave. Not with Ali's career at such a crucial stage.'

'And Ali doesn't know any of this?'

'Of course not.'

'Katie.' Rebecca interlaces her fingers with Kate's. Kate tenses. 'What exactly do you think she's going to do when she finds out? You can't keep it from her for ever.'

'Oh, Becs, I'm afraid I've done everything wrong, but I can't turn the clock back, I can't undo what's done and I can't do anything to put it right.'

'You could do some damage limitation. The way she found out about Victoria was bad – I'm guilty, I know, and I apologise. But you've got to stop it happening again. Once the competition is over, you must sit Ali down and be honest with her about her father. Next, you have to let him go. You'll be better off without him.'

'It's got to the point where I can't stand being in the same room with him, let alone the same bed. But it's been going on so long that I don't know how to change it. And if Ali wins Leeds, there'll never be a right time. Oh, God, how have I let things get so bad?'

'Hush, Katie . . . let me hold you.'

Kate flinches.

'Katie. It's not a big deal. We won't do anything if you'd rather not.'

Kate presses her hands to her face. 'Maybe it's not a big deal for you,' she says, 'but I've never slept with anybody except Guy.'

She looks at Rebecca's sinewy shoulders, her shiny, cropped hair, her open arms. Above all, the warmth in her eyes. The beseeching love that she sees there is real, and its existence casts her, spinning, into an unmapped solar system. Her instinct is to run. This is unfamiliar. Dangerous. Wrong, in a deep moral way.

Or is it? Is genuine love ever wrong? It's so rare. It's so precious; when you find it, how can you push it away? She can move forward, or she can move back. She's forty-eight years old, the mother of two young adults, yet she's trembling at the idea of touching another person for the first time. She begins to move back.

Then she moves forward. Normally, wanting anything so much makes her do the opposite, because it's too much to cope with. But now she understands she no longer has anything to lose. She lets herself go towards Rebecca; and she feels her silk blouse against her cheek and the gentle arms cradling her shoulders, and whatever is going to happen next, she's as terri-fied as if she's being led to the scaffold. Rebecca moves her mouth upon her own and for the first time the fear inside her begins to drown. Beyond the river is a new degree of hope that has nothing to do with her family, and everything to do with a self that she'd never known was there.

Adrian meets Anjali at Macclesfield station. It's Saturday, and as soon as he'd closed the shop, he'd hotfooted it to find her waiting for him near the ticket office. The blue gleam on her black hair, the sweetness of the light in her eyes when she sees him approaching, they thrill him every time. Adrian has gone out with plenty of girls, especially since he's joined the biking crowd and had a place and a salary of his own, modest though they are. But his little sister's best friend is different from the ones on whom he had, metaphorically speaking, cut his teeth. He'd lusted after pale bare legs, scarcely concealed by micro-skirts; midriffs gleaming beneath breasts enhanced with padded bras; straightened, lightened hair plastered with shiny stuff that reflects the glare in the clubs where they go to dance. Anjali is from another world.

She's a jewel to him, not just for the street cred he gains for being with an Indian girl, not just for her beauty, deepened by the tragedy that traces its shadow upon her face. He loves going to bed with her, even if he does have to take her home afterwards, but it's more than that: he loves her company. He likes having her beside him, with her sober expression that can unexpectedly blossom into a smile, her small hand resting quietly on his arm. How can she play the piano so well with such tiny hands?

After an hour or two in Adrian's bedsit, they take a shower together, then climb on to the bike and head up to the Cat and Fiddle for the evening. There they meet Josh and Charlie and their girlfriends, who are fascinated by Anjali's stories about the music school where she'd studied and her visits to her grandparents in India, where she'd had to avoid being matchmade. Adrian shows off about his sister, who's going to be on TV again – the Leeds semi-finals, in which she'll play tomorrow, will be filmed for broadcast on a BBC digital channel.

The evening had started warm. It is neither still summer nor quite autumn. The sinking sun melts gold over the moor and the scents of distant hay and damp earth are pungent in the air. The warmth vanishes with the sun and clouds start to blow in from the north; but inside the pub the group of youngsters is too absorbed in its conversation and its beer to notice.

Anjali sits with one hand on Adrian's leather shoulder. Their shadows on the wallpaper blend together, streamlined. The beer tastes malty and wheat-laden, refreshing after Adrian's long day minding the shop on his own (his boss is away in the classier part of Ibiza), not to mention the exertion of some fantastic sex. Tomorrow the guys are planning a race all the way across the moor. Adrian, Charlie and Josh talk biking gear and the crazy price of petrol. The girls swap stories about their summer holidays. Adrian sees Josh assessing Anjali. All he'll say will be 'Nice girl, that one,' but from Josh that's praise indeed.

A bell rings for last orders; after a final pint before closing time, they get up to go. The boys load the girls on to the backs of the motorbikes in the car park, where the rain has begun to form great puddles round them. The girls grumble about the wet weather; the boys steel themselves to be strong and capable.

'See you tomorrow,' Adrian shouts, waving to his friends.

'Mind how you go,' Charlie shouts back. Anjali, waving too, fastens the helmet that Adrian's lent her – it's a little too large, but then, as Adrian has joked many times, her head is a little too small.

'Hold tight, Anji.'

'Ready when you are!'

Adrian kicks the engine into gear and they're off on to the A537. It's almost midnight and the wind is rising. Her arms circle his waist, holding on tighter than usual. Adrian screws up his eyes; the road ahead is a blur of black Tarmac, sheep shit and rainwater. It's better travelling after dark, he always thinks, because at least when cars are coming you can see the headlights in good time. It's twilight that's truly deceptive, not the night.

'Slow down a little?' Anjali shouts through the wind, behind him.

'I want to get you home out of this rain!' he shouts back. He negotiates the trickiest bends in the road with his usual expertise; this is said to be the most dangerous road in Britain, but that's only because people do daft things on it, like over-taking in the wrong place. If you don't do daft things, you don't get into trouble.

As they twist and turn, Anjali's warm body presses into his back; the feeling arouses him and he wishes he could stop the bike and fuck her again right there. He's trying to get his head around a fact that bothers him badly: he's in love with this girl. He doesn't know how to tell her, even whether he should tell her. If she knows, if he gives her that power over him, won't she walk on him, use him and dump him? She'll go to uni soon, she'll meet other blokes, maybe more intellectual ones – all the pair of them really have in common is Ali. What will he do? He doesn't want to be without her. Things are hard enough already. Her father won't let him into the house.

'We've got to make a plan to deal with your dad,' he shouts through the helmet.

'I can't hear you,' Anjali shouts back.

'I said we've got to—'

Why it should be then that the animal appears, in the split second when Adrian turns his head the merest fraction to talk to Anjali, nobody can ever know. The sheep is large, pale as a ghost in the night, its face blank and unaware as it trots off the moor into the rainy road. Adrian doesn't even have time to swerve.

Morning streams into Rebecca's bedroom. It's been pouring most of the night, but no longer; now the ripening apples in the garden are brilliant with sun-trapping raindrops. The scent of fresh-ground coffee drifts up to Kate, who lies luxuriating under the duvet after the best night's sleep she's had in years.

'Here we go,' Rebecca says, carrying in a tray of oat biscuits and steaming mugs. 'This is my secret breakfast passion: dunking biscuits.'

'You're spoiling me,' Kate mumbles.

'You deserve spoiling.'

Rebecca is wearing a brown silk dressing-gown embroidered with a Chinese dragon. Kate gazes at the slender curve of her neck and shakes herself slightly. She can't believe she won't wake up a second time and find she's dreamed this entire episode.

'Here's your phone,' Rebecca says. 'It was in the lounge. It's beeping. You've got a message.'

Kate puts the phone aside. She sits up against the pillow, sips her coffee and dunks her biscuit.

'How do you feel?' Rebecca leans over and gives her a slow kiss.

Kate looks at her, smiling helplessly. She can't find the words. Rebecca laughs. The phone shrills out a signal, insistently indicating that Kate has missed four calls. 'It must be Ali,' she says. 'I should let her know I'll be there by lunchtime.'

'When's she playing?'

'Five. She's the last one this afternoon. Let me deal with the phone and then we can have some peace.' She presses a key to access her voicemail.

'Katie?' Rebecca says, watching her face as she listens.

Guy is hunting for his brown shoes in Emily's flat when the phone rings.

'Your shoes are here,' Emily shouts, running to answer it.

'Emily?' comes a strange woman's voice.

'Speaking.'

'Emily, this is Kate.'

'Hello, Kate,' Emily says. Guy, tying his shoe, freezes.

'I need Guy, urgently. It's bad news. Is he with you?'

Ingrid is whimpering and shouting, 'Mama!' in the back room; Guy knows that Kate will be able to hear her. He darts to the phone.

'Guy, sorry to call you at Emily's. Your mobile wasn't on. I found Emily in the phone book.'

'What's the matter? Where are you?'

'I'm in London, at Rebecca's. Listen. It's bad. Adrian's in hospital in Macclesfield. He came off his bike. He hit a sheep in the night. Anjali was with him.'

'Oh, my God.'

'He's unconscious, Guy.'

'I'll go right away. When will you be there?'

'I'm setting out now. I was going to go to Leeds for Ali's semi-final, but I can't.'

'Kate, we shouldn't tell Ali about this until after she's played.'

'Yes.'

'So you should be there.'

'How can I?' Kate's voice cracks. 'I have to go to Adrian. I can't not. Will you go to Leeds instead of me? Can you get away?'

'Tell Ali you've been held up, but that I'll be there. I'll go to the hospital now and when you arrive I'll go to Leeds. OK? Kate, he'll be all right.'

'He'll be all right,' Kate echoes. He can tell she doesn't believe it any more than he does. Dashing to the door, he realises he hadn't asked whether Anjali was injured.

'Darling,' Emily says, 'let me come with you. You mustn't go all that way on your own.' He knows she's silently terrified of the stress that this appalling development will put on his damaged heart. She doesn't want him alone behind the wheel of a car.

'Ingy,' he says.

'We'll bring her. I'm not letting you go on your own.'

'You're an angel. I'll call you from the hospital.'

'*No*, Guy, I'm coming too. I'll wait outside with her, if you prefer. But I'm coming too.'

25

Alicia is lying on the floor backstage, thinking herself into her music. Her récital programme is seventy minutes long, as required. First, Beethoven's 'Waldstein' Sonata, launching her in, cranking up the energy right away; then Chopin, two Ballades, popular but fantastic. Next, the contemporary piece that the competition obliges everyone to play; luckily she likes it. Last, French music: a group of Debussy Preludes and some Messiaen, her new favourite since she'd learned that he'd had synaesthesia. She's been devouring books about him, reading about how he visualised his delicious, scrunchy chords as orange, purple and grey flecked with pink. She wishes she could have met him; it's only twelve years since he died. Dan's been helping her, recommending articles and CDs. One day he'll be a marvellous teacher, like Professor Feinstein. She dreams: a circle of like-minded friends gathered round a wise professor and a piano, while outside the plains of the Midwest spread out to the far horizon.

A text message has told her that Mum is stuck in London with car trouble.

'Al?' Dan appears in the doorway. 'Your dad's here. I just saw him.'

'Cripes,' Alicia says, getting up. 'It takes a lot to get Dad away from his office.'

'It's not every day your daughter plays in the Leeds semi-final.' Dan winks.

'How long have I got?'

'You're on in ten. Break a leg, honey. I'm with you.'

'I know you are.' She kisses him and reaches for her brush.

Her hair hangs loose and straight down her back. She's wearing a plain, purply-blue dress, not too glittery for late afternoon; Dan's silk wrap stays round her shoulders until the last moment. She's cleared her mind of everything but the music. Nothing must put her off her stride today; even if she doesn't make it to the final, this will be her ultimate audition for Eugene Feinstein. She's playing today for him, for Dan, and – for once – her father. Perhaps her music has worked the magic it used to work when she was a small child: it's brought her father to her.

There's a crash of applause as she walks to the piano and bows. The hall is full; a quick sweep of her gaze suggests that every seat is taken. She glimpses a figure remarkably like Phyllida, but can't see Dad or Dan. She doesn't look at the jurors or the TV cameras. She focuses on the keyboard: her element, her home. She lifts her hands, feels the low C major chord starting to depress under her fingertips, hears the first bars in her mind, then leaps, plunging into the sea.

She knows from the first note that nothing can go wrong. She's flying. She's in complete control, showing the music to her audience, telling them the story of Beethoven's power and tenderness, the way he plays with the planets and speaks with the voice of spectral, eternal wisdom. She's fitted her own silent words to the final movement's shining melody: 'Sing out – the ancient story; sing out – the age-old song . . .' Its aural tapestry thrills her ears while her hands dance. She can feel the audience coming to her, giving back their love to refresh hers. She's soaring high as an eagle by the end; she can't wait to get back and play her Chopin. She sails through her two Ballades – No. 3 no longer conjures up riding over the moors, because now she knows that its rocking motion is simply the cradling tenderness of true love. No. 4 frightens her, but with a fear she adores: she imagines it as a great classical tragedy, like Dante's Francesca da Rimini, a crime of passion punished with eternal hellfire.

At the end the audience yells, wanting her to continue, but it's time for a break. She retreats backstage and lies on the floor for a few minutes, resting her arms, her back and, as far as she dares to, her brain, before the second part. She gets through the contemporary piece easily enough. Then she lets her beloved Debussy bathe her in mother-of-pearl and sparkling spiderwebs. And at last, her Messiaen, one of the most difficult pieces from his *Vingt Regards sur l'enfant Jésus* – 'Regard de l'Esprit de joie'. The spirit of joy. Alicia has learned a thing or two about joy recently and she lets rip. The piece is so complicated that it makes Balakirev's 'Islamey' sound like a nursery rhyme. She loves every note of it, has pulled it into herself until she can play it by instinct, not calculation. It's wild, volcanic, roaring with ecstasy, love physical and spiritual in equal measure, uniting her with the immortal soul that pulses through all humanity. Alicia flings the last downward flourish out to her audience and the final note resounds into the ether, deep, true and triumphant.

The sea surges about her, a crashing wave of crazy applause. She walks out of the water, damp, elated, exhausted. The audience is standing, stamping. Eugene Feinstein is smiling out from the middle. Dan is yelling, 'Bravo,' from the side. Leslie and Marina, who've been so good to her, are in the front row, tears in their eyes. Alicia raises her arms, radiating. She's never played better, which means that she's never been happier. Whatever happens next, even if she isn't allowed into the final, she's won her own war.

She walks offstage, her head filled with the ringing piano and the roaring audience. She puts down the flowers Leslie and Marina have sent her and waits for Dan. There's an agonising minute while she is entirely alone, forgotten. Perhaps nobody heard her; perhaps she hadn't played well at all. A second later, a figure in jeans and cotton shirt bursts through the door and she is in Dan's arms.

'You've done it!' He's overflowing with pride. 'You were unbelievable. The Messiaen was a complete knockout. The hall's going nuts and your dad's here, so come out quick as you can, OK?'

'I'll just be half a mo,' Alicia says, relief swamping her. He kisses her nose and hurries out.

She's about to change her clothes when the door opens again and there, to her delight, is Phyllida.

'Ali, you were incredible,' she says. She's filled out a little since Alicia saw her in hospital. Her image is coming back into focus.

'How are you? Are you feeling better?' Alicia hugs her.

'After hearing that, I'm on top of the world. You make it all worth it, Ali. All I want now is to get back to my desk and start fighting for you like there's no tomorrow.'

'I'm so glad you're here. Don't run away, I want you to meet my boyfriend.'

Phyllida lingers, but more and more people are soon crowding into the little backstage area; it's hard for Alicia to get away, and when things begin to calm down and she has done the requisite kissing, handshaking and small-talk, Phyllida tells her that she has to go home – 'Ali, come and see me in London, as soon as possible, OK?' Alicia doesn't want to let her go, but it's a long journey from Leeds to Tulse Hill, so she gives her another kiss and promises to phone to arrange a meeting, mother or no mother. After Phyllida has slipped away and the crowds have left her in peace, Alicia changes quickly into her T-shirt and jeans, then paces out into the hall.

Guy, listening to Ali, wishes that Emily could be beside him; she'd found a seat near the door in case Ingrid began to make a noise. He longs not to have to hide on such a day. Adrian is wired up and plastered over in the Macclesfield hospital; Guy stared aghast at the swathes of bandages round his head, the cage in which his right leg was strapped over the bed, while the doctor explained that he was out of critical danger but severely injured. Guy loathed the idea of leaving; but Kate – at her steeliest – had insisted on staying there herself and sent him away. 'I've failed him,' she declared. 'I'm staying. I won't fail him now.'

'Kate, you haven't failed anybody,' said Guy.

'Don't be ridiculous,' said Kate.

She left him no choice. If he, too, felt he'd failed Adrian, that was apparently not the point. It was the thought of the last time one of their children had been in hospital, fighting for life, that sent him into retreat, back towards the hospital's Victorian staircase, the cool afternoon and the drive over the Pennines to Leeds. He wonders how to break the news to Alicia.

Kate wants to hold Adrian's hand, but she can't: one of his arms is encased in plaster up to the elbow, while the other has been fitted with a clip to monitor something that she doesn't understand. Nor can she stroke his hair: his head, too, is heavily bandaged. She knows what may come next: manslaughter charges, court, possibly prison because he had no licence and no insurance. There's nothing she can do except sit beside him and say his name softly when he begins, at last, to come round.

'Mum,' Adrian manages to say. 'Ali?'

'She doesn't need me,' Kate whispers. 'You do.'

'Crap. Don't.'

'Hush, Adie. Don't try to talk. I'm sorry. I'm so sorry. It's my fault.'

'Not your fault. Mine. Stupid bloody me.'

'It *is* my fault.' Kate can't keep back the tears. 'I was so busy with Ali that I couldn't see how much you needed me.' His eyes close. He may be asleep, or losing consciousness again, but she tells him anyway. 'If I'd been watching, if I'd been looking out for you, this would never have happened. I should never have let you ride a motorbike without a licence. I should never have let you ride one at all. I gave up on you . . .'

'Bollocks.' Adrian is listening. 'Anji,' he says and tries to sob. His shattered bones will barely let him.

Kate can't take him in her arms and rock him like the baby he once was. Instead she rocks herself on her chair, sharing the tears that are all she and her son can share now.

In an aisle seat on the back row, Ingrid had sat on Emily's lap, thumb in mouth, watching the girl on the stage through her big silvery irises. All the way through the second half, even the noisy Messiaen, she'd been riveted, eyes on Alicia. She hadn't made a sound.

'It's incredible,' Emily says, when Guy wends an awkward way towards her across the standing ovation. 'She didn't budge! It's almost as if she could tell Ali is her sister.'

Guy, possessed with a rush of adoration for his two daughters, wonders what Ingrid will look like when she's Alicia's age. Despite her resemblance to Emily, she's not unlike Alicia at two and a half. At three, Alicia's perfect pitch had been discovered. Heavens, she'd been small. 'Do you want to come and meet Ali properly?' he ventures.

Emily crumples slightly. 'Oh, Guy,' she says. 'You know I'd love to. Let me think about it. But I'm desperate for the loo. Look after Ingy while I go?'

Guy takes his smaller daughter's hand, while the nervous Emily makes for the ladies' room; the queue extends into the foyer.

'It's Guy Bradley!' a voice exclaims beside him. He swings round and sees the dean of the university. 'You must be a proud man today,' the dean says, pumping his hand. 'And who's this young lady?' He smiles benevolently at the toddler beside Guy.

'She's the daughter of one of my journalists who's come to

hear Ali. I said I'd keep an eye on her for a minute.' Guy hates himself, but all this is, of course, perfectly true. 'How's life in the time of tuition fees?' he asks, to change the subject. He has interviewed the dean several times about the controversial changes that the government has been making to higher education.

'Hi, Guy! Wasn't she stunning?' comes another voice: Guy turns and sees Dan, his face full of love and excitement. Guy introduces him to the dean and, while he does so, Ingrid's hand slips unnoticed out of his own.

Ingrid is big and curious enough to be fascinated by the piano and the sounds that come out of it. She's also big enough, just, to wander away when her father is being distracted by grown-ups and her mother is queuing for the loo. She's been amusing herself recently by trotting off expressly against Mummy's instructions, to see how often she could do it before Mummy got cross. And she does want to know how the beautiful girl in the purple dress made those wonderful noises.

The hall stretches, vast, before her; her little legs take some time to carry her along its length. The piano is high up, on a great platform, glowering over her like a huge, spreading tree. She looks around for Mummy or Daddy, then finds she can't see either of them. She's on her own. Ingrid opens her mouth and starts to wail.

Alicia, coming out into the hall, spots Dan and Dad at the far end, talking to each other amid a bustling group of people. She's about to go over, when a distressing noise catches her attention. She looks down and sees a fair-haired little girl no more than two and a half or three years old, wearing a purple cotton jersey. The child is alone and big tears are rolling out of her strange, silver eyes.

'Hello, sweetheart,' Alicia says, crouching. 'What's the matter? Where's Mummy?'

'Mama went somewhere,' the little girl says doubtfully.

'She won't have gone far.' Alicia reaches out and takes her hand gently. 'She's probably waiting to go to the toilet. Mummies have to do that sometimes. Shall we go and look for her?'

'What's dat?' says the child.

'What?' Alicia follows her gaze. The little girl, whose tiny hand is warm and sweet in her own, is gazing up at the platform. At the piano. 'It's a very big piano,' she says. 'Did you hear the music?'

'I heared the music.'

'Did you like it?'

The child gives her a smile so wide and bright that Alicia is startled. It reminds her peculiarly of a photo on the piano room mantelpiece of herself at a similar age.

'That was me playing,' she says. 'My name is Alicia. What's your name?'

'Ingrid.' The word isn't clear enough for Alicia to catch it.

'Say it again? Very, *very* loudly?'

'Ingrid!' the child bellows, thrilled to have permission to shout.

'Ingrid? What a pretty name! You're such a poppet, aren't you? While we're waiting for Mummy, do you want to see the piano?'

Ingrid bounces up and down in a way that also seems oddly familiar to Alicia. 'Come on, then,' she says, leading the little girl up on to the platform. There's no sign yet of anybody looking for her. Who could have left such a small child alone at a piano competition? Who would bring such a small child to a piano competition in any case? Perhaps she's related to one of the contestants.

'You sit here—' Alicia sits down at the piano and lifts Ingrid on to her lap. 'Right in the middle. And you press the notes. Like this.'

Ingrid presses. A small note sounds. The Steinway's keys seem huge and heavy beneath her tiny fingers.

* * *

Guy is abruptly aware that Ingrid isn't with him. He'd been trying to avoid the dean, not to mention Dan, becoming conscious that the toddler was more to him than a temporary charge – but he's gone too far. Christ. Maybe Emily's come back and taken her? It's a vain hope, but as he's about to cling to it, he hears some odd, quiet noises coming from the piano. He turns.

Alicia is on the platform, at the piano. Ingrid is on her lap, little hands extended towards the keyboard. And Alicia is helping her to move her fingers and get a sound out of it.

Guy is transfixed. Ingrid looks like Emily and Alicia looks like Kate, yet Alicia and Ingrid look like one another. Ingrid looks like Alicia on the day they discovered her gift. And Alicia's radiance is perhaps not Kate's, after all, because Ingrid has it as well. He hears Emily's voice, calling, but glides on towards the stage, hypnotised by his two daughters.

Alicia, lost in the delight of showing her new little friend how the piano works, glances round and sees her father, white-faced, watching them. Behind him, the silver-eyed journalist is running up the aisle. Those eyes – that's where she's seen them before. She must be Ingrid's mother. Then she looks down at Ingrid. And she sees herself.

'Ali,' Dad calls.

When a train begins to move, it does so with the slightest shudder. A hint, a faint suggestion, then a gathering of pace as the energy feeds in and the speed begins to mount. And now Alicia's world shudders and starts to roll. The air flickers and spins. The hall pirouettes like a revolving door as her mind tries to go through it in one piece.

'No,' Alicia says.

'Dat my daddy,' Ingrid says, looking at Guy.

'Ingy, come here!' Emily calls, running forward.

Alicia gathers Ingrid into her arms and carries her down the stairs. She strides over to Guy, the little girl's warmth against her, soft and innocent. She stands face to face with him, and Ingrid laughs and reaches out her arms as she always does when she sees her father. Guy's gaze meets Alicia's as he takes the child from her. Ingrid settles happily against his shoulder. Alicia's legs buckle. She sits down on the nearest chair, speechless.

'Ali. Listen.'

'Listen to what?'

'I can explain everything,' says Guy.

Alicia glares from him to Emily, who is standing beside him, feet solidly planted. 'Dad, is Ingrid *yours*?'

'She is,' Emily cuts in, calm and firm. 'And mine. Alicia, your father and I are very much in love and have been for several years. We've never meant any harm, but we love each other and we have a daughter.'

'Dad?' Alicia manages to say.

'Yes, Ali. Ingy is your half-sister.'

Alicia glances behind them. Dan is hovering, anxious, wanting to reach her. 'No,' she breathes.

'Ali, darling, I meant to tell you. But—'

'But what, Dad?'

She has fallen out of the sky and is plummeting through cloud towards a mist-shrouded mountain. All the times he worked late. Sandalwood soap. Her mother's obsession with developing her career. Conferences in Denmark. Staying in Manchester because of not driving too much, because of heart trouble.

'So you've been lying to us for years.'

'I never meant to lie.'

'What about Mum?'

'Your mother knows everything.'

Just when you think it can't get worse, it does. They've both been lying. All the time. The recognition slashes across Alicia; the drop through the air brings her crashing into granite. The room lurches. She doesn't know why she's running or where to. She hears Dan calling her, and Dad, but she keeps going, past the concerned Leslie and Marina, past the astounded Fanny Waterman, out into the mindless dregs of the day. Night is falling and the sky, like Messiaen, is streaked with red, green and gold.

Her Renault is in the university car park. She locks herself inside and thumps her forehead with her hands, trying to wake herself up or at least beat out the consciousness that her life for the last few years or longer has been based on deception.

Her mother's transformation from lawyer and housewife into a loathed, over-ambitious music mother. Her father, shut out as Mum stood over her while she practised, instructing, helping, shouting, sometimes making her cry, every waking minute absorbed in what to do next for her gifted daughter. Especially since the one she'd loved best, the first one, had died. Another deception. What more have they kept from her? What further lies have they told her – just because she had to concentrate on practising the piano?

Her music hasn't brought her father to her. It's pushed him away, so much so that he's found another wife, another daughter, to be everything to him that she and Kate cannot be and maybe never were.

Why is she playing the piano in any case?

Alicia starts the engine. She heads west into the sunset, out of Leeds. Her mobile phone begins to ring; she lets it. What could she say to Dan now? Broad brushstrokes of Yorkshire, green and generous, spread round her in the twilight as she accelerates towards the open road. She's just given the best performance of her life – but what for? Why is she there? Why has she put her whole youth into the perfection of this peculiar art? What's the point, if this is the result? Right now, she can't think. A wall has collapsed inside her; it was never cemented.

Rain begins to fall on to the windscreen. She flicks a switch and the wipers swing in front of her. If only she could wipe away this discovery in the same way. If only they'd kept it secret. If only she'd never known.

No. That's wrong. Why can't people be honest? Her family is not the family she'd thought; and as she concentrates on the road through the hills towards Derbyshire, she can see, as clearly as if Dan's psychotherapist father had told her, that her parents' charade has been staged for her benefit, to create the illusion of a life in which her talent came first. As if she would ever put her music before her family! They'd never asked her how she felt. They wanted her to play the piano. None of them wanted her just to be herself.

What about Adrian? What does he know? More than her, presumably, because he'd left. Perhaps he's been hiding the truth too. No wonder he'd resented her. No wonder he cares not a jot for authority, since the authority in his life has always been too busy caring about her instead. And, as clearly as if Dan's father had told her, she understands that she has been living her bizarre life not to please herself, but to get her father's attention. Because it's the only thing that ever has.

She is eighteen years old, about – assuredly so – to be put through to the final of the Leeds International Piano Competition. If she wins, she'll have 'arrived'. The music-business machine will take her and grind her up: concerts, recordings, tours, aeroplanes. Stardom to the rest of the world; prison to her. Supposing they hadn't pushed her? Would she be there now, waiting as she soon will be under the TV lights to play the Rachmaninov Third Piano Concerto with one of the best orchestras in the country? Is that even her dream? Is it not, rather, theirs? A dream that she has to live for them, because they couldn't live it for themselves?

Alicia, watching the wet road, remembers her father holding her up to the window, remembers her little hands – just like Ingrid's – pressing on the glass that shielded her from the skidding raindrops. She'd imagined what it would be like to live inside one: a drop of water could be her whole world. Where

will she go now? What can she do? Will she, too, slide down
the window-pane and vanish into the gathering pools and the
moorland night?

Her phone rings and rings, its screen signalling DAN, but
she doesn't answer. She feels sorry for him, left far behind in
the blissful other world where she'd lived until Ingrid looked
up at her.

Alicia feels something splitting. She would rather not live at
all than live a lie. And what is her life but lies? Why live?

When she reaches the car park of the Cat and Fiddle –
where, mercifully, there's no sign of Adrian's bike among the
others – she has only one thought: she must attach the hosepipe
there to her car exhaust, put the tube through her window,
run the engine and go to sleep. It's the only way to dull the
pain.

The rain soaks into her clothes and her ankles feel damp
and icy under her jeans while she lugs the hosepipe towards
her car. The sheep look on – beastly things. Alicia realises she
hates sheep. She always has. She unravels the hose, holds one
end in both hands and approaches the exhaust pipe with it.

Of course, the two tubes are different widths. They don't
fit together. Alicia has heard that this is a way that people kill
themselves, so she'd assumed there must be some obvious
means of fitting one pipe into the other and keeping them
there while you let their smoke work its chemical magic through
your lungs. In the boot, she has water, chocolate, a torch and
a blanket spattered with dry grass from her open-air adven-
tures with Dan. But she has no tape, nothing with which she
can make a connection and hold it firm.

She tries to force it. She pushes the hosepipe deep into the
exhaust – it finally seems to engage with something – and
carries the other end to her window, which she opens only by
a slit. Inside, she closes the door quietly, then her eyes. She
turns the ignition key.

There's a bang and a horrible noise from somewhere in the

car's bowels. Alicia's stomach lurches with fear. No fumes come in. She switches off and tries again, but it's obvious that all she's managed to do is damage her car. As if things weren't bad enough already, she now finds she's too ignorant to commit suicide.

Stumped, she opens the boot, takes out the chocolate, then gets back in and ponders while she eats. She's losing it. She's lost the plot. She's going out of her mind.

Her phone shrills beside her. She reaches for it. Her hand feels heavy and clumsy.

'Al?' comes Dan's voice. 'Where the hell are you?'

'Darling,' she mumbles. She doesn't know what to say, so she rings off.

She munches the last of her chocolate. There's nothing more she can do. She's out on the moor, alone with nothing but her wrecked car and her wrecked life and a few bloody sheep.

She fetches the blanket and wraps herself in it. It reminds her of Dan and it helps to warm her despite her damp clothes, in which she's starting to shiver. She puts her head down on the steering-wheel and breathes deeply. The chocolate hangs, sweet and sticky, on her teeth. She's never felt so tired in all her eighteen years. She'll rest now, just for a few minutes. Then she'll decide what to do next.

26

Headlight beams wake her up, slamming into her eyes, dazzling her. Hours have passed; the motorbikes have gone; and she recognises, through a blur of unbanished sleep, her father's car. Someone is banging on her window. She opens the door.

'Al!'

Alicia jumps out of the car and Dan grabs her. She breathes his scent – suedey, comforting – and lets him cover her face with kisses. Faintly she can see Dad's dark figure waiting in the drizzle, exhausted and defeated.

'Oh, sweetie. Are you OK?' Dan pleads.

'I guess.' Alicia looks at him, remembering mysteriously how to smile.

'We didn't know where you were. You weren't at home so we drove out to look for you and we nearly went straight past – then your dad thought he'd seen your car. Thank God you're here.'

Dad comes towards them, dragging his feet. Alicia lets go of Dan and Dad gathers her up instead. He's been crying.

'I'm sorry, Dad. I didn't mean to worry you.'

'*Worry?*' Dan echoes. 'All of Buxton and Leeds have been out looking for you.'

Dad, though, seems unable to speak. Alicia notices the distress in Dan's face. 'What's the matter? What's happened? Where's Mum?'

'Sweetheart,' Dad begins, but he's overcome and turns his face away. Dan takes her hand. 'There's no easy way to tell you this,' he says. 'Your mom is in Macclesfield, because your brother's been badly injured and he's in hospital there. His bike crashed on the A537 last night.'

'No!' Alicia gasps. 'He's not dead?'

'He's going to be OK. But, Al – Anjali was with him. Apparently her helmet was too loose. They tried to get her to hospital, but she didn't make it. She died in the ambulance.'

'Oh, Christ. Christ. Christ.' Alicia closes her eyes, taking it in. Then she rounds on her father. 'You knew this earlier?'

'Yes, love. We knew this morning. We didn't want to tell you before you had to play.'

Arctic ice is spreading through Alicia. 'That's why I ran away,' she begins. 'The lies. The pretence. All supposedly to protect me so I can play the bloody piano. *I can't bear it.* I wish I was dead!'

'Hush, Al,' Dan pleads. 'Let's get out of here.'

'No!' screams Alicia. She'd thought she had nothing left inside her to scream with. 'Anji's dead and you didn't tell me! Because of the competition!' She swings round, lashing out towards her father. Guy backs away and Alicia, aghast at herself, pulls up short and covers her face with her hands. Anji. Sweet, serious, pure-hearted Anji.

'Al. We've got to get you out of the rain.'

Dan steers her towards her father's car and fastens her seatbelt for her. 'We'll go in convoy. I'll drive yours,' he says.

'I don't think it'll work,' Alicia mumbles. 'Something's happened to the exhaust pipe.'

Dan gives her one of his shrewd glances, but only says, 'OK. We'll take you home and worry about the car later.'

Dad pulls out of the car park. Drier yet drowning, Alicia pictures Adrian and Anjali in the pub, happy together as they should have been. Anjali. She'll never see her again.

Through her eyelids marches an array of people she's been too close to, then lost. People who'd dominated her life, only

to vanish. Mrs Butterworth. Lucien. Maybe even Rebecca. She
may encounter any of them again one day, but not Anjali.
She's dreaded death for her ageing grandmother and Cassie,
but Anjali was nineteen and for her to die was the greatest
injustice any cruel god could have devised. Everything moves.
Everything changes. You can't prevent time passing and the
world around you passing with it. The open air, the sunshine
under the hill, where she and Dan had made love. That was
their Garden of Eden. Why couldn't time have stopped there?

'You have to try to understand, Ali. I love Emily,' Dad says.
'I love you too, and Adrian. And, in a way, Mum. But things
have been going wrong for a long, long time. You must have
realised that.'

Alicia, in her dressing-gown, is sipping cocoa in the kitchen.
There's nothing like routine for comfort. She's given a concert
and so, even if it seems a century ago, she has cocoa. The only
time she hasn't had cocoa after a performance was the concerto
in Manchester – when she'd had something a lot better. Now
it's midnight. She's warming up gradually, the chocolate
working on her innards, but she's cried so much that she's
almost nauseous.

'Ali, you're in love. You know what it's like,' Dad says.

'Yes.' She glances at Dan beside her.

'So can't we talk about this?'

'That's not the problem, Dad,' she points out, acid. 'I know
you're in love. That makes it harder to understand how you've
let this drag on. You've been leading a double life. Why?'

'Because of something your mother said when I told her.'

'Which was?'

'Darling, she said that if I left, it might ruin your career,
your life. I couldn't do that.'

'And you *believed* her?'

Dan puts out a hand to steady her cup.

'How could I walk out on you? I couldn't do that.'

'It's all because of my piano. If I hadn't been "talented", if everyone hadn't gone around saying I was a "prodigy", none of this would have happened.'

'Ali, don't say that. It's not your fault.'

'I realised, up on the moor, that I'd only been playing as a kid to try to get your attention, Dad. That was all it was at the beginning. And then it took over. I had to be "*talented*".'

'Al,' Dan protests.

'It's true. Who's to say that if I gave up right now, I couldn't find a way to be much happier than I was this afternoon? And there was me thinking that that was the happiest moment of my life!'

'Al, please calm down,' Dan says. 'You're not giving up. No way.'

'Dan, stop it. You're as bad as them.'

The front door opens. Cassie glances up from her basket, which now lives in the kitchen because she can't manage the stairs. She doesn't bark. She's too old to get excited about every arrival at the front door, especially when her family can't pull themselves together enough to make a routine of it. If they can't be bothered, neither can she.

Kate blows in with the wind and runs to Alicia, who gets up to embrace her.

'How's Adrian?' she demands.

'He's going to be all right.' Kate had rung Guy earlier to tell him that Adrian had come round and that the broken bones were all mendable, given time. 'The first thing he asked was how you were getting on.'

'It's a long story, Mum. But I played OK.'

The fire in Mum's eyes has gone out. 'Thanks for looking after her,' she says to Dan. 'Would you like to stay tonight? I think she needs you.'

'"She" does,' Alicia adds.

'Thank you,' Dan says. 'That's kind. Yes, please.'

'Good,' Kate says. 'You're one of the family now.'

At the word 'family', Alicia shivers.

Alicia and Dan curl up in bed together with the curtains open and watch the clouds, above the sparse streetlamps, drifting by in what moonlight is left.

'Anji,' Alicia whispers.

'There's nothing we could have done.'

'But because of Adrian. On his bike.'

'Imagine how he must feel.'

'Sheep do that, you know. There aren't any fences on the moor, so they just go into the road. They're stupid, horrible creatures. They're the most dangerous things in the country-side. Oh, Dan. What do we do now?'

'We live. We make the most of our lives, for her sake, and for your sister who died, and for little Ingy.'

'She's so sweet. I always wanted a sister, but I never thought it could happen like this. It's funny, but part of me is actually thrilled about her.'

'Now this mess is out in the open, you can see Ingy when-ever you like. You'll be her idol, you know? Big sister Ali, at the piano.'

'Don't say that!'

'Al, you did the best performance of your life less than twelve hours ago. You didn't mean it when you said you'd give up?'

'I don't know. I just don't know. Because it's true: I wanted to please Dad, only I didn't realise it. It was Mum who pushed me, not him. But somehow, when I was little, the only thing I could do to get through to Dad was to play the piano. It made him notice me. Otherwise he was always too busy. That was how it began. And then everybody got inter-ested . . .'

'Come on, love. Try and sleep.'

★   ★   ★

Morning brings clarity of a kind, with the rain and wind leaving behind a silvered glint and a suggestion of faraway ice on the breeze. It brings clarity, too, from Leeds – a phone call from the administrator, concerned about Alicia's brother (the news has spread fast) but also telling her that she has been selected to play in the final, the last concerto on the last night, assuming that she wants to go ahead, under the circumstances. Dan fields an anxious call from Eugene Feinstein on his mobile, while Alicia switches hers off and tells Mum that if anyone calls she's practising.

Passing the bedroom door, she sees Dad standing by his cupboard, surveying suits and shirts. 'Are you moving out?' she asks.

He turns and gives her a straight answer. 'Yes, Ali. I'm going to live with Emily and Ingy.'

'Good,' Alicia says. 'I'm glad. Can I come sometimes and see my little sister?'

'It's your home too, darling. Come as often as you want. I'd like you and Emily to be friends.'

'Don't forget to pack your pills.'

Alicia, walking on down the stairs, breathes deeply. It may not be ideal. Her family may not be the perfect nuclear model that means so much to her mother, but honesty is a relief.

In the kitchen, Mum is on the phone, talking in a peculiarly intimate tone; listening the way she never listens; confiding the way she never confides. Alicia hovers. 'Dad's packing,' she says, when Mum hangs up and turns towards her, an odd, soulful expression on her face.

'I know, love.' Mum doesn't say who she'd been talking to.

Alicia sits opposite her, in the place she has sat thousands of times over the years. Mother and daughter gaze into each other's eyes.

'What I can't understand,' Alicia says, 'is why you thought I had to be kept from the truth. Or the truth from me.'

'Sweetheart, we're only human,' Mum says. 'Everyone makes mistakes. I did what seemed like the best thing at the time.'

Alicia has always seen her mother as all-powerful, controlling Mum. Not an ordinary woman, as confused and fallible as she is. She wonders who was on the phone.

She fastens the leash to Cassie's collar and takes her for a breath of fresh air; it hardly amounts to a walk. Gone are the days when they used to run together, pretending to fly. Cassie doesn't bark with joy any more – she's in too much pain, poor thing – and now Alicia runs for exercise, preferably with Dan, and likes the rain less than she used to. She walks past the spot where Matthew Littlemore stopped his bicycle and invited her to a party. Matthew's gone away to London, where he's found a job in a big department store. That's the trouble with small towns. People leave them.

When she comes back, Cassie limping at her side, Dad's car has gone. He, too, has left Buxton. Alicia goes into the front room, where Dan is playing the piano in her absence. She sits on his lap on the piano stool. Dan plays a tune and she picks it up an octave higher. They twiddle, improvising together without speaking.

'You couldn't have stopped it,' he tells her eventually.

'I'd never have wanted to. I wish he'd done this years ago. Poor Mum, living with him that whole time, knowing what was going on! And they did nothing about it because of *me*.'

'Don't be angry, love. Try to make the best of it.'

'I want to give up.'

'No, you don't. You're going on stage the day after tomorrow to win the bloody Leeds.'

'I'm going to phone them and say they've got to choose someone else.'

'They'll have a fit. They can't lose their only British finalist.'

'That's not my problem.'

'Al, wait. Think it through properly.'

'Why?'

'Come on. Let's go for a drive.'

The prominent, ship-like mound of Mam Tor presides over the hills and valleys, as it had when Alicia stood there with her father, pondering her future beyond another competition; as it had centuries before, in an age where there were no cars, no tourists, no National Trust to build flights of stairs and designate areas of Outstanding Natural Beauty. Until the Romantic movement, nobody would have paused to consider the Peak District beautiful, Dan says. Before then it would have been seen as wild and dangerous – chilly, muddy and threatening. Probably full of highwaymen, waiting to rob or murder you. And afterwards came the industrial revolution, the tentacles of its pollution curling round every hill and moor.

'But anyone can see this is beautiful,' Alicia says, lifting her face, the wind in her hair. 'If I have a home, this is it.'

Slivers of cloud like chiffon scarves wind through the valleys below them; the countryside is bronzing as the summer dies. Alicia thinks of Anjali. A tear slides down her nose. She glances round at Dan; his cheek, too, is, glistening with moisture.

'Can you throw it all away, Al?' he asks. 'When you think of the talent Anji had – and it's all gone. You've got the gift to bring beauty and meaning and wonder into people's lives. Can you ignore that?'

'What worries me more,' Alicia says, 'is that I can't do anything else. I've got hardly any qualifications. All I've ever done is play the piano. My future got decided for me when I was about five and now it's too late.'

'Nonsense,' says Dan. 'You're only eighteen. It's up to you. Nothing's too late – not now, and not ever.'

Alicia turns away and blows her nose.

'What are you thinking?'

'Just remembering. Anji. Adrian.'

'What else? Try free association. What's the next thing that comes into your mind?'

'Moorside. The night the moon turned red and we walked through the grounds. And Lucien said to me, "Your capacity to love is your own." He was saying that the way I love is up to me. Not anyone else. If you've got the capacity to feel love, he was saying, you can take it where you want to, where you need to.'

'And that's true of music?'

'I could take all the passion I put into music, and put it into working for a supermarket instead, if I wanted to.'

'*If* you *wanted* to. Exactly.'

'How do you mean?'

'The way you phrase it makes me think you don't want to.'

'I see.'

'What do you want, Al?' Dan asks.

She remembers standing on that spot years before while her father asked her the same question. At least the answer is clearer now. 'I want the freedom to make up my own mind and choose my own future, as a woman in my own right. And I want you. I want us to be together and take life as it comes. Don't take this wrong – I don't want to be pushy, I just want to be open.'

'I'd marry you today if I didn't know that we're way too young and that you've got other things to do first.'

'I do have things to do,' she says, nodding, 'but maybe not what you think.'

'Tell me?'

'I need to take some time out. I want to study and pace things a little more slowly. I'd like to come to Bloomington, if they'll have me, and study with Professor Feinstein. And if I have to cancel concerts, I'll cancel them. I know so little. I want to learn so much. I need to be certain I'm playing not for Mum or Dad, or even for you, but for myself. And I can't do that overnight.'

★   ★   ★

Adrian is flat on his back, his head bandaged, his leg in plaster held away from the hospital bed in something that looks like a cross between a cage and a cradle. Alicia almost cries out in horror, but a second later she's trying to embrace him through the mess. He smells of chemicals and his eyes are full of anguish, but not, she suspects, from his physical pain.

'Anji,' he says.

'Oh, Adie. I can't bear it either.'

'How can you forgive me?'

'It wasn't your fault.'

'No insurance. Nothing. I'll never forgive myself.'

'It was an accident. It could happen to anyone.'

'Can't stand it. Keep thinking I'll wake up and she'll be there . . .' Tears squeeze out of his eyes. His chest shakes. 'Ouch,' he says. 'Ribs. Broken.'

'You must rest and get better. We'll have you out and home soon.'

'I mightn't be home. I'll get sent down for this, Ali. I don't care. Can't live with myself now.'

Alicia strokes the part of his arm that doesn't hurt. She wonders how their parents can live with themselves, for they have a role in this too. 'You're going to be fine,' she insists.

'Prison. Manslaughter. God knows how long. I'm ready.'

'It *wasn't* your fault.'

'I loved her, Ali. I really loved her. She was the greatest girl, the sweetest, the most wonderful. Should have died with her.'

'Hush, Adie.' Alicia puts her head down on the pillow beside him and closes her eyes. They keep still there together, thinking of Anjali. Alicia imagines how she would feel if she had been driving the bike and Dan was killed, and the pain becomes so intense that she wonders how Adrian can breathe. 'You have to get through this,' she whispers to him. 'You have to. She'd have wanted you to.'

'I'll do my time, whatever it takes. She deserves that.'

'And you'll never ride a bike again.'

'You know what the best thing to do is when you come off a bike, Al? Get back on and keep on riding. Or else you never will.'

Alicia says nothing. She takes in his words. They're meant for her.

'Why? How?' she asks eventually.

'I've got a telly here and I want to see you on it tomorrow night, winning that prize. You've got just one chance and it won't come back. If you don't do it, you'll regret it for the rest of your life.'

'You mean, get back on straight away. And keep riding.'

'That's what I mean, lass. The world's your oyster. Go get it.'

It's a clear, sparkling day in the new year when a small group of people and an elderly, arthritic dog cross the teeming threshold of Manchester Airport. Alicia's hair has been trimmed to shoulder length. Behind her, her attendants dart about, helping. Her father loads three bulging suitcases on to a trolley. Her mother, wearing jeans and a leather jacket, runs through the list of things that Alicia must have remembered.

'Laptop.'

'Yes.'

'Rechargers.'

'Yes.'

'Brain,' Adrian teases, leaning on his crutch.

'Ali going 'Merica,' Ingrid pipes, holding Alicia's hand. Adrian smiles at Ingrid and does a Donald Duck impression. He's become very good at Donald Duck and Ingrid squeals with laughter.

Alicia checks in, loads her suitcases on to the belt with Dad's help and asks for a window seat. Her student visa is in place and the university has made a special dispensation to allow her to begin her studies in the year's second semester. Since she won Leeds, any door she touches seems to open. Maybe choosing should have been more difficult. But now, because she knows exactly what she wants, it's easy. As for her concerts, Phyllida has promised to carry out her instructions regarding her 'sabbatical'. Everybody will remember her when – if – she comes back, for no one will forget in a hurry the speech she'd made when she accepted her prize, dedicating it to the memory of her friend.

At the departure gate, everyone comes to a stop. Travellers throng round them, making for Africa, Australia, China, Brazil. Everywhere there are farewells, embraces, tears.

Alicia kisses them each in turn: Dad, Adrian, Ingrid, whom she hugs for ages. 'I wish I could take you with me,' she tells her. 'Will you draw me pictures sometimes?'

'Draw piccies,' Ingrid says. She's too small to understand what's happening, though big enough for Emily to have let her go out for a day with her father and his other family.

'Mum.' Alicia holds out her arms.

Kate steps forward and embraces her daughter. Announcements blare over the Tannoy: 'Last call for the last remaining passengers for Chicago.' Alicia and Kate, golden head to golden head, don't move.

'Call me when you get there,' Kate says. 'I'll be in London.'

'I will. 'Bye, Mum.'

Alicia bends and kisses the top of Cassie's head. She knows she's saying goodbye for ever to her dog. Then she picks up her bag and takes out her passport and boarding card. At the great glass gate, she turns one last time, hair gleaming, face radiant. With a wave, she's gone.

21 Leaders for the 21st Century

The right of Fons Trompenaars and Charles Hampden-Turner to be identified as the authors of this work has been asserted in accordance with the Copyright, Designs and Patents Act 1988

First published 2001 by
Capstone Publishing Ltd (A John Wiley & Sons Co.)
8 Newtec Place
Magdalen Road
Oxford OX4 1RE
United Kingdom
http://www.capstoneideas.com

British Library Cataloguing in Publication Data
A CIP catalogue record for this book is available from the British Library

ISBN 1-900961-66-0

Typeset by
Forewords, 109 Oxford Road, Cowley, Oxford
Printed and bound by
T.J. International Ltd, Padstow, Cornwall

This book is printed on acid-free paper

Contents

Preface

A generation ago, two world wars had so influenced our concept of leadership as to cast it in a military mode. To "lead" was to know sooner than others, and convince them, that harsh realities must be faced and sacrifices made. Winston Churchill, Charles de Gaulle, and Dwight D. Eisenhower, the rest of us followed. There was an inevitable feeling of certainty about those times. We were right, and the enemy was wrong. We all knew what had to be done, even if the doing was hard and dangerous. Our leaders had been the first to proclaim this necessity.

How much different are the circumstances now! Today, it is much easier to get things done. Gone are the blood, toil, tears, and sweat. Kosovo is bombed from a safe height. However, we are now much less sure about what *ought* to be done. We see people trying to lead, but question whether we should follow. Why go in this direction and not that?

Studies of leadership have attempted to duck the issue of what should be done by grounding themselves in what the leader was trying to do and not in the critiquing of values. The test became performance: Does this or that leader accomplish what he or she set out to do?

In 1983 Warren Bennis traveled across the United States proclaiming four universal traits of leadership:

- Management of attention (the leader just draws you to him or her, and makes you want to join the cause).
- Management of trust (leaders can be trusted because they are consistent – even if you disagree with their views).
- Management of self (leaders know their own skills and deploy them effectively).
- Management of meaning (leaders are great communicators).

This kind of prescription is largely value free and regards leadership as a skill or technique.

Hersey and Blanchard propose a "situational leadership" model. Styles of leadership are appropriate to different paradigms. The trick is to identify the paradigm and adjust your style to the attitudinal and knowledge stance of the Followers. This kind or prescription is largely reactive and unidirectional.

In *The Future of Leadership*, White et al. (1996), assert five key skills of a leaders gleaned from their observations:

- continually learning things that are hard to learn;
- maximizing energy as masters of uncertainty;
- capturing the essence of an issue to achieve resonant simplicity;
- balancing the long and the short term in multiple focus;
- applying an inner sense or a gut feeling in the absence of decision support data.

Many other authors and researchers have faced this struggle, and many prescriptions and explanations have been published. However, they lack any coherent underlying rationale or fundamental principle that predicts effective leadership behaviors. These models tend to seek the same end, but differ in approach, as they try to encapsulate the existing body of knowledge about what makes an effective leader. Because of the methodology adopted, these are only prescriptive lists, like a series of ingredients for a recipe – you can only guess at what the dish is going to be. There is no underlying rationale or unifying theme that defines the holistic experience of the resulting meal.

Such approaches create considerable confusion for today's world transcultural manager. Which paradigm should he fit into? Which meanings should she espouse: her own or those of the foreign culture? Because most of our management theory comes from the United States and other English speaking countries, there is a real danger of ethnocentrism. We do not know, for example, how the lists cited here fare outside the United States or how diverse might be the conceptions of leadership elsewhere. Do different cultures necessitate different styles? Can we reasonably expect other cultures to follow a lead from outside those cultures?

Part of the difficulty in researching leadership has been that, without an agreed-upon model of what effective leaders do, it is difficult to assess the value of this participant observation. To the interpreting observer, many of the best leadership behaviors are often inexplicable and are not the stuff of science. The observations are difficult to code, classify, and regurgitate. Can we know with certainty that a particular observed behavior would work for others?

Without an adequate theory of leadership, and therefore without any agreement on what makes good leaders, trainers revert to the tried and tested subject disciplines for which there is a documented and transferable body of knowledge. As Hunt, writing in the *Financial Times* of October 21, 1998, says, "In this way, we avoid the interpersonal aspects of actually managing, because we are not sure what they are."

The approach to leadership in this book is completely different. It developed from the convergence of two separate strands of thinking, one from each of the principal authors. The earlier research by Fons Trompenaars, developed since the early 1990s, was based on getting people to consider where they were coming from in terms of norms, values, and attitudes. This approach helped to identify and model the source not only of national cultural differences, but also of corporate culture likewise, how to deal with diversity in a local workforce. It helped managers to structure their experiences and provided new insights for them and their organizations into the real source of problems faced when they were managing across cultures or dealing with diversity. The second strand was work of Charles Hampden-Turner, who developed a methodology for reconciling seemingly opposed values. In his research, constructs such as universalism (adherence to rules) and particularism (each case is an exception) are not separate notions, but different, reconcilable points on a sliding scale. Universal rules are tested against a variety of exceptions and re-formed to take account of them.

The result of combining the two strands of research is that differences are progressively reconciled. Managers work to accomplish this or that separate objective; effective *leaders* deal with *the dilemmas of seemingly opposed objectives that they continually seek to reconcile.* As discussed throughout the body of this book, the contributing authors have collected primary evidence to support this proposition through questionnaires, workshops, simulations, and interviews. Furthermore, it is also confirmed that these behaviors correlate with bottom-line business results.

The 21 leaders described in this book were therefore approached deductively. The authors started with a proposition centered around the reconciliation of dilemmas and set out to demonstrate these concepts with evidence gathered from high-performing leaders. Thus, unlike other approaches that result from post-rationalizing observations into an *ad hoc* theory, they had the advantage of a conceptual framework when they approached and interviewed the target list of leaders. The author team believe this is the first hypothetico-deductive approach to leadership that tests its theory by opening this up to falsification. Thus the overall aim of this book is to render leadership practice tangible by showing how 21 world-class leaders reconcile the dilemmas facing their companies.

Peter Woolliams, Ph.D.
Professor of International Business
Anglia Business School, UK

The Structure of the Book

This text will attempt to explain reconciliation theory and make it more accessible. We seek to illustrate its principles through the practice of successful leaders and so demonstrate the vitality and power of synergizing values.

The book intends to help leaders:

* elicit and become aware of major business dilemmas in transcultural environments;
* see dilemma resolution as a crucial ingredient of strategy;
* utilize dilemmas as strategic contexts for action;
* learn the art of achieving one value through another in a virtuous circle (a process known as "through–through thinking"); and
* learn how transnational entrepreneurs take their stands (preneur) between (entre) contrasting values.

Here is a list of the Chapters, in order:

Chapter 1, "Transcultural Competence: Learning to Lead by
Through–Through Thinking and Acting, Part I"
(Fons Trompenaars and Charles Hampden-Turner)

In Chapters 1 and 2, we introduce seven dimensions that we habitually use in distinguishing between different national cultures. We seek to show that these dimensions also illuminate the way leaders think and act. Chapter 1 deals with the first three dimensions.

Universalism — Particularism
Individualism — Communitarianism
Specific — Diffuse

Chapter 2, "Transcultural Competence: Learning to Lead by
Through–Through Thinking and Acting, Part II"
(Charles Hampden-Turner and Fons Trompenaars)

Here, we continue our exposition with four additional dimensions characterizing the dilemmas faced by major leaders:

Affective — Neutral
Achieved status — Ascribed status
Inner directed — Outer directed
Sequential time — Synchronous time

Chapters 3–19 deal with major dilemmas faced by prominent business leaders the as twenty-first century begins. The chapter looks at the well-publicized personality and career of Sir Richard Branson the "Virgin Tongue in cheek." On these pages are reconciled a wide diversity of opposite endowments, so that Branson is both a critic of traditional capitalism and an agent of its profitable transformation. We start with Branson because he is living proof that enlightened leadership can change the whole spirit of capitalism.

Chapter 4 features the conscious design of a "hyperculture," a purpose-built corporate environment of superlatively high performance, created from the values of its participants (East Germans, West Germans, and Americans). In this particular case, the cross-cultural convenor, Martin Gillo, was familiar with dilemma theory and used it to design a culture of cultures, which broke all records. His own interpretations add to the theory expounded in Chapters 1 and 2.

Chapters 5–7 deal with the dilemmas and dynamics of corporate turnaround. How do those who save a company in crisis think and act? Each of three companies was suffering from a surfeit of its traditional strengths; it had overplayed a winning streak and found itself facing catastrophe. Philippe Bourguignon, of Club Med, had to save the company from the runaway costs of its own stylish hospitality. Christian Majgaard, of LEGO, survived a sea of red ink to restore "the children's toy of the twentieth century" to its former glory. Anders Knutsen, of Bang and Olufsen, saved the Danish company from its own technological perfectionism, which had scorned marketing and pricing.

Chapter 8 looks at how private enterprise provides a long-term public service; the chapter examines the deeds Gérard Mestrallet at *Suez Lyonnaise des Eaux*. Chapter 9 shows how Val Gooding inspires a corporate form that makes the private insurance of health work again.

In Chapters 10–12, we look at three global giants of the electronics and computer revolution, whose dynamism has outdistanced rivals. Jim Morgan, of Applied Materials, made a detailed study of, and even wrote a book on, Japanese electronics strategy, which is now widely copied throughout East Asia. Morgan's global strategy is based squarely on an East–West dialogue, in which the machinery made for microchip manufacture takes on various meanings in different cultures. Michael Dell, of Dell Computers, a latecomer to the maturing PC industry, has nonetheless thrust his company into the position of second in the world by direct sales over the Internet, on which all customers have their "premier pages." Finally, Stan Shih, of Acer, has shown what a company with a traditional Taiwanese management style can achieve in a global marketplace by adhering to, while reconceiving, its homegrown Taiwanese values.

Chapter 13 revisits the ferocious force fields and destructive cross-pressures described by the dilemma model. These are particularly severe in cultures that are in transition from communism to capitalism. We pick up the spectacular banking career of Russia's former Prime Minister, Sergei Kiriyenko, whose resistance to disintegrative forces within the system borders on the heroic.

Chapter 14 examines a rare, yet impressive, instance of changing a company by changing its values. Ed Bronfman, of Seagram, transformed the company's performance through a dialogue on values that all parties agreed to, committed themselves to, and operationalized, with notable success. Crucial to Bronfman's success was walking the talk and monitoring the results.

Chapters 15 and 16 examine two examples of "success" that the respective leaders realize cannot continue for much longer without important changes. Without waiting for a crisis to strike, Karel Vuursteen, of Heineken, and Hugo Levecke, of AMD AMRO Leasing, instituted changes that will stop the coming squeeze of future dilemmas.

Chapters 17 and 18 pick up on two companies in the fast-changing financial services industry. Merrill Lynch, symbolized by a bull's horns, confronts genuine dilemmas provoked by cut-price Internet brokerage services offered by Charles Schwab and other competitors. Should it beat them or join them? AEGON, the Dutch insurer, confronts a consolidating global industry. It must acquire or be acquired, but will it learn how to digest foreign acquisitions?

Chapter 19 tells the story of Rahmi Koç, of Turkey. Koç built a family business into a powerhouse that, by itself, makes up 6 percent of Turkey's GNP and pays 11 percent of the nation's taxes. The Koç Group, as the business is known, is admiringly referred to as Turkey's "Third Sector," behind the public and private sectors.

Chapter 20 shows that global activities generate dilemmas through conflicts with local cultures.

Chapter 21 looks at the dilemmas of three start-ups in family ownership. How do acorns become oaks? What are the dilemmas that kill off most small companies? Is it possible to "incubate" small companies so as to prevent their early demise? Three leaders tell their stories.

Chapter 22 seeks to generalize the particular models, frameworks, and discussion from the body of the text about the 21 leaders to a generic framework for reconciling each dimension of cultural values.

Appendix A provides background information about the construction of the dilemma database and the instruments used to develop the propositions on which this book is based. Appendix B describes the company that pioneered consulting on dilemma resolution. Appendix C gives short biographies of the main and the contributing authors. Appendix D provides references that support and supplement the chapter material.

Introduction to the Metatheory of Leadership

The main difference between managers and leaders is that some managers cannot sleep because they have not met their objectives, while some leaders cannot sleep because their various objectives appear to be in conflict and they cannot reconcile them. It goes without saying that, where objectives clash and impede one another, they will be difficult to attain, and no one will sleep! It is tough when you cannot "make it," but even tougher when you do not know what you should be making. When objectives are achieved, the problem disappears, but the dilemma of needing to combine objectives never disappears. You can reconcile a dilemma so that its "horns" are transformed into something new, but other dilemmas will appear and will have to be reconciled again and again. This challenge to leadership never ends.

A leader is here conceived as one suspended between contrasting values. So numerous are the value conflicts within large organizations, that their leaders must deal with the human condition itself. This idea was well conveyed by Alexander Pope in his "Essay on Man," whom he saw as

> Placed on the isthmus of a middle state
> A being darkly wise and rudely great
> With too much knowledge for the sceptic side
> With too much weakness for the stoic's pride
> He hangs between; in doubt to act or rest
> In doubt to deem himself a god or beast.
> In doubt his mind or body to prefer
> Born but to die, and reas'ning but to err
> Created half to rise and half to fall;
> Great lord of all things yet a prey to all
> Sole judge of truth, in endless error hurled
> The glory, jest and riddle of the world!

The reason that leaders must mediate values is that corporations have reached such levels of complexity that "giving orders" rarely works anymore. What increasingly happens is that leaders "manage culture" by fine-tuning values and dilemmas, and then *that culture runs the organization*. The leader defines excellence and develops an appropriate culture, and then that culture does the excelling.

Consider just some of the "dilemmas of leadership." You are supposed to inspire and motivate, yet listen; to decide, yet delegate; to centralize business units that must have locally decentralized responsibilities. You are supposed to be professionally detached, yet passionate about the mission of your organization; a brilliant analyst when not synthesizing other's contributions; a model and rewarder of achievement when not eliciting the potential of those who have yet to achieve. You are supposed to develop priorities and strict sequences, although parallel processing is currently all the rage and saves time. You must enunciate a clear strategy, but never miss an opportunity even when the strategy has not anticipated it. Finally, you must encourage participation, while not forgetting to model decisive leadership. No wonder the characteristics of good leadership are so elusive!

One reason leaders must know themselves is that they have to pick people to work with them who will supplement and complement their own powers. We all have weaknesses, but unless the leader recognizes his or hers, the team surrounding the leader will fail to compensate for that weakness.

To rise to a position of leadership is to experience ever more numerous and more various claims upon your allegiance. You are no longer in manufacturing, marketing, finance, or human relations, but *between* them. You must, of course, satisfy shareholders, but how can you do that without first sparking enthusiasm in your own people, who then delight customers, who in turn provide the revenues you all seek? Once again, you are between such constituencies, and you must learn how to reconcile their claims.

In several earlier books, the main authors have researched and described how different nations and their management cultures approach dilemmas, choosing one horn in preference to another and making choices that are mirror images of each other. Cultures also are more or less capable of reconciling opposed values. This book will demonstrate that outstanding leaders are particularly adept at resolving dilemmas, a process that has become our definition of good leadership.

Great psychologists have not agreed with each other on what vital entities the mind includes. Where they do agree is that the life of the mind is a series of dilemmas. Freud saw the superego contending with the id, a struggle mediated by the ego. C. J. Jung saw the collective unconscious contending with the libido, in a conflict mediated by the psyche. Otto Rank saw the death fear contending with the life fear. Brain researchers have identified opposed characteristics of the left and right brain hemispheres, generating conflicts mediated by the *corpus callosum* and the neocortex struggling against the limbic system. It can be said of leaders that they have voluntarily shouldered far more dilemmas than the life of their own minds presents to them. Along with psychic conflicts, they must struggle with all the oppositions identified by organizational thinkers: formal vs. informal systems, mass production vs. customization, competition vs. cooperation, Sociotechnical systems, adaptation to external reality vs. maintenance of internal integrity, and so on.

Among these many dilemmas is one vital tension around which this whole book is organized. Can you make the *distinctions* necessary to leadership, yet integrate these into a viable whole? It is to meet this challenge that *21 Leaders for the 21st Century* is offered. Our view is that value is not "added" by corporations, because only in the simplest cases do values "add up." Values are rather *combined*: a high-performing vehicle and a safe one, a luxury food *and* a convenient one. No one pretends that combining such values is easy, but it is *possible*. A computer of amazing complexity can, with difficulty, be made user friendly. It is these ever more extensive systems of satisfaction that successful leaders help create.

Main Concepts of This Book

Cultures consist of values in some kind of reciprocal balance, so it becomes important to ask what values are. Much of the life of people consists of managing *things*, and things are identified through a logic as old as Aristotle, a logic of noncontradiction. Two different things cannot occupy the same physical space at the same moment of time.

For example, we choose to buy this car or that, choose to live in one house instead of another, choose between airlines, and put out a contract and choose among the bids. But values are not things. You cannot acquire courage, hope, or innocence. You will not meet evil at the street corner, nor honesty, nor compassion. Values are *differences*, and any difference posits a continuum with two contrasting ends. For example, we can be honest or tactful, courageous or cautious, patient or insistent, trusting or supervising, and truthful or loyal. In many cases, it really does not make sense to say that one end of such a continuum is "good" and the other "bad." Should you be honest and hurt someone's feelings, or tactful and hide what you really believe? Should you trust a subordinate, or check up on him from time to time? When should you show courage, and when should you cautiously husband your strength? Is it better to be patient or insistent? In all such cases, good conflicts with good, and we face a dilemma.

Moreover, it would be ridiculous to live one's life continuously at one end of a continuum, forever proving one's courage and insisting on hard truths. Those who trust everyone on principle will surely get cheated – you might as well present your throat to a vampire. In fact, we *move to and fro* along the values continuum, now tactful and now honest, now trusting and now supervising.

Does this mean that all values are simply relative? Are they like a shell game, now you see it, now you don't? Fortunately not. There is a test of the skill with which one "dances" to and fro upon a continuum. At the end of this dance, the values at both ends of the continuum *should be stronger than they were before*. Here are some examples: as a result of your tact, you were able to communicate a more honest account; by cautiously conserving your strength and summoning help, your courage saved the day; in patiently listening to many points of view, you could insist on the best of them; your trusting a subordinate for a longer period caused your supervision to increase in significance; such was your loyalty to a colleague that she felt able to confide the truth to you.

In all these cases, the values continuum has been cleverly traversed to vindicate the values at both ends of the continuum, allowed seemingly opposed values to be reconciled, and achieved a higher level of integration.

The Example of Centralization–Decentralization

Values in tension, which appear, at first glance, to be negations of one another can, in fact, work in synergy (from the Greek *syn* and *ergo* "working together"). We illustrate this proposition in detail by the example of Centralization–Decentralization. This is a particularly important dilemma for leaders. On the one hand, they are responsible to shareholders for the combined profitability of the whole company, over which they exercise centralized control. On the other hand, the many business units must have the decentralized autonomy to engage their very different environments effectively.

At their simplest, centralization and decentralization are opposite ends of a "rope" or "string": each end represents contrasting characteristics. We can illustrate this as in Figure I-1.

When we draw the dilemma like this, our chief interest lies in the *difference* between centralized and decentralized activities. Typically, some people in a company will believe that it is overcentralized – a view common among outlying business units. Others complain that the firm is too decentralized – a view common with those supplying shared resources. Does the corporation risk disintegrating, or does it suffer from overcontrol? The "rope" is frequently stretched between rival factions as in a

Figure I-1

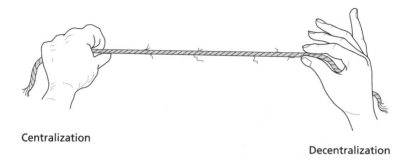

Centralization

Decentralization

tug-of-war, each believing that, to "save" the company, it needs to pull harder towards its own end – more centralization or more decentralization.

But conceiving of values as in opposition is not wholly satisfactory. After all, without decentralized activities, what is the purpose of centralized controls? Putting the two values so far apart misses the important connection between them. Is there anything we could do with our "rope" that would reveal this connection? We could join the ends of the rope to make a circle, as in Figure I-2.

Note that there is a subtle change of wording: "centralization" has become *centralizing knowledge*, and "decentralization" has become *decentralized activity*.

Figure I-2

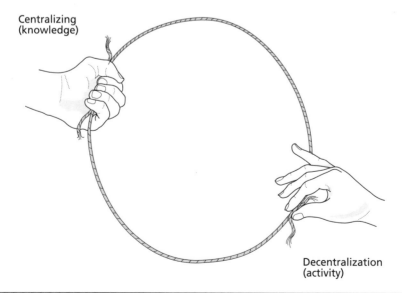

Centralizing
(knowledge)

Decentralization
(activity)

Control comes from the center, activity comes from the field. Instead of the two values negating each other, they complement each other. Now, even though our single dimension has become a circle, there are still two sides as we circle between the two former polarities. Can we do this? Of course! Who says that thoughts are static? The more we play with such constructs, the more we can see and grasp, while recognizing that what we have are merely variations on our original dimension.

The advantage of the metaphorical circle is that we can now see that central *controls* follow upon peripheral *activities*, and *vice versa*. You cannot have one without the other; they constitute a system.

So now we have two figures, each with a distinct advantage. Figure I-1 differentiates decentralized activity from centralized control. Figure I-2 integrates them. These are both useful viewpoints so is there some way of combining them in a single illustration? There is. First we take our original dimension and break it at a right angle, as shown in Figure I-3.

Figure I-3

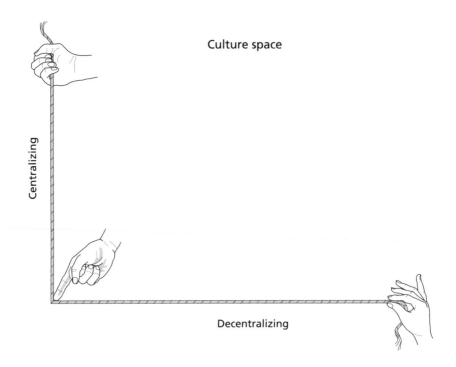

Culture space

Centralizing

Decentralizing

This conceptualization gives us two axes, or if you like two horns of a dilemma, that create a culture space; notice how much more freedom to move our thoughts have in two dimensions rather than in different organizations with different cultures deal with the dilemma of decentralizing and having to control decentralized activities in different ways: Some are afraid of peripheral activity, others accepting; some take delight in learning from peripheral activities, others suppress the very possibility.

We now are in a position to place our circle between the horns or axes, as in Figure I-4.

Figure I-4

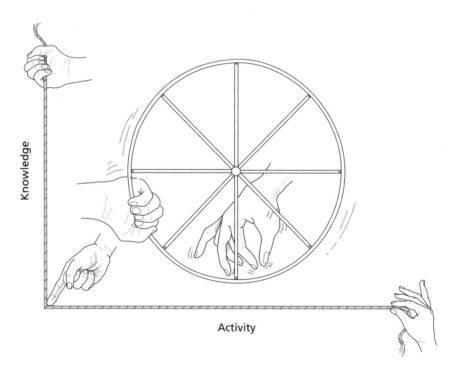

Knowledge

Activity

Decentralizing is now both *differentiated from* and *integrated with* centralizing in the same model, by the use of two variations on what was initially a straight line or single dimension. We now see that those performing the peripheral activity and those exercising the central control are different parties. (The control is about the activity and inquires into it.) Nor do the two processes occur at the same time. Rather, activity *precedes* control, which checks at intervals to make sure that everything is all right. But our model still has problems: it seems to lack all direction and purpose and goes around and around in one place. This is why we have suggested the effect of a treadmill, with activity recompensing the energy of central control. Is there some way of learning through this experience and making some kind of progress? Yes! We can add a third dimension, progression through time, to generate the synthesis between a circle and a straight line, called a helix. (See Figure I-5.)

Figure I-5

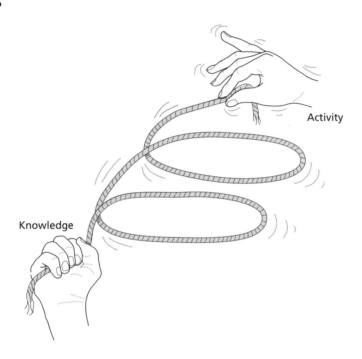

The helix shows how a circle looks from the side as it winds between our two polarities. Here, we decentralize to have more to centralize, and we communicate our conclusions about the myriad activities of the corporation to each business unit, so that it can compose itself to, and learn from, the activities of other units. Which have performed well, which badly, and why?

Helix-shaped molecular structures are the basis of life, so we should take this metaphor seriously. We can superimpose the helix on our culture-space in the manner illustrated in Figure I-6.

Here, our helix winds progressively between peripheral activity and central control of that activity. If a company is well led, its activities will become more and

Figure I-6

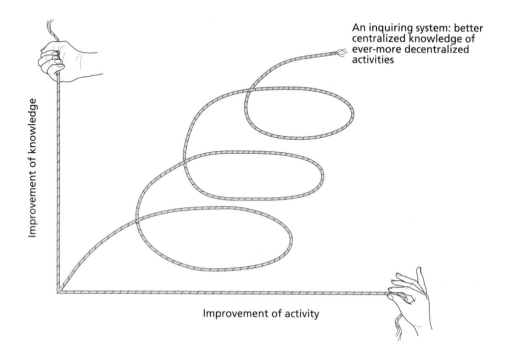

An inquiring system: better centralized knowledge of ever-more decentralized activities

Improvement of knowledge

Improvement of activity

both more decentralized and better and better monitored and centralized, with the center acting as does the central nervous system of a human body, which coordinates inputs from semiautonomous peripheries, such as the hands of an artist. What is being centralized is information about decentralized activities, which, by using this feedback, become more and more effective at achieving their goals.

Would we be better off if we were totally decentralized – that is, if we occupied the lower position in Figure I-6? Hardly: what is the point of being parts of one company and one system if we cannot learn from each other? The problem with total freedom not to communicate is that the poorer units no longer learn from the better ones, and the point of being one corporation generating a body of shared knowledge from multiple sources is then lost. There are many pathways to success. The experience of a hundred business units is far more valuable than the experience of any one unit.

Would we be better off if we were tightly centralized – if we occupied the upper left position in Figure I-6. Hardly: every business unit has a local market with key variations. The environment is constantly changing, and such changes will show up in some environments and not in others. Unless business units can adapt swiftly to changing customer demands, the whole corporation loses touch. The reason the center cannot give detailed orders to the business units is that the sheer complexity is too great. No single leader can process so much information; moreover, the center is further from customers than the local business unit is.

The answer has to be at the upper right of the figure: an inquiring system- and knowledge-generating corporation, which gathers information from scores of business units and transforms it into a body of knowledge, sharable with each unit, so that each peripheral part has the wisdom of the whole centralized system. As the saying goes, you must "act locally" but "think globally." Local actions provide the information from which global conclusions are drawn.

Our definition of good leadership is the capacity to reconcile such contrasting objectives and turn them into a single system that learns from its own activities.

Acknowledgments

This book is the result of much teamwork. Many people have contributed. First of all, we want to thank all our colleagues at Trompenaars Hampden-Turner Intercultural Management Consulting. All have acted as professional authors. They have interviewed many leaders with great care and have captured the essence of the fruits their subjects brought into existence. We have to thank Prof. Peter Woolliams for his ever-fresh enthusiasm and his great insights into many aspects of this complex field. We owe Dirk Devos for giving us the fruits of his interviews. Finally, we want to thank all the leaders who have contributed to the book. The majority also took the extra time to complete our Intercultural Competence Questionnaire – quite an effort, in view of their hectic schedules!

Fons Trompenaars
Charles Hampden-Turner
Amsterdam, August 31 2000

CHAPTER 1

Transcultural Competence

Learning to Lead by Through–Through Thinking and Acting, Part I

Time was when globalism was merely a question of extending American influence ever further across the globe, linked by the digital revolution. The world's sole remaining superpower had a universal methodology for economic development and leadership. Free markets were one with economic science. The American Way extended itself to social sciences in general and management theories in particular.

Then, some disturbing signs began to multiply. Why was China, although still communist, growing faster over a decade than any capitalist economy had ever grown? Why was newly capitalist Russia moving backwards toward total economic collapse? Why had Japan and East Asian economies grown "miraculously" for 30 years and then relapsed? The same business values that would appear to have given US businesses a new creative surge have had quite opposite effects elsewhere. Hopes of a world system of economic development have perceptibly dimmed.

This chapter will argue that business cultures are different, so different as to be in some respects diametrically opposed, and that, because business is run differently around the globe, we need different managerial and leadership competencies. Yet from these very differences, from that seeming Babel of discordant values, there is emerging a new capacity for bridging those differences. We call this *transcultural competence*. It has a logic that unifies differences. It is the logic that differentiates the manager from the leader and the successful leader from the failing one. The leader of the 21st century needs a new way of thinking, to which we refer here as *Through–Through* thinking. It is beyond *either–or* and even *and–and* thinking. It synthesizes seemingly opposed values into coherence.

For more than a decade, we have researched the cultures and values of managers in more than 50 nations. Recently, there has emerged a new phenomenon among those managers for whom crossing borders and engaging foreigners is a way of life. We will show that this competence can be described, measured, and identified for purposes of recruitment, selection, assessment, and training outcomes. We also believe that it reveals the competitive advantage of the managing of diversities of many kinds and origins. Most especially, it allows us to revisit the neglected field of values and ethics.

Before we can describe this competence convincingly, we must first dislodge the huge boulders of misapprehension, which block our path to understanding how values effect cultures. For at least two centuries, scholars have tried to give ethics a status borrowed from physics by pretending that values are like things or objects. Even industry has spoken of *goods* (good things). We were recently at a human rights conference where three speakers, inspired by each others' examples, pulled from their pockets a piece of the Berlin Wall, a stone from a Muslim temple destroyed by the Serbs, and a small rock symbolizing the steadfast nature of an insurance company. We seem to want our values to be hard, durable, solid, and exact. Yet, in truth, the attempt to reify our values and give them rock-like certainty has proved a disaster. Historians will almost certainly recall the 20th century as The Era of Genocide, in which rigid convictions clashed mercilessly. Many of those engaged in scientific inquiry have abandoned moral questions entirely. These are said to have no testable meaning, no reference to observable behaviors.

We view values quite differently: as information, as differences that make a difference to people communicating to each other. Values have no physical existence at all. They are not a bag of coins or jewels, but, like the binary digits in computers, they contrast 0 with 1. "Be flexible" means move down the Conviction–Flexibility continuum in the direction of flexibility and "be steadfast" means move towards the Conviction end – but, if we have been very flexible in reaching a position, we should become more convinced that it is right.

Leaders Recognize, Respect and Reconcile Differences

The main thesis throughout this book is that successful leaders reconcile value dilemmas better than those who don't. Leaders also face similar dilemmas. In our series of interviews with those successful leaders we have seen that seven basic dilemmas show up time and time again in different shapes.

Take the question of giving gifts. Suppose my American or West European HQ has a Code of Conduct banning gifts, which are considered forms of bribery. Suppose an important supplier gives me a gift of a piece of jade, not because he seeks to corrupt me, but because I mentioned over lunch that my young daughter collects jade figurines. The gift is small in value, a token of friendship and respect. It is even inscribed with birthday greetings. Should I "Follow the Code of Conduct" prescribed from 8,000 miles away? Or "Be flexible" and follow the norms of East Asian friendship networks?

At the moment, we lack the logic to decide such issues. British analytical philosophy tells us that values are mere "exclamations of preference," akin to liking or disliking strawberry ice cream. Economists tell us that all values are subjective and relative, *until* an objective price is fixed by markets, at which point their value becomes verifiable. The logic of dilemma resolution is circular or cybernetic. "Follow the Code" forbids all reception of gifts, but it needs to learn from SE Asian flexibility that *some* gifts are not bribes, but tokens of friendship – in short, that there are reasonable exceptions to this rule. So the rule is modified; now the prohibition is against accepting *bribes*, defined as gifts exceeding $75 in value. Note that the rule as qualified allows executives abroad *both* to "Follow the Code" *and* to "Be Flexible about friendship tokens." No longer do we have to insult gift givers by returning their presents and so lose business. Another variation is to accept gifts "equal to the value of an evening meal for two at a good restaurant" but no more. This makes sense, because Westerners tend to treat entertainment expense as a nonbribe; others do not make this distinction and are puzzled by our acceptance of meals and refusal of gifts.

The ideal of reconciliation upholds the important principle that the *best product* should win the business and that bribes distort this outcome – yet, service is also important, so small gifts may be used to show that friendship, consideration, and good relations are also on offer. Now, clearly, some gifts *are* bribes, but many are not. By thinking carefully about these exceptions, you learn to develop rules that will work in foreign countries, moving tactically upon the continuum of *New Rules–New Exceptions*. This is the way to make your rules better while appreciating the truly exceptional.

Consider two international businesses and how these confront two very common dilemmas of overseas operations.

Competing strongly   —   Making friends
Following rules   —   Finding exceptions

Let us suppose that one of our businesses is extremely successful and the other is teetering on the edge of bankruptcy. Can we explain their good and ill fortunes by the dilemmas they face? No, the dilemmas are the same. Can we explain it by the relative fervor with which they compete or follow rules? Not really; a failing company might be competing with desperate intensity and clinging to the rules as one would to a life raft. Feeling very strongly about any of these four values cannot distinguish triumph from disaster. So, where does the difference lie? Not in each value itself, nor in the strength of one or both. The answer lies *between* them, in the patterns of competing strongly and making friends, in the patterns of following rules and finding exceptions. In successful wealth creation, these two pairs of values are integrated and synergistic; hence the judgment that such leaders have "integrity." In wealth or value destruction, the two pairs of values frustrate, impede, and ultimately confound each other. We call the first pattern a *virtuous circle*, the second a *vicious circle*. The logic of the former is shown in the following diagram:

The Virtuous Circle

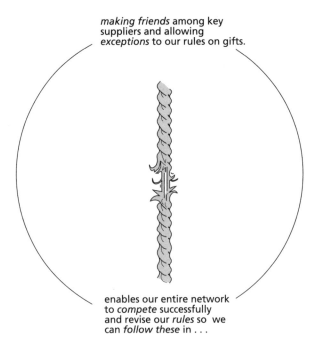

making friends among key suppliers and allowing *exceptions* to our rules on gifts.

enables our entire network to *compete* successfully and revise our *rules* so we can *follow these* in . . .

In the preceding example, making friends and competing fiercely on the merits of our product and service have been synergized, and the exception of gift-giving has been encouraged by revised rules, which allow genuine expressions of respect, but no bribes. All four values work together, but it could have turned out quite differently . . . as in the vicious circle:

The Vicious Circle

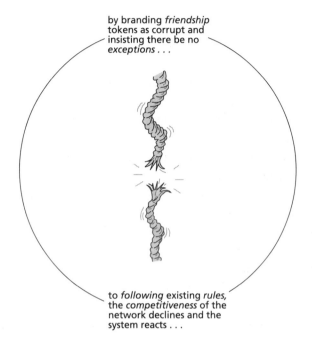

by branding *friendship* tokens as corrupt and insisting there be no *exceptions* . . .

to *following* existing *rules,* the *competitiveness* of the network declines and the system reacts . . .

In the vicious circle, one value sticking to the rules is deemed "right," the opposite making an exception for small gifts, is deemed "wrong." As a result, network competitiveness falls, business is in real jeopardy, and, in desperation, someone probably *will* pay a bribe, where friendship has failed! The result is a *downward* spiral: rules that exclude more and more of what is necessary to survive, and the failure of friendship, driving competitiveness ever lower, making friendship in its turn ever more costly and unwise. In virtuous circles, the values are mutually reinforcing and intensifying. In vicious circles, the values are split apart and provoke each other to ever further excess. A failing competitiveness under outmoded rules is extremely likely to swing over into flagrant illegality among crony capitalists. As the crisis looms, people grow desperate. As the values they once clung to fail, they veer to their opposites, which fail too. The vicious circle goes into "run-away," oscillating wildly from draconian rules to glaring exceptions, from competitive failure to conspiratorial cliques, as people attempt to save themselves from the consequences of that failure. When we communicate to each other about values, we are not uttering meaningless, subjective utterances. On the contrary, we can be helping each other to develop or damning each other to destruction.

This insight into how values connect or disconnect also helps us solve the age-old puzzle of whether values are absolute or relative. Cross-cultural researchers are often accused of cultural relativism – or say, equating the Taliban militia with Western democracy. Values are, of course, both absolute in one sense and relative in another sense, and we are healthier, wealthier, and wiser if we can combine these two senses. Adapting and following rules in some measure is absolutely necessary to wealth creation. In the absence of these values, no wealth will be created anywhere, ever. Yet the proportions in which these values are combined to meet this particular challenge are relative. They are acts of judgment, art forms. So, yes, we must have values to draw upon–the requirement that they be present is absolute – but, no, their expression is relative. They must be artfully combined in ever-changing syntheses appropriate to particular circumstances.

Take the question of loving and correcting your children. Both the value of love and the value of correction are absolute, in the sense that if either is not present, the child has no hope of growing up properly. Unloved or uncorrected children do not become effective citizens.

Yet, how loving and correcting are best *combined* remains an art form, relative to the challenge encountered. The way your criticism and support are expressed must vary with the child, with your relationship, with the seriousness of the situation. Whether your child *experiences* your anger as loving depends very much on skills of communication. Even with love and correction in abundant supply, you could get the expression all wrong and fail to convey your meaning. Hence, it is *absolutely* necessary both to love and to correct, yet the proportions of these in any communication are *relative* to the person being addressed.

In approaching transcultural competence, we have chosen seven major dimensions of difference, the first of which we have already touched upon. Each has contrasting value poles. These are selected because we have found that they best account for the major differences between national cultures.

The seven dimensions are as follows:

1. Rule-making   Exception finding
   (Universalism)   (Particularism)
2. Self-interest and personal fulfilment   Group interest and social concern
   (Individualism)   (Communitarianism)
3. Preference for precise, singular,"hard"   Preference for pervasive, patterned,
   standards   "soft" processes
   (Specificity)   (Diffusion)

Box 1 Fourteen Nations Compared

Universalism_____Particularism

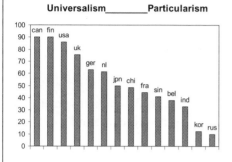

Individualism_____Communitarianism

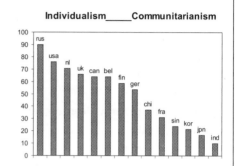

Specific_____Diffuse

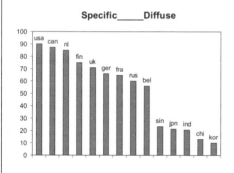

Internal_____External

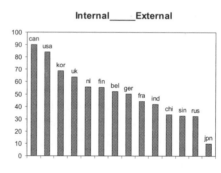

Achievement_____Ascription

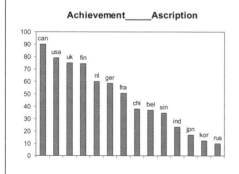

Overlap Present and Future

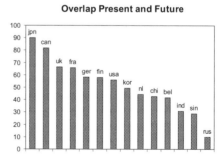

© THT Consulting 1997

1. Rule-making (Universalism)	Exception finding (Particularism)
2. Self-interest and personal fulfilment (Individualism)	Group interest and social concern (Communitarianism)
3. Preference for precise, singular, "hard" standards (Specificity)	Preference for pervasive, patterned, "soft" processes (Diffusion)
4. Emotions Inhibited (Neutral)	Emotions expressed (Affective)
5. Status earned through success and track record (Achievement)	Status ascribed to person's potential – e.g., age, family, education (Ascription)
6. Control and effective direction comes from within (Inner-directed)	Control and effective direction comes from outside (Outer-directed)
7. Time is conceived of as a "race" with passing increments (Sequential)	Time is conceived of as a "dance" with circular iterations (Synchronous)

The first three dimensions will be considered in this chapter. The last four will be considered in Chapter 2. Each of these seven dimensions can be polarized with each other, in which case we get spectacular, amusing, and sometimes tragic contrasts; alternatively, all seven can be integrated and synergized, in which case we achieve transcultural competence.

We will now go through the seven dimensions in turn and consider the following in each case.

(a)   the sophisticated stereotypes;
(b)   some typical misunderstandings;
(c)   what effective leaders know and have learned;
(d)   how we measured transcultural competence.

Before we proceed, let us explain what is meant by "sophisticated stereotypes." We mean by this term the stereotypes (or sociotypes) of a culture that have been carefully researched and found to be true. They are, therefore, not the product of prejudice or denigration, but they remain nonetheless surface manifestations. We cannot avoid stereotypes, for several reasons – mainly because cultures stereotype themselves: to sell popular culture, to sell tourism, to idealize themselves, and to contrast themselves favorably with perceived enemies.

Box 2: Chinese Particularism

Jorge Luis Borges offers the following excerpt from an early Chinese encyclopedia:

> Animals are divided into (a) Belonging to the Emperor, (b) Embalmed, (c) Tamed, (d) Suckling pigs, (e) Sirens, (f) Fabulous, (g) Stray dogs, (h) Included in the present classification, (i) Frenzied, (j) Innumerable, (k) Drawn with a very fine camel hairbrush, (l) Having just broken the water pitcher, (m) "that from a long way off look like flies."

We need have no fear for the variety and uniqueness of such a civilization, but some might doubt its rule-making and classificatory powers.

Source: Michel Foucault, *The Order of Things*, Editions Gallimard, 1966.

For 20 years or more, Geert Hofstede with his IBM samples and Charles Hampden-Turner and Fons Trompenaars with their dilemma methodology have classified respondents as belonging at one or the other end of various continua. Americans, for example, were Individualist, not Collectivist. The problem with sophisticated stereotypes is what they miss. How do Americans use groups, teams, communities? How do the Japanese create? Hiding beneath the stereotype is much crucial information.

We must therefore note the sophisticated stereotype, observe the trouble it causes, and move beyond it. This we will try to do by delineating transcultural competence.

Dimension 1. Rule-Making   vs.   Exception-Finding
(Universalism vs. Particularism)

The Sophisticated Stereotype

Here, the contrast is between the desire to make, discover, and enforce rules of wide applicability, be they scientific, legal, moral, or industrial standards, and the desire to find how to be exceptional, unique, unprecedented, particular, and one-of-a-kind.

As Box 1 shows, the USA, Finland, Canada, Denmark, and the United Kingdom are all high in their desire for universal rule-making. In contrast, South Korea, China, Japan, Singapore, and France are all relatively particularistic. One theme in universalism is Protestantism, which sees the Word of God encoded in the Bible; a second is the Common Law tradition; a third is the whole concept of America as The New World, with rules designed to attract immigrants. That America has 22 times as many lawyers per capita as Japan is one consequence of the universalistic preference. Well-known manifestations of high universalism are Scientific Management, Fordism, formula fast foods, benchmarking. "100% American," How to Win Friends and Influence People, and similar moral commandments. In contrast, a culture much higher in particularism is China. Box 1 shows an excerpt from an eighteenth-century Chinese encyclopedia that attempts to describe and to classify "animals." The particularity of detail astounds, yet the rules of classification are, by Western standards, very strange indeed!

Some Typical Misunderstandings

America, in her dealings with the world, tends to see herself as the rule-maker and global policeman. In her trade disputes with Japan, the USA tries to personify the rules of capitalism. "Rice is a commodity. It must be freely traded." The Japanese say, "But we are different. Rice is the sacred symbol of our culture, something very particular." Is the USA an "obvious" culture because it makes highly standardized "universal" goods – e.g. Levi's, Big Macs, Coca Cola? Or is France a "snobbish" culture because it prefers products of high particularity – e.g., haute couture, haute cuisine, fine wines? Such arguments can entertain, but they are unfruitful.

A famous dispute about sugar prices broke out between Australia and Japan in the middle of the 1970s. Japan signed a long-term contract to buy Australian sugar at a price below the then world market. Weeks later the bottom fell out of the market. Japan wanted to renegotiate a new contract, on the basis that its particular relationship with sugar exporters preceded contract terms. Australia wanted the original contract honored as a universal obligation to keeping one's word. Does particular partnership override the law? Or is legal conduct to be expected from true partners, however inconvenient?

What The Effective Leaders Know and Have Learned

As before, the secret of creating wealth lies not *in* the values of rule-making and exception-finding, but *between* them, for, of course, these values are complementary. How do you improve your rules except by noting each exception and revising your rules accordingly? – but this, of course, assumes that legislating better is your prime purpose. Suppose you were a particularist, seeking to be exceptional and unique. Would the same complementarity apply? It would, but in reverse order. How do you develop exceptional abilities except by noting the highest standards and exceeding them?

Either way, the transculturally competent leader can make a virtuous circle of rule-making and exception-finding:

A Virtuous Circle

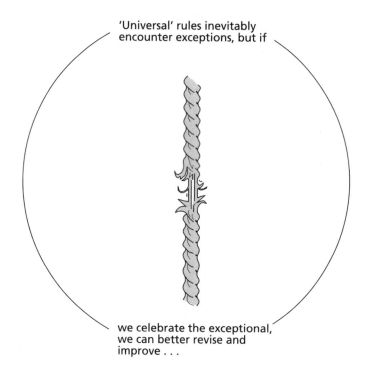

'Universal' rules inevitably encounter exceptions, but if

we celebrate the exceptional, we can better revise and improve . . .

Among famous examples of how particularism can be integrated into universalism are (1) Anglo-American case law and (2) the case method at the Harvard Business School, which begins with particular cases before generalizing. Such virtuous circles are much easier to conceptualize than to put into effect. The fact is, it is often infuriating to promulgate a rule and then discover an exception. If you are a boss, you feel defied. If you are a scientist, you believe you have failed. If you are a moralist, you are aghast at such sinfulness. All too common, therefore, is the vicious circle:

A Vicious Circle

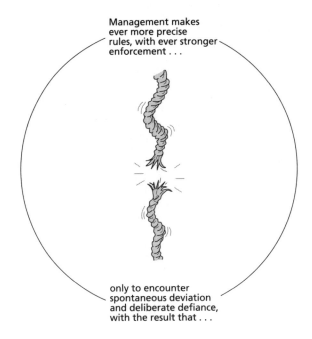

Management makes
ever more precise
rules, with ever stronger
enforcement . . .

only to encounter
spontaneous deviation
and deliberate defiance,
with the result that . . .

Once again, "the string has broken," and the system is in run-away. Attempts to enforce rules escalate and escalate, as do deviance and defiance; these only intensify rule enforcement, as "the snake devours its own tail."

A recent incident at Motorola illustrates how a vicious circle was avoided, only at the last moment, by a rule change. East Asian engineers were given a $2000 housing allowance so that they could live comfortably, adjacent to the plant. One day a senior engineer had to be contacted urgently at home and was found to be living in a shack. He had spent his housing allowance on putting his siblings through school. The corporation's first instinct was to fire him – had he not deceived them and misallocated funds – but their second thought was that he had put the money to better use than by isolating himself in relative luxury as the "kept man" of a foreign corporation. Was thinking first of one's own family an "offense"? The rules were changed. Today you can use the allowance for your own purpose and to implement local values. The corporation has learned from its environment about values different from personal affluence.

When a group changes its rules, we call this change *conceptual transformation*. There are several examples in this book of leaders who have learned from exceptions how to improve rules. In Chapter 3, Dilemma 5, Richard Branson of Virgin shows how a large organization, worth over $3 billion, with its own rules of operation, can nonetheless renew itself by spinning off numerous entrepreneurial ventures, each unique and particular. The trick is to let no unit grow too large and to quickly divide those that might do so. In Chapter 5, Philippe Bourguignon continues to protect the legacy that every Club Med vacation is a personal dream, a voyage into the discovery of an unfolding selfhood, with an *esprit* and an *ambience* that are unique and unrepeatable. Yet many of the elements going into that holiday can and must be standardized, globalized, and systematized, generated in high volumes and at low cost – all ingredients of a universal logic. You can create fresh scenarios of satis-faction *out of* standardized inputs. It is their *combination* which is unique, not the elements themselves.

In LEGO, Chapter 6, Dilemma 3, Christian Maygard faces the problem of how newly innovative companies, allowed the freedom to break the entrenched rules and norms of LEGO's core culture, can be integrated back into that core, as success models embodying new rules. Only when these innovators are confident enough and successful enough are their exceptional virtues used to update and revise LEGO's traditional rules.

In Chapter 10, Dilemma 4, rules have been Global and exceptions Local. Yet, Jim Morgan of Applied Materials has set up a system of transcultural learning wherein a series of discoveries about local and exceptional circumstances are used to *test generalizations about universally applicable knowledge.* Does this principle apply in all places or only in some? How important are the exceptions? *Might one of these exceptions become a new global rule, replacing existing rules?* "Global vs. Local" is transcended by "Glocalism," the process of modifying global rules through examining local exceptions.

In Chapter 13, Dilemma 4, Sergei Kirijenko, one-time Russian premier, confronted a Russian economy of chronic cronyism, of collusion and special deals with particular customers who used the size of their indebtedness to coerce. He was then head of NORSI oil, a major state-owned refinery. Kiriyenko obliged all parties to negotiate new agreements with the new entity he had created from the bankrupt shell, but, once agreements were forged, the parties *had to live by what they had promised.* The telephone crackled with threats, but Kiriyenko stuck to his guns. Renegotiation was possible, after a stated interval, but in the meantime the rules applied to everyone. The Russian economy was getting its first taste of particular requirements encompassed within universal rules of contract.

Measuring Intercultural Competence, Reconciling the Universal with the Particular: How We Did It, What We Found.

We now turn to the measurement and strategic use of transcultural competence and the results achieved thus far. Results were first accumulated with our "old" questionnaire. In these investigations, managers were given a straight choice between two conflicting values. For example, the issue of Universalism vs. Particularism was measured by posing the following dilemma.

You are riding in a car driven by a close friend. He hits a pedestrian. You know he was going at least 35 miles per hour in an area of the city where the maximum speed is 20 mph. There are no witnesses. His lawyer says that if you testify under oath that he was travelling only 20 mph, it may save him from serious consequences.

What right does your friend have to expect you to protect him?

Here, the responding manager must either side with his friend or bear truthful witness in a court of law. There is no possibility of integrating opposites, no opportunity to display transcultural competence by reconciling this dilemma. In our conversations with managers who had responded to this questionnaire, we kept encountering attempts to resolve the dilemma and some annoyance that we had pressed so stark a choice upon them. So we designed a more discriminating questionnaire, with five answers, not two. Two answers were the original polarized alternatives. One answer was a compromise between the two values. The last two answers were alternative integrations: one that started with universalism and encompassed particularism, and one that started with particularism and encompassed universalism. These are set out next:

(a)   There is a general obligation to tell the truth as a witness. I will not perjure myself before the court. Nor should any real friend expect this from me.

(b)   There is a general obligation to tell the truth in court, and I will do so, but I owe my friend an explanation and all the social and financial support I can organize.

(c)   My friend in trouble always comes first. I am not going to desert him before a court of strangers on the basis of some abstract principle.

(d)   My friend in trouble gets my support, whatever his testimony, yet I would urge him to find in our friendship the strength that allows us both to tell the truth.

(e)   I will testify that my friend was going a little faster than allowed and say that it was difficult to read the speedometer.

The logics behind these positions follow the accompanying figures.

The Basic Cultural Template – part one

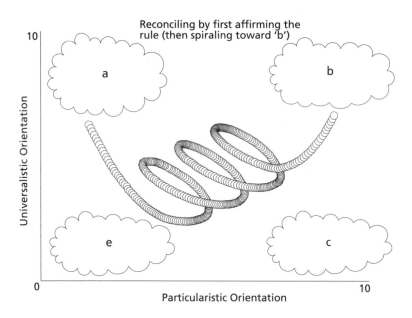

(a)   (1/10) This is a polarized response in which the law is affirmed, but the friend is rejected (Universalism excludes Particularism).

(b)   (10/10) This is an integrated response in which first the Rule is affirmed and then everything possible is done for the friend (Universalism joined to Particularism).

(c)   (10/1) This is a polarized response in which the friend is affirmed as an exception to the Rule, which is then rejected (Particularism excludes Universalism).

(d)   (10/10) This is an integrated response in which exceptional friendship is affirmed and then joined to the rule of law (Particularism joined to Universalism).

(e)   (5/5) This is a standoff or fudge, in which both the rule of law and the principle of loyalty to friends are blunted (Universalism compromised with Particularism).

The Basic Cultural Template – part two

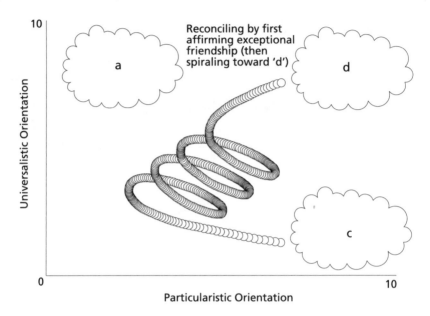

The underlying framework is as follows:

- Integrated responses (b) and (d) show more transcultural competence than polarized responses (a) and (c) and compromised response (e).
- American managers will typically put universalism first (adopting the anticlockwise spiral), and East Asian/Southern European managers will typically put particularism first (adopting the clockwise spiral), but each can integrate that priority with its opposite.
- From this, it follows that there are at least two paths to integrity, not "one best way."
- There are, however, better ways and worse ways.
- Transcultural competence will anticipate and explain success in overseas postings and will correlate with 360° feedback ratings.

What We Found

The questionnaire based on these logics has been administered to several groups: to US executives with both extensive and limited experience of international management at Applied Materials; to Chinese "high flyers" working for a US multinational; and to trainees attending the Intercultural Communications Institute summer school in Portland. What we found was that the capacity to reconcile rules and exceptions correlated positively and consistently with the capacity to reconcile several other dilemmas crucial to leadership and cultural effectiveness. Within Bombardier, the capacity to resolve dilemmas correlated positively with "promotions during the last three years," as opposed to lateral transfers and staying put.

Dimension 2.	**Self-interest and Personal Fulfillment (Individualism**	**vs.** **vs.**	**Group Interest and Social Concern Communitarianism)**

The Sophisticated Stereotype

Here the contrast is between the freedom of the individual, in which personal fulfillment, enrichment, expression, and self-development are championed above all, and benefits accruing to the group, community, or corporation. There can be no doubt where America stands. Her very population is formed by those who left the only community they had known to seek their fortune in the New World. Box 1 shows that Canada, the United States, Denmark, Switzerland, the Netherlands, Australia, and the United Kingdom head the national advocates of Individualism, while India, Japan, Mexico, China, France, Brazil, and Singapore head the advocates of Communitarianism.

In this matter, the USA stereotypes itself. Ever since Christian in Bunyan's *Pilgrim's Progress* shook off his pleading wife and child to journey alone to the Heavenly City, Americans have been making themselves, helping themselves, and accumulating on their own, lone rangers to the end. Did you ever see a Hollywood movie in which group opinion was proved right and the lone protagonist yielded to that view? Yet the superior judgment of he-who-stands-alone has been vindicated a thousand times! It was Hermann Melville who wrote,

> Take a single man alone, and he seems a triumph, a grandeur or a woe. But take mankind in the mass and they seem for the most part a mob of unnecessary duplicates.

The communitarian attitudes of rice-growing regions should come as no surprise. With less than a dozen people cooperating, it is simply impossible to survive. The self-aggrandizing schemes of war-lords have brought China to starvation again and again. France has progressed historically only when angry groups surged into the streets and manned barricades. The inspiration may have been individual, but the *force majeur* was communal. History shapes cultures. Country scores for Individualism–Communitarianism are in Box 1.

Some Typical Misunderstandings

American plans to "motivate" employees in foreign cultures typically fall foul of this crucial cultural difference. How many times has the "Employee of the Month" called in sick, rather than face an envious peer group at work? Individual incentives can be unfair if other members of the group helped you to succeed or if you believe that your supervisor deserves the credit for briefing and mentoring you so well.

There was a famous case of an error made in assembly work at Intel in Penang. One thousand units had to be reworked at great expense, yet the American boss could not discover who had made the error. The whole work group, even the plant director, took responsibility and apologized. They should have watched the worker more carefully, they explained, helped her more, trained her better. Where a whole community is dedicated to higher productivity and quality, you may be wise to leave well enough alone. Communitarianism has its uses.

What the Effective Leaders Know and Have Learned

The real limitation of sophisticated stereotypes is at its most obvious here. Yes, of course, Americans are individualists, but they have also created groups for a wider variety of purposes than most other societies: The Town Meeting, the Community Chest, the Protest Group, the Skunk Works, the Training Group, Teamworking, the Support Group, the Political Action Committee, and so on. The main purpose of this group may indeed be the advancement of personal interests, but it remains true that American individualism has important group expressions. For, once again, the wealth-generating solutions are not in values extolling groups or individuals, but in interactions between these values.

In this book, a large number of leaders have made artful combinations between individualism and communitarianism and between competitiveness and cooperation to create powerful learning systems. Richard Branson, Chapter 3, specializing, as Virgin does, in service organizations, looks first to the communities of his employees who serve the communities of customers; by taking back his company into private hands, he is able to moderate the demands of shareholders (himself) and take his gains in terms of growth, not dividends. A very similar strategy is pursued by Val Gooding of BUPA, Britain's premier private health insurer and provider,

Chapter 8. Without shareholders, she is able to invest all in staff, customer service, and rapid growth. This can be a crucial advantage for "caring organizations."

In Chapter 4, Dilemma 3, Martin Gillo has deliberately fine-tuned the individualism of Advanced Micro-Devices' American HQ with East German communitarianism. He set up rewards for individuals who contribute to team success and gave bonuses to teams for giving the best support to the initiatives of individual members. Both cultures joined enthusiastically in a system that respected their values, even if each preferred an opposite aspect of the system. In Chapter 9, we see how Suez Lyonnaise des Eaux has captured an astonishing 52 percent of foreign-owned water and treatment systems by combining the energies released by privatization with a social responsibility that returns to the served community full ownership and responsibility for its own municipal infrastructure after a 20 to 25 year overhaul. Rarely has private shareholder gain and responsibility for the integrity of a community been better combined.

Perhaps the boldest attempt to reconcile individualist and communitarian cultures, one that has been brilliantly successful, is by Jim Morgan of Applied Materials (in Chapter 10, Dilemma 2). Jim turned author to write a path-breaking book on Japanese business culture in the 1980s. The East Asian attitude toward electronics, microchips (the rice of industry), and computers was essentially communitarian. These technologies, contributing as they did to the community's industrial infrastructure in general, could not be allowed to fail and were accordingly nurtured by governments and banks. Jim realized early on that he had to give Applied Materials, Japan, the autonomy to locate itself at the heart of Japanese industrial policy, among the inner circles of industry itself. He has followed this policy in Korea, China, Singapore, and other major centers of communitarian consciousness. He has instituted an East–West dialogue at the apex of Applied Materials, in which the new freedoms of the electronic age converse with the priceless communitarian logics of accelerated learning for whole societies.

Finally, Stan Shih of Acer, in Chapter 12, Dilemma 2, built on the communitarian family-based Chinese culture of Taiwan. His "Dragon Dream" had a traditional appeal to the Taiwanese community aspiring to be a force in the wider world community, but he was very well aware of the individualism of the Western world as well as the incipient individuality of the Chinese. Accordingly, he has made Acer a public, national company in most of the nations it operates, with quotations on local stock exchanges. He also uses stock option plans for *all* employees, so that they can share as individuals in the regional success of the company. Acer applies that ratio of individualism to communitarianism preferred by the many cultures in which it operates.

It has been known for many years now that giving incentives, sharing gains, and rewarding the whole group is more motivating for individual members than trying to reward them directly. The virtuous circle looks like the following figure:

Virtuous Circle

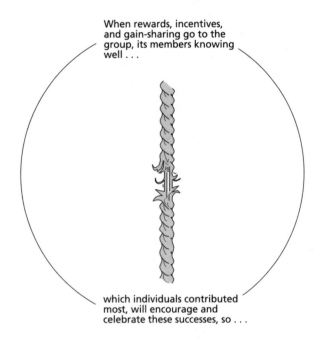

When rewards, incentives, and gain-sharing go to the group, its members knowing well . . .

which individuals contributed most, will encourage and celebrate these successes, so . . .

A group can make any one of its members feel like a million dollars. There may be nothing more satisfying in the world than being a heroine or hero to those who know you best – and who would grudge your subsequent promotion or pay rise, once you had steered your group to fame and fortune?

The transculturally competent know that "individualism vs. communitarianism" is a false dichotomy. The real art is to nurture individuals and individuals to serve groups, a process that Adam M. Brandenberger and Barry J. Nalebuff have called *co-opetition*.

An interesting example of this is Motorola's Total Customer Satisfaction competition. Teams that have "totally satisfied" their customers in any part of the world where Motorola operates gather together the evidence of their success and enter a worldwide competition in which they present their solution on stage, together with the results achieved. The contests teach all members how to compete fiercely, but note that this competition is about cooperating with customers and fellow team members. Once again, this is "collaborative competing" or co-opetition.

Virtuous Circle

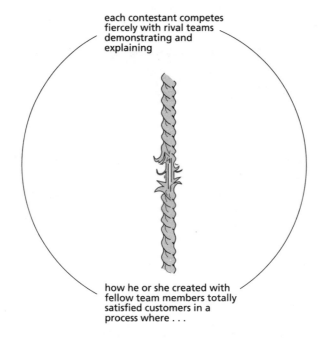

each contestant competes fiercely with rival teams demonstrating and explaining

how he or she created with fellow team members totally satisfied customers in a process where . . .

Among the advantages of this competition is that 8 hundred or so winning solutions surface, to be studied and disseminated by Motorola University. Competing differentiates ideas; cooperating integrates them. Knowledgeable executives have finely differentiated, well-integrated strategic maps of their terrains.

The dimensions do not exist in isolation from each other. We get powerful insights into Russia's current predicament in Box 1-3.

Measuring Transcultural Competence: Reconciling the Individual and the Group

We again turn to the measurement and strategic use of transcultural competence and the results achieved thus far. We have repeatedly asked leaders to choose between five options. Two are unreconciled answers, one is a compromise, and two are reconciled answers. (See Box 4.)

Box 3: Russia's Agony

What is clear from Russia's scores on our first and second dimension is that no viable system of social order currently exists. Civic order stems from two main influences, the combination of Universalism with Individualism, or "The Legal Harness of Self-Interest," and the combination of Particularism with Communitarianism, or "Special Deals for the Socially Responsible." If we cross our first two axes we find these two clusters:

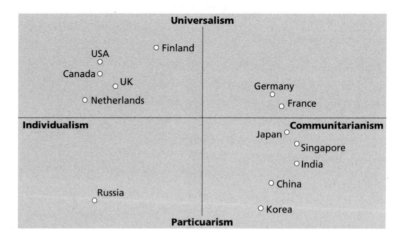

Box 4: Question 2. Jobs in your organization

Which of the following jobs is found most frequently in your organization?

(a)   A job that is part of an organization where everybody works together and where you do not get individual credit.
(b)   A job that allows everybody to work independently and where individual credit is received on the basis of individual performance.
(c)   A job where everybody works together in teams and where the teams are constantly stimulating individual creativity.
(d)   A job that allows everybody to work independently and where individual credit is given to the best team player.
(e)   A job where neither too much individual creativity nor excessive "groupthink" is the norm.

Answers (a) and (b) are unreconciled answers. Answer (e) is a compromise. Answer (c) is a reconciliation where we start with communitarianism, and answer (d) represents reconciliation that starts with the beauties of individualism. Again we have found that leaders that chose the latter two options were significantly more effective than those who chose the alternatives.

Dimension 3.	Preference for Precise, Singular, "Hard" Standards (Specificity	vs. vs.	Preference for Pervasive, Patterned, "Soft" Processes Diffusion)

The Sophisticated Stereotype

Here, the contrast is between the cultures that emphasize things, facts, statistics, units, atoms, analysis, and "hard" numbers and those cultures that emphasize relations, patterns, configurations, connectedness, synthesis, and "soft" processes. These contrasting styles have been identified with the left and right brain hemispheres. We call them Specificity versus Diffusion.

America's exaggerated specificity manifests itself in many forms, such as in "keeping your word" (as if there were only one!), in "bullet points," piecework incentives, straight-line forecasts, bottom lines, financial ratios, and other attempted distillations of virtue. We urge each other to "get to the point", and "not beat about the bush." Specificity is increased when we argue, by win–lose conflict which produces specific results and by debates between the respective advocates. Specific–Diffuse country scores are in Box 1.

Some Typical Misunderstandings

We well remember the fury of a young Israeli engineering salesman who had beaten the three other salesmen, all Japanese, in his department. Indeed, he had sold more than all three put together, while learning Japanese from his wife. When his Japanese boss gave him an "average" rating, he hit the roof. He appealed to the American HQ of the company, who backed his position. Now his Japanese boss was furious. "You shoot me, I shoot you," the latter hissed. From an American/Israeli perspective, this engineer's sales record said it all. Judged by specific criteria, he had done brilliantly. He had won the sales, worked longer hours, seen more customers, and not even bothered his boss. Yet, judged by diffuse criteria, he had failed. He had never informed his boss of his mounting success, nor allowed him to share in it. He had never passed intelligence or information to other salespersons or tried to improve the work process of the department. He had not contributed to relationships with his work colleagues at all.

Alfie Kohn recently compiled a long, sad dossier of what goes wrong with Pay for Performance. Many managers will recognize these problems, but still are reluctant to give up on the idea that, just as markets pull money and rewards towards successful enterprise, so should corporations. The problem with Pay for Performance is its exaggerated specificity. It assumes that superiors can know in advance how a task should be done, how difficult it is, and, hence, what pay should be attached to its performance, but increasingly, this is not possible. Work is too complex, too innovative, too subject to continuous improvement for superiors to know these things, much less to construct an elaborate tariff. Markets certainly do pay for success. This is their genius, but they do not tell you in advance what you should do or how much you will gain by doing it! Markets are diffuse, chaotic processes with some very specific and measurable outcomes. Let us count, by all means, but not shrink reality to what can be counted.

What the Effective Leaders Know and Have Learned

The answer lies, as before, between the preferences of those business cultures, such as in the USA and the Netherlands, with predominant specificity and of those business cultures, such as in Japan and Singapore, with predominant diffuseness. While Americans like to begin with forecasts, budgets, checklists, and plans and then start a process to hit these targets, East Asians typically value harmonious processes *(wa)* and the spontaneous flow of work and only later subject these to detailed feedback on specific indicators.

Some famous American gurus, among them W. Edwards Deming and Joseph Scanlon, had their ideas picked *over* in America, but picked *up* and massively implemented in Japan and East Asia, these imported back into the USA. Why was this? Because both Deming and Scanlon placed spontaneous action and the free flow of ideas and industrial processes ahead of the feedback and specifics needed to monitor, guide, and reward them. Deming's cycle of Act–Plan–Implement–Check starts with spontaneous action. The Scanlon Plan begins with the free flow of constructive ideas within work-teams. Once they are implemented, their impact on the input–output ratio is calculated, and specific gains from this process are shared among group members. This is a much better "imitation of capitalism" than Pay for Performance, because it sees that improvements are yet to be discovered and invented amid the "chaos" of work processes.

That employees are capable of self-organizing to form teams with their own flow and momentum is by now a truism. It could begin with a challenge or a definition of a problem by the sponsor of the team. Persons who care about this issue and have the skills and knowledge to address it select themselves or are selected by the regard of other volunteers. Note that the team is shaped by the profile of the problem and forms itself spontaneously to solve that problem.

Most leaders in this book developed ingenious ways of synergizing diffuse and specific processes. Philippe Bourguignon of Club Med was determined to build a "power brand" (Chapter 5, Dilemma 2). This requires millions of impacts upon the public of the Club Med brand, via an accumulation of specific "sound bytes" and fleeting images in the media, all of which reinforce the brand, via repetition. Yet, at the same time, the brand stood for a vacation that was dreamlike, playful, experimental, and without precedent in the customer's experience, a seamless, diffuse pattern of intense enjoyment, in which to reinvent oneself and rehearse new roles and different lifestyles. The specific brand stood for a cornucopia of novel experiences.

Val Gooding of BUPA, the British private health insurer and provider, realized that, in health provision, you have to go beyond specific medical crises in which you respond only after a diagnosis has been made. She instituted a policy of enhancing *wellness,* an extremely diffuse concept of living one of many healthy lifestyles, while avoiding emergencies by careful screening; see Chapter 9, Dilemma 4. Michael Dell of Dell Computers (Chapter 11, Dilemma 6), was one of the first to move beyond the supply of specific hardware or software to embrace process innovation via the Internet. Dell starts with why you want computers, what you want them for, and how you plan to mobilize information, and it helps you with that whole diffuse process of knowledge management. Eric Bronfman, CEO of Seagram's, launched a major program to change company culture. He saw culture as a diffuse process to be negotiated between leader and employees. The leader managed the culture, and the culture produced hard, specific results. What leaders cannot do is order up results like items on a menu. Hence, Bronfman developed a dual scoreboard for his managers: They were rewarded for specific results achieved and for exemplifying and managing the diffuse array of cultural values that guided the corporation and helped to define excellence.

A major issue having to do with strategy – see Chapter 6, Dilemma 3 – is whether strategy is a specific, codified plan of action, conceived in abstract and then implemented by staff, or whether strategy is a diffuse set of local initiatives arising from the grass roots and providing vital clues to success. Hugo Levecke of AMRO Leaseholding was able to show how powerful these two ideas are in combination. The organization learns from *first* appraising local initiatives and inquiring into their greater or lesser success and only then creating a specific strategy out of proven successful initiatives, generalizing from local to global gains.

Chicago psychologist Mihaly Csikszentmihaly speaks of the *flow experience,* in which teams or single competitors have so closely matched their skills with the attainment of their goals, that the boundaries seem to dissolve. They are their own challenge. The skier and the piste are one. The goal itself becomes a source of energy that speeds the team. Human beings and their teams, says Mihaly, are complex adaptive systems, capable of forming seamless, purposeful wholes.

In highly effective organizations, then, diffuse, "chaotic," creative teams receive specific feedback upon the success or otherwise of initiatives, managing, as it were, "on the edge of chaos."

Virtuous Circle

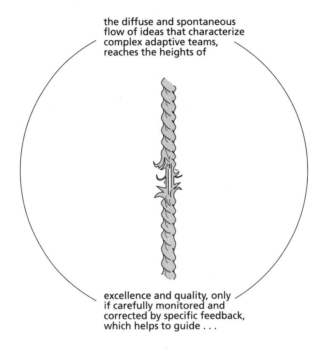

the diffuse and spontaneous flow of ideas that characterize complex adaptive teams, reaches the heights of

excellence and quality, only if carefully monitored and corrected by specific feedback, which helps to guide . . .

Box 5: Question 3. The best work environment

People have different opinions about how the work environment influences job performance.

Which of these alternatives best describes the work environment in your organization?

(a) People you work with know you personally and accept the way you are, both within and outside of the organization.

(b) Colleagues respect the work you do, even if they are not your friends.

(c) Colleagues know you personally and use this wider knowledge to improve job performance.

(d) Colleagues take some private circumstances into consideration, while disregarding others.

(e) The people you work with respect the work you do and are therefore able to offer to help you in private matters.

Measuring Transcultural Competence: Reconciling Specificity and Diffuseness

The 2500 managers who completed our transcultural questionnaire all considered five possible answers to the following ideas about what is the best work environment.

The Best Work Environment – part one

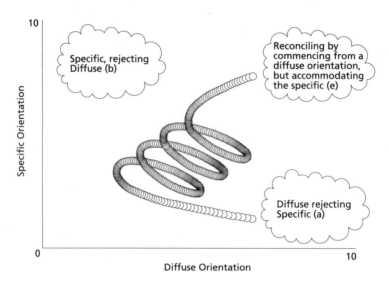

The Best Work Environment – part two

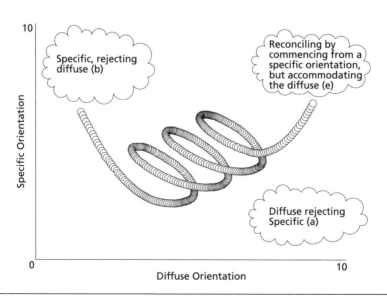

Here we see that the most effective work environments, (e) and (c), are those in which specific and diffuse sources of knowledge are combined – in either order.

This concludes the presentation of our first three dimensions. In each case, the recognition of dilemmas and their reconciliation helped us and our leaders to create a wider and more inclusive "integration of values." We submit that this integration, this bridging of diverse perspectives, is a vital aspect of creating wealth.

CHAPTER 2

Transcultural Competence

Learning to Lead by Through–Through Thinking and Acting, Part II

In this chapter we will consider our final four dimensions.

4.	Emotions Inhibited	–	Emotions Expressed
5.	Achieved Status	–	Ascribed Status
6.	Inner-directed	–	Outer-directed
7.	Sequential	–	Synchronous Time

Dimension 4.	**Emotions Inhibited**	**vs.**	**Emotions Expresse**
	(Neutral	**vs.**	**Affective)**

The Sophisticated Stereotype

It is well known that cultures display emotions to a greatly varying degree. The fury of the Frenchman when you nearly collide with his car and the way he uses his whole body to express his rage is legendary. In contrast, one can be forgiven for imagining that Japanese executives have gone to sleep during one's presentation. The posture of "half-eye" with the eyelid half closed can be very galling to those who do not understand "respectful listening." Equally unnerving are long silences following your statement. These might be read as "boredom," when in fact they are intended as evidence of thoughtful consideration.

This particular dimension has more subtleties and variations than most others, because, of course, there is strong disagreement about what one should be neutral or affective *about*. Americans, for example, show up as moderately affective, despite their Puritan origins of restraint in religious expression. They believe in showing enthusiasm for products, visions, missions, and projects, but are less expressive to each other. They approve of positive emotion (enthusiasm), but not so much of negative emotion (anger or grief). They will talk *about* emotion ("I'm feeling angry") in a vaguely therapeutic manner, but rarely explode or show physical signs of anger. The British use humor to release emotions and might begin a speech with a joke to relax the audience. Germans and Swiss could see this as unserious and frivolous. Japanese and Koreans reveal a desire for intimacy by getting drunk together; Germans prefer to bare their souls and share their philosophies of life. The patterns are extremely complex.

Some Typical Misunderstandings

The Swiss can be quite serious, especially during work hours. Humor is for relaxing moments before or after the seminar. The Dutch presenter used a cartoon to "break the ice." Dead silence. He used a second cartoon. Again, silence. Then a Swiss participant raised his hand: "Can we get on with the seminar, please?"

The Dutch presenter tried to make a joke of the intervention.

"You're a serious lot... Have you ever thought of going into banking?"

Silence.

In the coffee break, the senior Swiss manager approached the Dutch presenter.

"We didn't like to embarrass you, Dr. Trompenaars, but, in fact, the Swiss have been in banking for some time."

Note that both parties hung on tight to their conviction that jokes were or were not appropriate in this seminar. Those who saw humor as inappropriate could not even recognize the attempt! (Or perhaps they were being so subtly insulting to the presenter's intelligence that he justified their attitude by not catching on.)

Often, the same word triggers totally different associations. In a recent partnership negotiation, the Japanese and American sides both vowed to be "sincere." By this, the Americans meant outspoken, unreserved, and spontaneous, a trait the Japanese found insulting. By "sincere," the Japanese meant genuine efforts to create a climate of politeness, good etiquette, and gracious manners, a habit the Americans saw as "bull." The meeting proved a disaster.

What Effective Leaders Demonstrate

It is wise for a leader to make the greatest possible use of emotional range. There are wide variations in the fortunes of a company, and it is appropriate to have a mood that fits the occasion. As Robert Whittington wrote of Sir Thomas More,

> Where should we find a man of such wit, affability and lowliness? As time requireth, a man of marvellous mirth and pastimes, and sometimes of as sad gravity, as who say: A man for all seasons.

In the Bible, we are told in Ecclesiastes,

> To everything there is a season, and a time to every purpose under heaven.
> A time to be born and a time to die. . . .
> A time to weep, and a time to laugh: a time to mourn and a time to dance.
> A time to love and a time to hate: a time of war and a time of peace.

The effective leader operates in two contrasting realms, in calculated reasoning, which can require that emotions be temporarily suppressed, and in a wisdom of the heart, which knows that emotional expression evokes a resonance that can heal, inspire, enthuse, comfort, and calm those present.

It is perfectly legitimate to postpone the expression of emotion until you are in a place or in a presence where it is appropriate to communicate it, but temporary *suppression* should not lead to *repression*, where dangerous emotions are not admitted even to oneself. Persons with that tendency are likely to erupt into rage or grief, to tremble uncontrollably, or act maliciously and destructively. The effective leader trusts his or her body to convey appropriate feelings and strives to make good sense of, and logical deductions from, those feelings. Mind includes the body and the messages it sends to us.

A number of the leaders in this book managed neutrality–affectivity particularly well. Richard Branson, Chapter 3, regarded "*have fun*" as the surest recipe for an organization soon to serve its customers effectively. Good service should be a pleasure for those providing it, and, in its absence, something was wrong. LEGO put the switch from neutrality to exuberance and excitement to clever use by charging customers *before* they went into Legoland Parks, while they were still in a calculative mode (see Chapter 6, Dilemma 6), but the entrance fee gave families, and especially children, free access to all attractions, so that they could let their excitement rip, without clawing desperately at mother's handbag for one more treat. There is a time to seek entrance and a time to enjoy having done so; the first should be sober, the second joyful.

Bang and Olufsen was a family firm when it got into trouble. The roots of its problem lay within the family, in a needlessly expensive lifestyle and a preference for product quality over what the market could afford. (See Chapter 7, Dilemma 3). Anders Knutson was able to intervene and transform the company *both* because he was a son-of-the-house, trusted by the family, *and* because he brought with him a cool, detached professionalism that understood the cost savings essential to the company. BUPA and Val Gooding, in Chapter 9, Dilemma 1, had somehow to combine the cerebral calculations of a smart insurance company, which sees not people, but trends, aggregates, and numbers, with caring deeply about the One Life that each customer has. When the customer calls for help, after years of contributions, whether the company is "there" for him or her is a vital question. "I'm sick, I need you," says the customer, and the voice at the other end of the line will make or break that relationship by the swiftness, effectiveness, and empathy of the response.

For effective leaders, the virtuous circle of Neutrality–Affectivity reads as follows.

Virtuous Circle

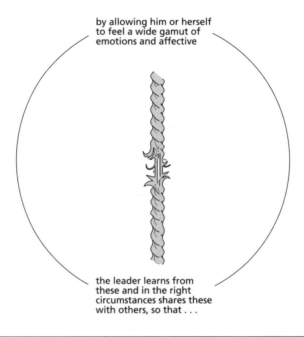

by allowing him or herself to feel a wide gamut of emotions and affective

the leader learns from these and in the right circumstances shares these with others, so that . . .

We might also pause to consider ways in which emotions are mishandled and leaders who are usually neutral might suddenly burst out with inappropriate emotion, uncontrollable anger, or self-pity. "You won't have Dick Nixon to kick around any more" is a famous example by a leader whose emotions could not be trusted by him or others and whose mental state was accurately rendered by "expletive deleted," a phrase punctuating the Watergate tapes. This illustrates a vicious circle.

Vicious Circle

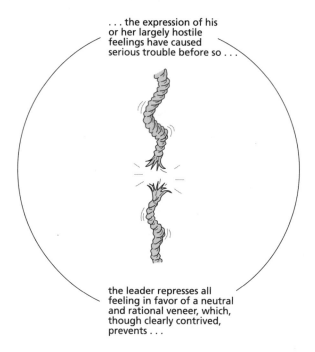

. . . the expression of his or her largely hostile feelings have caused serious trouble before so . . .

the leader represses all feeling in favor of a neutral and rational veneer, which, though clearly contrived, prevents . . .

It is such a leader that one hesitates to buy a second-hand car from and that is nicknamed "Tricky."

Measuring Intercultural Competence; Reconciling Neutrality with Affectivity

We can measure the extent to which meanings and emotions have been reconciled by comparing two polarized strategies with two integrated strategies and a compromise.

Emotions can be so strong as to obliterate thinking. Thoughts can be so calculated as to repress genuine feelings, but to think first and then let out the emotions at the right time, or to feel first and then think hard about how to express this to the best effect, are both pathways to integration.

Question 4: Upset at Work

In situations where you feel upset at work,

Which of the following behaviors are you most likely to adopt?
(a) Express your upset overtly so that you can become rational again as soon as possible.
(b) Express it overtly in a very moderate way so that your message gets across at least partially.
(c) Keep it to yourself. Expressing upset overtly serves no purpose.
(d) Keep it to yourself initially in order to find a more suitable moment to express yourself openly and in detail.
(e) Express it immediately. A good working relationship depends on open, honest communication.

Question 4 (my answer) – (how others in my organization would answer)

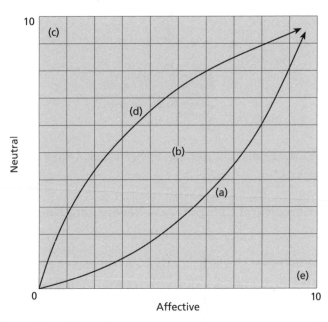

Dimension 5.	Status earned	vs.	Status ascribed
	through success		to a person's potential
	and track record		i.e. age, family
	(Achievement	vs.	Ascription)

The Sophisticated Stereotype

Here, the contrast is between being esteemed for what you do and esteemed for what you are. Status can be conferred almost exclusively on one's achievements. It can also be conferred upon one's being or potential. We may therefore expect more of males, of white people, of the college educated (which includes past achievement), of older people, of well-connected people, and of people of good family or class. Persons assigned to certain roles e.g., electrical engineer, might have higher status because the business or nation expects that such jobs will be crucial to its future.

American culture tries hard to mock all unearned privileges and distinctions, witness the recent move against affirmative action. "Ragged Dick" in the Horatio Alger stories was orphaned so did not even have parents to thank for his achievements – only himself! Andrew Carnegie famously remarked that British lords, dukes, and earls had done nothing, except to be born of ancestors who had done "dirty deeds for kings." Yet, ascribed status persists, and white males of northern European descent still enjoy higher status, even in America.

As we might have expected, Americans, Canadians, New Zealanders, and Australians, of immigrant nations all, have strong preferences for achievement. When you immigrate, you leave class and family associations behind you. Few in the New World care that you came from a "prominent family in Kent." Norway, France, Sweden, Ireland, and the UK are also high in achievement orientation.

Among cultures *ascribing* status are some with formidable records of economic growth in the recent past: Japan, Korea, Hong Kong, Taiwan, China, and Singapore. Are these against achievement? Surely not. They approach it in a different way. They ascribe high status to those entrusted with "catching up with the West," who are given prestigious posts within key projects. The idea is that these persons will achieve as a consequence of the trust placed in them.

Achievement orientations assume that what is being tried is *worth* achieving, but this is not always true. Rising to the top of a criminal conspiracy engaged in racketeering is a doubtful achievement. An American 1930's musical had a lyric entitled "You're the Top." The words have not stood the test of time.

"You're Mrs Sweeney

You're Mussolini
You're custard pie . . ."

There is something to be said for eyeing "achievements" critically to weed out fascist dictators.

Some Typical Misunderstandings

Societies in which people *achieve* status and those that *ascribe* it are often at odds in first encounters. When Americans visit East Asia with a product or proposition, they usually "put their cards on the table" and behave authentically as they see it. This is the deal. These are the costs. This is the size of the likely opportunity. With profits, on this scale should we not sink our differences? All this is "achievement talk," and, of course, it is deeply offensive to cultures that ascribe status. What these cultures seek to know is, who are you? With whom are you related and connected? What is your background? What family do you come from? They also seek to know whether you are inherently gracious, polite, and hospitable. By putting you in relaxed settings, they seek to establish trust. Many hours, and even days, might be spent on small talk, but the implications are not small. If you were pretending, you could not maintain the pretence. The scattered impressions would not be coherent. What, after all, is five days in a partnership lasting five years or more?

Attempts to get your partner excited about the product or the profit are deeply suspect. This is what conmen do. They appeal to your greed and exploitiveness. A partner too concerned with gain is likely to cheat you. A partner you can trust cares more about his reputation, the status ascribed to him by colleagues. Pressure tactics are equally repellent. If the American partner really trusted us, he would respect our judgment and seek concurrence.

If we look more closely at this misunderstanding, we see that it is really an issue of priorities. Once Americans have decided to do business with someone and feel that a deal is in the offing, then it is sensible to get to know the person, deepen the relationship, check his or her references. Once a Chinese or Japanese executive has got to know an American and deepened the relationship, then it is time to turn to business. Each accidentally offends the other by getting this sequence "wrong".

The reason it is so important to learn from other cultures is that "pure achievement" and "pure ascription" are *both* apt to fail. The British pensions industry faces a pensions misselling scandal in which tens of thousands of pensioners were induced to surrender their group pension plan for an individual portable pension, with significantly smaller benefits. The volume of this duplicity is a staggering £2 billion, with companies "named and shamed" by government watchdogs until they repay the difference. How could salespersons fan out across the country and talk luckless savers into a pensions provision worse than the ones they currently held? All too easily, we fear, because these sales staffs were being paid on commission only on what they achieved.

The signal this sends to employees is clear: "We care nothing for you as persons and will invest nothing in you personally. We will take a share in your performance." In other words, status ascribed 0 percent, status achieved 100 percent. What happened, of course, was that this attitude toward sales staff was passed on by staff to customers. "We care nothing for you or your pensions rights. You are there to help us achieve our sales targets." We must instead give status to simple humanity, to potentials capable of flowering in the future. If we think only of achieving, we risk trampling each other in the rush to succeed.

Pure ascribed status is similarly hazardous. Consider the loans made to relatives of President Suharto! No wonder the whole rotten edifice collapsed. Instead of money flowing towards success, it was flowing from political crony to political crony.

Most companies in the world, by a very large margin, are still family owned. Even in publicly owned companies, family concepts survive. One thinks of the Japanese term *amai,* meaning indulgent affection between mentor and subordinate, and *sempae-gohai*, a brother–younger brother relationship. Training your workforce and mentoring them is an investment in their potential, a form of ascribed status. That people who care for and respect each other go on to achieve is a natural consequence. The larger training expenses of several East Asian cultures speak for themselves. Japanese auto assembly plants in the United States give new workers 225 hours of training in their first six months. U.S. plants give 42 hours.

What Effective Leaders Know and Have Learned

The research findings in Chapter 1, Box 1 should convince us that cultures putting ascribed status first are still capable of rapid economic growth. Even with its present troubles, East Asian growth rates are the highest yet recorded in the history of economics. The reason for this is that ascribing status and achieving status are complementary. If you want someone to achieve, show him or her initial respect. In America, we keep stumbling over this fact, but, too often, "lean and mean" management ignores it. In the original Hawthorne Experiment, Irish and Polish immigrant female workers were given the status of co-researchers with Elton Mayo and Fritz Roethlisberger from Harvard. Instead of just assembling telephone relays, they were invited to investigate how telephone relays might be better assembled, a totally transformed job description. The fact that they were withdrawn from the factory floor into a small group meant that they could affirm each other's identities. Of course, they began to achieve. As productivity climbed, the startled researchers treated them with even more respect, and their achievement climbed again, as the virtuous circle took hold. What many dismiss as "The Hawthorne Effect" is in fact a learning dynamic of great power and influence.

Our leaders in this book also showed great skill in handling the Achieved–Ascribed dimension and using it to learn with. Richard Branson, in Chapter 3, Dilemma 1, starts by critiquing those industries in which he has decided to compete, that is by ascribing defective status to them and ascribing to himself the reputation of a reformer of those industries and an underdog in challenging them. Unlike many reformers, he then actually *achieves* superior levels of performance and so proves his original contention, using wide sympathy in the press and among customers to establish his case.

In Chapter 4, Dilemma 5, the issue is granting teams sufficient autonomy to *achieve,* without thereby diminishing the *ascribed* status of the senior manager who sponsors that team's efforts. Martin Gillo struggled with the need to have senior managers risk their senior positions by delegating resources and authority to problem-solving teams. Where these were successful, the sponsor's authority was actually enhanced, and the status ascribed to the team was used by it to achieve, and thereby add to, the sponsor's reputation.

In Chapter 12, Dilemma 5, Stan Shih of Acer had to make sure both that managers and employees achieved *and* that others were prepared to mentor that achievement, to describe, judge and celebrate excellence and, in that respect, rise above achievement, to assure that its ends were worthwhile. You cannot have everyone achieve; some must judge and consecrate the goals of that achievement, and some must ascribe status to, and be seen to symbolize the ends themselves. In Chapter 14, Dilemma 2, the CEO of Seagram's, Edgar Bronfman, had to decide whether a new culture was created by his ascribing status, acting top down, or by what his managers were actually achieving, bottom up. He sensibly opted for a dialogue and synthesis, so that culture expressed itself through action, but was also labeled and evaluated by his definition of what excellence constituted.

The Koç Group was another successful family company, in a Turkish context. Rahmi Koç, son of the founder, succeeded his father at age 53, relatively late in his career, see chapter 19, dilemma 5. Although his status was ascribed by his family membership, he was in fact sent to business school in America and was carefully groomed for succession. The pressure on those to whom status has been ascribed, to live up to their billing and up to the achievements of their illustrious forebears, can be intense.

If you are a very visible heir to a Turkish industrial dynasty with tens of thousands of workers and associated charities dependent upon your success, then the spotlight is very much on your performance. The nation has given you high status and respect in the fervent hope that you will justify this by achieving on behalf of the nation. Status is intended to be a self-fulfilling prophecy.

Virtuous Circle

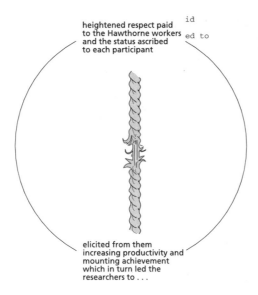

heightened respect paid to the Hawthorne workers and the status ascribed to each participant

id
ed to

elicited from them increasing productivity and mounting achievement which in turn led the researchers to . . .

That this was no coincidence has been found many times since. A common experience for any consultant who uses interviewing as a method of inquiry is that many executives have rarely had the experience of being listened to and that their morale and competence grow before your eyes. Royale Foote and colleagues tested the proposition that interviewing alone could boost productivity. In the Fairmont plant of Anheuser Busch, they trained each level of supervisors to interview the level below the top of the organization, to the very bottom, which was unionized by a tough Teamsters' local. Interviews were not focused on work issues specifically, but on whatever concerned the interviewee. There was no additional intervention. In the eight years of the interviewing process, the Fairmont facility climbed from almost the worst plant in the network to by far the best, on a score of hard measures. Something as elementary as brewing, canning, and trucking rests squarely on the status and respect ascribed to each member of the organization.

No less a luminary than Douglas McGregor taught that the respect and confidence we have in one another fulfills itself in subsequent achievement. He called this *Theory Y*. As Bernard Shaw put it in Pygmalion, "It's the way she's treated that makes her a lady." No wonder the Pygmalion Effect has been found in the workplace and the classroom. When teachers are told that a child will "spurt," the child does, although "spurters" were actually picked at random. It was the teacher's belief that spurred the child to achievement.

Measuring Intercultural Competence: Reconciling Achieved with Ascribed Status

There are two roads to integrating these values. You could argue that you must first decide *who* you are (ascribed status) if you are to go on to achieve in a way consistent with this; or you could decide that achieving at this and that is a good way of discovering who you are (ascribed) and what you were meant to stand for.

The following five responses were used to measure reconciliation vs. polarization.

Question 5. What is important?

Which one of the following best describes your values?

The most important thing in life is:

(a) getting things done, because in the long run it serves you best to think and act in a way that is consistent with the way you really are.
(b) that you are able to do things at some times and relax at others.
(c) to think and act in a manner that is consistent with the way you really are, because in the long run you will achieve more.
(d) getting things done, even if it interferes with the way you really are.
(e) to think and act consistently with the way you really are, even if you don't get things done.

Question 5 (my answer) – (how others in my organization would answer)
We plot these answers on the following grid

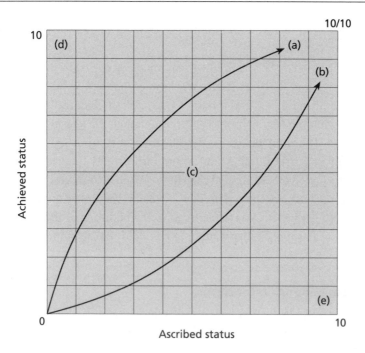

Dimension 6. | **Control and effective direction come from within (Inner-directed** | **vs.** | **Control and effective direction come from without Outer-directed)**

The Sophisticated Stereotype

Here, the question is about the source of virtue and direction. Is it inside each of us, in our "soul," conscience, or integrity – or outside us, in the beauty and harmonies of nature or in the needs of families, friends, customers? Is it virtuous "to be your own man," or "to respond to your environment?"

There are no prizes for guessing that Americans are inner directed; see Chapter 1, Box 1. Americans tend to plan and then to make those plans work, to rely on ability, not luck, and to prescribe taking control of their lives. The USA is joined in strong inner direction by Norway, New Zealand, Canada, Australia, and France. The latter, we might note, combines Communitarianism with inner direction, as in the group of fiercely convinced rebels seizing control of the nation's destiny. While inner direction is advocated by Judeo-Christian values, outer direction is sanctioned by Shintoism and Buddhism. Gods are believed to inhabit mountains, streams, storms, harvests, and winds. You mollify the gods by shaping attractive containers they will wish to inhabit.

On this particular bifurcation, we cannot evade the truth that American pop culture celebrates and satirizes itself. We have Superman vying with planes and bullets and overwhelming natural forces. We have Frank Sinatra "doing it my way" and even small children bearing arms against each other. *Fortune* magazine celebrates "America's Ten Toughest Bosses, " despite their very brief tenures. Alf Dunlap dresses himself in battle fatigues and ammunition belts to give an imitation of Rambo. Unfortunately, there are real casualties. When life imitates art, all concerned can escalate to absurd extremes. The flaw in celebrating inner direction is that for every boss "so tough he tells you when to go to the bathroom," there would have to be several American subordinates waiting to be told! It hardly improves effectiveness overall.

Some Typical Misunderstandings

No concept has ever taken American management theory by storm as powerfully as *strategy*. The metaphor is, of course, military, and it conjures up Alexander the Great's conquest of the known world. No concept better reflects the grip of inner-directedness upon the American imagination. It is the genius and conviction of business leaders that justifies their multimillion dollar salaries. Now, it is true that strategy can make or break a business. People Express grew to a $2 billion corporation when Don Burr slashed the costs of flying. He took out galleys, increased seats, sold tickets on board, and had passengers lift their own baggage into larger lockers. This enabled him to slash prices and get loadings (occupancy) above 80 percent; but strategy also defeated PE. American Airlines and United used management yield software to predict how full their flights would be on the day of travel and slashed fares to fill planes. Their flexible fare cuts beat PE's rigid fare cuts.

The problem with brilliant inner-directed strategies is that these are not confined to corporate HQ. Intelligence is widely distributed, and the closer you get to the interface with the customer, the better such strategies are informed. In a brilliant HBR article, Henry Mintzberg argued that strategies typically emerge from the grass roots of the corporation, where market changes begin. The problem with strategy designed at the top (or inner-directed strategy) is that top managers are typically furthest from the field and from customers.

The danger is that their strategy will be abstract and largely alienated from the culture of the corporation. At worst, the strategy will command the impossible. At best, it will command something that the grass roots of the organization has been doing for years without recognition. Top-down strategy says, in effect, "I think, therefore you act." It reserves for subordinates the role of putting their energies behind the superior thoughts of their leaders. In fact, nearly everyone has a strategy, and all of us want to think. This might help explain why outer-directed Japanese carmakers still register 28 implemented suggestions per employee per year, while inner-directed Western corporations register 1.8 at the best. It is prestigious to be outer directed in Japanese and most East Asian cultures; that is why superiors listen, while subordinates exercise initiatives, as hundreds of suggestions and strategies emerge. If you are really senior in a Japanese corporation, you hardly talk at all!

We are not, of course, claiming that outer direction is better. We do not even agree with Henry Mintzberg that emergent strategy obviates designed strategy or that it is worth holding debates between their respective advocates. We believe that top management can create grand strategies *out of* the initiatives emerging from the grass roots.

What Effective Leaders Know and Have Learned

The metaphor that best integrates inner with outer direction is the jiujitsu artist. He carefully observes the outer-directed momentum lurching towards him and deflects that person in the direction of his own choosing. Much of China, Japan, and East Asia tells the story of the Monkey King, which, unlike Superman, is physically weaker than other forces in its environment, but a lot more agile and clever. The trick is to harness your own aims to the external dynamisms and momentum of the market.

Our leaders in this book have shown remarkable skills in attaching their own deliberate aims to the swirl of the external world. In Chapter 4, Dilemma 2, Martin Gillo helped to build his "Fabulous Fab" by taking the high-risk, shoot-from-the-hip pragmatism of Advanced Micro Devices, with its inner directed drive, and combining it with an East German love for rationalizing and analyzing external environments. The two groups optimized their "opposed" values to an extraordinary degree. Bang and Olufsen had suffered from a perilous imbalance almost from its founding. Product excellence was what the founders defined it to be and if the external market disagreed, the market was simply wrong, consisting of a bunch of clods who failed to appreciate aesthetics and top quality; see Chapter 7, Dilemma 1. The company was inner directed to an unaffordable degree. Its models were displayed in New York's Museum of Modern Art, but too few customers could afford them. Not until costs were bought under control and customers outside the company were accorded the respect due to them did the company transform itself and take off. Inner and outer direction must be fine-tuned if inner convictions are to discover external acclaim.

Michael Dell was extraordinary for having challenged the very categories of "inside Dell" and "outside Dell"; see Chapter 11, Dilemma 1. By using the Internet,

Dell's "inner" deliberations were opened up to suppliers, subcontractors, and customers in an ongoing dialogue. Interested parties at any point in the network could gain access, so that parts suppliers could discover for themselves the company's inventory levels and take responsibility for making sure that customers never ran short and were supplied "just in time". Instead of ordering compliance, you share knowledge and the other responds. Knowledge accumulates whether its source is within Dell itself or it comes from a partner.

Sergei Kiriyenko (Chapter 13, Dilemma 1), trying to revive Russia's NORSI oil, found himself trapped between unions and his own managers, all demanding their "share" of nonexistent "earnings," and external creditors, tax authorities, and traditional recipients of its revenues. He obliged them all to negotiate with him and first favored those *inside* the organization, because he needed them to generate revenues, but as soon as these were flowing, he paid off *external* demands. Within two years, the refinery was in the black, and Sergei was famous and on his way to Moscow.

The transculturally competent whom we have measured can integrate outer with inner direction. Typical of their thinking is the next Virtuous Circle:

Virtuous Circle

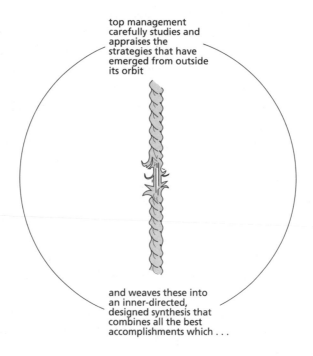

top management carefully studies and appraises the strategies that have emerged from outside its orbit

and weaves these into an inner-directed, designed synthesis that combines all the best accomplishments which . . .

Mintzberg calls this *crafting* strategy, as when the clay rises spontaneously from the potter's wheel, and hands lightly shape it.

Measuring Intercultural Competence: Reconciling Internal with External Loci of Control

We measure how inner directed vs. outer directed a leader is by considering the relative merits of "push" and "pull" strategies. Should you allow customers to *pull* you in outer-directed fashion towards their wishes, even where those wishes change, or should you *push* terms, conditions, and deliveries upon a customer in an inner-directed fashion and, having once won his or her agreement, carry through as promised? Following are the dilemma and some responses:

Question. Push or Pull?

Several consultants were arguing that you achieved greater customer satisfaction and quicker delivery times by using a customer-focused *pull* strategy and that *push* strategies were outmoded. Several other consultants disagreed.

Which position is closest to your viewpoint?

(a) A pull strategy is best, because it lets the customer reset the deadline and permits resources to converge upon the customer on cue. Remember, customers get behind schedule, too, and change their minds about the relative advantages of speed, quality, cost, and so on.

(b) A push strategy is best, because this commits the supplier and customer to a joint schedule, with costs, quality, and specifications agreed in advance. The customer can, of course, change his or her mind, but then the costs for altering the original schedule are calculable.

(c) A combination of push and pull strategies, so that the customer helps us to decide when not to push our products, and we tell the clients when we cannot meet their requests.

(d) A push strategy is best, because this commits supplier and customer to a joint schedule with costs, quality, and specifications agreed upon in advance. If you do as you promised, and you do it in time, then you cannot be faulted, and your record speaks for itself.

(e) A pull strategy is best, because it lets the customer reset the deadlines and permits resources to converge upon the customer on cue. The customer wants it when she wants it, and pushing hard can get it to her too early and at needless expense.

Question 23 (my answer) – (how others in my organization would answer)

The five possible answers are scored as shown in the accompanying diagram. Answers (a) and (b) are integrated, with outer-directed *pull* put first in the sequence in the case of (a), and inner-directed *push* put first in the sequence in the case of (b)

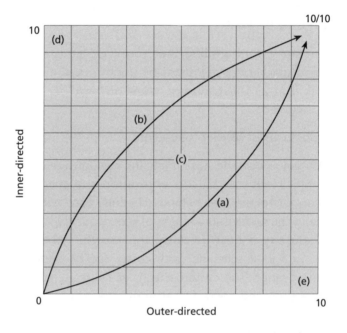

Answer (c) is a compromise; (d) and (e) are inner-directed and outer-directed polarities, which brook no opposition from the conflicting principle. Answer (d), for example, is concerned with the supplier is not being "faulted," not with satisfying the customer.

Dimension 7.	Time is Conceived of as a "Race" with Passing Increments	vs.	Time is Conceived of as a "Dance" with Circular Iterations
	(Sequential	vs.	Synchronous)

The Sophisticated Stereotype

The contrast is between two alternative conceptions of time: Time cannot really be seen or touched, so culture looms large in its definition. *Time-as-a-race* sees time as a sequence of passing increments. An aim of life becomes doing as much as possible within time limits. *Time-as-a-dance* concentrates on timing, or synchronization, so that one moves in time with other persons or processes.

Chapter 1, Box 1 shows that American managers take a sequential approach to time, in common with Brazil, Ireland, Belgium, Italy, and the Philippines. Japan and China take a mostly synchronous view, as do Hong Kong, Korea, Singapore, Sweden, and France. Orientation to time is part of America's self-satire and stereotyped view of itself. There are time and motion studies or "racing with the clock," as workers sang in *The Pajama Game*. Benjamin Franklin said, "Time is Money," so it is no wonder that Americans seek "to make a quick buck." Andrew Marvel, the Puritan poet, even chided his bashful mistress that "Time's winged chariot" was overtaking the slow pace of their love life.

America's time and motion studies have made a priceless contribution to the efficiencies of mass-production, but so, too, have the Japanese conceptions of *just-in-time* and *parallel processing*. The former is clearly sequential, the latter synchronous. Before we consider how modern manufacturing combines these viewpoints, let us consider conflicts arising from the clash of expectations.

Some Typical Misunderstandings

One of the authors was buying a book at the Singapore airport. The clerk took his credit card, wrapped the book and proceeded to serve the next customer, the card and the book being both in her possession. When the purchaser objected, she explained, quite reasonably, that she was saving time. It would take several seconds for the credit card company to respond. When the credit had been cleared, she switched her attention back to the original purchaser. In practice, few cultures are as well balanced between concepts of time as Singapore.

A more usual experience is that sequential cultures regard synchronous cultures as "rude" because they typically run late and then overstay to "make it up to you." Synchronous people dislike waiting in line for service and often form a scrum. They also interrupt your work and are themselves highly distractible, seemingly doing several things at the same time. Synchronous cultures might regard sequential cultures as "rude" because they respond not to you, but to some "inner clock." They stride hurriedly from one place to the next, occasionally waving at you, but never stopping, and are so immersed in their work that they ignore people. They seem to want to stand behind you or in front of you, but not by your side. They refuse to abandon their plans in the face of unexpected meetings. Politeness makes them impatient.

Synchronous cultures have a logic of their own. You "give time" to people important to you, and, if these abound, you will be delayed. Top people deserve more scope to synchronize their face-to-face engagements, hence, they enter the room last after juniors have assembled. Synchronization is often symbolized by bowing, nodding, or making exclamations of assent. It is as if you were all on the same wavelength and practicing the coordination of your inputs. Pure sequentialism leads workers and employees to be machine timed and dehumanized, but purely synchronous cultures seem haphazard and inefficient, episodic, and lacking purpose. Sequentialism is typically short term because deadlines need to be close by to have much effect; but synchronous cultures might or might not be long term – if they lack direction, there is no long-term goal.

What Effective Leaders Know and Have Learned

We can identify transcultural competence by giving respondents an opportunity to integrate sequential with synchronous views of time and seeing whether they take this opportunity, because, of course, modern effective manufacturing practices must combine both concepts. Neither is sufficient by itself.

It is self-evident that you will complete a process sooner if you speed it up. The gains from synchronous thinking are less immediately obvious. One source of considerable timesaving is to take a sequence 80 yards long, divide this into four 20-yard sequences, work on these simultaneously, and then assemble the four parallel processes. No wonder the workers at AMD sing "Doing it Simultaneously"!

What has happened historically is that costly sacrifices have been made to continuous process machinery. These symbolized speed. Sequential movement was what it was all about, so cheap workers doing simple operations were hired to keep the machines moving. Other sacrifices were equally serious. The machines had to be buffered by large inventories of supplies and work in process. In some plants, 80 percent of products were not being worked on, but remained in large piles tied up in such inventories.

Enter Taichi Ohno and the Toyota Production System. If you think synchronously as well as sequentially, the huge inventories and the semitrained workers doing dumb, repetitive tasks are suddenly seen as limitations. Inventories are cut to a fraction by JIT (just-in-time), and you need multiskilled workers of considerable intelligence to ensure the smooth synchronization among parallel processes. All this the West has known for a decade or more, but cultures are stubborn patterns to change.

There are few sequential–synchronous issues in this book, in part because we have not looked much at manufacturing. In the case of LEGO's turn-around (Chapter 6, Dilemma 4), Christian Maygard was particularly concerned that every stream of ideas meet its own "window of opportunity." The ideas themselves were neither right nor wrong; they had a *rendezvous*, that shaped their destiny. Either synchronized with the needs of the market, or the windows closed in their faces. It needed *good timing* to dart through the window.

Stan Shih of Acer was also engaged with this issue, as explained in Chapter 12, Dilemma 6. He promulgated his "fast-food model" of computer production and marketing, even likening his company to McDonalds. Just as fast-food outlets concentrate on rapid sequences of high-quality components, so they concentrate on getting them to customers in just the combinations ordered *just in time,* or, in Acer's case, three months from order to delivery. Shih reckons he borrowed speed from the West, but timely delivery from his Taiwanese homegrown culture.

Reconciling a sequential concept of time with a synchronous concept of time can give you the advantages of both and the limitations of neither. Each corrects for the potential excesses of the other. Ever faster sequences with ever finer synchronization is what modern manufacturing is all about. The virtuous circle below illustrates this point.

Roughly the same rules apply to reducing "Time to Market." The traditional approach has been sequential, with "progress chasing" and a push strategy to get projects through faster. Analog Devices even culled those projects that were behind schedule by more than the permitted margin, so that the remaining projects would "run for their lives."

A recent innovation at Motorola University has substituted a synchronous "pull strategy." This strategy adopts the deadline and the viewpoint of the customer and pulls resources, people, and products into the development process in the volumes needed to make the rendezvous with the customer. More resources will be needed for late projects, fewer for those ahead of schedule. When customers themselves fall behind schedule, such delays can release resources needed elsewhere. Here *just-in-time* means "synchronization with the customer's latest deadline."

Virtuous Circle

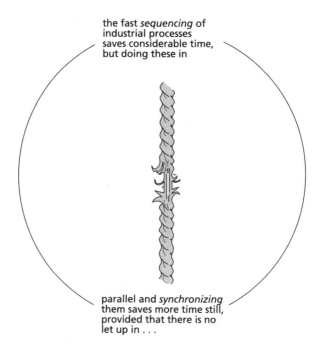

the fast *sequencing* of industrial processes saves considerable time, but doing these in

parallel and *synchronizing* them saves more time still, provided that there is no let up in . . .

Measuring Intercultural Competence: Reconciling Sequential with Synchronous Time

In the following dilemma, a somewhat haphazard and synchronous fashion house is frustrating a sequential and time-conscious wholesaler.

Question 6. How to speed up latecomers

As a manager of a wholesale distributor of a fashion company, you are getting very worried about late delivery times to your clients. The summer did not allow you to deliver high-priced goods within a week of the scheduled delivery date that is the accepted norm in the fashion industry. You have tried many ways of solving the problems of late delivery. You still have not made any progress. You are now also in conflict with the transport firm, because a contract was signed and the fashion supplier denies any responsibility.

Which of the following most closely describes what you would do?

(a) You need to explain your problem to the supplier while appreciating the excellent quality of the goods. This will most probably lead to better adherence to deadlines.

(b) You need to order early and ask for the goods two or three weeks before you need to distribute them to the shops.

(c) Recognize that the fashion business is highly dynamic, artistic, and in constant turbulence. Accept the fact that sometimes goods will be early as well as late. What difference does another week make anyway?

(d) Your partners have a flexible-time mind-set, and you will not be able to change that. You need to talk to your clients in order to prepare them for a possible late delivery and give them a discount in case it occurs. Separately, you need to negotiate a premium for punctual delivery.

(e) You need to know the suppliers personally. Try to avoid problematic issues, and during the visit emphasize how important it is for the clients to get on-time deliveries.

Question 6 (my answer) – (how others in my organization would answer)

We classify the responses (d) and (a) as integrated, (b) and (c) as polarized, and (e) as compromised.

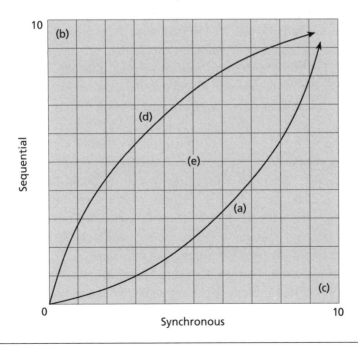

This concludes all seven dimensions of difference.

Summary of chapters 1 and 2

1. We first contrasted rule making and exception finding and argued that they can be integrated. You use exceptions to improve rules and rules to recognize what is genuinely exceptional. We call this learning *revising rules to accommodate exceptions.*

2. We then contrasted competitive individualism with the requirement that communities cooperate and argued that these could be integrated. It is possible to compete at cooperating with customers or, cooperating within your team. It is possible for communities to develop and at the same time to celebrate their outstanding individual members. Competing helps us to differentiate best practices. Cooperating helps us disseminate and adopt the best. We called this learning *co-opetition.*

3. We contrasted the preferences for analyzing issues into specifics with the preferences for synthesizing and elaborating issues into diffuse wholes, and we argued that these could be integrated. You have to allow self-organizing knowledge, values, and team processes to flow diffusely and then supply detailed, specific feedback on their effectiveness. We called this learning *co-evolution with corrective feedback.*

4. We contrasted *neutral* and *rational* with *affective* forms of expression, in which feelings are fully owned, and argued that these could be integrated. You cannot think about your emotions unless they are owned, expressed, and shared, but you also have to control yourself until the right moment and circumstances. We agree with Pascal that *the heart has its reason.*

5. We contrasted two sources of experienced control: that from inside us, which is inner directed, and that from outside us, which is outer directed. Strategy, for example, could be designed from inside a company's top management, or it could emerge from the company's interface with customers, outside top management. We argued that these processes could be integrated. Top managers could use their inner resources to design and reshape the strategies emerging outside them, which had already pleased customers. We called this *crafted strategy*, in honor of Henry Mintzberg, who likened it to the rising of clay spontaneously from the rotating potter's wheel.

6. We contrasted status earned through achievement with status ascribed to the person's potential – for example, age and family – argued that these could be were integrated. The more you respect people's potentials and the more you

Box 6: The Seven Dimensions in American Pop Culture

The recent popular film *Armegeddon* might well be viewed as having been constructed with the seven dimensions in mind.

In the film, the mission is nothing less than to save humankind (universalism) from a giant meteorite. Two spaceships, the *Freedom* and the *Independent* (individualistic), are operated not by astronauts, but by rugged roughneck oil drillers, who will drill into the meteorite and explode a nuclear bomb. All this requires elaborate detail and precision (specificity), including a slingshot around the moon. Luckily, their leader and his men are tough as hell. They never quit and (amazingly) have never failed (achievement), except of course in their social lives. They must drill in an incredibly hostile terrain of granite spikes, yet they prevail over nature (because they are inner directed).

The film also features seven digital countdowns (sequential time), with time running out before spacecraft ascend and before nuclear bombs kill our heroes. Americans are affective, especially in this film, in which roughnecks shout, "I love you, man!" above the dust and din and the characters are much given to domestic endearments on the edge of doom.

invest in training them, the more likely they are to reciprocate by achieving on behalf of the company. We called this *mentored achievement.*

7. Finally, we contrasted a sequential view of time as some kind of race against the clock with a synchronous view of time as timing, as in a finely choreographed dance. We saw that these could be integrated, as when, by synchronizing processes just in time, you "shorten the racecourse" by way of parallel processing, before combining results in the final assembly. We called this *flexible manufacturing*, or, in a market context, "pull strategy."

Not only do these seven integrations constitute Transcultural Competence; they represent a model for valuing in general, wherein the preferences and stereotypes of a culture are relative, while the need to integrate values is absolute and essential to civic society, as well as to the creation of wealth. The danger of stereotyped cultural imagery is that it hides this necessity from us. It follows that foreign cultures could arouse what is latent in our own values, to remind us that what is perhaps overemphasized in their culture is underemphasized in ours. We have the preferences of foreign cultures within our own, albeit in a weaker state.

Measuring Intercultural Competence: How We Did It, What Others Have Found

We administered our questionnaire to the Intercultural Communications Institute summer school near Portland and to several European samples. The following trends are already evident.

There is a capacity to deal with and reconcile values in general. Respondents who reconcile dilemmas are likely to employ similar logics across the board, as do "compromisers" and "polarizers."

Transcultural competence, as measured by our questionnaire correlates strongly, consistently, and significantly with all of the following:

(a)   extent of experience with international assignments;

(b)   rating by superiors on "suitability for" and "success in" overseas postings and partnerships;

(c)   high positive evaluations via "360° feedback." Arguably, this reconciles Equality vs. Hierarchy, since the verdicts of peers, superiors, and subordinates are compared.

Moreover, there is a surprise: With the exception of Chinese "highflyers" who recently have been influenced by American training, the transculturally competent do *not* put their own cultural stereotype ahead of foreign values in a logical sequence. For example, American Transcultural Competents (TC's) are as likely to argue that good communities and teams generate outstanding individuals as the reverse proposition. TC's can begin with the foreigner's sociotype and join it to their own. This probably reveals skill at negotiating and entering dialogue, where one shares an understanding of the other's position in the hope of reciprocity. It may also reveal a case-by-case adoption of foreign methods in which such skills are considered appropriate, along with curiosity about "the road less traveled" by one's own culture.

Finally, we would like to suggest that transcultural competence might be only the tip of the iceberg, representing the most visible manifestation of human diversity in general. The role of leaders and managers is increasingly to manage diversity per se, whatever its origins in culture, industry, discipline, socioeconomic group, or gender. If there is indeed a way of thinking that integrates values as opposed to "adding value," the implications are far reaching.

In Chapters 3 through to 21, we show how our 21 leaders manage knowledge by integrating dilemmas and discuss these concepts in some detail. We refer again to the wider database in our summary in Chapter 22 and give further details of the analysis and underlying modeling in Appendix A.

CHAPTER 3

New Vision of Capitalism

Leader: Richard Branson (Virgin)

A lmost no one has taken the art of being British to a higher level of national popularity than Sir Richard Branson. The cultivation of a pleasing personality has been a British art form for several centuries. The gentleman was traditionally "socially pleasing," although *what* pleases and what does not has changed dramatically since the Sixties, and Branson is very much a child of that era. Although the traditional gentleman, with his verbal fluency, formality, aloofness, strangled emotions, and chronic understatements, has been in decline for many years, the photogenic "media personality" has risen to replace him. Branson is very much the outrider of this new order, the celebrity of free enterprise. He turns his fascinations into businesses.

If British entrepreneurialism is being reborn, as many now believe is happening, Richard Branson is very much the role model of this new style and the symbol of this resurgent vitality. He is much more than a business leader, famed for making money; he is the exponent of a new lifestyle in which business activity expresses the personality of its founder: irreverent, cheeky, ironic, enjoyable, and reformist. In a business environment whose exponents increasingly live in order to work, Branson works in order to live, and he is seen by his culture as enjoying himself and expressing his own personal convictions through his various feats and adventures.

The Key is Personality

In many chapters, we will show how business leaders reconcile values, but we must first ask where these reconciliations are stored and how they are deployed. An important repository for reconciled values is the human personality. There is about the personality an inherent fascination. At its best, it has surface and depth, changeability and constancy. It can dazzle with its multiple facets, yet impress with an underlying integrity. By turns sad and joyful, serious and humorous, tough and tender, idealistic and realistic, it is the peculiar power of personality to bring unity to myriad aspects, what Joseph Campbell called "The Hero with a Thousand Faces."

To an extent almost unprecedented in world business, the Virgin brand *is* the personality of Richard Branson. While Disney is symbolized by a giant mouse or duck, McDonald's by "Ronald," a red-haired clown, Shell by a scallop, and Michelin by a fat, inflated man, Virgin is personified by the colorful, living personality of its chairman and founder.

There could be some danger in this policy. Personalities can come apart. Founders die. Masks may slip. Scandal might reveal that a person is not what he seems. Branson has recently been forced to sue a biographer. The media profits when its stars rise *and* when there fall, a process they aid and abet, but Branson seems able to charm even seasoned hacks, and his press is largely favorable. A pleasing personality is almost infinitely capacious. Branson has received repeated warnings from marketing men that his brand cannot stretch to so many diverse activities. Yet, are they right? When a company's image is contrived, its stretch is limited. Would you want Ronald McDonald to fly you across the Atlantic? Would you entrust your savings to Mickey Mouse? A living personality as versatile as Branson's, however, can brand all Virgin's two hundred companies, from bridal shops, to Cola, to condoms, to MGM cinemas, to insurance, to pensions, trains, books, and music.

The Search For Moral Enterprise

The now-conventional view is that Mrs. Thatcher ended Britain's "hate affair" with business enterprise. Whereas the British were once ashamed of "trade," they now demand more profits than other cultures. There is some truth in this, but no culture changes so completely or so fast. The British still believe that business enterprise needs redemption: witness the popularity of the business writer Charles Handy, who has profiled Branson among his select on moral grounds. Shareholders in Britain are among the most demanding, yet admiration is still withheld from profit providers. "Rip off Britain" is still a common accusation. Alan Mitchell, another business writer, said of Branson, "Somehow his values and style allay our nagging doubts about the morality of modern capitalism's means and ends."

The secret of Sir Richard's popularity is his knight-errant attitude towards consumers. The Virgin on his shield blesses not his personal enrichment but the creation of wealth for the larger society by improving service to consumers. He turns business enterprise into *moral* enterprise. He began by backing new, countercultural stars in the music industry. He beat British Airways on the quality of service and tweaked its tail in the law courts. When the AIDS crisis struck, he supplied cut-price condoms. He even offered to run the National Lottery at no profit, thereby maximizing revenues for good causes. He challenged the pensions industry with cheaper products, offering higher yields and entered the insurance industry with Virgin Direct, which cut out selling and brokerage costs. He has set up an Internet company to import cars cheaply into Britain from the continent, where prices are generally lower. Finally, he plans to use his "light-ships," airships illuminated from within, to detect and destroy land mines, thereby redeeming a pledge to the late Princess Diana.

Branson's appeal is, however, not exclusively to the post-1950s generations. There is something traditional in his derring-do reminiscent of *The Boys' Own Paper*. He broke the world record for crossing the Atlantic ocean in a speedboat and tried to circumnavigate the earth in a hot-air balloon, at some risk to his life. All this harks back to the age of intrepid explorers, to Scott of the Antarctic, to Sir Richard Burton, and even further back to Sir Francis Drake. No wonder that one poll of youth culture discovered that Richard Branson was among the very few people trusted by respondents to rewrite the Ten Commandments!

The Use of Irony and Humor

What makes Branson such an elusive target for critics and competitors is that he does not take himself seriously. He makes far better fun of himself than satirists have succeeded in doing. Irony and humor in the personality have a very important bearing on the capacity to reconcile dilemmas. It takes a sense of irony to acknowledge dilemmas in the first place. Hitler, Stalin, and Mussolini, for examples, were all notoriously humorless.

Arthur Koestler pointed out that laughter arises from an accidental collision between two frames of thought that connect incongruously. The "punch line" surprises you to produce a "ha ha" reflex. Take for example, e.e. cummings' quip, "She was a good cook as cooks go, and as cooks go, she went." You rarely laugh if the joke is familiar. While laughter is not the *reconciliation* of contrasting ideas, it often greets their *juxtaposition*. Because you must juxtapose ideas if you are ever to reconcile them, irony and humor can be regarded as *approaches* to reconciling values, necessary, but not sufficient, conditions. Branson's tongue-in-cheek "virginity" may therefore be a vital clue to his leadership skills in reconciliation. He tells wonderful stories on himself; see Box 1.

The style is a quintessentially British way of releasing tension and disarming critics. For example, Branson called his first flight from Gatwick in June 1984 "The Maiden Voyager, " changed from "The Maidenhead" at the last minute. The plane was packed with celebrities, notably English cricketers Ian Botham and Viv Richards,

---

Box 1: "I puffed out my chest..."

Richard Branson had just won his libel action against British Airways and was being lionized by the British media. To escape the photographs and applause, he took his family to Majorca for a vacation.

> "I was lying by the side of the pool one morning, reading all the press cuttings about Virgin which had been faxed over to me and trying not to let everything go to my head, when a young couple came up to me. They coughed nervously to attract my attention. 'Excuse me,' they said, proffering a camera. 'Would you mind? We'd love a photograph.' I smiled at them. 'Of course not,' I beamed, standing up and grinning. I brushed back my hair. 'Where do you want to take it?' 'Just here would be nice,' they said. I went and stood with my back to the swimming pool, puffed out my chest and pushed back my hair. 'About here?' I asked them. To my surprise, they were looking confused. They whispered together. Instead of pointing the camera at me, I realized they were holding it out towards me. 'Sorry,' the husband said. 'We were hoping that you could take our photograph. I'm Edward and this is my wife Araminta. What's your name?'

> Source: *Losing My Virginity: Richard Branson, The Autobiography*, London: Virgin Publishing, 1999.

---

and the crossing was one long party, hosted by "The Grinning Pullover" himself. Branson's motto is "Do Business, Have Fun." He thinks nothing of dressing up in drag and serving his own customers in flight. "Fun is at the core of the way I like to do business," he explains. "It has informed everything I have done from the outset. More than any other element, fun is the secret of Virgin's success. I am aware that [this] goes against the grain of convention."

When he launched his first flight from Heathrow in July 1991, he posed for press pictures in front of BA's proud model of the *Concorde* outside terminals 1–3. He wore a pirate outfit and had draped a banner entitled "Virgin Territory" in front of the *Concorde*. Nearly every British newspaper and newscast featured the publicity coup. Lord King, chairman of BA, who had originated the "pirate" epithet, was reportedly so furious that he broke his own sound barrier. His "Virgin Bride" chain of bridal shops is clearly tongue in cheek. How many brides are still virgins on their wedding day? He invites them to share the joke.

We will now consider six important dilemmas that Richard Branson has reconciled. These are not the dilemmas simply of one company; they are, in most cases, the dilemmas of conducting business in the United Kingdom itself and of how to appeal to its consumers, media, and establishment. The dilemmas as follows:

1. Making money vs. Critiquing and reforming the economic system
2. Gains for shareholders vs. Gains for employees and customers
3. Specific aims vs. Diffuse contexts
4. Fierce haggling vs. Benign branding
5. Large established business vs. Everlasting entrepreneurialism
6. The Victorious Antagonist vs. The Proverbial Underdog

Dilemma 1: Making Money vs. Critiquing and Reforming the Economic System

Ever since Adam Smith poured scorn on the idea that businessmen might serve the public interest consciously, making money has been regarded as an act of personal aggrandizement, connected to public benefit only by the inadvertence of the Invisible Hand.

"I have never known much good done by those affected to deal in the public," sneered Smith, taking a sideswipe at his patron, the Duke of Buccleuch. "It is an affection indeed not very common among merchants, and very few words need be employed in dissuading them from it." Quite so; this is the kind of businessperson with whom we are all too familiar, and the attitude helps to explain British ambivalence toward wealth creation in general.

Branson is demonstrably different. He campaigned against corporal punishment and "fagging" (younger boys acting as servants to older boys) while still a schoolboy. These battles are now won. He marched on the US embassy in London to protest the Vietnam War. He founded the nonprofit Student Advisory Center, because his girlfriend could not get an abortion. The center published *The Student Magazine*. This came to the rescue of a student on whom the police had planted drugs, and, in retaliation, they prosecuted the journal under a nineteenth century law forbidding any published reference to venereal disease. Branson was fined £7. He was prosecuted again in 1971 by HM Customs and Excise for selling cheap Jimi Hendrix records. They had been diverted from an export consignment. He spent one miserable night in prison with a filthy blanket and recalled his mother's adage that your most precious asset is your reputation. He repaid the excise due on the records and escaped conviction, but he has guarded his reputation ever since. He says of this incident, "Undoubtedly that created one of my values. I have told myself I would never enjoy being accountable to anyone else or not being in control of my own destiny."

Earlier that year, the postal strike had forced Branson to switch from mail order to his first record shop in Oxford Street. This was his first step into the music business, in which he promoted artists whom the music establishment had shut out. Among his successful discoveries in the ensuing years were the Sex Pistols, Boy George, and Mike Oldfield. He considered the two major record retailers at that time, W H Smith and John Menzies, to be stuffy and hostile to new styles of music.

By 1978, he was opening nightclubs, where many of his studio performers gave live concerts. In 1984, Branson challenged British Airways' (BA's) near monopoly of the British-based airline business, flying from Gatwick with Virgin Atlantic Airways and Virgin Cargo. He remarked, "I see something done badly which I know could be done better like the airline. No one was offering their customers a decent service. I was sure that whoever did so would not only have a successful company, but change the whole industry."

In 1989, in the teeth of the growing AIDS crisis, Branson marketed MATES Condoms, a challenge to Durex and considerably cheaper. His hilarious commercials, in which a salesgirl in the drugstore, shouts a query from a shy purchaser so that the whole shop hears, were accompanied by public service messages, on the multiple chances of getting AIDS from the partners of each partner. All profits were donated to AIDS charities.

In 1990, Virgin Lightships, using helium was formed. The initial purpose of the aircraft is advertising. In 1992, Branson alleged "dirty tricks" by BA against Virgin Atlantic passengers, who were being poached and misinformed about alleged "cancellations" of Virgin flights.

In 1993, Branson won a libel suit against BA for claiming that his allegations were invented for purposes of self-publicity, forcing BA's chairman, Lord King, to make a public apology. Damages and costs reached a record £5 million ($8 million). Virgin Atlantic was voted Executive Travel's Airline of the Year for the third year running.

In 1994, Branson took on Coca-Cola and Pepsi Cola with Virgin Cola, against all marketing advice about the entrenched positions of these giants. In 1995, in the midst of the long-running pensions misselling scandal, in which Britain's major pension businesses were forced to repay more than a billion pounds to purchasers they had misled, Branson launched Virgin Direct Personal Financial Service. In the same year, amid growing complaints that Hollywood had a stranglehold on movie distribution via the ownership of movie houses, Branson bought MGM cinemas and promised to give independent producers a better chance.

In 1996, when an ailing conservative government broke up British Rail and sold off the pieces, Branson started Virgin Rail Group. This is often cited as his one major mistake of judgment. The rolling stock was obsolescent, and the track was in very poor condition – a situation that only Railtrack, another company, could remedy. Virgin is among the poorest performers in the whole industry, a problem likely to persist until new rolling stock arrives and Railtrack gets around to Virgin's part of the network. In the same year, he launched Virgin Brides, a chain of retail bridal shops, Virgin Express and a short-haul airline, and Virgin Net, a Internet service provider that soon offered free access.

In 1997, Branson launched Virgin Direct, an alternative telephonic and Internet banking service and a response to persistent press reports of stealthy increases in bank charges by the major clearing banks. In 1998, Branson won a libel action against G-Tech's Guy Snowdon, who had sued Branson for telling the media that Snowden had offered him a bribe to withdraw from the competition to run Great Britain's National Lottery. G-Tech was the prime contractor for Camelot, the successful bidder. Branson's bid was finally unsuccessful in highly mysterious circumstances, though he greatly reduced the profits of the winning bidder by submitting a not-for-profit bid.

In 1999, Branson announced a £4 billion ($6.5 billion) investment in high-speed tilting trains for Virgin Rail, he launched Virgin Mobile is with protections against radio waves affecting the brain. In February 2000, Virgin announced an Internet-based car-buying service designed to combat the exorbitant prices of new cars in the UK, with prices 18% to 30% above those of identical make on the European continent. He hopes to use this competition to get British car prices down.

In March, 2000, Virgin announced that its light-ships service, using remote mine-sensing equipment developed by the Ministry of Defense, was planning a major clearance of millions of unexploded mines, which were bankrupting farmers in thousands of acres of the world's war zones.

All these examples share a single theme:

- There is an injustice, an abuse of power, a scandal, an overcharge, or an important need not met.
- Richard Branson allows press, politicians, and the public to do most of the moralizing.
- What he does is offer a lower-price, higher-quality alternative, thereby becoming the consumer's champion and the media's darling. If customers

wish to avoid being ripped off, they should switch to his brand, increasingly identified with Branson's personal integrity, so much so that he jokingly suggests he should call himself "Brandson."

The dilemma that Virgin has so artfully reconciled is illustrated in the following diagram:

Dilemma 1. The Reforming Millionaire

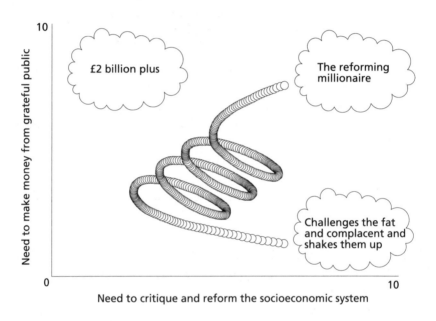

Branson is frank about his strategy: "I can't walk past a fat, complacent business without wanting to shake it up a bit." When he entered the personal pension (PEP) market, he sold £400 million in the first year and £1 billion in the second. "If you go for big, fat, lazy brand leaders, it is often easy to offer better value for money."

"Life insurance?" everyone snorted when they heard the idea. "People *hate* life insurance...It's a terrible industry." "Exactly," he said, "It's got potential."

Branson has certainly grown rich. His personal fortune is estimated at over £2 billion, yet his riches have been gained by his rescuing customers from "fat and complacent" overlords. He has a critic's view of most British business. Instinctively, he I felt that the world of financial serves was shrouded in mystery and rip-offs and that there must be room for Virgin to offer a jargon-free alternative with no hidden catches. "Apart from a few exceptions, he says, postwar Britain has bred a domestic commercial culture that is anticompetitive, cartel based, and patriarchal."

He explains that one should never go into an industry, with the sole purpose of making money. One has to believe passionately that it is possible to change the industry, to turn it on its head, to make sure that it will never be the same again with the right people; with that conviction, anything is possible. "Whenever I see people getting a bad deal, he observes, want to step in and do something about it. Of course, this is not pure altruism – there's profit to be made, too."

Dilemma 2:   Gains for Shareholders vs. Gains for Employees and Customers

Richard Branson has very cleverly adjusted a serious imbalance in Great Britain's economic system, at least as far as Virgin companies are concerned. After going partially public in 1986, he and his managers bought back the stock in 1988, making Virgin once more into a private company.

This was done in part to evade the grip of institutional shareholders and the heavy emphasis that the financial interests nicknamed "the City of London" put on the rights of shareholders. One result of the dominance of Britain's financial sector over the rest of the economy is that the pound is kept strong, interest rates stay high, and profits are squeezed out of industries, often at the expense of employees and customers. Hence, Britain remains, compared with the European Union, an arena of low wages, high prices, and high profits, with interest rates for the pound sterling considerably above those for the Euro.

Branson believes that customers are very important and that you cannot reward them if the morale of your employees is low. Hence, satisfied employees are a precondition for satisfying customers, which in turn, is a precondition for making profits. If external shareholders are pressuring you for the lion's share of trading surpluses, it is hard to avoid the erosion of employee and customer interests.

Once Virgin was converted back to a private company, Branson could spend his profits as he wished and he wished, to benefit *all* stakeholders, not just himself. He explains his view: "Virgin staff are not mere hired hands. They are not managerial pawns in some gigantic chess game. They are entrepreneurs in their own right."

You look after people because at least some of them will invent your own future. As Branson puts it, "I get the best people. I ask questions, and then I say, 'Let's have some fun'." It is simply not possible to enjoy yourself if your job or career is under threat. Virgin is fueled by exuberance; for that, employees must be happy and secure. "Staff should come first," he says. "If it means making £5 million less, then that's the right decision to make."

He believes in a "share the wealth" philosophy that the City would not tolerate, but *how* he shares it is ingenious. There are two levels of shareholding: in the group as a whole and in the individual business units. Branson is generous with the shares of each unit, but 60% of the shares of the whole group is still in his own hands and is likely to remain so. That way, he controls the relative shares of all stakeholders and the clamor to harvest profits and squeeze other resources cannot grow, so far as to wreck the system. The dilemma is illustrated in the accompanying figure.

Dilemma 2. Stakeholders United

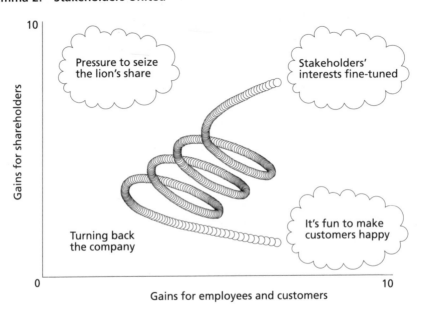

Branson's assumption is that *it is fun to make customers happy*. You do not have to bribe employees to do this but you do need to sustain the morale and enthusiasm they bring to their work and to their clients. If any one kind of stakeholder gets too much, tensions will grow, and common purpose will suffer. Virgin is pledged to give consumers a better deal, and this goal is endangered by siphoning off jointly generated funds. "But the difference is that I'm prepared to share more of the profit with the customer, so that we're both better off."

Dilemma 3:   Specific Aims vs. Diffuse Contexts

One of the major dimensions discussed in Chapter 1 was the dilemma of specific vs. diffuse criteria for judgement. Some cultures are "bean counters." They ask, "What is the bottom line? Cut the crap and give me the *results*! Give me the facts and *only* the facts. Get to the point." Other cultures are broad and inclusive in what they deem important. People work to improve their relationships with peers, superiors, subordinates, contractors, and customers. Through such relationships, they learn. Indeed, information is stored in rich networks of knowledge. Concepts such as morale, ambience, atmosphere, good will, fun and *esprit de corps* are all diffuse and hard to pin down. Branson refuses to be pinned down to any "business philosophy." "I generally won't do so, because I don't believe it can be taught as a recipe." That Branson associates hard work with being loved may have originated with his mother, who thought up challenges for him and would drop him by car some distance from home so he would find his own way back. She also taught the secrets of contributing to a family.

There is another interesting reason that Richard Branson's approach is so diffuse. He has been dyslexic since childhood and left Stowe, an English "public" (i.e., private in U.S. parlance) school, at age 16, having repeatedly failed mathematics. It is not that Branson ignores specifics or fails to value numbers and contract terms. After all, a Virgin bank either gets its sums right or fails its customers, either a Virgin plane is properly serviced, or disaster awaits. It is rather that he has always needed *other people to do the specifics on his behalf.* What he excelled in was creating trust, knowing whom he could trust and whom he could not, and reading human rather than written characters. His own critical weaknesses could be overcome only by high levels of social intelligence. That he had problems double checking his accountant's figures made it all the more important for him to know that person so well as be able to deduce that he would not be cheated.

Branson has to be diffuse for other reasons. Work cannot be fun unless you invest it with all or most of your personality, humor, gaiety, romance, and social life. Satisfying customers means reading their thoughts and needs – realizing that an airline passenger is exhausted and wants a quick snack before the longest possible sleep, could do with a back massage to relax him, or needs a cough drop to ease an itchy throat. Branson also believes that people *define* themselves through their taste in films, music, travel, vacation and so on. Service must be broad enough to cater to such self-definitions.

Branson's early attempts at creating diffuse systems of service sometimes went too far. His early West End music store was designed for people to hang about in, chatting with the staff, trying out records, and sitting and listening to the latest music, but he had reckoned without some of the parasitic characteristics of the Hippie culture of that time. People were using the store to party and to listen and, but to buy. Branson solved the problem in his own gentle way. A doorman reminded each visitor that this was a shop, not a pad. If no one bought, the shop would have to close. Sales, which had dropped to a quarter of those in the opening week, picked up again, and the Virgin chain of music stores – later Megastores – prospered. Branson is well known for elaborating rather than streamlining services. His multiplex cinema chains make clever use of the heavy human traffic around movie houses, and his plans for railway stations on Virgin lines would turn them into small shopping centers, such are common in Japan.

Virgin Atlantic beats BA and other carriers year after year in the standard of its service, as judged by travellers' associations and journals – especially its service in upper class and premium economy. Branson learned early on to look at "the big picture." He was unable to raise $10 million to put videos in every seat back, but he *was* able to raise $4 billion for 10 Boeing 747-400s, which had the videos thrown in as an inducement. That's diffuse thinking!

One of VA's few rivals is Singapore Airlines, with its diffuse, East Asian custom of care for the whole person and of catering to the total experience of travel. Somewhat surprisingly, Singapore Airlines has purchased 49% of Virgin Atlantic, thereby uniting two of the world's most diffuse, elegant, and sophisticated airline services. In the joint venture with Singapore Airlines, an East Asian tradition has merged with a British one. The combination is well epitomized by Raffles, Singapore's famous English Colonial hotel and restaurant. Business class on Singapore Airlines is called "Raffles Class." So long as a corporation is willing to pay for it, the British executive likes to be treated as if he were dining in his London Club or his country estate. Style may even be valued over substance. Fiddling with money to pay for each drink or headset is regarded as vulgar. Service is, ideally, seamless. That Branson has captured the diffuse ambience of East Asian and British service and epitomized it in upper class is beyond question.

Virgin Atlantic is also very effective at getting you to and from your aircraft. If you live within a 60 mile radius of London, Virgin's limousine service brings you to Heathrow or Gatwick, and another limousine picks you up at your destination. A driver for Virgin told the Dutch author, who asked whether wages were good, "To be honest, no, but the passengers flying Virgin Atlantic are so thrilled with the service level that they always give very good tips. Therefore, it's OK that our basic salary is not that high. And I always have happy people in my limousine." Finding yourself in the safe hands of a driver who knows your destination when your body clock has passed midnight is an agreeable and restful way to reach America.

Diffuse social processes are also essential in order for Branson and his top managers to *learn as they go*. We might well ask how a music shop and recording studio boss expects to run an airline, much less an insurer, a bank, a lottery, a railway, a cinema chain, nightclubs, hotels, real estate, a condom supplier, and a chain of bridal shops. (There are many, many more.) The answer is that Virgin enters joint ventures with people who have mastered the specifics of these industries, hires in needed experts, and funds a proposal that includes those specific resources and people as parts of the project. Branson dissents from the "stick to your knitting" school. If you sell records in shops, but do not know the Internet, the latter will ruin you. You need to be well dispersed.

In an important sense, Branson is forever trying to complete the education interrupted at 16 by taking on a series of "learning journeys" into new industries and magical mystery tours into unknown territories. He avoids high-tech or science-based industries, where success cannot be learned from social interactions alone, and sets up diffuse communication patterns in which experts can teach him the specifics, while he teaches experts how to learn from the diffusely spread network of employees and customers. You learn faster from those you respect, from those you trust, and from those you treat as equals. His affable, easygoing style is the key to learn as you go. As he puts it, "What I like most of all is to learn. When I feel that I've learned what there is to know about telecommunications, or airlines, or cosmetics, . . .then I move on to something else. It's like being at university, which I never went to, and taking crash courses."

Several observers have noted how well women and minorities do in Virgin and how relatively numerous they are, but Branson declines to moralize about this success

Dilemma 3. Specific Aims vs. Diffuse Contexts

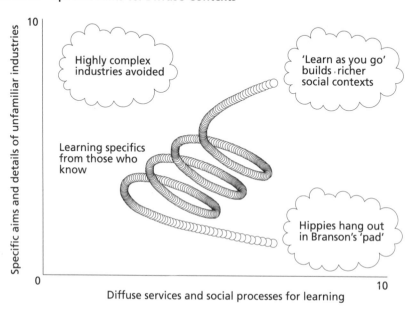

or even proclaim the statistics. You "have fun" meeting lots of different people. Of course, Virgin would be culturally diverse, in the same way that consumers are. Is not variety the spice of life?

For Branson, the rules of sociability link all his businesses: "If you know how to motivate and deal with people, it doesn't matter if you are taking on the airline industry, the soft drinks industry, or the film industry. The same rules apply."

What makes Virgin into one coherent company, despite all the disparate tasks it undertakes, is an underlying social intelligence that builds information-rich contexts in which all concerned learn fast.

Dilemma 4:   Fierce Haggling vs. Benign Branding

There are many who cannot stomach the seeming contradictions of Richard Branson's personality. Perhaps he only *pretends* to be nice and, inches beneath the surface, is a ruthless workaholic and scheming self-publicist who can bring even BA to its knees. Many people, social scientists among them, are threatened by any hint of anomaly. Economists, especially, deem people to be *essentially* self-seeking and profit-maximizing, with a false veneer of altruistic and social concern muddying the clear waters of causation. In this reading, Branson is all façade, with a machinating mind behind a false front.

Much is made of his love of haggling. He enters joint venture negotiations with little but his grin and his pull-over and emerges with the best of the deal. Tim Jackson, in *Virgin King*, refers to Branson's "street-trader's aptitude for negotiation, knowing exactly when to talk and when to stay silent, when to press his counterpart on a point and when simply to walk away." According to Des Dearlove, "Charisma and affable charm belie a calculating business brain. . . ." These (affable) attributes "are complemented by an appetite for haggling that would put a Turkish carpet salesman to shame." Branson also has a propensity to renegotiate contracts when relationships have changed. Does any of this throw doubt on his reputation as a nice guy?

For those writing this book, a haggling competitor and a benign brander are wholly compatible. Any effective personality alters with circumstances. An Olympic wrestling champion strains every sinew against a strong opponent, but does not go home to tie his wife, children, and neighbors into knots. "For all things, there is a season. . . ." Why would *not* Branson haggle with competitors and woo customers?

Indeed, if we look more closely his benign branding is what makes his haggling so effective. Norwich Union (NU) gave him the secrets of the life insurance industry, while he gave NU a brand far better than its own. "Goodwill" and "brand recognition" being notoriously difficult to value, Branson would be failing in his job were he not brash about his brand's advantages. After negotiating with him, you realize just how formidable is that brand, which is co-extensive with his personality. He and it are utterly persuasive, so, of course, he would come out on top.

Branson calls this "reputational branding." He explains, "I'd like people to feel that most of their needs in life can be filled by Virgin. The absolutely critical thing is that we must never let them down." He points to Japan, where corporations like Mitsubishi and Yamaha are seen as benefiting the Japanese culture and people, whether by banking or by supplying pianos, cars, or motorbikes. The reputation is for fair dealing, consumer service, and high-quality employment opportunities. These are attributes, not of manufactured things, like "Speedy" Alka-Seltzer, but of effective social processes. Ninety-six percent of Britons are aware of the Virgin brand, one of the highest recognition scores recorded. Thirty-eight percent reported that they "liked and trusted" the name and were therefore more likely to buy its products.

Virgin seeks to provide "a lifetime relationship" of service and trust. Will Whitehorn, director of corporate affairs, has expressed it well. "At Virgin, we know what the brand means, and when we put our brand name on something, we're making a promise. It's a promise we've always kept and always will. . . . Virgin sticks to its principles and keeps its promises."

The reputation that Virgin promotes and keeps is that the company to be all of the following:

Dilemma 4. Benign Haggling

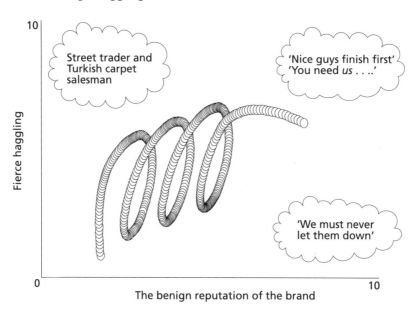

- genuine and enjoyable;
- contemporary and different;
- a consumers' champion; and
- first class at a business-class price.

Armed with this world-class reputation, Branson is in a very strong position when it comes to haggling. When his opponents find their reputations tarnished by their own ruthlessness, it only goes to prove how much more they need Virgin than Virgin needs them. "You need *us*. . . ." No wonder Branson grins. As Dearlove puts it, "Nice guys finish first."

Those who have spent their lives in big corporations are often surprised when they confront a market trader. They have travelled so far from the actual coal-face that its cheery, grubby countenance is a rude shock. It occurs to them too late that they have sold their expertise at a knock-down price.

Dilemma 5: Large Established Business vs. Everlasting Entrepreneurship

One reason Richard Branson has such fun is that he is *both* the founder–owner of a large, established business *and* an everlasting entrepreneur, always starting enterprises, always renewing himself, always exploring new territories. How is it possible to have the best of two worlds – to maintain a schoolboy's enthusiasm for fresh experiences while presiding over a business empire? Why does he not become stuffy, pompous, staid, and arrogant like so many others with early achievements behind them?

One reason can be found in the organizational structure of Virgin. It is simultaneously large and small. The network is large, but the HQ is small, barely 20 people, and most of the business units are small also, although not all of them. Sir Richard clearly identifies with the start-ups and new ventures in his portfolio. It is this that imparts a Peter Pan quality to his character and style. He is always renewing himself, always starting again from scratch, and he has the openness and humility of a novice in strange environments, an approach that is genuine, not contrived. He really *has* to discover new vistas, *has* to listen to people who know a certain field.

Sir Richard no longer dreams up projects by himself. His conviction that employees are entrepreneurs is no posturing. He receives 50 proposals *a week* from within and outside his network and is obliged to pass up 90 percent of them. His major energies and his enthusiasm are reserved for these new departures, and he will see them safely off the ground and into the air before turning his interest to newer launches. "I immerse myself in them [new ventures] for three months [and] then back off." He subsequently looks in on going concerns once or twice a year.

"The idea for Virgin Bride came from a flight attendant from Virgin Atlantic. After a single conversation, she was set to work in the new company, and the first Virgin Bride retail outlet opened its doors in 1996," stated Branson.

All projects are run on a profit-sharing basis by those who dreamed them up and are passionate about the realization of their ideals. Sir Richard poses questions, points out obstacles, identifies pitfalls, helps locate the experts, and then sets the project free to "have fun" and go for it.

He might start a new business because an older one is getting too big. With a hundred or fewer people, first names are the rule, and groups are capable of spontaneous self-organization, made possible by the knowledge persons have of each other's skills and attributes. But where a business grows above such numbers, bureaucracy sets in, rules must be instituted, procedures must be followed, and the division of labor segments employees into mental compartments.

Branson struggles to prevent the onset of business formality by keeping units small and quick on their feet. Small airlines or train companies might not be economically feasible, but the units that compete most effectively – for example, the cabin staff aboard an airliner – *are* small enough to take a spontaneous interest in passengers and care for them. It is a cabin crew that enjoys *one another* that can bring enjoyment and genuine hospitality to passengers. Branson explains, "Every time a business gets too big, we start another one. Keeping things small means keeping things personal; keeping things personal means keeping the people that really matter." He clearly wants personalities to develop and bloom under his aegis, which is why he favors start-ups. It is interesting to note what he does *not* do: grow by acquisition or seize, dismantle, and sell off large bureaucracies.

Des Dearlove has called Virgin "The Atomized Empire" – an empire broken down into chunks made manageable by face-to-face relationships. The company eschews office blocks and prefers to locate itself in one-time residential blocks around Holland Park, in Regency houses with ample space for conviviality. Such housing encourages the integrity and identity of each business unit. Each business has its own board of directors and substantial independence.

Sir Richard is nonetheless constantly on the lookout for new combinations of strategy. For this reason, business units are also *clustered* according to the markets they serve. A trading drinks cluster includes branded vodka and cola. A travel cluster includes two airlines, aviation services, and a travel company. A new idea by any one business unit in a cluster could require the cooperation of another unit. For example, travel magazines on Virgin trains might feature tourist destinations owned or serviced by Virgin, helping to create a network of care for tourists. Joint ventures within clusters are encouraged. Creativity requires new combinations.

In fact, it is new ideas and exciting ventures that catalyze the Virgin network. Out of seeming chaos comes a spontaneous tendency for people to self-organize around ideas that excite them. It is in this way that new order keeps emerging from a party atmosphere and Virgin's "aimless" socialization generates new projects. Bureaucratic order always faces backwards to past production processes. The trick is to generate new orders appropriate to the novel tasks envisioned. Improvisation and quick adaptability are the keys. New processes must be invented to deliver novel products and services.

Dilemma 5. Creative Microcosms in a Large Network

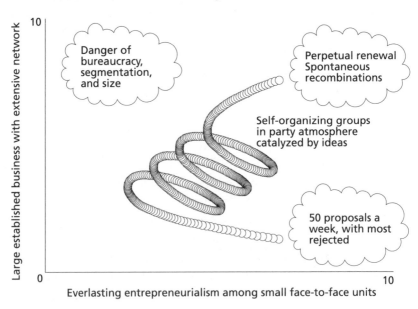

The overall effect is rather like splashing water onto a tangle of live wires, sparks leap across connections, flames flare up, the possibilities of new circuits are realized, power jumps across gaps, everything crackles with new energy, and a mess takes on new meanings.

Dilemma 6:   The Fierce Antagonist vs. the Underdog

Sir Richard Branson is a fighter, and many are the businesses that have regretted taking him on, but he has escaped the reputation of a bruiser or a vexatious litigant by

Box 2: "Saved from Suicide"

Richard Branson was such an unpromising student that he had to be sent to "a crammers" (a school specializing in getting backward students through exams). Unable to recognize dyslexia, the headmaster beat him instead. However, young Richard succeeded in attracting the headmaster's daughter, Charlotte, aged 18, but he was caught climbing out of the bedroom window and was summoned before the headmaster, who promptly expelled him, telling his parents to take him out of the school the next day.

"That evening, unable to think of any other way to escape the wrath of my parents, I wrote a suicide note saying that I was unable to cope with the shame of my expulsion. I wrote on the envelope that it was not to be opened until the following day, but then gave it to a boy who I knew was far too nosy not to open it immediately."

"Very, very slowly, I left the building and walked through the school grounds towards the cliffs. When I saw a crowd of teachers and boys beginning to run after me, I slowed down enough for them to catch up [to me]. They managed to drag me back from the cliff and the expulsion was overturned."

"My parents were surprisingly relaxed about the whole episode. My father even seemed quite impressed that Charlotte was 'a very pretty girl.'"

Source: *Losing My Virginity: Richard Branson, The Autobiography*, London: Virgin Publishing, 1999.

choosing his opponents carefully and by setting the scene of his confrontations so that he is clearly the underdog, likely to attract public sympathy. If he wins, he wins, but even if he loses (as in his failure in the bid to organize the National Lottery), he wins sympathy and (in this case) the jury's verdict against Guy Snowden of G-tech. Richard is the boy "who picks on someone bigger than himself." Whatever the outcome, his reputation is intact. Branson's skill at "underdogism" revealed itself at age 13; see Box 2.

He has taken on Coca-Cola, Pepsi Cola, the giant clearing banks, the pensions industry, the US gambling industry, BA's 95 percent of the UK-originated airline traffic, the motor car cartel (which used Britain's right-hand drive to overprice domestic vehicles), and the closed system of movie distribution. Under normal circumstances, these big boys would swat Virgin like a pesky fly. Distributors of Coke have huge muscle, which has sent a long series of would-be interlopers packing. These are simple products, and they stay on top by controlling shelf space, slashing prices, and crushing rivals.

What appears to have happened is that Virgin's big competitors prefer to leave Branson with a small foothold rather than drive him out, because attacking Branson can be a public-relations disaster. He is brilliant at using the press to his own advantage. He disguised himself as a can of Virgin Cola at Shinjuku Station Square in Japan. A BA plane that landed in Kuwait a few minutes after the Iraqis invaded thereby stranded itself, its passengers, and its crew. It was Branson who sent one of his planes to get the people out. BA drops you in it; Virgin organizes your escape. It was a PR triumph.

So was the coup against Pepsi. "When Pepsi recently spent US 500 million on telling the world that its cans had turned blue, Virgin announced with a grin that it, too, had introduced new cans, which would turn blue on their expiration date. We got a huge amount of publicity and didn't pay a penny for it," according to James Kydd, marketing director of Virgin Cola. Virgin hitches rides on other companies' expenditures, by reframing their expensive publicity.

Big bureaucracies are hopeless at public relations. Spokespersons read prepared statements in a flat monotone with the script shaking in their hands, as if they expected their lies to blow up in their faces. The text has been written by a committee dominated by lawyers and designed to admit nothing, while tediously espousing public virtues. Once accused, top managers in large bureaucracies will look to exculpate themselves and defend their own positions, with rival leaks to the press and crumbling credibility for the company as a whole.

All these symptoms afflicted BA's defense of Branson's libel action against the airline. The public had to choose between, on the one hand the honest indignation of one man, in alliance with investigative journalists, speaking off-the-cuff in response to late-breaking news, and on the other hand, the denials, protestations, and contrivances of PR consultants and political fixers rearranging screens around the scandal. Having misled the public, BA officials were reduced to disowning the acts of their subordinates and offering Branson £11 million if he agreed never again to mention the sorry affair. (He refused.) The jury's award of £500,000 to Branson and £110,000 to Virgin Atlantic was the highest in the history of uncontested libel settlements in the UK. *Branson gave it all to his employees*!

Lord King was forced to retire prematurely and departed, glowering at the media, like a villain in a Victorian melodrama, cursing his own disgrace. It was game, set, and match to the spontaneous powers of personality over the artificiality of contrived stratagems. Sir Richard the Lionheart had won again.

Several commentators have suggested that Branson's artlessness is in fact high art. Tim Jackson and Des Dearlove have both proposed that his motto should be *ars est celare artem* "art lies in concealing art." This seems unnecessarily cynical. To have a highly developed personality and reveal it spontaneously is no super stratagem; it is simply to be yourself before others, striving always to reconcile, but, when that is impossible, pointing out your anger at the dissembling of opponents and asking witnesses to choose between your testimonies. Some people can *trust* their own reactions and do not need to rehearse their moral positions. Others hire an army of advisors to dress them up before the battle in armor so heavy and cumbersome that it weighs them down and forces upon them absurdities of posture.

There is also public sympathy for the wronged individual confronting a collectivized assailant, part of Dilemma 2 in Chapter 1. Branson does, to be sure, head a large organization, but, before public opinion, he is a man alone facing servants of power – a personality against an institution. In individualistic cultures like the UK and North America, the individual is going to win the PR war every time. It is part of our folklore that groups conspire against individuals.

In the chart below, Branson starts from his underdog position and uses the sympathy generated to win his fights against compromised corporations in David-and-Goliath battles.

Dilemma 6. The Victorious Underdog

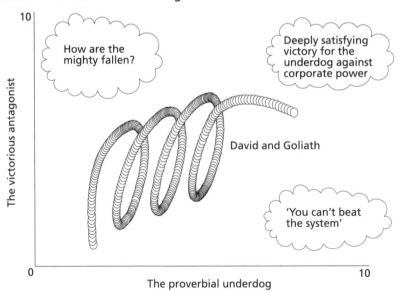

Now that we have looked at the six dilemmas that Sir Richard Branson has successfully reconciled, what can we learn from his potent example? We can draw six important conclusions, one from each dilemma he has confronted:

1. Social criticism answered by social remedy is saleable in a "moral market place." A world in which we can offer our convictions and our life-styles for public approval could change the face of capitalism and bring new meaning and motivation to work.

2. There might be a limit to the level of profits shareholders can demand from business enterprises. By remaining a private company, Virgin appears to have redressed the imbalance between investors, the one hand, and employees and consumers, on the other.

3. As we move into a service economy ever richer in information, Branson's diffuse style of management, in which employees learn as they go, appears to produce ever greater effectiveness. We must learn to cater, not so much to numbers and bottom lines, but to whole people in whole scenarios of satisfaction. Has it taken a dyslexic school dropout to show us the way?

4. "Brand-son" is a fascinating example of the fusion between a brand and a human personality, with all the stretch, versatility, humanity, humor, and tenacity that a living person can bring to a corporate logo. A brand as a promise made by a company to its customers – a promise that can include an extraordinary variety of businesses – is a new and profound phenomenon.

5. Equally important is the idea that a company can perpetually renew itself and avoid growing up into a segmented, soulless bureaucracy of roles and statuses instead of a team of people. Virgin shows that entrepreneurialism need never end, that we can remain forever curious, forever open, impulsive, and exploratory, and, in that sense, forever young.

6. Traditionally, business has supported the top dogs and the powers that be. Even the great dictators had business on their side. Branson has shown the viability and the great strength of becoming a champion of consumers, an advocate of the underdog, and a proponent of a better deal for the public. If we learn these lessons, we could transform capitalism profoundly and vastly increase its powers of social provision. Perhaps Branson has started a revolution in the form of capitalism. Are we on the threshold of "buying" the social character of product and service-related organizations? Could the Internet be used to monitor the conduct and responsibility of moral enterprises? Has Branson started something having momentous consequences?

CHAPTER 4

Creating a Hyperculture

Leader: Martin Gillo (Advanced Micro Devices)

What does it take for a firm to stake its future success on a huge, groundbreaking decision? Clearly, it requires a convinced and passionate CEO with a daring vision and the stamina to see the project through its tribulations to success. Fortunately, AMD had that kind of CEO in Jerry Sanders, plus a courageous board of directors that backed him on this important strategic decision. It also requires a team of top managers to support him. Among these are key players, whose hands are on the levers crucial to the company's strategy. This chapter will focus on the account of one such key player. As of the time of this writing, the story is still in progress.

Advanced Micro Devices (AMD), a large US chip maker, made an audacious move when it decided in 1995 to pursue CEO Jerry Sanders's vision to build a Mega-Fab (factory) in the region of Dresden, in the former East Germany for producing state-of-the-art microprocessors at least equivalent, and, in a number of ways superior to those of Intel®. To give a sense of the degree of courage, at the time, the product was not yet defined; the processes for manufacturing were not yet spelled out; suppliers were still developing the production machinery; the company had no experience in manufacturing chips outside the United States; the employees would be totally new; and East Germany had the challenge of an inferior infrastructure compared with that of the West.

Funding was very attractive, as is usual for such a kind of investment around the world, so the key issues quickly focused on the people questions. Would it be prudent for the company to risk so much on this challenge? AMD has always defined itself by the motto "People come first, products and profits will follow." Here was an opportunity to put that commitment to the ultimate test. Would the formula work in this context? Could an American high-tech firm carry its approach to the deepest parts of East Germany and win? Could the Silicon Valley spirit of passion, of time pressure, and doing the impossible with limited people be brought to life in a region that had to live for decades under the communist system? What about the work ethic?

Would the West German executives try to show the East how to win in their way? How would the different cultures work with each other? Here, three cultures were going to come together: US, West German, and East German. There are significant differences between the latter two. In fact, our research data base shows that there are larger differences between East and West German cultures than between West German and other European countries.

The project could become a smashing success if it unleashed needs long latent in the East German workforce, but not yet given expression. It could also be a disaster – a snake pit of resentments. When the first explorations about the viability of this program were made, the company approached Martin Gillo, its director of human relations (HR) for Europe, with an avalanche of questions. There were many skeptics at the outset.

In our opinion, Gillo is a key example of someone who contributes to success through recognizing that, when it comes to people solutions, *where one places the leverage point* is often more important to the outcome than the magnitude of the force applied. A principle of minimalism is present in reconciling dilemmas. If you really understand the force fields, it might take only a nudge to create a virtuous circle. Martin Gillo was a fortunate find for AMD. He had spent half of his life in Europe, half in the United States. German by origin, he had studied and taught at US universities before moving into HR in the consulting and management fields. He had contributed nine years at AMD's headquarters in California as HR director before spending 10 years as AMD's head of HR in Geneva.

Some teased him, at the outset, that Dresden couldn't be done successfully. As it turns out, the more he studied the situation and the dynamics of the region, the more he became one of the key supporters of the project; and he got ever more involved, becoming one of four managing directors (*Geschäftsführer*) of Dresden AMD and moving to Dresden in 1999.

That said, an American, Jack Saltich, whose excellent leadership during the first three years of the project was crucial to its eventual success, managed the project. Jack and Martin were two of the four general managers. Hans Deppe, head of operations and slated to become CEO for Dresden, and Jim Doran, the expatriate CEO for Dresden at the time of this writing, are the others.

Gillo was well placed to help unify the three cultures of AMD Dresden. His case is different in another regard. Nearly all of the leaders featured in this book had no foreknowledge of dilemma theory. Their ways of thinking were their own. But Gillo had studied our earlier work and had appeared with us on occasion to explain its use. He had used it in earlier years to help AMD's European organization understand its opportunities for marketing in cross-cultural synergies. We have consulted with the AMD Europe marketing organization and also briefly with AMD in Dresden and Austin, to help present the ideas of cultural dilemmas and their resolution.

That Gillo used some of our ideas detracts in no way from his accomplishments. Dilemma theory is no set formula. It is not a technique to be applied with guaranteed results. Rather, it is a way of organizing and utilizing your own judgments and is useless unless those judgments are sound. Martin also is a longtime enthusiast of the work of University of Chicago psychologist Mihaly Csikszentmihalyi, who advocates the creation of "flow states" in personal life and in the workplace – states of total group engagement in the task to be solved, so that the boundaries between task and solution collapse in an experience of transcendence or "flow state." We share his enthusiasm for these concepts and assisted Gillo in using them.

The Dresden location benefited from some crucial advantages. Most obvious were the sizable grants offered by the German state government for locating in this area. Also significant was the fact that East Germany's former communist government had designated Dresden as the center of microelectronics for the whole German Democratic Republic (GDR). Indeed, much of the former Eastern Europe has well-educated professional class, a numerate and literate workforce, and, yet, seriously deficient industries.

It is crucial to grasp that the perceived East German "backwardness" under the communist regime was by no means uniform. For example, the University of Dresden had been specializing in high technology for 30 years before reunification and was an established center of excellence. The educational part of the communist blueprint had always worked better than the industrial part, and the theory had outshone the practice. In fact, one could argue that in some crucial respects East Germany was ahead of West Germany. In technical education, the former GDR awarded degrees for highly skilled manual labor and had a long-term apprenticeship program aimed at placing people in high-technology jobs (e.g., *Halbleitertechniker*, or semiconductor technician, a craft that was eliminated because it did not exist in West Germany). Ed Crump, a German-speaking American HR executive, considered the local technical high schools to be superior to the community college system in California. Given the chronic level of unemployment in Saxony when AMD began to hire, there were very well educated employees lined up to take advantage of the opportunity of working for the company.

The local *Bundesland* (state government) was heavily committed and invested financially, politically, and psychologically in the success of this Fab. At stake was the whole vision of "Silicon Saxony" as a microelectronics cluster. If AMD (and Siemens nearby) succeeded, other multinational companies (MNCs) would likely follow, and Saxony might recapture the wealth and magnificence of its history. The phoenix would rise from the ashes.

The deal to move to Dresden was hammered out between Jerry Sanders, founder and chairman of AMD, and Professor of Economics Kurt Biedenkopf, popular and visionary governor of Saxony. At the very outset, the deal was not widely popular in AMD. There were strong opinions about Germans, about communists, and about German laws on unions, work-councils, and codetermination. With Siemens already there, doubts were expressed about timing. The decision had been intensely difficult. Under Governor Biedenkopf's leadership, however, the Ministries of Labor and Economics had been combined, so that all industrial partners cooperated in *one* ministry at the highest levels of government to reindustrialize the region. The administration and agencies followed suit. Although Germany is a country of laws and countless regulations, AMD never lost a single day's work by having to wait for a permit. All permits applied for were delivered punctually. The workforce proved flexible and highly motivated, out to demonstrate that Saxony was world class. Saxony is very much a source of the Protestant work ethic. The elector of Saxony was the first German prince to endorse Martin Luther's reformation, and the state was at the core of the Reformation down the centuries.

A word should be said about the critical dimensions of a fabrication plant for microchips. Manufactures of the chips consists of large, highly automated processes with extremely exacting standards of quality. Modern transistors are made of layers, some of which are only a dozen atoms in thickness. The key measure of success is the "yield," that is, the percentage of silicon not wasted during the production process. Yields typically are low when operations first start, but they ramp upward over time in a steep learning curve.

Profit and loss depend crucially on this rising curve. A plant with a disappointing yield can lose millions of dollars a week and exhaust its energies on breaking even. A plant with a yield rising quickly to record levels is not just a feat of intercultural competence, but a highly profitable outcome for the company. In such circumstances, misunderstandings, breakdown, in communication, and mutual resentment between those of different national cultures or between managers and workers are potentially catastrophic in their consequences. A series of fine balances is easy to upset by any dissatisfied party. Harmonious working requires the fine-tuning of all efforts. The overall process is extremely delicate and vulnerable to disturbances. The business is a hostage to the continued high quality of cross-cultural communications.

Given the well-known, but often denied or "repressed," antagonism between

"Ossis" and *"Wessis,"* and given the varying approaches to business of Americans and Germans, the whole project had to be considered hazardous. Might AMD be bled dry by interpersonal conflicts carried out thousands of miles from the United States in a language it did not speak? Jerry Sanders had put his reputation and the company on the line. On the other hand, if AMD succeeded, it would have the invaluable experience of a highly successful foreign operation under its belt. The stakes were very high.

The Dilemmas that Martin Gillo Perceived

Our interviews with Gillo elicited the following major dilemmas confronting the Dresden Fab.

1. Neither One Culture nor Another Dominates: the Creation of a Hyperculture
2. Beyond Reason and Pragmatism
3. Beyond Individualism and Communitarianism
4. Learning from Errors and Corrections
5. Skill vs. Challenge: The Flow Experience
6. Sponsoring the Empowered Team

We will now consider each of these six dilemmas in turn. But first note an important word of introduction to the case study that follows: When talking about differences between groups, cultures, and peoples, we must remember that we can talk only about trends and about quantitative, not qualitative, differences between them. There will be many Germans who act and think in some respects more "typically American" than "typically German," just as there will be many Americans who think and act in some respects more "typically German" than "typically American." The reader needs to keep this in mind or be at risk of seeing only a world of stereotypical caricatures in black and white, not the real-life world of shades of grey. Yet, when we are dealing with cultural differences, we are dealing *only* in shades. Having said that, we are ready to explore this case study's ideas for creating a hyperculture.

Dilemma 1: Neither One Culture nor Another Dominates: the Creation of a Hyperculture

From the very beginning, the AMD team realized that trying to import and to impose AMD's American culture on Dresden would be a mistake. In no way can one culture reproduce an exact copy of another, even if it wants to – and it rarely does. A large number of German engineers visited the existing Fabs in Austin and facilities in California. This was not to indoctrinate them, but to provide various models of operation and give them the feel of an operational Fab. 250 Germans visited American operations, and most loved it. It was a whole new world of self-organizing systems. Their right to organize themselves when they got home was not questioned.

America still retains its tradition of openness and hospitality to strangers. Several German visitors were moved to tears by the genuine welcome they go to. Not that the visit was free of misunderstandings: when the Germans presented their annual vacation plans upon arrival, as German law and custom decree, this action was misconstrued! Here they were, on their first day on the job, already thinking about vacations.

The numbers alone show why American culture could not be imposed. The Dresden Fab would soon be 98 percent German–90 percent East German. You can command people up to a point, but not their culture, their shared mental programming. Even the German employees were themselves "singing" at times from "different sheets"; many of the senior managers, were West German, while virtually all the workers and some managers were East German. Our research shows that cultural differences between West Germany and East Germany are *at least* as wide as between other European countries. Many East Germans saw Americans as examples of best practices, open-mindedness, optimism, and can-do conviction. Many West Germans expected an American company to adopt their views on how to succeed with people in all of Germany.

It was for this reason that Martin proposed early on that Dresden AMD should cocreate a new *hyperculture* of its own. The company would borrow and synthesize from the cultures of America, East Germany, and West Germany. It would copy no one culture but would rather distill that which was best in each of them and most relevant to the task at hand. This was a crucial decision, because it prevented each of the cultures from having to defend itself or from insisting on its own ways. The sterile jousts between *"Ossis"* and *"Wessis"* or between US culture and German culture were broken up and sidelined. For the truth was that the work to be performed jointly was in advance of, and more complex than, that which *any* culture had yet achieved anywhere. The new Fab would exceed the performances of all AMD's current Fabs, because it included all the latest technology. It was also dedicated to producing the 6-copper-layer K-7 chip (entered in the market under the AMD Athlon™ brand name) to within a tolerance of 0.18 micron, a feat never before accomplished.

The hyperculture was organized around a task like no other and must of necessity be unique. It followed that, although several national cultures could contribute to a solution, no one culture owned it. A hyperculture is precisely tuned to its corporate objective and exists in order to excel. The dilemma looks like this:

Dilemma 1.   Creating a Hyper-culture

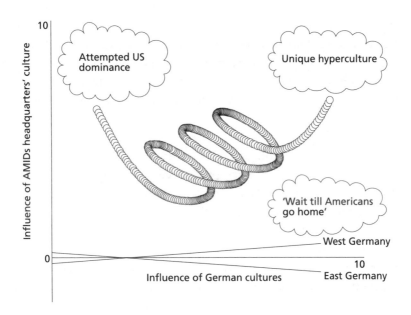

Creating a hyperculture was not without its tribulations. When some Germans felt unhappy, they would say, "Wait till the Americans go home!" The 10 percent US presence in Dresden during the preparatory phase quickly dwindled to 2.0 percent or lower. Long before that, the American influence could be squeezed out. Its dominance must fade with time and with the preference of Californians and Texans for their own patch.

Dilemma 2:   Beyond Reason and Pragmatism

A famous German-American dilemma is the distinction between solving problems by reasoning and logical insight on the one hand and by empiricism and pragmatism on the other. We picked this up ourselves when interviewing German engineers recently sent to Austin, Texas, who were still sensitive to culture shock.

Here was the situation as seen through some German eyes:

• Americans were very often in team meetings discussing this or that initiative.

- They kept changing tack and trying something new, instead of keeping to agreed avenues of inquiry.
- Americans rarely spent any time alone *thinking through* their problems and coming to rational conclusions.
- On some occasions for which German engineers had carefully prepared their positions and were ready to present them, the objectives had been once again changed and their efforts had been wasted.
- If Americans did not joke, kid around, and change their minds so often, work could finish at a reasonable hour. It was a question of discipline and keeping to schedules. German engineers had their families to consider, who were having to deal with strange environments and were often lonely at school because of language barriers

The tension here, according to Gillo, is between *high-risk pragmatism*, favored by Americans, and *lower-risk rationalism*, favored by Germans. From the German point of view, the Americans "shoot from the hip" without taking careful aim; German engineers, by control coming as they do from expert cultures, like to solve problems by rational and cerebral means. In extreme cases, Americans even criticize German engineers for "paralysis by analysis." You don't have forever to find solutions when definitions of problems are changing quickly. However, the dilemma is not that simple, nor are Germans or Americans so homogeneous. What surprised Gillo initially was that East Germans were, in this respect, closer to Americans than to West Germans, although the reasons for that were intriguing.

Because of the decades of extremely limited resources in the old GDR and the frequently unreliable delivery of necessary supplies, and because prices for electronic goods had been arbitrarily fixed in Moscow, often at unrealistic levels aimed at exploiting the Warsaw Pact countries (the old Eastern Bloc), East Germans had learned to improvise, to substitute cheaper components at the last minute, and generally to scramble to remain solvent. The joke about centralized planning was that it spawned local improvisation on a massive scale because the plans were so rigid. In any event, many of the East Germans took to the American pragmatic style as if they had been born to it. Sudden changes of tack were what they were used to, and they suffered much less than West Germans when parameters were suddenly changed. Moreover, it gave them equal footing with their West German peers. This was a "new game," and all came to it afresh.

We must, nevertheless, take care not to put rationality down. It saves us from reinventing wheels. German engineers learned much by analyzing the operation of

American Fabs. Without analysis, the Dresden Fab could not have done as well as it did.

The value that the AMD Dresden team strove to endorse was *Systematic Experimentation*. The *systematic* part was designed to appeal to German rationality, the *experimental* part to American (and East German) pragmatism (and improvisation). The dilemma is set out in the following diagram:

Dilemma 2.   Reason vs. Pragmatism

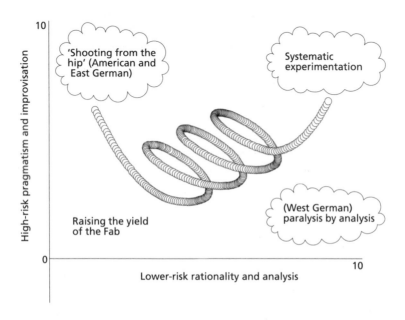

Systematic experimentation is monitored by raising the yield of the Fab progressively. What works pragmatically is retained; what fails is discarded. Rationality remains crucial in providing insights into what works and what does not. This holds true even more for painstaking systematic experimentation.

Dilemma 3:   Beyond Individualism and Communitarianism

One dimension on which the former West and East Germany still disagree is the relative salience of individualism and group orientation. While much of the former Eastern Bloc now claims to be more individualistic than Americans and to extol the ideology of the West, many East Germans still reject the "arrogance" of the West Germans and their perceived tendency toward consumerism and superiority, according to Wolfgang Wagner's research. The courage it took to survive the

Box 1: Individualism vs. Common Good

	West Germans	East Germans
Description	are more oriented toward individualist and pluralist community of interests; decision making through dissent, conflict, and compromise	are community and group oriented and are disappointed by the individualistic Western society; decision making through consensus about the common good
Advantages	all can find happiness in their own ways	more cohesion, more clarity, and more dependability
Characterize themselves as	independent, casual, lonely, uptight, pleasure oriented	overwhelmed by changes, group dependent, family oriented
Characterize others as	bourgeois, kind, trusting, narrow minded	independent, arrogant, cynical

Source: Wolfgang Wagner, *Kulturschock Deutschland* (Hamburg: Rotbuch Verlag, 1996).

oppression of the Stasi (secret police) and the high price of resistance is rarely honored in the new Germany. The East retains a solidarity based on a suffering that few in the West wish to understand or appreciate. Martin Gillo likes to cite recent surveys comparing "Wessis" with "Ossis" that saw West Germans embrace a form of individualism and East Germans an identification with the common good; see Box 1.

The latter descriptions in this box give a flavor of the East German mood of resentment toward their Western compatriots and other outsiders. "How shall we deal with such differences?" asks Gillo. He rejects cultural colonialism ("Follow us"), the melting pot ("Fondue"), and tolerance (the cultural mosaic), because in all these cases there is no genuine engagement between the integrity of one culture and that of the other. "Follow us" ignores the East German culture. "Fondue" opts for one sticky mass. Tolerance follows the discredited policy of separate but equal, a result that almost never eventuates, because the weaker of the separated cultures wilts.

The AMD team's answer was *cultural symbiosis*, or *synergy*, a process by which West German culture, East German culture, and American culture combined their preferences. The resulting symbiosis is individualistic because the USA and

West Germany are involved, yet communitarian because East German employees constitute the large majority of the participants. Both values are joined together, but at higher levels of intensity, not in a fondue mix, but by catalytic conversion to higher levels of energy and power.

"We go through five steps," explains Gillo:

1. Recognize that the cultures are legitimately different.
2. Respect those differences; there is no "right" or "wrong."
3. Locate the cultural differences on a dual axis, as illustrated in the following figure.

Dilemma 3.   Individualism vs. Communitarianism

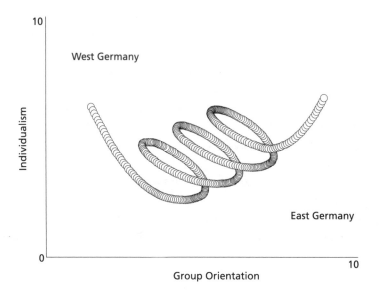

4. Caricature both extremes to make them unacceptable: "Look out for no. 1" (individualism); "only society counts" (group orientation).
5. "Symbiotize" (as on might call it) both values. That is, strengthen one value *through* the other. For example, the symbiotic combination of East and West helps create the climate of a communitarian culture, whereby the groups work extremely closely together and the individuals are encouraged to take initiatives and risks for the best interest of themselves *and the group*. (Communitarianism has been outlined in the United States in recent years by authors such as Amitai Etzioni.)

"The truth is, individualism and group orientation are complementary, not opposed, provided that we can fine-tune them," Gillo continues. "The group can, if it so desires, nurture individuality, whereupon the individuals so formed contribute to that group, all the more effectively because of their independence of judgment and opinion."

But you cannot just announce this philosophy and hope that it sticks. You have to treat employees according to its tenets. You have to reward individuals *as* individuals for their support for the team, and you can also give them a bonus as a team for supporting and championing the initiatives of individual members. Between them, these rewards encourage individuals to improve teams and teams to develop individuals.

In this overall dynamic, each culture tends to see its preferred value. East Germans tend to prefer the "descending arc" on the right. West Germans and Americans tend to prefer the "ascending arc" on the left. What all cultures should be able to recognize, whichever arc they prefer, is that the *entire cycle* is necessary to enhance both individualism and communitarianism in symbiosis.

A second dynamic is to let individuals or groups compete in friendly rivalry until a team emerges that can *cooperate around that winning formula*. For example, one team's initiatives might produce a better yield than another's, but most crucial is the capacity of the whole community to adopt those winning initiatives. The ideal is *collaborative competition*.

To achieve that ideal, once again we stigmatize the extremes: "tooth and claw" is corrupted individualism, and "cozy collusion" is corrupted communitarianism.

Note that the term "co-opetition" has had to be coined recently in order to convey a symbiosis that dictionaries still do not acknowledge. Only the Japanese, to our knowledge, have an accepted term for "cooperating while competing."

Gillo does not confine his concept of symbiosis to these two values alone, but sees golden opportunities for the reconciliation of numerous dilemmas. To three more of these we now turn.

Dilemma 4:   Learning from Errors and Corrections

Let us look more closely at the unique challenges of building a prototype Fab. You cannot reason, because it is not possible to gain a clear definition of all of the problems to be solved. Reasoning assumes the preexistence of a logical solution to a definable problem, but building a Fab is less a definable problem than a nest of interdependent problems, each of which affects and changes the definitions of the other problems. You have to start somewhere, but, depending on this choice, the remaining problems rearrange themselves spontaneously. One bottleneck once removed, for example, creates several more. The task itself constantly evolves along with those who perform it, a process Gillo calls *coevolution*, in which we change the environment, which in turn throws up fresh challenges to be met anew. It is less the survival of the fittest than the survival of the *fittingest*. We keep on reengaging the environment in ways that ever increase the yield; however, this improvement quickly changes the competitive environment itself and thereby triggers the need for never-ending virtuous cycles of improvements. This is not unlike to an *error-correcting system*, in which you zero in on improving yields by *successive approximations* to ever-increasing levels of expected quality. W. Edwards Deming made this process famous.

Yet, conventional wisdom tells us that errors are somehow "evil" and must be extirpated, while corrections are "good." Good must then "conquer" evil to create a world that is perfect and pure of all contaminants. The problems with this view are that it makes learning from our mistakes almost impossible and that it assumes that what is best can always be known before we act.

Conventional morality is a serious impediment to the *discovery* of better ways by trial, error, and continuous improvement. How to build a K-7/AMD Athlon™ Fab is not like a search for the Holy Grail, where the object is ideally "out there" to be found in all its perfection. Rather, a high-yield fab is the culmination of thousands of

Dilemma 4. Error, Correction, and Coevolution

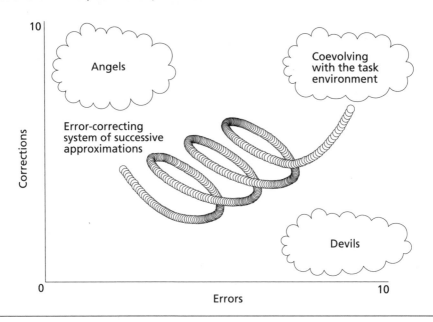

(Graph with vertical axis labeled "Corrections" (0 to 10) and horizontal axis labeled "Errors" (0 to 10). Cloud labels read "Angels," "Coevolving with the task environment," "Error-correcting system of successive approximations," and "Devils.")

continuing trials that successively improve on earlier attempts. "Error" is no devil; it records what was once good enough, but now is surpassed because we aim higher. The dilemma is shown opposite.

Included in the coevolution are all the cultures involved, plus the remaining resistance to a heightened yield contained within the environment of the whole Fab. Persons, tools, tasks, and work environments evolve together.

Dilemma 5:   Skill vs. Challenge: The Creation of "Flow" Experience

As mentioned earlier, for many years Gillo has been fascinated by the results of over 25 years' research of Mihaly Csikszentmihalyi, especially his description of "flow states." Even before moving to Dresden, Gillo had published his own in-house pamphlets to promote the idea of a continuous flowing engagement with the task at hand, one that learners find all-absorbing and intensely stimulating. (The original research was into the state of happiness itself.)

Flow states, sometimes called *peak experiences*, occur when the team (which could be one person) confronts a problem that almost exactly matches its combined potentials and skill sets, so that, provided that these potentials can realize themselves, the solution is (just) within the team's reach. The intensity of pleasure comes from stretching toward and reaching new levels of attainment, discovering strengths within the team that were formerly aspirations, and crossing additional barriers to attainment. Csikszentmihalyi's work, together with the valuable extensions by the Swiss consultant Martin Gerber, have important ramifications for self-organizing teams. The work suggests that people gravitate to the problems they want solved and believe they can solve together and that they spontaneously match their skills to challenges, not just to get past the problems, but to discover more about themselves and what they can accomplish. At the moment of their triumph, the barriers between the problem and the people dissolve. They *are* the challenge they have met.

The word "solution" holds the key to this dilemma. The word means both *the answer to a puzzle* and a combination formed by dissolving something into a more fluid medium. When a solution is found to a problem, the hard edges of that problem dissolve, and the separate identities of skills and challenges are transcended. The one flows into the other like an onrushing stream of energy, as the team rides upon the momentum in a surge of excitement.

We took Martin's insights into flow dynamics, combined them with a dual-axis diagram of challenge vs. skill proposed by Csikszentmihalyi himself, and created the following image.

Dilemma 5. Skill vs. Challenge

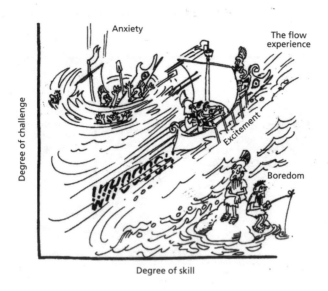

Where challenge (the vertical axis) is greater than skill (the horizontal axis), you get anxiety; where skill is greater than challenge, you get boredom (bottom right); but where skill engages challenge to realize its ideal and actualize the person, you get a *whoosh* of excitement and a flow experience (top right). All of a sudden, the skills and the challenge that *were* formerly in conflict (the first seeking to surmount the second), are suddenly one, so that the very strength of the challenge now testifies to the skills developed. These moments of ecstatic attainment can be fleeting, as when we look back nostalgically, say "Then we were happy," and wonder how we can recapture the feeling.

Dilemma 6:   Sponsoring the Empowered Team

Progress is not equal on all dilemmas facing AMD in Dresden. Work still needs to be done, in Gillo's estimation, on the process of sponsoring groups or teams so as to empower them. "Group sponsorship" needs to be defined.

Dennis Roemig, working on team effectiveness in AMD's US manufacturing plants coined the phrase *semiautonomous team*. His research found that such teams were a lot more effective than either totally autonomous teams or closely supervised teams. (We shall see why in a moment). So successful was the team approach that had worked in Texas and California, that it was defined as a nonnegotiable aspect of

Dilemma 6. Sponsoring the Empowered Team

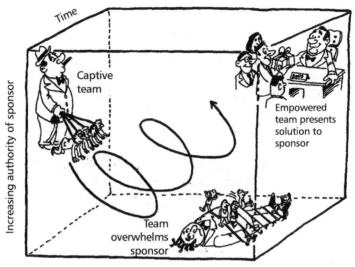

Empowerment of team

operations at the new Dresden Fab. Teams are vital because problems have grown in their complexity beyond the expertise of single professionals and even beyond the mandate of top managers. They may know there is a problem, know it must be solved, know the solution when they see it, but *not* know exactly what has to be done to solve the problem or improve the yield. Problems in a Mega-Fab need to be *discovered*, and it takes a team to do this and to work out the remedy as quickly as possible.

It is sponsorship of a team by a leader that renders the group semi-autonomous. The sponsor describes the problem to be solved, allows the group to form spontaneously around the problem profile, and makes sure all the required skill sets are present. The sponsor then delegates authority to the group and gives it the resources that are necessary. Finally, the sponsor *sets the group free to complete its task*.

However, this "freedom" is a question of degree. The team must report back in weeks or months, so that autonomy is measurable *by the time interval between supervisions*. If the team is left alone for months, the autonomy is great and the risk is high. The team might go off course and waste time and money. If the team is left alone only for days and is seeded with the leader's spies, the autonomy is low and so is the risk, but so also is the likelihood of the team coming up with anything remotely innovative or significant.

Note that Gillo has added a third dimension, time. It was he who wrote to us some years ago to insist that *all* dilemmas were resolved over time.

The authority of the sponsor is on the vertical axis and the empowerment of the team on the horizontal axis. If the sponsor hangs on to authority for dear life, the team remains on a short leash, captives of its leader's doubt and distrust (top left), but if the team is *totally* autonomous, it could deviate from, misinterpret, or defy its sponsor's charge and use its newfound power to bind its sponsor to developments neither sought nor intended (bottom right). After all, the team has the delegated authority and the resources given to it and *could* diminish both. In this event, the sponsor's authority is seriously weakened.

Alternatively, the charge could be so clear, the problem so important, the team so motivated and in such a "flow state" that the sponsor's problem is solved, and this solution, along with part of the credit, goes back as a gift from the empowered team (top right). In this event, all concerned are better off. The sponsor's judgment and authority are vindicated and enhanced. The team's morale is sky-high, and its power and influence are enhanced. The semiautonomous nature of the team is indicated by the gaps between the spiral loops. How often must the team check back with its sponsor? Too often or too seldom can both do damage, but "just right" makes the team into a strong investigative arm of its sponsor, an invaluable way of uncovering new facts and testing propositions.

The problem – in this case – could be with traditional German culture, East and West, which places the sponsor's expertise above the team's initiative in the organization's hierarchy. Sometimes, German sponsors are less willing than American ones to delegate their authority to teams and to trust in developing capacities for problem solving. Yet, given the nature of new fabrication plants, delegating might be the only way. Sponsors rarely know the answer for which the team is searching, and it would be a waste of the team's time and effort if they did.

The Dresden team does everything possible to preserve and develop "natural work groups" – that is, groups that have learned and experimented together and in whose relationships much crucial information is stored. Gradually, these natural groupings are growing in their reputations for discovery and problem solving. In the continuing coevolution of natural work groups, it could turn out that they benefit from constitution like protective boundaries and explicit role clarifications for the groups and their sponsors. The same could also apply to the owners and to the internal as well as the external customers of the problems to be solved. Of all the dilemmas, this last is turning out to be the most stubborn so far.

How Has the Dresden Fab Fared?

We cannot give figures for AMD's yield at the Dresden Fab (they are commercially confidential), yet the signs of significant success are everywhere. As of this writing, the 0.18-micron copper version of the AMD Athlon™ microprocessor is the most ambitious and the most advanced in AMD's worldwide operations. Gene Conner, a senior vice president of AMD, pronounced Dresden "the most successful start-up in the history of the company." Learning curves by which yields climb can be steep and rapid or shallow and slow. The Dresden learning curve was the steepest and fastest among all the start-ups of AMD's Fab. That the Fab we have been discussing was a Mega-Fab employing a thousand people to produce a chip of unprecedented complexity and sophistication merely made the feat more remarkable. That Dresden was chosen to produce the AMD Athlon™ was an occasion for regional rejoicing, a triumph not just for the plant, but for Saxony, where ancient castles were selling for $1 if the owner would only restore and then properly maintain them. Gillo comments, "We now run two day shifts and two night shifts. The plant never sleeps. At 3:00 A.M., several engineers will still be there. This is their baby. Employees have rights to unionization and a works council under German law. So far, these have not been organized. I like to think this is in some part because we look after everyone's needs. We all share the great adventure of improving the world's most advanced Fab. We want to hear everyone's voice. We are determined to give their opinions and cultures the weight that is due to them. We are a *partnership-oriented* company indeed."

CHAPTER 5

Recipe for a Turnaround

Leader: Philippe Bourguignon (Club Med)

It is a particular pleasure to write about Club Med, because one of us (FT) has taken his wife and family to its village resorts at least 10 times. To study the company is to begin to understand the intensity of our enjoyment, but we are not simply indulging ourselves. Club Med caters to an international clientele with a prodigious mix of international staff. Vacationing is the world's fastest growth industry, and within that industry, which is the best known brand? Club Med.

So, while one of us, at least, is a Club Med fan, quite capable of playing the fool at the Club's nightly evenings dancing in a tutu or otherwise frolicking, the recently interrupted success of the company has its serious side as well. Our memories of Club Med's French stylishness; its easy camaraderie; its well-trained staff, seemingly also on vacation while eating, dancing, and flirting with the guests; the sports; the buffet; and the free wine among the gregarious mix of nationalities are unforgettable. We even thrived on those hand-waving Club sing-alongs ("Hands up! Gimme, gimme, your heart!").

Yet all these fond memories might have been nonrenewable had it not been for Philippe Bourguignon. Until 1997 he had been busy trying to turn around the fortunes of Euro-Disney. Even while he was thus engaged, the fortunes of Club Med were ebbing as it descended ever further into financial trouble, with annual losses of $200 million, until, in February 1997, Bourguignon was asked to take the helm. It was said at the time that the Gulf crisis had hit hard at the company's "villages," several being too close to the fighting. But the real problems were more endemic to the system.

Radical action was needed to stop the losses, and Bourguignon had to move fast. Among other things, he closed 8 of Club Med's 116 sites and renovated 70. He imposed high quality standards on the remaining sites. Before we can understand the subtleties of his many strategic moves, we have to look at the history of Club Med and the troubles into which the company had descended by early 1997.

Early brilliance that lost its way

Club Med was founded in 1950 by a Belgian, Gerard Blitz, a former Olympic water-polo competitor. He was soon joined in partnership by a Frenchman, Gilbert Trigano who, as a member of the French communist party, saw Club Med as breaking down class barriers. That summer, they introduced their "all-inclusive vacation," consisting of a military-surplus tent village in Alcudia, Majorca. The concept of the Club was born in a prewar context, where people had to learn to live together in mutual trust again. This package holiday was a major innovation for its time, now so usual that we rarely inquire into its origins. In 1954 the first concrete apartments were built in Greece, followed by the first winter village, in Leysin, Switzerland. The company was years ahead of its time. It pioneered the exclusive hotel and resort facilities, as well as the concept of "Club membership" with accompanying brand loyalty. Today Club Med has 116 resorts or "villages," plus 11 villas across the world, and serves 1.6 million vacationers a year from 40 different countries, largely in winter and summer seasons. It also features a three-mast cruise ship, The Club Med 2, launched in 1992.

We can trace the company's extraordinary success to key features of French culture and to its capacity to combine values not previously integrated by its competitors. The all-inclusive package differed from those of its more standardized competitors by combining freedom and choice for the vacationer, with prearranged bookings and accommodations and extensive opportunities for conviviality and generosity.

The Club goes out of its way to attract families, while providing an opportunity for parents and children to be separately entertained and relieved from each other's company for periods of time, including relief from the parental chores of cooking, housekeeping, and baby-sitting. The Club also reconciles the improvisation and informality of camping with the luxury of good food, wine, and entertainment. Blitz refers to this as "a strange cocktail of château life and wild life."

Blitz intended his company to restore the values lost in modern tourism: "Adventure is dead and solitude is dying in interlinked systems of tourism. The individual doesn't like promiscuity, but needs a community. Therefore, we offer him flexible vacations to which he can adhere himself at any moment or avoid it." The village provides a "base camp" from which those seeking solitude and adventure can roam, with or without guidance and companions.

Gilbert Trigano claimed that Club Med was aimed deliberately to straddle "the contradictions of French life," to make up for what was lacking in work life: "Vacations result in a kind of liberation that enriches the rest of the year. The Club has crossed some borders by giving serious people the right to be ridiculous and to try out almost anything. Therefore, the villages were initially designed to respond to typical French contradictions: Sophistication versus Back-to-Nature, Individualism versus Camaraderie, a mix of sports, sensuality, culture, and exotically strange decors, a yearly escape from the barriers and tensions of society in a utopian brotherhood. As the company's own history puts it, Club Med members "spent their days frolicking in the Mediterranean sea and their nights sleeping under army surplus tents supplied by the Trigano family."

France, as our research shows, is perhaps the most communitarian nation in Western Europe, and, to a great extent, Club Med celebrates this fact. Each table accommodates eight people, room enough for your own family and one you have met during the day. Every evening there is live entertainments, which brings families together and in which the audience can participate. But during the day different people can follow any one of dozens of sporting or adventure activities, with special interests of particular family members catered to and supervised within "clubs."

Now, it would not be French unless the conviviality had real style and *panache. Les Gentils Organisateurs* (The Gracious Organizers, or GOs) set an example of social grace, hospitality, and exuberant spirits, making sure that everyone is included,who wants to be, and usually helping to provide the evening *"spectacle."* On Friday evenings the GOs help to arrange *spectacles* featuring the children of *Les Gentils Membres* (The Gracious Members, or GMs), who perform for their parental audience in elaborate costumes the numbers they have rehearsed. You pay up front, and everything else flows and bubbles with the wine, as spontaneous communities self-organize to have fun and to exhibit their talents to each other.

We can summarize the reasons for Club Med's initial success by listing the dilemmas that it helped to reconcile:

Dilemma	Resolved by
1. Many separate bookings vs. One shared experience	The all-inclusive, all-paid holiday
2. Preorganized holiday vs. Adventure, autonomy	Individuals explore around their base camp
3. Attract the family vs. Give members a rest from each other	"Clubs" in which children have separate daytime activities and evening reunions

4. Improvisation and informality vs. Luxury of food and entertainment	"Cocktail of château life and wild life"
5. The individual's solitude vs. The need for community	Attach or detach yourself at will
6. Serious people vs. The liberation to have fun and enjoy losing yourself	*Spectacle* and Camaraderie
7. Sophistication vs. Back to Nature	*The Noble Savage* (Jean Jacques Rousseau)
8. Exotic decor vs. Barriers and tensions of society	Utopian brotherhood of mutual self-expression
9. Guests as audience vs. Guests as entertainers (especially children)	Freedom to do what you want when and where you want
10. International diversity vs. *Les Gentils Organisateurs*	GMs celebrate their common humanity through GOs

In the preceding table, we have tried to give a resolution or reconciliation for each contradiction; most were provided by the two founders, but some by us and one by Jean Jacques Rousseau. France is perhaps the only country in the world where "contradictions" – what we call dilemmas – are considered to have intellectual status as recognized societal phenomena.

So What Went Wrong?

Given this feat of *bonhomie*, it seems surprising that Club Med could get into trouble. Yet success, like God, is in the details, and even as the GOs and GMs were celebrating each other, certain crucial details began to slip.

The trouble began as early as 1993. Club Med's prodigious growth had overstrained as well as obscured its antiquated management structure. It had become intoxicated by its self-celebrations, week after week, and was not keeping track of costs or logistics. What Bourguignon called the *infernal spiral* (vicious circle) was kicked off through a series of uncontrollable accidents and worsened during the 1993 global recession. The company's downward spiral had begun. Meanwhile, some holiday makers copied Club Med's concept and took some market share from it. Combine these up with bad management, leading to a series of expensive, faulty investments and a decreasing number of innovations, and it explains higher prices and lower perceived quality. One of the core values of Club Med, "generosity," was not affected by the down-turn swing best expressed by lower occupancy rates. No company survives for a long time, under these conditions, but maladministration drove Club Med further under. Resorts were not profit centers, and several had lost money without anyone being aware of it, or of opening too early in the season or not early enough and closing too early or too late.

Moreover, hospitality had simply been increased, with no awareness of diminishing returns. The choice of 40 different sporting activities was too many, requiring too many experts in each sport and smaller membership of Clubs. The food and wine expenditure had escalated too far. Too many GMs were aging friends of the founder's families, with an average age of 50-plus, Club Med's strengths had been extended to the point of weakness and indulgence. In the meantime, the rest of the tourist industry was catching up, and Club Med was soon seen as too expensive. It responded to lower bookings with higher prices, and the downward spiral intensified.

Philippe Bourguignon Takes Charge

Bourguignon took charge in early 1997 and started by making a tour of the villages around the world. On his first day, he showed up in a village in Africa rather than in the more established life of the headquarters in Paris La Villette. He was very clear in his objective to find out the keys to why the Club was hitting bad weather financially. "It is typical of Bourguignon that he refused the best bungalow of our village on the Ivory Coast which I, as *chef de village,* had dedicated to our new president, says Vincenzo Del'Zingaro, one of the 100 *chefs de villages,* or site managers, of Club Med. "Bourguignon loves luxury, but his job was to find out how local sites were operating. Therefore, he wanted a standard bungalow. When I asked him how he was doing in the morning after a terrible night of storms, he said it was OK, except for the water on his floor and the fact that the temperature of the shower didn't rise beyond room temperature. But he was very factual about it and just suggested that he had bad luck. Even when, the next day, his new bungalow was unexpectedly surrounded by nudists from the neighboring hotel, he just responded by saying that it was quite an interesting experience."

By the end of his tour, in July 1997, Bourguignon had a pretty good idea of the mess his company was in. The annual report for 1997 listed the weaknesses he had uncovered, and it was typical of his straightforward behavior that he pulled no punches. The brand had not responded to the entry of new players. Prices were too high, driven by failures in cost containment. Excessive choices at each village diluted the experience of sharing, as well as pushing up costs. Villages should specialize more instead of offering everything. Many villages were shoddy and in disrepair. Lack of investment had taken its toll. Finally, the communications system among villages and to headquarters was seriously deficient.

Bourguignon was faced with a powerful, once-successful Club culture, proud of its history and its pioneering tourist attractions. So many of these traditions were valuable and right, that he did not want to attack them. How could this unique way of serving and satisfying people make money once again?

Behind every great strength lies a potential weakness. Those who excel at lavish hospitality and gentle sociability are rarely the best accountants or "number crunchers." Bourguignon set about analyzing the profits and losses for every individual village and resort and discovered monumental waste. He closed 11 losing resorts in Greece, Ireland, and Switzerland and sold off a cruise liner, *CM1*. He built 10 new resorts, renovated 70, and extended opening and closing times to increase the overall room capacity, until every week was profitable in itself. He adjusted prices to reflect demand through a simplified price policy, a reduction in the number of advertising promotions to improve the discount factor, and the implementation of yield management.

He kept the Chefs de Villages and replaced some GOs as heads of departments and country managers in headquarters functions with colleagues he had known at Euro-Disney, Accor, or other companies like PEPSICO and Danone, but the test was always performance and an understanding of culture, not favoritism. A delicate touch was required in order to create a renewed management team of 49 new managers out of 86, combining new skills with existing talents, but Bourguignon emphasized and celebrated the mission that had made Club Med great. You entertain people with their children in varieties of activities, including sports, and give them excellent accommodation and food in a beautiful site, with charming and entertaining hosts.

As an outsider and a turnaround specialist who earned his spurs at Euro-Disney, Bourguignon, could be more drastic about severing old relationships. One European GO observed, "In a French company, you need to be a relative outsider to be able to take tough measures like closing a site or asking people with 20 years of experience to leave, because they are unwilling to change. Previous management couldn't do this. They were too much attached to existing relationships and traditions."

Bourguignon was clear that Club Med's values were not wrong *per se*, but they had in many cases been taken so far that they were hurting, not helping, the organization:

"All companies have strengths that are weaknesses if you take them too far. The Club's strengths are its unique formula, whereby GOs eat, sport, create shows, and dance with GMs. [The Club] offers a vast variety of sports, some 60 in total, which we keep extending. We are the largest sports institute in the world. We are located in some of the loveliest places, and our miniclubs for kids are a great success, as is our cuisine. This triangle of GO, GM, and site in an atmosphere of generosity and living together needed to be reassessed and rebuilt in an affordable way. . . . but all these were also expensive and came at the cost of other luxuries and attentions, at higher-than-necessary prices. HQ was too large. Relationships to HQ were too hierarchical. We needed to empower villages by giving them the information on how they were doing and the authority to act. Every unit is now a self-conscious center which knows the costs of its activities and can estimate their value."

Before his first year was over, Bourguignon had coined a new watchword *Être-Re, or Re-New*. Club Med's traditional values would not be abandoned but rather would be renewed in their attractiveness and impact on customers. Renewal had four strategic axes, all built on past accomplishments.

1. *Re-Focus* the product by renovating villages and featuring this strategy in a marketing campaign.
2. *Re-Store* the brand and the product as the all-inclusive vacation, with a brand entity aligned with its perception.
3. *Re-Gain* price competitiveness: Reevaluate price policies by more closely tracking and responding to peaks and troughs in demand.
4. *Rationalize* management and organization, the way operations were done in HQ and in each site, in a way that takes advantage of what is common to all sites and hence emphasizes what is unique and special to each site.

In implementing these strategies, Bourguignon employed the famous French axiom *Plus ça change, plus c'est la même chose*, or literally, "Everything changes, yet remains the same." He wanted Club Med as an idea and a set of values redefined in changed circumstances.

We will now examine these four strategic thrusts and consider what dilemmas they addressed and how those dilemmas were reconciled.

1. The Dilemma of Refocusing: The Unique, Seamless, Personalized Vacation vs. The Reliable, Affordable, Segmented, Standardized Global Product

The need to refocus comes from the fact that the unique, personalized vacation presided over by GOs who get to know you well and concentrate on creating an unforgettable experience is not enough. This means that more effectiveness needed to be created. The worst that could have been done would have been to offer a little bit of everything. It is like offering nothing. The *Re-Focus* program was aimed at "an increased offering by focusing on what you offer." This was done on all levels: sports, food, shows, and so on, with all the operational risks that come along with it. Less lyrical issues like occupancy rates and how to improve them must be considered at the same time. You cannot be "gentle" only with those who turn up. They will not turn up if they do not expect a standard of service they seek at an affordable cost. Little inexpensive things to create a "personal touch" are details like memorizing your first name and a previous occasion where GO has met the GM. This is what refocusing is all about.

Bourguignon has concentrated his offering into four categories (hut villages, 2, 3, or 4 trident) instead of six levels of luxury. He created this arrangement by renovating 70 of the 100 villages and classifying them all. The two main markets are young couples and families, the latter generally wanting more luxury and services than the former.

Quality control has also been brought to the subject of sports and evening spectacle levering shows. Top tennis professionals are available at some sites, are featured in marketing, and help bring sports specialists at villages up to scratch.

Club Med had always emphasized the life and pleasures of the body to the exclusion of the life and enjoyments of the mind. Starting in North America, summer forums were held in which writers, intellectuals, artists, and agents of change could discuss weighty topics such as globalization, cultural diversity, literature, and similar issues. One purpose was to drive a stake into Club Med's reputation as a swinger's paradise. The plethora of clubs "swinging" in alarming ways for people with esoteric tastes had made this market inaccessible to Club Med and potentially dangerous.

Bourguignon wanted an appeal much broader than hedonism, with multiple themes to enlighten the human spirit: "People can come to Club Med to rediscover their body, to rejuvenate their mind, their family, their friendships, themselves. So far, I am pleased with the results of the preliminary efforts in this area. A classical music series at a Portuguese resort in 1999 helped boost attendance in June, a low season. Likewise, a Christmas festival at a Moroccan resort in November of the same year helped the company to lure vacationers in what are usually seen as the resort's slowest months."

Club Med has also professionalized its *spectacles*. There is now a creative center where shows are devised and produced by professionals with the help of village impresarios, who are inspired to higher standards. The original shows varied from brilliant improvisation to amateurism. Costumes, scripts, scenarios, and new ideas (from kids' fashion shows to Asterix the Gaul) are offered to participants, who can borrow whatever is most relevant to their village and type of customers. So successful has been the creative team that Club Med is thinking of turning it into a business in its own right and offering shows to impresarios and to organizers of parties and festivities.

An important aspect of Re-focusing is improving access to the company by would-be vacationers. IT systems that work out travel itineraries for customers, along with rental cars and other amenities, replace work done previously by travel agents, with the company getting commissions. This arrangement allows for a total view of each customer's plans and renews the concept of inclusivity. Early in the year 2000, Bourguignon launched Club Med On Line, allowing customers to make on-line bookings where vacancies exist, as well as setting out the sheer range of choices available, along with comments by other customers on the attractions sampled.

The Web site will also feature services linked to Club Med offerings such as fitness, sports activities, music, and film, along with such branded Club Med products as sun wear, swimming costumes, luggage, skin care, and perfume. In order to integrate these products with vacation scenes, distribution agreements with *Carrefour*, a large retailer, will feature its products in the context of vacation themes and offerings.

Says Bourguignon, Club Med needs to refine the art of placing immaterial experiences above the bits and pieces of the material world. The wholeness of experience with its *esprit* and stylishness is vital. What fills empty beds is not concentration on each separate bed, but an overall impression of dreamlike intensity and sensual satisfaction. With ever-advancing living standards, the separate elements of luxury and good living are available to more and more people. What is often missing and is more elusive is the integration of these elements into a diffuse sense of satisfaction, a *savoir vivre*. We no longer manage villages, but a shared spirit, a seamless scenario of satisfactions, an *ambience* or atmosphere, as Planet Hollywood or Starbuck's Cafe started doing for restaurants and bars, but more discriminating, less harsh, and augmented by food and wine.

"Our new city sites in Club Med World allow us to create 'menus' of city attractions, restaurants, cinemas, museums, lectures, libraries, and stores concerning which we are the guides, the gourmets, and the connoisseurs, arranging transport, dinner, theater, coffee, brandy, and safe return, a flawless series of fulfillments. . . . But all this would be prohibitively expensive if we did not boost density, volume, and throughput. So many customers choose our favorite haunts and consume the same sights and sounds, that we achieve volume. In one sense, the experiences and products we line up are global objects, but, when synthesized with the help of choosy customers, they are transformed into novel blends of experience in which the client participates. We operate on these two levels simultaneously, a reliable world of high-standard objects and replicated services and an exotic world of unique personal experiences organized around each customer."

The dilemma of the Unique, Seamless, Personalized Vacation vs. the Reliable, Affordable, Segmented, Standardized, Global product is set out in the following graph:

Dilemma 1.   The Global Ingredients of a Personal Dream

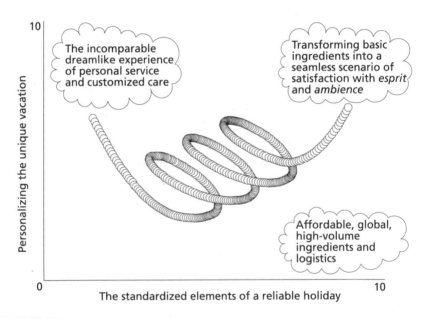

Note that the *specific* ingredients that go into the making of these *diffuse* experiences (Dimension 4 in Chapter 2) can coexist simultaneously at different levels of analysis. They are each part of a whole.

Club Med's tradition belongs at the top left of our chart. As a vendor of incomparable experiences, it has to find renewal in a fiercely competitive world of superficial impacts. What Bourguignon has done is move toward the bottom right, to segment the market, to reduce vacations to the standardized units out of which they are constructed, and to offer affordable high-volume sales of these units.

However, he has not abandoned Club Med's founding values. These standard ingredients are used to create an *esprit* and an *ambience*, which represents a transformation of those ingredients into seamless scenarios of satisfaction. He has pushed down the costs of the parts, while elaborating the value and the luxuriousness of the whole – no mean feat.

2. Restoring the Brand and the Product: Building a "Power Brand" through Repeated, Multiple, Itemized Impacts vs. Dream play, Experimentation, and New Experiences

Club Med is a branded service, and Bourguignon saw that as his challenge to restore and renew the brand. The brand had become blurred and ambivalent. Club Med was appreciated for its guest orientation, yet increasingly criticized for its prices and poor plant. Its physical assets were run down. "When I started my job with Club Med," he says, "what I found was exciting and frustrating. On the positive side, I inherited a strong brand with huge awareness and a huge international presence. But the image was anything between blurred and ambivalent. There was a strong culture that was extremely guest oriented, but there were operational inefficiencies and the physical assets had been run down. Over the years, our guests had built up expectations that were integrated into the brand of Club Med. Over the years, we have seen a wider gap developing between the brand, its identity, and perception."

One criterion for judging a brand is its authenticity. Is it revealing the company honestly, or is the impression false and contrived? Bourguignon decided on the theme of *regeneration*. Club Med was being reborn so that customers could be reborn in unforgettable milieux. Regeneration was a theme capable of being shared by the company and its customers. If customers were regenerated, the company would similarly arise. In Bourguignon's own words, "We want to make the brand breathe again, and we want it associated with regeneration. We want people to renew, to rejuvenate, and to recharge. We want Club Med to be the place where people rediscover their mind and their body, where they reacquaint themselves with families and friends."

When people are briefly and intensely thrown together with strangers for a limited time, in highly usual environments, an opportunity is created to experiment with new identities, to offer and confirm new strengths, and to live out dreams that the work world has suppressed. If your new capacities are confirmed by intimate companions, it could lead to permanent change – to the regeneration of underused aspects of your personal repertory.

Historically, Club Med had undermarketed itself. It had an aura and an atmosphere, but with too few saleable products attached. Its reputation was seriously underutilized. "We have enormous brand awareness, with scores of 80 percent spontaneous awareness in France, Australia, and Brazil," Philippe points out, "while we are only a $1.6-billion-turnover business. Where awareness is high and sales low, there are fantastic opportunities. We need to become a *power brand*. Nike does not sell just shoes. Disney sells more than Mickey. Club Med is a better way of life."

It is for this reason that Club Med is busy expanding its range of products associated with vacations. All villages now carry branded produce. There are advertising partnerships and joint campaigns with Coca-Cola and Konica. In America, Club Med is featuring the family and family values. Aquarius, a discount subsidiary of Club Med, has been reintegrated into the single brand. The total environments that Club Med consists of can be used to encompass other products, like BMX bikes used to climb walls and for trick cycling generally. Club Med is busy wrapping its own logo around some of the most enjoyable pursuits it can devise. It is increasingly a backdrop for other distinguished products.

As you might expect from a man who once ran Euro-Disney, Bourguignon sees endless repetition and multiple impacts as essential to the creation of a power brand. Yet such brands can have hidden depths, and elusive qualities that invite further exploration. You can recognize a brand while still wanting to discover the experiences it stands for. Bourguignon summarizes his re-branding as follows: "We need to approach this from a broad historical perspective. Man is not just *homo faber* (man the worker), but *homo ludens* (man the player). Free time allows you to 'play' at what you might be, a person with new physical, emotional, and intellectual resources.

"The leisure industry has become the largest industry in the world. In 1998, 290 million European tourists travelled abroad, spending $225 billion. In the year 2020, there will be 1.6 billion tourists leaving their country to enjoy vacation, three times as many as today. Tourism and travel represent an economic power that is bigger in Japan than the economy represented by electronics and bigger than the automobile industry in the United States. Our business is responding to large sociological developments during this century; a society of consumers has become the information society, a mass society has become a society of diverse individuals with a myriad pursuits. A society oriented by norms and rules has become groups of players rehearsing new roles for themselves. A society built on exclusion has become a society seeking connection around chosen themes of interest.

We have to be more than dreamers; we have to dream of *new realities*, new forms of fulfillment which we can then try out in everyday life. We need to regenerate old talents and find new ones. We are no longer enjoying ourselves on the side, we are bringing new enjoyments to our *being* in this world. These are the values we must integrate into our brand.

"Add to that that we have to develop a worldwide power brand integrating universal values with a Club Med product that still has many local perceptions. For example, it is seen as rather expensive in the Netherlands, focused on the family in the UK, but rather adult in Germany and Belgium. Our regeneration needs to be focused on the integration of these varieties of orientations."

It is difficult to diagram such a rich and nuanced philosophy without simplifying it, but here is our best effort.

Dilemma 2.   Rejuvenating Customers and the Brand

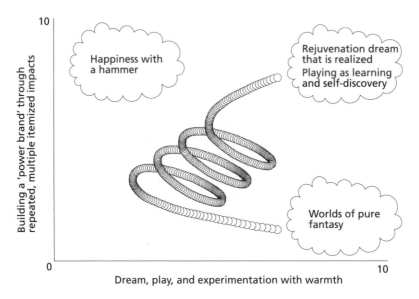

If hammering on about happiness were all Club Med did, it would finish up as just so much noise, signifying little but its own bangs and crashes. But creating worlds of pure fantasy for short ersatz "honeymoons" will soon be lost in a world of inquiry and serious information. The dream will fade in the routines of daily work. What *can* be of lasting significance is *serious* play – playing to learn about yourself, rehearsing undiscovered aspects of yourself among new friends, dreaming and then realizing those dreams, and rejuvenating yourself. Club Med wants no less for its brand than it wants for its customers. Wherever people rediscover their own powers through play, the brand is reinforced.

3. Reevaluating Price Policies

If you have an experience that is basically pleasurable, then the more people who pass through it, the better the word-of-mouth advertising. If you have high investments in plant and equipment or fixed costs, you need increased utilization of those premises. If you have a slow season like Christmas or late autumn, you need to and create reasons for coming to you during those times. Stage a major event, or engage a sporting hero.

Club Med found that boosting off-peak occupancy increased the demand for expensive peak occupancy, too. There was a "halo effect." It paid to drop prices, as long as you were not losing money. Thus, a 30-percent off-season cut at the Moroccan resort of Al Hoceima pushed up peak bookings by 38 percent and sales for that village by 73 percent over the year.

In many resorts, seasons were extended by charging less and featuring new attractions. With cheaper, last-minute Internet transport, spare places could be filled. In making each village a profit center, the local management soon learned how to match demand with supply and use its assets more intensively. Another strategy was to win a greater proportion of the vacationer's total outlay, gaining increased shares of air travel, car rental, equipment purchase, branded Club Med products, and fees for joining clubs affiliated with Club Med.

There is no real dilemma here, save perhaps the well-known crossed axes of supply and demand, which are elementary economics. But we must not underestimate the extent to which this dream-selling company had lost touch with economics, until Philippe Bourguignon and his tough-minded controller, Henri Giscard d'Estaing, reengaged with market forces and decentralized responsibility for that engagement.

4. Rationalize What is Common to Appreciate What is Unique

Philippe Bourguignon's success at Euro-Disney inevitably led to his being stereotyped in France as "too American," as sacrificing people for profits. He had spent some years in the United States earlier on, and his rescue of Disney's highly mechanized and globalized amusements was seen as one more example of the American invasion of French culture, now aided and abetted by a Frenchman. Some would have preferred Euro-Disney to fail.

Bourguignon introduced process reengineering into Club Med, putting 500 *Gentils Organisateurs* through a process not known for its gentleness. He modernized the global reservation systems and supplied all sites with up-to-date financial data. That he rationalized the system from top to bottom is undeniable, but does this of necessity militate against human concerns or subtract from sensuous experience? Bourguignon would argue that to rationalize what is amenable to rationality allows you to concentrate on and appreciate the uniqueness of what Club Med provides – and there are plenty of those unique characteristics. First of all, there was a significant discrepancy between the actual functioning of people and sites and their creative reporting. This was partly due to the fact that the Club had an oral tradition, not a written one. Many creations of the mind are possible that couldn't be written down. Add to this that the typical *chef de village* acts as an "artist" rather than a manager. He likes to be creative and would rather "reinvent the wheel" than adopt a solution provided by an outsider. Finally, the complexity that arises from operating as an international firm in both Western and non-Western countries created quite a challenge for Bourguignon.

We can see this most clearly where his reasons impinge on people, in the area of human resources. He insisted that the age distribution must be rebalanced. The organizers were much older than most customers. He wanted more mobility between sites, so staff would learn faster. He wanted new kinds of expertise, so as to keep pace with what customers wanted to learn, and he wanted those at the site to be held accountable for its operations. They could ask for help, but that, too, was their responsibility.

Above all, the staff had to professionalize. Experts in sports had to be of recognized competitive ability. Those in the arts must have respect in their fields. Those looking after kids must be competent, all-around generalists. All GOs of any kind are assessed by customers and peers.

Evaluation of a kind had long been practiced, but rather than being a "balanced scorecard," it was perilously *unbalanced*. The *chefs du villages* had long competed fiercely in the quality of their food, wine, *spectacles*, and costumes and of the fireworks let off at the end of the week at great expense. Each chef wanted to win the village oscar, an election based on the votes of GMs.

Such was the rivalry that best practices were not shared or learned, nor were scripts revealed or ideas discussed. Villages did not want other villages to beat them, and individual ambitions were pursued at the expense of the wider company. Outstanding performances and the reasons for them were village secrets. In effect, competition had got the best of cooperation and learning together.

Bourguignon rebalanced the scorecard by measuring both customer acclaim *and* the performance by chefs on targets, budgets, and profits. In frantic attempts to win, chefs had earlier squandered money on food, wine, fireworks, and *spectacles*. The new scoreboard demanded that they delight customers *while* making profits for the company, they had to integrate these objectives to win the contest. Each chef is evaluated on these opposite measures of effectiveness. Pay was also reorganized to more closely reflect performance, and the success of the unit or village became the measure of the leader's success.

Bourguignon is not happy with the accusation of being "American." He believes that France needs American disciplines, just as America needs French aesthetic appreciation and sensuous satisfactions.

"I am not an American, but French, and proud, for example, of the changes that we have made in Euro-Disney. I am not trying out an Americanized version of Club Med, but if being rigorous and professional is American, then I am American. Club Méditerranée is not, and will never be, a reflection of American culture. It has values that are strongly embedded in all its key processes. After the Second World War, the Club represented freedom and the lowering of social thresholds – later, freedom and the release from old *moeurs* (customs). Today, it represents the freedom to rediscover and redefine yourself. It stands for the family and the community, both still stronger in France than elsewhere.

"Take McDonalds', whether you like it or not, it is the number-one restaurant in France. If an organization has so much success, it is because these restaurants are clean, hygienic, and without problems, which is not the case in many of the French bistros. The day when the French bistros, while keeping its ambience that accounted for their success, become clean, that formula could be exported to the States. This would be the best way to react to our fear of the world becoming Americanized."

The dilemma diagram that follows represents Bourguignon's view that America and France share between them the reasons for Club Med's newfound organizational effectiveness. You cannot exclusive be rational or exclusively constitute unique experiences; you have to confront this contradiction and reconcile it.

No European wants a "hamburgerized" McWorld or Mickey Mouse entertainment (10/1). They can occur where global rationality seeks to be an icon for all possible tastes. On the other hand, French indulgence in being unique and incomparable gets you into trouble, too. The improvised bistro is no match for McDonald's, even in France. Where every *chef* has to excel at lavish hospitality, costs go through the roof. It was the scorecard balanced between profitability and customer delight that helped turn Club Med around and symbolized Franco-American organizational effectiveness.

Indeed the company has prospered under its new leadership. Occupancy rose to 73.5 percent in the 1999 financial year, from 66.9 percent in 1996. Other results have also improved markedly.

In fiscal-year 1999, attendance rose 5 percent, to almost 1.6 million. The

Dilemma 3. Franco-American Effectiveness

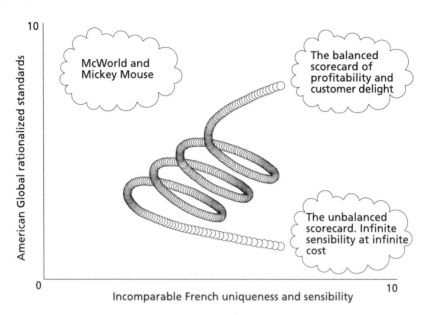

company earned $39 million, against $26 in 1998 and losses of $130 and $215 million in 1996 and 1997, respectively. In 1999, sales went up again, to $1.5 billion. Perhaps Club Med is now positioned as a brand rather than an experience, but the company wants to revolutionize the leisure industry in the new millennium just as it did 50 years ago. "We have a global concept, with global clients," says Bourguignon. "No other company is developed internationally as we are, and nobody is looking at leisure time in a global way."

Sadly, the remaining founder quit, lamenting that the spirit and soul of the organization were gone. We believe rather that the spirit and soul were *qualified* by some apparently contradictory values, which actually strengthened them. One of us (FT) went back to Club Med last summer and lost whatever remained of his dignity and reserve!

CHAPTER 6

Recapturing the True Mission

Leader: Christian Majgaard (Lego)

L EGO, the Danish supplier of children's construction toys, recently faced some difficult choices. Was it selling to children or their parents? The answer was "both." Were the children just playing or learning? "Both." Should the idea be to supply children with implementable construction kits, so that the kids became, in essence, part of the assembly process? Or was the point to stimulate children to create something unique, as one does with vocabulary? Was the company in the plastic bricks business, or was it the promoter of intelligent and constructive play in general? Once again the answers were "both." The task of being constructive might *start* with plastic bricks, but it goes beyond such materials into the creation of an integrity upon which the future of the company depends. LEGO is an assembler of customer satisfactions, and the broader this synthesis, the greater are the prosperity and success of the company.

One of us (DD) went to Schipol airport in June 1999 to meet Christian Majgaard, the member of LEGO's Group Executive Team personally responsible for global branding and business development. He looked relaxed and cheerful. He was travelling from Billund, the small town were LEGO was founded in 1932, to an international executive conference in Nice, where he had been invited to expound on LEGO's heroic saga of innovation. He and the author spent most of the day conversing and produced the origins of the account that follows.

LEGO had recently survived a rough passage. Majgaard, who worked closely with Kjeld Kirk Kristiansen, the CEO, was on the front line. Kjeld and other team members had forged the World Wide Fitness Programme, designed to weather the storms they faced. The year 1998 had brought the collapse of Southeast Asian markets, followed by the Russian market, resulting in a loss after taxes of DK 194 million (194 million Danish kroner or over US $24 million).

It was this crisis that convinced the company it was carrying too much "ballast," which prevented timely changes of direction and the speed necessary to escape episodes of turbulence. It was time to ask the crucial questions with which this chapter began. What did LEGO stand for? What kinds of innovation would renew its brand image and recapture the meaning the company had long had for children and their parents? The values for which LEGO stood were eternal, but new ways must be found to realize them, using modern media and materials.

Majgaard and the Dutch author found an easy rapport and a shared appreciation of the values that had made LEGO. These values did not just join interviewer and interviewee; they had helped LEGO's executive team surmount the recent crisis. The values are lived out in the actions of team members, all of whom know the following words:

LEGO Vision

The LEGO name shall become universally known and shall be associated with the following concepts.

IDEA	EXUBERANCE	VALUES
Creativity	Enthusiasm	Quality
Imagination	Spontaneity	Caring
Unlimited discovery	Self-expression	Development
Constructiveness	Unreservedness	Innovation
		Consistency

Lego is also distinguished by what it has avoided – any war toys inconsistent with peaceful construction – and what it includes, 5 billion compatible LEGO bricks with none unusable.

Mission and Scope

Children are our vital concern. Our basic business concept and the foundation for all LEGO products and activities is that we take children and their needs seriously. As a dependable partner for parents, it is our mission to stimulate children's imagination and creativity, and to encourage children to explore, experience, and express their own world, a world without limits. As a quality leader, we will do this by offering creative, developmental, and enjoyable play and learning materials, experiences, and brand values, all bearing the LEGO logo, to children all over the world. By the year 2005, we want the LEGO brand to be the most powerful brand in the world among families with children (measured among brands with children as a part of their target group).

Today, the LEGO Group is a family-owned and family-managed business employing 9000 people and selling products in more than 130 countries. LEGO is the clear leader in the construction-toy sector. In addition to the core business (LEGO bricks), LEGO has developed the following new categories:

- LEGOLAND Parks: development and operation of family parks (Denmark, United Kingdom, United States, Germany)
- LEGO lifestyle products: license agreements for clothes, watches, and other compatible products
- LEGO media products: software, music, video, books, and film for children

LEGO has decided to globalize geographically and strategically, within a single global marketing strategy. According to this strategy, quality is deemed to be more important than speed, and the notion of quality – the conviction of what LEGO stands for – has to come from LEGO people themselves in dialogue with the executive team. Kjeld Kirk Kristiansen believes that success will come from this redefinition of core values.

The History of LEGO's Innovation

Before we reengage with current issues, it will be useful to chronicle LEGO's history.

- 1932. The Depression forces a change in the nature of the business. Formerly serving the agriculture industry with carpentry and joinery work, the company switched to wooden toys made by hand.
- 1934: The name LEGO is chosen; it comes from two Danish words, "Leg Godt," and means *play well*; later it was discovered that in Latin it means "*I study*", or "*I put together.*" Core value and ambition of the company: "Only the best is good enough."
- 1942: The LEGO factory is burned, but production of wooden toys is resumed.
- 1947: Plastics and injection molding are adopted. Plastic toys are produced.
- 1949: The first plastic brick is manufactured.
- 1955: The LEGO system of play is instituted.
- 1958: The quality of the LEGO brick is improved, with tubes placed inside the brick.

- 1960: Fire guts the LEGO warehouse with wooden toys: The company makes a strategic choice: produce plastic toys only.
- 1963: A new type of plastic replaces the old plastic.
- 1968: LEGOLAND Billund, the first family park, opens to the public.
- 1974: LEGO figures make a hit with both boys and girls.
- 1979: Kjeld Kirk Kristiansen is appointed president and CEO of LEGO A/S.
- 1995: Kjeld Kirk Kristiansen's father dies.
- 1996: LEGO goes on the Internet and the first family park outside Denmark is opened.
- 1997: Computer games, software, and LEGO MindStorms learning center are featured.
- 1998: License agreements are reached with Lucasfilm/Star Wars and Walt Disney Company. The Next Generation Forum is created.

From this historical overview, we can glean the following insights:

- Enabling technologies have played a major role in LEGO's development (1947, 1963, 1996, and 1997).
- Crises had a major impact on the company (1932, 1960, and 1998).
- Visionary leadership leads to decisive moves (1932, 1934, 1955, 1958, 1960, 1968, 1996, 1997, and 1998), including the idea of a system (1955) in which the child is active.

It is in this context of brands, markets, products, ideas, people, and relations that Christian Majgaard and his colleagues have revitalized the tradition of innovation.

Christian Majgaard's View of Strategic Innovation

Christian Majgaard has been championing strategic innovation at LEGO for some eight years. Most of the new initiatives, including the Fitness Programme, bear the stamp of his way of thinking. During his daylong stopover in Amsterdam, he explained to the interviewer the five main themes with which he was struggling.

1. *How can the business system be restructured to realize ideas?*
2. *How can we form teams with a diverse mix of members?*
3. *How can we achieve distance from, yet gain an understanding of, the core business?*
4. *How can we seize each idea's fleeting window of opportunity?*

5.   *How can we ensure that all new departures and innovative projects eventually are welcomed by, and integrated with, the core of the company?*

1. How Can the Business System be Restructured to Realize Ideas?

"The problem is not the availability of new ideas, says Majgaard," we have plenty of ideas. Nor is the problem getting funds to develop these ideas. The problem, is and always has been, that the business system can get in the way of good ideas being realized. I have learned that the person who has the idea should be given the resources, and the people and the freedom to develop it into a viable product. It can be fatal to split the idea from its implementation. The board often comes up with ideas, and because of the influence and status of its members, the idea gets implemented, but by persons other than the originator, which leads to the idea and its underlying assumptions not being properly challenged and critiqued.

"A case in point 10 years ago was the idea to create small indoor entertainment centers of less than 8000 square meters, unaffected by seasonal climate and attractive to commercial partners in the same mall or complex. But when we searched world markets for an example of a small, profitable entertainment center, we could not find a single one! Still, we were reluctant to negate an idea coming from the board level, so we hired consultants. It was one of them who explained that entertainment centers were where children were left off. When adults sought adventure jointly with their children, they typically went *out* into the wider environment.

"Hence, this idea would violate one of the key principles of LEGO: that children and adults are joined by constructive appreciation. It had taken us an inordinate time to turn down a nonviable idea, which, as it turned out, originated in Australia and had everything to do with a local initiative to upgrade shopping malls. I learned not to separate ideas from their originators."

"But our time investigating entertainment centers and theme parks was not wasted: We discovered that those who charged a sizeable entrance fee did much better than those who charged for each separate ride or amusement. Why was this? We came up with two possible answers:"

- When you pay upfront you act when the excitement of children and adults is at its height, and once you are inside, everything is free. You can stop calculating. You do not have to say "no" to excited children or let them bankrupt you, and there is no restraint on their enjoyment.
- When you pay extra for each attraction, the conflict between adults and children is exacerbated, and resentment at the company that has driven your

children to "extravagance" is keen. Adults are caught between guilt and unaffordable outlays and cannot control their spending.

"Anyway, this intelligence caused us to change the pricing policy at our new Billund theme park. Suddenly, receipts soared, and what we had regarded as a mainly promotional activity became an important new concept. The family park is now in four countries, and we have plans to expand globally."

"What I learned was that the business system must facilitate, not impede, the flow and refinement of ideas, so that they can be realized."

2. How Can we Form Teams with a Diverse Mix of Members?

"When you have too similar persons on a team, the knowledge the team has is limited," says Majgaard. On a team, opposites are needed, six people in a group is optimal, with both genders and various nationalities and backgrounds represented. In strategic innovation projects, people from the new industry and people from the original company should work together. And that's the hard part of it: How can you make such a group of people work together effectively?

The key is to realize that if people are different, they have more to say to each other – have information to communicate that is more likely to be novel and illuminating. Of course, *dis*agreement is more likely, too. So, use process theories, group dynamics, and anything that facilitates interaction.

Giving people a superordinate goal that contributes to a shared "win" is very important. A common destiny also helps bind a team of diverse talents, and it is smart to include younger people who have a reputation to make rather than to protect. Perhaps most important is a shared passion for turning a common vision into a powerful reality, to gain ownership of an important initiative.

3. How Can we Achieve Distance from, yet Gain an Understanding of, the Core Business?

"The older the core business, the less likely it is to be able to reinvent itself, opines Majgaard." The business is too brittle for new life to emerge. Strategic innovators often condemn these aging cores. What is needed is a greater understanding. Only then will we know what to do. Any organization with a long history has established rules that protect its core values. "Do this and you will succeed. Don't do that or that, we tried them once and they failed." These prohibitions accumulate with time until the core is left with a severely limited number of possible moves.

Reinventing yourself may require doing something prohibited, so the core stagnates. We are not talking about good or bad people, but about entrenched belief systems, many of them not consciously examined. As with driving a car in the UK, you have to concentrate hard on not moving instinctively to the right-hand side of the road. Because it is painful to change ingrained habits and responses, you can innovate successfully only if you can achieve some *distance* from the belief system of the traditional core of the corporation.

However, being "distant" from beliefs that stifle innovation is not enough: you also have to understand why the traditional core thinks and believes as it does. You have to understand this because, in the end, you are one company. You have achieved your distance in order to *serve* the core, not abandon it.

4. How Can we Seize Each Idea's Fleeting Window of Opportunity?

Ideas are not good or bad in themselves. They are, under certain circumstances, practicable, but, when those circumstances change, no longer practicable. For many ideas, there exist windows of opportunity that can open and close quite quickly, so that timing is everything. An idea can fail because it is too early to try it – the creator is ahead of the market. Or the idea might fail because it is too late: your competitors have moved, costs are rising, and diminishing returns have set in. This is why speed is important and timing all-important. You have to keep learning, so that, when the window opens fleetingly, you are ready and prepared to jump. Those who thought up the idea might not be the right people to train others or to pounce. Those who pounce successfully might not be the right people to exploit the opportunity and push for the big numbers.

If the opportunity turns into a sizeable one and you find yourself in a race to meet demand, then you will need your core organization.

5. How Can we Ensure that All New Departures and Innovative Projects Eventually Are Welcomed by, and Integrated with, the Core of the Company?

We have already seen that innovative strategies must maintain their *distance* from the company's traditions if they are to escape being caught in thickets of prohibition (theme 3) but, sooner or later, innovative business units initially separated from the old core need to be integrated with it to restore a sense of a single company. Some units had a prolonged separation (LEGO family parks). Some were integrated quickly (LEGO software). It helps if the success of the unit is spectacular.

LEGO software generated net sales of 500 million DKr, and the core was proud of it. But some early integrations, like robots, approached the core because they needed its financial support. So integration is not a "must" in the short term, but it is a question of the health and survival of the innovative unit.

What is more important is that the entrepreneurs in the innovative units be treated as the heroes they are. All too easily do the old core and the old values gang up on the newer ones. Some very balanced old-timers say disparaging things about new initiatives. If the success has been spectacular, there is rarely any opposition, but new projects that need support to be genuinely successful can have trouble finding it, and that leads to cruel disappointment. "I'm fighting for the future," these innovators say. "Why can't they see this?" Successful innovators should be offered a promotion and public recognition. That sends powerful signals about their entrepreneurial qualities. We have to make the core not just tolerant of, but enthusiastic about, strategic innovation.

Dilemmas at the Heart of the Five Themes

Each of Christian Majgaard's five themes is, for us, a key dilemma that has to be reconciled if LEGO is to grow and prosper:

- Theme 1 is the dilemma of *the Ideal vs. the Real*: how can the business system help realize the ideas generated by employees?
- Theme 2 is the dilemma of *Diversity vs. Harmony among team members*. Are members sufficiently *different* from each other that novel information is processed, but sufficiently *unified* to turn that novelty into solutions?
- Theme 3 is the dilemma of *distance* from the traditional core of the company and one's *relationship* to that core. Paradoxically, you can contribute more to LEGO's core if you are independent of its toils.
- Theme 4 is the dilemma of *originating* ideas and *seizing the opportunity*, often fleeting, to implement those ideas. The key is timing. Every good idea has a brief window of opportunity, which then closes in your face. You can be too early or too late.
- Theme 5 is the *creation of innovative strategies vs. the integration of their instigators into the core culture of the company*. Innovation will soon dry up, unless LEGO's best entrepreneurs find honor and reputation within the company.

There is in fact, one more fascinating dilemma, which we may introduce as a footnote to theme 1: In exchanging satisfaction for payment, should *payment precede satisfaction*, or should *payment accompany the choice of each event?*

Can any of the seven dimensions help illuminate LEGO's own dilemmas?

In Chapters 1 and 2, we introduced the seven dilemmas, or dimensions, we use to research various national business cultures. Are there any connections between the themes or dilemmas Christian Majgaard defined and our own dilemmas? We hope to show that added insights are achieved by connecting LEGO's definitions to our own.

Theme 1

LEGO's Model: The Ideal vs. the Real
Our Model: The Individual vs. the Community

Majgaard pointed out that there was no problem with finding enough individuals to generate enough ideas. The problem lay with the "business system" or community, which had to translate those ideas into the reality of viable products and services. Not infrequently, the community or system would impede the realization of good ideas, especially when they came from senior people. Juniors were expected to do implement the ideas.

The dilemma could be diagrammed as follows.

Dilemma 1. The Path to Realization

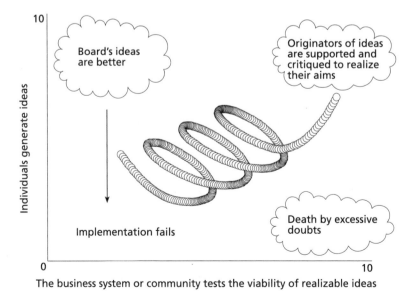

10

Board's ideas
are better

Originators of ideas
are supported and
critiqued to realize
their aims

Individuals generate ideas

Implementation fails

Death by excessive
doubts

0

10

The business system or community tests the viability of realizable ideas

From the diagram, we can see that, while ideas originate with individuals, it is *not* a good idea simply to pass the ideas down for subordinates to implement. The latter are inhibited in their criticism, and consultants have to be hired to legitimize skepticism. Instead, the originator must work *with* critics, implementors, and builders of working prototypes to help to debug the idea whenever it is necessary. (This is why the helix periodically winds back toward the individual originator.) Futhermore, it is unwise to give higher status to the idea than to its implementors, otherwise, defective ideas will persist to disappoint their backers. Realization is at least as important as idealization, and the two must be reconciled (at the top right of the diagram). You must also beware of testing ideas to destruction (bottom right).

Theme 2

LEGO's Model. Diversity vs. Unity in Teams
Our Model: Competing as Individuals vs. Cooperating as a Community

Here, we have once again used our second dimension, Individualism vs. Communitarianism, but in a slightly different form: Competing vs. Cooperating. If we combine these with Majgaard's insight that the membership of teams must be *diverse*, consisting of people whose values and talents are opposite, and yet these teams must achieve a *unity* of purpose and shared solutions, then we can diagram the

Dilemma 2. The Search for the Unity-of-Diversities

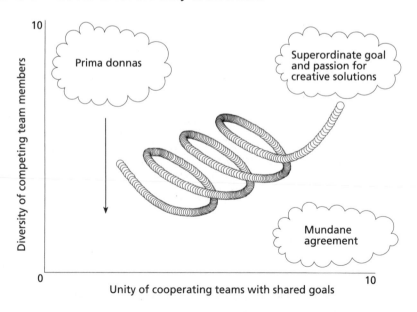

dilemma as follows (once again, we have two polarized failures, but also the potential for coming up with a solution that has benefited from diverse viewpoints and novel input).

The problem with having highly diverse, competing individuals is that they might behave like so many prima donnas, singing their own praises. The problem with emphasizing unity and team spirit above all is that diverse and novel inputs get squeezed out.

Majgaard's reconciliation, which we heartily endorse, is to make the superordinate goal so exciting, and the process of creating new shared realities so passionate and enjoyable, that diverse members overcome their differences to realize a unity of diversities, which makes the solution far more valuable.

Theme 3

LEGO's Model. Distance (from Core) vs. Relationship (to Core)
Our Model: Particular Exceptions vs. Entrenched Rules

Here, we may recall, Majgaard argued that strategic innovation had to maintain a distance from the core of the company, otherwise it might find itself impeded and opposed. Later, it might be able to reestablish relationships and might have some very significant innovations to bring to LEGO.

Dilemma 3. The Return of the Exile

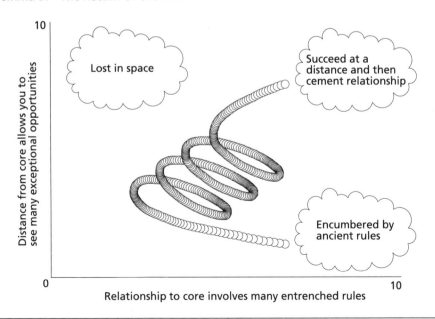

10

Distance from core allows you to see many exceptional opportunities

Lost in space

Succeed at a distance and then cement relationship

Encumbered by ancient rules

0

10

Relationship to core involves many entrenched rules

Majgaard also explained how this impedance occurred and how we could come to understand it without hurling accusations. Over time, a residue of entrenched rules accumulates around the core of the company, things that once failed and are therefore not permitted. Those at a distance from the core see many exceptional opportunities and particular chances to succeed, but those closer to the core have a learned inability to break old rules. They regard the history of the company as teaching universal prohibitions against certain avenues of exploration. The dilemma is shown above.

The distance can be too large (Lost in Space), or too small (Encumbered by Ancient Rules). What you have to do is "exile" the innovator and the idea temporarily, as when Jesus went into the wilderness or Odysseus went on his odyssey, and then return them either with notable success or with elements of success. What "exile" gives you is freedom from the prohibitions that have petrified the core.

Theme 4

LEGO's Model: Ideas vs. Fleeting Opportunity
Our Model: Time Sequences vs. Timely Synchronizations

Majgaard argued that all good ideas had a fleeting "window of opportunity" allowing for their realization. It was a question of preparing and educating yourself and then of pouncing at the opportune moment. We have a similar concept: Time as a

Dilemma 4. Leaping through the Windows

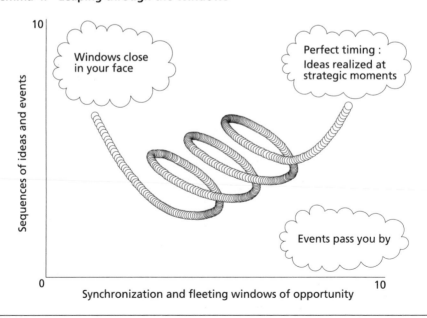

sequence of events vs. Time as seized moments of opportunity, a timely synchronization of the ideal and the real; only when the window opens do you dart through it.

Events rush past you in sequences, and you need to pounce when there is a *rendezvous* between idea and opportunity. Mistime your leap, and the chance is gone forever, with a new product or technology replacing the one you had in mind. Business is unforgiving. You can actually *change* reality in your own favor if your intervention is timely, but if you mistime your intervention, the windows close in your face or events pass you by, as the diagram above shows

The helix starts with a sequence of ideas and events, but requires that the best of those ideas be realized precisely at strategic moments, so that you "leap through the window of opportunity."

Theme 5

LEGO's Model: Strategic Innovations vs. Integration with the Core of the Corporation
Our Model: Specific Initiatives vs. Diffuse Relationships

Majgaard raised the issue of innovative business units, which had kept their distance, and would later need reintegrate with the core of LEGO. Unless this was done, so that successful entrepreneurs would receive the honor due to them, the core values were unlikely to change quickly enough. We have combined this insight with our own dimension of specific vs. diffuse phenomena. LEGO could score many specific successes via business units created for a particular purpose but, unless this new knowledge permeates the whole organization, the units will be better off as independent small businesses, and the new enlightenment will fail to spread. The center of the organization needs to learn which of its units are succeeding and why they are. In this way, strategies are tested, reviewed, replicated, and revised. What is learned by one business unit is communicated to all, giving each a much wider spectrum of strategic information than that which would be enjoyed by independent businesses. The dilemma is depicted in the following diagram.

At the top left, even successful initiatives remain isolated. At the bottom right, all units are welcome, but they must abandon ideas and information that do not fit. Only at the top right are many specific innovations registered, compared, and celebrated, and then communicated to the entire company, which becomes the champion of entrepreneurialism.

Dilemma 5. Diffusely Integrated Specifics

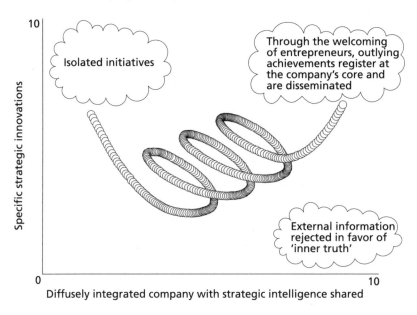

Theme 6

LEGO'S Model: Pay as You Go vs. Pay Up Front
Our Model: Affective vs. Neutral

This was originally a subissue of theme 1, but it is important enough to receive special treatment. LEGOLAND Parks transformed their balance sheet by moving from Pay as you Go to Pay up Front, or, as we should say, by getting the neutral calculation out of the way at the beginning and leaving the children free to be as affective and exuberant as they wish and to sample every amusement available. With payment up front, parents do not need to limit their children's enjoyment; they do not have to face the painful dilemma of either overspending in response to a clamorous child or refusing that child. The calculated decision to spend a certain amount on getting in can be made in a neutral environment, and, following admission, pleasure can run riot and vindicate the original decision by exploiting it to the utmost. The dilemma looks like this.

Dilemma 6. Calculated Enjoyment

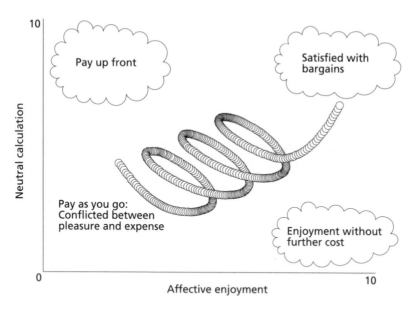

When you pay up front (top left) you make a neutral calculation without being pressured, because the children have not yet sampled the treat. You then move rightward along the affective enjoyment axis, and as the children rush joyfully about, you become satisfied with the bargain you paid for.

In the middle of the diagram, next to the X, we see the fate of "pay as you go," in which your children's exuberance costs, you and their very excitement cuts holes in your pockets. The greater the children's pleasure is, the higher become the parents' costs. LEGO's mission to enrich parent–child interaction is frustrated.

The pay-up-front solution closely models LEGO's celebration of unlimited imagination and creativity, spontaneous enthusiasm, and lack of reserve, all of consistent quality and innovativeness. Once parents have paid, children should get to express their exuberance without hindrance.

Which is Where we Begin . . .

We began this chapter by asking how LEGO reconciled parents and children, play and learning, solutions suggested to children with solutions found by children themselves. We also asked whether LEGO was a plastic-bricks company or a company dedicated to intelligent, constructive, and creative play.

LEGO's latest strategic moves have answered the last question. The company is in the business of constructive play, with putting plastic bricks together being one form taken by such play. Using software, reading books, viewing films, and playing games are other ways of playing. It is within LEGO's core purpose and mission that innovations are generated.

. . . With What Results?

Let us recall that in 1998, LEGO was in the hole, with an after-tax loss of DKr 194 million. By the end of 1999, LEGO were back in profit by DKr 560 million (after restructuring costs of 700 million). Sales were up 22 percent. Christian Majgaard, Kjeld Kirk Kristiansen, and their team colleagues had vindicated their judgments. Every incremental step toward those top-right-hand corners on our diagrams could be worth millions.

Postscript

On January 30, 2000, LEGO was voted "Toy of the Millennium" in a poll of international retailers and consumers. It beat the teddy bear and Barbie doll to win the prize.

CHAPTER 7

The Balance between Market and Product

Leader: Anders Knutsen (Bang and Olufsen)

In this chapter, we will examine another feat of leadership. Anders Knutsen assumed the leadership of Bang and Olufsen, the Danish audiovisual company, at a point of severe crisis. He rescued a tradition of immaculate design and engineering, so "perfect" that fewer and fewer could afford it! It started with a bang. It nearly ended in a whimper, but, thanks to Knutsen, the Bang is now bigger than ever.

From a Whimper to a Bang

When someone creates and invents a new product, the market is in his or her mind's eye. The person thinks, "I love this product I have made, and others will soon come to appreciate its beauty and its quality." That is a supposition which sometimes comes true, but often does not. The creator can be too subtle or too aesthetic for the customers "out there," and finer sensibilities do not come cheap. Customers are expected to pay for ineffable qualities they do not understand and cannot fully appreciate.

This had long been the trouble with B&O (as professionals call it). When we inquired among potential customers, they told us they "loved its looks and sound" and were keen to buy a product "when I can afford it." When, in 1972, the company sent its catalogue to the Museum of Modern Art in New York City, no fewer than seven of its products were chosen for the museum's permanent collection of modern design. It was a great tribute, in a way, but, as one customer put it, "I can always visit a gallery for something as beautiful as this. I want something that plays music to high standards, not an artwork."

Products Emphasized, Markets Neglected

B&O began in 1925, when two young engineers met in Quistrup. Svend Olufsen and Peter Bang were intrigued by a new radio that Peter had obtained in the USA. Their second factory was blown up by retreating Germans in 1945, but it was reassembled by volunteer Danish citizens in the weeks that followed, so that the company became a symbol of postwar resurgence.

In those days, Peter Bang was the creative technologist and Svend Olufsen the extroverted salesperson. It might be significant that Svend died as early as 1949 and Peter lived another eight years, until 1957. In any event, technical prowess thereby gained ascendancy over marketing, and so it continued. Among B&O's "firsts" were giant Loudspeak Cars – perhaps an extravagance, but in many respects the company was consistently ahead of its time, creating the first fully transistorized radio (in 1964), advanced movie projectors, the Beocord 844, and the wire recorder, forerunner of tape recorders. As early as 1957, B&O launched the first stereo pickup for music recording.

All monies made were immediately reinvested in more product development. After Svend died, Peter brought in a financial specialist to "fight the fires" that distracted Peter from the "real" business of new products. P. H. Jensen kept the company solvent, but sales and marketing were no longer among the firm's strengths. After Peter's death, Jens Bang, his son, took charge of product planning until 1984, working with brilliant freelance designers Jacob Jensen and David Lewis; thus was created the elegant synthesis between design and high-fidelity performance for which B&O is famous. A synthesis is, however, only as viable commercially as its weakest link, and in the process of celebrating two forms of product excellence, the customers' needs and preferences for lower prices started to be ignored. The delights of modern art had captured the company's imagination, but how many affluent music lovers are *also* connoisseurs of modern design and seek to gaze at their equipment?

B&O's problem was symbolized by the creation of System 6000, a quadra-phonic hi-fi music system. There was only one flaw: No one had made any records to play on it. In those days, there were seven corporate identity components: authenticity, auto visuality, credibility, domesticity, essentiality, individuality, and inventiveness. All were characteristics of the product. The cheapest product with these sterling characteristics cost $2,500. Outside Denmark, sales staff were in some despair at such prohibitive prices.

The Neglect of the Market Leads to Crisis

Senior managers had developed some expensive habits during the 1980s, believing that an aristocracy of good taste entitled them to aristocratic lifestyles among the few who could afford their products. However, it was not simply that B&O headquarters was divided from the humbler people of Struer, a village of 14,000 in Jutland; rather, R&D was divided from Marketing and Sales, and Finance was also a separate kingdom. The principal casualty was logistics. It took so long to get spare parts that many customers gave up and switched to other systems.

Anders Knutsen realized he had little time. Upon taking over leadership in July 1991, he proposed emergency action. The company was facing the prospect of accelerating losses in the near future. His plan was to focus on the following:

(a)   growth and profit;
(b)   the most important strategic opportunities that produced growth and profit;
(c)   a reduction in service and maintenance activity by rendering it almost unnecessary; and
(d)   the identification and prioritizing of activities that produced a surplus.

These items were emergency actions, but they did not blind Anders to the deeper underlying problem, which was the disconnection of Sales and Marketing both from R&D and from Production. His "butterfly model" saw these opposite wings of the organization as in urgent need of coordination and reconciliation. Of the two wings, the product side had long been dominant. "We knew we had a great product," Anders explained, "but we did not always have a market for it. We knew we were creative, but could we afford the costs and subsequent price? This company had to think numbers and business, *without* losing its creative traditions. The right brain had to be reattached to the left, or the whole would suffer."

Early attempts at cutting costs by shutting down noncore activities like cables did not restore profitability on the scale intended. Anders launched a plan called "Break-Point" to restore harmony between the feelings of customers and the undoubted excellence of design and technology, without losing either. It was this balance that found favor with markets.

Professionalism or Family Membership?

The Break-Point program was very ambitious. It had to be. Costs had to come down radically. Of the 3300 employees at the Struer HQ in late 1992, only 2100 were left by the end of 1993. Seven hundred people lost their jobs in a small town in which B&O was the principal employer.

Anders Knutsen explained that he was able to do this because he had convinced so many people of the necessity of doing so and because the management team backed him to the hilt, but interviews among colleagues revealed that he was able to perform so unpleasant a duty because he was seen as "a son of the house." The son of a company foreman working in Vejledalen he had joined B&O as an economist and had directed the radio factory in Skive before successive promotions to CEO. He had never behaved like the "aristocrats" who had pushed the company costs sky-high in the 1980s. For years, he had owned a rusty Citroen and then an aging Alfa Romeo. This frugality, and his friendships at all levels of the organization, saw him through.

B&O *could* have brought in an outside professional hatchet man with no ties to those he fired, but there would almost certainly have been strikes, and quite probably B&O would not have been Danish any more. It was *how* Knutsen managed this difficult downsizing that was the secret of Break-Point's success. He described the crisis with frankness and courage and then outlined the remedy, so that everyone could follow the logic to its culmination. The objective was to save the company and its contribution to audiovisual excellence. The price was steep, but surely it was worth paying, given the alternative.

Knutsen was helped considerably by the steadfastness of the five-man board of management. They supported him publicly and energetically. Each agreed to play a part in communicating the solution and all kept their promises. There was near-unanimity on what had to be done to survive. At the end of what was a traumatic experience for everyone, the workers themselves erected a portrait of Anders Knutsen in their factory. It was their tribute to a truth teller, the person who respected them sufficiently to put them in touch with reality. Per Thygesen Poulsen, a local journalist, marvelled at the event and wrote about it.

Although Knutsen was an economics graduate, you do not readily impress the people of Jutland with higher degrees. What impressed them was his honesty, his realism, his long-established concern with keeping down costs (now seen to be vindicated by events), and his encouragement of workers' development and creativity (which had always been combined with a tough negotiation stance on wages). Now that the company was running out of money he was the man of the hour.

From Technology Push to Market Pull

The second major challenge was to develop some understanding of the market and of the patterns of demand before aligning B&O's own products with them. "We had to teach people how to think in business terms, without sacrificing their pride in their creativity and their products," Anders recalled. "Beauty, style, and technical superiority were everything. No one had been paying attention to development costs or commercial success." The product had actually taken the place of the persons who were supposed to lead. Knutsen regarded this imbalance as so serious that he made himself the head of Marketing and Sales until an internationally experienced VP could be found. In this way, he was able to discover facts that the company had long ignored. By the time Ebbe Pelle Jacobsen had been hired from IKEA, Anders believed that he had diagnosed the problem. Jacobsen agreed and was able to give us the following account.

"B&O thought communication was a one-way process and that its customers were dealers, not consumers. Of course, the dealers were passing on our arrogant treatment to the final customers." Anders had discovered that dealers used the B&O aura to upgrade the image of their dealerships, while putting most of their energies into selling rival products better suited to the market, including Philips, Daewoo, Sony, and Grundig. These appeared reasonably priced compared to B&O's expensive, upmarket offerings. "There was a radical disconnection between the product and the market," Anders recalls. "It was as if we communicated to the product and not with the people."

In the mid-1980s, B&O had moved out of stand-alone products into integrated systems. It made sense visually and acoustically to use B&O for all system elements, but it meant that customers had to abandon many existing purchases and start again, and it meant pricing systems from $2,500 upwards. Many younger buyers were put off accumulating the elements of a B&O system over time and were faced instead with an unrealistic price threshold.

The first move was to change distribution channels. B&O actually *reduced* the number of dealers from 3200 to 2200 in the EU, yet sales climbed from $250 million to $400 million in six years. B&O did not insist on exclusive dealerships, but it did insist on certain sales staff being dedicated to its products, so that they could listen to and learn from the firm's customers. The substitution of dialogue for monologue revealed to what extent B&O values were shared and how sharing could be increased.

B&O also defined carefully the niche in the market to which it was appealing and the customer segments it aimed to reach; then it made sure the message was consistent internationally. It also introduced a computerized system of direct ordering through its own shops with a guaranteed delivery date, so that customers could essentially build their own system, using a wide range of alternative B&O components.

Technical Excellence and the Emotional Climate

The third and last major challenge that Anders Knutsen saw himself as confronting was that of technical excellence and the emotional appeal of products. The latter was a subtle and diffuse concept. Beautiful audiovisual information had to be conveyed on instruments worthy of their content, in the same way that the instruments of an orchestra carry the spirit and express the feeling of the composer. "Time is in our favor," Knutsen believed, "The world is flooded with discount junk products that strive to become classics; products with emotional value will be strongly placed in our 'throwaway' culture." In the history of B&O, both technical excellence and emotional climate had been important, more so than sales or marketing, but even these leading values had not been reconciled or harmonized. First one was dominant, then the other, and their fight for dominance had made the product that resulted unaffordable.

So Knutsen extended "Idealand," a nonlocalized space where engineers, music lovers, designers, and others, both within R&D and outside the company in the community of experts, could engage in a dialogue that would stimulate and balance ideas. Another balance is between the audio and the visual, which come together in digital sound pictures. Carl Henrik Jeppesen, a senior colleague, explained: We send development teams, usually to the USA, to study what sounds and sights are being made and consumed. They go to concerts, music studies, discotheques. You need someone to champion the original sound picture and the emotions generated therefrom and someone to champion the technologies of recording and playing those sound pictures. It is this creative clash between the artists and engineers that gives you optimal integration. In the old days, one competence would dominate the others, but no more. There came the day when Anders Knutsen and his team refused to sponsor a prototype product because the costs were out of line. That was a real shock for all of us. It had never happened here!

"With Break-Point, the culture changed dramatically, but values were retained and began to strengthen one another. In one sense, the B&O secret is integrated seamlessness – every part of the system has to work with every other part – and now this became true of our values as well.

"We now test our product with our customers, and if they like it, sales start at once, with a projected product life of 10 years. We position ourselves in the market in such a way that confirms or fails to confirm the hypotheses developed in Idealand. The latter is no private muse, but a testing laboratory for viable ideas, a set of hypotheses to which our customers say *yes* or *no*."

Analyzing B&O's Dilemmas

According to the information we received, B&O faced three major dilemmas, which they defined as follows:

(a)   the disconnection of Sales and Marketing both from R&D and from Production, and the elevation of the latter functions to a dominant position, so that commercial marketing considerations were largely ignored;

(b)   the prospect of laying off almost a third of the company's workforce at HQ without violating the culture and family spirit that made B&O such a friendly and creative community;

(c)   the reconciliation and integrity of two important traditions: an aesthetic and emotional commitment to the beauty of sights and sounds recorded and played, and an engineering and technological commitment to brilliant solutions.

B&O would not have survived the Break-Point of 1993 without the solution of the first two dilemmas, and it would not have turned around into substantial growth and profitability without the reconciliation of all three. We will try to diagram all three. As in Chapter 2, we will compare the client's model with our model and use both to try to deepen the insights obtained.

Dilemma 1

The Client's Model
Research, Development, Production — Market, Sales, Customers

Our Model
Inner-directed individuality — Outer-directed community

The company had all the classic symptoms of technology push by inner-directed, individualistic, genius entrepreneurs who built a company that celebrated their own notable strengths and downplayed what, after the death of Olufsen, they lacked. Neglected were the market, sales, customers, service, and effective distribution – everything, in fact, that lay outside in the wider community. From these, B&O took little or no direction. The dilemma can be diagrammed as shown on the next page.

In the grid, the Museum-type exhibits and System 6000, built without any records to play on it, are two symptoms of excessive emphasis upon the vertical axis at the expense of the horizontal axis. The Break-Point Plan, is the culmination of this chronic imbalance, as B&O faces a cash-flow crisis. Anders realized that he had to move towards the marketing "horn" of the dilemma, or the horizontal axis. He appointed himself marketing director *pro tem* and discovered that distributors were using B&O's reputation for quality as a backdrop window dressing for selling rival products. His answer was the Butterfly Model, with products and marketing to the

Dilemma 1. Market Orientations

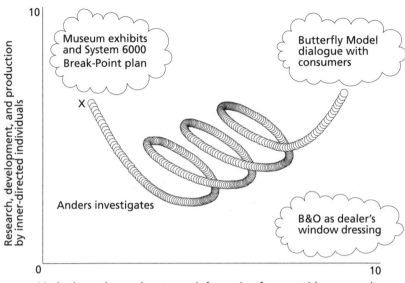

Museum exhibits
and System 6000
Break-Point plan

Butterfly Model
dialogue with
consumers

X

Anders investigates

B&O as dealer's
window dressing

Research, development, and production
by inner-directed individuals

Marketing, sales, and customer information from outside community

final consumer as two coordinated "wings" of the same operation. Having fewer, but more dedicated, distributors facilitated dialogue with the consumers and the company. Consumers could order directly from retail outlets, building up a modular system over time.

Dilemma 2

The Client's Model

The ethos of a family with trusted — The ethos of cool professionalism
parents and the resilience   and realistic commercial decision
to face common adversity   making

Our Model

Affectivity and concern for   — Neutrality and the application of
particular people's hardships   universal accounting principles

Our model combines our dimension 4, Affectivity vs. Neutrality, with our dimension 1, Universalism vs. Particularism. As before, the combination of the client's model and our own deepens an understanding of the dynamics.

B&O was a relatively small family-owned company that loomed very large in the small town of Stuer. It had many of the advantages of a family – friendliness, a human scale, generativity – and some of the *dis*advantages – expensive lifestyles for a privileged few, traditional prejudices against outsiders, and "poor relations" who were largely ignored, such as Sales and Marketing. Charismatic leaders tended to deemphasize those activities which did not interest them or in which they were not proficient. There was a desperate need for business realism, for economic calculations independent of family feeling, and for someone to face the facts, however unwelcome to the community the facts were. Dilemma 2 gives the picture:

Dilemma 2. The Trusted Family vs. The Indifference of Cold Logic

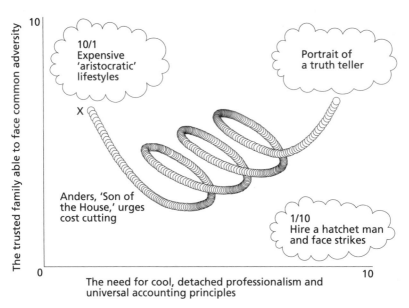

Y-axis: The trusted family able to face common adversity (0 to 10)

- 10/1 Expensive 'aristocratic' lifestyles
- Portrait of a truth teller
- X
- Anders, 'Son of the House,' urges cost cutting
- 1/10 Hire a hatchet man and face strikes

X-axis: The need for cool, detached professionalism and universal accounting principles (0 to 10)

When the Break-Point Plan was launched in 1993, B&O was close to the "X" in the diagram and suffering from years of inattention to cost control. Had the company swung to the opposite extreme and hired an outside hatchet man to axe employees, strikes and protests would surely have erupted, and claims to be a family of employees would have been forever forfeited. It was crucial that the cost cutter be associated with the family – not necessarily a relative, but a metaphorical "Son of the House." Despite the cruel circumstances in which over 900 people had to go, this necessity was explained with such honesty and such shared pain that Anders was seen as the rescuer he was, not as an executioner or an itinerant hatchet man. The cost cutting was done by the "family," in the context of the family, to save the family. It was because the employees understood the need for surgery that a portrait of Anders was erected in the factory. The workers may have hated the medicine, but they appreciated the cure, and they admired the person who had shared the truth with them.

Dilemma 3

Client's Model

An aesthetic and emotional commitment to the beauty of sights and sounds, recorded and played

— An engineering and technological commitment to brilliant scientific solutions

Our Model

Particularism of art — Universalism of science

Diffuseness of experience — Specificity of solution

Affective — Neutral

The client's model actually touches on three of our dimensions: the diffuse and affective experiences of particular art forms and the specific neutrality of scientific and universal solutions. B&O had two strong traditions that were often at odds with

Dilemma 3. Two Strong Traditions

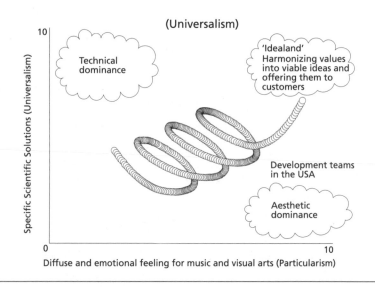

one another tilting the balance of power now this way and now that. On the vertical axis of the figure for Dilemma 3, we have the engineering commitment to *specific scientific solutions*, on the horizontal axis the aesthetic and emotional commitment to *music* and *visual art forms*.

To counterbalance the strong influence of scientifically oriented R&D, teams were sent to the USA and elsewhere to try to capture the ineffable qualities of new sounds and sights, so that they could be faithfully rendered. You have to love what you are trying to reproduce in high fidelity in order to convey the genuine experience. It is in "Idealand" that various values meet, clash, and achieve a final harmony. Each group champions its own values until they find inclusion in a larger system and in a more creative synthesis, watched over by a *principle of parsimony* that seeks to cut costs to the bone. The values' synthesis must be spare, rich, elegant, and "price wise."

Though the kind of thinking portrayed in this chapter, B&O was able to turnaround from a company in very serious financial trouble to a profitable niche supplier, showing strong growth and quality leadership in the international industry.

CHAPTER 8

Private Enterprise, Public Service

Leader: Gérard Mestrallet (Suez Lyonnaise des Eaux)

There is an ongoing public debate about what private enterprise can and cannot do – about the limits of privatization and whether "public goods" like clean water and sanitation can be safely trusted to profit-making enterprises. A ringing endorsement of the capacity of private enterprise to dedicate itself to public goals is provided by Gérard Mestrallet, who built upon the achievement of Jérome Monod, the long-time leader of Lyonnaise des Eaux. Monod pioneered the internationalizing of water distribution and treatment. Mestrallet's grand vision is of a transcultural, "one-stop" provider of utility systems and infrastructure, now including (in addition to water) electricity, gas, and telecommunications. This was a classic meeting of minds. The provision of water and other basic necessities is an issue of geopolitical significance.

Gérard Mestrallet has the academic pedigree of much of the French industrial elite. A graduate of the *Grand École Polytechnique* and the *École Nationale d'Administration*, he began his career in 1978 in the Treasury Department of the French Ministry of Economic Affairs and Finance, typifying the close intellectual ties between the public and private sectors in France. Among his mentors was Jacques Delors. In exchange for lifelong status guaranteed by elite schooling, the individual dedicates himself to serving the broader community, even beyond France itself. Yet Mestrallet is of modest origins. His father was a *patissier–traiteur* in Montmartre, in Paris. He is a merit scholar who has made good.

This capacity to adapt to new environments led him, after he joined *Compagnie de Suez* in 1984, from the post of senior vice president of the *Société Génerale de Belgique* to the position of its CEO in 1995. Following the merger with *Lyonnaise des Eaux*, in which he and Jérome Monod were the prime movers, Mestrallet became head of the merged company, *Suez Lyonnaise des Eaux* (SLDE), in

1997. The global ambition of this new group was immediately recognized by the international press. *Lyonnaise des Eaux* had already had a 50-percent world share of foreign-managed water companies. "SLDE's new mission is to conquer the world," commented *The Times* in April 1997.

Favorable press comment also greeted Mestrallet's early years at the helm of the new group. *Le Nouvel Économiste* named him the French "Manager of the Year 1998." From 1994 to 1999, with the addition of Lyonnaise des Eaux, group turnover at Suez rose from $15 billion to $35 billion. Martine Aubry, writing in the same journal, observed that "With the speed of light, the CEO of SLDE has completed his mission: transforming two companies into one coherent industrial group with global ambitions." A reported compliment to Mestrallet was overheard at a public ceremony. "You know where you want to go, but you make certain not to travel alone." It is this capacity to bring people with him on ambitious journeys that captured public attention. Mestrallet gave to the whole company a strong industrial focus and a genuine service strategy. His vision, although Europe based, is broadly multicultural.

Joining the Histories of Two Venerable Companies

The merger could not have been a success without respect being paid to two quite different, yet equally distinguished histories of the two companies, each more than a century old. We see their histories side by side on SLDE's Web site. *Suez* was the former *Suez Canal Company*, founded in 1858 to build the Suez Canal, thereby joining the Mediterranean to the Indian Ocean. *Lyonnaise des Eaux et de l'Éclairage (Water and Lighting)* was founded in 1880 to distribute water, gas, and, later, electricity. Both companies internationalized early, *Suez* from its inception and *Lyonnaise* from 1914 onwards, largely in French colonies. Both were used to long-term time horizons in the provision of infrastructure. Typical of this approach was the 25–30 year contract for the building, operating, and management of utility systems, which would then revert to local control and ownership. These concessions were originally made by French or colonial administrations to the company concerned, but the vision of returning a vastly improved infrastructure system to independent communities was postcolonial in its inspiration and a charter for the freedom of developing nations.

The vision has proven immensely popular, and, aided by French diplomacy, LDE especially has dwarfed its international competitors. It was a vision worthy of Jérome Monod. Public health and low infant mortality rates are important foundations for economic takeoff and social development. LDE would put an end to cholera, typhoid, and diseases due to polluted water supplies. It would train an echelon of indigenous professionals to operate and maintain the system and then depart. A private company would help developing people to help themselves and leave their destiny in their own hands. This is an undertaking that cannot simply be shifted from one location to a cheaper one, like electronics manufacturing. You are committed to that locality for a generation, and inevitably, you lose some and win some. Yet you are not free of competition simply by virtue of having a long-term contract; the instability of local politics is a constant threat, and you must justify your performance to critics. It was Jérome Monod who wrote in 1999, "You cannot live without a grand vision, and only those who see the invisible can realize the impossible."

Mestrallet's challenge has been to translate that overarching vision and timeless quality into clear goals that stockholders can grasp and monitor periodically. His success can be gauged by a June 16, 1999, headline in *The Financial Times*: "Utilities Group Has Crystal Clear Aims." His five-year objectives were bold and unambiguous. The water business was to become a world leader, not just in market share, but in profitability. To that end, he acquired Calgon in the USA in 1999, that country's third-largest water-conditioning company, and, just two weeks later, Nalco Chemical, the biggest water-treatment company, which turned SLDE into the world's number-one water conditioner. For SITA, the waste-management unit of SLDE, the objective was to double its sales, an aim accomplished within a year by the acquisition of all of the units of Browning Ferries Industries outside the USA. This made SITA the world leader outside North America. In the same year, Mestrallet gained full control of Tractebel, its Belgian electricity and gas subsidiary, and was therefore in a position to use it as a launch vehicle for acquisitions in the energy industry.

Mestrallet is personally very gentle, courteous, and unassuming. His *courtoisie* is much remarked on, but it covers a steely determination and an unswerving pursuit of the goals he has set for his group. A veritable Boy Scout in his demeanor, and charmingly intelligent, he nonetheless is unswerving in the pursuit of objectives. He told his senior staff, "The road we have chosen is hard and passionate. Therefore, let's internalize Leonardo da Vinci's beautiful motto: obstinate rigor". A list of what Mestrallet sees as his major challenges is as follows:

- "Globalization," or, more precisely, building a transnational corporation, global in scope, but rooted in every region.
- Meeting the sheer variety of requests from countries at every stage of development.

- Creating new, up-to-date forms of urbanization and basic infrastructures for multiple utilities.
- Deregulation of public monopolies in the supply of, for example, water and energy to create new opportunities for industrial customers.
- Privatization of public utilities, opening them up to world financial investment and increased capital.
- New ways of safeguarding the environment and monitoring its quality.
- Combining a constancy of purpose with the capacity to make quantum leaps in technology and service, with the aim of strengthening the whole.

The Search for Complementarity

Mestrallet's first task was to get two very different companies working in tandem. This was not easy. Both companies were old and effective operators, with deeply ingrained habits for achieving success, which had strongly etched their cultures. Neither had reason to defer to the other in the area of its own expertise.

Lyonnaise des Eaux was a well-regarded national number-two in local public services, desperately in need of capital to develop its infrastructure. *Suez* was strong in the very finances Lyonnaise needed. Despite such complementarities, the cultures were very different. LDE was oriented toward projects and led by engineering. The concession model necessitated a 20 to 25 year commitment to build, maintain, and operate water and sewage treatment facilities and pipelines in far-flung locations, with the municipality as a customer. LDE was largely intuitive in its assessment, because of the large number of uncontrollable variables in regions far from HQ. The company also depended substantially on relationships of trust and confidence between local officials and French engineers on the ground. Foreigners assuming command, however temporary, of local water supplies is a potentially tense issue. That which falls from the heavens upon a community is surely its own. LDE's triumph had been one of diplomacy – its own and that of the French government. Such skills were highly localised and decentralized, with no two problems alike and with few safe generalizations possible about the best practice.

In contrast, *Suez* was a highly capital-intensive company, with a financially oriented culture. It had the knowledge and skills in banking and financial services, in evaluating profit and risk, and in structuring finance and raising money at low costs. Mestrallet's first move was to sell off all noncore activities, including, the making of *paté de foie-gras* and the extending of consumer credit. He also divested *Suez* of companies in other financial services, concentrating on capital investment in, and the operating of, water, waste, and energy activities. The aim was to make a 14-percent return on global investments.

Dilemma1:   LDE's Search for Complementarity

LDE's search for complementarity is captured in the following diagram:

Dilemma 1.   The Search for Complementarity

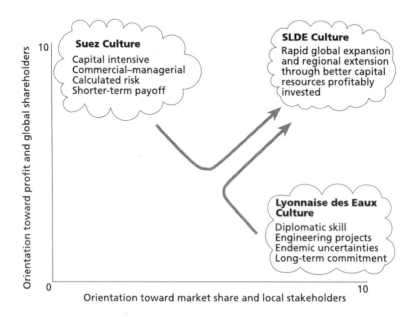

LDE's ability to open up ever more varied opportunities across the globe had been immeasurably enhanced by cheaper and more plentiful capital. Jérome Monod was travelling ever more widely. Commitments to stakeholders can be longer still and larger where the company is well financed and profitable. When you are putting in energy pipelines, you can leave room for water, and vice versa. With good management, you need lay these infrastructures only once.

Dilemma 2:   Socially Responsible Privatization

It was Mrs. Thatcher who first beat the drum for Europe-wide privatization, yet, paradoxically, it was the French who were best positioned to take advantage of this. Why? Because, for many French managers, the proper conduct of private enterprise has never been without a sense of public duty and social obligation to the wider community. In Chapter 1, we saw that French managers, to a greater extent than most other Europeans or Americans, saw in business the opportunity "continuously to take care of the needs of your fellow man."

It follows that privatization, as practiced by French companies in general and SLDE in particular, is less likely to lead to local communities' being taken advantage of and more likely to be seen as an opportunity to care creatively. Fresh water supplies and the proper treatment of wastes have historically been responsible for doubling life expectancies in affected communities. A company dedicated to these tasks is not easy to find in *laissez-faire* economies, where self-interest is sovereign over public services.

This helps to explain why there are over 55,000 municipal water companies in the United States, only 15 percent of which are run by private enterprise. Only 9.0 percent of US water treatment companies are in private hands. Clearly, for Americans, "responsibility" means small, local, and nonprofit. If you are *of* the community, you can be trusted to take care of it, but unelected out-of-town operators, going for profit, have been insufficiently trusted up to now. Moreover, the five-year concessions mandated by federal regulations were too short to attract private investment.

Now that the regulations have been changed to 20 years or more, the race is on, and the opportunities for SLDE are vast – provided, of course, that communities across America come to trust SLDE's heritage of public service. For while being small and local assists the taking of social responsibility, and while a five-year concession assures that the contractor can do nothing much wrong without quickly losing that concession, the system was chronically inefficient, lacked economies of scale, and afforded disincentives to investment.

Today, the chance for SLDE to be locally responsible *and* a big, efficient investor is too good to miss. "The company sees great opportunity in the fragmented US market," explained Mestrallet. Here is a chance to show that privatization is not just technically and economically superior, but also matches the concern for the local communities shown by contractors on a short leash, forever lobbying for the renewals of their five-year concessions. SLDE is targeting big cities in which their professionalism is appreciated. It has projects going in Atlanta, Indianapolis, Gary, Milwaukee, and San Antonio, among others, and the comments have been favorable. "SLDE's tap water may not yet taste like Perrier, but it is just as French."

However, deregulation is not pure gain. It pushes down prices and puts profitability under pressure. For this reason, "we need Monod's talents to develop all corners of the planet, from Casablanca to Djakarta. Here the desperate need is for drinkable water."

The dilemma of *Socially Responsible Privatization and Deregulation* can be diagrammed as follows:

Dilemma 2. Socially Responsible Privatization and Deregulation

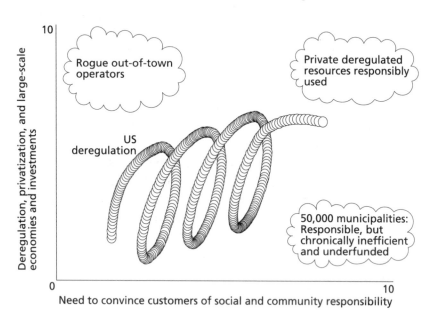

In a world where political controls over corporations are weakening and where utility companies are "natural monopolies," it becomes increasingly important not to abuse this power and behave like a *rogue operator*. Deregulation has perhaps started a stampede, but it will take dedication to customers and communities to avoid injuring them in this stampede.

The future of privatization is *not* necessarily secure. Much will depend on how private companies conduct themselves. Some developed nations have declined to take this path, the Netherlands, for example, where water is an issue of national survival, argues that private companies push for "cheap solutions" that leave out less prosperous citizens. The UK has had occasion to criticize its privatized water companies severely, and there is some dismay with foreign ownership. Privatized electricity companies in the UK treat their large users very well, their small users far worse. Norway has suffered large price fluctuations, with price rises during droughts, because of the domination of hydroelectric power.

The idea of making profits from rain and rivers still sticks in many voters' throats, despite the value and technical challenges of water treatment. France itself is nationalistic about water and about privatization involving foreigners. It also has a long tradition of government influence in industrial affairs. SLDE may find its foreign operations curbed if its base country does not become more hospitable to foreign investment in its infrastructure; nor is France privatizing fast enough, according to Mestrallet: "In France, we are losing time now. It takes too long to privatize important industries. Just look around you. We cannot maintain this idea that France can be a small laboratory apart from the rest of the world. Of course, we must preserve our unique history and traditions, but we cannot be blind to developments around us. There is a real risk of a 'back to public service' spirit if private companies make too much money while contributing too little to communities. *Le Mal Française* with its state-influenced rigidities, its suspicion of flexibility and initiative, and its tendency to politicize all decisions, is still a threat to us."

All these factors make it even more important that SLDE commit itself to those communities and municipalities it serves. If the tide turns against privatization, there is still a chance that SLDE could be regarded as an exception and a future model, one of the few global operators that serves its customers with honesty and dedication, thereby creating an oasis in a spiritual desert. It is this kind of caring, which Jérome Monod's vision described as "invisible," that Gerard Mestrallet is determined to demonstrate in the company's results. It is to this dedication that we now turn.

Dilemma 3: Enriching Shareholders vs. Sustaining the Poor, the Underdeveloped, and the Environment

One might well ask how SDLE can *afford* to pursue social goals, save at some cost to its shareholders, who might object to this use of their money. One answer is the very large gain from network accelerated returns. Much fuss is currently made over the economic advantages of the Internet and the huge share prices for still unprofitable companies. But investors know that networks can produce accelerating, rather than diminishing returns. This is because every additional member of a growing network lowers the costs for serving all existing customers. By simultaneously expanding the base and lowering per-unit prices, a utility precipitates a *virtuous circle*, with ever more customers at ever lower per-unit costs, which in turn gives access to ever more customers, even the very poor. SLDE's policy is to *share these gains with the communities it serves*, all of which have produced "net gains." The Internet is only the latest of several networks.

For example, in Buenos Aires, the state utility company was widely unpopular and financially troubled, and it reached too few people. SLDE invested $1 billion and reached 1.6 million *more* people, with upgraded equipment. And did all this without raising water rates! In Santiago, Chile, the company worked with the government to provide "water stamps," so that even the poorest people became paying customers and were involved in consultations about better service. Finally, popular participation and suggestions elicited from poor customers in La Paz, Bolivia led to costs being cut by two-thirds.

Mestrallet likes to make Monod's caring more visible than heretofore, just as he likes to make strategic objectives clear. To that end, he created an ethics charter and employs an in-house deontologist (a practitioner of the branch of ethics concerned with duty, obligation, and good intentions, much influenced by Immanuel Kant.) The values embodied by the company include professionalism, partnership, *esprit de corps,* respect for the environment, and the creation of genuine value.

The impact of these ethics must be viewed in the context of taking over inefficient, overstaffed, and sometimes even corrupt municipal services, upgrading these services over 20 years or more, and then returning them to the local control of trained, professional, indigenous managers and workers. In these circumstances, the following ethical principles guide policy:

- Fire as few people as you can and try to get unions on your side and acting responsibly.
- Where downsizing and layoffs are unavoidable, demonstrate as soon as possible the improvements in service and the impacts on public health arising from them. Write measurable improvements in water quality into your contract, and extend services wherever you can, to get costs down. Sponsor surveys of public health, so that improvements are publicized and preventable illnesses are seen to become less frequent.
- Build long-term partnerships by improving efficiency and by holding or lowering prices to the customer. Hence, in Budapest, raising prices at less than the level of inflation, which is a net lowering of prices, is written into the contract. Efficiency includes energy *saving*, so that customers' key appliances use less.
- Focus especially on poorer people, their employment, and their access to water, electricity, and other utilities.
- Assist the environment through recycling and separation of glass, tin, and so on from other wastes, with rewards for the apprehension of illegal dumpers.
- Learn to respond to dire emergencies. For example, in the destructive storms in France in 1999, SLDE staff rode to the rescue of many communities cut off from water and electricity. Mobile water treatment units were installed, and individuals and small and medium enterprises were helped to get through local electricity distribution emergencies.

An important insight into the success of these policies, comes out of the dilemma theory we have been using. Why, for example, does it benefit SLDE to persuade customers to *save water and energy?* Conventional economic thinking would scoff at this strategy. After all, you are *selling* energy, so the more customers that use and pay for, the more money you make. Why save energy at all? Should not your shareholders be angry? Why provide water for the poor, who are "uneconomical" to serve? These might indeed have been the attitudes of the municipal water and electricity authorities in underdeveloped economies, which SDLE replaces temporarily, but if we look at the situation as a values *system*, the reasons for social responsibility become clear. If you lower energy costs for a pizza maker with two ovens, he or she can cut costs and use the proceeds to buy a third oven, which consumes the electricity you supply in greater quantities than before. You are better off, the pizza maker is better off, and more customers are served. If you pipe clean water to poor people and collect in payment "water stamps" that the government cashes, those people will no longer dig up the pipes and sell them, no longer have to sit up all night with a cholera-stricken child, and no longer absent themselves from work because of illness. Again – *everyone* is better off and lives longer.

The same is true of sustaining the environment. It is not the "fittest" who survive, but the *fittingest*. The unit of survival is the person *plus* the environment. They survive together or not at all. In the end, those who pay for pollution are the poor, pushed into the dirtiest corners of the urban sprawl and picking over the piles of trash.

In short, joining people to networks for the supply of such mass utilities as water, electricity, gas, telephone, and telecommunications produces network economies *shareable among all parties*, including shareholders and stakeholders. Such networks create the infrastructure for economic takeoff and accelerating returns to that community. The dilemma is reconciled as in the following diagram.

At the top left, we have the monopoly supplier, like some of SLDE's US-based competitors, widely blamed for environmental pollution. At the bottom right, we see that infrastructure might actually be destroyed by people too poor to pay their rates. What is necessary are gains and solutions for the whole national and regional network. These can be paid for only if all citizens participate, because a whole network can be sabotaged by a desperate minority. As Monod put it, "We are only world leaders when we help to solve problems on a world scale: like the future of Lake Aral now crippled by salination."

Dilemma 3. Enriching Shareholders vs. Sustaining the Poor and the Environment

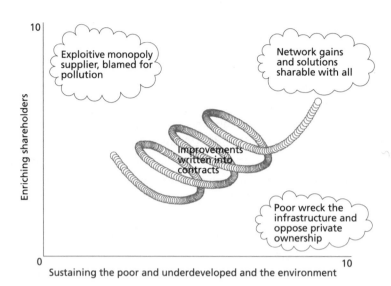

Mestrallet agrees: "To be a world leader, you must think about the problems of humanity, about making the desert bloom, [and] about how to treat water in large urban agglomerates."

For this reason, SDLE sees environmental organizations as its partners, not its enemies. It installed a Water Resources Advisory Committee, established in February 2000. The committee consists of a group of international experts established to brainstorm on major water resource issues. The committee will be consulted on social and environmental issues raised by major SLDE projects, as well as on basic principles related to public – private partnerships, and it will be asked to help in providing answers to water supply problems. The committee includes experts in water-resource issues throughout the world: Europe, Asia, Africa, and North and South America.

A "laboratory" for trying out new ideas is Casablanca, where SDLE has a multiutility concession. The project includes the inspection of systems, the improvement of network efficiency, the reduction of electricity use and water wastage, and the cleaning of 50 km of piping every month. Since taking over the responsibility for sewerage in Casablanca, SLDE has now been protecting the city's population a key priority. Part of the project has been a major stormwater-drain infrastructure, because regular flooding used to disrupt city life.

SDLE has also sponsored Aquassistance, an association of volunteers trained to deal with floods. Since 1994, Aquassistance has intervened in many stricken countries. Along with the Water Resources Advisory Committee, SLDE published an environmental charter in which the company pledges to universalize best practices, to optimize energy use, to control CO_2 emissions, to guarantee potable water, to recycle household waste, and to train disadvantaged communities to collect and reuse wastewater.

This is why SDLE is expanding rapidly across the globe. China has been a market since the late 1970s. Its huge population has urgent needs for water treatment and infrastructure. As recently as September 1999, SLDE signed a deal to build and operate a $23 million water-purification facility in Shanghai and a $28 million incineration plant in the Pudong zone. There is a $20 *billion* water and sewerage network for Buenos Aires and a $3 billion multiutility project for Casablanca. Contracts have been won in Manila, Budapest, Jakarta, La Paz, and Potsdam. SLDE is linking with Vivendi to jointly bid for the $1 billion water-system privatization in Rio de Janeiro, and in a consortiumwide project for Santiago, various utilities cooperate on installation costs.

To the extent that developing nations have an effective networked infrastructure sustaining their health, rapid economic development is that much more likely. To the extent that the poor and the environment are included in a programme of sustainable development, all citizens will contribute to common objectives and all forms of "development" coincide.

Dilemma 4: Differentiated vs. Integrated Service Provider

Providing added value via multiservice, multiutility offerings challenges SLDE to establish synergy between its three main businesses: energy, water, and waste services. According to Mestrallet; "Our very ambitious strategy is possible only because there is complementarity between our diverse activities. Clients are on the same terrain, and our partners are often cities, states (nations), and regions. We all manage complex sets of activities, frequently buying companies that are privatized, and we are all, in a large number of cases, the project managers for the public service. We are all in the same business: delivering basic necessities to our customers' doorsteps. The future is in one-shop service: water, electricity, gas, heating, cable services, and the collection and treatment of solid waste and wastewater."

The added value is not just in applying the same concept to the different services. SLDE's capacity to design, finance, build, and manage can be used to offer unique integrated services, such as combining the activities in "waste" and "energy" in "waste to energy" projects or combining the activities in "energy" and "water" in desalination technology. Integrated service provision is especially relevant for "late-developing" nations or regions. One advantage of being a "late-developing" nation or region is that your utility infrastructure is brand new and can be built from scratch. Instead of having water pipes here, gas pipes there, telephone wires overhead, and sewage everywhere, it makes sense to build a multiutility pipeline and distribution system with all utilities in single channels, laid side by side, often under large curbstones that need only be lifted to avoid the necessity of digging up the roadway to make serial repairs.

While such combinations are ideal, they are also quite rare. One example of an "ideal" multiutility system is SLDE's concession in Casablanca, where the firm is installing water, energy, sewerage, and telecommunications simultaneously. The problem with extolling such opportunities is that they seldom recur; what is needed is a viable model for more common patterns of customer demand. The multiutility pipeline is an "engineer's dream," but most engineers working for SLDE have to alter their course and do something else that customers want. Nonetheless, the search for integration is strategically important: For example, when running a desaliniation plant, you generate steam, and it makes sense to use that steam for heating or for generating electricity. Such dual functions are more economical than separated functions. If you are laying pipelines anyway, billing customers anyway, treating water anyway, it typically pays to integrate such activities so that you treat water *and* supply it *and* supply electricity or steam from this process.

Attractive though the multiutility concept is, it applies largely to the downstream delivery of services. Electricity has still to be generated, water has still to be treated, and these activities usually are separate, specialized functions, requiring very different technologies. Upstream integration is relatively rare. Even the process of generation is changing. Mestrallet explains, "We are moving from a centralized energy-generation system to an increasingly decentralized one with smaller and smaller plants. At the same time, gas-fired turbines are growing smaller, too. Today, we can supply a hospital with its own 10-MW turbine. Soon, individual gas-fired turbines will be sold to personal clients."

These trends intensify the differentiation of the company, which provides different utilities, on different scales, in different places. The commonest situations are utility systems in chronic disrepair, which need overhaul, extension, and proper maintenance, but *not* rebuilding from scratch. Accordingly, SLDE faces every variety of system in greater or lesser crisis and has to call upon a wide repertory of skills. Perhaps more relevant to the integration of this variety is SLDE's still small, but growing, telecommunications business. This is very much more than just an additional service, an extra cable, sharing the same trench. SLDE is in a position to include telecommunications in its multiutility offerings in order to turn a vision of "total housing service" into reality. In January 2000, Mestrallet announced that SLDE would accelerate its communication activities: cable services, the Internet, satellite television, terrestrial TV, and mobile phones, including applying for a mobile telephone license for the new UMTS norm, which supports convergence with the Internet. "Our cable activities are full of promise," he says, "To connect just Paris on the Internet through our cables is a jump start. Many investments can be gained back in these new e-commerce times. There progressively develops a demand for bytes. Digital quality is part of an explosive growth. Next to that, we are extending our services on the cable, including speeding up the Internet by a factor of 1000 compared to the telephone. Here also, we manage the infrastructure."

This initiative in communication is not just helping SLDE create value for its shareholders; it also can help SLDE get closer to its final customers: Call centers and e-commerce implementation will give advantages in offering new services and billing. In addition, the initiative can help SLDE reconcile the dilemma between differentiation and integration of its services. All this gets the company much closer to its final customers, via home information systems, that switch on, switch off, monitor, and economize on the utilities entering the house. Mestrallet's phrase *"one-stop service"* has two meanings: "one stop" for the ultimate household customers, who can get a simple readout of how all their utilities are performing, and "one stop" for SLDE's distributor customers out in the regions, who require only one major contractor to advise upon and provide many different utilities, in just the proportions required by the situation. "One stop" means that SLDE can do it all: you need only one consultation and one contract. We can draw the dilemma as shown on the next page.

At the top left, we have the typically overdifferentiated approach, with "chimneys" or "silos," the digging up of the road once a month to fix faults and the blocking of traffic for half a year. It is hard to overcome this, because it is typical of many urban centers in the West, where utilities have been installed by accretion over time and some of the systems date from the turn of the last century. The *tabula rasa* of a city like Casablanca, where it is feasible to start from scratch and build an ideal up-to-date system, is not so much wrong as rare, too rare to act as a model for most of the company. By far the commonest situation is that in which each region has its unique problems, yet their solution draws from SLDE's wide skill base and resource base. In Budapest, for example, 99 percent of the population gets piped water, but its quality has deteriorated. In parts of Latin America, there is no infrastructure where poor people live. In many cities, the municipalities are employers of last resort, hiring the relatives of politicians. What is needed here is professionalization and training. You stop once to consult with SLDE, which will provide for your particular situation.

Dilemma 4. Differentiated vs. Integrated Services

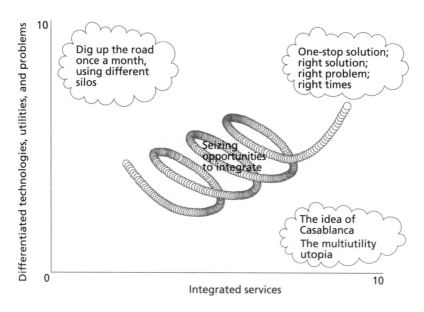

Dilemma 5:   Globalism vs. Multinationalism: The Ideal of Transnationalism

SLDE is very much in a race to globalize. Already, it has concessions for over 50 percent of the world's foreign-run water companies – although that makes up only 4.0 percent of all such companies, so the race has barely started. SLDE has made a fast break. Mestrallet emphasizes this: "Essentially, I believe that internationalization is our next important challenge . . . the process has only just started. It does not make sense to stop water, waste, or energy development at borders. All these businesses will change their shape. Unfortunately, the French do not have a strong tradition of needing foreigners and tend to stay within home markets. Even so, we have managed to move from 50 percent of turnover being French in the early 1990s to 73 percent being foreign today. Tractabel, our energy company is number three in the world among independent suppliers, although it, too, is home grown, with 95 percent of the Belgian electricity market."

Mestrallet's vision is of a transnational organization, in which any one of 100 countries in which SLDE operates could inspire the rest, much as Casablanca's multiutility model is an inspiration to those installing an infrastructure for the first time. Local solutions might remain local, but they could also lead to powerful, global generalizations.

Mestrallet announced in 1998 that he wanted to develop the organization according to the transnational model: "We need to take advantage of our Franco – Belgian base, quite equally shared in terms of business. We are in the process of building a truly transnational organization with multicenters of excellence – for example, in Paris and Brussels. We need to utilize the possibility of having a financial center in Brussels and Hong Kong, while R&D and Legal Services are cited in Paris. However, it is impossible to be active in 100 countries or so without having a strong home base in France and Belgium – or rather, Europe. In our business, being international is significantly more than just a process of exporting. If we enter a new market, in most cases a nation state, we do this for 20 or 30 years. Every franc of nondomestic business is generated outside of France by people who are locally distributing water or electricity or who manage waste. We need a much larger time horizon than many other industries do. We need to have a very fundamental knowledge of the economic workings of a country, as well as of its sociopolitical and cultural life. In our business, we can't take a power plant or the network of water pipes on our back and leave a city or country. We are condemned to the physical place, so we had better do a good job. Because we can't easily pack our bags, we do our best to develop long-term relationships and assimilate with local partners. Both in water and electricity, we have to face local authorities and laws. Once you decide to codevelop a region that is politically unstable, you have to combine a long-term view with a tremendous amount of political and social risk-taking. We are coresponsible for creating the wealth of a country or region. Therefore, we need to have a total integration of our and our clients' interests. We are not able to abandon any of our countries. Furthermore, it is impossible to organize ourselves as a multiregional company. We need to be there locally. The main dilemma is to be present globally anywhere in the world, but nowhere in particular. Our base is European, but our growth potential is elsewhere. And we need to deal with former local monopolies in many cases if not all. We need to understand the country's culture."

Mestrallet clearly tries to build upon SLDE's traditional strength of an informal, pragmatic approach: building contacts, networking, forging unique political and personal relationships with municipalities and governments at various levels, and fostering the culture of understanding what the problem is. As he said in a speech in 1998, "The development of the French model of outsourcing is an answer to the present world situation." The French particularistic approach can definitely be a strength in comparison with, for instance, American companies, which tend to see the civil service as inferior to them and don't build-long term relationships. However, the informal and pragmatic approach can also turn into a weakness. The group spirit in SLDE at the operational level is very much based on a personal network of French expatriates. This monocultural, often monolingual, group is good at sharing and exchanging knowledge in an informal way and at encouraging an entrepreneurial spirit and networking. However, this strength often goes together with a weakness in formal planning and decision making. Globalization inevitably requires more formal control.

If SLDE is multinational by necessity, working on the ground in scores of long relationships with foreign regions, then what needs more emphasis is linking these sites with a transnational learning system in which up to a hundred contracts and concessions are monitored and studied for the lessons they will yield, for each other, and for the system as a whole. But there is an additional way to globalize effectively. Next to local public authorities, industrial clients are becoming more important for SLDE, if only because developing with global industrial clients will help SLDE to globalize itself. You follow an industrial client from operating site to operating site throughout the world, so that all plants, for example, benefit from recycling systems, waste disposal, and incineration, wherever in the world the plants are located. In short, you use the globalism of client companies to expand your own operations.

Industrial outsourcing is rapidly becoming a new market, combining storage, transportation treatment structures, and control over consumption. SLDE is well positioned for these types of activities, with its combination of urban water services, industrial water services, turnkey project engineering, and huge opportunities to sell electricity to industrial clients after deregulation. SLDE applies this model to waste management with its industrial customer, Ford. Waste-management systems for a car company are highly specialized. You must typically get into the production processes themselves if less waste is to be generated, and much of what remains recycled. The similarity of this expertise helps SLDE to integrate itself as one company, with bodies of core competence available at all sites. Essentially, such learning is part of the partnership with Ford, a form of coevolution in which manufacturing skills and waste-control skills develop together. Once these are learned, the client company would be foolish not to apply them at all its plants.

The dilemma of how to be multinational and regional but *also* global and centralized, is reconciled in the following figure:

Dilemma 5.   Globalism vs. Multinationalism

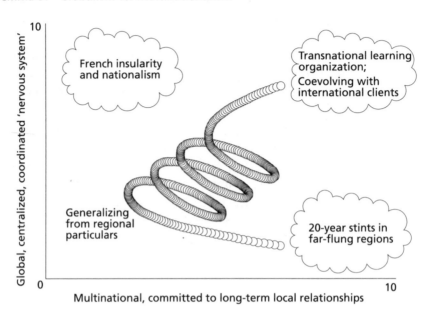

Mestrallet has forced himself to overcome French insularity (at the top left) and uses the far-flung regional concessions in foreign lands and the many information points, sending news of greater or lesser success to the company's "central nervous system" in Paris and Brussels. It is from here that well-informed strategies arise.

Being committed to a regional site for at least 20 years challenges SLDE to learn. The ideal of transnationalism allows any country in the international network to influence others. A solution in San Antonio could have vital lessons for 30 other sites around the world. Resources needed in Jakarta might have to come from a dozen other sites. In addition, the company is learning and coevolving with its international customers in developing methods of production that are more friendly to the environment. This alone could win contracts in several other regions. SLDE made huge steps in building further on the transnational model in 1999 and 2000, as part of the integration of Nalco and Tractebel. Chicago was designated as the global center for water-treatment activities, Brussels as the global center for energy activities. Mestrallet made an effort toward putting global project teams together for projects at one location (e.g., in Berlin and in Casablanca) and toward knowledge management.

The need for global marketing and global account management immediately leads to the next dilemma, related to SLDE's public image. SLDE does not have one global brand name at the moment, although a global brand name would help in building a global reputation. On the other hand, SLDE has strong local brand names such as (in Belgium) Tractebel and Electrabel and (in France) Lyonnaise des Eaux (water business), Elyo (energy business), and SITA (waste business). It would be a pity to lose these and even a risk for the French market situation: having SLDE operate under one brand name would make its presence in France too dominant. Mestrallet says, "We face a dilemma: we risk having to balance between our local interests and international interests for years."

The question whether the name *Suez Lyonnaise des Eaux* is sufficiently international is often asked. Mestrallet replies, "On the question of whether our name is sufficiently international, no– I think that it is necessary to think about an evolution."

Conclusion

Suez Lyonnaise des Eaux is in many ways an extraordinary case, emphasizing as it does not just the "social responsibilities" of private enterprise, but the international communal *advantage* of using private finance and technology to solve environmental and social problems on a world scale. What is required is a leadership that approaches world statesmanship and vision. These are the legacies of Jérome Monod and Gérard Mestrallet. They have taken their French heritage of civic and municipal responsibility for public resources and extended it across the globe. They have given new meaning to privatization. They have provided networked infrastructures that lay the foundations for economic takeoff itself.

The ambition of *Suez Lyonnaise des Eaux* is to become the world leader in businesses that are at the heart of mankind's essential needs: energy, water, waste services, and communication. Mestrallet's great passions are a reflection of SLDE itself. SLDE is a company that delivers basic necessities to the customer's doorstep; Mestrallet, as a youngster, wanted to become a farmer, being attracted by the great forces that the earth exerts. His second major hobby still is horseback riding. Mestrallet's great passion is a reflection of SLDE itself, in that it aspires to be close to the basics of life. "The most important [thing] is that I work for the interest of my company," he says, "but my real happiness is my family and friends. Today, obviously my passion is my work, but tomorrow I could start anywhere else. One day, without any doubt I will return to the earth, and I will take care of my horses. I will become a farmer – not a gentleman farmer like now, a real one."

CHAPTER 9

Leading One Life

Leader: Val Gooding (British United Provident Association, BUPA)

Val Gooding has been chief executive of BUPA, the British United Provident Association, since 1998. BUPA is the United Kingdom's largest private health insurer and provider, with around 40 percent of the private health insurance market – that is, nearly 3 million members. It is the second largest employer of nurses and medical staff, after the National Health Service, Britain's giant state-sponsored medical system, free at the point of delivery and paid for from tax revenues. BUPA's interests extend to home care, health screening, fitness, occupational health products, and a private medical insurance business overseas.

Val Gooding, who is married with two children, came to BUPA after a distinguished career with British Airways. As head of cabin service from 1989 to 1992, she was involved in BA's famous transformation in customer service, in which cabin staff engaged customers in "Moments of truth," according to a philosophy first enunciated by Jan Carlzon of Scandinavian Airlines. (We shall explore the significance of these "moments" later and trace their impact on Gooding's leadership.) She rose from this position to Head of Marketing (1992–93), thence to the director of business units (1993–94), and finally to the position of director of the Asian Pacific region of BA. At BUPA, she was briefly managing director UK before becoming chief executive in 1998.

Val Gooding appears to have been something of a late developer. In a recent graduation speech, she identified with the tortoise in the fable of "The Tortoise and the Hare." She herself did not spring spectacularly from her school starting gates, but she did make solid, steady, and impressive progress in corporate settings. It was, then, with quiet satisfaction, that at one point in her career she assumed a leading role in an organization that had refused her a place as a student intern some years earlier. That people do much of their learning and development at work has been both her own experience and her credo as CEO.

Asked about the major dilemmas she faced as BUPA's new leader, Gooding identified the following major issues.

1. An Effective Insurer vs. the Carer for the One Life Customers Have
2. The Quality of Business Systems vs. the Degree of Staff Caring and Morale
3. Free Universal Provision vs. Allocation of Resources by Free Markets
4. Responses to Medical Crises vs. Wellness as Preventive Medicine
5. Nationally Based Services vs. Globally Expanded Services
6. For-profit status vs. Nonprofit status

She would have to grapple successfully with these or see her efforts undone by cross-pressures in the business environment. This chapter will describe, in a paraphrase of Val Gooding's own words, the dilemmas that BUPA faced and how she resolved them.

Dilemma 1:   An Effective Insurer vs. The Carer for the One Life Customers Have

In some respects, Val Gooding's background in BA was an excellent preparation for BUPA, and she was grateful for what she learned with BA, but in one important respect, BUPA turned out to be very different from an airline service. Its biggest business is health insurance, although it also provide, direct care to patients in acute-care hospitals and to elderly residents in nursing homes. In the *insurance part of the business* BUPA is guided to a certain extent by actuaries, by aggregates, and by statistical projections of likely future demands on services. Above all, an insurance culture is averse to risk. It tends to think of customers as claimants, people trying to get money out of the company – and, of course, it does have to be legal and contractual in its orientation. Members have paid exactly so much money for exactly so much coverage, and the company cannot afford to go beyond stipulations if it is to be fair to all its customers.

Like so many insurers, BUPA tend, to be internally focused on its own procedures, numbers, rules, and limits. Its millions of customers are viewed, in general, as trends and probabilities, *not* so much as particular people, with one life, infinitely precious to that person. Gooding noticed early on that BUPA missed the 'little' things, things that on closer inspection were not really little at all. When she looked at how BUPA answered customer complaints, there was courtesy, often under trying conditions, but there was also a culture of self-justification. It was as if BUPA had to be right on everything all the time and had to convince the complainant of this. It was as if the smallest admission of error would be used in evidence against it. BUPA needed claimants to endorse the way it thought, instead of the firm's understanding them.

Also, BUPA was oddly cold and formal in manner. Gooding had not read "Thank you for your letter of 15 inst." for more than 10 years before joining BUPA. She insisted on a change in the whole style. It was not possible to give key staff the kinds of financial bonuses they could get elsewhere, so it was all the more important to create a culture like no other: BUPA *despite* being an insurer and having to think like one, identifies with the one life each member has.

Another key strategy arose from BA's seminars for cabin crew and the importance of Carlzon's "moments of truth" concept. This held that most passengers interacted with cabin crew for only about 20–50 seconds throughout a long-haul flight, but that, from such fragments of interaction, they drew conclusions of wide generality about the airline. The "moments" might be very brief and specific, but "the truth" inferred from them was sweeping and all-embracing. Yet the "truth" about an airline is of minor consequence compared with the truth about a medical service upon which a person's health and very life depends. According to Gooding, it's a moment of truth when you have been paying out premiums for years to BUPA and now suddenly you need the company to reciprocate. How does the person on the other end of that telephone behave? Are they immediately and authentically concerned with *you,* or are they concerned mainly with their own categories and rules – with how they should conceive of you in the abstract? Are they trying to save your life or reduce their own costs? Now that *you* need *them,* are they warm, welcoming, considerate, moving with the same alacrity as when they accepted your premium?

Those first 30 seconds on the telephone are not just moments of truth, but moments when you calculate your survival chances, when you thank heaven for BUPA or curse the day you heard of it. BUPA makes its reputation in those moments – good or bad. BUPA has to create a culture acutely conscious of the one life on the other end of that line.

Of course, Goodling *tells* people this, but it is not enough just to tell them; she, models the behavior she wants others to show: *servant leadership,* consisting of doing it yourself, serving others as you would have them serve the customer. She is to model nonarrogance, noncomplacency, dissatisfaction with progress thus far, and a willingness to learn from one's environment by listening.

She judges that she needs to be "at the coal face", where those "moments of truth" are happening. Accordingly, she attends surgical operations (as do the other senior managers), talks to patients before and after, visits call centers, takes calls herself, and talks with those continually on the front line with anxious inquirers. She used to hear some skeptical comments: "She won't keep *that* up for long..." and "New brooms sweep clean...." But she has been at it for four years now and has no intention of stopping. And staff remember. "I saw you at Staines," they tell her. She does it for herself, too, to remind herself what all this is about: that three million people have placed their lives in BUPA's hands and the company has to be there for them.

BUPA has a new training program called Leading One Life. It's not like other programs. Participants do not go "through it" like sheep being dipped and having some substance deposited on them. Instead, it inquires of participants, *"Who are you as a person? What are you outside work? Is there any part of that 'outside' you that you could bring to the workplace, to members and their concerns?"* The more of themselves and the more of their personal experiences they can bring to the workplace, the better they care and the more ways they have of caring.

Early on in the program, the participants form groups, which self-organize around the central concerns of members. How can we be of more help and enjoy that experience? What are the recent high points, and how can there be more of them? they ask. They share with each other the zest of being able to do more for customers, of being there for them, of finding just the right words, of sheer gratitude for their *own* health and good fortune and the feeling of having lent their strength, experience, and adulthood to others.

These teams also come up with very practical suggestions and solutions: for example, a special *health line* for those facing bypass surgery. On line were people who were specialized in the operation and would patiently explain the preparations, the producres, the aftermath, and the odds on surviving. There is another specialized line for breast cancer, with an experienced nurse. Customers are extremely appreciative of these developments. Any person or any team can write up a suggestion and be financially and socially rewarded when that suggestion is implemented. In sum, no set formulas or prepared spiels are going to train you to deal with people whose health and lives are unexpectedly threatened. What is required is nothing less than the totality of your personal experience and all the compassion you can muster from within yourself.

We are now in a position to diagram the first of Gooding's dilemmas.

Note this important point: BUPA *remains an insurer*, with the disciplines and categories of an insurer. You cannot evade this reality, but you can treat members in life-threatening situations as suffering human beings and not just as claimants shaking you down. This need of members for succor, potentially overwhelming for carers, is another level of reality – a pit of despair that most insurers keep away from if they can. It needs "emotional muscles" to move from where BUPA was in 1998, at the top left of the diagram, toward that pit to help those in crises.

Dilemma 1.   An Effective Insurer vs. The Carer of The One Life Customers Have

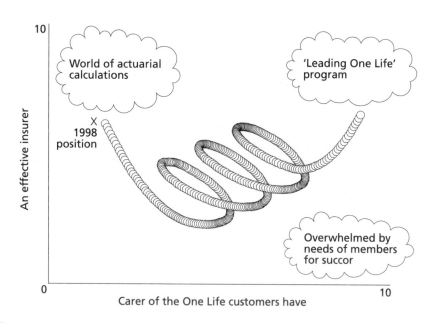

The Leading One Life program and policy *relies* on a sound insurance basis and then these uses very strengths and resources to reach out to members in peril. It is scary to try, but wonderfully satisfying to succeed, to be the voice at the end of the line that made everything happen. This helps explain why the Leading One Life program is not a "data drop," but the elicitation of the carer's powers to be fully present for others.

Let us stay for a moment with the metaphor of a reservoir of skill, compassion, and concern. In order for staff at BUPA to have this, they have to receive it from somewhere, absorb it into themselves, and pass it on. This brings us to the vital issue of staff morale.

Dilemma 2:   Quality of Business Systems vs. The Degree of Staff's Caring and Morale

There is simply no emotional reservoir to invest in frightened customers, no patience or understanding, if those same qualities have not been received by service staff. In the mid-1990s, BUPA staff morale was poor. When Gooding took over in 1998, it had improved, but not enough. Certainly, there were too few emotional riches to share with members. Val Gooding saw at once that increasing staff morale was a top priority. Yet her view of the problem was typically tough minded. She saw staff morale as not simply a "human relations thing": You treat other people with the kindness and consideration you yourself have received, but it is not that simple. Professionals work through the tools they use, and if the tools are neither the best nor the most relevant to the customer's needs, then, even with an abundance of caring, one cannot do an adequate job.

Imagine a call center. The caller is distressed – that's par for the course – and you are eager to help, but without good systems, you are in serious trouble. The caller expects you to know who he or she is, to have details at your fingertips, and to have speedy answers to some pretty urgent questions on such things as eligibility, costs, and appointments. Can you imagine trying to help when you have poor equipment or software that answers the questions of the insurer, but not the insured? It is hopeless, stressful, and infuriating.

Gooding learned this lesson at BA when she was head of cabin crews. Her section fought for and finally won the right to upgrade the galleys on long-haul flights. It meant taking out a couple of business-class seats, so you can imagine the opposition to that move! But it had a phenomenal effect on cabin-crew morale. Pushing a trolley with a wonky wheel or handling hot food in painfully confined spaces can totally destroy one's morale. Workers will believe nothing you say if you leave them to suffer with defective equipment. What Gooding found at BA proved even truer at BUPA. The staff are trained professionals, whose equipment is bound up with their pride and identity. If that equipment does not work properly or takes the staff away from its customers, instead of helping to focus on them, then morale is going to drain away and the number of complaints will rise. If the software is not right, if you can't get the customer's history and situation right there in front of you while the customer is begging you for answers in a voice strangled by anxiety and panic, can you imagine how awful the staff person feels, how helpless and angry? If the screen does not contain plain English, if it does not address the question the member is asking, but is full of in-house jargon, helpfulness is impeded. There was a need to change training, software, and even hardware.

In its state-of-the-art call centers at Staines and at Salford Quays, BUPA now has a "calming room" to which staff can retreat after highly stressful calls. BUPA trains staff to recognize the stress in a caller's voice and bring it down. The company has invested heavily in the environment of call centers: the soft fabrics to dull noise, the curved desks arranged in clusters so that team members can call on one another for help, the specialist resource people and help lines that can be relied on. Managers are right there in the center to provide help and guidance, not in privileged corner offices where they can hide away. There are restful, muted color schemes, a gym, a staff restaurant, and recreational facilities. Whatever horror stories one has heard about call centers do not apply at BUPA. Help is available in depth, so if staff get distressed or must go away to find answers, there is backup.

BUPA monitors service carefully: 80 percent of calls are answered by the fifth ring – that is, in 20 seconds. BUPA learns, especially from its corporate clients, how service can become better. When an institution deals with individuals with their own worries, there is no time for feedback or suggestions about improvements, but corporate clients tell the firm exactly where it succeeds and where it fails.

All this upgrading of the tools BUPA works with has been expensive, but absolutely necessary to staff morale and to the credibility of One Life programs. "If you are not going to back your people up, then talk of care is so much rhetoric. And now we are getting the results . . .," says Gooding. Her second dilemma is reminiscent of the socio–technical systems described by Eric Trist and Fred Emery. You cannot, they argued, consider technical systems in isolation from social systems, and you must always bear in mind the social meanings and implications of technology. If the equipment in use says "only profit counts" or "let the cabin staff suffer," then conflicts between systems doom even the best intentions, and the advocates of each system are frustrated. The dilemma looks like this.

Dilemma 2. Quality of Business Systems vs. Degree of Staff's Caring

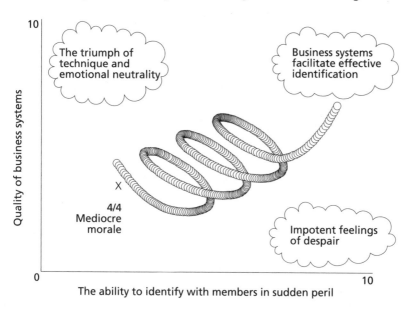

At the top left we have the triumph of technique and emotional neutrality, a trap that several giant insurers have fallen into. At the lower right, there is plenty of identification, but it gives rise to impotent rage and despair because poor technology cripples the capacity to care for members effectively. In 1998, the authors located BUPA roughly at the X, lacking up-to-date equipment and with insufficient feeling actually reaching members in trouble.

Val Gooding's move was to invest in more customer-relevant technology, which thereby allowed more identification to be expressed, symbolized by the virtuous helix moving upward and to the right toward a reconciliation in which business systems facilitate effecting identification.

Now, this achievement has to be measurable. Gooding thinks not only in terms of offsetting measurements; she speaks of a "balanced scorecard," where gains on both axes can be monitored. BUPA measures levels of complaints and then follows up to see how the complaints were dealt with. BUPA measures health outcomes: how hospitals and surgeons have fared in curing patients, how patients benefited from surgery and how quick their recovery was, how their initial calls were dealt with, how swift appointments and diagnoses were and how soon intervention followed, and how well the patients were prepared for their ordeals by those who counselled them. But the key is never to rest content, always to ask how you can do better, and never to be deflected from the task of continuous improvement.

Dilemma 3:   Free Universal Provision vs. Allocation of Resources by Free Markets

Everything BUPA does is in the shadow of its huge state-owned neighbor, Britain's national health service (NHS), financed out of general tax revenues and dedicated to free universal provision at the point of delivery. Neither Conservative nor Labor governments choose to envisage the failure of this, the UK's most ambitious social experiment. Cradle-to-grave *entitlement* to medical care is now programmed into the British political psyche. Inevitably, the perceived effectiveness of the NHS, and the extra tax revenues pumped into it under pressure from voters as elections approach, will affect the decision to take on medical insurance. Were the NHS a perfect provider, medical insurance would be unnecessary. BUPA thus relies, to a certain extent, on the shortcomings of the state system. Under Margaret Thatcher, herself privately insured, BUPA grew apace, but the private medical insurance market has never really recovered after the recession of the early 1990s.

BUPA is having to decide whether there is a future for private health care. At the moment, the market is flat in numbers, but slightly up in value. BUPA's future is very much tied in with that of the NHS. Gooding believes, it is up to BUPA to make the market grow, by offering what the NHS and other insurers do not provide. The difficulty is that BUPA benefits from the shortcomings of the NHS – especially its long waiting lists – so people see BUPA as an alternative and hence as "opposed" to the NHS. The company cannot help being an alternative model to which people turn when the NHS is being criticized, but it does not behave in a rivalrous way, and it does everything possible to help and supplement the NHS.

In Gooding's view, BUPA acts as a valuable adjunct in several ways. When elderly people in "acute" beds are not acute any more, but are not ready to be sent home because no one is available to look after them, BUPA can provide facilities for care and convalescence that free up emergency beds. BUPA is also in a strong position to shorten NHS waiting lists, especially for routine procedures such as eye surgery for cataracts. Cataracts are progressively disabling; you can experience significant loss of vision while on the waiting list, for want of a relatively simple operation. BUPA's actuaries worry about such offers of help, since cataracts are one of the main reasons people turn to it, and so BUPA is relieving a fault that could win it many members. But Gooding is personally determined to show that BUPA *complements* the NHS, whose service would cost British taxpayers "one hell of a lot more but for the seven million people who use private health insurance" and make no claims on the NHS.

What handicaps BUPA is that the NHS is itself quite fragmented into local hospital trusts. As a result, BUPA has many local *ad hoc* arrangements with various trust hospitals, but there is no national policy that would entrust it with key support functions. BUPA would love to pilot NHS policies and spearhead its innovations, but there is no central decision making in this area.

BUPA has certainly undertaken some important initiatives. At the Bristol Royal Infirmary, patients recovering from heart surgery do so at a nearby rehabilitation unit run by BUPA and are joined by outpatients further on the road to recovery, who attend weekly physiotherapy sessions. A similar arrangement is in operation at the East Surrey NHS hospital at Redhill. Patients recuperate in a nearby BUPA facility. BUPA also takes the strain when it comes to elderly care: More than 70 percent of the residents in BUPA homes are state funded, and some would certainly have to be in NHS hospitals but for BUPA's skilled carers. In Cambridge, BUPA has a joint venture with Addenbrooke's Hospital to provide an additional MRI scanner for both NHS and BUPA patients. Training has been offered to radiographers working for the NHS in other hospitals. There are many such examples, but they are scattered, and they depend on the not always positive attitudes of trust hospitals. The private sector as a whole contributes £240 million to NHS pay beds and local authorities.

Val Gooding appears to be of two minds about whether the NHS might render private medical insurance obsolete or vice versa. One of the main arguments in favor of the NHS becoming obsolete is that massive investments, far greater than tax revenues allow, will be attracted to the health field by people becoming more used to the idea that they must provide for some of their own personal and social needs. One way this might happen could be piecemeal, with failing hospitals (like failing schools) turned around by private sector intervention. Another way is to privatize the provision side, with more and more private services brought in. Yet another route is to give employers incentives to provide health insurance, to make private health insurance tax deductible, or to provide insurance out of savings.

Why might the NHS, for all its fame and political support, be unable to continue providing comprehensive health care? For one reason: because demand rises faster than resources. Resources are finite, but demand is infinite. Already, the NHS is dependent on the private health-care market to ease an otherwise intolerable burden. Gooding points out that the private health-care market is small (in the UK) in comparison with the NHS. Six and a half million people, or 11 percent of the population, commit themselves to private health through taking out medical insurance. It is worth noting, however, that the private sector carries out 20 percent of all heart surgery and 30 percent of all hip replacements in the UK. Without it, the NHS would have another half a million surgical operations a year.

The mood of voters about paying higher taxes has not been favorable, and British state health care is inferior in its outcomes to that of most developed countries in Europe, who pay more for their health. Although Britain is pledged to close this gap, whether it can do so without losing votes through tax hikes is highly problematical. One way or the other, the private sector is likely to have to provide the answers.

Another important consideration, discussed later under Dilemma 4, is that health services under pressure are obliged to focus more and more on crisis medicine, accidents and emergencies, and life-threatening illnesses. Everything else must wait. But exclusively emergency medicine is not good medicine, failing as it does to catch the onset of preventable conditions and to help patients keep from falling ill in the first place. It is not even economic on its own terms, since the dangerously ill are expensive to treat.

Although Gooding is unsure about whether the future belongs to private medicine, currently in a 10-year lull, or to the NHS, plagued by hostile media and party politics, she has few doubts about BUPA's best strategy: to *complement* NHS services wherever possible and to join with that service in a *partnership to raise overall standards.* This is one of the key gains from competition – that standards rise and, with them, public and political expectations. That was the gist of BUPA's recent submission to the House of Commons Health Committee in January 1999. BUPA sought to raise quality, to extend regulation and monitoring, and to create clinical indicators of quality. It offered to contribute to the measurement of outcomes.

There is an underlying method in these proposals that might do more than anything else to assure the future of private health care. BUPA and other private health suppliers are in a position to use these outcomes to award contracts to health care professionals or to withhold the contracts from them, depending on the monitored quality of their services. This has always been the secret of free markets – that they reallocate funds from the least to the most successful. With information about outcomes, BUPA can *learn* who is best and what works best and move its support in the direction of those activities.

Dilemma 3 is described next. Val Gooding notes that BUPA confronts "one of the most famous mandatory health insurance systems in the world and one that has been emulated by a number of other countries. . . . It is a service in demand, more demand than it can cope with." The very existence of BUPA and other insurers is, to those who extol the NHS, a reproach and a means of siphoning off the will to maintain universal coverage.

The dilemma looks like this:

Dilemma 3.   Free Universal Provision vs. Allocation of Resources by Free Markets

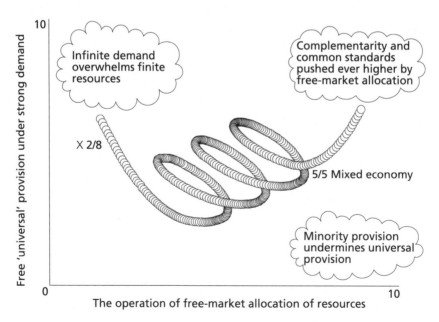

As of now, about where the X is, BUPA is with very high demand on the NHS and a relatively small, flat market for private care, where the reallocation of resources to the more competent is working on a modest scale. Gooding's strategy of complementing NHS services wherever possible and cooperating on nationally monitored standards is the "level playing field" on which BUPA then hopes to excel and to start to move resources towards successful outcomes (upper right).

The fear, of course, is that good medical service will be available only to the wealthy, who will be influential enough to make a mockery of universal provision, by voting down taxes. Somewhere in the middle is the mixed economy, which, unless it learns from its own indicators, will muddle through as a compromise solution. Whether private medical insurance proves more effective and learns faster than state sponsored medicine depends crucially on which system can best *keep people well.* It is this issue that we now turn.

Dilemma 4:   Responses to Medical Crises vs. "Wellness" as Preventative Medicine

The greater the strain on the NHS becomes, the more likely the state-sponsored system is to fall back on "crisis medicine." Those under immediate threat, whose plight can be readily publicized by the media, are bound to receive the bulk of public resources. Increasingly, the system will be geared to forestalling scandals and avoiding the expensive litigation that scandals bring. It makes sense, after all, to use limited resources for the most urgent cases.

There are other strong forces pushing toward crisis medicine. Generally speaking, medicine is rewarding to those who are most specialized and most professionally qualified therein. Disease is interesting in a way that health is not. In a system full of doctors, but without paying customers, crises get more attention than routine care. Crises evoke "heroic" interventions in a male-dominated profession and are part of the struggle of life against death, in which doctors are the field marshals.

Another good reason for crisis medicine is that it maintains the power of doctors in any conflict or dispute. If lives are at stake, the doctor's authority is supreme. If patients are flat on their backs while doctors are steady on their feet, not much argument can ensue. "Patient" comes from the Latin *pati*, to suffer. Our roles are to suffer patiently: the doctors is to decide. Recent scandals, especially at the Bristol Royal Infirmary, where the majority of children died in high-risk operations, could not have occurred without this tradition of absolute command during crises. Crisis intervention also maintains medical specialization, since one part of the body usually gives way first. Unfortunately, good overall health is not subdivided: a cure in one speciality will often cause symptoms handled by another, and you start to make your rounds of hospital departments.

The problem with focusing more and more on crisis medicine is that it loses sight of one of the mainstays of a healthy, long, and zestful life, which is to *avoid getting ill in the first place* and, if at all possible, to avoid going to the hospital, where disease entities inevitably congregate. It is for this reason that BUPA puts prime emphasis on *wellness*. Val Gooding explains that there is only one way out of this bind (posed by finite resources and infinite demand): people must take responsibility for their own health and lifestyles. By "take responsibility," she does not mean only "take out medical insurance," although that is obviously vital to BUPA. She also means taking responsibility for how you live – your diet, exercise, stress levels, and way of work – and doing the same for those one loves. BUPA is actively committed to wellness. This is not just a state of wholeness involving mind, body, and environment; wellness is an independence of living, a personal commitment to remaining able to make your own choices.

Of course, wellness is also an elusive term. Ill people have stereotypical diagnostic symptoms, which easily lend themselves to classification. In contrast, the ways of wellness are many and varied. Those who dare to describe them are easily dismissed as quacks. Those ways are liable to fashion – like most lifestyles – and easy to discredit as fashions change. The invocation to holistic health means that many different variables are included, so precision tends to suffer. BUPA's *Guide to Healthy Living* resembles a magazine supplement. Health consciousness *can*, in other hands, become narcissistic and self-indulgent.

From all these objections, however, there can be salvaged a central truth, that health grows out of personal commitments through yourself to others, especially family and coworkers. In short, health is a *stance*, not just a safety net, a demand, an entitlement guaranteed by government – not even just a restorative, to be used when your lifestyle has let you down. Health begins, paradoxically, with a determination *not* to suffer patiently, but instead to engage, while on your feet, those who can help prevent illness in the first place. It is there that BUPA is strong and the NHS is woefully weak. Indeed, in a curious way, a crisis bureaucracy *needs* you to be helpless. Instead of rewarding those who rise above their condition, systems based on welfare psychology tend to punish such fitness. Hence, a seven-year old amputee and sufferer from meningitis hopped on his remaining leg with such cheerfulness and energy that he was nominated for a Child of Courage Award; yet the Child Benefits agency has stopped his £369 mobility allowance, leaving his single mother without a car to supervise his hopping. Welfare and crisis systems have difficulty working *with* the process of recovery rather than against it. The system provides incentives that prolong crises.

BUPA started its sixth business unit, Wellness, in 1999, to provide services to both personal and corporate customers. The unit combined a new acquisition, Barbican Healthcare, with BUPA's existing health screening and occupational health activities, providing health assessments and screening at over 50 medical facilities around the United Kingdom. Up-to-date screening devices include a bone-density scanner, able to detect early signs of osteoporosis (in which bones become brittle and break easily), the cardiorespiratory exercise bike test, and a resting EKG. Over 60,000 people have had problems detected in time for early treatment.

It is perhaps in the corporate sector that the greatest opportunities lie. It should not be too difficult to prove that employees who share a vision, an exciting strategy, or a super ordinate goal have better reasons for reporting to work every day and work more creatively as a result. For health is, above all, a state of mind. Those who can locate themselves in a context of meaning that transcends their own lives have that much more to live for.

You can start modestly with occupational health and then add, one by one, the variables that make a difference. You might well end up with a corporation, not unlike BUPA, in which case the model you seek to build is already within you. You begin with "saving on absenteeism" and end with the meanings of work itself, and the more meanings you find, the healthier and more effective the workplace becomes.

The two axes of Dilemma 4 are *Responses to Medical Crises* and. *"Wellness"*

Dilemma 4.   Responses to Medical Crises vs. "Wellness" as Preventative Medicine

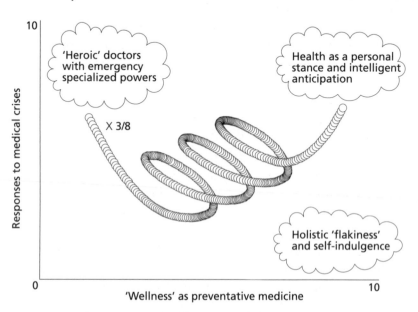

as Preventative Medicine. Britain is currently biased towards responding to crises – hence the location of the X.

It is important, when moving from BUPA's position at the top left, not to fall into the trap either of health fads *or* of believing that your mental state can "conquer" all illness. The right response to crises, which we all face before we die, is intelligent anticipation of inevitable failings. You do not ignore crises; you act to preclude and delay them. That is why the helix is counter-clockwise: first prevention, and then a timely response that escapes the worst. Health is a stance that invites your body to sustain you until necessary activities are complete.

Dilemma 5: Nationally Based Services vs. Globally Expanded Services

A final reason that either the personal or the group insurance model might prevail is that the world of medicine, although slower to globalize than other industries, is at last doing so. While the National Health Service, concentrates on the mandate to serve British citizens and tourists at a price, BUPA is engaged in some 180 countries across the world. It can mobilize world resources at the behest of its members, and many of those members are foreigners to the United Kingdom. Val Gooding is articulate on the subject.

> Globalization is upon us. There are giant health insurers 'out there,' and before too long, our members will be able to purchase their operations anywhere, while the members of other insurers will buy them from us. Already there are people flying to India for cataract operations, because even with the airfare, it costs less. Waiting lists are shorter in France, and UK patients could attempt to make appointments there. When the Internet gets properly utilized, there will be a giant market for various procedures, and Europe, which outspends the UK on health, is sure to attract many customers.

She goes on to say that BUPA is importing more nurses from overseas and once again, it has the advantage of its existing foreign contacts and operations. The weakness of the NHS is in ancillary staff and those able to look after the frail, not necessarily the ill. BUPA hopes to be able to remedy skill shortages by importing key staff in various fields.

BUPA International recently undertook an £8.5 million relaunch, including a Web site with on-line price quotations and with enrollment and claims forms for brokers. Bill Ward, general manager of BUPA International, made the following pledge: "Wherever you are in the world, whatever time of day, we are seven seconds away, and we will deliver on our promise. If you're in trouble, we will get you out." BUPA now has four million customers worldwide and assesses 4,000 requests a week from 180 countries. Much of the international coverage is via multinational businesses, concerned about getting expatriates home in emergencies. Even so, there are 115 nationalities among BUPA members, and there are many foreign companies with activities in the UK. Since 1989, BUPA has owned Sanitas in Spain, with 830,000 insurance customers and a capacity for 135,000 accident-and-emergency admissions. A joint venture with the Primal Group in Mumbai (Bombay) runs a health-care-services clinic in that city. There is an insurance joint venture with the Nazer Group in Saudi Arabia, and BUPA health-insurance companies exist in Thailand and Hong Kong.

Crucial to a global health system is "telematics," the means for communicating medical information between countries and hospitals and for obtaining readouts of members' medical histories. Telematics will allow procedures to be carried out safely in many parts of the world and will bring prices down through competitive tendering. If it plays its cards right, BUPA should be able to capitalize on some of these opportunities.

Dilemma 5. Nationally Based Services vs. Globally Expanded

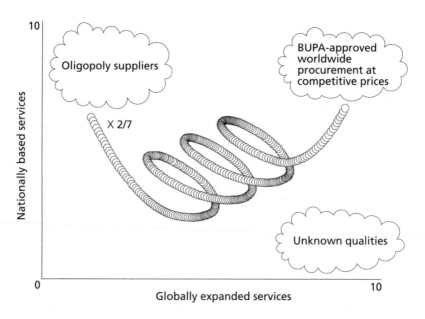

The problem as of now is the relatively few (oligopolistic) suppliers for highly specialized British-based procedures. Hence, in the diagram of Dilemma 5, we have located BUPA as of 1998 at the X. The strategy, as the authors understand it, is to expand services globally, while avoiding the purchase of items of unknown quality by means of rating procedures available via the Internet and by approving only the best and most reliable suppliers. Competition should make prices fall, and members could be offered the most appropriate procedures.

Dilemma 6:   For-profit Status vs. Nonprofit Status

There is much ongoing speculation about whether "care" should or even could be effectively delivered by those seeking to make profits therefrom – profits that match rising returns, increasingly common in the UK stock martket. Should a "care home" yield 25 percent profit to shareholders and have to compete with high-tech stocks and Internet companies "to make a killing"? When the customer is very old and frail or when investments in facilities take several years to pay off, some other corporate form would seem preferable to the shareholder-driven private company. For this very reason, BUPA has no shareholders, but is a *provident association*, an interesting hybrid, hovering between "for-profit" and "nonprofit" status. It differs from a for-profit company by having no shareholders to demand their cut, as a price for not raiding the company. But this condition does not mean that surpluses are not generated and cannot be reinvested in making the company more provident still. In fact, BUPA is well positioned to acquire other companies in part *because* it has no shareholders to pay off and can use *all* its surplus to expand and acquire. Nor is there any reason that BUPA cannot feature profitability or surpluses among its principal goals. Unlike the members of mutual societies, BUPA's members are *not* its owners, so the company is free to invest where it chooses. Val Gooding regards provident status as a strong advantage, at least if she can furnish the stimulus for growth and risk that would otherwise come from shareholders. She explains that her problem has been how to get the sense of urgency and constant striving for improvement that shareholders often bring. BUPA can plough *everything* it earns into new investments, provided that the will is there and that the firm is determined to proceed along commercial lines. That is where she deems her predecessor so valuable. It did not always make him popular, but he turned BUPA into an organization that aimed to generate surpluses in order to succeed and to expand.

In a provident association, the customer is unambiguously the top priority, and because it takes high staff morale to keep customers happy, employees become the means of satisfying customers. Furthermore, a provident association can invest for the long term; BUPA has made investments in upgrading equipment and call centers that will take 10 years to justify themselves. Most stock companies, having impatient shareholders, cannot do that, which is why several in the elderly care businesses recently quit. The short-term pressures on them were simply too great.

It takes time to build a genuine reputation for caring, but, as a provident association, BUPA can afford to take time to win customers and make that caring pay. But it's not all plain sailing. Provident companies can be laid back, lazy, risk averse, and self-congratulatory about their noble intentions. BUPA's board has to take the role usually played by shareholders: to set targets, provide incentives. and get people to stretch their capacities. Yet Gooding can't do it with stock options, because BUPA has no stock. Therefore, she has to create a culture second to none, a place where people want to stay and to which they choose to give their working lives.

The dilemma looks like this.

Dilemma 6. For-profit Status vs. Nonprofit Status

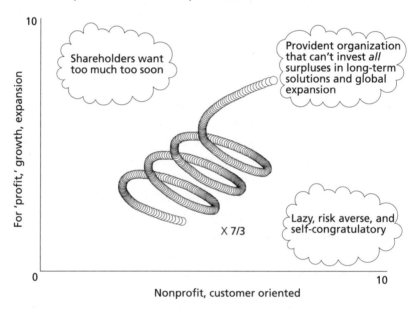

Val Gooding has taken BUPA from roughly the vicinity of the X, as a company that is somewhat risk averse and too noble of intention to try hard to succeed, into a company eager to grow as fast as its success allows, with no need to pause for private enrichment, but dedicated to worldwide customers and willing to invest in its long-term welfare. It is a vision of capitalism serving social ends in which the human meaning of the work is its own reward and all join in celebrating the one life we have in common.

Sadly, Val Gooding is the only woman leader with a chapter in this book. Women leaders will not, the authors' in view, ever "make it" by being exclusively kind, gentle, and compassionate. Business is too predatory. But they will and can succeed by reconciling hard and soft, by possessing and expressing an iron will, and by exerting a relentless push to care deeply and sincerely for their customers. Val Gooding has toughened her compassion with hoops of steel, and she has brought closer the day when "nice gals finish first."

With what results?

The 1990s were a mixed decade for BUPA, but since Gooding's arrival, things have been looking up. By 1999, the company turned a profit, staff morale had soared, and BUPA had hit the acquisition trail. The firm's newspaper, *BUPA TODAY*, carried the following editorial from Val Gooding.

"We have seen the first-quarter results for 2000, and we are on course to meet the challenging targets we have set for this year. . . . Profits are up and there is no dividend to be paid. I was able to tell the annual general meeting that, through the hard work of our people, all BUPA business units are doing well in their markets."

CHAPTER 10

Pioneering the New Organization

Leader: Jim Morgan (Applied Materials)

Fons Trompenaars was fortunate enough to be invited to the Applied Materials Quarterly Global Management Meeting in Palo Alto, California, in 1997. Applied Materials is the world's largest manufacturer of semiconductor-producing equipment, the machines that make the circuits. It is also the most transcultural company we have yet encountered, a microcosm of world cultures. The authors have a broad experience of American "global" companies; many are American at the core and foreign only at the fringes. Even when group photographs are taken, the foreigners somehow gravitate to the edges of the picture; the beards and darker countenances surround the paler center. Here, however, everything was different. The core management team spoke English in a variety of accents. President Dan Mayden was an Israeli scientist. Chairman Jim Morgan was an American business executive. Korean and Japanese officials were prominent. In all, the top fifty managers represented 30 different nations.

So we sought an interview with Jim Morgan, chairman and CEO. We wanted to know what it feels like to bestride such high degrees of global diversity. How does one lead such a mosaic of nations, such a cosmopolitan mix of talent? What he had to tell us is described under the following heads:

1.   the history of Applied Materials
2.   the transcultural reach of Applied Materials
3.   what Applied Materials learned from East Asian cultures, and the resulting core values
4.   a value-driven corporation
5.   reconciling eight paradoxes

(a) Errors and Corrections
(b) Extensive Participation with Satisfied Customers; Quick Decisions and High Efficiency
(c) Excellent Technology and Effective Production Outcomes
(d) Local Fit and Global Reach
(e) Stable Continuity and Flexible Change
(f) Growing Bigger, yet Remaining Small
(g) Leaping Up and Diving Down

1. The History of Applied Materials

Think about it – we touch almost everyone's life. Every time you log onto a PC, surf the Internet, send an e-mail, or make a cell phone call, you use technology made possible by Applied Materials' chip-making equipment. Applied Materials makes the systems, that make the chips, that make the products, that change the world; that's why we say, "The Information Age Starts Here."

When Applied Materials was founded in 1967 in Santa Clara, it started with five employees and a little over $100,000. Companies in the budding semiconductor industry preferred to build their own manufacturing equipment in-house and treated their systems as proprietary, so Applied Materials started by supplying them with materials and components for their homegrown systems. The problem with those systems, however, was that no two were alike – or performed alike – yet, in semiconductor manufacturing, uniformity and reliability are essential. Seizing the opportunity, the founders of Applied Materials began offering turnkey chip-making systems with performance guarantees based on rigorous testing in the company's own laboratory. It led to more standardization of the manufacturing process, which revolutionized the semiconductor industry.

The strategy paid off. By 1972 the company was shipping systems to every major semiconductor manufacturer in the open markets of the world. That year, with sales of $6.3 million and 155 employees, Applied Materials, Inc., made its first public stock offering.

During the 1970s, Applied Materials continued to broaden its markets and diversify its product line, stretching its resources dangerously thin. As the new CEO of the company in 1977, James C. Morgan refocused Applied Materials on its core business: semiconductor manufacturing equipment. The timing was just right.

In 1980 Dr. Dan Maydan joined the company from the prestigious AT&T Bell

Laboratories. Following him were Drs. Sasson Somekh and David N. K. Wang. This trio developed and commercialized many successful innovations, beginning with the Precision Etch 8100 and 8300 Hexode Etchers. In 1987 the company marked its twentieth anniversary with what industry observers hailed as "the most successful product introduction in the history of the semiconductor equipment industry": the first of the Precision 5000® series of single-wafer, multichamber processing systems. In 1989 Applied Materials reported annual revenues of over $500 million, and in 1990 the company broke into the ranks of the Fortune 500. On March 3, 1993, the first-built Applied Materials Precision 5000 was inducted into the Smithsonian Institution's permanent collection of Information Age technology, next to the first transistor and the first semiconductor chip.

In 1992 Applied Materials became the top semiconductor-equipment manufacturer in the world. It has held that position ever since. In support of manufacturing efforts, the Austin Volume Manufacturing Center became the volume manufacturing site for the company. With over one million square feet of dedicated manufacturing space, the site produces nearly 90 percent of the company's products. In further recognition of the company and its leadership, James C. Morgan, Chairman and Chief Executive Officer, was the recipient of the 1996 National Medal of Technology, America's highest honor for technological innovation, awarded by the President of the United States.

Distinction is also given to the company through frequent rankings as a well-managed organization and an employer of choice. *Fortune* magazine rates Applied Materials as one of America's most admired companies, as well as one of the 50 best companies for the employment of Asians, Blacks, and Hispanics. *Fortune* also highlights Applied Materials as one of the 100 best companies to work for in America. Today, the Company's worldwide sales, service, manufacturing, and tech-nology-development capabilities remain unrivalled in the semiconductor-equipment industry. Forecasts indicate that the markets it serves will continue to develop into the next millennium. Applied Materials is positioned to grow right along with those markets.

2. The Transcultural Reach of Applied Materials

In addition to corporate facilities in Santa Clara, California, Applied Materials maintains research, development, and manufacturing centers in the United States, Israel, Europe, and Japan, as well as technology centers in South Korea and Taiwan. To support a growing worldwide customer base, sales and service offices are located in the United States, Europe, Israel, Japan, South Korea, Taiwan, Singapore, and the People's Republic of China.

In 1997, Applied Materials entered the metrology and inspection market by acquiring Opal, Inc., and Orbot Instruments in Israel and integrated them into its Process Diagnostics and Control Group. AKT in Japan (formerly a joint venture with Komatsu), which produces fabrication systems for flat-panel displays, has been fully owned by Applied Materials since 1999. Applied Materials employs 13,000 people worldwide in more than 95 locations in 14 countries. Financial highlights for fiscal year 1998 show net orders of $3.1 billion, revenue of $4.0 billion, net income of $230.9 million, and ongoing net income of $437 million. Investment in research, development, and engineering for 1998 was $643.9 million.

Applied Materials' 1998 worldwide sales demonstrate its global capability: North America sales yielded 38 percent of its revenue; Japan, 17 percent; Taiwan, 20 percent; Europe, 16 percent; South Korea, 4 percent; and Asia–Pacific (China and Singapore), 5 percent.

3. What Applied Materials Learned from East Asian Cultures and the Resulting Core Values

The first foreign market that Applied Materials engaged with and learned from was Japan. At the time, Japan was *the* major threat to US economic hegemony, at once the culture most different from that of America *and* the most successful among those of East Asia. Since the 1980s, the threat from Japan is somewhat less, but that from the Chinese diaspora (Singapore, Hong Kong, Malaysia, Taiwan, etc.) is considerably greater. Morgan is not just a CEO, but an author. He wrote *Cracking the Japanese Market* in 1991 with his son Jeff Morgan and has since switched his focus to the burgeoning economies of East Asia generally.

Globalizing should, ideally, start with those cultures most *unlike* your own. If a US company can "crack" the way those cultures think, despite the fact that their views are virtually the logical opposites of its own, then differences found in Europe, the Indian subcontinent, Latin America, and the Middle East are unlikely to shake the company's composure. Japan, a culture the early Jesuit missionaries deemed "devilish" on account of its contrariness to their own views, is an acid test of cross-cultural sophistication. If you make it in Japan, much of the rest of the world will hold fewer challenges in comparison.

Scores obtained by using the TH-T data base for the United States, Canada, and Northwest Europe on the one hand and for Japan, Singapore, Hong Kong, China, and Malaysia on the other hand are summarized in Box 1, Chapter 1, for all of our seven dimensions detailed in Chapters 1 and 2. It can be seen at a glance that the scores for most of the world fall between the scores of the United States and Japan. To "crack Japan" was not simply to come to terms with America's foremost competitor, but to span some of the widest cultural divergences on record.

Morgan's book is perhaps the most insightful account of Japan written by a working foreign executive. He likens the Japanese market to the *fugu*, or blowfish, a delicacy served at only a few select Japanese restaurants, which have been licenced by the government to prepare it for eating. The reason for this is that the blowfish has poison-secreting glands which must be carefully removed before cooking and serving. If you do not know the fish well, you can do yourself great harm. If you know and understand it, you derive great benefit. Morgan sees *fugu* as a metaphor for the impact of Japanese culture on American corporations.

"*Fugu* can be used as a symbol for the Japanese market," he explains. "When approached properly, it is a market that offers great opportunity for wealth, but, approached improperly and without care, a venture in Japan can prove ruinous." Applied Materials's Japanese adventure began as early as 1979. In those early days, it was a relatively small company ($42.6 million in sales), the first wholly foreign-owned company to secure funding from Japanese Development Bank. But once the company was in, the momentum was unstoppable: Applied Materials rode the wave of Japan's eighties economic miracle, leading the huge expansion of the electronics sector, which spear-headed and underpinned that nation's prodigious record of growth.

Finding himself at the very center of Japan's catch-up strategy, playing a crucial part in the effectiveness of chip manufacturers nationally, Morgan and Applied Materials received a crash course in what it meant to be an insider, working within government "guidance" in producing chips, "the rice of industry," to the highest possible specification, in order to create "mechatronics," the fusion of mechanical with electrical engineering. Morgan learned, for example, that instead of the customer "coming first" or being "always right," *the customer was God*. Morgan had a bond of trust and service not just with specified chip producers, but with *their* customers and with Japanese chip users as a whole. As a typical "horizontal technology" (a technology cutting across the economy as a whole and used in many industries), chips constituted the infrastructure of the economy itself, the yeast in the rapid rise of the economic cake.

Morgan observes, "The Japanese use the word *anshin* (trust from the heart) to describe the type of relationship they want to have with their suppliers and business partners. . . . Vendors are loyal to their customer, and in return, they receive loyalty back. Japanese customers are much more demanding in terms of expectations of quality, service, and delivery schedules. The relationship is an ongoing process of problem-solving and opportunity creation. What Japanese look for in a supplier is the strength of the company that makes its personal history and track record." Whereas in the United States a customer will typically run suppliers against each other and create a relationship with the winner, in Japan you first create the relationship and then pressure your partner to turn in a winning performance. This pattern is common in East Asia, Southern Europe, and Latin America.

Morgan explains how Applied Materials used its Japanese experience to cement relations throughout the world: "We have since used the relationship model to build relationships with other customers throughout the world. Applied Materials has been successful by globalizing what we've learned from competing in Japan." Applied Materials also learned from its Japanese experiences to improve its relationships with its own suppliers. Part of this is the notion that it is the customer's responsibility to help the supplier achieve excellence. The Trompenaars Hampden-Turner group, responsible for this book, has benefited from Applied Materials's relationship philosophy. Morgan is thinking of a new book, called *Cracking the Asian Market*, detailing how the lessons learned in Japan can be applied more widely, especially in China's huge market.

South Korea was another crucial lesson for Morgan and for Applied Materials. In some respects, South Korea outdoes Japanese expectations. For example, South Koreans expect discounts from list prices for their own "particular" company, a variation of Universalism (same price for everyone) and Particularism (special price for friends). Koreans also expect free service and training support until the machines supplied are being used effectively. If you have not factored these costs into your initial offer, you are in trouble. Applied Materials Korea (AMK) sold only two or three machines during its initial sales pitch, but it sold hundreds once it had figured out how to offer discounts and give support. Between them, just two South Korean companies, Hyundai and Samsung, produce 40 percent of all DRAMS sold on world markets. It pays more to get close to them than to anyone else! South Korea's export of semiconductors has passed $20 billion semiconductors and are their single biggest export product.

In East Asia, relationships last a lifetime, and when a local economy is in trouble, you discover who your friends really are. During the Japanese recession of 1985–1986, employees of Applied Materials Japan (AMJ) were assigned to more prospering regions of the globe instead of being laid off or dismissed. In the Korean recession of 1998, this pattern was repeated. Furthermore, Young I. Lee, President of AMK, avoided many layoffs by increasing training and development budgets. A time of slack demand was an opportunity to learn as well as to bounce back from the recession with renewed vigor.

It did not take long for Morgan to discover that foreign companies in East Asia, especially firms from the West, had a reputation as fair-weather friends, so he determined that Applied Materials would be different. Semiconductors are not a product for on-again, off-again investment. East Asians continue with these products, even during times of loss, because electronics undergirds industry in general and renders more profitable any product with an advanced chip inside it. East Asian economies therefore continue to make semiconductors for the leverage this gives to all their industries and do not insist that every product pay for itself.

Applied Materials's work is therefore essential to these entire economies, and it is crucial that the company be seen as a rock of reliability and a steadfast ally of Korea, Japan, Singapore, and the other Asian Tigers, as well as of the companies actually involved. Morgan hates to see them making chips at a loss and tries to reward their persistence by steadily increasing quality and decreasing costs. He can make these heroic efforts because the mutuality of commitments is so strong.

"We try to do a good job so that they do not feel the pressure to [manufacture at no profit]. That's why we put so much emphasis on being a local company and a loyal friend, a committed supplier who hangs in there in good times and bad. With our global view, our low cost structure, and our breadth of technical understanding, we can really help them."

4. A Value-Driven Corporation

Morgan sees the company as driven by values, certain attributes that grow stronger and stronger over time and are subject to continuous increase, and by paradoxes requiring resolution, which we address in the next section. Here we will deal with the values that power Applied Materials's global success.

Applied Materials, Morgan insists, must *demonstrate world class performance in everything it does."* But that is possible only if Applied Materials *keeps very close to the customer*, who defines what its "performance" must accomplish and whether it has been delivered. A final value is *practicing mutual trust and respect* in a world of multiple sources of expertise. Applied Materials has to be good so that its customers can produce superlative products, so that the industries using those semiconductors in turn can succeed. Applied Materials's own success depends upon the success of those it supplies, on the success of the customer's customer's customer. Mutual trust and respect is what integrates the improving performances of all suppliers and customers, who succeed in combination, not separately. Applied Materials strives continually to adopt the principle of carefully listening to one another to try to understand different perspectives.

The aim of the Total Solutions approach is to provide a "total solution" to the customer's problems – one that can then be used by the customer to focus on its own customers. "We strive to walk the talk of these values every day, in our Total Solutions approach, to systematically meet our customers' needs worldwide. In 1998 our team focused like a laser beam on leveraging every one of our assets to the benefit of our customers, through Total Solutions. At Applied Materials, Total Solutions is expressed in our innovation, product line breadth, equipment productivity, human and intellectual capital, and global service and support."

Asked what characteristics his company would need in the twenty-first century, Morgan answered at length: "In the twenty-first century and the evolving Internet economy, leadership companies will have to develop a core set of success characteristics to survive and win. Let's consider some of these elements. First, you will have to be global. Applied Materials led the way in going global, because we realized early on that the Information Age had no borders. This revolution is about borders and walls falling down, to enable the free flow of ideas, people, and capital. So, while many companies, including some much larger than us, are just now grappling with globalization and all that that entails, we've been global for decades.

"Second, you must be lean and fast. The accelerating pace of change, particularly in our industry , and the unpredictability of markets means there is less time for correcting errors and no time for hesitation; and, because narrow windows of opportunity are open only briefly, you can't let yourself be too heavy to squeeze through.

"Third, in the Internet economy, you must be knowledgebased. This means unlocking and using all the knowledge that resides within your team and your global organization. At Applied Materials, we're working full time to connect all the centers of excellence we've already developed . . . in product, support, and regional organizations. Further, we are linking to our customers and to our suppliers to help them and to help Applied Materials. The goal is to build an Internet-fast knowledge organization that uses all its global knowledge to meet customer needs.

"This leads me to a subject I'm going to be talking about in this millennium. As we change the world, and the world changes around us – as change accelerates and markets move faster – our products must move from imagination to production in ever-shorter time frames. In the Internet economy of the twenty-first century, business success will depend on a company's ability to demonstrate leadership in times of change – the ability to thrive on unceasing waves of change and the ability to both manage and capitalize on rapid change. The new global economy offers both unparalleled market opportunity and risk. As Asia's boom and gloom have shown us, the global market can be rich and volatile. Driven by the instant information of the Internet, the global economy rewards speed, resilience, and, most of all, courage. In this new world, where capital, information, and goods flow almost friction free, the old rules of the physical economy apply less and less.

"Leadership companies in the fast new global economy will need to compete on speed, innovation, and differentiation. Those organizations which can't keep up, and which aren't creative, will have to compete primarily on cost. The upending of the old physical economy means that many economies that once competed from regional strongholds or on brand loyalty will find themselves in a commodity gulag. Meanwhile, fast innovators will rewrite the rules. To avoid this pit, leadership companies will work to ensure that they are high-change companies in high-change industries. In the fast new economy now being born, you will want to work for, partner with, and invest in companies with the ability to change, adapt and grow – leveraging their fundamental strengths to take advantage of new opportunities. These companies will succeed because they have clear vision, a focused mission, shared values, an ability to deal with dilemmas and paradoxes, and a sense of unfolding history."

It is to these paradoxes and dilemmas that we now turn.

Reconciling Seven Paradoxes

Errors vs. Corrections

In a world where speed is crucial, you cannot wait to get everything right the first time. Fast learning involves pouncing on mistakes and improving fast. It involves reclassifying what was acceptable last month as unacceptable this month and doing better. Errors never go away, because the bar keeps rising and because you keep trying new things to see what works better. Another reason for being close to "godlike" customers is that you need their feedback to improve rapidly.

The successful corporation of the twenty-first century, according to Morgan, "will foster a culture that is resilient in the face of setbacks, [a quality that] also rewards success. They encourage taking risks and they forgive failure, because mistakes will be inevitable in the new world. People will require emotional intelligence to survive disappointment and then rally quickly in the face of tough times. In a market of ideas, some will work spectacularly and some won't. It takes courage to live with your mistakes so as to transcend them and move on, learning as you go."

This dilemma can be drawn as follows:

Dilemma 1. Learning Fast through Mistakes

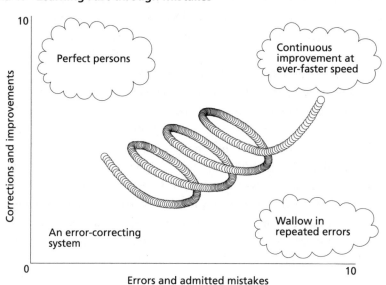

W. Edwards Deming, an American consultant largely vindicated by Japanese auto manufacturers, showed how to set up error correcting systems of continuous improvement and ever-rising standards. Every error is an opportunity to improve, rather than the cause of shame or disgrace. People must be empowered to monitor and improve themselves, reflecting on their work and rethinking it. No one can be a perfect person (upper left on the diagram) first time around, and there is insufficient time even to attempt this. At the same time, you should not wallow in repeated errors (lower right). The idea is *not* to make the same mistake twice, but to *learn*. We tend to learn fastest by making smaller and smaller mistakes, successively approximating to an ideal. This process is not without pain, and emotional tensions are strong, but beyond this tension lies the capacity to improve continuously and even to redefine "improvement."

Extensive Participation with Satisfied Customers; Quick Decision and High Efficiency

The ideal of rapid decision making has almost a military flavor. When danger abounds, when emotions run high, when panic is a potential hazard, the clear voice of authority from field headquarters helps forge an army into a fighting weapon. There is no time for debate or hesitation. If decisions are delayed by even a matter of seconds, the day may be lost. Controversy is tantamount to indecision. Argument, in its power to sap morale, can amount to treachery.

Fortunately, or unfortunately, the design and supply of machines for making semiconductors is on a level of complexity much higher than that of most battlefields. Moreover, those at the top do not have all the necessary information and have goals more elusive than winning at the expense of an opponent. They have to create multiple winners, not force losses on an adversary. You cannot help someone else "win" unless you know what their problems are and what their customers' problems are. The Total Solutions emphasized by Morgan are for the satisfaction of multiple players. Inevitably, these players must be consulted widely and must participate in decisions. So how do you make quick decisions, while consulting and participating widely with interested parties? How do you maintain outstanding efficiency, while still satisfying multiple customers?

It certainly is not easy, but it is possible. The first point to grasp is that, although customers have many, varied concerns, the same themes recur: they *all* need to be as efficient and cost containing as they can. Morgan explains

"We work for some of the best companies in the world: Intel, Samsung, IBM, and so on; companies like these are increasingly looking to us to take a more active role in the totality of the manufacturing process, because they trust us. With our global capabilities and their global reach, they continue to offer us more and more opportunities." Applied Materials's industry is changing as the twenty-first century dawns. "First, chipmaking is increasingly process intensive: more circuits, more layers, more fabrication steps. As the semiconductor industry evolves toward future generations of smaller devices, using new materials like copper and larger wafer sizes, our customers will demand that we provide a broader set of innovative solutions that add increased value. Worldwide, chip demand is growing, so more fabs are being built. One of the top priorities for chipmakers – our customers – is to maximize the return on their existing capital investments and to contain operating costs. Applied Materials is committed to leading the way– and rightly so."

That particular solutions have been devised for other customers makes all Applied Materials's customers concerned about staying abreast of developments. To lead, or even survive, in chipmaking, you must have up-to-date fabrication equipment, at least as good as your competitors'. "Because Applied Materials has the largest number of installed systems in the world, it represents a global standard of which customers dare not fall short. In an industry where the sale of a hundred systems is a major milestone, we recently celebrated the installation of the 5000th Precision 5000 system. Applied Materials systems reside in virtually every production fab in the world."

Customers have a huge stake in the equipment already installed in their fabs. "Therefore, we are making an all-out commitment to protecting our customers' sizeable investment in our family of advanced products. . . . Perhaps the most significant issue our industry [is facing] is the changing relationship between chipmakers and equipment makers. Given the scale of their opportunity and the speed at which they must perform, our customers are increasingly focusing on their core capabilities as their key source of advantage. They bear down on chip design, architecture, and engineering, and they look to us for solutions in the manufacturing process. Our history shows that, over time, customers have asked equipment companies to take responsibility for more and more aspects of the chip-making process, thus increasing our market. And today we see that trend accelerating. In effect, we are becoming process partners in the business of chipmaking.

"This is the most fundamental and important shift in the past 30 years of our industry. With the pressures they are under to perform and compete, chipmakers today can afford – and should expect – no less than total solutions from their process partners. First, you must provide a set of unique process solutions. Second, make systems that work reliably, and back them up around the world. Third, design compatible products that work together and can be integrated. Fourth, invest mightily in leading-edge capabilities to keep solving new customer problems. In short, Total Solution products are unique, cost effective, compatible, and, increasingly, integratable. And they are fully supported on a worldwide basis for maximum uptime performance. We have been the first to recognize what our customers need in this most dynamic, demanding, and fluid of markets – and the first to offer solutions to them."

The dilemma or paradox that Morgan is describing can be diagrammed as shown on the following page.

Applied Materials moves from consulting widely among top world competitors to designing Total Solutions that will upgrade the race in general. Given its ready access to the most creative chip designers in the world, the company has unprecedented and unmatched levels of knowledge about how global competition is shaping up – about who is winning and why. You cannot create a machine for fabricating a superchip without knowing its design, purpose, and performance. Hence, Applied Materials has a grandstand view of the race for global supremacy in different forms of chipmaking. It is in the position of a coach helping most of the contestants in a race and is even virtually the race organizer, who provides the contestants with their equipment. It is as if many competing vehicles in the Grand Prix or Indy 500 had the same constructor and were competing for his time and attention. Applied Materials is in a *very* strong position.

Dilemma 2. Organizing the Race

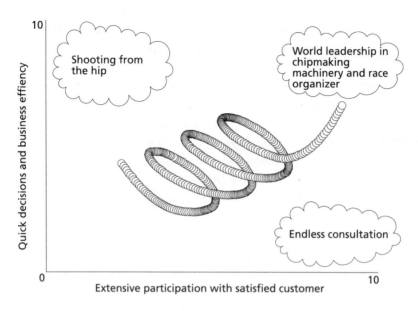

Its high level of extensive participation is what *informs* the company's swift decision making and what upgrades the efficiency of its machines. Because chips can be designed *for* cheaper and higher-quality manufacturing, Applied Materials soon becomes an expert on design and a consultant on manufacturability. The real secret of combining participation with decision making and consultation with efficiency is *leadership*. Having consulted widely, you discover who and what is best, and you learn that key performance standards, which you make your own, lead the industry.

Excellent Technology and Effective Production Outcomes

From a strictly legal point of view, Applied Materials supplies the technologies of manufacture to customer specifications. If customers misuse, misunderstand, or misapply that technology, thereby failing to derive full benefit from it, that could be considered *their* look out, but Applied Materials does not operate that way. Its responsibility does not end with world-class technology or even a conceptual solution. It ends when customers can use their new equipment to the limit of its powers. Applied Materials has completed its success only when the customer has achieved a successful production outcome and the fab is up and running with a record high yield (the proportion of silicon not wasted). This is necessary because billion-dollar fabs are involved, capable of catastrophic loss or soaring success. Because chips are themselves the intelligence in several hundred varieties of product, it might well be that nothing less than national economic priorities and strategies is at stake. If the chip fails, so does "the food chain" for countless products. Chips are a "catalytic" technology, the secret ingredient that transforms a product's value by rendering it responsive to its environment and capable of communicating information.

It is necessary to distinguish product innovation from process innovation. If a product is innovative, it might have to be manufactured in a new way, and that can vitiate its value; but even if the *product* is not new, an innovative way of *manufacturing* it can give a substantial cost advantage. Process innovation involving the reduction in a number of manufacturing steps is one of East Asia's principal advantages. Applied Materials concentrates on Total Solutions that actually work *in situ*. As Morgan puts it, "Our customers have voted for our solutions by making us the leader in etch, metallization, thermal processes, chemical mechanical polishing, and installed base support services and by supporting our efforts in emerging markets. In our industry, it takes quite a time to develop a new technology, and we are trusted for that persistence by our customer partners in business. Applied Materials's success is very much based on our ability to translate these developments into operations, and we were better able than many of our competitors to commercialize it."

The dilemma that is resolved is as follows:

Dilemma 3. Responsibility for Outcomes

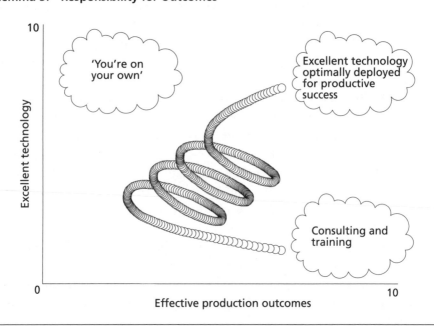

We see from the diagram that it is not enough to supply superb equipment that operates to specifications. You and your customer assume joint responsibility for how well that equipment works and the outcome it achieves. The customer has to be able to exploit innovation, not just be in receipt of it, and to make the whole system operational is an aim to which Applied Materials is dedicated.

This is similar to the Specific–Diffuse distinction introduced in Chapter 1. The excellence of the machinery has been specified in advance and either meets or fails to meet those specifications. But *actually making the machinery work* is a much broader, more diffuse process, including person–machine interfaces and effective human adaptation to new work routines. Customers feel genuinely supported when Applied Materials's acceptance of responsibility extends to jointly determined outcomes.

Local Fit and Global Reach

How does Applied Materials succeed in constantly extending its global reach, while simultaneously improving its local fit? Can a company be sufficiently diverse to solve each region's particular problems and at the same time pursue a global strategy of offering the best to all comers? One answer is to have powerful regional influences. Young I. Lee, head of Applied Materials Korea, showed his courage early in life by crossing the Demilitarized Zone (DMZ) between North and South Korea on his own as a young man. Very much a national celebrity, he has attracted top talent to work for AMK. AM Japan has been similarly fortunate in attracting strong local leadership, not always available to foreign companies in Japan. It is Applied Materials's key strategic importance in regional chipmaking policies that attracts top talent to the company.

Applied Materials's attitude toward the various countries in which it is engaged is that every country has something to contribute, and lessons to teach, to the wider global community. You learn "chipmaking as infrastructure transformation" from East Asia, as well as the pursuit by whole nations of greater knowledge intensity – an old Mandarin value. (China had a civil service chosen *on merit,* through written exams, four centuries after Christ.)

The Israeli semiconductor industry is among the most innovative in the world, so that what is "local" to Israel today could be "global" only a few years hence. Every new development has to start *somewhere*, and it is through this diversity of "somewheres" that Applied Materials keeps ahead of its competitors and in touch with new departures. With the acquisition of Opal and Orbot in 1996, Applied Materials has direct access to Israeli R&D. Morgan observed, "We learned so much in Japan and now apply it in all other, much less complex corners of our business. I think Israel comes in a good second in complexity."

Imitating Japan and Korea does not mean that America has got it wrong; it means that there might be one strategy for early-developing, pioneer economies like Britain and the United States and quite another for a late-developing, catch-up economy. Certainly, semiconductors and electronics are major targets for catch-up economies. Applied Materials's aim is to be effective in the circumstances faced by different kinds of economies, using different strategies for fast economic development. The chip world is in a "learning race" mentored by Applied Materials.

We asked Morgan how he had developed his broad cultural tastes and his appreciation for diversity. "It might have to do with my early managerial and business exposure," he answered. "I was working as a manager in the seasonal food and agriculture business. I had to supervise people twice my age, and I taught myself two important lessons. First, never judge people on their age, gender, or racial background, but only on how they add value. Second, look at how individuals fit into larger teams. Complementarity is of utmost importance. That is perhaps why I have a management team of so much diversity. I learned how to make tough decisions when being young, around those crucial issues."

This brings us to a crucial issue in reconciling globalism and localism. Slogans are not enough. "Act locally think globally" is a cliche by now, as Morgan sees it. You can talk "glocal," but talk by itself will not conjure the synthesis of globalism with localism into reality. What is needed are *transnational teams* that knit together local contributions and global trends. The importance of teams is that they place diverse people in close, face-to-face relationships. It follows that resolving conflicts on a team – say, between American and Japanese members – is a dress rehearsal for resolving conflicts between the two companies. The diversity within the team gives vital clues to the diversity between the companies, and because team members have a track record for successful cooperation, they can usually provide clues as to what has gone wrong and find agreed-upon solutions to any problems. The Applied Materials relationship at the very top of Applied Materials, between President Dan Mayden, an Israeli, and CEO Jim Morgan, an American, is international in itself.

A cross-cultural team is, at its best, a *microcosm of the diversity within the company.* If the team can reconcile its own conflicts, there is at least a chance that it can mediate successfully in more attenuated relationships between remote sites. The team also symbolizes the fact that agreement is possible when people take the trouble to get to know each other – in other words, that cultural conflicts are the result of ignorance and misconception, not some everlasting chasm between values. A transcultural team also admits all concerned to the status of "insider." There are no outcasts. It is of considerable significance that the cross-cultural team is *at the top* of the organization, an example to all subordinates.

The dilemma looks like this:

Dilemma 4.   Generalizing Local Discoveries

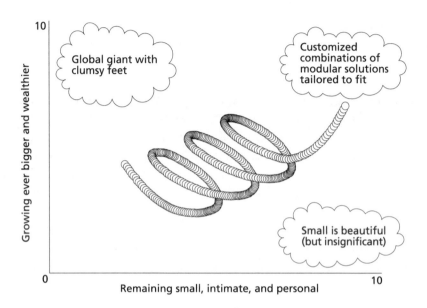

Morgan emphasizes the importance both of local circumstances that *cannot* be generalized (lower right diagram) and of global issues without relevance to local circumstances (upper left). But once one has categorized both of these, there remain issues that originated in particular localities yet can now be globalized, as well as global issues still underexploited in particular localities. No doubt all customers are different, but not all customers are equally effective and successful. Applied Materials is in the enviable position of being able to discover *the difference that makes the difference* and to inform everyone who still wants to learn. Every culture wants to succeed in its own way, but these "ways" do not all lead to the best results. Applied Materials helps various cultures "keep score" and discover the strengths, as well as the weaknesses, of their cultural values. No wonder that so many different accents are found at the heart of Allied Materials (an observation made in the introduction to the book).

Stable Continuity and Flexible Change

Morgan understands that, paradoxically, you must change if you want to remain the same and must pursue a stable continuity of core values if you want to experience continuous change. He elaborates on this theme: "In our business, change is a strategic weapon, and change management is a survival imperative. The world that Applied Materials envisioned decades ago is now coming to pass – perhaps even faster than we imagined. While other, much larger, richer, more famous companies sweat through implementing change programs to deal with the coming new world, anticipating and preparing for change is already deeply wired into our culture, our thinking, and our strategies. Ours is a dynamic business, and that's the way it has to be. We're on the cutting edge. The semiconductor chip market has always been fast moving, and we've come to expect changes. We thrive on them. At Applied Materials, we believe that change is the medium of opportunity."

In other respects, however, Applied Materials has to remain true to its core beliefs: always close to the customer, always technologically efficient, always learning from mistakes, and always practicing mutual trust and respect. Indeed, the more Applied Materials changes in some respects, the more it must remain the same in others.

Morgan believes that he knows the trajectories of change: more fabs, more complexity, more responsibility for the supplier of manufacturing equipment. But some linear projections will not extrapolate as planned, and that is when you have to be flexible – to take Asian booms and busts in your stride and hang in there with your customers. The clearer and more definite your conjectures, the more vivid and

Dilemma 5. "The More Things Change . . ."

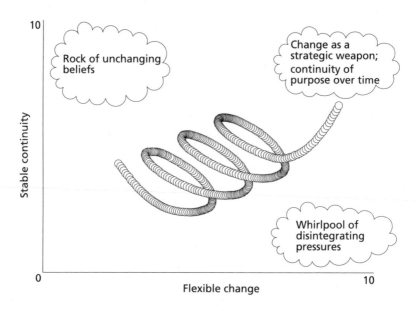

memorable is any refutation. Just as you learn from mistakes, you learn when your expectations do not pan out and must be revised. To be true to your own values through turbulent times is to keep your nerve and not go into shock. Cultures without values to which to be true are disintegrated by external change. Change is a great opportunity only to people and companies that know who or what they are and what it is they stand for.

We draw Morgan's fifth paradox as shown on the previous page. By steering between the rock of unchanging beliefs (upper left of the diagram) and the whirlpool of disintegrating pressures (lower right), Applied Materials uses change as a strategic weapon, maintaining a continuity of purpose over time and changing to preserve that continuity.

Growing Bigger, Yet Remaining Small

This is an industry in which size is a definite advantage. Morgan made the point clear: "In this industry, you need to be big because you need a large amount of cash for R&D in order to be able to continuously introduce leading products, you need global service capability, you need to have an extensive product line, including full process modules, and so on. At the same time, you need to be small to meet your customer's demands: be easy to deal with, flexible, work with customers on their needs as if we were a small enterprise, be fast to react, and be able to deliver single systems as well. Because we are big *and* small, we have the capability for rapid introduction of leading products. Our message to the industry is clear: Applied Materials is the Total Solutions company. With suites of interactive products covering six of the eight essential manufacturing steps, with a global support and service infrastructure, and with pace-setting investment in research, development, and engineering, Applied Materials is the leader in delivering total solutions worldwide – and we intend to remain so."

This fusion of bigness and smallness is achieved by *modularity*. The totality of Applied Materials's offerings can be broken down into modules, each one a Total Solution. Customers interface with a relatively small local supplier, of human scale, who can offer whatever module or combination of modules that particular customer wants. It is because Applied Materials has so many solutions to call upon, through its sheer size, that it can customize offerings locally and behave like a small, friendly job shop to create just the solution asked for. Customizing solutions allows each business unit to exercise high degrees of autonomy: to have Koreans serving Koreans, or Israelis Israelis, while being able to draw on a global network of accumulated know-how.

The sixth dilemma looks like this:

Dilemma 6.   Small Modules, Large Combinations

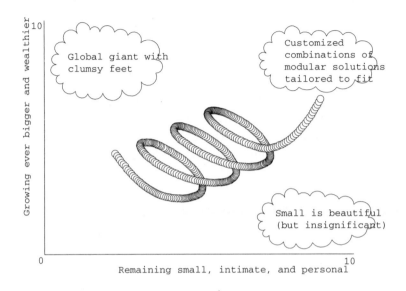

"*Can Giants Learn to Dance*" asks Rosabeth Moss Kanter, or are they doomed to trample on intimate, one-to-one, small-scale relationships? Perhaps this is the wrong question. The trick is create your "giant" out of hundreds of modules, each viable in its own right, yet capable of joining with others in customized combinations. In this way, you enjoy vast economies of scale and a wide variety of solutions, while being able to get the best-fitting solutions to the customer in a personalized way. That small is beautiful is a common experience. We want service that is of human scale; but small by itself can be insignificant in global commerce. We want right-sized solutions from a corporation big enough to customize itself globally.

Leaping Up and Diving Down, Porpoise Style

We come finally to Jim Morgan's distinctive "porpoise style"-leadership. Is this also the reconciliation of a dilemma or paradox? It is. The most admired of Morgan's leadership traits is his strategic foresight and long-term planning abilities, but he is also capable of rapid tactical shifts and is master of the moment. It is the combination of these traits that has stimulated rapid growth. "We are always among the first to enter and invest in potential new markets, which reflect our long-term business strategy," Morgan comments. "I respond to short-term crises not by throwing money at the problem, but by asking what business advantage to the firm can arise from this crisis? Where should we be positioned at the end of it?"

Morgan tries to take a "big-picture" view of the industry, which looks from above and sees far ahead. While doing this, he delegates responsibility downward and empowers his staff to act in his absence. Yet he also makes periodic plunges into the detailed workings of the company and examines key issues up close. This is less to check up on his subordinates than to learn (or reacquaint himself with) the fine details of the operation. "I have confidence in myself and our product," he says. "Hence, I feel comfortable delegating responsibility and empowering [my] staff . . . but this does not mean that I wash my hands of day-to-day minutiae and never examine [anything] up close. I ask many questions and look carefully at whether standards are being maintained. What I don't do is tell my staff how they should perform or operate. Rather, I look at the results, on occasion 'with a microscope.' It is this mix of a long, large view and short, sharp examinations that leads me to form generalizations that work on the ground in many concrete instances. I call this the porpoise style: diving into the business to stay close, before gaining height once more. You can get a lot done in a hurry."

We can use this porpoise analogy to summarize all seven paradoxes, since Morgan is explaining to us how he moves in sequence up and down between two contrasting sets of values. (See Illustration 1.)

Illustration 1

**Axis X (a) Correcting (b) Quick deciding (c) Excellent technology
(d) Global reach (e) Continuity (f) Growing bigger**

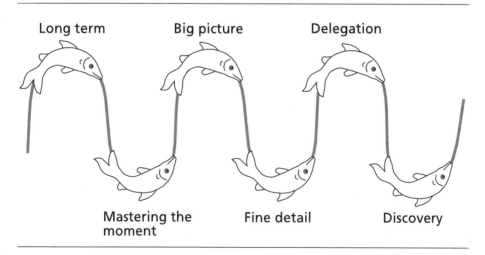

Long term   Big picture   Delegation

Mastering the   Fine detail   Discovery
moment

**Axis Y (a) Erring (b) Participating (c) Effective outcomes (d) Local fit
(e) Flexible change (f) Remaining small**

On our X axis, the vertical one in most of our diagrams, we see that Applied Materials corrects quickly, decides fast, excels in its technology, and so on; on the Y axis, the horizontal on most of our diagrams, we see that Applied Materials errs, participates, jointly seeks successful outcomes with customers, and so on. Jim Morgan, adopting a porpoise style, jumps and dives from one axis to the other.

We can, of course, express this dilemma in the same style as the other six, thus:

Dilemma 7. Leaping and Diving

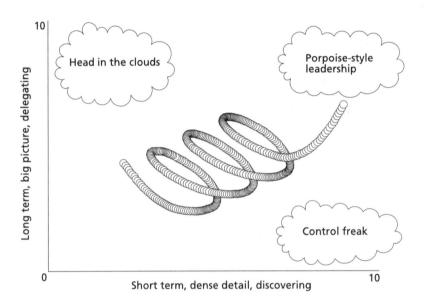

By constantly moving between the two axes, Morgan escapes both control freakery and having his head in the clouds. Indeed, the porpoise pattern of bobbing up and down is simply another way of expressing the virtuous circles or helices we have been using throughout this book. A frequency wave is a rolling circle.

Applied Materials well exemplifies the unexpected 1990s renaissance of US business. If the twentieth century was the American century, then the twenty-first century is apparently going America's way, too. Morgan's company has shown its readiness to learn from Japan and East Asia, rather faster than those regions have learned from the United States. This is a triumph of transcultural competence as well as of technology. Morgan has encompassed East Asian values into a more inclusive whole and has mastered this novel synthesis.

CHAPTER 11

The Internet as an Environment for Business Ecosystems

Leader: Michael Dell (Dell Computers)

The computer industry stands at the summit of the new "information economy." The future belongs to those enterprises which can receive, organize, distribute, and utilize information most effectively and most swiftly.

As James F. Moore has pointed out, we have moved beyond competition and cooperation to the creation of business ecosystems – that is, whole economic communities of interacting organizations and individuals. Informational goods and services are produced *by* and *for* ecosystem members. The most effective strategy is to position yourself near the center of the web or ecosystem and make your enterprise indispensable to its major transactions. As the ecosystem develops, its principal modes of transactions grow with it, often faster than the ecosystem itself. Wherever an enterprise is a node in a system, every new member increases nodal transactions, which grow exponentially. Thus, the tenth member of a group produces nine additional relationships, all of which might pass through the nodal enterprise. The quantum leap "beyond competition" is shown on the next page.

Note that competition and cooperation have jumped to a higher level of complexity. Whereas employees once cooperated *within* the firm to compete against those *outside* the firm, now the companies composing an ecosystem cooperate *within* that ecosystem to compete against *outside* ecosystems, which could even include replacements for the computer itself – not an impossible scenario. But unless and until such a challenge takes place, the computer industry remains a powerful and burgeoning ecosystem. If we compare computer ownership with that of telephones, and consider how much more versatile the computer is and its possible links with telephones, we see that computers could still grow massively, especially with the cost

Dilemma 1.   The Emergence of Business Ecosystems

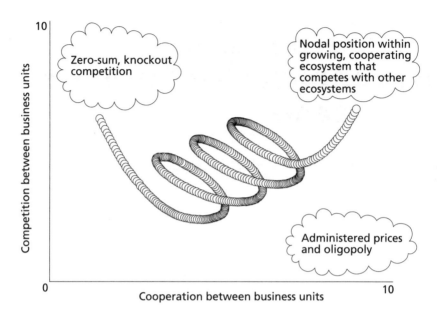

of million of instructions per second (MIPS) falling year after year and Intel and Apple charging around half a dollar for each million of capacity.

Also crucial is the convergence of telecommunications and content – for example, entertainment, education, business, and news – all of which will need computers to store a wealth of information. But the biggest catalyst for the spread of the computer is the Internet and the World Wide Web, which currently require computers to receive, store, and communicate information.

Michael Dell, the Successful Late Starter

Michael Dell's feat in taking on the giants of the computer industry from a late start and succeeding so spectacularly that Dell is now the world's number two computer firm in terms of global sales, deserves careful examination. The company's growth has indeed been phenomenal, even by the standards of a mercurial industry. It is a major player in a major market, and we shall show how it embraced fundamentally different rules of operation in order to flourish in a fast-changing marketplace. We shall examine Dell's approach to the new global economy in the light of the dimensions of culture and values and show how Dell brought about a grand reconciliation of seemingly opposing values to harness the true power of the new economy.

Short History of Dell Computer Corporation

Michael Dell founded Dell Computer Corporation in 1984 with $1000 of start-up capital and an idea unprecedented in the computer industry: bypassing the middleman and selling directly to the consumer. This was dubbed the Dell Direct Model. The idea caught on. Dell Computer Corporation is now one of the top vendors of personal computers. In 15 years, company sales have grown from $6 million to $25 billion. Dell now has sales offices in 33 countries and sells its products in 170 countries. It has manufacturing centers in the United States, the United Kingdom, Ireland, Malaysia, China, and Brazil. By 1995, shares of Dell stock, originally priced at $8.50 in 1984, were selling for $100.

The fundamental competitive advantages of the Dell Direct Model were enhanced by the advent of the Internet. In 1996, Dell customers were able to buy a Dell computer via the Internet. By 1997, company sales via the Internet reached $1 million per day. Also in 1997, Dell shipped its 10-millionth computer, and the per-share value of its common stock reached $1,000 on a presplit basis.

By 1999 sales via the Internet had reached $30 million per day, representing 40 percent of overall revenue.

Michael Dell is chairman and chief executive officer of the company he founded. When the company was added to the Fortune 500 list in 1992, he became the youngest CEO of a company ever to earn such a ranking. His strong belief in the power of information technology to improve productivity and to change entrenched methods of working has been the driving force behind the company. He realized early on that information was capable of changing the economic models of the new global era, and he was one of the first to latch onto the power of the Internet.

Dell's Direct Business Model

Because Michael Dell came late to the computer industry fray, he *had* to do something entirely different, something that would distinguish him from competitors and something that would get around the fact that distributors were stuffed full with rival products, so that to dislodge the major brands was an apparently insuperable task. It was not simply that channels of distribution were blocked; the seas of information, service, and support surrounding computing technology were ever more expansive. Even if distributors could make room for Dell products physically, could they absorb the additional information, service, and support, master it, and pass it on?

So Michael Dell decided to bypass distributors entirely. He would sell directly to customers, thereby establishing a unique advantage over other computer vendors and creating his own ecosystem apart from theirs. Direct selling had some crucial advantages:

- Manufacturing to order would minimize the capital sunk into inventory, especially obsolete inventory that had become unsellable as a consequence of technological advances.
- Speaking directly with customers, instead of using intermediaries, brought information on changing customers needs to the company more quickly and with greater clarity and urgency. It was possible to learn at first hand the strategic aims of major corporate customers.
- With inventory turning over every six days, innovative technologies can be introduced very swiftly, along with needed refinements to new models. The quicker this feedback loop, the finer the adjustments to the detail of customer requirements.
- A process of *mass customization* became possible, by which standard components were assembled in those unique configurations that customers demanded. In this way, economies of scope were combined with economies of scale.
- The model of direct selling received a welcome and powerful boost from the Internet, which was first used to sell a Dell computer in June 1996. Today, there are more than 40,000 customized home pages, called Premier Pages, especially for corporate customers. These pages contain not only the details of customized configurations and instructions, but also a total record of past and current transactions between Dell and each customer.
- One consequence of this direct link is that Dell becomes privy to far more information about its customers than would otherwise be the case. When configuring a customized package, you can serve the customer better by knowing why it is wanted and how it will be used.

Dell's Dilemmas

We hope to show that Michael Dell has brilliantly and intuitively solved several crucial dilemmas facing the computer industry. It is the quality of his reconciliations that has elevated the company to its present powerful number two position in global sales. We will consider the following dilemmas, numbered starting with "2" because the first problem, how to break into the business at all, was solved by Dell's Direct Business Model and its creation of an ecosystem:

2.   Broad Spectrum vs. Deep Relationships
3.   Porter's Dilemma: Low-Cost Products vs. Premium Products
4.   Face-to-Face Selling vs. Internet Selling
5.   Uniting Inner and Outer
6.   Virtual Integration of Product and Process
7.   Premier Pages: The Bridge between Gift and Sale

Let us consider dilemmas 2–7 in turn.

A Broad Spectrum of Customers vs. Deep, Personalized Customer Relationships

This dilemma was exacerbated by Michael Dell's youth, which made him the latecomer in a maturing industry in which he faced the prospect of pushing into a crowded field, full of existing attachments, some of long duration. Could Dell push entrenched competitors out of their dug-outs? It turned out to be unnecessary, because the Direct Selling Model had the advantage of being simultaneously very broad and at the same time quite deep, personal, and customized. The conventional wisdom is that you can aim either for many customers, broadly distributed across the field, *or* for just a few clients with complex problems and specialized needs, who desire deep, ongoing relationships of service. The first strategy is cheap, but rather

Dilemma 2.   Broad Spectrum vs. Deep Relationships

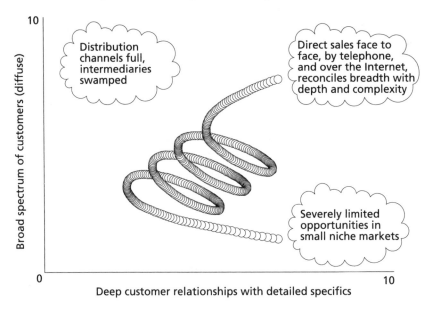

superficial. The second strategy is intimate and personal, but typically niche oriented and expensive, because of the detailed attentions necessary. The dilemma is illutrated above.

The genius of direct selling via the Internet is that you reach an ever-increasing spectrum of customers *and* you can use the Net to give personalized, detailed, information-rich services to those customers. As long as you assume that distributors are necessary, you are stuck with the fact that existing channels are full and that no intermediary's brain is capacious enough to hold the details and information about several rival products and their accompanying instructions.

It is only when you let go of the whole idea of using distributors that the processes of direct selling via the Internet commend themselves. The Internet is uniquely suited to information-rich products, which can be embedded in an ongoing community of discussants and can be woven around with dialogues on details and special opportunities. You can serve the whole spectrum of net users, *and* you can go deeply into any specific problems. This dilemma is close to Dilemma 3 of our seven-dimensional model, described in Chapter 1. It was the dilemma or dimension of Specific–Diffuse. You can get down to each customer's problems in *specific* detail, *and* you can serve a *diffuse* array or spectrum.

The "Michael Porter" Dilemma: Low-Cost Product vs. Premium Product

Michael Porter's two "generic" strategies (meaning "of their own kind") are of very special interest to Michael Dell. Porter claimed that these strategies were exclusive: *either* you went for low-cost products, *or* you tried to give the product a special premium that would make it unlike competitors' products and so earn higher returns. Dell sounds skeptical about Porter's warning that if you tried both strategies, you could muddy the consumers' perceptions and achieve neither aim effectively: "I believe that Dell has continued to grow at three times the market rate by doing both. We have provided the lowest overall cost to our customers, and since our cost structure is less than half of our competitors', we can sustain our advantage in pricing.

"We have also offered superior service based on our differentiated, direct customer relationships. Further, I believe the Internet era provides Dell the opportunity to not only sustain its costs and service advantages, *but* also extend them."

Dell's premium, customized direct service is not only of higher quality and more complex, it is cheaper at the same time, thereby transcending "Porter's Dilemma." One important reason that Dell can do both is that it orders its components in mass quantities from its suppliers, thereby achieving economies of scale, but it also codesigns its computers with its intended customers, so that all these cheap components are assembled in unique, customized configurations.

Joe Pyne has called this process *mass customization*, first introduced by the Japanese automobile industry and now widely imitated. Through the delivery of components "just in time" to a central assembly line, 30 to 40 varieties of automobile can come off at the end of the assembly line, with little loss of speed or momentum. Information systems devise each configuration in advance, and components are dispatched to make a synchronized rendezvous with the vehicle in the process of assembly. The dilemma can be drawn as follows:

Dilemma 3.   The "Michael Porter" Dilemma: Low-Cost Product vs. Premium Product

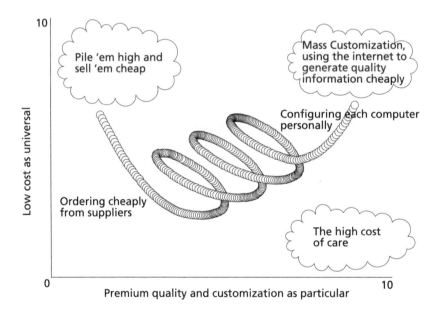

How does Dell deliver high-quality service *cost-effectively,* thereby reconciling "Porter's Dilemma" and steering between Pile 'em High . . . (top left of diagram) and The high cost of care (bottom right)? First, there are no distributors' margins to pay. Second, information via the Internet grows cheaper per instruction per day. Third, an economy of scale makes *components* cheap, while economies of scope allow every detail of every customer to be attended to on-line. What made customized service so expensive originally was the labor intensity of personal visits and the ensuing face time. Problem-solving over the Net is considerably cheaper. Furthermore, the Net has helped Dell's service to be much more sophisticated at this point, as it connects customers directly to a technician, after special intelligence embedded on the computer motherboard has self-diagnosed – either ruled out or identified – common problems. At Dell, this service is known as *e-support*.

In any event, compared with its other major competitors who use distributors, Dell is *both* competitive on cost *and* more customized. Note that there are elements of Universalism – Particularism (Dimension 1 in Chapter 1) in this dilemma. Low cost is a universal appeal, one that works only if all units on offer are substantially similar members of a universe. By contrast, premium products appeal to particular and unique sets of requirements. At Dell Computers, the two have been powerfully combined. Essentially, Dell has created (and now dominates) its own ecosystem, one that competes with the ecosystem of those companies using distributors. The distributors are a bottleneck that Dell has cleverly eliminated. Without these bottlenecks, information flows more freely and grows to greater and greater complexity. Dell's competitive advantage is in being more capable of managing knowledge than are rival ecosystems. It first orders components en masse and more cheaply from suppliers. Then it uses the Net's mastery of details to customize each sale at highly competitive prices.

Face-to-Face Selling vs. Internet Selling

The Direct Business Model preceded the use of the Internet by several years, so the almost limitless opportunities supplied by the Net came as a very welcome surprise and challenged Dell's capacity for quick adaptation. Dell's sales force initially felt threatened by the Internet. Because the Internet was capable of creating dynamic and complete customer–client relationships, down to the purchasing of a computer, sales teams felt that their role in the era of the Internet would be drastically minimized. Field-based account managers, who "own" customer relations, were especially sensitive to how the Internet could supplant their role.

Dell management knew it had to educate its sales force to work alongside the Internet and seize a new kind of initiative. The Internet was an inevitable and incredible development. Rather than fight it, sales representatives would need to know how to use the power of speeded-up information channels to gather better information and further enhance valuable customer relationships – so Dell invested heavily in education and training. He explains: "Not only did we teach them to use the Net, but we jointly invented ways to make them more effective by managing more relationships while providing value-added services for the customer as well."

The most crucial change was to start valuing and rewarding the communication of knowledge, rather than the mere registering of sales. It is not that sales are unimportant, but rather that knowledge applied successfully to customers is the origin of *subsequent* sales. The first is prior to the second. Under the original face-to-face system in the industry, knowledge of customers' needs tended to get hoarded by the local agent and the field office. Sharing this information with others puts your own office at a competitive disadvantage. You reported your sales, not the *reasons* for them or the changing *patterns* of customer demand discovered in your territory. Knowledge was considered proprietary. After all, you had visited the customer personally and gained choice insights into how computers might be used to advance a new strategy. Such knowledge is hard earned.

Sales teams were instead now rewarded for entering this knowledge on electronic forms, accessible by all other sales teams. The more valuable potentially this information was, the more the team was rewarded. For example, a new use of software could spread rapidly through particular industries. If Dell was alerted from the moment this process started, it could help spearhead the new trend elsewhere. Also, customers are not usually confined to single sales regions. To know that district 7 of company *X* has tried a new approach successfully allows you to spread the same system to all company sites. In these and many other ways, knowledge of what customers are strategizing about can be systematically computerized.

Sales representatives soon stopped seeing the Internet as an adversary. They found that the Internet could be a source of highly qualified leads, as a result of which they could close a deal with fewer calls and have greater reach within existing accounts. Rather than being intimidated by the competition provided by the Internet, they could use the Internet to add a dynamic dimension to unique customer relationships. Again, Michael Dell explains: "We wanted the Internet to become a key part of our entire business system. We wanted to make the Internet the first point of contact for every customer and prospect. . . . Our information technology perspective was – and still is – to reduce obstacles to the origin and flow of information and to simplify the systems in an effort to really maximize our processes."

Brushing aside fears that employees would make "improper" use of the Net, Dell encouraged browsing and information collecting. You could make much better use of "face time" if you were properly briefed on a computer before a meeting and if you kept careful track of the success of previous initiatives. "If you are preoccupied with the ways in which your staff might abuse technology, you're going to miss out on the benefits while your competitors run away with the future. For us, the issue wasn't whether people would waste time on the Internet, but whether they would use the Internet *enough*. Not to become completely familiar with a transformative business tool like the Internet is just foolish – especially when it is an integral part of the company's strategy and competitive advantage."

The dilemma Dell solved was to make personal, face-to-face knowledge, which had earlier been confined to and hoarded by single sales agents, into highly relevant *networked knowledge* in which the deep, personal insights of local agents become the potential inspiration for the entire community. The dilemma is set out in the following diagram:

Dilemma 4. Face-to-Face Selling vs. Internet Selling

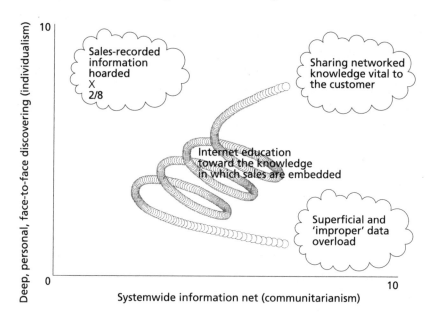

At the top left, we have the old competitive system, wherein agents compete on sales, but refuse to share their secrets. At the bottom right, we have Internet overload of superficial and even "improper" data. Dell was unafraid of this, because his people had much important information to communicate and he was rewarding them for communicating it. Thanks to Internet training and education, and thanks to the emphasis given to the knowledge contexts in which sales occurred, Dell has succeeded in sharing networked knowledge, all of which was vital to at least one customer and could be generalizable to some or all customers. E-relations (electronic relationships) do not substitute for personal relationships, but recording what was communicated, agreed upon, and planned enables later understandings to be built on earlier ones.

We may note in passing that this dilemma is a variation and special case of Individualism–Communitarianism. The Internet makes possible cheap, communal links, earlier undreamed of. It allows an entire community access to the vital knowledge of a single member.

Uniting Inner and Outer

Of crucial importance to Michael Dell was bringing the "outside" of the company into the "inside" and letting the "inside" go "out." He observed, "One of the things that makes the Internet so exciting is that it brings the outside in. In today's marketplace, you cannot afford to become insulated in your own activities." It is a characteristic of modern business that information is increasingly stored in relationships – but *where are* these relationships located? Dell's relationship with an automobile systems supplier is neither "inside" Dell nor "inside" that supplier, but is carried via electronic impulses between the two. It is simultaneously accessible by interested parties from any point in the system. It is everywhere, yet nowhere in particular.

What the Internet can do is host an entire ecosystem of suppliers, customers, partners, and subcontractors. Instead of ordering spare parts from its suppliers, Dell allows its suppliers to discover for themselves the current state of inventories and by how many units new orders from customers will draw down those inventories. This is done to make sure that Dell never runs out of components, while minimizing its carrying costs. Suppliers have the information to deliver "just in time," exactly as their supply contracts specify. All elements in the ecosystem adjust themselves in coevolutionary patterns of mutuality. According to Michael Dell, "By virtually integrating with our suppliers in this way, we literally bring them into our business; and because our entire production is built to customer order, it requires dynamic and tight inventory control. By working virtually with our company, we challenge our suppliers to reach new heights of quality and efficiency. This improves their process and their inventory control, which creates greater value for them, as well as for us and our customers."

Instead of Dell instructing partners, suppliers and subcontractors what to do, it provides and shares with them the knowledge on which those instructions would have been based. The partner can then combine sources of information to make even more intelligent decisions. The ideal is to cooperate seamlessly – to use knowledge from the whole system to enable each node to behave autonomously. Once again, Dell manages this cooperation with a high degree of sophistication. Metrics of supplier–partner performance are agreed upon jointly every year, and these can be reviewed through Dell's secure Web portal for suppliers, valuechain.dell.com. Through this portal, each major supplier has, in essence, its own equivalent of the customer premier page. The portal also allows suppliers to link into Dell's own procurement orders, factory flow, and other useful sources of information.

Moreover, new levels of mutual understanding and greater joint intelligence are achieved when you and your partners share the same bodies of information and can follow each other's reasoning. Everyone has the same "inside information" and can draw the attention of either party to something the other may have missed. The dilemma looks like this:

Dilemma 5. Uniting Inner and Outer

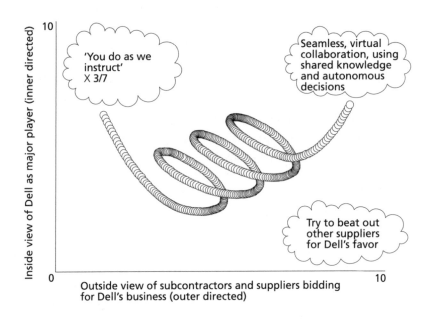

Economic value in this model stems from speed, effectiveness, and complexity. Instead of arguing about who is right or wrong, each party cites the information that informed its decision. In this way, you share mental models and get across to the minds of other players, and make decisions that have been mutually qualified by the players.

Virtual Integration of Product and Process

The computer industry initially organized itself along vertically integrated lines. This was the ticket to creating maximum value and establishing a sustainable scale of operation. Suppliers were not well established, and computer companies had to design and manufacture their own products and components. Proprietary technology and physical assets and products could be priced at a premium. Product differentiation was, in these initial stages, a key to competitive advantage in the marketplace. But as the industry matured, product differentiation gave way to process innovation. Dell came to the conclusion that any successful company would have to move from vertical integration to virtual integration in order to survive and succeed.

Michael Dell argued for virtual integration along the following lines:

1. Seek to establish direct relationships that close the gap between customers, manufacturers, and suppliers.
2. Place yourself strategically in an ecosystem of cooperating players.
3. Discover and define the value you intend to add, and then focus on that distinctive competence and contribution.
4. Choose and help develop partners who are equally good at what *they* do. Make them part of a single system that measures its own effectiveness by agreed metrics.
5. Think of the Internet not as an add-on, but as the environment in which you operate, an integral part of Dell's strategy. Only then can you achieve virtual integration and surpass more traditional companies.

The Dell Direct Model was the basis of this virtual integration, allowing customers to make purchasing decisions that were better informed, more involved, and more elaborately detailed and specified. It integrates physical with virtual assets to configure the whole better.

Dilemma 6. Virtual Integration of Product and Process

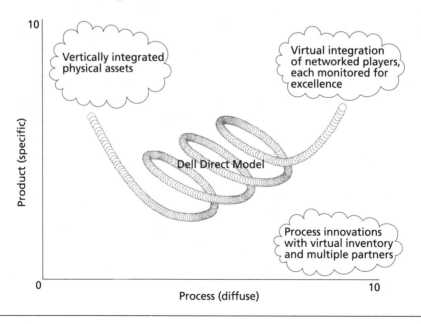

The changing shape of the computer industry and its transition from vertically integrated products to virtually integrated networks is illustrated in the above figure. The traditional part of the computer industry is stuck at the top left of the diagram, maintaining necessary coherence by vertical integration, in which the computer maker "does everything." Dell used its Direct Model to develop several process innovations that created a novel *virtual integration* of key suppliers, manufacturers, and component specialists, each selected for excellence and each connected to the Internet ecosystem. The entire system is self-evaluating and self-monitoring, and all parts jointly agree on the metrics by which the system will assess its own, integrated performance. Note that Dell is *still* a supplier of computer hardware-specific products that customers buy in greater or lesser quantities. But these products are embedded in information about strategic aims and purposes. You buy a Dell computer because it is an effective means to your ends. Virtual integration is about understanding those ends and thereby customizing and deploying the products appropriately.

Michael Dell's dilemma or challenge in creating virtual integration is similar in some respects to the third dimension in Chapter 1: Specific vs. Diffuse. Products like computers and their components are specific, but the oceans of information in which they swim are diffuse. You have to understand the ocean currents if you are to move your own hardware.

Premier Pages: The Bridge between Gift and Sale

It was Romeo who said to Juliet, "The more I give you, the more I have." This has always been true of love relationships, but only recently has it become more and more true of relationships between business partners. We are not talking here of wellsprings of positive emotions, but of sharing seminal information and allowing the combinations of that information to create new knowledge and new synergies, usable by all parties to the interaction. Michael Dell is typically eloquent on this topic: "The real potential of the Internet lies in its ability to transform relationships within the traditional supplier–vendor–customer chain. We are using the Internet to share openly our own applications with suppliers and customers, creating true information partnerships. We are developing applications internally, with an Internet browser at the front end giving them to our customers and suppliers."

Dell computers are an integral part of the information and knowledge communicated, as well as a means of storing, receiving, retrieving, and sending knowledge, so the more this knowledge is "given away," the more necessary it becomes to purchase the computers to which the knowledge refers and by which it is organized. Several Internet entrepreneurs made their fortune by giving away programs, browsers, or tools and asking users to make a donation if they found the gift useful. Their subsequent enrichment was largely or entirely the result of voluntary reciprocity. Similarly, if Dell supplies you with vital information, then buying the company's computers is a rational response and a means to keep that information coming.

Instead of arguing whether this is "really" a gift or "really" a sale, we need to understand that cogenerating knowledge on the Internet transcends this dichotomy and that gifts and sales facilitate one another. The bridge that Michael Dell has built between Dell, its customers, its suppliers, its partners, and its subcontractors are the Premier Pages, password-protected Web pages that serve the special information needs of business customers and technology partners. There are over 40 thousand Premier Pages, and they serve as a dynamic interface for customers and partners to access relevant information. For a corporate customer, this could include information on global accounting, preapproved pricing and configurations, technical white papers, product road maps, and so on. At the click of a mouse, the corporate client has immediate access to a complete picture of its purchasing channels. For a particular client, this could be the number of computer systems bought at its European operation, or details of standing orders, or preapproved configurations and discounts. Of course, customers have to be willing to share information with Dell and its suppliers in order to benefit from better-informed relationships. Many purchasing departments are secretive by habit, but they learn that being more transparent can lead to more attractive and better customized deals.

What Dell does is to model the transparency it seeks from others and waits for them to reciprocate, so that confidences are mutual. Michael Dell explains: "Driving change in your own organization is hard enough; driving change in other organizations is nearly impossible. But we believed, and still believe, that the Internet will become as pervasive as the phone. We knew it was too important to our business, and potentially to our customers' businesses, to wait for them to figure it out for themselves. What teaches parties to reveal more about themselves is experience: the more that is known about your needs, the better others can serve you."

The value of Premier Pages soon became evident. Companies no longer had to work through purchasing channels every time they needed to purchase a computer. Dell made it a point to have this kind of information up and ready from the very beginning. Dell's Premier Pages have resulted in massive savings, and companies have told Dell that they are saving millions of dollars by ordering their products and getting support in this way. Michael Dell is persuasive about the economies achieved: "Early on, Ford Motor Company estimated that it saved $2 million in initial procurement costs placing orders through its Premier Page, and Shell Oil saved 15 percent of its total purchasing cost. Premier Pages also allows us to deliver critical service and support information directly to our customers, based on the specific products they buy and use. This information is drawn from the same databases our own technicians and engineers use. This doesn't necessarily result in major cost savings for Dell, but it has resulted in significant cost savings for our customers, enriching their relationship with Dell."

Premier Pages are also a bridge to research and development between Dell and its partners: "The Internet is changing the way we work with our technology partners. We are moving to truly collaborative research and development models, using the Internet to share information openly and work together in real time. We can also engage our customers in our product development, giving them the same level of access to critical information as our own people have. For example, we were able to develop and introduce an award-winning line of notebook computers, using the Internet to keep a common set of notes by engineers in the United States and Asia. By making the same information available to critical partners, we were able to close the information loop. A traditional, vertically integrated company would have spent months, if not years, designing parts and building them."

Dell has built supplier Web pages for its top 20 suppliers, covering 90 percent of its procurement needs. These pages allow Dell suppliers to provide Dell with rapid information on its capacities, up-side capabilities, inventories in their supply lines, component quality as measured by Dell's metrics, and current cost structures. Dell passes on to the supplier direct and immediate customer feedback, gathered in part through its customer Premier Pages. The feedback covers such areas as quality in the field, current forecasts and future demand, special technical requirements, and end-use market pricing.

This type of collaborative partnership, exemplified by Dell Premier Pages, is a starting point, or a portal, for future innovation in the era of the Internet. Any innovative process will have to begin from a point where time and distance have been shrunk and where development speed is unimpeded. The quality and directness of the relationship, the speed with which you can channel information, and the dynamic forces that you thereby create will determine the long-term sustainability of your position in an industry with notoriously short life cycles. Like Dell, you will have blurred the traditional boundaries between buyer, seller, and supplier, and you will have created a radically new creative enterprise.

The process by which Premier Pages become the bridge between the gift and the sale is depicted in the next figure:

Dilemma 7.   Premier Pages: The Bridge between Gift and Sale

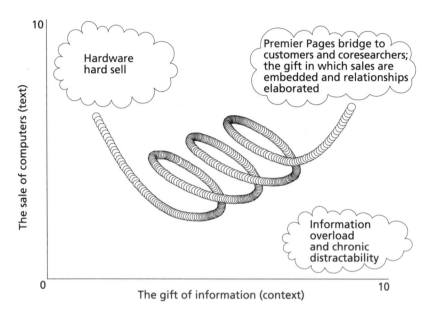

What Dell has done is leave behind the hard sell of hardware and, by gifting to all members of its network the relevant information, promote computers and the relationships that convey that information. The computers are the text within the context, helping to structure and move information across the bridges of knowledge that join all members of Dell's ecosystem. In the progressive, mutual revelation of deep needs, these bridges become preferable to all others. The wealth of knowledge that ties together members of this network would be very hard to duplicate or reconstitute. The net binds its members by hundreds of threads.

CHAPTER 12

Global Brand, Local Touch

Leader: Stan Shih (Acer Computers)

The Taiwanese computer company Acer is perhaps the best example of a globalized ethnic Chinese company. Acer's success made company cofounder, chairman, and CEO Stan Shih one of Asia's most admired businesspersons of the 1990s. By 1989 Fortune had already mentioned Shih as "one of the 25 people you ought to know when doing business in Asia," and Shih was selected by *Business Week* as one of the top managers of the year for 1995. Despite recent difficulties as a consequence of the East Asian financial crisis, Acer seems to be well positioned for the twenty-first century, and Acer's strategy is often quoted as a model for other East Asian companies. This makes it interesting to study Shih's globalization strategy: gaining competitive advantage by reconciling cultural differences. Does this help Acer in exploiting opportunities, neutralizing threats, and adapting to the fast-changing environment of the global IT industry?

Acer has been recognized as having a unique globalization strategy since the beginning of the 1990s. Vogel (1991) mentions Acer as an example of a "world-class company". Kao (1993) cites Acer as an example of an ethnic Chinese company that became a "global player" while retaining key elements of traditional Chinese business culture. *World Executive Digest* dubbed Acer's strategy "the fourth way of globalization," to differentiate it from the American, European, and Japanese ways. Although recent literature pays attention to a "Chinese model" of management, it is not well documented in comparison with Western and Japanese management models. Management guru Peter Drucker pointed out that Western organizations could learn from Chinese models: "Chinese companies will be an important object study for Western managers; just [as] the Japanese succeeded in changing the modern corporation into a family, I think that the overseas Chinese will succeed in changing the family into a modern corporation."

Traditional Chinese business consists of small companies with intense familial network connections. The challenge for network organizations in a globalizing world is to cooperate as small units in such a way that knowledge circulates freely and that they keep their autonomy, but at the same time gather sufficient power to become a "global player." Stan Shih seems to have succeeded in creating such a flexible network. Acer, originally founded in 1976 as Multitech, is arguably the most globalized of all Taiwanese companies. It has more than 28,000 employees, is an important player in more than 30 countries, and belongs in the top 10 global computer companies. The interview with Stan Shih reveals that his successful strategy has been less about changing the family into a modern corporation and more about reconciling aspects of traditional Chinese business culture and Western corporate culture. Shih, born in 1944, is not a Westernized Asian businessperson. He studied at a Taiwanese university and made his career in Taiwanese companies. People describe his character as modest, tolerant, and generous. He ascribes his own success to his willingness to learn not only from positive examples, but also from negative teachings, and to his willingness to trust his employees and appreciate different opinions. About solving conflicts between subordinates, Shih says, "I never make a decision before I understand the overall situation. I involve subordinates in the reconciling of their differences."

In 1993 Stan Shih emphasized (Kao, 1993) that many of the strong points of Acer, such as its stability at senior levels, are related to elements of traditional Chinese business culture, relying more on intuition and opinions of trusted employees than on figures and on establishing work relations with other ethnic Chinese companies. Characteristics of traditional Chinese business culture are well documented (Tai, 1989; Serrie, 1986; Rothstein, 1992; Redding, 1996). An analysis reveals that these characteristics reflect orientations on the seven dimensions of the Trompenaars model. It turns out that those orientations fit very well with the Chinese cultural orientation according to the TH-T database (and are opposite to American cultural orientations).

Universalism — Particularism

Traditional Chinese business culture is *particularist*. Chinese managers are proud to be extremely flexible and adaptable. Not much value is attached to a formal organization chart. The people who form part of the organization, interpersonal relations, and informal contact between managers and staff are much more important. Particular circumstances and relationships are stronger than abstract rules.

Individualism — Communitarianism

Traditional Chinese business culture is *communitarian*. Companies often started as family companies or at least have family-company characteristics. People regard themselves primarily as part of a group and not as individuals. This reveals a strong communitarian orientation with important consequences for how business is organized. For instance, meetings in traditional Chinese companies are not places to make decisions, but are places to check opinions.

Specific — Diffuse

Traditional Chinese business culture is based on *diffuse* relationships. An essential concept in traditional Chinese business is "guanxi": networks in and between companies, on the basis of trust between people with family ties or people from the same region or language group. The networks are used to obtain easy access to capital, to establish business contacts, and to share and disseminate information. All aspects of the relationships in these networks are interwoven, and the "diffuse" whole is more than simply the sum of its parts.

Affective — Neutral

Traditional Chinese business culture is emotionally *neutral*. There is a strong orientation toward making money by working extremely hard and an emphasis on frugality and discipline. Being able to control emotions is considered an important quality of managers and leaders.

Achieved Status — Ascribed Status

Traditional Chinese business culture is oriented toward *ascribed status*. Status is attributed to leaders who adopt a paternalistic style. The development of human potential takes place on the basis of belief in the "educability" of employees and the ascribed status of knowledge. The spoke-and-hub style of many ethnic Chinese companies (spokes around the "hub" of a powerful founder) allows for a traditional leadership style in which the leader combines the roles of ruler, father, and teacher.

Sequential Time — Synchronous Time

Traditional Chinese business culture is characterized by a *synchronic time orientation*. There is not much attention to formal planning. Making quick decisions is the key.

Internal Control — External Control

The Chinese are willing to make exceptions and to make many *ad hoc* decisions to cultivate long-term relationships with customers. Traditional Chinese business culture is *external-control* oriented. Chinese businesspeople are inclined to adapt to external forces instead of resisting them. Chinese businesspeople are the entrepreneurs in many Southeast Asian countries. They are famous for entrepreneurial skills, based on the ability to see business opportunities in their environment and the ability to translate new developments into the satisfaction of customer needs.

These business culture patterns traditionally determine the way of working of small and large Chinese companies and have been an important factor in their success (Deyo, 1978; Goldberg, 1985).

A Short History of Acer

Phase 1

Stan Shih cofounded Multitech, the predecessor of Acer, with five friends, among them his wife. He wanted to let go of the traditional Chinese family-owned style of business, but when he lists the success factors in the early years of Acer's internationalization, it becomes clear that the success was very much based on a Taiwanese style that made use of traditional Chinese characteristics. Acer's success factors in this *"Phase 1"* (between 1976 and 1986) were the following:

- Extreme flexibility and adaptability to the needs of customers. Stan Shih stresses that flexibility has been an essential Taiwanese survival characteristic for centuries, because of Taiwan's "immigrant culture." *Flexibility* and *adaptability* are key terms in Taiwanese management in general. The background of the claim that "members of the Taiwanese workforce have an educational preparation and a cultural background that make it easy for them to adapt to new situations" is that there are no standardized rules for management practice in Confucianism. Management is based on highly personal and particular relationships between employers and employees. Taiwan's economy is based mainly on small and medium sized enterprises, in which management can easily work without standardized rules. In "Phase I," Stan Shih's Acer was very much a typical Taiwanese company with an emphasis on *particularist* values.
- Shih's philosophy of "Creating the Dragon Dream," intended to motivate Acer's staff (at this stage, almost exclusively ethnic Chinese). "Creating the Dragon Dream" refers to Shih's dream of being instrumental in creating what was to become the first multinational Chinese firm, which reflects the Chinese *communitarian* orientation.
- Collective entrepreneurship, consisting of exchanging opinions, reaching consensus at the management level, and taking risks together. These were possible because of the *diffuse* relationships in the network of Acer's managers.

- Acer's "poor young man's culture," the term used by Stan Shih to emphasize his focus on low cost, frugality, and discipline (reflecting a *neutral* orientation).

- The capability of forming fast decisions, because of clear mentoring relationships. In the early days, Acer's employees referred to their superiors as *shi-fu*, literally meaning teacher–father, reflecting the *ascribed status* orientation.

- Acer's "first followers principle." Shih's product strategy for Acer was to be not the first *on the market*, but the first *to follow*. Being a quick follower of competition and "cloning" competitor's products instead of focusing on his own product planning was a key factor in Acer's success. Shih explains, "We would rather wait until technology becomes mature and then quickly follow up." Speed was of the essence to be successful with this strategy. The speed of change within the information technology industry played right into the hands of a company like Acer, where staff was used to a *synchronic* time orientation, working in short bursts and quickly changing directions in an *externally controlled* manner.

- Manufacture under Original Equipment Manufacturer (OEM) agreements – that is, equipment made to another firm's specifications and marketed by that firm under its own brand names. OEM business is characterized by low margins and low risk, because the marketing risk and stockholding risk are taken on the customer side. In OEM business, margins tend to be small, but as long as the quantities are large, it is possible to make a good profit. OEM business fits very well with the Chinese saying, "The capital has to be big, the risk small." Stan Shih made use of Acer's externally focused environment when he chose this strategy. During the 1950s and 1960s, Taiwan's economic development was very much dependent on American support. Major US multinationals were stimulated to use Taiwanese companies as OEM subcontractors. The establishment of export processing zones in Taiwan after 1966, where regulation was minimal because production was for export, led to a boom in Japanese investment and a boom in electrical and electronic goods. The presence of many small and medium-sized enterprises stimulated a network economy with an export orientation. The focus on OEM contracts, exports, and external markets in Acer's first stages of development fits very well with Taiwanese *external-control oriented culture.*

The use of aspects of traditional Chinese culture likely was a strength in the first phase of Acer's international development; the threat was that they would become a weakness when further globalization was required. Particularism, communitarianism, and ascribed status orientation, taken to the extreme, often make Chinese organizations too dependent on the charisma of the founder and on personal relationships. Having few rules and procedures and many exceptions can become a problem when the company starts to work with Western employees who expect job descriptions, personnel manuals, and standard criteria for promotions.

The focus on particularist behavior is also responsible for the problem that Chinese companies generally have in finding enough skilled managers for global marketing. Focusing on OEM strategies was not good for the brand image of Taiwanese companies and made it difficult to get rid of the low-quality, low-price image of "Made in Taiwan." Speed can be an important source of competitive advantage for a company like Acer, but it can be a hindrance to globalization as well. Taiwanese companies are used to *ad hoc* decisions and to moving people around a lot. For foreign staff, changing all the time can be very confusing. They are used to more stability. Taking the external control orientation to the extreme can lead to a lack of direction and of long-term focus. The Chinese saying, "People are never poor for three generations, and people are never rich for three generations," reflects the experienced difficulty of sustaining long-term success. The perception of Western staff is sometimes that the Taiwanese management has no clear direction and just follows the external environment with a "we sell everything" mentality. It was clear that further globalization required change. The implementation of a new strategy led to a difficult Phase 2 in Acer's development.

Phase 2

Phase 2 of Acer's development (1986–1992) was marked by an aggressive globalization strategy and the hiring of outside managers. Stan Shih hired a former IBM manager to be Acer's president, and Acer made such major acquisitions as the American company Altos. The former IBM manager's confrontational style was in contrast to Acer's consensus style. This phase ended with the departure of the former IBM manager from Acer, a restructuring operation that included the layoff of employees in 1991–1992 and the merging of Altos into Acer America. It was clear that trying to copy the strategy of big Western companies had been a failure. According to Shih, "The logic of success that worked in large companies was not viable for us." The operational costs for high-paid (American) *individuals*, the absence of a sense of crisis, the blurred division between authority and responsibility as well as between reward and penalty, and the inability of employees of acquired companies such as Altos to adapt to Acer's corporate culture had been important stumbling blocks.

Looking back, the choice to adopt Western business practices seemed to be correct, but problems arose because there was no connection between the successful strategies in Acer's first phase (building on traditional Chinese business culture) and Acer's strategy in the second phase (trying to emulate the success of big Western companies). Shih recognized that he was confronted with a dilemma, but he was still optimistic about solving the crisis: "When we are forced into a dilemma by our opponent, we either make a wrong move and lose the whole game or take a smart move to solve the crisis." He recognized that, to be successful in the long term in a globalizing world, Acer required a different strategy. "Following the footsteps of first-class companies will only make us second-class or third-class enterprises. To conduct effective globalization, we have to develop a management model of our own." The implementation of his own management model marked the start of the third phase of Acer's development. This "fourth way of globalization" (as *World Executive Digest* called it) could also be described as a reconciliation strategy. An analysis of Acer's globalization strategy in its third phase of development shows that Stan Shih intuitively reconciled aspects of traditional Chinese business culture with aspects of Western business culture on all seven dimensions.

The Fourth Way of Globalization

Phase 3 (1992 to the present) saw the development of Shih's own management modes and turned him into a global player by reconciling global practices with elements of traditional Chinese management. This was done in seven principal ways.

Reconciling universalism and particularism: Acer's global brand–local touch strategy

Stan Shih saw the need to implement more universalistic elements in Acer's strategy, such as making Acer known as a global brand name, while retaining the company's strong particularist elements. He therefore designed the "global brand – local touch" strategy. There were many difficulties to overcome. Taiwanese companies are traditionally not strong in establishing trademarks, channel structures, structured market research, and sales policies. Marketing and price setting are traditionally based on personalistic networks, and loyalty is based on mutual obligations. Even an already internationally oriented company like Acer did not have strong marketing policies, because of its tradition in OEM, in which the responsibility for the marketing is on the purchaser's side.

A history as a small to medium-sized company and a family business made it even more difficult for a Taiwanese company like Acer to establish a brand name in the international market. Building a global brand image required building up that image over a long period, customer service, and dedicated staff available to answer the questions of customers. Taiwanese companies traditionally used price competition as their main marketing strategy. However, frequent lowering of prices is not conducive to establishing a prestigious brand.

Taiwan has suffered for some time from a reputation for low-end products and inconsistent quality. "Made in Taiwan" used to have the image of "low price, low quality." The reputation for cloning had led to an image of "Me, too" manufacturers, imitating designs and compromising to keep prices competitive. Stan Shih managed to make Acer Computers the first Taiwanese manufacturer that changed the image of "Made in Taiwan" for the better. For some time, because of the bad image, Acer was forced to use creative ways to avoid putting "Made in Taiwan" on its products. Then Acer started with its "global brand–local touch" strategy: the development of Acer as a global brand name with a good reputation, in combination with local assembly, local shareholders, local management, local identity, and local autonomy in marketing and distribution. Acer is now Taiwan'ss most famous branded product. "Global brand–local touch" is a good example of the reconciliation of particularism and universalism in business strategy. The particularist "local touch" part of the strategy consists of the following elements:

- Localization of the business structure: Acer's strategy is to have a majority of local shareholders at the beginning of the twenty-first century. Shih wants the majority of ownership of the local operations to be in the hands of local investors. He envisions a company owned by local investors and quoted on national stock markets. The final goal is a "worldwide alliance of borderless global companies" within the Acer group: the "21 in 21" concept, or 21 companies for the twenty-first century (for instance, Acer America, Acer Peripherals, Acer Europe, Texas Instruments Acer, Inc.) – publicly listed companies with local shareholders in the majority, each with access to the full Acer group technology, but each following its own marketing strategy: "Global coverage, local-focused regional offices."
- Local assembly: Acer reversed the trend toward centralized manufacturing centers. Instead, it seeks to have local assembly centers close to the customer. Nationally based, highly autonomous companies combine quality ingredients according to local demand.
- Local identity and local management with local autonomy in marketing and distribution (*Far Eastern Economic Review*, Jan. 26, 1995). Stan Shih demands of his local managers that they be pragmatic and accountable, a good example of reconciliation between Taiwanese particularism and Western universalism.

Diagrammatically, Acer's reconciliation can be conceived of as follows:

Dilemma 1, The Fourth Way to Globalization

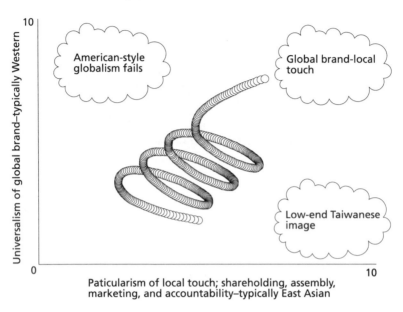

Universalism of global brand–typically Western (y-axis, 0 to 10)

American-style globalism fails

Global brand–local touch

Low-end Taiwanese image

Paticularism of local touch; shareholding, assembly, marketing, and accountability–typically East Asian (x-axis, 0 to 10)

It is crucial to grasp the fact that Acer and Stan Shih have *universalized their own preference for particularism.* They have assumed that most other countries want Acer to be particular and exceptional also, in their ways of investing, assembling, marketing, and so on. One country of refugees and immigrants is appealing globally to migrant cultures, who are the creators of so much wealth. With one-third of all Silicon Valley's wealth being created by Indian and Chinese immigrants to America since 1970 (Anna Lee Saxenian, 1999), Acer's strategy looks like a winning one.

Reconciling individualism and communitarianism: individual stock ownership and the Dragon Dream

The Chinese family form of communitarianism has never been without strong individualist features. After all, families are small, and family members benefit individually from the success of family businesses. Shih's initial appeal to "realize the Dragon Dream" was an attempt to move community pride beyond the family and make the Chinese "dragons" a force in the world community. This worked well in the early stages of growth, but less well as Acer spread from continent to continent. Making a Taiwanese company world famous was not the first thought in the minds of American and European employees. Some other way had to be found to give non-Chinese protagonists a stake in Acer's prosperity. A generous stock option plan for all employees gave them ownership of local stock quoted on local stock exchanges. They were part of Acer America or Acer Europe, with an individual stake in their local community, even as they built the Dragon Dream.

Shih continues his strong support for the local communities in which Acer is based, through the Acer Foundation, but in addition, each employee (and his or her family) has a personal financial stake in the success of a regional company. The reconciliation between individualism and communitarianism can be diagrammed as follows:

Dilemma 2. Dragon Dream with Personal Stakes

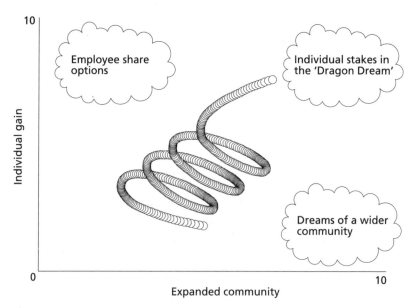

The Taiwanese communitarian orientation that Acer starts with is widened still further, but as Western economies are included, each individual is given an additional personal stake in the Dragon Dream.

Reconciling specific and diffuse: Acer's "client–server" structure

Stan Shih designed a flexible "client–server" model to make Acer's network organization structure work. *Client–server* is the term originally used for the computer structure in which the connection of several PCs in an office with servers performing different functions leads to the establishment of a complete and flexible network. Client and server are closely, but flexibly, connected to each other. PCs act as independent clients, and the servers on the network are ready to provide the appropriate resource. Shih used the client–server relationship as a metaphor for Acer's structure: the product/technology oriented business units (servers) provide technology and products for the regional business units (clients). The most basic principle is that each unit accomplishes what it can handle, asks for support from other units for more complicated matters, and is ready to act as a server and to support other units at any time.

The client–server structure allows each business to become an independently and separately operating "client" as well as a support-providing "server" for other units. Both the product groups and the regional units have autonomy and specific targets, but the relationships between the business units are diffuse, and all units have direct access to the support of the Acer Group. There are no superior–subordinate relationships between units. Each unit is in an equal position and can conduct business without having to go through headquarters. Acer even has a separate department, Acer Open, that occupies itself with the sales and marketing of products of other Taiwanese companies. The loosely knitted client–server structure leads to many ambiguities and apparent contradictions. There is internal competition between different units. Acer Open and a regional unit, for instance, may compete with each other in the same market. If the management of a local region does not want the components of a product unit, because these are no longer the best, the latest, and the least expensive, it is allowed to pick other suppliers with better terms. The idea is that this will help each unit to maintain competitiveness, also in the internal market.

The different units should manage their relationship with the view that "My benefit will be my partners' benefit, and in the end we will be able to share the benefit." Stan Shih compares the role of the CEO in this network with that of the operating system of a PC. The center of the network defines a few general features, such as pricing and brand name, and stimulates the units to establish cooperative relationships and work effectively for their common interest. If a unit is not competitive anymore or refuses to work in partnership, the client–server structure makes sure that Shih will discover this in time to reverse the trend.

Acer's Aspire computer was an example of a successful cooperation between different business units, where communication did not go through headquarters. The ambiguity inherent to the structure doesn't seem to disturb Shih. If the resolution of a contradiction is difficult, he does not appear to push himself hard to untangle it. Instead, he tries to think up a way that would permit him to live with the contradiction until the timing is right for the settlement. This approach requires time and patience. Shih observes, "Never make a decision before you understand the overall situation. If unnecessary, make no decision at all."

This client–server culture has the structure of *collaborative competition* (co-opetition). Specific servers compete to cooperate diffusely with clients. It can be diagrammed as follows:

Dilemma 3.   Collaborative Competition

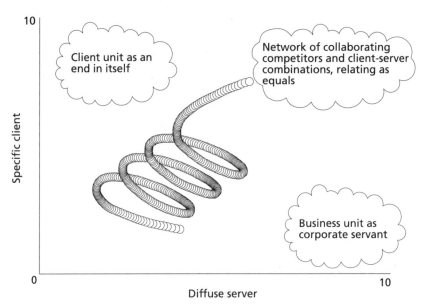

Reconciling Frugality with Kindliness

Not every reconciliation achieved by Stan Shih follows our seven dimensions exactly. It is important to give credit to the leader's original thinking rather than our own model. We see our model as a reflective theme, not as a surefire technique that has only to be followed. Shih and Acer gave great prominence to what they called "a poor young man's culture." This phrase was difficult to translate literally into other languages, and there were several misunderstandings when that was tried. Perhaps the closest equivalent in English would be "young, lean, fit, and travelling light," very much the value of the Chinese immigrant who carries his or her most important possessions between the ears and comes without land, baggage, or attachments beyond the family. The immigrant is "poor" in the sense that young people and students are poor in possessions, but rich in potential.

After several unsuccessful attempts to convey this idea, Shih settled for "a Commoner's Culture," people without privileges, eager to earn their own way in the world. At the same time, commoners' frugality and economizing were balanced by kindliness towards all employees. They were there to contribute to prove themselves, but kindliness was facilitative of quality and excellence.

There is a partial correspondence with our fourth dimension, Neutral vs. Affective, but Shih is really saying something more, and the subtlety of his distinctions is catured in the following diagram:

Dilemma 4.   A Commoner's Culture

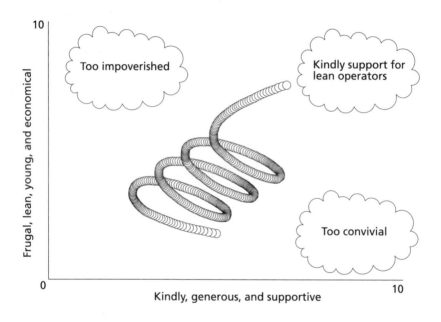

By giving kindly support to those who travel light and who economize, Acer has built a fit and lean culture for effective operations.

Reconciling achievement and ascription: Managers are mentors who conceal nothing from their pupils

One of the mysteries of East Asian business success is how nations so much given over to ascribed status can nonetheless create such successful learning organizations. Surely, to ascribe people a status instead of letting them earn it through achievement is counterproductive? Not necessarily. A vital metaphor for business in this part of the world is the mentor–learner relationship. If your main purpose is to impart knowledge that leaves your pupils wiser and more independent, then the ascription of *tutor* or *mentor* is both effective and benign. This is a form of ascription that stimulates, and is vindicated by, the achievement of learners. You are mentoring *for* achievement. Stan Shih advocates a leadership style that he describes as "being a tutor who conceals nothing from the pupils." This leadership style still has paternalistic elements, in the sense that a leader is supposed to know all the details of the work. However, entrepreneurial achievement is encouraged and rewarded by giving employees the running of small business units. The Chinese expression, "Better the head of a chicken than the tail of an ox," reflects the view that leadership of a small unit is preferable to subordination in a larger one.

Shih is famous for his tolerance of errors, which he calls "tuition payments," provided they are not repeated. Error and experience are the best teachers; hence, authority must be delegated downwards as far as possible, so that subordinates have the opportunity to err, learn, and succeed on their own. The employee's learning and self-advancement will directly help the company. Errors have important information content and memorability, so they should be studied, not swept beneath the carpet.

The dilemma is diagrammed in the next figure.

Dilemma 5. The Path to Realization

Every move to the left involves action. Every move to the right has mentors and learners reflect on that action. Instead of oldsters clinging to past achievements, we have dedicated tutors eager to pass the torch to the "poor" young men and women coming up behind them.

Reconciling sequential and synchronic time orientation: Acer's fast-food business model

Stan Shih's "fast-food model" is a perfect example of reconciliation between sequential and synchronic time orientation. He also refers to it as the "McDonaldization of the manufacturing process," in which Acer's "boards and drives" substitute for "burgers and fries." The idea of "McDonaldization" came to Shih's mind when he had a meal in a McDonald's branch on a business trip. He realized that a computer company can learn from the McDonald's system and apply it to the manufacturing and sales of computers. McDonalds has a unified brand name, a simple menu, and systematic, consistent operation. The differences from Chinese restaurants struck Stan Shih; they are also inexpensive, but they are not known for consistent quality from one to another. Acer combines standard ingredients (the PC components: hard disks, CPUs, memory chips, software packages, computer housings, keyboards) with a consistent quality and assembles the computers in a flexible way, locally adapted to customers' tastes and needs. The components come via different routes, depending on the extent to which their specifications change because of innovation. The result is a low risk of inventory depreciation and "freshness" of essential components:

- Motherboards, which change rapidly in design and price, are shipped by air from one global factory ("the central kitchen") to other sites, mostly in East-Asia.
- Hard disks and CPU and memory chips come in from a regional supplier.
- The computer housing, power supply, and floppy-disk drives, which do not change rapidly in their specifications, are shipped by sea to the local assembly factory.

The consequence is that the local branches always have the newest technology available and become a "fast-food store" that assembles fresh PCs. Acer has some 40 assembly centers, all over the world. The final assembly of the PCs takes place under a modular assembly system, according to standard procedures, ensuring the quality of the product. Parallel supply processes (synchronic) are combined with a sequential assembly process. The result is that the customer gets "fresh" PCs and that Acer has lower inventory costs.

Acer's secret formula for success in the "fast-food business model" is speed, as it was when the company's focus was on OEM business and on cloning IBM PCs. Speed is also behind the success of Acer as a PC-component manufacturer. When a computer manufacturer makes a change in the CPU of a chip, changes in the motherboard will inevitably follow. Waiting until the specifications for a new motherboard are officially released, and going step by step through all the various procedures, means that it will take about 6 months from the time that specifications for a new CPU are revealed to complete a design for a new motherboard. But Acer can put out a design in only three months. This is much more efficient and reduces the time it takes to get new products to the market.

Acer component manufacturers grasp the first opportunity to design a product in order to have a competitive advantage, even though the first design might not be perfect. Sometimes they can begin production after only a few small changes. This small investment risk is necessary to be the first in business.

Acer is happy with the competition that exists between Taiwanese firms to lower their prices and deliver yet speedier service. This competition has always forced them to develop new competencies. Acer now promotes its "global logistics management systems," which it had to develop when a "just-in-time" OEM supplier for global players. Coordinating business between big suppliers requires the ability to reconcile a sequential with synchronic time orientation, and Acer made that ability one of its strengths.

Sequential time has to do with sheer speed; cutting three months out of the time needed to design a new motherboard is an example of time cut in half. Synchronous time is about *timing*, getting a product there when the customers want

Dilemma 6. Speed, yet Synchronicity

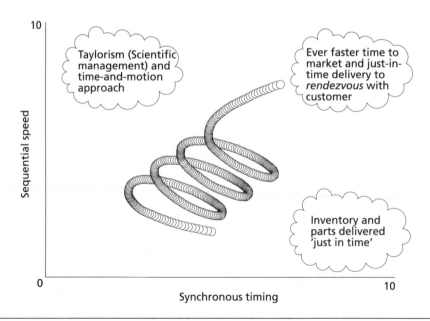

it, neither sooner nor later, so as to save on inventory and carrying costs. Acer has borrowed an emphasis on speed from the West and an emphasis on precise timing from the East, particularly the Japanese, and then reconciled these two visions of time. The dilemma is illustrated in the diagram above.

The reconciliation is to speed your and your customer's *time to market*, yet get it there *just in time*. Even the customer might fall behind schedule, so the trick is to "pull" products toward an agreed *rendezvous* in the future, adding or subtracting resources so as to catch up or slow down. Acer appears to have mastered this art.

Playing Go: Acer's reconciliation of internal and external sources of control

Stan Shih uses the traditional Japanese boardgame *Go* to describe Acer's successful globalization as the "*Go* game strategy." *Go* fits an outer-directed orientation: "I will gradually encircle and constrain your moves." In *Go*, you first occupy peripheral positions, especially the corners of the board, before surrounding your opponent. You can control the corner with fewer resources, yet still be able to surround your opponent. The game is won when your opponent can no longer move. Shih says, "An entrepreneur should secure a firm foothold in a small market before entering a big market."

Acer adopted a globalization strategy in which the firm started in small, but growing, markets that were not immediately interesting for the big players – markets where Acer could win with fewer resources. Thus, Acer managed to obtain top market positions in countries such as South Africa, Malaysia, the Middle East, several Latin American countries, India, and Russia. These are countries that were not seen as priorities by American, European, and Japanese major PC firms. The strategy worked out well, and Acer became a global player by starting from the periphery. When investing in Russia, Acer took the idea of playing from the corner even one step further. Most other international computer companies invested in Russia itself, thereby facing difficulties and risks involved in transport, customs, regulations, government intervention, and opening local offices. Acer built an assembly operation in Finland, close to the Russian border. Russian distributors would collect the products at the factory. Acer thereby avoided many troublesome issues.

Stan Shih developed his strategy as a *response* to the moves of the bigger players, gaining undefended ground and growing *with* the often rapid rates of economic development in emerging economies. Because computerization is an important part of infrastructure development, these emerging nations would associate Acer with their own economic "miracles" and breakthroughs, and Acer could become a permanent, even traditional, part of their growth and strength. Not only is it easier to penetrate an emerging economy, but also, you are carried along on its dynamism and momentum – a typical outer-directed strategy.

The company has built successful local partnerships in Mexico, South Africa, Brazil, Chile, Thailand, Malaysia, and elsewhere. Shih is famously unconcerned with losing control to foreign partners – a feature of outer-directed characters. He believes that wherever his equipment is good enough, Acer's influence will usually be enough. "I would rather lose control of the company and make money, than wrest back control and lose money," he explains.

Acer's reconciliation of inner with outer control is illustrated in Dilemma 7. While long experience working for OEMs on a contract basis has made Acer outer directed, recent experience with original design manufacturers (ODMs) also has made Acer more inner directed. The diagram looks like this:

Dilemma 7.   Riding the Dynamisms of Growth

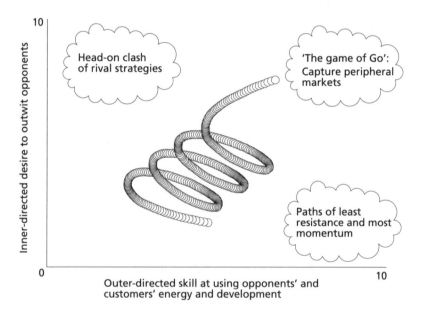

It goes without saying that *Go*, like chess, is a game you aim to win. It is the *means* of winning, the choosing of those "corners" where the influence of a small investment of force can be relatively high because defenses are relatively weak, that illustrates the outer-directed paths to an inner-directed goal.

Despite these seven forms of reconciliation that have made Acer so successful and Stanley Shih so adept a leader, scores of interpersonal difficulties and misunderstandings typical of any global company remain. Westerners still complain that the "playing field" is not properly marked out and refereed, that they have no clear criteria for promotion, and that Taiwanese senior managers are relentlessly ambiguous. Shih's reluctance to make decisions, his means of forcing others to take up this responsibility, is still misconstrued as abdication. Feedback on how well a job has been done is insufficiently warm and definitive, say Western employees. That your superior is your mentor, not your boss or judge, is sometimes misunderstood, as is the indirection of many of Shih's policies.

That Taiwanese-type management can reverse many Western conventions, and that these mirror-image priorities work as well as they do, tells us that "East is East and West is West," but perhaps the twain can meet after all.

CHAPTER 13

Weathering the Storm

Leader: Sergei Kiriyenko (former Russian Prime Minister)

In our quest for leaders for the twenty-first century, we venture beyond the world of the established economies to the former Soviet world. How has reconciliation been practised here? We decided to concentrate on Russia, the largest entity of the former Soviet bloc, motherland of the majority of the Slavic people and the cradle of both the Russian Orthodox Christian faith and Soviet socialism, a huge country, in economic distress, but with a population of 150 million people taking pride in its rich history, its norms and values – its Russian soul.

How can one go about being successful in Russia, where, according to Western observers, the social fabric is ruptured, and the economy and the people crave stability? In most of what we hear and see about "successes" in Russia, the reconciliation of value dilemmas seems to play a marginal role. Where can one find successful leaders, managing by reconciling value dilemmas, in this vast (and still overwhelmingly) Byzantine-style empire – managers who can lead the change Russia is going through? With Russia's isolation finally breaking down, thanks to language education, the Internet, and travel, many of the new generation must be developing respect for values that differ from the Russian ones – respect necessary to bridge the gap dividing them from their political and economic counterparts in the West. We decided to interview one of these Russians.

On the precious advice of our friend Dr. Jurn Buisman[1] and with his extensive introduction, we were particularly fortunate to interview Sergei Kiriyenko. He is, of

---

1   Dr. J. A. Buisman is director of the Benelux branch of the Foreign Investment Promotion Center (FIPC) of the Ministry of Economy of the Russian Federation. The FIPC was created by the Russian Government in 1995 to stimulate foreign investment in Russia and to bridge the (cultural) distance between Western business initiatives and the Russian federal and regional government institutions at the top decision-making level.

course, best known as former prime minister of the Russian Federation, appointed at the astonishingly young age of 35. Before that, he was founder of the Social and Economic Bank Garantiya, where he was so critical of the management of NORSI oil, and that the governor made him president so he could demonstrate his own advice! He moved from there to government circles in Moscow, where he was briefly first deputy minister, minister of fuel and power, and then prime minister. He was elected to the Duma (Parliament) in 1999 and retains his reputation as a brilliant financial reformer.

Our reason for seeking out Kiriyenko and featuring him is significantly different from our criteria for selecting other leaders in this book: We wanted at least one case in which the dilemmas confronting a leader were overwhelmingly fierce and intractable. However important conventional business success is, we must also pause to admire those who fight against force fields and dilemmas of ferocious intensity that would disable lesser persons.

By interviewing Sergei Kiriyenko, we were satisfying our search for a leader caught in a maelstrom of conflicting political pressures. Even if he did not "succeed" in the conventional way (although he did so brilliantly at first) and as a manager, he could give us a graphic account of the dilemmas that menaced him. Tragedy has always been a lesson full of drama, because dilemmas reveal a soul in purgatory and are clear and forceful, "To be, or not to be. . . ." In Kiriyenko, we sought such a Russian soul who could vividly describe the trials inside the maelstrom of Russia. How do you "manage" in a country where that concept barely exists? How do you "reform" in so weak a democratic tradition? In our quest to discover his tribulations, we were not disappointed, but we were also surprised to discover a brilliantly innovative leader, who thoroughly deserved his promotion to his country's premiership, even if that position proved impossible to deal with.

We broke our own rules in another way in this interview, although doing so had a fortunate outcome. We usually try *not* to reveal the models we are using, so that the leaders who talk to us are entirely independent of any suggestions we have planted. In this case, Kiriyenko was hesitant to speak to us at all, so, to intrigue him, we had aspects of our model translated into Russian and sent to him. When he turned up for the interview in Stockholm, not only had he read some of our work, but he had begun to organize his own experiences and memories along our dual axis, to which he took like the proverbial duck to water. Indeed, much of what he said was structured around several of our dimensions. We were surprised and rather flattered.

Kiriyenko at NORSI

Analysis

Kiriyenko began by taking an unusual position on one of our dual axis charts and by writing in the parties to the conflict, as shown in the following figure:

Dilemma 1. Crisis at NORSI

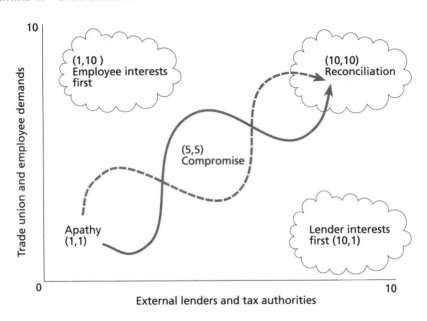

To our surprise, Kiriyenko immediately went for the apathy position at the lower left of the chart. This was the mood he had encountered in assuming leadership of NORSI Oil. In our own experience, apathy is more notional than real, since the very presence of a dilemma usually means that someone is excited about something. If apathy were total, it is difficult to see how we would discover a dilemma in the first place. The person would be too bored to tell us anything! But Kiriyenko insisted. When he took charge of NORSI Oil, the several interests were uninterested and apathetic, and that was the main problem. He explained, "Because, in Russia, the skills needed to reconcile [a difference of opinion or a conflict] barely exist, and because you can lose badly if you try to gain something at someone else's expense, apathy is extremely common. You just hang on to what you have, trying to change nothing for fear of making things worse. The compromise position at 5/5 was *not* so common. In order to compromise, you need two defined positions in the first place, and the parties did not have that. They just wanted things to stay as they were and not get any worse. Actually, the culture is not good at compromising either. For that, you have to have expectations and then be willing to split the difference. Instead, typically, positions are not taken, so there is nothing to compromise, nor was there any surplus to be divided."

Of course, the other side of apathy is the trauma of a fierce fight between interests, with one or perhaps both sides losing everything. Apathy is chosen because the alternative, conflict, is so dangerous and so traumatic, especially with gangsterism on the rise. Russia had been moving *backwards* economically at the time of our interview. There was less for everyone, unless they began fighting, and then there might be nothing at all. We asked for more details. Kiriyenko complied:

> The Nizhmy Novorod Oil Company (NORSI) is one of the biggest refineries in Russia. When I assumed its presidency, I already knew it was bankrupt. There were the following dilemmas: the monthly costs exceeded the income; the trade union tried to raise the salaries, as did the management; the authorities wanted to raise taxes; the creditors wanted the debts to be paid; and the oil suppliers wanted lower refining costs. It was a vicious circle. For example, the trade union wasn't willing to talk about reducing the expenses for the social security system or reducing the cost of the numerous social enterprises around the refinery (blocks of apartments, holiday retreats, hospitals, etc.). Fifty percent of the costs had no relation at all to the refinery production. The authorities were unwilling to reduce taxes. Debts surpassed the value of the plant by 1.5 trillion rubles, but at the same time, authorities objected against the plants going bankrupt because, as a result, 10,000 people would lose their jobs. Finally, the managers didn't want to change course; they would just borrow more money, thus creating a classical debt pyramid. This, by the way, increases the power of the director, because he can decide which debts to pay – thus creating an additional possibility for corruption! As for the oil suppliers, they are interested only in their own businesses. The more complex the shipping of the refined products, the easier it is for the oil suppliers to make a personal deal with the director. Worst of all, nobody wants to normalize the situation. You can try to mark the different positions on the graph, but there is no wish to find a compromise. No one is even going to look for it.

It was not just apathy, but paralysis! The system was slowly subsiding into a wealth-diminishing spiral of disequilibrium, but to rock the slowly leaking boat was to risk catastrophe. Everyone clung to a bit of the boat, as the subsidence continued, and no one bailed.

Radical Action

"You have to accept where people are now," said Kiriyenko, "and that was at [the lower left of the diagram]. We had to break them out of that state. The only way was to abolish the whole company. Because the system was in apathetic equilibrium, with no one daring to let go, we decided to end the existence of what they were clinging to. I got the agreement of Governor Nemtsov that everyone be told that the plant was closing. We set up a new management company with a controlling stake in the share capital of the plant and signed an agreement that this company would control everything, such as the flow of commodities and finances, and would have final management responsibility."

The immediate result was *more* apathy! Whereas *before* no one had *wanted* to move, *now* no one felt *able* to do so. There *was* some regret expressed that they had not tried to reach agreement earlier and that this was the consequence. They had forfeited their chance to influence events; now Kiriyenko acted unilaterally. He formulated new rules. On December 1, 1996, all debts were frozen: salaries, taxes, debts to old lenders, debts to oil suppliers, and so on. He stated that new money, generated from refining new oil, could not be used to pay and service old debts. Fifty percent of this new revenue would go into the improvement and maintenance of the plant, so that it would become more productive, and 50 percent would go to defray debt in a publicly transparent manner, via a Council of Lenders, which published its decisions. In this way, NORSI would stop the steady erosion of its effectiveness and could start to make progress. These rules were strictly applied. Kiriyenko would be in trouble if he broke his word. Everyone and everything was hanging on this new dispensation.

He deliberately paired off the parties and got them to negotiate with each other, seeing that there was not enough for everyone to get all of what was owed him or her. Negotiating at least moved them from apathy to compromise. For example, the trades unions were forced to negotiate with the tax authorities and lenders. After all, if no one earned anything, no one could pay taxes, so, unless the authorities relented somewhat on the company's back taxes, there would be nothing to collect from employees. Lenders and suppliers were also invited to negotiate. If the former were to stop lending, the company would be unable to pay its suppliers; if the suppliers were to cut NORSI off, the demand for loans would dry up.

Even with Kiriyenko's encouragement for them to negotiate with each other, they often could not do it. So, he offered agreements to individual interests: if they agreed, they got some of their claim; if they did not agree, they had to wait. It was just as well, because NORSI did not have the money at that time to meet all claims – even compromised ones – so those who held out actually helped it over its cash flow crisis.

Gradually, however, all parties began to accept agreements. Kiriyenko presided over the agreements and over the resulting flows of funds. In the early stages, he favored the unions and employees, because he needed allies, he needed the company to cohere, and he needed production to improve quickly. As things picked up, however, he swung to the side of the suppliers and creditors. Now that NORSI could generate some income, it was its turn to be repaid. At all costs, he had to prevent everyone from reverting to apathy. If he could help the various interests to create new agreements, and if they discovered that skill in negotiation made a difference to their futures, then they would begin to gain some mastery over their fates and to see that each interest needed the other to cooperate.

The Upward Movement on the Chart

Whereas all had earlier been clinging to shares of the refinery's meager and diminishing income, now NORSI generated more income to share around. Production had increased 350 percent. With 50 percent of income being ploughed back into improvements in plant operations, NORSI was at last adding value. At long last, there was something to compromise *about*, something more than continued failure of which no one wanted a share. In fact, several parties got a smaller *percent* share than they had received before, but because the income had grown so much, they actually did much better.

The next chart tracks NORSI progress.

Dilemma 2.   Progress at NORSI

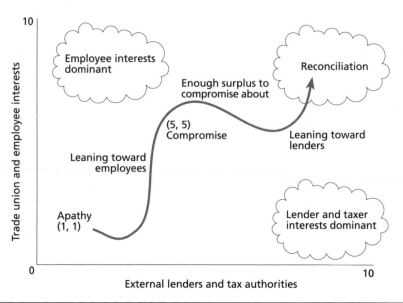

We see that Kiriyenko's first move was toward unions and employees. He had to get them productive. No sooner had they begun to generate a surplus, however, than he leaned the other way. Suppliers and lenders had to be paid, and taxes were needed to shore up the crumbling infrastructure. But above all, there was *now something worth agreeing about,* a greatly enlarged income stream, even if the result was a compromise at (at the center of the chart). This was a huge gain over the earlier apathy. We marvel at Kiriyenko's intuitive skills (and cold-blooded determination). With no tradition of management studies to inform him, he had grasped that he had to wind his way between internal and external interests in order to provide them with reasons for negotiating with one another. With a surplus to distribute, the system came to life.

After six months, he got all the interests together around the table and confessed that he had had to play them off against each other and that those who had not agreed had had to wait. His next move was just as bold:

> As of now, my individual agreements with them would cease. They would get what they had agreed upon with each other. I think it was a new experience for them, to strike a new bargain with their environment and live by that agreement. If those agreements were fair, the income to be shared would grow. They had grown up under centralized coordination, with rules not agreed among parties, but imposed from the top, so they had had no practice in reaching agreements and no motive to do so. When centralized imposition from above began to disappear upon the breakdown of the Soviet system, the various interests just froze into apathy. Nothing in their experience had taught them to reach agreements independently.
>
> Their initial attitude toward change was not that it might improve productivity, but that one of the other interests was 'after our share' and had lobbied me to that purpose. They would therefore oppose all change on principle and hang onto the remnants of what they had. What we taught them, I believe, was that they could build up a business via voluntary agreements and jointly take charge of their destinies. Instead of waiting for a *ukase*, an edict from above that was traditional since tsarist times, they could realize that no more edicts were coming. They were on their own. They had an autonomous company created by their own interests.

External vs. Internal Control

Kiriyenko found one of the dimensions particularly apt for the situation NORSI faced: inner directed vs. outer directed (dimension 6 of Chapter 2). The Russian people, in general and historically, have had their fates decided by external powers. NORSI Oil was just one typical example of this trend. Even the amount of money to be spent on the company's kindergarten was decreed from hundreds of miles away, not by parents, unions, or managers on the spot.

We asked Kiriyenko whether the old archetype of the fatalistic Russian was true. "My hypthothesis is that, at present in Russia, what motivates people is changing. The main thing for the middle and older generation is to avoid mishap. That means that, to break the immobility, you might need, if not a shock, at least a threat – and maybe sometimes a shock. The younger generation and the successful businessmen are now motivated by success, and for them we need a positive stimulus – not a stick, but a carrot."

At NORSI, therefore, Kiriyenko had to make things worse before they could get better. He had to abolish the company *and* the *ukase* on which everyone was dependent. He had to say, in effect, "There is no company or edict coming to save you – only what you yourself create." In November 1996, NORSI was *losing* 25 billion rubles a month. Six months later, when Kiriyenko left to become first deputy minister for fuel and energy, NORSI was *making* 25 billion rubles a month. He had totally turned around the enterprise, by eliminating that on which everyone was trying to depend. This is illustrated in the following figure:

Dilemma 3. Cutting the Apron Strings

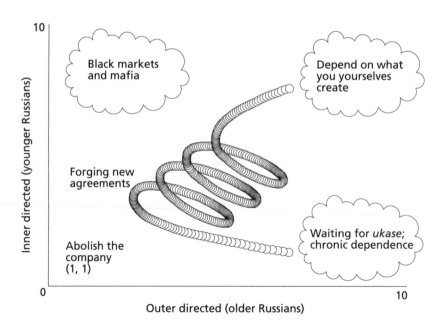

The act of abolishing the company forces everyone to negotiate, for mere survival, new and better agreements through which they can halt the losses or even profit.

"There is even an application of your rules vs. exceptions dilemma," Kiriyenko explained (Universal Rules vs. Particular Exceptions – Chapter 1). When he took over NORSI, several of its creditors were getting paid in preference to others. In fact, owing people money, if you are a large strategic company, is a power game. You pay your favorites and ignore the rest. You force loans from banks by threatening not to repay earlier loans. Those you like can creep to the head of line and collect money that belongs to others. Why would NORSI avoid chronic indebtedness when that gave it so much power to make or break lenders and suppliers?

When Kiriyenko brought in new rules and cancelled and then rescheduled all of the old debts, there was an outcry. He was cursed, blackmailed, sued, and threatened with physical assault! As some saw it, the rules had been abrogated, and they resorted to physical coercion. But he promulgated new rules, drew everyone's attention to them and refused to be intimidated by anyone. One by one, they came around, until everyone was playing by the new rules.

The situation is outlined in the following diagram:

Dilemma 4. From Cronyism to New Rules

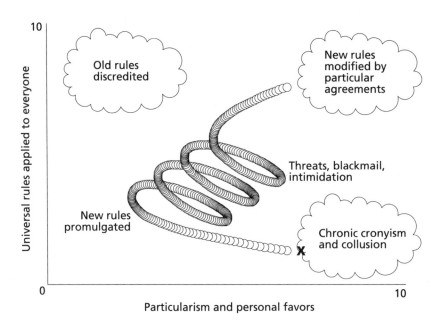

The system was at point X when Kiriyenko took over. There was chronic cronyism and collusion between NORSI and "special" creditors. The old rules were discredited, so personal favors ruled the roost. Kiriyenko promulgated new rules, whipping up a storm of threats, blackmail, and intimidation, but by letting these rules be legislated by the interests themselves, he gradually won acceptance for a homegrown, profitable system, in which rules covered the particular concerns of all parties.

After Sergei Kiriyenko left NORSI to become first deputy minister in Moscow, oil prices hit bottom, and NORSI was struggling again, but he was credited with creating the cushion that allowed the company to survive. "When I was received by Prime Minister Chernomyrdin, he asked how things were going at NORSI Oil. Classic bore that I am, I told him. It took 45 minutes to answer what was, on reflection, only a polite inquiry! But even if his initial impulse was politeness, I succeeded in intriguing him, because he had once worked at the Orenburg refinery. When I had finished, he said, 'I wonder if we could do for the Russian economy as a whole what you did at NORSI Oil?' I thought he was kidding at the time, but when I became Russian premier some time later, I discovered he was serious."

At the national level, the debt pyramid and the cronyism were the same, only on a vaster scale, and so was the solution. Could he get the interests bargaining with each other and creating new rules, originating within those interests themselves? As it was Russian prime ministers came and went with Yeltsin's constant changes of tack. Kiriyenko had to plead to keep the key experts essential to long-term change. Thanks to the combined efforts of Chernomyrdin, Kiriyenko, and, later, Primakov, some continuity of reform survived even as prime ministers were chopped and changed.

Earlier Experiences in the Social and Commercial Bank Garantiya

Sergei Kiriyenko's ideas for turning around NORSI did not come out of the blue. After graduating from the Academy of National Economy in Moscow with a degree in Banking and Finance in 1992, he founded the Social and Commercial Bank Garantiya in 1994. The very name suggests that Kiriyenko was seeking a balance between Western commercial imperatives and the social objectives to which the old Soviet system had given lip service, but singularly had failed to provide. His university studies had convinced him that banks had, for the most part, ill served their depositors and customers, and that trust was at a very low ebb and had to be restored if the banking system was to serve the Russian economy. He believed in making money *through* the fulfillment of social objectives, so he deliberately set out to create a bank worthy of social trust, which made money only insofar as it satisfied its depositors.

Russian banks had for many years served specified industries and had an oligopoly if not a monopoly, in key industries. They perpetuated a closed shop. You could not get into an industry without financing. Finances however, were typically in short supply, with banks being prisoners of debtor customers that did not want any new enterprises in their industry and that dominated those banks via their very failure and continued indebtedness. Like drowning men in a pool, they clutched each other in a lethal embrace. It was an example of the vicious circle and destructive vortices typical of unresolved dilemmas:

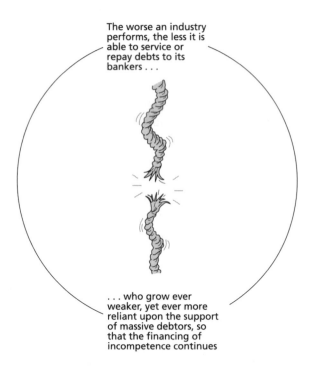

The worse an industry performs, the less it is able to service or repay debts to its bankers . . .

. . . who grow ever weaker, yet ever more reliant upon the support of massive debtors, so that the financing of incompetence continues

Kiriyenko realized that he had to start from scratch with a customer base not already captive to failing institutions. From his youth, as the secretary of Young Communist Leagues in the Red Somorva Plant and in Gorky, Sergei had retained a youthful idealism. It should be possible to serve the people and, at the same time generate a surplus so as to serve even more of them. Banking was the field in which status was mostly *ascribed*, he told us, using the fifth of our seven dimensions. Bankers simply "were" officials of a highly centralized system. That bankers might *achieve* by intelligent, well-judged lending, and grow bigger thereby, was very new to Russia at that time, and very rare.

A Bank for Those Most in Need

In any event, Kiriyenko chose as his new customers some of the most exploited and distressed of his fellow Russians. He targeted older citizens with pensions, savings, and retirement income. Although many of them had worked all their lives, inflation had reduced their pensions to pittances, if indeed they were paid at all. Many industries were defaulting. Many pensioners had fallen victim to pyramid schemes, in which those at the apex increasingly exploited the levels below, until the whole collapsed in scandal. "Elderly people tended to save more, so that they were a source of income for us, but they were also more bemused by economic changes, more likely to be cheated, and more distrustful of banks," said Kiriyenko. Our social research showed that these customers needed more than a safe place to deposit their savings: they desperately needed someone to advise, protect, partner, and represent them. They needed a financial institution to trust with what remained of their savings.

So we began to specialize in the support of Russian pensioners, training our staff especially for that purpose. This included the delivery of cash to the pensioners' homes so that they would not have to venture outside if they found that difficult or risk being robbed in dangerous areas. But we still needed a bold initiative to distinguish us from other banks – to guarantee that we were on the pensioners' side and would stay there. So we set up a supervisory council to represent depositors and other customers. This was our guarantee that we would not do – indeed, *could* not do – anything against the depositors' interests, because the council had to approve any move we wanted to make.

At that time, interest rates were very much an issue, because they could go up or down, and if they did not stay ahead of inflation, depositors could lose. These were times of financial turbulence. Among the specific duties of the supervisory council was approving or, as it happened, disapproving, changes in our interest rates. I was not at this stage aiming for reconciliation. I was still fighting apathy and the accompanying despair. Many of our depositors had been through hell. What I was aiming for was a fair compromise between the interests of those who were relatively powerless and our own interest in building up the bank and increasing the number of our customers.

"The way the supervisory council behaved, routinely siding with our customers against us, was costing us a lot of money. Other banks could adjust their rates to market conditions better than we could, but I was not prepared to disempower depositors or abrogate the decisions of the council, even had that been legally. No one else was even compromising with depositors; all were rather taking advantage of them. That the council was standing up for depositors' rights was winning a lot of attention, and the number of our customers increased rapidly.

"Even so, it was a classic compromise along a straight line. What depositors won, we lost. Had we won, they would probably have lost. But I cannot overemphasize what compromise meant to the parties concerned. We were making money as a bank and the gains were being shared between bank and customers. That was a rare event in the economy of that time, and it still is. That we had some gains to divide up between us, that pensioners did not lose, as routinely happened, that their council got its way and we backed off – all these were rare events, and people took notice." We could diagram the situation as follows:

Dilemma 5.   Compromise and Beyond

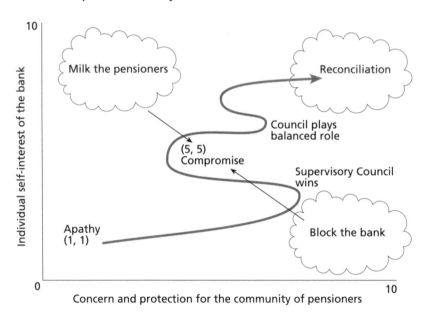

There is a straight-line compromise between bilking the pensioners and blocking the bank, with the bank on one side, pursuing individual self-interest (Individualism), and the supervisory council on the other, upholding the community of pensioners (Communitarianism). The S-shaped line first moved from apathy rightwards, as the supervisory council was encouraged to win several disputes. Unless this had happened, no one would have believed that the council was anything but a front for the bank's own interests. After the council had won two or three rounds, Kiriyenko approached it and had it examine the numbers. He showed what the council's "victory" had cost the bank on at least one or two occasions and pointed out that these monies had also been lost to depositors, to whom they rightly belonged. When the council was making its judgments, inquired Kiriyenko, could it look more broadly at the prosperity and survival of *all* parties, the bank included? If the bank went bust, the pensioners would lose their only friend in the financial world. Surely it was in the interest of all that survive, the council and the bank included.

A Sensible Long-Term View

After that talk, the council stopped acting only in the short-term interests of the depositors in all conflicts and stopped merely maximizing the pensioners' immediate returns. It saw the sense of making interest rates responsive to the changing markets and began to achieve a vital balance between different interests. Perhaps it was not exactly reconciliation, but the bank was on its way! It had moved beyond the straight line of win, lose, or compromise. The bank made it clear that it was concerned for pensioners, so their council should be concerned for the bank, if only because such concern would help the bank continue to cooperate and extend aid to some of Russia's most exploited people.

In place of the vicious circle describe earlier, there was now a virtuous circle:

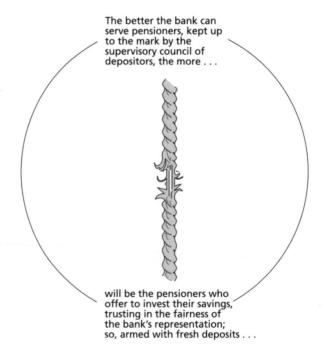

The better the bank can serve pensioners, kept up to the mark by the supervisory council of depositors, the more . . .

will be the pensioners who offer to invest their savings, trusting in the fairness of the bank's representation; so, armed with fresh deposits . . .

The Pension Oil Scheme

An extension of the activities of the Social and Commercial Bank Garantiya was the Pension Oil Scheme. "Because it had started with pensioners' personal deposits, it was not long before the bank started providing services to the Nizhny Novgorod branch of the Russian Pension Fund, which appreciated that its own depositors trusted the bank more than they did other financial institutions. It was extending the rapport that the bank had achieved with its own supervisory council. The bank was asked to look into a major problem faced by the fund. There was a conflict between Tyumen, a major oil-producing region with many refineries, and Moscow, where the central fund for pensions was located. Tyumen was a net contributor to the pension fund because of the concentrated industrial activity there, while Moscow was a net recipient because money was sent there for distribution throughout the Federation. Unfortunately the oil companies were not paying on time, so the pensions were not being paid on time and the economic knock-on effect for the whole country was disastrous, not to mention the emiseration of pensioners themselves. The oil companies would be fined for making late payments, but this only reduced their volume of contributions and delayed these for longer periods.

"So we set out to study why payments were in arrears. The problem turned out to be not a shortage of oil but a dearth of buyers for that oil. The economy had slowed appreciably and there was not the money to pay for the oil. If the pensioners had agreed to accept oil in lieu of pensions there would have been no trouble but of course they could not. Another problem was the under-capacity in the refinery industry. At the NORSI Oil refinery insufficient amounts of oil where being offered for refining, because the parties were not confident of being paid and there was no one to make payment guarantees."

Kiriyenko at once saw that here were some potential clients for the bank, NORSI, the government of Nizhny Novgorod close to where we were located, the Russian Pension Fund, and the oil companies of Tuyumen. Unfortunately, they were all fighting with each other, and all were thereby perpetuating a crisis in which pensioners were being starved of their entitlements. The bank did not have a solution for the whole federation, but it did have a local solution: the governor of Nizhny Novgorod would guarantee that, when oil from Tuymen arrived at NORSI, the proceeds from refining it would be contributed in part to Nizhny Novgorod pension fund, via the Central pension fund in Moscow, which distributes the monies, and in turn the pension fund in Tuymen would get its money too.

Through the governor's guarantee all parties win. Oil companies are no longer fined for delayed pension contributions. The refinery's under-capacity is solved because customers offer it their oil. The local administration gets its taxes paid and the pension fund administrators get paid because they have met their obligations.

Of course, as long as only the Nizhny Novgorod region makes this guarantee, it becomes the main benefactor of the improved relations while the Central pension fund in Moscow has still to deal with unreformed regions, but Moscow is still better off than it would have been otherwise. The oil pension scheme certainly won many new clients for the bank.

Russia's Major Problem: Change at the Center, Not the Periphery

"The problem in the Russian Federation is that social and economic changes can be organized at the center, or the 'inner circles' of the system, but we have so far failed to bring with us those beyond the first few circles of influence. It was because pensioners were being neglected and a whole group of older people were being forgotten that I set up the Social and Commercial Bank, but when I moved into government it proved

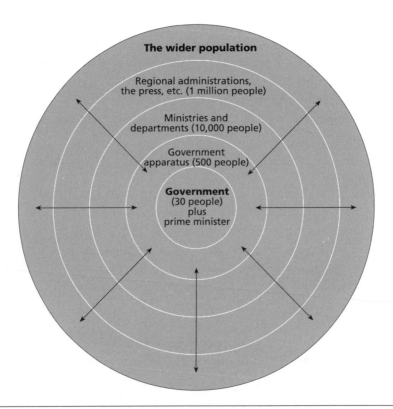

Concentric Circles of Governance

impossible to reach out to ordinary people and influence these in the same way as I had with the bank.

"It is because we do not have the wider public with us that it is so easy to dismiss senior politicians and blame them for disappointing results. Here, let me draw for you the Circles of Government. At the center are the Prime Minister and perhaps 30 people.

"When you get into government you can with great difficulty and some skill, influence two circles beyond your own, about 11,000 people. But the regions typically oppose you and the wider population suffers and blames you, so that a succession of Prime Ministers are dismissed to appease them.

"The unreconciled contradictions and dilemmas between the inner and outer circles are just too many and too severe. We failed to mobilise public support for what we believed had to be done and so the pressures, shown by the converging arrows was too strong to withstand.

"You do not just have people in the outer circles pushing, you are also pulled apart by interests who want you to do opposite things. I guess that is how dilemmas operate. You cannot satisfy everyone and they keep demanding that you support their interests against the others.

All this time you also had to satisfy the IMF, whose loans we could not do without, but which set conditions, which some Russians regarded as subversive of the nation's values. Russians are living in an apartment which we are simultaneously trying to repair and the mess is everywhere and everyone complains. The coordination of economic interests present in the first two or three circles is relatively simple, because you have the rationale of creating more value to guide you and attracting outside funds. But as you get into circles 3, 4 and 5 it is more and more politics and here the rivalries are fierce, unforgettable and set in solid rocks of hostility. These people are not creating wealth between them but keeping ancient animosities alive. They at once oppose any suggestions acceptable to a rival.

"Russia is very much tossed on the horns of Individualism and Communitarianism (dimension 2). We desperately need new ideas, new businesses, new initiatives, but when these are offered they are characterised as 'selfish' and 'opportunistic,' as they sometimes are. Reform is not trusted. Western ideas are seen as destructive of society. To get caught in these arguments is to be destroyed politically. Both sides turn on you."

Thus went the stellar rise of Sergei Kiriyenko to the premiership of the Russian Federation. Sadly some systems are simply too much for even the most talented of leaders. What used to be called "the contradictions of capitalism" and might now be called "the contradictions of post-communism" were finally too strong, for this one of its ablest administrators. For in the end, only *some* dilemmas are within our own cognitions, many lie *between* us and other people in our cultures. The force fields within cultures can be fearsomely strong and divisive. The would-be reconciler is among the foremost casualties.

CHAPTER 14

Toward a New Spirit

Leader: Edgar Bronfman (Seagram's)

It is no coincidence that we hear so much today about the missions of companies, their values, their cultures, and their purposes. We are advised to study *The Living Company* (Arie de Geus, 1998) and companies *Built to Last* (Collins and Porras, 1994). This is much more than rhetoric and public relations, for the fact is that leaders can no longer tell subordinates what they should do. Problems and challenges are too complex and too numerous. There is insufficient time to refer most issues to the top of the organization, and no mind is so capacious and knowledgeable as to be able to solve hundreds of judgment calls a day.

What has to happen is that leaders manage the *culture* of the corporation: its values, mission, purposes, strategies, and aims. Thereupon, autonomous agents within the context of this culture will make decisions that respond to those cultural aims. Rather like a director shooting a film, the leader does not tell the actors how to act, but describes the setting and the meaning of the situation and lets the characters loose to interpret their roles. The leader also recognizes quality in performance and moves on to the next take when quality has been achieved. The leader may not know how to handle a camera, but he or she knows good camera work. The leader might be incapable of rigging lights, but knows when a set is properly lighted. Values are used to set parameters (or soft goals), so that initiatives can be taken within these.

Shared meaning, values, and culture are all the more important when sites and operations are geographically dispersed. When the industry is in flux, when environments are turbulent, and when times are tough, it is even more important to know who you are, what you value, and where you intend to go. Edgar Bronfman, CEO of Seagram's, faced just such a situation. In addition, he was convinced that the firm's culture and its values would have to change if the company were to engage its changing environment successfully. What follows is an account of Bronfman's program for change.

What Bronfman Faced

Culture and Values: What are they?

Values are embedded in culture. The culture of an organization is the pattern of *what actually happens* on a routine basis – what has been seen to work well and is therefore admired and rewarded, what achieves internal integration and external adaptation, and what is passed on to newcomers as "the way we do things (or don't do things) around here." This definition is taken from Ed Schein, and it has some implications. Culture is *not* just what a CEO dreams up, extols, or tells people to do. The values espoused by an organization might or might not be realized in practice. What managers say they do, what they actually do, and what customers experience are not necessarily the same. Not all talk is walked. Not all aspiration is realized.

Seagram's Challenge: The Necessity of Change

Joseph E. Seagram and Sons, Inc., is a major player in the global beverage industry and recently has diversified into entertainment. The history of Seagram was a classic example of a company whose founding values and implicit practices seemed outmoded and counterproductive in the face of significant marketplace challenges. The Seagram Company was founded in 1924 with a single distillery in Canada and became a major player in the beverage industry for more than 70 years. Seagram developed a loyal consumer following with premier products and premier brands, such as Chivas Regal, Glenlivet, and Mum Champagne. Primarily operating in North America and Europe, Seagram has successfully positioned itself in these growth markets for decades.

By the late 1980s, however, the entire $16 billion industry was facing a "new sobriety." Young, up-and-coming executives and entrepreneurs drank water, especially at lunch. The new "high" was work itself and achievement. Spirits, being highly intoxicating, failed to keep pace with wine, and a health-conscious public turned to wine and fruit juices. Seagram acquired Tropicana in 1988 to keep up with this trend, as liquor sales fell. Higher taxes, campaigns against drunk driving, and social criticism of the marketing of spirits proved major challenges to the industry. Bronfman began to repeat his message throughout the company: "Better business results cannot be achieved by business as usual." His vision for Seagram was that it should be "the best-managed beverage company." When he assumed the roles of president and CEO in February 1995, he told 200 senior managers, "I have a vision and a belief that we will be best managed. We will be focused on growth, be fast and flexible, and be customer and consumer oriented. We will honor and reward teamwork; we will lead, not control. We will be willing to learn. We will develop, train, and motivate our people. We will be honest with ourselves and each other. We will manage on the basis of the values we articulate and share."

To realize this vision, Seagram would have to transform itself radically, change the way it thought and acted, reposition itself strategically, diversify, and "reengineer" its processes. Values were to be the medium and the currency of these changes. Over the next five years, values were to play a major role in transforming culture. What had been a proud and successful culture of individualism, entrepreneurship, authority, functional pride, and personal relationships was "in transition" to a new culture built around such new values as teamwork, innovation, and a consumer focus. Indeed, the value of innovation would become very dramatic as major strategic changes – multibillion-dollar acquisitions into the entertainment industry – were later to emerge as strong evidence that change was sought.

Seagram's success in the future would derive from this very different portfolio of businesses and a far more global enterprise. Its young and visionary CEO had visibly taken significant risks and laid major new bets for the company. To succeed would require aggressive development of their brands, products, and people to exploit their new businesses and improve old ones. But as the plans for reinventing Seagram were being fashioned, it became more and more clear that the company had to change every aspect of the way it had been managed. Indeed, it was then that Bronfman set the goal of being the best-managed company and a growth goal of 15 percent per year – both highly aggressive targets. Toward those twin ends, he was very clear about the need to reconcile top and bottom, hard and soft, and the long and the short term, but before being able to integrate and reconcile these orientations, the company needed to be reengineered.

Reengineering the Company while Developing Its Values

Bronfman was quick to grasp that reengineering was no magic formula. You cannot change industrial processes without the guidance and understanding that values bring. "It was essential from the outset that we would integrate the hard and soft sides of the change process," he said. "Reengineering *per se* is useless. Just looking at values and behavior is not much better. The combination with the right timing is what makes a winning team."

Dilemma 1:   Hard Reengineering vs. Soft Values

Seagram engaged the Boston Consulting Group in the mid-1990s to assist them in a major reengineering effort. The initial goal was to manage Seagram's business processes and operations more effectively and to reduce costs, yet there came to be increasing recognition that significant barriers to progress existed. The new processes required numerous changes in how people behaved and interacted with each other – indeed, a new culture. Seagram would have to unlearn its old culture, typified by silos, risk aversion, a rigid hierarchy, and limited communication. And the company would have to learn how to be more innovative, cooperative, communicative, and customer focused.

Bronfman articulated the conviction that, in order for values to change in any permanent way, *behavior must first change.* People value what they have experienced as accomplishments. They value the results of the accomplishments, the rewards for the results, the admiration received as a consequence, and the processes involved; but the key remains behavior, because the way aspiration is transformed into reality is via behavior. Seagram would finally consummate its values when it began to perform, and Bronfman's target was growth to 15 percent per year, a very sizable improvement on what he had inherited: virtually flat, even declining, performance.

The dilemma Bronfman faced and which his statements recognize is that reengineering without values to guide it, makes employees into "retrofitted mechanisms." (See same on chart for Dilemma 1.) But merely espousing values might not work either if the underlying hardware is not being used effectively. "Love-in on the *Titanic*" (see chart) should remind us that if the ship's present course and speed are going to sink it, then all the culture in the world and all the beautiful people on board will not keep that from happening. Your relationships must give you access to the wheelhouse, or they are doomed.

Dilemma 1. Culture as Patterns of Valued Behavior

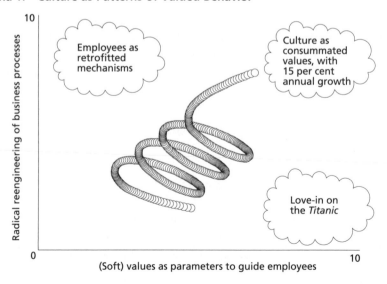

The helix moves clockwise, because you start with soft values and then realize them through the reengineering of hard processes, which in turn makes the soft values operational. Culture arises from values consummated through action. In this case, Bronfman made his 15-percent growth target.

Dilemma 2: Top Down vs. Bottom Up

If you want your core corporate values enshrined in actual behavior, you cannot impose that by fiat. Bronfman had the right – even the duty – to propose the values that Seagram should serve, but then these had to be negotiated and discussed with those whose conduct he was seeking to influence. He engaged in an intensive top-down *and* bottom-up process to reach agreement on the right wording and the right implementation. Bronfman explains, "I found it crucial to start conceptualizing the basic values myself. I knew where I wanted the company to be heading, but I couldn't do it alone. So we developed a very time-consuming, but effective, process that included all employees at Seagram."

Thus, the output of the management conference was refined and redrafted by the top 15 executives. This in turn was reviewed and critiqued by over 300 employees through 8- to 10-person focus groups. These employees represented a vertical cross section of the entire company – all businesses, all functions, and all levels. They were asked not only to give feedback on the values draft, but also to identify behavioral examples of the values in action and make suggestions about how to introduce and communicate those values. The employee version of the draft was much simpler and shorter than the original and was more understandable to all levels and all cultural backgrounds. These inputs were then fed back to the top executives, who once again redrafted the values. With this draft, the company appeared ready to finalize the six values: a consumer and customer focus, respect, integrity, teamwork, innovation, and quality. (See Exhibit 1.) Along with the values, there was a summary of "values in action," a checklist of behavioral examples for living the values. (See Exhibit 2.) There also was a strong view that the values had to be measurable in order to be practiced.

One might reasonably ask why employees would take so much trouble to discuss, negotiate, and finally agree on the core values inscribed in the two exhibits. Are they values not largely rhetorical? With the generalizations so wide and abstract, what we have is not a solemn agreement on the desirability of motherhood and apple pie? Many corporate missions might indeed be so abstract as to mean almost nothing and to constitute mere frosting on the cake, but we would be unwise to put Bronfman's in this category, because something else is happening here – something

Seagram Values

As Seagram Employees We Commit To the Following Values:

CONSUMER AND CUSTOMER FOCUS
Everything we do is dedicated to the satisfaction of present and future consumers and customers.

RESPECT
We treat everyone with dignity, and we value different backgrounds, cultures, and viewpoints.

INTEGRITY
We are honest, consistent and professional in every aspect of our behavior.
We communicate openly and directly.

TEAMWORK
We work and communicate across functions, levels, geographies, and business units to build our global Seagram family. We are each accountable for our behavior and performance.

INNOVATION
We challenge ourselves by embracing innovation and creativity, not only in our brands, but also in all aspects of our work. We learn from both our successes and failures.

QUALITY
We deliver the quality and craftsmanship that our consumers and customers demand - in all we do - with our products, our services and our people.

BY LIVING THESE VALUES,
we will achieve our growth objectives, and we will make Seagram the company preferred by consumers, customers, employees, shareholders and communities.

Exhibit 1

Seagram Values in Action

 Consumer And Customer Focus
- We demonstrate through our actions that consumers and customers have top priority in our daily work.
- We treat each person we deal with as a customer.
- We work continually to understand our consumer and customer's requirements and anticipate future needs.

 Respect
- We seek ideas and contributions from people, regardless of their level.
- We have a climate where issues are openly discussed and resolved.
- \We have a balance between our professional and private commitments.

 Integrity
- We deliver what we promise.
- We disclose facts even when the news is bad.
- We make decisions based on what's best for the company, rather than personal gain.

 Teamwork
- We share across borders, across affiliates and across functions to learn from one another.
- We work together to achieve consistent, shared goals
- We consider the impact our activities have on other areas of Seagram.

 Innovation
- We create an atmosphere where continuous improvement and creative thinking are encouraged.
- We look for new ways to remove layers of bureaucracy to enable speed and action.
- We have patience with new ventures and recognize there will be failures.

 Quality
- We produce results that consistently meet or exceed the standards of performance our consumers and customers expect.
- We consistently improve our processes to better serve our customers.
- We get the job done accurately and on time.

Exhibit 2

that helps to explain the alacrity of the negotiators and the 15-percent growth target later achieved. The values *are* indeed soft and *do* leave latitude for interpretation, but *therein lies the autonomy of managers and Bronfman's delegation of responsibility to them.* With broad parameters, you have considerable discretion from the bottom up in satisfying customers and for realizing the values via several alternative means. What these values call for is not obedience to set procedures, but self-generated solutions. To focus on customers and their satisfactions leaves all managers with considerable latitude in how these satisfactions are best delivered. The leader is not directing specific actions to be taken, but rather is indicating a process of discovery in which customers are *the* vital source of information. The values support a process of inquiry into what the environment wants and how those wants are changing. Bronfman is *modeling* the same bottom-up elicitation of knowledge that he wants his managers to employ with customers. The reconciliation of top down with bottom up is diagrammed in the next figure.

Dilemma 1.   Confluence of Top Down with Bottom Up

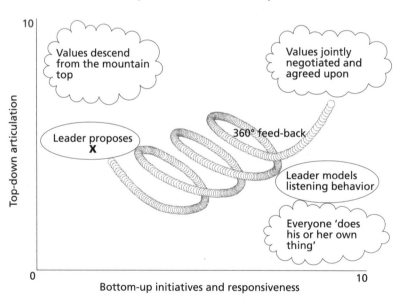

Note that Bronfman has led the process of defining values. The helix starts near the top left position on the chart, but this is no imposition: he proposes a set of values, and his managers come back to him with their own revisions and suggestions. Bronfman listens to them just as they should be listening to customers and incorporates many of their requests. Exhibits 1 and 2 are jointly negotiated and

Value Total		
Total	4.14	
Supervisor	4.57	
Peers	3.96	
Director of Reports	4.21	
Self	4.71	

6. This executive is approachable and friendly.		
Total	4.67	
Supervisor	5	
Peers	4.75	
Director of Reports	4.5	
Self	5	

1. This executive seeks ideas from people regardless of their level in the organization		
Total	4.44	
Supervisor	4	
Peers	4.5	
Director of Reports	4.5	
Self	4	

3. This executive is careful to consider another person's idea before accepting or rejecting it.		
Total	4.11	
Supervisor	4	
Peers	4.5	
Director of Reports	4.5	
Self	4	

4. This executive explains issues and answers questions when communicating.		
Total	4.11	
Supervisor	4	
Peers	3.75	
Director of Reports	4.5	
Self	5	

5. This executive treats people fairly when they make a mistake.		
Total	4.11	
Supervisor	5	
Peers	3.75	
Director of Reports	4.25	
Self	5	

2. This executive support people in their efforts to balance their professional time with their private lives.		
Total	3.78	
Supervisor	5	
Peers	3.75	
Director of Reports	3.5	
Self	5	

7. This executive provides periodic feedback to tell others where they stand in terms of performance.		
Total	3.78	
Supervisor	5	
Peers	3.5	
Director of Reports	3.75	
Self	4	

Exhibit 3

agreed upon, with the result that managers will try to live up to what are *their own* values.

Focus groups met at several levels to gauge the reaction of managers and employees to the statement of values. At "cascade meetings," local chiefs would meet with their direct reports, and comments, suggestions, revisions, and redraftings were collected. One theme emerging from the focus groups was whether "management is really serious about living the new values themselves." In short, workers were waiting to see whether their supervisors were going to *behave* differently or whether getting the workers' reactions was all a verbal exercise to make people feel good. To make the values statements operational and credible, a 360° feedback system based on the values was designed and administered to everyone. (See Exhibit 3.)

Three-hundred-sixty-degree feedback consists of asking peers, supervisors and workers to give feedback on the individual's demeanor – in this case, the individual's capacity to "live the values." The advantage of this tool is that it highlights upward, downward, and lateral styles of communication and identifies both those with a tendency "to bow to the wishes of authority and tread on the people beneath them" and those who organize the grass roots against those in authority. Bronfman used a virtuous circle to encompass the entire culture of change:

Bronfman's Virtuous Circle

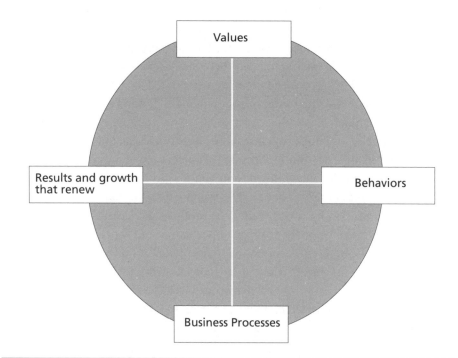

The concepts at the opposite sides of this learning circle were in tension with each other: values vs. business processes and behaviors vs. results. Each acted as feedback for the other. Values led to improved business processes, which in turn confirmed new values. Behaviors led to better results and increased growth, which habituated those behaviors which had proved effective and eliminated those behaviors which had not.

Dilemma 3:   Values Training as a Form of Consultancy and Learning

The new focus on values was also incorporated into training programs; toward this purpose, *the Center for Executive Development* in Cambridge, Mass., USA designed two values training programs, each of four days' duration. The first program, "Leading with Values," targeted Seagram's top 200 managers; the second program, "The Seagram Challenge," reached approximately 1000 middle managers. Each program focused on the meaning and application of the six values in everyday Seagram life and in best-practice standards from other companies. Participants discussed small case studies of Seagram situations in which the values were effectively put to a test. In addition, participants received 360° feedback about their own behaviors related to each value, were provided a private coach to discuss their findings, and were encouraged to develop personal action plans. Finally, each value was assessed on a companywide basis in terms of the perceived amount of "talk" about it and the perceived amount of "walk." Participants were asked to summarize their recommendations for improvements for the company, to close the gap between the walk and the talk as well as the gap between "today's walk" and the desired amount of "walk." The recommendations were presented to and discussed with, one or two senior executives, often Edgar Bronfman himself, during the last half-day of each training program.

Traditionally, training programs simply impart a lesson that senior managers wish their workers to learn. But in this case, seminars were designed so that trainees could consult with senior management and could assess and monitor the ongoing progress of the values project. That kind of training does not happen "on the side," but is part of a process by which leaders learn along with participants. In effect, training is one more opportunity for supervisors and workers to exchange "top-down" and "bottom-up" information to negotiate their differences.

Bronfman commented, "These discussions are very useful. The only way to translate values into behavior is to challenge ourselves as leaders continuously and to allow ourselves to be challenged by those who want to follow us. As leaders, we need to keep on pointing at what is valued behavior and what is not. People should not learn this from being fired when the message comes too late for them, but from many small ways in which we celebrate what is consistent with our values and discourage what is not."

The dilemma of how to train workers while also educating the educators or "talkers" is set out in the next diagram. Educators present and reinforce the values, but trainees explain how and why some of these values are difficult to translate into action, and they make representations and recommendations on how to "walk the talk" more effectively. Each side has half the answer. Educators know what values they are trying to instill. Participants in the seminar know the practical difficulties and pitfalls in the way of making some of the values viable. What happens, for example, when customers want something different from what they should get? How are staff in the field to mediate conflicting loyalties? Training continues the process of making values work in practice. It is a conduit through which customers communicate with the top of the corporation via managers in the field.

Dilemma 3.   Training as Consulting to the Corporation

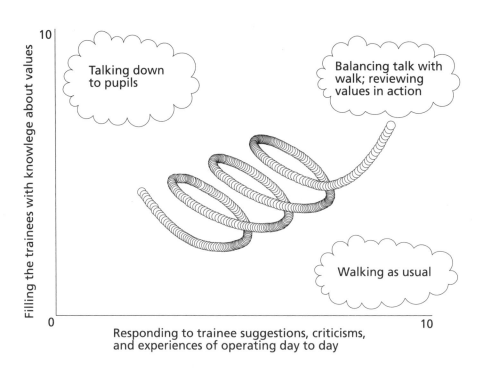

Dilemma 4:   **Those Who "Succeed" but Violate Values:**
Reconciling "What" With "How"

Many participants in values seminars take it as a sign of Bronfman's seriousness that those who violate values, however "successful" they might be according to traditional criteria, are sanctioned for their violation. Suppose your commercial results are good, but you acted in the wrong way – breaking promises, hiding facts, and conning the customer? Bronfman had a chart, borrowed from Jack Welch at GE, that dealt with this issue. (See Exhibit 4.)

Make the numbers	Type I Former Heroes	Type II New Heroes
Miss the numbers	Type IV Newly Unemployed Executives	Type III Potential Heroes
	Inappropriate values	Appropriate values

Exhibit 4

People could *make the numbers* or *miss the numbers*. In the old dispensation, that was all there was to it. Those who *kept* missing would soon *go* missing. Making the numbers was everything. Top management was not too fussy about how this was done or whether values were violated. Under the new values-driven system, the "former heroes," or Type I, were to be disciplined on account of their inappropriate behavior, while those who fulfilled the values, but had yet to make the numbers, were "potential heroes" of Type III. Those who *both* missed the numbers *and* violated values now had two reasons for unemployment, as in Type IV, while the "new heroes," Type II, both made the numbers and personified the values in the ways they behaved.

We have reproduced Exhibit 4 in the exact style Seagram uses, but in fact, it can easily be represented as a dilemma without altering its sense. We thereby illustrate – if more illustration is needed – that outstanding leaders think in terms of dilemmas, as shown in the following figure.

Dilemma 4. Reconciling "What" with "How"

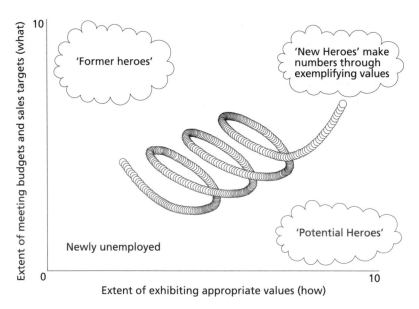

The helix is counterclockwise and moves first to the right, because Seagram wants managers to start by modeling its values. Then, *through* modeling the values, the managers go on to make their numbers. The "former heroes" may have short-term results to their credit, but they have achieved them by violations of good conduct that, before long, will weaken the organization and harm the development of its people and customers. Together, these visible symbols of the rewards for exemplary values behavior and the costs of values violations were crucial actions to reinforce and sustain the values. There were always disagreements as to who truly deserved an over-and-above award or who deserved to be fired, but the signal was sent that there would be consequences to living or not living the values.

Several issues are still in the process of being discussed. Should those "living" the values be rewarded for this alone – even the Potential Heroes? Is it not true that living by values is its own reward and should not gain additional compensation? Should the entire work-force below management be participants in the values discussions?

Results

Communication of Values in Action

Finally, the corporate and business unit communications managers developed plans to highlight the values in executive speeches, corporate magazines, off-site conferences, annual reports, and letters from the CEO. For example, the quarterly corporate magazine, called *Premiere*, included stories of successful values in action – highlighting one or two values in each edition. Even as times and individuals changed, terms such as "Team Seagram," "consumer focus," and "innovation" appeared regularly through the end of the decade of the 1990s.

What Happened? Outcomes and Results

There was no formal evaluation of the impact of the values culture change, but there are several data points – qualitative and quantitative – that together add up to a qualified success overall. What follows are comments made by Seagram executives in interviews.

> Reengineering did not just spot gaps in our knowledge and processes, it also discovered a host of hidden talents, roles, and capabilities. We are already reaping the benefits of reengineering, in terms of improved business practices and working culture, as well as cost savings, as part of a continuous drive toward excellence.   (Donard Gaynor, reengineering leader)

> Cultural change was crucial to improving our performance as we seek to be flexible, innovative, and fast to market. For this to happen, people need a common denominator and clear reference points for behavior – hence, our values-in-action program.
> (Steven J. Kalagher, president and CEO, Seagram Spirits and Wine Group)

> Regarding teamwork, there has been more cross-departmental cooperation. Employees from sales and manufacturing areas have come together in workshops and learned about one another's job challenges and responsibilities, which has led to a greater respect among and across departments.   (A Seagram manufacturing manager)

> Our surveys of customers have shown that Seagram's external customers are more satisfied, validating our commitment to the value of a customer and consumer focus.   (A Seagram marketing manager)

Some of the traditional, militaristic methods that were a common complaint among employees have been replaced by flextime options and casual workday attire This is a big part of what the respect value is all about.

(A Seagram employee)

In addition to citing these comments, one can point to some quantitative factors of success. Customer satisfaction surveys, training workshop evaluations, and the innovative acquisition of new businesses all indicate market improvements in Seagram's performance. The values have served as a critical impetus for all these initiatives. Indeed, the overall growth rate of the company – attributable to many more factors than the values, of course – has increased in the late 1990s. Finally, all the values workshops and discussions have sparked enthusiasm in a group of employees who have the potential to become future leaders and key contributors to the company's success.

Now, expectations have been raised – and by no means always met. Despite some of the positive changes that had occurred in Seagram since the values program was implemented, there remained some underlying skepticism among employees. Despite the fact that this four-year initiative – continuing to date – has been the longest in Seagram history, employees still question whether their managers are truly living the values. Conflicts between day-to-day behaviors and decisions based on some of the Seagram values continued to exist and understandably sent disheartening messages within the organization.

For example, to some of the old guard at Seagram, respect means keeping your mouth shut and your head down and treating those who rank above you with awe. Some of the newer, younger, and more innovative thinkers interpret respect differently and feel *themselves* to be disrespected by their elders. Another value that is subject to some criticism is teamwork. For some, the existing bonus system still essentially says, "Rank has its privileges," and, as a result, "Team Seagram," which is meant to cut across vertical and horizontal boundaries, appears unachieved – as yet.

In sum, the experience to date with values and with reengineering has created a lot of good results, but some obvious gaps remain. The reinvention of Seagram's business strategy and business processes is palpable. Seagram has become both a beverage and an entertainment company. It has transformed numerous fundamental business processes through reengineering. But in the creation of a new "genetic code," labelled as values, there is still work to be done. Indeed, this is hard work that takes many years to bear fruit, and Seagram has made undeniable progress to date. However, as was stated at the outset of this chapter, it is easier to focus on the restructuring, the buying and selling of businesses, and the cost-cutting efficiencies than it is to change the daily work habits and attitudes of thousands of employees. Nonetheless, the long-lasting results of change will occur only when the values are indeed the instinctive habits of the new company and, as such, become institutionalized.

Discussion and Implications of the Seagram Case Study

Seagram's example provides an in-depth look at how to implement values by using management as a critical component in a restructuring and reinvention effort. The details of the process were examined because it is by the details that the success or failure of an effort is determined. What are the general lessons from all this? There are two ways to put this example in perspective: one for the pragmatic practitioners and the other for the reflective practitioners.

What differentiates successful from unsuccessful values-based management? What is common to companies that succeed, and what is common to those that fail? The way a company implements its values program is a critical determinant of whether the program succeeds or fails. Implemented properly, a values program can become the very essence of a company. Implemented improperly, it can become the subject of mockery and make the shortcomings of the company only more glaring.

Successful values-based management efforts tend to share some characteristics. First, value systems cannot be imported; they have to be homegrown. In doing so, first and foremost, a company must make sure its values are aligned with its strategy and are seen as a vehicle to help a company build competitive advantage. Second, values are typically balanced between "soft" and "hard" issues. This balance ensures that values are linked to real business and customer issues. Third, proposed values are discussed in detail and their relevance to the company is debated. If employees contribute to the process, they are far more likely to support and live the values. Richard Pascale, in *Managing on the Edge*, supports these observations as well:

> Experience teaches us that an effective statement of vision, values, and guiding principles cannot be hammered out by the public relations staff or the human resources (personnel) department. Nor do they blossom from crash efforts of an executive task force. Values are truly a "no pain, no gain" proposition. If top management doesn't agonize over them and regard them as a psychological contract between itself, employees, and society, such statements are little more than empty words. But if hewn from discussion and introspection, values come to be internalized as honored precepts of behavior.

They serve like the North Star: as valuable guiding lights that orient an organization and focus its energies.

Once they agree to a set of values and aspirations, people must be equipped, trained, coached, and reinforced to live the values. In the case of Seagram, there was a clear evolution of training efforts to help reinforce the values. In the beginning, there were the Leading with Values and Seagram Challenge programs, which were designed to create awareness and build commitment. Then the Living the Values program was instituted to provide a forum for employees to talk about values, and later the Seagram Discovery program emerged to address specific "how-to's."

In putting all these elements together, one can see that the implementation of values-based management ultimately requires a broad repertoire of change levers, all of which are aligned and all of which are crucial. Exhibit 5 summarizes the key elements discussed here and serves as a road map for practitioners of change. The exact sequence and, obviously, the specific details vary from company to company. However, it is by the effective use of these levers and by disciplined execution that the success of values-based management is realized.

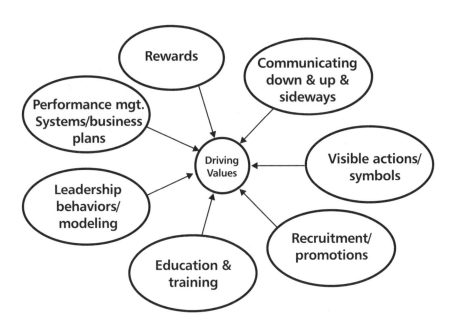

Exhibit 5

Dilemma 5:   Values Can Evaporate like Spirits – How to Keep on Connecting

More recently, the question has arisen of how to keep up the momentum. When everyone has agreed on the *values in action*, and after most have been through seminars and raised issues of implementation and practicality, where does Seagram go from there? One direction was to create additional learning initiatives. A program called Living the Values provided a forum for ongoing discussions. Those who had taken the seminar 3 years earlier faced new challenges on the ground. Because challenges had not yet been exposed to the values test, the executives who had taken the seminar could benefit from a refresher course, while the values themselves could be assessed for their relevance to new markets and new developments.

A program called Seagram Discovery targeted new recruits to the company: those who had not attended the original seminars. The values were supposed to be the keys to better performance, but simply believing in them was not, by itself, going to raise performance. Values had to be imaginatively deployed and mobilized. New *ways* of "respecting the customers" had to be discovered and tried. The values "came to life" when they made a major difference in the performance of a job. Values could also be interpreted from a variety of viewpoints and perspectives. Ronny

Dilemma 5.   Multiple Interpretations of Core Values

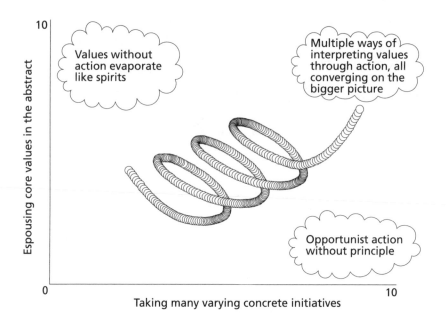

288

Vansteenkiste, head of organizational learning and change and the designer of Seagram Discovery, said, "This program forced people to put on a different lens and see things from other angles. We needed to expose people to such a program in order for us to become innovative. They needed to see the bigger picture."

The process of integrating values with behavior and walking the talk is not a once-only breakthrough. You do not "get it" and then keep the new knowledge safely in the bosom of the corporation. The task of reconciling values with actual conduct never ends, and it keeps coming apart unless it is carefully maintained. Bronfman recently likened values to spirits, which all too easily evaporate into a heady sensation in your nasal passages. Once again demonstrating his instinct for dilemmas, Bronfman condemned both "vaporous spirits" *and* "acting without principle" – that is, acting without knowing or asking yourself why you are behaving that way. The previous diagram illustrates the dilemma.

What helps to integrate the many ways of serving customers is the underlying principle of respect. The search for new ways of grounding values in new realities never ends. Values need to be renewed in all their manifestations.

Commentary

Measuring the Driving Values

There is an old adage that what gets measured in a company literally "counts," but values are typically too soft and vague to measure and are accordingly "of no account." Values are given lip service, but, when all the data come in, you either have made the numbers or you have not; your unit either is profitable or is not. Unless the attainment of values is measured with equal rigor, it can become so much "noise."

Values-Based Management as a Trend among Successful Companies

The companies that have engaged in values-based management the longest, such as Johnson and Johnson, have shown that it is indeed a combination of balancing the effort to reinforce with an effort to reinvigorate. Every few years, J&J has engaged in a companywide exercise to challenge and improve its credo of corporate values. The words, ironically, seem to end up largely the same, but the dialogue that occurs serves to refresh and reinvigorate, and thereby enable people to recommit to the values. Thus, there emerges a delicate, but effective, balance between *preserving* what people believe to be critical standards of behavior and decisions and continually *challenging* how to improve them.

Ironically, then, values-based management can both help to create change in organizations, as was stated at the outset of this chapter, and itself be subject to change and challenge. For most companies, the challenge of instituting and living values is itself formidable, but the ultimate challenge for the most successful companies is how to keep the values alive through refreshing, reinterpreting, renaming, and reiterating. These "re" words are therefore just as applicable to values-based management as they are to the companies that themselves are facing change pressures and opportunities. Thus, Motorola's "Individual Dignity Entitlement" has no fixed definition, but evolves over time through structured dialogues between the supervisor and the person supervised. It is a process of values renewal.

There are many such indicators if you are determined to identify and use them. For instance, *communicating up, down, and sideways* was measured by the 360° feedback instrument already touched upon, but this concept had to be gradually eased into use, because its verdicts can hurt the managers assessed. The discovery that your subordinates dislike you – that, say, women or minorities find you arbitrary and unpleasant – can be quite a shock. Accordingly, in the first year of operations, a manager's score was a private affair between that manager and his or her coach, but, in the second year, scores became known to the manager's superior and became an official part of the assessment. This meant that, in effect, everyone had a year's grace to put right negative feedback on values in action.

Visible Actions and Symbols

Another way of supporting *values in action* is to bestow public praise on those whose measurable performance best exemplifies core values. Which field office has been rated best by customers on the basis of what criteria? Not only should measures of customer satisfaction be publicized, but those with the highest ratings should receive honor and acclaim.

Recruitment and Promotions

The process of recruiting to Seagram must advertise for people willing to serve described values, and during the interview process potential recruits can be asked about initiatives they envision that would fulfill those values. Can they think of ways of making their values work in practice?

Assessment and promotion should employ instruments based on the values. In the case of Seagram, several managers were put on "probation," not for underperformance, but for not exemplifying the values. This had a profound effect on the culture; values were important after all.

In our view, all micromeasures should themselves be in dilemma format. Hence, when assessing a manager, you ask "How bold was your aspiration for the previous year?" "How well did you meet those aspirations?" "What did you achieve?" and "How did you achieve it?"

Education and training has already been discussed. Suffice it here to say that the presentations to top management at the end of the seminar should be an occasion to reward the best. Furthermore, there is no reason that initiatives should stop at the door of the classroom. Good presentations can be repeated to key groups of decision makers, and smart teams can be kept together to champion their solutions.

Finally, *leadership behaviors need modeling.* Apart from what you say, fellow managers notice what you do. Indeed, there is much to say for changing your behavior *first* and then, when you have colleagues intrigued with your new conduct, explaining your reasons. If you want staff to listen to customers, it is more effective to listen to staff yourself than to preach a sermon on listening. If you want punctuality at the office in the morning, look to your own arrival times. Actual behavior is much easier to measure than the utterance of noble sentiments.

Performance Management Systems and Business Plans

Among the easier values to measure is quality. How many broken cases? How many returns? How many late deliveries? What about in-process inventory, carrying costs, and inventory turns? How many customers complained? Do they now believe that their complaints were respected and the problem remedied? Which were the outstanding teams in the last quarter? Who do those teams believe were their most valuable players in enhancing team performance? Who *sponsored* the most successful teams, empowered them, and delegated authority to them? Who were chiefly responsible for recognizing the innovative capacity *of others?*

The more ways you can find to measure values, the more reliable will be the pattern that emerges. How and why does a certain person repeatedly sponsor a team, give it a goal, and get wonderfully innovative solutions out of it? We know the values involved: respect, integrity, teamwork, innovation, and quality, but they do not tell what crucial judgments the sponsor has made to keep getting superior results. The behaviors that serve these values need constant rediscovery. How do you set goals that "stretch" your group without exhausting or disappointing its members? Values are the avenues of inquiry at the end of which lie realizations of that inquiry.

Rewards can take many forms, but it is perhaps inadvisable to dangle carrots or wield sticks, because these may detract from the logic of discovery involved in bringing values to life. Most values carry their own rewards; your customers will reciprocate your respect for them, and teams can make their star members feel ecstatic about themselves. Rewards are very important for another reason, also: Any group or person solving a problem deserves the attention of the corporation, so that the solution can be taught. Rewards are not so much the motivators of problem solving or of learning in themselves as they are *signals about who has succeeded and who should now get additional resources to follow up that success.* Those who have brought core values to life need to be highlighted so that others can learn to emulate them and duplicate that feat.

Conclusions

We have seen that values-based management is essentially a participative process in which managers negotiate wide degrees of freedom and latitude in exchange for being assessed according to behavioral indices of how those values have been exemplified in practice. Managers are judged both by results and by the process used to achieve those results. They must "make the numbers" by methods that clearly derive from the core values involved.

Throughout the entire change process, there must be a reconciliation of re-engineering with values parameters (Dilemma 1), of top-down articulation with bottom-up initiatives (Dilemma 2), of filling trainees with values with responding to their criticisms and day-to-day experiences implementing those values (Dilemma 3), of *what* has been achieved commercially with *how* it has been done socially (Dilemma 4), and of the abstract core values being espoused with an ever-increasing variety of initiatives that bring those values to life in different ways (Dilemma 5). Bronfman's record speaks for itself.

An Ironic Postscript

Most of our chapter have "happy endings," with all indicators pointing up. In June 2000, Vivendi, the French entertainment group, made a successful bid for Seagram, so that once again all is uncertainty; but values-based management is well designed to help business units survive such experiences – to know, amid the turmoil, who they are and what they stand for.

CHAPTER 15

Change within Continuity

Leader: Karel Vuursteen (Heineken)

Karel Vuursteen, president of Heineken, took control of a company that had been successful for a number of years, but the prospects of continuing that level of success were less certain, without a renewal of the values of the company. He could not afford to let go of a profitable past, but neither could he continue without significant changes. He faced the problem of redefining his company in fast-changing circumstances – the ever recurring dilemma of change with continuity and the challenge of renewal.

Karel Vuursteen: A Professional CEO

I (DD) met Karel Vuursteen, Heineken's president, in Amsterdam, at his office, looking over the canal and facing the old brewery, now a museum and the site of Heineken's new business academy. Although he sits amid the elaborate carvings of the Heineken dynasty, Karel is the first CEO to run the company without family members on the supervisory or executive board. Yet, he must somehow reconcile the interests of that family with the professionalism required and expected of a CEO who has been chosen for his merit, expertise, and achievements. He has been spectacularly successful, as we shall see.

Heineken's *Global Leadership Platform* recently flagged some serious problems. There was growing pressure on prices and margins in the firm's retail food outlets. The company's capacity to influence consumers was limited, especially in hotels, restaurants and other outlets. Much of the growth was in less attractive markets. The fragmentation of markets had raised marketing costs.

Heineken undertook an extensive exercise in postulating scenarios. Two axes of uncertainty were the relative strength of retailers and the globalism vs. regionalism of markets:

The following table describes the scenarios in more detail.

Scenario	Environment	Beer markets
World Shopping Center	Continued globalization Free trade Solid economic growth	Powerful global brands Strong local brands Few global brewers
Back to Identity	Strong regionalism Strong tariff barriers Slow economic growth	Stable global brands Strong local brands Network of viewers
World of Retail	Mediocre economic growth Powerful retail chains Cheap, fast-brewing technologies	Strong private-label brands Stable local brands Low-cost producers

In facing these alternative futures, whose salience would probably be a question of degree, the Global Leadership Platform saw several strategic dilemmas.

• What would be the consumers' strength of preference between high quality and low cost?

- Would free trade be stronger than protectionism, or *vice versa*?
- Would regulation facilitate or restrict the beer business?
- Would consumer behavior be group and community oriented or more individualistic?

We will leave these issues for the moment, to pick up on the leadership dilemmas described by Karel Vuursteen, but we will return to them in the light of his concerns to see how the reconciliation of certain key dilemmas can contribute to the reconciliation of other ones. Vuursteen and I discussed three major dilemmas that the leader saw himself confronting and needing to reconcile:

1. Rapid growth vs. the shareholding interests of the Heineken family
2. A premium, branded global product vs. a cheaper, local–regional product
3. Stability and tradition vs. innovative products and markets

Finally, we shall turn to issues flagged by the Global Leadership Forum and the exercise in postulating scenarios and ask what else might need to be done to meet the concerns expressed in these issues.

Dilemma 1: Rapid Growth *vs.* The Shareholding Interests of the Heineken Family

The company is still controlled by the Heineken family, and Karel Vuursteen's duty remains to the family (as well as to public shareholders). He is an agent of owners, obligated to serve their interests, but the owners are of two kinds: private and public. The family-held shares constitute a majority. The members of the family see Heineken as a legacy to their children, grandchildren, and great-grandchildren – indeed, as a legacy to the nation and to the global beer industry. Short-term positive results are welcome, but these occur in the wider context of the Heineken contribution to economies and lifestyles and its overall reputation and market position.

"Clearly," Vuursteen states, "I'm not hired by the Heineken family[1] to dilute its share in the company, so there is a very exciting tension that I have to manage: not dilute the interest of the Heineken family, yet grow fast enough to satisfy my public shareholders while remaining world class. I have to be both a caring father and a champion of high earnings." Some people, including certain colleagues in the

---

1 The role of the family and business is discussed further in Chapter 19, when different family business sociotypes are considered.

company, find his policy too cautious. They believe he should sell more shares to the public, increase investment funds, and go for growth at all costs. They think him insufficiently daring. But his aim is for controlled growth, for sustainable returns, and for being true to Heineken's origins as a family company that aims to improve the human condition. He is not about to attenuate the family's control of what it built over three generations.

He continues, "There is a way of satisfying both sets of obligations, and that is to increase our value per share. That way, both public and private shareholders are better off."

Karel Vuursteen's success in this policy should not be underestimated. Since he joined Heineken, net profits have tripled from dfl 300 million to almost 1 billion. The company's nominal growth since 1980 has been 14 percent per annum, or 11 percent when corrected for inflation; that amounts to doubling in size every seven years. Above all, earnings and value per share have risen since Vuursteen took charge. The dilemma looks like this:

Dilemma 1.   Growth vs. Family Interests

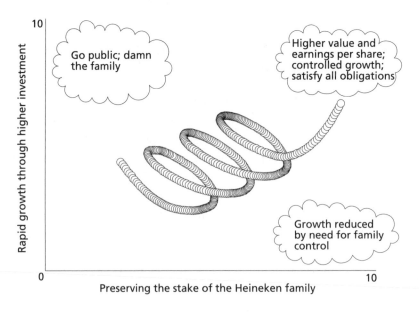

By making each share more valuable and boosting earnings per share, Heineken rewards public shareholders, yet the Heineken family remains in control of its legacy and tradition. Those who originated the company and shared its fate for three generations have rights and obligations, superior to those of a pension fund that bought the shares last week and might well sell them next week. Vuursteen has to mediate between these very different stakes.

Dilemma 2:   A Premium, Branded Global Product *vs.* a Low-price, Regional or Localized Product

We have elaborated this dilemma slightly by melding Vuursteen's chief concern, *brand vs. brewer*, with the Global Leadership Platform's concern about *premium quality vs. low cost* and with the issue arising from the scenario-postulating exercise about *globalism vs. regionalism*. The successful brander tends to earn a global premium, while the successful brewer has a more regional, word-of-mouth appeal, based on production processes that initially delight only neighborhoods nearby, although their popularity may spread.

Vuursteen explained to Dirk Devos that the marketing of beer is quite complex. Heineken is the only premium lager beer brand with a truly global presence. At the same time, it must be aware every day of the importance of local roots for beer marketing. Every country, every region, has its own beer tradition, and this specific tradition largely determines how to integrate a beer portfolio into the existing traditions of the local market while adding the Heineken brand on top of it as the international premium brand. "We surf on the power of the local beer roots when we enter a new market," says Vuursteen. Heineken believes it has good reason to do it this way. "Look at Coca-Cola in Brazil," urges Vuursteen. "They never got the soft-drink position Coca-Cola has obtained in other markets, because they neglected regional tastes. We should be aware that local responsiveness is connected with local eating and drinking habits that are deeply rooted." Yet sheer volume and economies of scale are crucial in the beer business, which operates by a very simple logic:

profit = **operating profit** per hectoliter (22 gallons) × **volume** of hectoliters or gallons

Heineken believes that it has the best brewing technology in the world, but the throughput from using this technology is vital also; it has to push volume through high-quality processes. In 1886, the company developed the famous Heineken A-yeast, which gives its lager a distinctive taste and is the core of its brewing process to this day. Heineken was the first export beer in the United States to offer lager in small bottles, making that move in 1933. With Prohibition just ending and the number of refrigerators in the home increasing, the firm won a sizeable share of the US market.

Heineken's typical strategy for expansion reconciles the company's premium brand with local brewing traditions. Heineken acquires regional breweries, and it is good at transferring its brewing know-how to them while still maintaining the taste that won them local acceptance. Using their outlets, their customers, and their goodwill, Heineken continues their brewing traditions while superimposing its own premium brand. This strategy enables Heineken to encompass both low-cost products and premium products and to convert some consumers to the latter while the company supplies a wide spectrum of demand. Both premium and lower-priced brews push up total volume. In those countries where Heineken cannot command high volumes, it aims for a niche position among premium beers and strives for leadership.

Compared with its competitors, Heineken uniquely combines branding strategies with brewing strategy. Interbrew and South African Breweries are typically strong in brewing, investing chiefly in production and distribution. Anheuser-Busch is among the top branding companies, with its powerful Budweiser brand. Heineken invests heavily in both branding and brewing; its brewing technology gives it economies of scale, and its brands, global and regional, constitute a family, each member having both a local identity and enough autonomy to grow beyond local roots to a broader presence.

Traditionally, Heineken followed the American pattern of earning premiums via "export lager." In that multiethnic society, imported European beers had a special cachet as the authentic flavor of the old countries. Now, however, Heineken is challenging this entrenched belief, on the grounds that local product and local sourcing give it regional advantages, without the sacrifice of premium qualities. The company exports know-how, not necessarily or always beer. Over time, Heineken has switched from *central control* to *decentralized coordination*, which reconciles branding with brewing and globalism with regionalism. When Vuursteen took over the company, he had a discussion with his predecessor, who advised him, "If I were to choose between brewing and branding, I would have to choose branding."

That was in the early 1990s. Vuursteen is now glad that he did not make a definite choice for either one. When you go through a scenario-building process, you realize that you might have to rely more heavily on one than on the other, but you cannot predict which will be more effective. You then see that you require both, with the relative emphasis dependent on circumstances. In a "world shopping center," for example, you need branding above brewing, but in "back to identity" you need all the brewing expertise you can muster. It is irresponsible not to develop both themes.

Can we diagram Karel Vuursteen's dilemma, together with the dilemma seen by the Global Leadership Platform? We believe we can. The conflicting values read as follows:

Dilemma 2.   The Branded Brewer

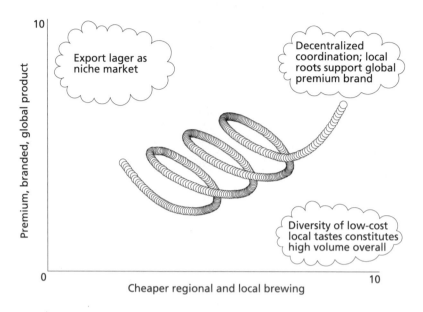

The actual process is a bit too complex to be captured by this diagram. Roots in the local community give Heineken immediate knowledge of local beer-drinking habits and distribution networks. These are then reorganized to deliver not simply staple brews, but also premium, branded products. The mix of local and global brews maximizes volume throughput, while advanced brewing technologies make quality relatively cheap. More of this complexity can be captured by devising a virtuous circle, as shown on the next page.

Dilemma 3:   Tradition and Stability vs. Innovative Products and Markets

The Heineken tradition is incredibly valuable, but also potentially frail. For over a hundred years, it has appealed to people's taste buds, but these sensing devices do not explain why they enjoy Heineken and what commands their loyalty. Because this patronage is in part mysterious, Heineken interferes with it or introduces sudden changes only at its peril. When you are unsure of what you have, you can lose it quite easily. When changes must be made, it is unclear what is fundamental to Heineken's reputation and what is peripheral. Historically, the company's reputation has been maintained at great cost.

Vuursteen provides an example: In 1993, Heineken had a problem with glass

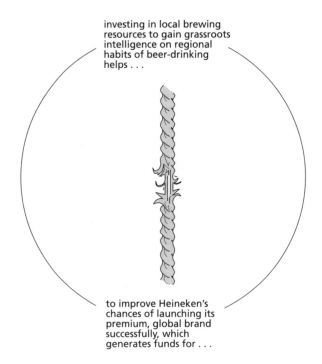

investing in local brewing
resources to gain grassroots
intelligence on regional
habits of beer-drinking
helps . . .

to improve Heineken's
chances of launching its
premium, global brand
successfully, which
generates funds for . . .

particles in its bottles. It needed to decide whether to recall all the bottles from all its distribution channels in 21 countries. Heineken had no data on how much this operation would cost. Nor could it judge the risks, because experts came up with different views. Vuursteen faced one question: Should Heineken recall all these bottles, yes or no? The decision had to be made without any knowledge of the consequences. He isolated himself and, one hour later, decided on a full recall action. His reasoning was that if even one human life was endangered, that would be too much risk. He also saw some possible benefit in quickly admitting a mistake, even if it was that of the bottler, and accepting full responsibility for the consequences. Perhaps ready admission would lead customers to trust Heineken more in the long run. Those hundreds of millions of bottles carried its brand, so the brand had to act responsibly. Heineken survived that crisis with greater respect for itself and from other people.

In its early days of export to the United States, the Heineken family promised its American agents that all profits from its operations stateside would be reinvested in the export business: 50 percent in Heineken advertising and 50 percent in Heineken USA. That pledge, together with the bond it created, is part of Heineken's heritage and tradition. It will not lightly be destroyed. That is an example of how Heineken's approach to innovation is cautious. It changes one thing at a time and watches carefully for negative impacts. Of course, we are talking less about facts than about perceptions and appearances. Vuursteen's view of change is that it must maintain continuity: There are lots of changes out there, but Heineken must remain true to what people like about it, even as markets and environments shift.

Vuursteen continues: "In a funny way, we are still searching for what has always been important in our appeal to consumers. We know we are successful, but we don't know just why.The real fight is for consistency to maintain whatever our attraction is. We may have to change to remain consistent. This applies especially to processes. Can we do things better, cheaper, and quicker, with the same results as before? Can we draw on more talents to preserve our quality? We recently launched a design competition on the Internet for the improvement of beer-can designs. We received top-quality work."

One way of innovating that is not dangerous is to clear a space for a totally new approach, one that is separate from Heineken's existing success and will not endanger it. Look at the Volkswagen Beetle: in the early 1970s, the Golf (Rabbit) was created. It was the first expression of a new archetype. It was needed, because the Beetle was outdated. So when somebody comes to Vuursteen and says, "I want to create something totally new in the beer market," he is inclined to say, "Go ahead, do it; let's create the free space you need and create this new world, but don't touch the heritage and the present success of our leading products and brands."

This dilemma can be expressed as follows.

Dilemma 3.   Don't Mess with Success

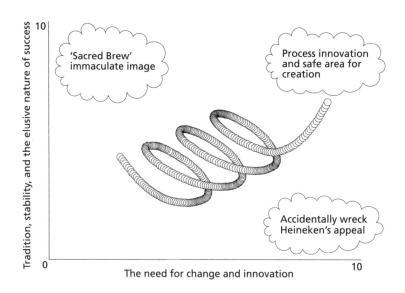

Heineken is highly successful, but the reasons for this success are elusive. *That* customers like the brand is clear; *why* they like it is less clear. Vuursteen might decide to change nothing, for fear of damaging the "Sacred Brew," or he could embark on wholesale innovation and accidentally wreck Heineken's appeal. Instead, he has very cleverly embarked on two forms of innovation that are relatively safe: *process innovation* searches for better and newer means of creating the same result, and *reserving a safe area for creation* allows new beverages to be invented from scratch, without involving Heineken's premium product in these experiments, much as the Golf grew up beside the Beetle.

This completes our discussion of Karel Vuursteen's three principal dilemmas, but, in addition, we can observe an obvious affinity between our second dimension, individualism vs. communitarianism, and a very similar concern expressed by the Global Leadership Platform on how consumer behavior might evolve.

Individualism vs. Communitarianism in Markets

Traditionally, beer brands are heavily advertised via TV to the *mass market* (a market of aggregated individuals who do not know each other, but who share a liking for Heineken's products). Heineken's export lager grew up in America's age of mass marketing and is one of its outstanding success stories. Surveys show individualism growing in affluent parts of the world. Do we need anything more?

The story Vuursteen told about the glass particles in bottles suggests another side to the company. Most economists will tell you that self-interest and individualism are sovereign and superordinate in commercial affairs, but that is *not* how Vuursteen behaved in the crises he faced and not how Johnson and Johnson behaved when a deranged person put cyanide in bottles of Tylenol. In both cases, *all units of the product were withdrawn and the company took responsibility for the errors of others.* When the chips were down Heineken was a family company concerned with families of customers. Its *first* duty was to the safety of those customers; only second did its duty to enrich shareholders come into play. Crises teach us what our real values are; as Johnson and Johnson remarked, all the money due to shareholders comes from satisfied customers.

In both of these cases, the community judged the companies by the social concern they exhibited. For both, sales climbed rapidly after the crises were resolved. Vuursteen had to ask himself what the Heineken family would want and what he himself stood for. In both cases, the answer was the coherence of community and individual concerns. Individuals benefit as a consequence of first caring for customers. In crises, you learn what economists do not teach.

The dilemma can be drawn thus:

Dilemma 4. Community concern vs. self-interest

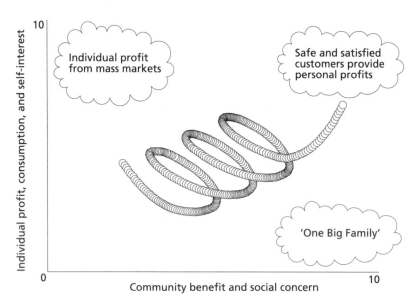

The conventional economic view is at point X, where there are short-term profits to be made from mass-market appeals, but, when a crisis struck, Vuursteen was challenged to understand that his prior obligation was to the community. "Prior" is not necessarily the same as "most important," though prior means "before." Before you make profit, you take good care of customers, so that the flow of custom is restored; then you integrate community with individualism once more. Vuursteen was correct in his belief that this crisis might, in the longer run, turn to Heineken's benefit. What customers infer from such incidents is the supplier's commitment to *them*. They are impressed, as well they might be, by sacrifices made to protect them. We tend to judge others by their intentions, not by the absence of any mistakes. We have learned this from our fourth dimension: Specific – Diffuse. Mistakes are specific, but if they occur in the diffuse context of continuing care and good intentions, we often forgive them.

What are the prospects for the balance between individualism and communitarianism in the future? In our view, the Internet makes it much easier for customers to discuss and form opinions about a corporation's social conduct. In the future, it might well be that a reputation for social responsibility and good, neighborly conduct will be at least half the battle.

CHAPTER 16

The Challenge of Renewal

Leader: Hugo Levecke (ABN AMRO)

I (DD) have known Hugo Levecke, the chairman of the managing board of ABN AMRO Lease Holding, for 17 years. Over that time, Levecke's reputation had become formidable: whenever he was given a leadership task, dynamic growth, improved service, and superior financial performance resulted. For the purposes of this book, we met at the Okura hotel in Amsterdam, where we discussed strategic innovation and its inherent dilemmas. Levecke took the lead, warm and enthusiastic as always. The largest part of ABN AMRO Lease Holding's business is in car leasing: 72 percent of the company's profits come from it, and 78 percent of the firm's assets are in it. Lease Plan (AALH's core brand) is among the founders of the car-leasing industry in Europe. The "open calculation concept," whereby the costs of leasing are broken down, compared with those of outright purchase, and shared with the customer has been widely imitated and has contributed significantly to the success of the industry. In many markets, Lease Plan was the first to offer global systems to manage the entire fleet of a company's cars. Together with *GE Capital*, ABN AMRO Lease Holding is one of the few international players with a global presence.

ABN AMRO started as a team of 25 entrepreneurial front-runners some 20 years ago; now 5000 strong, the company faces some major challenges in a changing industry, for the car-leasing industry is in the throes of transformation. One can see from a list of its 1000 top clients that more than 60 percent are international companies. There is a tendency for transnational harmonization of car-leasing policies and a pressure for cost management. Margins and fleet-management fees are under pressure, and customers expect tight control on exploding car-leasing and maintenance costs.

On top of all this car manufacturers are becoming players as well and have started their own car-leasing businesses. In mature markets, the fleet-management product tends to become a commodity, and operational risks, especially the decrease of the residual value of the leased vehicles, are increasing. The introduction of the euro and of e-commerce will make markets much more transparent than they ever have been ; price comparisons will become easier, and operational risks will increase.

As early as 1996, Hugo had warned the company's directors about these turbulent changes. In his speech at the directors' meeting in Rovaniemi, he discussed a number of options with his colleagues. His purpose was to raise issues and pose questions, not to propose solutions. Among the options, should the group . . .

- switch to commodity pricing and positioning? While doing so would match market conditions, it would waste all previous efforts toward becoming a highly profitable market leader.
- fully exploit the remaining differentiation options and new-product extension strategies? Will clients really notice the difference and will they be prepared to pay for it? It could be too little too late.
- aim for market expansion strategies, bringing in higher margin business from new markets to offset the lower margin business from older markets? This strategy risks being slow and expensive, and evenually one must run out of new markets.
- create product development strategies, opening entirely new markets and channels as a toehold to new industries and new profits?
- focus on internal cost productivity? By working in a different way, one may be able to liberate capital resources that will fund innovative, breakthrough projects, enabling new margins to develop. However, this would completely depend on the willingness and ability of the existing team to change its daily way of working.

Although these arguments and reflections were well heard and acknowledged by the directors, nothing really changed. ABN AMRO Lease Holding was cocooned by its strongest competitive force: the very autonomy and entrepreneurialism of its business units. The company had grown up in this way, so why change a winning formula? The freedom of each local company to respond to local conditions had proven highly effective in the past.

Two years after the Rovaniemi meeting, Hugo was asked to chair the managing board. He was convinced that the company should reinvent itself, and he realized that the major challenges were (1) to persuade the very same leaders whose local autonomy had been the recipe for past successful reinventions of the company and (2) to develop new patterns of mutual assistance and information sharing. The company needed a single global strategy, although with local adaptions where necessary; all units had to cooperate in its realization. The strategic goal was to be among the top three automobile-leasing companies worldwide *and* in each local market where the company did business. The new overall strategy would encompass an integration of new-product development with internal and external cost-cutting strategies. An example of a new product is Fleet Management Consultancy for transnational accounts. An example of a local adaptation is consumer leasing as it has been introduced in France. CARPLAN is a joint venture with Carrefour, the biggest megastore of France. The distribution of the product is the key factor in success. Manufacturers are very surprised by this development.

As we sat together in the Okura hotel in Amsterdam, Levecke asked me, "What will happen when brains meet emotions?" He had been strategizing for nine months with unit heads, and he believed that the rational case for what he proposed had now been made and accepted in principle. But what of the emotions? Could they bring their hearts to this far more interdependent way of doing business? Had they not *earned* their autonomy by skill, hard work, and results? All this was a dilemma for Levecke himself. He had been part of this group. Many directors were his personal friends. He had personally recruited nearly half of them and urged them toward autonomous decision making. Indeed, he was part author and exemplar of the present paradigm of radically decentralized operations. Now he was asking them to change their patterns of work. They would be reporting to him, at least on questions of shared strategy. His relationships to them would change, and some of the trust and mutual respect they developed over the years could be put into jeopardy. Might relationships turn sour?

Together, Levecke and I inventoried the key changes necessary – the shift from left to right in the following table:

From	Toward
Managing an operation	Leading a transition
Working on issues that we know rather well	Discovering new issues that we don't know so well
Exploiting a success formula	Reinventing a success formula
Local entrepreneurship	Transnational leadership

Levecke said, "I realize that this is demanding a huge transformation of the business. It is about changing our deeply held beliefs, our daily habits, the way we are used to working. There are no easy or secret tricks. Business transformation will require personal transformation in the way we all lead, and each of us is going to hurt inside emotionally – and that includes me. No one will be privileged. We are going to have to go through an intensive leadership development program with our minds open and vulnerable. This is not a linear progression or a rollout of tested techniques, but a process of trials and errors, and of mutual support and understanding for the lessons learned therefrom. From time to time, all of us will be asking each other, 'Why are we doing this?'"

Listening to Levecke, I appreciated his honesty and his care for his friends in their directorship roles. But had he underestimated new ways of tapping into their entrepreneurial energy, new sources of pleasure in risk taking? Might not this new paradigm have additional sources of satisfaction for all concerned? So we talked the four core transitions over and considered them in turn. Looked at more closely, the four transitions were really dilemmas, because *leading the transition* could not possibly replace *managing an* (existing) *operation* (which would have to follow rapidly upon any transition). The same applied to the other three. The group must, for example, *reinvent a success formula*, but it would then have to *exploit the* (new) *success formula*; nor could the group stop *exploiting the* (old) *formula* while it was *reinventing* it.

Managing an Operation vs. Leading a Transition

How can our operational qualities help us to better lead the transition? And how can the transition improve our operational qualities? Leading a transition while managing operations is rather like playing simultaneous chess games. The leaders of ABN AMRO Lease Holding needed to drive current business along with key projects, while connecting at a transnational level and forwarding the transition process. How was this to be wrought? An important clue is contained in Chapter 1. There, Fons Trompenaars and Charles Hampden-Turner discuss Centralization–Decentralization and argue that both can be achieved simultaneously, *provided they operate at different levels.*

The levels that concern us here are those of action and information. Activity of an entrepreneurial kind must remain radically decentralized, as has always been the case since the company's founding. In this respect, the company does *not* have to change. *Managing an operation* proceeds as before, with local judgment, the skill and autonomy as strong as ever – perhaps stronger! In contrast, the new centralization, which *leads a transition* takes place at the level of information. ABM-AMRO Lease Holding *acts locally but thinks globally.* No one's right to act innovatively is infringed upon, but the information from all such initiatives is shared by all. A "scoreboard" is created that records everyone's autonomous activities and the results they have achieved. We now know and share what was tried, what succeeded, what failed, and, most especially, *what was learned* from this initiative.

The answer, then, is not to work *harder* but to work *smarter*. Before you make a deathless decision and put your reputation on the line, you have the benefit of studying similar or identical initiatives that tried to achieve the same goals. In this way, you do not have to repeat mistakes and may be able to steer around pitfalls.

In addition to a companywide scoreboard that records initiatives and results, it is important to have periodic *meetings*. It should be the right of any director to call in any other director for, say, five "consulting days" per year. You form teams, consisting of directors or specialists reporting to them, who have had *the experiences most similar to the initiatives being attempted by a business unit.* Hence, the French director who pioneered CARPLAN with Carrefour in France is a member of the strategy teams trying to do something similar in Germany, the United Kingdom and The Netherlands. Teams must always have a strategic purpose and seek to move information from one successful project to help create another. These meetings are not committees of people representing other people who have to report back, but persons empowered to act so that the team takes direct responsibility for the strategies it recommends. The dilemma and reconciliation can be illustrated as follows:

Dilemma 1. Using Information to Learn

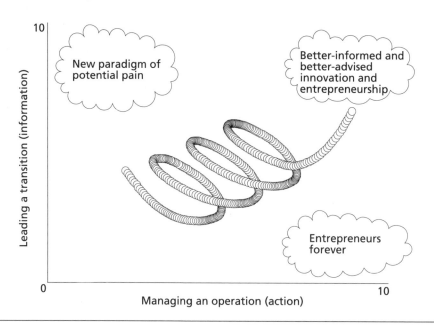

There is no reason for the sense of entrepreneurship to be any less simply because each director now has an intelligent audience to admire and critique each initiative. There will always be local variations in what needs to be done, but the shared global strategy means that any initiative by a local business unit could become a potential breakthrough for all of them. Now the initiatives of each have ramifications beyond their own country.

Working on Issues That We Know Rather Well vs. Discovering New Issues That We Don't Know as Well

How can we know that we do not know? How can what we know already help us to explore? We must follow Gary Hamel's advice in his *Manifesto for Revolutionaries* and "challenge the orthodoxies." There are a number of ways to open yourself up to what is new, to what you need to know and to which of your assumptions deserve to be challenged. We have already discussed the "scoreboard," which compares strategies with the results achieved. What we now need to do is *interrogate that strategy and those results.* Ask those attending team meetings to set the agenda. They might see different priorities or read the information available in different ways. One advantage of asking questions is that you develop hypotheses, which your data then confirms or rejects. Data should not be confused with information or knowledge. Information is a *response to a question.* Knowledge is a response so important that it can have wide applicability to many processes, markets, and customers and is therefore stored and shared across the business. For instance, a vital issue in any networked company is *who knows what.* There might be a vast array of experience, information, and success based on these initiatives across the company, but unless you know where such knowledge is located, you will not be able to bring the right people to the crucial issues.

Finally, you have to ask what the current results posted on the strategy "scoreboard" *dis*prove. What might no longer be true, judged by the most recent achievements? You cannot keep planning without "*unplanning,*" without saying, "Well, that turned out to be wrong!" A final advantage of a knowledge-creating company is that errors and failures are useful information, which other business units can learn from and which do *not* have to be repeated.

The dilemma looks like this:

Dilemma 2. Interrogating Strategic Results

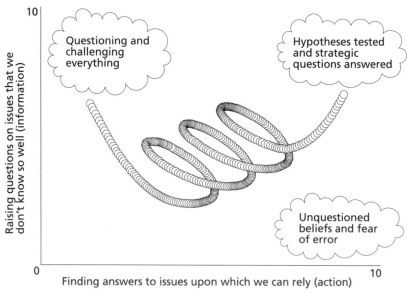

In this model, all business units share and compare their results, which are systematically interrogated, to see whether they fall short of the strategy *or* the strategy fails to illuminate and model the results. We can improve our performance, revise our strategy, or do both.

Exploiting a Success Formula vs. Reinventing a Success Formula

To some extent, this dilemma is resolved by our two earlier reconciliations. Giving each business unit entrepreneurial freedom to maximize returns on the *open calculation* concept was the original success formula. Now, we must reinvent our formula by investigating what these businesses have discovered that could be generalized across the whole group and again lead to a fundamental breakthrough in the car-leasing industry.

Hugo Levecke recognizes in his strategy for the future that car leasing has a life cycle of birth, growth, and maturation. It is possible for mature businesses in developed countries to anticipate the growth pains and advantages of countries following behind. Many of these emerging countries may seek to leapfrog the earlier stages of development and go straight to leasing in its more sophisticated forms. Nothing decrees that we should all make all the errors of all our predecessors. It makes sense to cut straight to the leading edge. Perhaps the quickest way of learning is to regard *all* successful entrepreneurial initiatives as potential strategies for other business units to follow – what Henry Mintzberg has called *emergent* strategy. These successful initiatives could be more than local successes; in rare circumstances, they could be *strategic models that can be generalized to other units* and that can be used in the *design* of a megastrategy. In short, entrepreneurial success can have something to teach us and can have principles that inform us. Within local *success formulas* could be a *new reinvented formula* for global success. The dilemma looks like this:

Dilemma 3. Tradition and Exploration

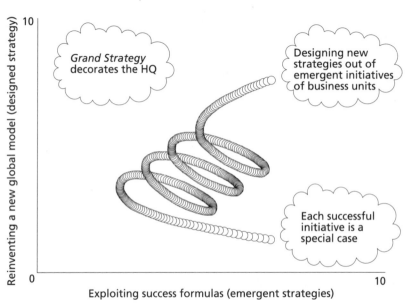

At the top left, we have the "Grand Strategy" as a decorative flourish by company HQ. Given Levecke's values, there is little danger of that. At bottom right, there *is* the danger that every regional success will be regarded as unique testimony to entrepreneurial genius, never to be repeated. In fact, all successful initiatives *have something to tell us about the success of other units.* They might well be based on principles of success that can be generalized. Ideally, Hugo should design his global strategy *out of* the successful initiatives of business units.

Local Entrepreneurship vs. Transnational Leadership

How, then, can the power of local entrepreneurship help us to develop transnational leadership? And how can the development of transnational leadership reinforce our local entrepreneurship? We have already seen that local successes can have lessons for a global strategy – that, with many business units, the good and the mediocre can learn from the best and replicate at least some of their moves – but the process also works the other way around. Transnational leadership can become a repository for models of success and, armed with these solutions, can think through problems and dilemmas. HQ is a kind of *central nervous system* integrating into one brain the news coming from all localities and able to communicate this knowledge to each business unit. HQ celebrates and enshrines what some business units have done and stretches and motivates others.

In addition, there are also huge cost savings to be made from one HQ's buying 200,000 cars a year from manufacturers and sharing IT facilities and strategic training. The more these costs are pushed down and shared, the more competitive every business unit can become. *Through* a bulk-purchasing agreement, every unit can be more competitive in its local markets. *Through* success in local markets, HQ becomes better and better informed about what works and what does not.

The following dilemma illustrates the point:

Dilemma 4. Leading Transnationally

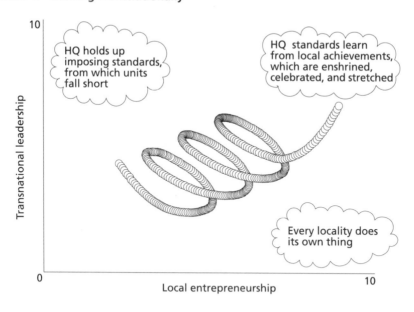

At the top left, HQ upholds such imposing standards, that business units fall short. At the bottom right, each unit "does its own thing" to remain incomparable. The ideal is for HQ to have standards inspired by extant achievements, to celebrate those achievements, to encourage emulation, and so to excite the ambition of all other units to excel in turn. Hugo Levecke seems to have intuited all these processes. HQ and the business units have shared responsibility for all of the following:

- *Stretching ambitious goals.* This is achieved by using the "scoreboard" to show what level of improvements is possible and by urging businesses to aim high. It is motivational to have your achievements recorded and advertised.
- Accepting the *discipline* of comparing all actions with results and all ideas with real outcomes.
- Developing the *trust* of people you learn from, teach, evaluate, and applaud, advising them and sharing consequences with them.
- Coming to *support* other business units with similar problems and challenges – business that can benefit from your successes, learn from your errors, and be encouraged by your understanding.

In a few years time, Hugo Levecke has redirected his company from being a financial services provider towards the global number one position in the fleet management industry, with a portfolio of 12 million cars.

CHAPTER 17

Keeping Close to the Customer

Leader: David Komansky (Merrill Lynch)

This chapter features a leader who is prominent in global financial services, Dave Komansky, CEO of Merrill Lynch, one of America's premier investment bankers. Three or four American-based investment banks now dominate global markets, with the weight of American shareholders behind them.

The Historical Context

The Bull at Bay

Merrill Lynch's symbol, the Bull, which stands outside its Wall Street offices, is famous throughout the world. Its two horns serve to remind us of the dilemmas that face business leaders, of the Bear that shadows the Bull, and of Merrill Lynch's latest dilemma: its confrontation with discount brokers using the Internet, especially the challenge posed by Charles Schwab.

The Wall Street Journal was recently analyzing one of the greatest dilemmas that the management of Merrill Lynch has faced in its existence of over 70 years. Company founder Charles Merrill believed that the opportunities of the financial markets should be accessible to everyone. His life's mission was "bringing Wall Street to Main Street." Indeed, Charles Merrill revolutionized financial services in the twentieth century with the simple, yet powerful, promise that the client's interest would always come first, explains Herbert M. Allison, Jr., president and chief operating officer of the firm. "Today we are pleased to show how we'll carry that vision into the twenty-first century, as the preeminent financial advisor for client achievement in what is fast becoming a 24-hour-a-day financial world. This is a natural extension of the client-focused strategy that has attracted over $1.5 trillion in client assets worldwide over the past several decades."

Yet there were still unresolved issues in early 1999 that sparked much discussion and debate within the organization on how to prevent a loss of market share to competitors. What was urgent was to *renew* Merrill's mission of keeping closer to customers than did its rivals. The Internet could be an additional means to this closeness; hence, in the spring of 1999, colorful brochures entitled "Key Things You Can Do with Merrill Online!" were mailed out to clients. This led to the following comment in *The Wall Street Journal*:

> Customers can transfer funds between Merrill Lynch accounts. They can view their statements. They can track gains and losses in their portfolio, and read Merrill research reports. They can even shop via direct links, from books from Barnes & Noble and vines from Virtual Vineyards. Buy and sell stock? Uh, no. To do that, they still need to call their Merrill Lynch stockbroker and pay fees that often are several times the cut-rate commissions paid by investors using Internet accounts from a growing number of upstart firms.

The consequences soon became clear. The frequency of calls to Merrill Lynch brokers declined sharply. Clients who wanted just 1 or 2 trades had figured out that they could make 5 to 10 trades for the same price with discount brokers. Most did not close their Merrill Lynch accounts, but used them for long-term holdings that they rarely traded.

Merrill Lynch's lack of on-line trading facilities had started a serious erosion in its market share during 1998. The issue had come to a head by May 1999. It was clear that Charles Schwab, a relatively new and dynamic discount broker, was training its customers to be their own brokers and traders, using the Internet. This was clearly a problem for Merrill Lynch, which, with 15,000 brokers all earning at least six-figure salaries in US dollars – and some seven figures – was the world's largest brokerage house, charging its customers millions in fees for the advice of top professionals.

Charles Schwab's appeal goes beyond discounted fees. Indeed, compared with rival discount brokers, it is not among the cheapest. Schwab's appeal is that it *transfers its own professional expertise to customers.* It is that rarity among professionals, a firm that educates customers in its own secrets so that they can, in time, if they wish to, become fully independent. This could be a losing strategy if it did not draw an ever-increasing number of "pupils" eager to be taught, who replace those who have "graduated." Schwab is in the "customer mentoring" business, as opposed to the financial services business. For many elderly Americans and people between jobs, managing their own share portfolios is their "last and most meaningful employment," providing funds they can leave to their families to ensure their continuing influence. Schwab was helping customers to help themselves, in the time-honored American tradition.

Dave Komansky saw that this challenge would have to be met, yet he could not risk alienating his army of professional brokers. Increasingly, however, financial services were being unbundled: you could buy top information and research and then pay as little as $5 per trade on the Internet. This was far less than the brokers' inclusive fee. Furthermore, brokers' judgments are not infallible. In the hurly-burly of stock fluctuations, it is not unknown for the Dow Jones average to outperform professionally managed portfolios. Luck is quite a leveler.

Merrill Lynch's response to its dilemma was to refocus its efforts on reconciling new technology with customer service. Its strategy was announced by John Steffens at the Forrester Conference in May 1999: "By combining technology with skilled advisors, clients are given the convenience of interacting when, how, and where they want."[1] Dave Komansky clarified the policy: "Anyone, anywhere, at any time, can log into the Internet to get free quotes, market data, and stock picks from a variety of chat rooms. Yet, at Merrill Lynch, we are confidently making unparalleled billion-dollar investments in our financial consultants, research analysts, technology, and products. We're doing this because we know that success in the on-line world – as it was in the offline world – will be defined by *meaningful content* for the individual. Only, now, in a world with almost unlimited access and bandwidth, this content can be delivered in more effective ways – and its value grows exponentially. That is why we are confident in our investments and bullish on the future of financial advice."[2]

The Importance of Personalized Service

What the new technologies made possible, besides the opportunity to lower costs, was the personalization of service. John "Launny" Steffens, Merrill Lynch's "Mr. On-line," created for the company a Trusted Global Advisory System (TGA), which would synthesize more than 50 data sources and make possible a process of matching the requirements of customers with the latest market opportunities. ML's financial consultants would have this information at their fingertips and could create optimal client advice within minutes.

Dave Komansky spoke of "leveraging technology to deliver value" and of "elevating advice to a new level through a collaborative platform modeled on choice and empowerment." While the TGA is for consultants, not clients, Merrill Lynch Online is a Web site for clients to discuss investment issues. The company has found

---

1   John Steffens, "The Role of Online Advice," Forrester Conference, Princeton, NJ, May 24, 1999.
2   *Ibid.*

that informed clients are better customers, asking better questions and getting better answers. On-line dialogues grow deeper and more intelligent. It helps to empower clients. Komansky seeks to improve and multiply these dialogues and conversations by moving some of TGA's resources to Merrill Lynch Online. An additional tool is the Global Investor Network, which allows clients to join discussions through video and audio channels. These links are just beginning, but the goal is to make every tool that facilitates the investment process available on-line. Despite this, the value of skilled financial consultants is meant to increase, and they are to hold onto a valuable share of the market by catering to a diversity of individual needs by a willingness to spend more or less time on investment decisions.

"On-line," Steffens points out, "there is no single type of advisory relationship that will serve all clients well. Clients can inform their financial consultant as to what kind of advisory relationship they seek. At one extreme, we have clients with little time or interest in managing their own financial affairs. They wish to be kept informed, but for a professional to decide. It is a question of time, that perishable asset. Investing is better left to those with the means to inform themselves in minutes, while the client is freed up for his or her own favorite activity."[3] At the other end of the spectrum are clients who actively manage their investments and come up with their own investment ideas. For them, the financial consultant serves as a sounding board, an educator, a personalizer of information, and a source of new ideas.

A computer cannot, by itself, provide the level of service, the dialogue, and the personal focus of a human advisor. Only advisors can attain the wisdom, judgment, and habit of personal service that views each client as a whole person having dreams and ambitions.

Clients are not confined to one advisor. They can speak with specialists and consult experts in particular fields. Quality advice is not "consumed" in the usual way. Rather, it enlightens clients and provides access within Merrill Lynch to the most qualified persons available to improve the clients' investment opportunities.

From Phase I to Phase II
Dave Komansky sees two distinct phases in the Internet revolution. Phase I is reconciled by asking, "How will on-line services revolutionize existing service models?" To that end, *Merrill Lynch Direct* was launched in late 1999. The service offers after-hours and in-hours direct trading. Investors can buy or sell stocks at $29.95 a trade. But Phase II is already upon us; it is reconciled by asking, "How will on-line services themselves be revolutionized by ever-higher client expectations?" It is a mistake to think of technology as the sole driver; clients want more. Steffens

3   *Ibid.*

explains: "If you don't maintain a laser focus on helping your clients thrive and find freedom in a complex financial world, no one is going to stay at your party very long. We are looking outside our walls to bring better execution and extended hours of trading to our clients. We're doing all this – and we're doing e-commerce – because the big picture matters to clients, and sweating the details counts. The relationships we're building through these efforts are sticky, rich, and profitable. A lot of people doing business on-line are more than happy with what they've found, but there's another segment that's mad as hell, and they are not going to take it much longer. It's in Phase II of the Internet revolution where clients will ask, "What have you done for me lately?' They will demand a richer level of content and a higher level of service than are currently offered by many on-line services."[4]

An important characteristic of the Internet is its density of information. Complex products, like books on Amazon.com, sell well on the Internet, because reviews, comments, and discussions revolve around them. Giving clients access to this wealth of materials about investment, along with a means of navigating through that knowledge, could be Merrill Lynch's priceless advantage. Once again, Dave Komansky is articulate on the topic: "I believe the trump card to these bundles of information will be *access* to trusted advice. Choice and openness are vital, but not enough, because the choices are so limitless that you are overwhelmed. What is hard is to find personal meaning among all the data and to guide the client through this morass so that direction and commitment are possible."

While it is still too early to discover whether these strategic syntheses of technology and personal service have worked, early indications are positive. Wall Street seemed impressed by Komansky's newly built strategy. As of late 1999, Merrill Lynch had pulled even with the market capitalization of Charles Schwab, having briefly lost its place to its archrival. Merrill Lynch's new policy of "click and mortar" has won many admirers on Wall Street, and Forrester Research placed the company's Web site second among a dozen or so on-line competitors in "effectiveness for investors." In the words of the report, "Up to now, Schwab has been setting the pace in on-line brokerage. Merrill, though, is a bolt from the blue."

Despite some hostile comments, Komansky has launched Merrill Lynch's campaign for its services by highlighting the "human achievement" of the investment advisory process. As one ad put it, "Computers are plastic and metal and sand. People are brilliance and discernment and vision." That is intended not to put computers down, but to emphasize how well they are utilized and by whom. Merrill Lynch believes that it is creating a comprehensive framework that will revolutionize

4   John Steffens, "The Internet Revolution: Phase II," Jupiter Communications Online Financial Services Conference, San Francisco, CA, September 27, 1999.

the concept of personal financial services in America. Clients will be able to customize the global power of the company for their own purposes and preferences. Merrill Lynch is proud of the versatility of services available under one roof, backed by its history and reputation and by its globalism, intelligence, and financial strength.

We are now in a position to diagram the dilemmas that Merrill Lynch has recognized and reconciled. We are also in a position to suggest a dilemma that the company might *not* yet have recognized or reconciled. Finally, we consider an ingenious idea and, turning around our usual procedure, ask, "What dilemmas does this reconcile?"

The dilemmas are as follows:

1.   Low-cost, specific data and transactions versus Rich, meaningful, diffuse personal relationships
2.   Individuality of the client versus The concentrated power of Merrill Lynch's global community
3.   The profit-maximizing model versus The client-mentoring model
4.   The influence of London versus the Influence of the Regions
5.   Capitalism versus the ideals of democracy
6.   The private sector versus the publicly funded education sector

Low-cost, Specific Data and Transactions vs. Rich, Meaningful, Diffuse Personal Relationships

The challenge to Merrill Lynch has come in part from the unbundling of services into specific pieces. You can buy information, research, trading facilities, and advice from separate sources, yet find the combined fees perhaps less than those paid to Merrill Lynch's six- and seven-figure professionals. The Internet is overflowing with *data,* but that is not the same as having knowledge or information. We are *informed* by facts relevant to our questions and concerns. We *know* when we get answers to our propositions and hypotheses. The vaster the Internet becomes, the more customers will need a guide to what is relevant to their concerns.

Instead of relationships being eclipsed by the Internet, they will become more and more important in interpreting data flows, as what is available keeps growing ever larger than what is relevant to each client. Hence, in Phase II, we will discover that intelligent dialogue about the bewildering complexity of financial markets forms and changes the Internet, rather than that the Internet changes the financial markets. We need *high tech*, but we also need *high touch*. The more those numbers rain down upon you, the more you need to talk to someone about them.

The dilemma can be defined as follows:

Dilemma 1. Guidance through the Maze

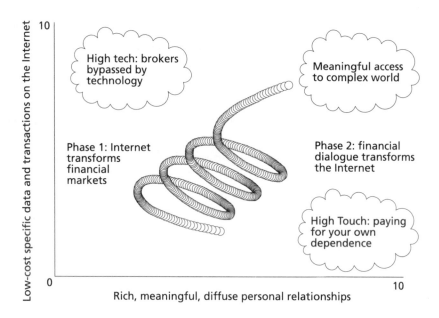

In 1998–99, Phase I was in full swing, with the prices of specific trades and reports falling and Schwab and others making inroads, but in 2000 and 2001, Phase II is setting in, with a complexity so vast that meaningful access via professional relationships becomes vital.

The dimension of Specific–Diffuse is the fourth of the seven dimensions introduced in Chapters 1 and 2. In this case, it is heavily qualified by other considerations.

The Individuality of the Client vs. The Concentrated Power of Merrill Lynch's Global Community

One good reason that the Internet will not sweep all before it simply by communicating data is that every customer is different. Some want high risks, others low; some want growth stocks, others dividends. Some have specialized interests in, perhaps, technology, media, energy, or engineering; others feel more secure with diversification. Some have ethical concerns about tobacco or armaments; others rely on the invisible hand of the market to provide the greatest good for the greatest number. Some investors would say, "I do not keep a dog and bark myself" that is, they employ professionals to do what they do not personally want to do or are not qualified to do. Some investors want to participate in or influence the professional's decision; others want professional advice on choosing for themselves. Just as there are degrees of participation, there are degrees of transparency vs. privacy. Some customers would *like* other people to know just how wealthy and successful they are; other customers use professionals to keep their affairs private. They believe it boastful or dangerous to flaunt their wealth and might even ask for their mail to be sent to a post office box or to be bundled up for personal collection.

Whichever way you look at it, customers vary in a myriad of ways and might treat their brokers like the Buddha or as butlers. It is because customers are so diverse individually that it takes a global community to bring satisfaction to each person, and it requires deep relationships of mutual respect to find, amid that community, just the people and resources the client most requires. Within any networked community of professionals, there are literally thousands of meanings for individual investors, rather than one message for everyone who can download it cheaply.

Merrill Lynch's strategy has been to devise two parallel systems: TGA, to inform professional brokers, and Merrill Lynch Online, for investors. This division ensures that investors get better and better informed, but that the professional community retains an important edge in sophistication and expertise and is not second-guessed on the basis of the same information. The likely success of the

Dilemma 2. The Search for Personal Meaning

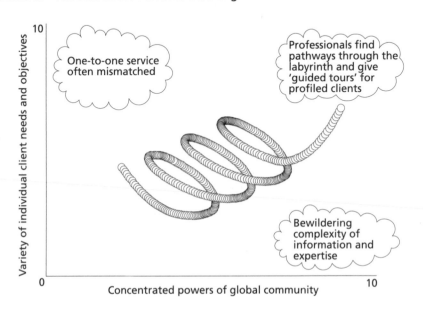

strategy depends in part on how well individual customers are profiled. Do they want someone to talk things over with? Do they aspire to professionalism themselves? Do they want someone they can trust to get on with things, without bothering them? What is their trade-off between security and gain? Customers of a particular type need appropriate service. They have the right to set their own goals and objectives and have these pursued. The dilemma can be diagrammed as in the above figure.

Given the vast expansion in world trading, Internet information, initially intriguing, will rapidly become overwhelming with a host of contradictory opinions making it harder, not easier, to decide. Far from substituting for professionalism, this complexity and chaos will increase the demand for "guided tours" through the labyrinth by professionals aware of client idiosyncrasies (upper right of the figure). One-to-one service (upper left) is not enough, because the client and the financial consultant can be mismatched. Nor does the overflow of information (lower right), however easy to access, guarantee understanding and relevance; rather, professionals earn their salaries by "managing chaos" on behalf of individual interests.

The Profit-maximizing Process vs. The Client-mentoring Process

We come finally to a dilemma that Dave Komansky has perhaps missed, but that could be crucial to the competition between Merrill Lynch and Charles Schwab. We say "perhaps" because Komansky certainly knows more than he says within our hearing.

It seems possible that Charles Schwab is not just a discount broker, but an *educator* of those who wish to develop professional expertise. The job of advising on investments has two different tests of effectiveness. There is the profit-maximizing process, in which you look at how effectively stocks perform and ask whether the input of costly professional advice pays for itself in better returns, and there is the client-mentoring model, which involves the transfer of professional expertise from experts to clients, with the purpose of turning those clients into experts in their own right. The latter process can be cheaper, because it involves clients acting themselves, rather than paying others to act, but that is not the main attraction. What attracts clients is that *their autonomy and expertise is being developed to put them in charge of their own wealth.* The fees are less commissions than they are tuition fees. The outcome sought is not "to have my money work for me" but "to have me work with my money."

This helps explain why many other "discount brokers" have made little headway against Charles Schwab, which is by no means the cheapest. If clients believe they are paying "tuition fees," then they will pay more now to benefit more later, and their satisfaction will come from steadily increasing their autonomy in managing their own wealth and from steadily increasing their responsibility for the size of their wealth. (This is very much "the American Way," and Schwab's appeal perhaps cultural.) Now, clearly, this does not appeal to *every* client. Many have more enjoyable things to do with their lives than trade stocks. For others, however, that is a job from which they cannot be retired or fired, and to do it well is very important.

Merrill Lynch should not surrender this market to Schwab, and no one should underestimate the significance of this development. Traditionally, professionals have kept their secrets from their clients, profiting in part from the esoteric nature of professional jargon to make clients dependent upon them. Schwab might well be the first to make a determined attempt to *professionalize clients themselves.* George Bernard Shaw once said, "All professions are a conspiracy against the laity." All but one, perhaps? The revolution in customer service might involve sustained mentoring and education. Although such customers will eventually cut their ties, could each be replaced by two or three who are eager to learn? We have tried to convey this in the next figure.

Dilemma 3. Professionalizing the Client

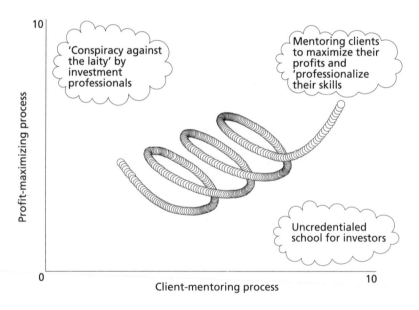

Provided that you make it clear that you are emancipating your client in the longer term from continued reliance on Merrill Lynch, you can legitimately charge educational fees. The criterion of success is still profit maximization, but *the agent of investment decisions is the client himself,* your pupil (upper right of the figure). The "conspiracy against the laity (upper left) sees professionals scheming to stay ahead by withholding from clients all that they know. The uncredentialed school (lower right) is committed to tuition, but makes no effort to compare its efforts with performances by seasoned professionals. "Pupils" should not be encouraged to "graduate" and go solo until they have proved their capacity to perform against the best. The internal "league standings" would be part of the education and part of the thrill.

If capitalism is *really* to work at full potential, we need ever more sophisticated investors in ever more specialized areas. We believe that Merrill Lynch has yet to counter Charles Schwab's major appeal. In the discount issue, Merrill Lynch has started a false hare.

The Global Investment Challenge: A Simulation

Sometimes there are ideas so good that we instinctively applaud them. Only later, often through the disciplines expounded in this book, do we realize *why* they are so good and just how many dilemmas they resolve. The test of a *really* good idea is its simultaneously and multiply resolving dilemmas facing a whole industry. Let us consider such an idea that was recently implemented at Merrill Lynch in the United Kingdom and then use dilemma theory to assess it.

The company recently launched an investment simulation, or game for schools, called the Global Investment Challenge (GIC). Any secondary school in the United Kingdom is free to enter and play. Each team of players, supervised by a teacher, is given a hypothetical £1 million ($1.6 million) to invest. All teams compete with one another in the gains achieved by their portfolio of investments. The winners get an all-expenses-paid trip to Merrill Lynch's New York HQ. In this game, no one can lose (money), but the winners get treated to the Big Apple. Yet much of the thrill is in the process, not the prize. Each team and its teacher receive a packet containing stock and bond information, instructions on how to play, and forms on which to enter a portfolio of selections. The game is publicized, and local teams are reported on and supported by local newspapers. Investments are global in range and in scope, so students must be aware of world trends and events that could affect prices, and they must become aware of the sheer diversity of possible investments.

Teams buy or sell shares on five occasions during the course of the game, and in making these choices, they have access via free phone service to Merrill Lynch's leading analysts in the fields in which the latter specialize. These analysts advise the team approaching them, much as they would a genuine client. Probably, the analysts concerned want "their team" to win the trip to New York. Throughout the contest, it is possible to discover where you stand in relationship to rival teams, with last-minute changes in prices tipping the balance. Excitement runs high.

In 1997, 75 students from 16 schools participated, and valuable publicity was gained when Steven Byers, secretary of the Department of Industry, awarded the first prize, in Newcastle, to a team from a local Newcastle school. By 1999, three games were being run, for 1700 students from 133 schools.

So, what might this game accomplish for Merrill Lynch? It could help to reconcile at least three dilemmas:

(a)   the balance of relative influence between London and the regions;
(b)   the tensions between capitalism as a system and the ideals of democracy;
(c)   the tension between the private sector and the publicly funded education sector.

The Influence of London vs. the Influence of the Regions

The United Kingdom is notoriously overcentralized, with London, a magnet for world money, overshadowing the regions and the provinces. This is especially true for towns like Newcastle, once the site of great shipbuilders, but long since in industrial decline. Such regions not only need help with their educational efforts; they also need an understanding of world competitive pressures. They need to understand how and why investments are flowing from their own capital city to enterprises the world over. If regional school pupils can learn to think like investors, they might also learn what *attracts* investment to their region and what does not. At the height of Britain's industrial revolution, such provincial "capitals" as Liverpool, Newcastle, Glasgow, and Sunderland were models of civic pride and prosperity. Can they rebuild their fortunes? Although the GIC is a modest contribution to a huge historic imbalance within the British economy, where financial services ride high and manufacturing struggles, every little bit helps, and a proper general *understanding* of investment flows could be the key to future policy.

Merrill Lynch sees its game as an attempt to repay the communities, where much of the company's talent is nurtured and subsequently drawn upon. The demand for workers with knowledge is exponential. Komansky calls this "good citizenship." Among the advantages accruing to the company is a greater brand awareness in the regions, which have been slower to take up investment opportunities than have London and the "home counties" (the areas adjoining London). Merrill Lynch recently set up a number of regional offices.

The dilemma can be illustrated by the following figure:

Dilemma 4. The Relative Influence Between London and the Region

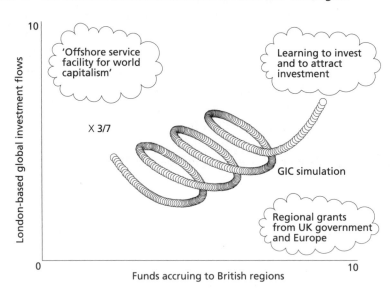

London-based global investment flows

'Offshore service facility for world capitalism'

Learning to invest and to attract investment

X 3/7

GIC simulation

Regional grants from UK government and Europe

0

10

Funds accruing to British regions

London's somewhat ambivalent reputation is as an "Offshore service facility for world capitalism." In a world where geographic contiguity no longer matters, Taiwan might get much more investment from London than does the Northeast region of the United Kingdom, including Newcastle. What such regions *do* get are government grants and European funds for regeneration – monies for which their relative poverty qualifies them. Yet these measures are only stopgap solutions to the problem – the lack of attractive investment opportunities – and this is where Merrill Lynch is helping. The GIC simulation is an enjoyable way of learning about the real world of capital flows and about how to get your share to your region.

The Tension between Capitalism as a System and the Ideals of Democracy

The next two resolutions are ones that we as writers consider important, even if Merrill Lynch has not specifically cited them. A lot of leadership ability is tacit, not explicit. Leaders can be better than they know.

All democratic nations today are also capitalist, but not all forms of capitalism are democratic. For example, in Chile, Argentina, Greece, and Spain, for at least periods of recent history, capitalist economies and repressive governments have cohabited. American slavery was once defended as a sacred property right. Capital investment, which reallocates funds from losers to winners, is not necessarily democratic in its outcomes: there is a marked tendency for the rich to get richer.

In order to reconcile capitalism with democratic ideals, certain steps must be taken. First, shares must be *widely* held, so that most citizens own them. Second, the citizen must *participate in the investment process.* Pension fund capitalism, in which the citizens' retirement resources are managed by professionals, is *not* enough to build a property-owning democracy. So long as investing is the activity of relatively few, the capitalist system will appear alien and elitist to many of the world's citizens. They will not understand why their parts of the world are not as affluent as others and will blame investors. The dilemma looks like this:

Dilemma 5. Capitalism as a System and the Ideals of Democracy

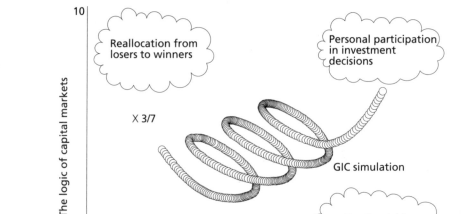

The reallocation of resources from the less to the more successful has antidemocratic possibilities, *unless* investment in those successes is widely distributed through the population. This is more the case in the United States than in the United Kingdom and more the case in the United Kingdom than in most of Continental Europe, but most citizens need more than a financial stake in investment flows – they need understanding of those flows and the ability to exercise personal judgments in where to invest. It is here that GIC simulation makes an important contribution. As of now, the idea is perhaps more important than its present impact, which is relatively small. But "investor education" might be essential to making world markets not unjustly skewed against poorer regions. The fact is that you must understand this system in order to share in its advantages.

The Tension between the Private Sector and the Publicly Funded Education Sector

In most developed nations, general education is paid for by public funds, raised out of taxes. This has given teachers and their unions an ambivalent attitude toward capitalism. They judge with some justice, that idealistic, nonmonetary reasons for a teaching career are routinely exploited by low salaries. The dynamics of supply and demand are such that markets punish teachers for having dedication to people rather than to financial objectives. "Idealism plus peanuts" is a teacher's typical reward. Not surprisingly, education professionals and associations show a preference for left-wing political parties and hesitate to educate their charges about the potential of capitalism. That one of the purposes of schools is to prepare students to take their places in a capitalist economy is regarded with some distaste.

The dilemma is laid out in the next figure.

Dilemma 6.   Synergy of Mutual Respect

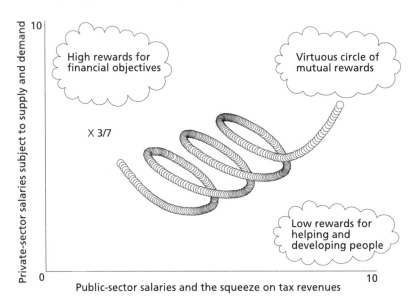

We do not wish to pretend that a simulation game for children is "the answer" to the historic antipathy of the teaching profession to those multitudes in the private sector who are much better rewarded for comparable skills. Resolving this societal dilemma will require much more effort and money, but the GIC simulation is at least an indicator of what creative solutions can accomplish. Every teacher won around to exploring what investment flows can teach is a gain to that economy and that region.

It is not Merrill Lynch's mission or responsibility to change the world, but those with the ambition to do so *could* benefit from studying these examples of artful reconciliations.

CHAPTER 18

Managing the Internationalization Process

Leader: Kees Storm (AEGON)

K ees Storm, now CEO of AEGON, the Dutch insurance giant, devised his own system of management back in 1990, when he was responsible for AEGON's Dutch market. He called it "Management by Betting." The system consists in estimating what was genuinely possible for the company to achieve and then having Kees make a friendly bet that the managers could not do it. If Kees lost, the company won anyhow. It was a win–win situation. Forecasts tended to be very conservative, with managers anxious not to fail and so aiming low. Kees wanted to throw down a challenge. "I'm betting that you fail; show me differently!" He wanted to take the trauma out of failure and give pleasure to those confounding him. The bets were usually symbolic – a good bottle of wine – but this strategy has lasted 10 years.

AEGON has certainly put on a winning performance. Its share price rose 173% in 1998 and is up more than 400 percent since 1997, and more than 3000 percent in the last 10 years. The price stands at 40 times earnings and 6 times book value. AEGON is one of the highest rated insurers in the world, second only to AIG in overall market value. AEGON is number 2 in the USA. The company's total assets have passed $200 billion.

AEGON avoids both hostile take-overs in the glare of publicity and auctions. These tend to be expensive for shareholders when you have to beat all other bidders and offer a price that no one else will top. Storm prefers private negotiations, out of the limelight.

The Process of Internationalizing

AEGON is internationalizing rapidly. Members of its boards recently held American, British, Dutch, German, and Belgian passports. The company has come a long way

331

since the 1980s, when an American colleague remarked, of AEGON's culture, "If you ain't Dutch, you ain't much."

Internationalization has been accomplished by radical decentralization. Storm explains:

> We have a very decentralized company, and our units have almost complete freedom to decide what is good for their own business. We manage our company together with our main-country managers. We meet four times a year to discuss the framework of our plans. Local freedom is high, because we have jointly internalized some shared rules of the game, like "Make a plan and stick to it." Financially speaking, our acquisitions are quite simple – simpler than those in other industries. We have a minimum ROI of 11 percent after tax in mind, so in our quite stable piece of the service industry, we can calculate these numbers with quite some certainty. The real challenge lies in the social and business integration of the acquired company. Our portfolio is nicely spread between insurances that thrive on longevity and those which don't. We have funeral insurances, so-called home services, and pensions. They nicely balance each other. The intermediate salesperson has regained a position in our service industry by extending the scope of what he or she offers. It is almost becoming a full financial consultant.

Fitting into Local Markets and Regional Opportunities

AEGON operates in five key countries: the United States, the Netherlands, the United Kingdom, Hungary, and Spain. The country units operate in such an independent way that each of them could decide to go beyond its own borders. AEGON USA, for example, started a joint venture with the largest Mexican bank, Banamex. AEGON The Netherlands started to sell certain specialized types of financial services in the German and Belgian markets. AEGON started to sell insurance services in Taiwan and the Philippines and is represented in China and India.

Storm sees decentralization as essential because of the diversity of local laws and customs: "Our local approaches are a result of the dependence of our services on local laws and cultural habits. We have taken this very far. Despite the fact that we are very Dutch in our roots, we have no Dutch men or women in our foreign activities. Each local business unit has a unique knowledge about the markets and knows its opportunities. The *management of this knowledge* is therefore crucial for the success of our decentralized business. In our internationalization process, we have no intention of just putting as many flags on the globe as possible. We rather focus on some 10 large markets where we can grow significantly. I think it is important for the members of the management team to be physically available in the countries in which we do business. This is particularly important in the start-up phase of a new acquisition. We will internationalize in a restricted and focused way. We are now listed at six stock exchanges: Amsterdam, New York, London, Frankfurt, Zurich, and Tokyo. That is very important for capital-funding needs of the company. At the present moment, more than 75 percent of our people work outside of the Netherlands. In order to be able to attract the best people for the top jobs, we have introduced English as our working language at AEGON."

Integrating and Managing Knowledge from All Regions

AEGON doesn't focus on regions only: each business unit is concentrated around one specific segment of the market, one specific country, and one specific distribution network. At AEGON, there are many examples in which the local experience in a new service area was quickly used in another part of the organization. This is made possible by an excellent IT and communication system and a strong shared corporate culture that enjoys the exchange of ideas. Selectively moving a number of people across business units reinforces this culture.

What follows in this chapter are essentially Storm's reflections on AEGON's role in internationalization.

AEGON developed so-called inner circles – networks of specialized managers (IT managers, financial specialists) whereby knowledge is exchanged across business units. Moreover, it established a way for all its 30,000 people to get a chance every three years to communicate with all executive board members. Every three years, the board pays a visit to all the company offices, meets the people there, and presents and discusses future plans. It is amazing how many people ask questions in a variety of areas on these occasions, and the board hears what issues are alive in AEGON's family. In a program it calls "Optiek," AEGON is trying to minimize hierarchical layers just by meeting people around the globe in a personal way.

AEGON HQ derives principles of global strategy by studying local successes and discussing to what extent they can be generalized across the world to other regions. The value and relevance of these global strategies are widely debated. AEGON is probably one of the very few organizations – maybe the only company of its size – that organizes all-ranks meetings in every country to give every employee a chance to meet the members of the executive board in person at least once every three years. It also gives everyone the opportunity to hear the group's strategy explained from the horse's mouth. Global strategy would not work unless employees had a stake in global success and cared how units in other regions fared. Accordingly, employees are encouraged to join a global stock option program. More than 90 percent have chosen to do so. Stock options also give the whole company a stake in being consistent and in implementing methods proven to work in one or more regions.

AEGON has a very loyal group of people with close relationships and respect for cultural differences. It tries both to radiate consistency, by having its strategies, goals, and results as comparable as possible, and to have its people challenged by the achievements of its best groups. AEGON wants quick feedback about what is working and what is not, and what feels good or bad. If people make plans, they should stick to them, otherwise they cannot learn about any shortcomings or even determine whether the plans were too modest. As usual, Storm bets that the people cannot beat their targets, and they rise to the challenge. AEGON also has "bonding events," such as marathons and golf tournaments – whatever works."

Stick to Your Knitting

So complex is this process of studying what works, what does not, and why, from region to region and across numerous insurance products, that AEGON could not possibly make sense of it all unless it *stuck to its knitting* – that is, operated in the insurance industry business alone. Of course, there are connections to industries like banking, but these are tactical and *ad hoc*. Storm explains: "We date banks, but do not intend to marry them. We are trying to prove that this is best for the organization. Many banks have merged their activities with insurance companies. Up until now, not doing this has paid off [for AEGON]. I think merging banks and insurance companies is *the mistake of the century*. It would be like driving two cars at the same time. It is the convergers who end up against a tree. Therefore, we stick to our knitting – which, by definition, does not make us contrarian, but consistent. We also believe that giant mergers or takeovers resulting in companies that employ hundreds of thousands of people will prove to be unmanageable and will fall apart sooner or later. We will gladly pick up some parts if that happens in our industry."

The Importance of Stakeholder Value

Storm has strong views on the folly of being narrowly fixated on shareholder value, although paradoxically, AEGON is often regarded as an exemplar in this regard.

AEGON is often seen as an Anglo-Saxon company, because of its focus on shareholder value. Storm has "never heard such a stupid dichotomy as shareholder versus stakeholder value." Value creation starts with the customer. AEGON's primary task is to fulfill the needs of the client and to extend the circle of satisfied clients. This can be achieved only if you have motivated employees with the resources to do their work properly. And to have the proper resources, you need to have access to the capital markets. For AEGON, that is crucial. This access can be created only by rewarding the capital resources properly. Value creation is a process that involves many stakeholders, and leadership consists of trying to find a balance between all the stakes. Whenever one stake prevails, the whole circle becomes vicious. Instead, Storm intends to create a learning spiral "resembling a Catherine wheel, in which all rockets combine to rotate the display." He sees this balance of stakeholders "firing together" as a form of democracy.

Storm is one of the very few leaders we have run across who was very explicit about reconciliation of values. "This famous discussion between stakeholder value versus shareholder value," he said, "should be finished, in my opinion. Value creation starts and ends with the client, and to satisfy your clients and to keep them satisfied, you need motivated employees. Where you have motivated employees, you will make great returns for your shareholders. If you then tie the stakes of the shareholders, employees, and customers together through our famous share options, you will create a value circle that increases its revolving speed continuously." All this results in an ever-faster Catherine wheel.

This notion of the Catherine wheel can be diagrammed as follows:

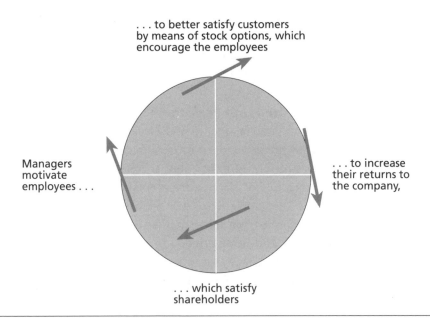

Dutch Codetermination

AEGON was much influenced in its employee participation efforts by Dutch codetermination laws and by the institution of workers' councils. Storm: AEGON did not have to institute them in countries where they were not mandatory, but its Central Works Council gave AEGON such good advice that it exported the spirit to the whole global system. Industrial democracy is so much a part of how the firm exchanges ideas and shares experiences that AEGON does not always need to give it legal expression. Among its most enjoyable activities are friendly competition between business units to see which has the better ways of working. AEGON learns a lot that way. The company uses IT to "keep score," but nothing beats personal contact and meeting people in other units. AEGON's slogan is "Respect people, make money, and have fun."

While being interviewed by *The Scotsman* on March 21, 1999, Storm had to leave in a hurry on other urgent business. He left behind a giant doodle of intersecting circles of roughly rectangular placement, all overlapping at one central point. The newspaper wrote of "an urge to interpret the doodle as a subconscious expression of his strategic thinking." Each circle was presumably another business unit, largely free, but joined to the center.

Dilemma Analysis

Two dilemmas stand out from various interviews and accounts of AEGON given by Kees Storm. We call these *Learning from Decentralized Unit Performance* and *The Synergy of Stakeholder Value*. Storm probably intuits the resolution of many more dilemmas, but his statements give us clues to at least these two conscious reconciliations.

Learning from Decentralized Unit Performance

All units are radically decentralized in order to fit the legal and cultural requirements of particular markets. They are encouraged to make plans, to beat the bets Kees makes that these plans are unattainable, and to record their best possible performances, which are then studied, discussed, and emulated by the company inner circles, which ask, "What is comparable across such performances and what is unique to one?" Differences are respected, but the search for consistency never ends. Can best practices be followed and duplicated – if not precisely, then at least approximately? And what do these many successes have to teach us all?

We diagram this dilemma in the following figure:

Dilemma 1. Learning from Decentralized Performance

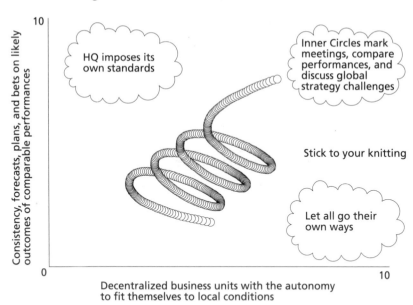

On the vertical axis is the combination of the drive for consistency, comparability, and betting on targets. On the horizontal axis is the combination of the high level of decentralization, autonomy, and fitting to local conditions. Each of these emphases would fail were it exclusive of the other. You cannot make *everything* consistent when regional conditions are so varied. The company rightly shuns an HQ that imposes its will, but you cannot let every unit diverge and lose itself in noncomparability.

Thanks to the Inner Circles, the all-ranks meetings, and the forecasts (matched to results) on which Kees lays his bets and gets others to do so, AEGON discovers many ways of succeeding and consistently seeks to have units inspire and learn from each other's examples. However, this learning process is *complex*, so AEGON must "stick to its knitting" or lose track. You cannot add to the existing degree of diversity by mixing the contrasting cultures of insurance and banking.

The Synergy of Stakeholder Values

Storm sees nothing but foolishness in extolling shareholder value above the rights and duties of stakeholders. This is because the outcomes for all the stakeholders are interdependent, and you cannot emphasize any one stake selectively without damaging the whole system and precipitating a regressive spiral. Once again, we must not confuse "importance" with "priority." You can argue that shareholder value is most "important" to you – that is a question of ethics, and we prefer to leave it to those in touch with divine inspiration. But if we ask which has "*priority*" – which value must logically come first – then there is no doubt that motivating employees to satisfy customers, *precedes* "Increasing returns and paying profits to shareholders." The reason for this order of precedence is that customers supply the monies that shareholders later receive. If employees are, for any reason, *not* motivated and customers *not* satisfied, then there is no money for shareholders to receive. The dilemma is illustrated in the following diagram:

Dilemma 2.   The Synergy of Stakeholder Value

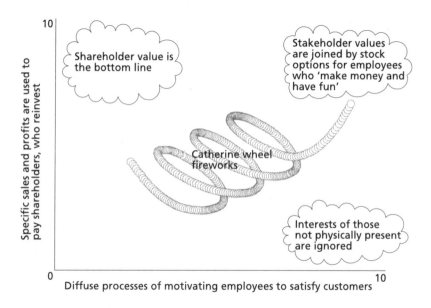

Note that the *clockwise* spiral is, in this case, obligatory: the money customers pay you for satisfying their needs is given to shareholders, who reinvest it, allowing the processes of motivation and satisfaction to continue. We have also reintroduced our own Dimension 4, *Specific* vs. *Diffuse*. Shareholder value tends to be specific and countable; motivation and satisfaction are more diffuse. Diffuse processes can too easily be overlooked.

In the diagram, *specific* sales statistics and profits for shareholding are on the vertical axis, and *diffuse* processes of motivating employees to satisfy customers are on the horizontal axis. The bottom line (upper left of the diagram) can be taken too far, but it is also possible to ignore the interests of those not physically present [i.e., the shareholders (lower right)]. By operating his "fireworks display," illustrated earlier, Storm first motivates employees to satisfy customers and thereby raises sales and profits for shareholders, who reinvest in AEGON as a result. Stakeholder values are synergized at the top right, by stock options that give each interested employee a stake in the shareholders' profits, so that employees "make money and have fun."

It was Storm himself who warned against the "vicious circle" of celebrating shareholder value too exclusively. We next diagram one way that could happen:

The ship sinks by the stern (where the employees are), but everyone else later drowns as a consequence, even shareholders, who in the end are worse off for being favored above the rest.

CHAPTER 19

A Corporate Dynasty

Leader: Rahmi M. Koç (Koç Group)

It is not often that you'll find a profile on a Turkish business leader. Almost as rare is the large-scale, family-owned conglomerate known as the Koç Group (KG). If we want evidence that the ways of capitalism are very varied in different parts of the world, we need look no further than KG. Extraordinarily successful within the Turkish cultural context, KG is sometimes described as "The Third Sector," after the public and private sectors. Koç businesses employ 45,000 people and constitute 5.5 percent of Turkey's GNP. The group is also a significant contributor to charities and to education. We interviewed the Koç Group because we were particularly interested in the effects of globalization on a country that is at the crossroads of Europe and Asia. We also wanted an insight into how a business leader behaves in a very pronounced family culture.

Rahmi M. Koç succeeded his father as chairman of the board in 1984 at age 53 when his father died in 1996 at age 94. The difference between family ownership and public ownership could not be more clearly drawn. The head of the Koç family and the founder of KG, Vehbi Koç, remained at the helm for some 30 years after most business executives retire. He had towered over Turkey's business sector for three-quarters of a century. The Koç Group is a business dynasty, only two years younger than the Turkish Republic itself.

Now Turkey is eager to become a member the European Union and has taken the first steps by joining the customs union. How, then, will Rahmi M. Koç and his group fare in the global economic system they are in the process of joining? Will the group prosper in the new environment? In this larger world, conglomerates are recently out of fashion, and large, family-owned companies are looked at with some skepticism by financial markets. When we spoke to Rahmi Koç in the elegant old Harem Building, with a magnificent view of Istanbul, he spoke of the following dilemmas:

Dilemmas that Face the Koç Group

1.   Whether to continue with family succession or transform into a public company.

2. Whether a "National Champion" with strong regional loyalties can withstand the competitive pressures of global rivals.

3. How to find the correct balance between the private sector and the public sector.

4. How to reconcile the pressure on Turkey to be democratic and to practice free trade with playing its cards effectively so as to catch up, particularly with the rest of Europe.

5. How to take into account both the Turkey that is a marginal state and the Turkey that is a tinderbox of conflicting loyalties.

6. How to reconcile local success with the search for new directions for the nation.

Dilemma 1: Family Succession vs. Public Ownership

Rahmi Koç has only been head of the company since 1984. He had no choice; it was his destiny. The company had grown up since the 1920s in a relatively closed economy. It won the "first mover" advantage in several fields and was preeminent in the Turkish economy in energy, construction and mining, banking and financial services, retailing, consumer durables, automotive supplies, motor vehicles, and tourism. Koç has now succeeded his father, but ironically, he faces another succession crisis, that characteristic of the third generation of a family. Only 18 percent of US and 25 percent of European family firms make it into the third generation, and it will be interesting to see whether the Koç Group succeeds. His three sisters run different parts of the business, but what remains to be seen is whether the next generation and the one after that want to rise to the challenge. Unfortunately, as Koç observes, loyalties of non-family executives are not as strong as they once were.

One obvious alternative to grooming successive generations of family members to serve the company is to switch to public ownership. But this has turned out to be more complicated than expected. Koç has a reputation in Turkey for its leadership, integrity, corporate culture, nationwide production, distribution, aftersales service, and its Foundations. Though Koç is quoted on the exchange in Turkey, the company withdrew from an IPO in the United States in 1998 because it did not agree with the valuation put on thecompany.

A local reputation does not always travel well to global centers of finance. In 1998, the markets were in shock from the East Asian meltdown and the Russian default, and the IPO was so long in preparation and so badly timed that international investors declined from investing in emerging markets such as Turkey. The firm was valued at $2.2 billion, as against the $5.6 billion KG is generally valued at today on the local stock exchange. It was a moment of truth – the way the markets treat an offering they do not really understand from a region thought to be in turmoil and hence risky. Many of the virtues of a family company do not register with shareholders: long-term commitment to the nation, concern for the environment, the value of a reputation for integrity, and especially years of loyalty between customers, consumers, and the family. It was a shock to see these intangibles so disregarded and so undervalued. The team responsible for this débâcle was released from the company. KG felt that it had let the company down in the eyes of the world.

We should note here that another possible reason for the low valuation was the market's known dislike of conglomerates, but probably more importantly, Turkey's high rate of inflation. All in all, the transition from family to part-public ownership for a company of this size is not easy. Western shareholders do not understand the reasons for the strength of family ownership in Turkey or the suitability of this form to local conditions. KG believes that its hard-earned reputation for integrity is in no way inferior to the so-called transparency of public companies, all too often contrived by creative accountancy.

We can illustrate Rahmi M. Koç's dilemma with the following diagram:

Dilemma 1. Family Succession or Public Ownership

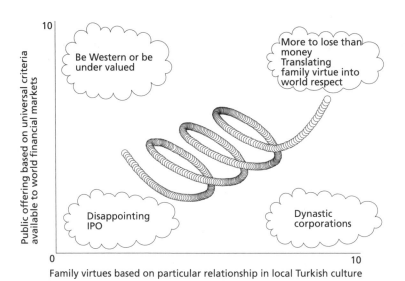

Public companies are judged by universalist criteria, allegedly transparent. They supply the same "facts" to everyone. Family companies are judged by particularist criteria; allegedly revered and trusted in their own cultures, they are more opaque and have very special relationships to key persons, whom they sometimes treat differently.

What Rahmi M. Koç has to do is make the strengths of his family dynasty *appeal* to public shareholders, despite the differences between Turkey and Wall Street. Educated in business administration at Johns Hopkins University, Koç is no stranger to American ways and is determined to demonstrate the virtues of his company to the world markets. One handicap is that Turkey still lacks financial rating agencies, so it is not always clear how the wider world will regard KG or what its criteria of judgment will be. The story that has to be told is how one preeminent Turkish family constitutes both the backbone of, and the gateway to, the Turkish economy and would deserve respect for that reason alone (although there are many others).

Those that have more to lose than money – that is, their reputation, a good name with neighbours – can be expected to act honorably, and the Koç group has a track record of 75 years of fair dealing. A word should also be said about the dismissal of the IPO team. When a family's reputation is at stake, together with that of the Turkish nation, those who embarrass it in public bring censure down on themselves; even if circumstances are beyond their control, there will be no emotional resolution until someone suffers.

Dilemma 2: Can a "National Champion" with Strong Regional Loyalties Withstand the Competitive Pressures of Global Rivals?

The Koç group is very much a homegrown champion. Can it, despite its impressive but local size and great resources, stand up to the competitive pressures of truly global players? The sheer amount of charitable donations, including the Vehbi Koç Foundation, with assets of over $650 million, the Rahmi Koç Foundation, and the Suna and Inan Kiraç Research Fellowship, is impressive; can a company so immersed in giving *also* satisfy shareholders and customers, or will it fall victim to global rivals with lesser obligations to national infrastructures? The truth is that Turkish markets have not been truly open in the last 20 years or so; the danger is that KG might be outclassed by global competitors that have been under more pressure to be efficient.

Rahmi M. Koç believes that KG can meet this competition head on and either do something no one else does or do something better than others do. He believes that his joint partnerships with such global giants as Ford and Fiat are truly equal and mutual in their benefits, and that those partnerships can help guarantee that Koç shares global strategies with the big boys. For Fiat, Koç manufactures the Palio, Marea, and Brava family of cars at Tofas. For Ford, the Ford Otosan venture with Koç is unique. Otosan will be the sole manufacturer of Ford's brand new light commercial vehicle, aimed especially at regional markets. Exports are due to start in 2001. The Koç brands Beko/Arçelik (durable goods) and Ram Store/Migros (supermarket and retail chain) are extremely successful in Western Europe and CIS countries respectively.

KG's strength lies in traditional ties of loyalty. Some of its long trusted dealers are also in their third generation of ties between respective families. Can this last? Will the rising generations feel the same way? Will they prefer a relationship with KG, which does so much for Turkish society, or will they prefer to ally with a global player vying for KG's markets? Koç was not sure of the answer, but we pointed out that Japanese consumers pay from 20 to 30 percent above world prices, in part because national companies are public benefactors and major contributors to learning and development. So long as KG commanded local loyalties, it would be difficult for a global giant to enter the Turkish market without a respected local partner. The family cannot renege on its charitable giving at this point; the only viable strategy is to utilize the loyalties won by this generosity and make it hard to enter local markets *without* the guidance and the blessing of KG. The partnerships with global players would help win respect and make KG privy to global strategies. The dilemma can be illustrated by the next figure:

Dilemma 2. Global Competition vs. Local Loyalties

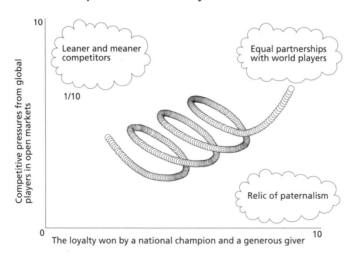

The danger is that the leaner and meaner competitors (top left) will tempt Turkish society to abandon its loyalties. The converse danger is that KG could become a relic of paternalism (bottom right), still giving generously, but less and less able to afford such kindly concerns. Koç's answer seems to be to partner global players and, in this process, become their full equals and learn all about their thinking and strategy, their manufacturing techniques, and their market intelligence – above all, his aim is to join them in exporting, so that KG grows into a genuinely global player itself, rather than just a national powerhouse.

Dilemma 3: The Private vs. the Public Sector: Finding the Right Balance

Like many countries left behind by the wave of industrial revolutions that transformed Western countries in the nineteenth century, Turkey was mobilized and had its fortunes revived by government. Kemal Atatürk was the founder of the new Turkish Republic, which arose from the collapse of the Ottoman Empire, and the English expression "Young Turks" is a lasting tribute to the reforming zeal of Turkey's new republicans. In a pattern that has repeated itself among nations that found themselves behind industrially and then started to catch up fast, these efforts were orchestrated by government. The original ideal was a good one, Koç explained. Governments could *start* things going, but then spin them off to the private sector before they ossified and became bureaucratic. Alas, the ideal was not always adhered to. Had the government sold its telecom business several years ago, it would have been worth much more than it is today. Quite soon, the springboard becomes dead wood.

In Turkey, the state is the largest employer and constitutes a large portion of the economy. The government is not merely the employer of last resort; it also needs to keep its electoral supporters "on its side." For many years, due to extensive budget deficits, lending to the government has been a guaranteed source of profit for Turkish banks. In a recent scandal, several failing banks due to be taken over by the government gave generous loans to selected cronies, safe in the knowledge that the state would take over their debts. One thing that prevents timely spinoff of government initiatives to private enterprise is the sheer number of politically motivated deals. In this regrettable situation, Rahmi Koç seeks to redress the balance within his own publicly oriented initiatives. The money given to charity – to universities, hospitals, schools, and museums – is, whenever practicable, managed by his own employees. He does not believe in dropping money into public institutions, where it falls through the cracks. If he does not actually manage a school he endows, he makes sure it is close to one of his plants so that trusted managers can keep an eye on it. The Turkish nation has not yet given its private sector the scope or the people to be effective, but at least the Koç Group is doing its best to redress the balance. It has shown most dramatically, by its own example, that public projects are best performed by private initiatives and that the public interest is safe in the hands of at least one corporation. It is not just a matter of charity and meaning well, but a matter of good management and the effective use of funds. There is no good reason for social caring not be to businesslike, and the Koç foundations have demonstrated this truth. The dilemmas involved can be illustrated as follows:

Dilemma 3

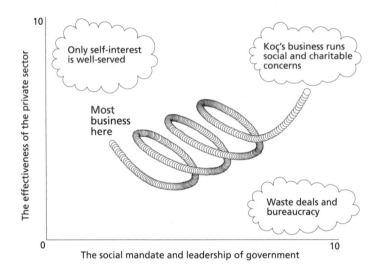

Most businesses are near the upper right of the diagram – effective but narrowly self-interested in their aims. It has been the achievement of the Koç Group and its foundations to combine business with social caring and to show the nation that big government might not be necessary after all.

Dilemma 4:   Pressure on Turkey to be Democratic and Practice Free Trade vs. Playing Turkey's Cards Effectively, so as to Catch Up

We put the proposition to Rahmi Koç that *no* nation has ever made it to economic leadership through free trade. The United States, for example, hid behind the Monroe Doctrine of disengagement from Europe for much of the nineteenth century and then became an arms' supplier in two World Wars. Its Cold War defense expenditures were massive and subsidized its airlines, its microelectronics, and high tech generally. Free trade is the slogan of nations once they have reached supremacy and want no markets closed against them. Singapore, South Korea, Malaysia, China, and the Pacific Rim have all grown rapidly by radically modifying the free-trade doctrine. What should Turkey and the Koç Group do about this dilemma?

Koç answers, "God has given every country some cards to play, but Turkey's situation is particularly difficult. We have cheaper labor, but are accused of 'dumping' when we use it strategically. Global companies tend to dictate terms, especially the price of raw materials. They can and do dump on us, to gain market share. At the moment, global companies, with exceptions, are transferring their profits and wealth to their home countries. When this is reversed, the pressure on Koç will become intense.

"I agree that certain nations have come from behind quite successfully, but most of these are a long way from being democratic. South Korea has been in a condition of martial law (justifying it by the threat from an aggressive northern neighbor) for 35 years or more. Singapore is not genuinely democratic and has been ruled by a benevolent for most of its years since independence. Because East Asia was a frontier in the Cold War and has weak democratic traditions, considerable variations from orthodox free trade were tolerated. China, as of now, manages to have a communist government alongside markets partly open to the West.

"None of these concessions are offered to Turkey. We are expected to be a European-style democracy and a full signatory to human rights legislation as a condition of entry to the EU. This includes following the rules of the World Trade Organization and letting global players into our markets. South Korea has created by government policy vast economies of scale and powerful concentrations of high tech, but if Turkey or the Koç Group were to attempt a similar action, it would almost certainly be ruled illegitimate. The irony is that Europe itself is not really liberal in trade and erects barriers against the outside world; nor is it genuinely a single economy or single market. Turkey *does* have cards to play, among them a highly skilled workforce with excellent manufacturing quality, but whether we will be allowed to play these cards remains to be seen. At the moment, we are expected to live up to free trade and democratic ideals that our competitors have not consistently attained themselves. In order to join, we have to be better than those we are joining! It is a tough assignment. Someone gets drunk and makes a lot of noise in the middle of the night, waking up his neighbors. When asked to be quiet, he replies, 'We live in a democratic country.' When he gets arrested, he then complains that his human rights are being ignored! We are trying, but it is hard."

The truth is that, to take off, infant industries need a period of protection as they grow their muscles to be ready for world competition. Current trade rules render this almost impossible to achieve, save informally by "nontariff barriers" erected by customer loyalties. Turkish industries could be subject to head-on assaults before they are ready to meet them. The dilemma illustrated by the next figure presents the bind in which Turkey, as a culture and economy, along with the Koç Group, finds itself:

Dilemma 4. Pressure for Free Trade vs. Playing our Cards to Catch Up

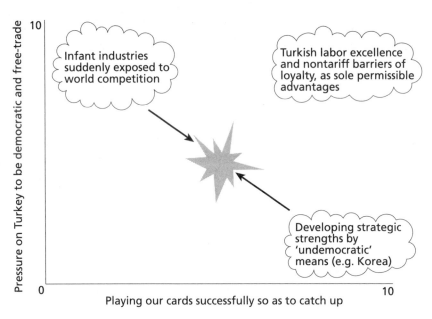

On the vertical axis, we see that the price of admission to the EU is to behave in a way that European democracies have idealized, but not fully attained. On the horizontal axis, we see that nations like South Korea have been allowed to "cheat" on the probably unrealistic rules of free trade because of their continuing state of emergency and a frontline position against a communist state. Turkey is debarred from the use of such strategies. We should not think of dilemma theory as always enabling reconciliation. Too often, the external forces are too great, and whole nations are tossed from one horn of a dilemma to the other. The two incompatible pressures collide in the center of our diagram; in truth, the Koç Group and the Turkish economy might well not have enough cards to play. What the Koç Group *does* have are some very skilled workers and some fiercely loyal customers who realize that the fortunes of KG and those of the Turkish nation are closely bound together. Whether this will be enough remains to be seen.

Dilemma 5:   Turkey as a Marginal State vs. Turkey as a Center of Potentially Conflicting Loyalties

Turkey is a nation situated on dividing lines. It is on the very edge of Europe, yet it was a loyal ally of the West throughout the long years of the Cold War. Turkey is where Islam meets the West.

Two views are possible. The first is that Turkey and the Koç Group are "marginal Europeans," on the very frontiers of European economic wealth and "civilization." It is in Turkey's interest to join the club of relatively wealthy nations, despite the fact that it may always be regarded with some suspicion as not "really" European. The opposing view is that Turkey is a potential tinderbox, vulnerable to the fate that befell Lebanon, which, after years of peace, turned into a nest of religious and ethnic hatred and burned itself down in internecine strife. It is such fears that lead Turkish business to be labeled "high risk." Although Turkish culture presents the moderate face of Islam, some fear this may not last – religious differences may tear at the country, so that Turkey lies not just on a geological fault-line (having suffered terrible earthquakes in recent years) but on a cultural fault-line as well – *Jihad* clashes with "*McWorld.*"

Rahmi Koç is particularly insightful and visionary on this issue. He sees the future of Turkey as a "peaceful Lebanon," the dream that once was but then died. He points out that many "crossroads" nations have prospered: Switzerland, historically; Austria, when it bordered on the Iron Curtain; Hong Kong, which gave access to China; and Finland, which was linked to both the West and the Soviet bloc. At their best, crossroads states allow different cultures to mingle peacefully and engage in trade. Turkey stands at the frontiers of the Middle East, of Islam, of Russia, and of Europe. As a secular state, it could reap the benefits of multicultural, multireligious membership, a safe bridge over potential fault-lines.

Turkey is multilingual. It has adopted the EU's legal framework, particularly the defense of intellectual property. It is also developing a hugely popular tourist industry, evidence that people feel safe while visiting this exotic clime. Such schemes as duty-free car rental are highly successful and help to earn foreign currency.

The dilemma and its reconciliation may be expressed as follows:

Dilemma 5. Turkey as a Marginal State vs. Turkey as a Center of Potentially Conflicting Loyalties

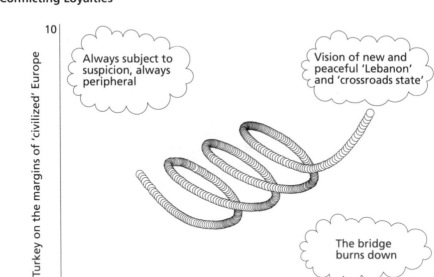

Although this is very much Rahmi M. Koç's vision, he is not very hopeful that the Turkish government will help bring it about. "Governments have been nationalistic rather than cosmopolitan. Liquor and tobacco are still monopolies, though salt and beer were demonopolized to a large extent some years ago. As of now, I doubt that we have the strategy to be like Hong Kong." There was a fashion in the 1970s for pushing up the birthrate to become 'Big Turkey,' with a population growth rivaling those of India and Pakistan. Then, following a change in policy, measures have been taken to bring the rate down to 1.2 percent.

"On the export front, incentives have been on again, off again, and we have been accused, increasingly in my view, of 'unfair competition' with Europe and have been subject to anti-dumping regulations."

Dilemma 6:   Local success has Reached its Limits vs. Finding New Directions

Rahmi Koç's last dilemma is less about Turkey than about the Koç Group, although the fortunes of the two are closely intertwined. KG's large market shares in the national economy – in several cases reaching 50–60 percent and rarely less than 35 percent – mean that there is not very much more "success" to be had locally

Dilemma 6. Domestic Success vs. New Directions

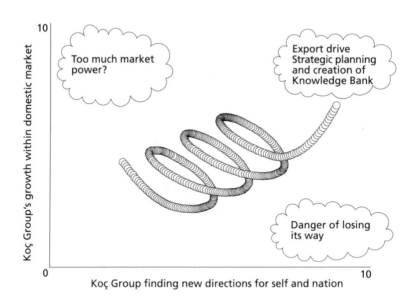

without so dominating various industries that KG is undone by its own market power and is accused of oligopoly. Although it is difficult, and perhaps even undesirable, for the Koç Group to increase its local size, there is still much to be done in export markets by the development of local brands that can withstand competition. (That Rahmi knew what he was talking about was strongly suggested at the end of our interview, when he took a call from the Turkish Prime Minister himself.)

What is urgently needed, as he sees it, is to close the gap between education and the workplace. On-the-job training should begin when someone is still at university, so that what is learned there can be tested, developed, and renewed in the world of work. The Koç Group recently divested its relatively low-knowledge textile business and is concentrating on helping the Turkish nation manage sophisticated knowledge, so that this informs new products and services. To that end, the New Business Development department of the Koç Group (a part of the Strategic Planning Group, which acts as an internal investment bank for the group) is determining long-term strategies and looking into alternative futures. One possibility is a trans-Caspian pipeline project, which could carry natural gas from Turkmenistan under the Caspian Sea. Another is to bid for the state telecom monopoly, Türk Telekom. Another ambitious project is a standardized and integrated customer database of literally hundreds of thousands of the business customers of the Koç Group. When complete, this should be an invaluable source of intelligence about who does what in Turkey.

Whatever it decides to do, KG hopes to mobilize a sizable part of Turkish business to follow its lead in the twenty-first century. Schools, hospitals, museums, research centers, and businesses will, among them, organize the knowledge that will be the core competences of the new millennium. The dilemma and its resolution can be illustrated as in the previous figure.

As a major player in Turkish economic development and a potential mediator in what has recently been dubbed *the clash of civilizations*, Rahmi M. Koç looks down upon the Bosphorus with a keen vision of what the twenty-first century might bring.

CHAPTER 20

Leading through Transformation

Leader: Mark Moody-Stuart (Royal Dutch Shell)

Mark Moody-Stuart (now Sir Mark), became a member of the Committee of Managing Directors (CMD) of the Royal Dutch Shell Group of companies in 1991. By 1998, he was chairman of the CMD. He was fated "to lead through interesting times," although just *how* interesting (and just how turbulent) came as a surprise to everyone, himself included.

During these years, Shell was totally transformed. It closed its major national headquarters in Rotterdam, Houston, Hamburg, Paris, etc., and Shell-Mex house in London, and reorganized itself internally. Senior Shell managers think in terms of dilemmas, so the word is not strange to them. One of us (C.H.-T.) wrote "The Dilemmas of Planning" for the CMD in 1984, and the idea of confronting dilemmas and reconciling these, as a challenge of leadership, appears to have stuck. Speeches made by senior officers are full of dilemmas.

The Dilemmas of Royal Dutch Shell

Mark Moody-Stuart confronted the following issues:

1. Internal vs. external orientations and the trauma of Brent Spar
2. Truth and communicability. The judicial murder of Ken Saro-Wiwa in Nigeria
3. Excessive decentralization and the need for global action
4. Trust me, tell me, show me
5. Shareholders and stakeholders
6. The multicultural, multivalued meritocracy

We will look at these events one by one.

Dilemma 1:   Internal vs. External orientations and the Trauma of Brent Spar

Before we spoke to Mark Moody-Stuart we had received extensive briefings on background issues from some of his senior officers. Some of what they told us can be paraphrased in the passages that follow.

The oil industry (Shell included) has long tended to look inwards. Shell's ear was not to the ground. It had integrity, and a Calvinist conscience, but it was *insider* integrity, insider rationality, and insider judgment that was more expert than anyone else's and more likely to be correct. It would always come as a shock to Shell when the oil industry was criticized. Shell managers saw such issues as ones of technical expertise, and about that they knew better than any critics. After all, they had the facts and outsiders did not. These facts were typically technical, not social issues, and had the rational–empirical substance that engineers love. Of course, it was recognized that the decisions would have social impacts, but that only made it more important that they be technically sound. That sociopolitical events in the external world had logics of their own was not always clear to Shell in those days.

In part, this came about because upstream was more profitable than downstream: exploration and production were much more profitable than retailing. Shell divsions made money in inverse relation to their proximity to consumers, and this fact reinforced an inward-looking technological bent. In addition, there was a cultural tendency for the engineers to be Dutch and the accountants Scottish, so that the profitability of upstream activities was widely known and admired. The British tended to be more commercial, trading on the back of the old empire. It was this inner-directed technological mind-set that got Shell into trouble over the Brent Spar, a massive, obsolete oil storage and loading buoy in the North Sea that Shell planned to dispose of by sinking it in a deep part of the Atlantic.

Shell had done its homework, costing out all the options for disposal and calculating them from multiple points of view, including environmental aspects. As far as Shell could measure the impact, disposal in a relatively deep undersea trench was best for all stakeholders, compared to the alternatives. Safety of the operation was a big concern. Of course, getting rid of a huge metal structure is not going to be trouble free: there are always some costs. The British government had endorsed the calculations, and its Department of Industry was on Shell's side. Shell had consulted widely. What could go wrong? Plenty, as it turned out. Moody-Stuart takes up the story himself:

"We allowed ourselves to be placed in a false position, and this made it imperative *not* to sink the buoy. Greenpeace had accused us publicly of leaving 4000 tons of oil sludge and sediment in the core of the spar. Because Greenpeace had dramatically occupied the spar, the world assumed that that organization had looked and measured the amount of sediment. We knew that this report was wrong, but had we sunk the buoy we could never have disproved the accusation, and we would have been blamed ever after for polluting the water as the oil seeped out. On top of this accusation came another from a German expert that toxic pollutants were to be dumped at the same time. He claimed in an affidavit to have sealed the drums himself! We knew the charge was crazy, but once the spar was sunk, we would be accused of drowning the evidence. We could refute these charges only if the spar was open to inspection.

"So our famous 'U-turn,' which gave the appearance of our being irresolute and unsure of our position, was forced upon us by false accusations and the need to establish our credibility. We had to withdraw from a solution we believed – and still believe – to be technically correct. Were we right? Within our own logical framework we were, but there are other frameworks out there in the world external to oil. And these we were slower to grasp. Admittedly, they were emotional arguments, but they also had a logic of their own.

What really had a big effect on me was a statement by the Swedish minister for the environment. She said, 'Actually I believe Shell's arguments. I accept them completely. But how can I talk to our school children about the importance of recycling materials, when one of the world's largest companies simply topples its own huge wastes into the sea?' And I saw at once what she meant – that her logic was impeccable also, albeit different from ours. I learned that one can be absolutely right technically, but that real decisions must take account of personalities, agendas, emotions, beliefs, symbols, and appearances.

When people ask me, 'Don't you think you were right all along?' I cannot entirely agree with them. Decisions must take into consideration how the people with whom you are consulting think. And because people think about and value things differently, there is always a dilemma – a need to reconcile diverse logics."

Sinking the Brent Spar in the vicinity in which it had originally stood could convince the watching world that Shell was a huge litterbug, dumping that for which it had no more use, at minimum inconvenience to itself. In this context, wild stories about the poisonous contents of the spar gained a credibility they did not deserve. It must have seemed as if Shell were hurrying to dispose of the evidence of its "crimes," except that there were no crimes and the process had already taken years, with the actual sinking being only a culmination.

However, it is crisis that sells newspapers and attracts audiences to TV, so when the disposal was only hours away, the furor intensified. When Greenpeace finally apologized for its wildly inaccurate report about the oil platform it had occupied, it was too late. The audience had shifted its attention.

There are two dilemmas here: inner-directed technological expertise vs. the outer world of sociopolitical appearances, and truth vs. communicability. We will deal with the first of these two now and postpone the second until after our discussion of the Nigerian crisis.

Shell's inner-directed technological expertise is far stronger than its grasp of sociopolitical appearances. This dilemma is a slight variation on the inner-directed vs. outer-directed dimension discussed in Chapter 2. The situation is set out in the next figure.

Dilemma 1. Internal vs. External Orientation

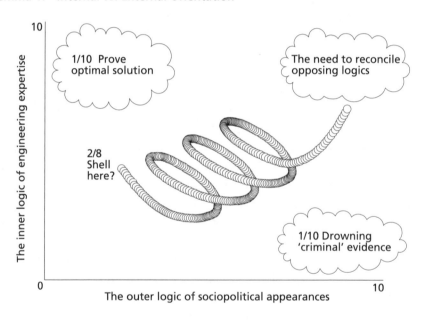

We have tentatively located Shell toward the upper left of the diagram, indicating that the company is strong in inner-directed technical expertise, but much weaker at understanding the external world of sociopolitical appearances. Organizations such as Greenpeace require scandals to "raise consciousness" about environmental issues and recruit members. Boarding the Brent Spar amid crashing waves made them look like "cockleshell heroes," braving the elements to discover "the (unfortunately false) truth."

Shell is relatively unsophisticated in this world of heroic postures and media "spin." While enraged protestors vent their righteous wrath, Shell spokespersons read the deliberations of a committee from prepared scripts. Even if the second is more truthful than the first, the first *seems more authentic and spontaneous.* It is the utterance of the underdog "thinking only of the environment," as against the might of a profit-making giant corporation.

What Moody-Stuart is calling for are decisions that take into consideration *all* logics (upper right on the diagram): the internal logic of inexpensive, safe disposal *and* the concern of the Swedish minister of the environment, trying to teach schoolchildren not to throw debris into the environment we share. All major corporations take public positions, if not on purpose, then by default. Shell must learn the logics of such positioning.

In that connection, we can now come to the second scandal to plague Shell: that of the execution of an environmental campaigner by the Nigerian military junta.

Dilemma 2: Truth and Communicability: The Judicial Murder of Ken Saro-Wiwa

The execution of Ken Saro-Wiwa had to do with two conflicting issues: the truth of what actually happened and the communicability of that truth. When you speak the truth, will you be believed by the Nigerian government, by your own employees, by the indigenous people, and by the world community? Dilemmas are not just a mental exercise for resourceful leaders; they can be murderous crosscurrents in world politics that drag under anyone caught between them. Saro-Wiwa was the chief victim, but Shell's reputation suffered, too, even if only in lesser degree.

Ken Saro-Wiwa was an environmental activist and the representative of a minority Nigerian tribe not favored or represented by the Nigerian military junta. The junta had seized power from an unelected civilian regime. Installed by the previous military government, it was in the process of being expelled from the British Commonwealth. The environment in which Saro-Wiwa's tribe lived was allegedly polluted with crude oil; and prompted by Ken Saro-Wiwa and the environmental campaigners who supported his cause, world newspapers and TV programs were full of pictures of stagnant pools and twisted, broken pipes, although the extent of the real damage was questioned by *The Times* and *The Independent*. The latter pointed out that Shell controls only about 10 percent of the Niger Delta, which puts the reported "devastation" in perspective. Here, then, was a brave, lonely African protester, imprisoned and charged with treason for protesting an intolerable state of affairs. Was this ghastly tangle of leaking pipes Shell's work? If so, was Shell also complicit in the death of this "troublemaker," who drew attention to the company's environmental record? Was this not an unholy alliance between a junta, caring only about its royalties, and a company seeking profits, which decided that Ken was in the way? In a world that judges by appearances, Shell was in the dock of world opinion.

We asked Moody-Stuart for his view of this dilemma. He was typically forthright. Commenting on our background interviews, which had revealed that the locals sabotage the pipelines themselves, he demurred at the word "sabotage." "I don't think that is the right word. These people are totally excluded from the benefits of their society and get virtually none of the massive oil revenues we pay their government. It is their frustration at not getting any share of this wealth, while living in the midst of the disturbance it causes, that drives their behavior.

"If there is a mess," says Moody-Stuart, "we pay them to clean it up, and the more the mess, the more we pay. They break up the pipes for many reasons, sometimes only to get back at an arbitrary and illegitimate government, not of their people. Perhaps if that government loses enough revenue, it will make concessions. Getting your money directly via a foreign company, which keeps its promises, is infinitely preferable to hoping that money paid to your overlords will eventually reach you. A stinking environmental mess is preferable to not earning and not eating at all, and these are desperate circumstances."

We asked Moody-Stuart whether he had noticed these appalling conditions when he himself was in Nigeria in the late 1970s and early 1980s. His voice grew lower and softer: "Oh yes. . . . There were community disruptions when I was in Nigeria. At that time, Shell's effective tax rate was 98.5 percent. Of every million units of local currency we generated, we kept barely two thousand. I remember the community coming to me in a rage, saying, 'It's not fair. Unless we, too, receive something, we'll just shut down this operation.' I used to pull out my charts on which the division of income was presented, but they said to me, 'You are like the millionaire's son. We know *you* don't have the money, but if we hold you for ransom, maybe the millionaire will notice us.'

"So I used to say, 'I promise you I will pass on your message. I absolutely guarantee to repeat what you tell me to government. But if the government clamps down and if the population is provoked, we could all lose.'"

Our background interviews revealed to us some of the reasons that the Nigerian government might continue to ignore its own people, even when an oil company passes on the message. Oil companies are, after all, among the residues of colonial eras. They are not political organizations, and no one elected them. They are tolerated for one reason only: their technical prowess at locating and extracting oil.

The difference between the best and worst companies is several hundred millions in revenue, so you choose the best and try to forget that they are part British.

Why white technicians should be thought influential with black politicians about Nigeria's sovereign interests is very hard to explain. That white foreigners are campaigning for Ken Saro-Wiwa is rather a reason for *executing* him and emphasizes the effectiveness of his "treason": "He has set the world against us!" The political impotence of a white technical expert in a former colonial country should be highlighted. If the expert asks for a political objective, someone will make sure that he or she does not get it. To "fight for the life of Ken Saro-Wiwa" is to seal his doom! No astute black politician will be seen making concessions to former colonial masters.

What Shell did was try to influence the junta "behind the scenes," a tactic that did not succeed in halting the execution, but just about the only avenue of influence that would not be gleefully snubbed. Moody-Stuart continues: "Brent Spar and Nigeria both acted as magnifying glasses that clarified where we were not succeeding. We were not connected to the several publics with which we interface on issues that were highly symbolic.

"On many such subjects, the public mind is itself schizophrenic. On the one hand, it wants instant, clean energy, on the other, it also seeks the freedom and independence of traveling when and where it wants. We wish to be wealthy, but bewail the gap between rich and poor. We want to grow economically, but not at the expense of the environment. Between these opposing views, Shell finds itself situated. Until the parties agree with each other, we are liable to be the football between contending sides."

The underlying dilemma is between truth and communicability. Not everything that is true is easily communicable. The sheer enormity of the gap between the Nigerian government and its own people, who, in their desperation, break up pipelines, is true, but not easily communicable, because no constituencies want to hear that message – no groups gain from publicizing it. There are no heroes opposing villains; instead, there are victims turned villains, as the legacy of past oppression lingers. We can draw this dilemma as shown on the next page.

The uncomfortable truth is that military rulers in Nigeria will kill for the vast riches of "black gold" supplied by oil companies, and the profits will be sent straight to Switzerland or Luxembourg to fatten overseas accounts. The truth is bitter and ironic. What the press wants are people to love and to hate. Heroic Ken vs. the "complicit" company, not the "exploited turned exploiter." The fact is that Mahatma Gandhi, Nelson Mandela, and Martin Luther King, Jr., are exceptions; most exploited people *bite back* when they get the chance! Mobutu repeats King Leopold in plundering the Congo.

Dilemma 2.   Truth and Communicability

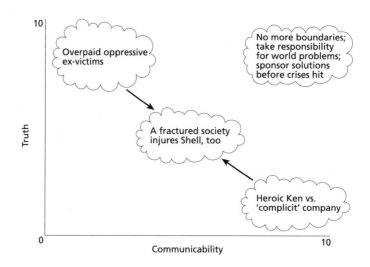

From our background interviews, we got some idea of what Shell is planning to do about situations such as that just recounted. These ongoing dilemmas must be publicly discussed with press, politicians, and the public before the crises that are symptomatic of the dilemmas strike.

You know something is likely to go terribly wrong if you are the only visible white agent of an increasingly oppressive government. On the other hand, you know jobs and income will be lost to other nation's oil companies if you simply pull out. These dilemmas must be engaged before they explode in Shell's face. Shell is prepared to sponsor an examination of the problems. So long as the public itself is fragmented into mutually hostile shards, though, Shell is likely to be cut.

Moody-Stuart has changed the whole mood of the company in this regard. He explains, "If our society is fractured, then this is no good for us. I say to our people, 'If someone comes to you with a problem, never say, "That's not *my* problem; I'm a businessperson."'" If it's a problem of our society or of the world community, it's *our* problem too, and sooner or later we'll be caught in the middle if we are not prepared to deal with it. The question is, What can I contribute? All those comfortable boundaries are gone. It is not a 'Nigerian problem,' a 'technical problem,' a 'matter for the government.' It's *our* problem, because we are abroad in the world.

"You can no longer say, 'We pay our taxes to the Nigerian government. We run an open, honest, audited business.' It isn't that we are responsible personally, it is that we are part of the process, and if the money is siphoned off for illegitimate uses, that social system will eventually fracture, and we will be in the middle of it. Pulling out is no answer either. These countries have a single chance in their entire histories to use their oil revenues for economic development. If they blow it, that is forever. We have to give them that chance.

"You cannot give up talking to any regime you are enriching; we have to keep trying. We have an obvious personal interest in fair and stable elected governments, but we cannot hector them. We rather point out our shared interest in a peaceful, prospering nation with shared wealth."

Dilemma 3: Excessive Decentralization and the Need for Global Information and Action

So how did it happen that Shell shed so many of its national headquarters?

Shell is justly famous for its scenarios, which consist of three or four "alternative futures," each one coherent, persuasive, and reasonably probable. In the early and mid-1990s, the scenario writers were telling the leaders of the Shell Group that there were three contending visions of capitalism: that of North America and NAFTA; that of East Asia, using a more cooperative model of catch-up capitalism; and that of the euro zone, soon to be unified by a single currency.

No one tells Shell managers which scenario to believe. The whole point of scenarios is to be ready to engage *whatever* future emerges. What *does* happen is that group decision makers check from day to day on which vision of capitalism's future is becoming more nearly true and more influential. It was soon obvious that American-style global capitalism was the type most in the ascendancy, by virtue of the long boom and the sustained success of the US economy, whose ceaseless innovation appeared to have ended the cycle of boom and bust. In contrast, East Asia suffered a financial crisis, and the euro lost ground to the dollar.

In this emerging new world, was Shell's traditional model of decentralized multinationalism the right one? There were excellent reasons for Shell's traditional decentralization. The automobile had come into its own between World Wars I and II, when nations were divided by steep tariff barriers. Oil has long been regarded as a strategic commodity, and it was advantageous for nations to have their "own" oil supplies. That Shell took on the coloration of different localities was long regarded as a competitive advantage. If the Hague was under German occupation, London was not. During the Vietnam War, Shell was, to many, the most acceptable oil company – for instance, Shell Oil of Houston was separated from Royal Dutch Shell.

But times change. Moody-Stuart takes up the story:

"The old Shell business model served us well and was well suited to the world as it was 30 or more years ago, with strong, autonomous national business units, with money accumulating to those units which managed their regions, and so on. That was right for a world in which communications were still slow, boundaries were firm, tariff and nontariff barriers were still high, and governments were influential in economic affairs. It was demonstrably successful, because we started way behind Exxon and caught up. The problem we faced in the 1990s was that boundaries and barriers were falling. Communications were instantaneous, markets were globalizing, and you had to respond far faster than before.

"One key point was that we neither decided nor intended to 'sacrifice local marketing' in the process of centralizing and globalizing. I sincerely hope we have not done so. The strategy is not to diminish our local reach and intelligence, but to centralize information about those local initiatives. A great many things are best done locally, but we must think globally about them and respond globally, where necessary, to events anywhere in the world. The old system was too slow to react. Something happened. There were many different opinions, and by the time we had an agreed-upon policy, the situation had changed yet again.

"What we have done now is to vest executive authority for a business and non-executive authority for all the other businesses in the country on one person so that he or she, say, is both in charge of our exploration, production and gas business in the UK and also as country chairman represents all Shell businesses in the UK in dealings with the government. When closing the Norwegian refinery, it was the country chairman, who happened to be the executive responsible for our EP business, who handled all the government public relationships. He knew all the local players. You cannot parachute someone from the center into Norway to do that kind of job.

"When we closed national headquarters, we did not thereby withdraw from our involvement in those countries. Instead, we moved *closer* to actual customers and to local operations and made sure that they informed our global strategic activities as to what was happening on the ground. The offices are now closer to customers and retailers and are no longer located in big towers."

In fact, Shell embarked on a process of making each of its research units justify itself in terms of the customers' demands, instead of assuming that any piece of interesting research would eventually pay off. All research staff were exposed to courses in "marketing for nonmarketers," which showed how to estimate the value of your own activities in market terms. Each project became a profit center looking for customers and had to look to its own bottom line. The fact that you are decentralized in your localities does *not*, unfortunately, mean that you look outward to customers and markets.

Mark Moody-Stuart believes that the move to greater centralization and globalism was the right decision, but he believes it could have been communicated better. "The old habits of patiently negotiated consensus and voluntary compliance with suggestions proved just too slow, especially when it was these very practices that were to end. There was the usual resistance – the usual talking in circles. We finally decided we just had to change and could not wait for everyone."

The dilemma of centralizing the previously decentralized structure is illustrated in the follwing figure:

Dilemma 3. Centralizing Decentralized Activities

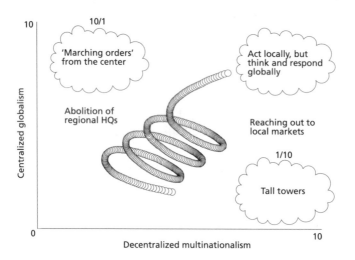

The figure shows how Moody-Stuart aims to increase centralization *without* reducing the group's range, scope, or local flexibility. His aim is nothing less than to increase Shell's outreach to customers, while better coordinating the knowledge that flows from such operations. This will enable the group to act swiftly and in concert.

Dilemma 4:   Trust Me, Tell Me, Show Me

It is an axiom at Shell that the world is changing from "Trust me, I know what I'm talking about and my business is too complicated to explain anyway," through "Tell me – explain to the world what Shell is doing," to "Show me that you are doing what you say you are doing, so I can check up on you." The original formulation was by Sir John Jennings, a senior officer in the group, but Mark Moody-Stuart saw it being used by a union speaker at a UN conference called by Kofi Annan to launch his "Global Compact," where industries, unions, and NGOs came together to support the "Compact." He was fascinated to see the distinction come back to him via a union spokesman, who said we had moved from a "Trust me" to a "Show me" world and that unions and NGOs now wanted to be shown. It gave Moody-Stuart pleasure, because it was a sign that Shell had engaged the public world of opinion formation, to which it has so long felt itself a stranger.

Moody-Stuart sees *Trust me – Show me* as a dilemma, but one readily reconcilable by making Shell's operations as transparent as possible. It is how he plans to run his restructured organization. Managers are held publicly responsible for cost containment and better capital utilization, with clearly defined targets, and are encouraged to show each other, the corporation, and the public what they have done.

Shell is now a "three-legged stool," with objectives having to do with return to shareholders, environmental audits, and social impacts, but all three are in the "show me" world. It is not enough to do something; you must also arrange for its verification and demonstration. Moody-Stuart explains that there are *two* levels of "Trust me": "Trust me without looking at the evidence" and "Trust me because you have seen the evidence repeatedly and do not want to bother rechecking." He explains, "But [it] is a different form of trust; it is a trust based on complete openness – absolute transparency of reporting – so people trust you because they can see what is happening. So, very interestingly, you come back to trust via the show-me tactics."

The dilemma can be illustrated as in the following figure:

Dilemma 4.   Trust me – Show me

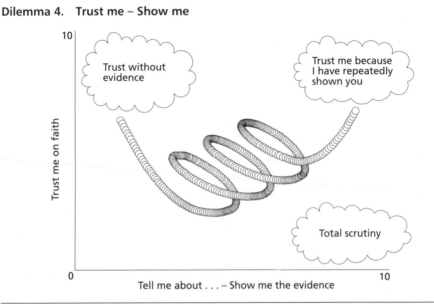

What this means is that Shell's knowledge and reports must be in demonstrable form, open on request to outside scrutiny.

Dilemma 5:   Shareholders vs. Stakeholders

Among the rude shocks that rattled Shell's foundations was the dramatic incident in 1998 when the financial markets wrote Shell down from $180 billion to $140 billion. Moody-Stuart had been chairman of the CMD for just a year. It was a shock for him and for everyone. Shell was being challenged by the shareholder community.

In fact, the financial markets had their reasons. Several Shell competitors were making a 15–17 percent return on assets, while Shell had been languishing in the single digits. A sizable part of the oil industry was making less than its cost of capital, and shareholder protest was a matter of time. Even so, $40 billion was a swinging reduction in the group's estimated value and, characteristically, Sir Mark fought back.

Exxon stood for the model of capital efficiency, whereas the model of flexible public recognition of the need to change patterns of oil consumption was BP. Moody-Stuart decided that Shell was going to be as capital efficient as Exxon. Our background interviews also suggested movement on alternative sources of energy, which is BP's rhetorical position.

Moody-Stuart explains that Shell unashamedly looked at Exxon's example of capital efficiency. For years, Exxon had been making the same net income as Shell, but with $25 billion less capital. That is not true any more; Shell has closed the gap. Moody-Stuart agrees with Lee Raymond of Exxon that, in this way, Exxon has given us all a lead and shown the industry what is possible.

Nonetheless, Moody-Stuart insists that pleasing shareholders is only part of his task. His three-legged stool includes social ramifications and environmental impacts. He does not want Shell to be like Exxon in all respects, as there are other areas where he believes Shell to have the lead. He judges that BP has been a great communicator – a great packager of the message.

Moody-Stuart immediately set to work to increase Shell's capital efficiency. The closing of national HQ offices was not unconnected to this issue, because each office had a grandeur of its own, with all the trappings of national pride, not to mention prime urban sites. Value was not created by these monuments; it was destroyed. BP had abandoned its London HQ much earlier. Moody-Stuart explains that the commitments Shell made to the outside world were very simple. "(1) We are going to sort out our portfolio and remove unprofitable and less profitable activities. (2) We are going to increase our capital efficiency by cutting capital expenditures and by completely changing the capital allocation process, so that the higher expected returns outcompete the lower ones, rather than having all proposals try to reach a threshold. We no longer optimize locally, but compete globally. 3) We have targets to cut costs and continue cutting while improving operations."

Here is where the *Trust me – Show me* dilemma joins with the *Shareholder – Stakeholder* dilemma. Mark is adamant that transparency is internal to Shell, so that outsiders can peer inside: "What has changed is personal accountability. Every bit of the cost structure, from the top downwards, is broken up into pieces and is allocated to specific individuals. We are not so much concerned with blame and punishment as with everyone knowing who is responsible for which cost reductions and realizing that this is being accomplished on all sides. We want to be sure that the person with the responsibility also has the power – the levers of change – in his or her hands. It rapidly becomes clear if responsibility and power are mismatched, and then changes can be made.

"When everyone starts to use these powers effectively, the whole process accelerates; savings made in one place have ramifications in another, and it becomes easier to save money. The move to *Show me* comes full circle back to *Trust me* – trust that everyone is working hard to use the assets more effectively. These methods are not confined to the capital-allocation and cost-cutting processes. Indeed, we aim to show the same kind of thoroughness and attention to detail with the other two 'legs of the stool': environment and social impact. Here, too, responsibilities are individualized. An NGO would not bother to speak to us a few years ago because it did not trust us. Such persons are now *shown* by the persons responsible what is being accomplished, what the targets are, and when these will be met. If Shell cannot make these targets, those responsible explain why and how much longer it will take, but it is rare that we do not keep their promises."

Moody-Stuart comments, "NGOs are increasingly working *with* preferred oil companies, in order to prove to industries and governments that social and environmental targets can be met at reasonable costs. We want to be chosen by these NGOs, and we want to join with them in proving what is possible. If they have a big enough stake in joining with us to get things done, maybe we can count on their support in future crises. Part of increasing our social intelligence is to work with those who have personal agendas, so we understand the crosscurrents of opinion in the world."

Every year from now on, Shell will make a tripartite of reports: on finances, on the environment, and on the social impact of its operations. None is to be sacrificed to the others. The funds saved by better capital utilization can be spent in all three areas. As Moody-Stuart wrote in his message from the chairman in *Shell Report 2000*,

My colleagues and I are totally committed to a business strategy that generates profits while contributing to the well-being of the planet and its people. We see no alternative.

The image he uses is that of the surfer who does not know which of the big waves moving toward him or her will hit; Shell is ready for all three scenarios and the crises associated with each. The trick is to keep your balance in heavy seas. The dilemma can be visualized as follows:

Dilemma 5. Shareholders vs. Stakeholders

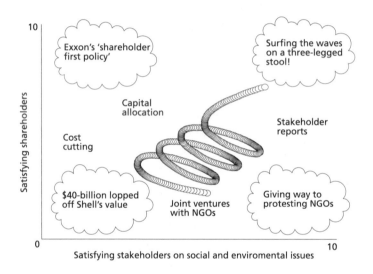

"Surfing the waves on a three-legged stool" is, of course, a mixed metaphor, doubtful in terms of literary quality. But we must accustom ourselves to such hybrid concepts if we are to appreciate fully the need to reconcile values generally believed to conflict with each other. The mixed metaphor is the gateway to the realization that shareholders and stakeholders can both be satisfied. Literary elegance will have to take a back seat to creative resolution.

Dilemma 6:   The Multicultural, Multivalued Meritocracy

Mark Moody-Stuart is passionate about meritocracy, but also concerned about the framework against which "merit" is judged. Traditionally, Shell has attracted some of the finest minds in core disciplines, and they do not stop learning when they come to work – in fact, they have barely begun. The big payoff of scenario planning was never the accuracy of the predictions made, but the fact that every manager who used them had three or four guesses about future outcomes, rather than just one. You learn by conjectures and their refutations. With three or more guesses, refutations come thick and fast, and learning is accelerated. But Moody-Stuart knows better than to believe that "merit" is universally understood across the globe and that we all agree easily on what an employee "deserves":

"When I talk about getting genuine national and cultural diversity into Shell, people remind me that this is a company run on merit. What I am 'really' talking about, they claim, is quotas – getting so many people from this or that place, based on ethnicity. If you go out to fill a quota, you will get some people who would not have made it otherwise, and that harms the merit principle."

Actually, Moody-Stuart is not talking about quotas at all, but a much more subtle issue: *Who says what merit means?* People succeed in different ways, in part because their personalities are different, but largely because different cultures value different attributes. Shell has to see that merit itself is culturally defined. So when an Anglo–Dutch corporation claims to promote people on "merit," these yardsticks are defined and invented by the founding nations of Royal Dutch Shell. These are asking a world of diverse peoples to succeed *as they define it.* That is not something to be ashamed of – every company sets standards – but it is something to be aware of. To what extent has Shell accidentally narrowed the definitions of competence? Is an element of being global of diversity, not just of people, but also of standards, so that multiple forms of intelligence can find the respect due to them?

Shell does not have Nigerians on the CMD, or most other nations for that matter. Genuine diversity is not a race with multinational entrants and Dutch, British, and American judges. It is crucial to discover what different cultures most value and to ask whether these values could benefit the Group. That is a genuine meritocracy, with multiple definitions of "merit" so that employees can excel in their own ways.

And Shell is making progress – generally, better progress than its rivals. There are 96,000 employees, speaking 51 different languages, from 135 countries. Seventy-one percent of its employees, well above the average for big corporations, say "Where I work, we can question our conventional way of working." Sixty-eight percent endorse the view that "Leaders in my unit trust the judgment of people like me."

Moody-Stuart continues, "Shell must move toward being a dialogue of national and cultural groups. I had an American journalist ask if he could write up an interview in a personalized way as it was easier for both him and his readers if things were personified. I agreed (there is not much choice with journalists!) as long as both he and his readers understood that it was a gross oversimplification. You cannot run Shell, or even work in it, without depending on thousands of other people. If X wants to be an individualist, fine, but other people must provide the other values. The CMD filled in the Myers-Briggs indicator some time ago, and I'm proud to say we were all over and at different ends of the four continua. That's how it should be: unity from diversity."

Moody-Stuart's sixth dilemma is illustrated in the following diagram:

Dilemma 6. Multicultural Merit

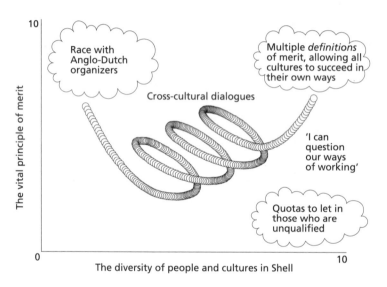

At the top left, we have the present situation, which is fairly open and quite competitive, but the standards come mostly from two or three cultures, and the judging is Anglo–Dutch and Anglo–American. At the bottom right, we have the quotas that Moody-Stuart has rightly rejected. At the top right is the reconciliation, a multivalued world of multiple competencies and forms of intelligence in a perpetual dialogue.

Let the last word be the peroration of Mark Moody-Stuart's report:

> Compiling and verifying this report makes us measure our progress in a rigorous way. Our aim is to give you the necessary information to form a view. This year we have combined the group health, safety and environment report with the Shell (financial) report to provide you with a consolidated overview of our activities. Read on. Judge for yourself and then tell us how we stand.

CHAPTER 21

Keeping the Family in Business or Keeping the Business in the Family

Leaders: Stuart Beckwith, Tim Morris, and Gordon Billage

> *There is scarcely any less trouble in running a family than in governing an entire state.*
>
> Michel de Montaigne (*Essais* [1580], 1.39)

Today's major corporations have a world presence so strong that we are tempted to believe that multinationals rule our lives and our economies. Each has a host of smaller service industries feeding off it. Even education, training, consultancy, and research are being organized by large players. We might be led into thinking that the only place for world-class leadership is among these giants. But we would be wrong. Most of the world's corporations and most employment are within family-owned companies. It is the entrepreneurial sector that creates most new jobs and that is the major engine of innovation. Even when a small company ends up being acquired, it remains a creative nucleus for the economy as a whole. This chapter will address four major topics:

1. The small or family-run business as a genre
2. Stuart Beckwith, an entrepreneur who is a consultant to other entrepreneurs
3. Tim Morris, an entrepreneurial support service provider to small businesses
4. Gordon Billage, who had to lead the founding division of his company into new areas of business.

The Small or Family-Run Business as a Genre

Small businesses are, in many cases, the "acorns" from which the "giant oaks" grow. In new environments with new logics, like the Internet, recent start-ups dominate the medium. This is because the giants have difficulty *unlearning* the assumptions that made them great originally, while entrepreneurs think and act afresh.

The governments of the G8 and other countries are busy incubating or otherwise facilitating small businesses with various enabling measures, including tax concessions, industrial parks, and rule waivers. Considerable resources and effort are, therefore, being focused on supporting and helping small-to-medium-sized enterprises worldwide.

There is some difficulty in defining what is meant by a small, or family, business. In the United States, the term *family-run business* (FRB) can be synonymous with the term *small-to-medium-sized enterprise* (SME). In Europe, the latter term usually refers to organizations that employ fewer than 200 people and that have an annual turnover of less than £15m. We can also identify some larger successful corporations with only a few major shareholders, all of whom are members or descendants of the original family. Finally, we can identify these small-to-medium-sized businesses in which a small team of principals is in continuous intimate interaction, even though they are not actually related (as in a true family). Whichever definition we choose, the statistics remain impressive and remind us that we ignore small business at our peril.

The Economist (1996) reported that SMEs account for 40 percent of the US GDP and 66 percent of Germany's, while employing 60 percent of the workforce in the United States and 75 percent in Germany. A slightly earlier study found that SMEs account for 70 percent of Portuguese companies, 75 percent of British companies, 80 percent of Spanish companies, and 85–90 percent of Swiss companies.

Even when a family-owned company goes public, the influence of the family can persist, by virtue of significant shareholding and managerial standing within the company. Donelly (1995) found that 20 percent of the Fortune 500 manufacturing companies retained a significant family influence.

Family-influenced businesses have several characteristics that public companies are criticized for having lost. They are usually managed for the long term, because the family itself seeks to perpetuate its line and its wealth. There is a tendency for employees to be regarded as family and for top management to seek to leave a legacy to the generations that follow. The family might also seek to make a lasting social contribution to its town, State, or nation.

Under the broad definition of an FRB used by Goldberg (1995), some 95 percent of all businesses could be so described, although many of these are small and employ under six people. Figure 21-1 shows the percentage of all businesses that have been categorized as FRB. (Grant Thornton, 1999). SMEs are in addition to these percentages.

Figure 21-1

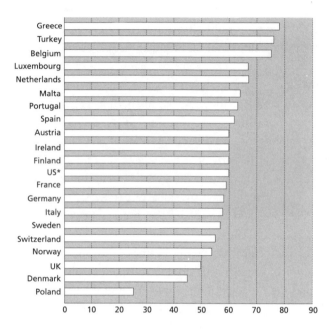

This pattern is replicated across the globe, with China, Japan, South America, Australasia, and Africa relying even more on the family. China's "town and village enterprises" are typically originated by prominent families, with the assistance of local community members. These enterprises, not the state-owned behemoths, are the ones responsible for nearly all of China's record growth rates. Taiwan was the country least affected by the recent Asian banking crisis, in part because of the predominance of small family firms, which are largely self-financing.

Family-run companies have also been shown to outperform public companies on the stock market. Leach (1994) cites a number of longitudinal studies by Stoy Hayward carried out between the 1970s and 1990s, showing that, during that period, $1 invested on the Dow or Financial Times Stock Exchange in 1970 would have grown to $8.72, whereas $1 invested in a family business would have risen to $11.11. Westhead et al. (1995) suggest that the main reason for this higher financial performance originates from a tendency to be more focused than nonfamily counterparts on seeking to maintain and enhance the lifestyle of their owners.

Buried within the myriad of small businesses across the globe, then, is an enormous number of successful leaders. Some are known as successful and effective leaders only by their immediate family and friends. Many employees and local economies owe their whole lifestyle, prosperity, employment, personal finances, and career to these leaders. Rarely do the leaders appear on the world stage, in the world's press, or in the media. Some do receive publicity, but often only in the local newspaper, perhaps as a result of some charity or other philanthropic event.

Characteristics of FRBs/SMEs

Before we consider leadership in small businesses, we must first ask how such businesses differ from larger corporations. We find them different from other businesses in that their directors, managers, and other employees often share a family relationship, the ethics and behavioral pattern of which are to a greater or lesser extent carried over to the workplace. In many, the family subsystem dominates the business management system. This effect is seen by some researchers, such as De Vries (1998), as a built-in Achilles heel that can render the interaction between the family and the business incompatible and cause friction and conflict.

On the other hand, it is often said that family businesses are more human places to work than the stereotypical bureaucratic organization. Generally, there is more concern for the welfare and the satisfaction of employees and the community, and family businesses usually pay higher wages than the industry norm. Yet, family businesses are often risk averse. Donckles and Frohlich (1991) concluded that FRBs tend to be more successful when they are positioned in niche markets. Leach (1995) attributes this kind of success to this genius of the founder, whereas Degolati and Davis (1995) disagree, reasoning that the small size of most FRBs keeps them from competing on the basis of economies of scale, so they instead search for a niche wherein they can rely on customer loyalty.

In this chapter, we will consider three leaders as representatives of this important community of FRBs/SMEs. We have chosen them to illustrate how many of the underlying concepts, propositions, and frameworks on which this book is based apply to that world as well. In drawing these comparisons, we note the following facts:

1.   FRBs and SMEs are like the early stages of large organizations. We can seek to derive generalizations that will be applicable to any type of organization as it develops.

2.   In many large corporations, what actually goes on at the top is like a small family business. Members of the senior executive team are in continual close and personal contact with each other. Often, their contact with other staff and other parts of the organization is limited, and they behave like family "insiders" despite being involved in feuds with wider interests.

Stuart Beckwith, an Entrepreneur Who Is a Consultant to Other Entrepreneurs

Stuart Beckwith is the founding entrepreneur and managing director of the BCIF group of companies. His organization provides a "one-stop" center for business training, consulting, and recruitment, one targeted mainly at small or family-run businesses. Over the last 15 years, BCIF has grown from nothing, while helping more than 9000 other new businesses become established. Beckwith has both grown his own organization and helped to grow thousands of sole traders or partnerships to viable, self-sustaining businesses. The corporate ethos of BCIF, deriving from his own style and personality, has been to synergize the contribution his organization can make by cooperating with the many other (often government-initiated) agencies that provide help to small businesses. BCIF works in close partnership with these government departments and with staff agencies, accountants, tax and planning advisers, and banks and venture capitalists. In an earlier career, Beckwith was a senior lecturer at a major UK business school, specializing in small-business entrepreneurship. In the early 1980s, he left the security of his tenured post to face the challenges of the commercial world. This chapter will provide some extracts from an interview with him by one of the authors.

PW: Stuart, how would you cope if you were starting out today, rather than 15 years ago? Wouldn't it be much more difficult in today's much more competitive world?

SB: In fact, I think it is easier today. There are so many sources of help, many of which are free (i.e., publicly funded). Also, technology means you can quickly position yourself on the Internet, across the world, with e-mail and accommodation addresses, and give the impression that you are already established and successful, almost from (and with) nothing.

PW: So, what have been the main dilemmas you have faced or you have observed with your customers?

SB: Without doubt, it is the interaction between the demands of the family and those of the business. I have observed families breaking up through the demands of their business and businesses failing through the demands of the family. In our business, I employ some of my sons, and my wife is also a senior executive. I have always been conscious of the need to find ways to integrate these apparently competing demands.

Typology of Family-Business Sociotypes

If we examine these opposing values, we find the following dilemma occurring frequently:

Dilemma 1. Four Sociotypes of Family Businesses

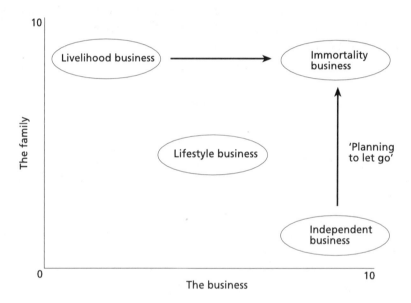

The diagram provides us with a typology that explains the appearance of small-business sociotypes (after Swaffin-Smith, Woolliams, and Tomeko, 2000).

Let us consider these in turn.

The Livelihood Business

In a *livelihood business*, the family is dominant. For some family members, the activity might not even be recognized as business. Because the demand of the family is paramount, the prime concern is to accumulate personal assets rather than retain profits in the business. In many cultures, it is often the womenfolk who take the key roles, with a man taking the "front man" role. Many pass the business on to another member of the family when it has fulfilled the needs of the family in terms of funding the upbringing of children. Even more frequently, the business withers or dies and doesn't pass to the next generation. Often, in developing countries, an FRB is subsidized by family members who work overseas, on condition that it employ other family members who otherwise would not have employment, might not have a specific role, and might not be the best people for the job. Terms of payment for nonfamily employees are usually not comparable to those of family members working for the business. Children can be under pressure to join the family business, to "carry on with your father's mission." Other FRBs discourage their children from working in the family business or employ low performers to insulate their children from the demands of the external job market. Children often work in the business as they grow up simply by virtue of being a member of the family. Sometimes, they work for their keep and are not paid enough salary to make them independent of the family.

Investment funds are often borrowed from friends and family, who see them as a stake in the family's future. The meaning given to this funding is as a personal loan to an individual, with little or no expectation of an economic return. In many cases, the lenders realize they are making a gift, but it is easier to regard it as a loan, making it a vote of confidence. The financial and control systems are simple, with emphasis on cash, not profit. Cash generation is required to cover living costs and investment in personal assets. In many cases, the balance sheet does not differentiate between personal and business wealth. The next generation often finds it difficult to enter and develop the business, because there has not been enough investment to grow it.

FRBs often have no real management systems. Intuitive decisions are often based on dealing with people who are known intimately. Families decide for themselves which of their members become involved in a business decision. A manager in a larger corporation might play tennis with fellow employees during lunch hour, but is able to separate these personal relationships from necessary business decisions. If these sports partners had to be dismissed or relocated, the clean disjunction of work from play would help the manager in making the necessary decisions on purely business grounds.

In a livelihood business, the equivalent situation is the owner–manager's playing tennis or soccer with employees to whom he or she is probably related – perhaps by marriage. Here, the relationship is not separate from the business. It is more difficult to return to the office and make decisions injurious to a member of the family. Investments might have been made on the expectation that family members would be provided with employment. Any damage to one relationship could have ramifications on others. A family firm has all its eggs in one basket. A conflict originating in the bedroom or the boardroom will affect both, but it is the family that will be put first, even if the business suffers.

Independent Business

The *independent business* has its own identity and makes demands on its members and on the family to support that business, even at the cost of some family relationships. There is a clear distinction of the family from the business. The business is often well financed from a range of sources, but with an emphasis on medium- and long-term returns. There are well-developed financial procedures, with review by representatives from all major stakeholders. The accountancy function is generally performed by a professional outside practice.

There is usually a clear business strategy, which is clearly positioned for growth. There is a greater tendency towards strategic thinking, having budgets associated with it, and motivating a shared attitude toward achieving sales targets. Family members are entitled to *opportunities* for success and promotion, but not to *automatic* preferment. The system is meritocratic, and ownership, management, and control stakes are frequently traded for diversity and growth.

The demands of the business often place stress on relationships within the family. Family members who are less well educated or less effective in business (e.g., they fail to meet sales targets) might be replaced by external employees who are skilled or experienced personnel. These decisions can easily give rise to rifts, to close family members not speaking for years, and even to the breakup of marriages. Once again, the eggs are all in one basket, but here the survival of the business is put first, and the family could be sacrificed.

The Lifestyle Business

We see the *lifestyle business* operating as a compromise between the competing demands of the family and the organization serving as a market. As with any compromise, there is always some loss on both sides: family life has to give something, yet business performance never reaches its full potential. It could be that what is essentially a hobby or a form of self-expression is generating income. These small businesses can be primarily backdrops for how the principals present themselves publicly and might only secondarily serve family or business values. Some are extensions of the "life spaces" of protagonists.

Those involved might argue that their main concern is to fulfill themselves and earn enough to subsidize a degree of self-actualization. The contribution they can make to the building up a wealth both in the family and in the business might be limited. The business is often financed through personal assets or through not having to pay domestic or other personal bills. Cash (survival) to maintain the lifestyle and sustain the enterprise is the main issue. The lifestyle business can move towards independence over time if funds exceed lifestyle requirements. It usually dies with the person whose lifestyle it enhances.

Products or services vary considerably, originating as they do from individuals' interests or hobbies and therefore are wide ranging. The initial focus of the business might be on the short term, fulfilling personal achievement through producing the best. Many take high risks because of their dream visions of themselves, and the business could have an uncertain future through aspirations exceeding achievement. Grand plans are part of the lifestyle. We return at this point to more comments from Beckwith.

PW: Do you observe that the businesses you interact with tend to follow one of the preceding three sociotypes?

SB: Very much so, and I have always been conscious of the need to avoid conflict between family and business demands in my own companies.

PW: To probe the nature of these relationships, we sometimes ask, Would you expect your employees to help you paint your house or give you support for a domestic event outside of work?

SB: I think I can safely say that there wouldn't be any dilemma on the part of my staff. In fact, we had a move recently, and many people offered to help. There was no recording of who helped and who didn't. Some nonfamily members helped, and some family members did much less. It just wasn't an issue. No one, I am sure, felt uncomfortable about the situation – except perhaps me! I didn't want some people to see inside my house and see how much expensive furniture I might have! On another occasion, different members of our team would help.

PW: So how does your style of leadership bring about this integration between the business and family values.

SB: It is no one simple thing. It is about continuously striving to bring this integration about. It is more than just policy or a decision framework. I make sure my sons, for example, have clear roles at work – yet we have a drink afterwards on several evenings. We can discuss business when being together socially, and we can discuss family matters during work time. In fact, I would say that the family bonding has helped develop the business and that the business has helped strengthen the family.

PW: Do you foresee the time when you will need to step down or retire?

SB: Yes, and I am conscious of the problem that many founders won't leave their next generation to get on with things. The original owner wants to stay on and interfere. I see this all the time. They try to use their status and family position (probably now akin to a grandfather or "godfather") to get their own way. This often conflicts with younger middle managers who have new ideas, recognize changes in the marketplace, and are keen to exploit new technology.

PW: So how have you resolved this tension between your role derived from your status and the technical competence of the high-performing managers you are developing?

SB: I recognize the importance of "planning to let go." I can use my "status" to ensure that we do have succession plans in place and that the business will not depend on my personal prescence in the future. I also recognize the need for change and that BCIF in the future will be much different from what it is now.

The Immortality Business: A Plan for Letting Go

So we can identify a fourth stereotype: the *immortality business*. Here, the demands of the family and business and the tension between the aging founder and younger achievers are reconciled. The founder achieves immortality of a kind by living through his successors. Unlike most family businesses, they won't suffer the "Italian syndrome," in which family businesses tend not to survive to the third generation. In fact, most small businesses don't even survive the loss of the founder.

We observe that family members often own a part of the business in a custodial role. They are willing to forgo short-term profit to ensure that the business continues, and their family history is intimately tied up with the history of the business. They share power and build up assets, both in the business and in the family. There is a possible opening in the business for all members of the family who want it, and, importantly, they recognize that fairness is not the same as equality. They might even consider unrelated staff as "sons (or daughters) of the house."

Family members play a variety of roles. They can be owners (shareholders) and members of the family, but not working in the business. They can be family members working in the business, but with no ownership stake. They can be just family members, but related to owners or people working in the business. They can have a strong psychological attachment to the business. What they have to pass on are "genes" of knowledge and experience. Even so, letting go is very difficult; even the most loyal progeny mix your ideas with their own.

Some family members might try to originate policies, using professional managers qualified in particular functions to carry them out. Such policies include both agreed-upon relationships between family and professional rights and obligations. "Inside" decisions can be routinely checked against "outside" advice.

In the end, our only lasting powers come from our influence and from the organizations that empower our ideas. A family business aspiring to "immortality" must ask, "What is our legacy?" and must give subordinates the autonomy to renew that legacy in a new century. Pressure for change will come from changing market conditions, from family members who want to do more (or less), from those seeking to withdraw or add capital, and from major nonfamily contributors who feel they are being shortchanged for their efforts. The "right" balance is an ever-shifting one.

The number of family businesses to be found in each category will vary from culture to culture, usually with the relative importance the culture places on the individual and the family. But there is little doubt that all values find fulfillment at the top right of the diagram repesenting Dilemma 1 and that the struggle to reconcile is a crucial aspect of value creation as such.

Tim Morris, an Entrepreneurial Support Service Provider to Small Businesses

In an earlier career, Tim Morris worked in banking for one of the larger banks providing corporate lending to client companies. In those days, the bank was interested only in covering its own risk on the borrower's home and savings. Morris led a change toward lending on the basis of professional risk assessment and understanding and helping to develop a better business plan.

Later, he left banking and became managing director of the Greystone Group. Greystone was originally in the business of purchasing and managing service stations (gasoline filling stations). Morris excelled at this venture and gained a reputation with the major oil companies as a highly successful entrepreneur and a shrewd (station) operator. He was able to develop and lead an extensive team that would seek out service stations that were underperforming. He would complete a comprehensive review, including customer and traffic surveys in the vicinity and a study of local planning developments, prior to purchasing a station. He would add a retail store to the business of basic gasoline sales. Revenue would grow quickly, while the relative costs of operations fell.

It wasn't long before the Greystone Group owned a string of service stations. Reflecting on the classic question "What business are you in?" led Greystone to realize that it was in the property-development business, rather than in gasoline retailing. The value of each service station purchased had increased beyond the rate of property-price inflation or gasoline revenues. The codirectors wanted to diversify Greystone into purchasing hotels and residential property, but they reached a point at which their quest for growth outstripped the scope of their own specialized expertise. At the same time, the property market looked increasingly uncertain. For this reason, Morris made his exit and established a new venture he could have control of himself. He is now the founding entrepreneur and managing director of MMP Business Management, Ltd., which he established some six years ago. MMP is a business management company that provides the back office for a range of diverse organizations that want to grow a distinctive competence full time.

For example, a local restaurant might be started by a restaurateur or a chef. Such persons know about serving people, about good food, and providing an ambience that will give diners a satisfying experience. What they don't know about (or simply are not interested in) is how to connect an electric cash register to a local area network of PC computers, so that the next morning they can see the business results of the night before. Here, Morris's company helps: It provides all such know-how and services that are necessary. Let's talk with Morris about how he does this.

PW: Why is your MMP business so successful after such a short time, Tim?

TM: There are many reasons, but it is clear that people want to get on with what they know best and leave the rest to someone they can trust. Banks don't help anymore – they just want to rip off their clients. Traditional accountants are useless and think their only job is to produce a set of accounts at the end of a year to satisfy the tax authorities. So we have a wide range of clients and help them to execute their business. It may be companies selling replacement windows, electrical contractors, small manufacturing or engineering companies, etc. They may be sole traders or larger SMEs employing up to 100 people. We are their "office." We also act as intermediaries between banks, the tax authorities, and problem customers, negotiating prices and terms with suppliers, all on behalf of our clients.

PW: What was important when you started?

TM: We recognized that technology was and is going to play an increasingly important role in all business. Although I (and my core team) were IT literate, we knew we needed to get up to speed with the very latest – and keep up to date. We needed this enhanced technical competence fast.

We also needed some instant credibility. New, young, and hungry entrepreneurs we wanted as our clients don't all play golf. Yes, we want to develop relationships, but we needed some instant status.

PW: Did you see the need to get both instant technical competence and status to be a contradiction –even if it was just because of what you could afford at the time?

TM: Yes, at first. We thought of expensive offices, a prestigious address, and high-quality printed literature and promotional material. We also thought of attending our local university and colleges that could give us the enhanced technical competence –although it would take a little time.

PW: So how did you reconcile this dilemma between novelty and credibility?

TW: I decided to set about studying for and passing the Microsoft exams. The course material is available electronically, and what we needed was a high level of capability in Microsoft Office products, networking, Internet, e-mail, databases, etc. I also knew that if we were successful in passing the exams, we might get Microsoft's approval.

After a three-month, very intensive study period, both I and my wife passed a range of Microsoft exams. As a consequence, our company became instantly "Microsoft approved." We were able to use the status of Microsoft by branding all our literature as "an approved Microsoft solution provider." This immediately brought us clients who thought we must be good (and differentiated from other, "cowboy" companies). Because we were technically up to date, we could indeed provide them with the technical help they wanted and solve their technical problems. This was more than just basic PC awareness. We were competent with hardware (bar codes, scanning, and networking) and software (accountancy and office systems). This instant "status" gave us initial inquiries, but the clients stayed with us because of our technical competence. In fact, even Microsoft passes on business leads to us in our specialist area. Many follow the typology you describe. Our clients may be lifestyle, livelihood, or independent businesses.

PW: What sort of contract do you have with them?

TM: We don't have a written contract. They pay us a fee each month for our services. We may renegotiate the fee if the volume or scale of what we do for them changes. If they are not happy with our service, we just tell them to stop paying for it.

PW: OK, so you take away the hassle of the administration. Is that it?

TM: No, it is much more. It's all about control. We are continually surprised at how many small businesses don't know how much cash they have in the bank, what payments (to creditors) are due in the near future, and what debtors they have. They seem to be trying to catch a flight with last month's departure screen display board! I couldn't sleep at night if I didn't know exactly where my business was! On the other hand, we find owner–managers who are obsessive about being in control. Just because they started the business and it has been running successfully in the past, they think it will go on forever if they continue to apply their "magic formula."

PW: So are you a control freak?

TM: No, it is a matter of avoiding the extreme. For those who are all fatalistic and think that everything depends on luck or the economy, we try to encourage them to get their business in control. We produce a daily (or sometimes weekly) snapshot of income and expenditure and exactly where they are. This gives them a greater degree of control. We do the same thing for our own business, of course. At any time, at the click of a mouse, I know exactly our cash bank balance, our creditors, and our debtors.

Conversely, for those who think they are in control, with simplistic administrative systems, we try to show them that they are not – because in the medium term they may be vulnerable to the external environment.

PW: So does this mean you are concerned with overall concepts and a holistic view?

TM: Yes and no. We also need to be concerned with details.

I remember, in our gas stations, fuel was delivered by volume. One hot day, I realized that we were getting less in our delivery from the oil company supply because of the thermal expansion (and therefore lower density) on hot days. We assessed this and negotiated volume and cost corrections due to temperature variations on deliveries to us. What we thought was simply a matter of principle and of scientific interest turned out to be significant in real revenue terms over a year. It's being concerned with this level of detail that makes being in business for an entrepreneur so exciting. Knowing you have made things sharper, more profitable, and more efficient is where we get our kicks.

In the end, it's not just about money – we can eat only three meals a day. You can be an entrepreneur only by doing it, by making and learning from your mistakes. The buzz comes from doing something your own way, with no one else around to tell you how. In our MMP business today, we are continually using small detailed costings and margins to make the overall company more efficient. In turn, by making the overall company more efficient, we can focus on the smaller things that make a difference.

PW: So is your business (and your clients) concerned with the short term or the longer term?

TM: In fact, and if the truth be known, we often get new clients because they are in trouble. They may be overtrading or facing a cash-flow crisis. There is a temptation to focus on the short term: How are we going to pay the workforce next week? How can we pay the next tax bill due? Implementing only short-term emergency measures would mean that we could never climb out of the hole. Similarly, if we only take a medium or longer-term view, a creditor may petition to suspend the business from trading.

We have to use the short-term emergency actions to set up guidelines for longer-term sustainability. Just because we produce cash position statements each morning for our clients when we take them on doesn't mean we stop doing that when the crisis is over. We still do it every day. The short-term action becomes the long-term operational characteristic – so they don't get caught unawares next time.

In the same way, we identify where they want to be in two or three years' time. We then use the long-term goals to encompass any short-term emergencies. The long term must *include* the short term.

It pays to be honest, believe me. We make a point of keeping our promises and never letting people down. If it is good news or bad news, I like to be straight. I like to have a relationship with my clients that is more than just a business relationship. This means I can tell the truth even though it hurts. Take it from me, in the long run, it pays!

PW: How do you benefit from all of this?

TM: Apart from monthly fees that start to come in from month 1, we often try to negotiate an equity stake in the client's business. It also means we accumulate wealth in the longer term, rather than fees being just an alternative to salary earnings.

PW: What next?

TM: Although some of our clients (or their businesses) may not be here in the future, we certainly shall. We think the world of work and business is changing faster than many pundits think. While technology is one of our unique selling points, we accept Dale Carnegie's view that only 15 percent of financial success comes from technical business knowledge and that 85 percent is skill in human engineering. It is our ability to lead people in what really helps our clients, and as we help our clients, MMP grows from strength to strength.

Analysis of MMP's Dilemma Resolution

Tim Morris and his company have a keen eye for one of the central dilemmas of entrepreneurship: that most entrepreneurs are interested *in only the most original aspects of their enterprise.* They have an idea; they want to make that idea a reality; the other aspects of organizational existence –keeping accounts, filing taxes, meeting payrolls are felt as almost an affliction, a necessity dragging the entrepreneur away from the work that he or she finds most exciting. There is a desperate need to find someone willing to do such "boring" and "routine" functions. Those surrounding the entrepreneur and identifying with him may be equally bored with maintenance activities, so that such activities frequently are done badly by a marginal person not liked or admired in the organization. This helps explain why MMP tells clients not to pay their monthly invoice if they are dissatisfied. In truth, very few clients can afford to do without help, so this generous attitude is very rarely exploited. The dilemma is between what the entrepreneur *likes doing* and *dislikes doing.*

Dilemma 2 . Likes and Dislikes

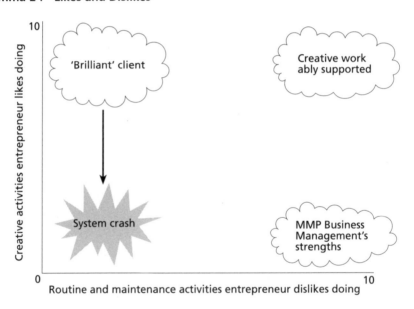

In the preceding illustration, we see that MMP provides a strength and reliability that *complement creative work,* allowing it to continue without the system crash (bottom left) to which "brilliant clients" (top left) are prone.

We should be careful of our labels. What is "boring" for a high-tech entrepreneur is interesting and challenging for MMP Business Management. Microsoft Office is an exciting field of new applications for those wrapped up in it, and Tim Morris and his wife are entrepreneurs, too. They get their thrills in their own ways. Nonetheless, clients benefit from getting on with the leading-edge aspects of their own work, while gaining high-quality support for necessary functions.

Tim Morris is also extremely insightful regarding two contrasting types of entrepreneurs: those who *over*control and those who *under*control. (See Dilemma 3.) For each kind of client, he has a different treatment. The undercontrolling client we have already encountered: The attitude is "Leave it to lesser beings." There is important and creative work, and there is support work, of less importance, done by lesser persons. Such entrepreneurs leave the control to others and disparage control *per se.*

Dilemma 3.   Under and Over Control

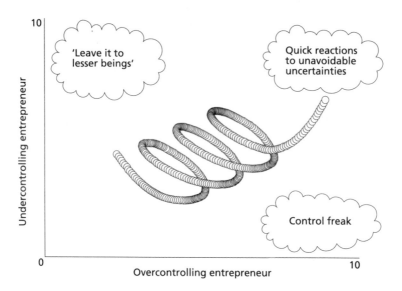

There is a second, contrasting tendency. Many an entrepreneur has "made it" because a set of original ideas was mobilized within a single mind. These ideas could be ordered and sorted, with perfect control over their disposition; all of this resulted in breakthrough success. It is very easy for such entrepreneurs to associate any success with their own total control of key elements. As the company expands, those "key elements" come to include other people, and we have the makings of the *control freak* (bottom right). Morris moderates "control freakery" by constantly informing the entrepreneur of variables beyond his control –variables that *cannot* be changed or countermanded, but *can* be responded to and taken advantage of. He moderates the "leave-it-to-lesser-beings" entrepreneur by compensating for this snobbery through innovative office products. He is also privy to *very* important, inside information, and should he choose to invest in his clients, there is probably no other investor with his quality and accuracy of information. There are advantages in being both underestimated and concerned with detail!

Famous examples of the two types of entrepreneur are Edward Land of Polaroid, who tended to disparage and neglect all functions save his own inventive leadership, and Henry Ford, who ended his reign as an avid supporter of Adolf Hitler, keeping his factories full of management spies, informers, and gangsters hired to beat up unionist activists.

A final reconciliation for Morris was between the newness and riskiness of his own enterprise and the continuity and security his customers would expect. After all, he was accepting responsibility for some very private and privileged information. They would need to be able to rely on him. Of these two contrasting characteristics, it was the second that posed more difficulty. His company was young and daring by definition; how could it also become trustworthy and reliant? His ingenious solution was to get himself certified and approved by Microsoft Office, thereby borrowing the prestige of an industry giant and even getting clients referred by Microsoft. This also gave him ever more efficient and economical ways of running an office.

Morris's reconciliation of this Novelty – Reliability dilemma is set out in the next diagram.

Dilemma 4.   Novelty vs. Credibility

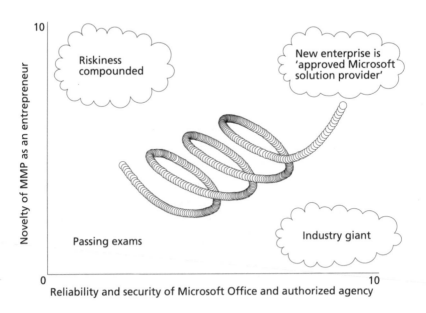

Morris had essentially gained access to an unending stream of innovative office management tools. Unless Microsoft itself fell behind, he would be able to surf on its success. What the client thought of as "support" was, for Tim Morris, continual innovation in its own right. The obvious danger is at the upper right of the diagram, where riskiness is compounded by having one fledgling company rely on another. By passing exams and getting his company guaranteed by Microsoft, Tim Morris gets the best of both worlds (upper right). Note that this is superior to a direct relationship with an industry giant (lower right), because so large a company probably would not bother with small, risky enterprises of the type MMP tries to help.

Gordon Billage: Leading the Founding Division of his Company into New Areas of Business

Gordon Billage is CEO of Clifford-Thames (Holdings), Ltd., a successful, dynamic, and growing SME employing some 300 people. Under Gordon's leadership, Clifford Thames has grown from a printing company to a printing and communications company and is now repositioning itself as a 'support services enterprise.' Gordon is leading a major push, away from traditional print and toward technology data management and the delivery of information across a variety of media. The current overall objective of the group is to realize a shareholder value of £25 million by March 2003. We now present parts of an interview with him.

PW: How would you classify Clifford Thames?

GB: We are not a family business, but most of our senior management has been in place for many years after our buyout, and we operate as a personal and closely knit team. We have climbed out of the traditional very small business and we are now a substantive SME, with sales of approximately £20 million a year. The last few years have been difficult trading, but I am anxious to lead our team into the next phase.

My problem, as ever, is that I know what we want to do, but cannot always see how to do it. Corporate culture and change have exercised my time over the years.

PW: Let's go back a few years. You were founded as a "high quality printer" but by 1993, you already had a range of diverse operations. What has been your corporate culture?

GB: While printing was always rather authoritarian – you get an order and carry it out as instructed –our communications company warranted a more open and participative style of management. Reconciling these with the group has been –shall we say –interesting. We introduced a Total Quality approach back in 1991, mainly because certification was required by some of our major customers. It didn't come from the heart.

PW: How did you lead the workforce?

GB: Commencing in 1994, we introduced an annual employee survey to involve the workforce and to provide an input to our decision making and planning. In early surveys, people saw it as a chance to air their grievances. However, over time, the feedback became more constructive and has been a major factor in getting everyone committed to a shared vision. By 1996, we were described by one of our major clients as the furthest advanced in quality operating systems in Europe. We took this to mean furthest: "continuous improvement" rather than simply obtaining ISO 9000 certification.

PW: So does your certification bring customers because of the status of ISO 9000?

GB: Meeting ISO standards helps us to acquire and satisfy other customers who do not actually insist on them. It shows we have processes and procedures to meet customer requirements that we follow. Because we maintain this thrust and constantly review what we do, this in turn means that we can position ourselves as a star "Quality Company."

PW: Did you just follow standard TQM procedures to introduce this philosophy?

GB: The original steering committee was a mix of strong personalities. Some wanted change, and some wanted to keep things the way they always were. Attendance at meetings was variable. Many things we tried showed up opposing value systems. "Management by walking about" was welcome, but also criticized. ("What's he doing? It's not a Royal Tour!")

PW: Did this lead to the in-house publication *Prospect*?

GB: We already had *Prospect*, but saw that we could use it to improve communication between management and the workforce. We carried several articles over a period about the competing demands of change versus stability, following procedures, and including everyone.

PW: What about the technology of printing?

GB: We are all aware of the changes in this industry. On the one hand, we have the advances in digital typesetting and printing, resulting in lower costs and faster turnaround. At the other extreme, high-quality, high-volume printing presses are enormously expensive. It's only when they run 24 hours a day, 7 days a week, that return on investment becomes achievable. New technology means greater efficiency and leaves us with less margin to compete at price levels created by the more efficient presses. It also means more flexibility and a quicker setup for short runs.

PW: So which did you choose?

GB. Both! We are continually upgrading and replacing our major presses, as well as digital low-cost systems for lower-volume jobs. We have to have both because our customers want solutions, and we have to have the range of options to satisfy their needs.

PW: It appears that you have had to reconcile change with stability, high-cost volume technology with low-volume, low-cost technology, and the status of ISO certification with achieving results by continuous improvement. Is this still the position now?

GB: At this stage, the real dilemma originates from our role as the parent company in the degree to which we direct and dictate to our operating subsidiaries or adopt a more passive coordinating role.

PW: Centers have the potential to add or destroy significant shareholder value. The key question, therefore, is How does one go about designing and creating a center that can fully exploit common opportunities without damaging the individual integrity of units?

GB: There is little general advice or guidance as to the role and structure of a corporate center. Even traditional research in university business schools tends to focus on functional activities and does not appear to have any general frameworks. Given this, many centers opt for a simple rationale that small is best. This tends to produce an atmosphere of cost reduction rather than value creation.

Many organizations have struggled to transform headquarters. In my experience, it is not simply a matter of deciding what is best, because what is appropriate changes continually and shows up at the unit level.

PW: How do you see your leadership role at the center of Clifford Thames?

GB: My role is to *continually* reconcile the universal needs for growth, to follow the corporate plan, and to achieve universally agreed-upon organization goals with the particular needs, talents, and circumstances of the operating companies.

I believe that the center's influence should be positive, so that strategic value opportunities can be exploited. For this, we need to stay sharply focused. Compromise alone is insufficient and tends to drift toward the traditional role of administrator.

PW: What are the general principles by which you lead?

GB: The agenda must follow corporate strategy. Recently, we undertook an exhaustive strategy review for 1999–2003. We must be lean, responsive, flexible, and benchmarked. We translate "pressure" into business unit goals. Overall, we are creating a partnership of expertise within our organization. We see our customers as having a series of continuing relationships with us over time –not just a quick sale, but a valuable source of information for improvement.

I see my CEO role not as simply designing the center, but as leading that continuous improvement, which we learned from our earlier days with TQM under John Cumberland's stewardship. Together with our chairman, Ed Hough, we must now seize opportunities and learn from and instruct our operating companies, while maintaining a "feel" for the uniqueness of each business. If we can continuously reconcile these objectives, we can create additional value that easily outweighs the two- or three-percent cost of the center.

Although we have achieved growth in the last few years, trading has been difficult, and bottom-line profit has not kept up with our growth. Unlike some of our competitors, we have survived, and we are increasingly confident of the future as we continue with our business transformation. It is the pride and passion shared by members of my senior team that will deliver results and that makes our success also theirs.

Small Business and Entrepreneurship

We selected the leaders in this chapter as representatives of successful entrepreneurs in small, but growing, businesses and because they could comment about others as well as themselves. Had there been space, we could have included many others in small-business enterprises, the following among them:

- Hashem Al Refaei, from the United Arab Emirates, who integrated his technical knowledge of IT with his status by virtue of his family relationship with his sheikh ruler.
- Starn Landi from Pisa and his coffee bar, frequented by the older generation (pensioners) during the day and yuppies by night.
- Su Yo Kuk (Taipei) and his interest in fish; in his shop, he sold not only fish for cooking and eating, but also aquarium fish for pets, and many more.

Most previous rigorous research studies of entrepreneurs and of leadership by entrepreneurs attempted to identify their psychological characteristics. However, these approaches ignored the interdependencies between the leader and his or her staff and how the crucial dilemmas are reconciled. We cannot study these leaders in isolation, investigating only their personal characteristics. It is not a case of *what makes an entrepreneur*, but of *what an entrepreneur makes*. The real leadership component of entrepreneurship is understandable only in context. We must be concerned with the interaction between their followers and the more general processes through which purpose and commitment are generated and sustained within the evolving organization.

It is frequently found that entrepreneurs have not had a formal academic education; often (especially in their mature years), they wonder whether they might have been even more successful if they had been to college or received some other relevant business education.

However, education traditionally recognizes only a Cartesian approach, one which supposed that all problems need only more time and money to be solved and that managers (rather than leaders) can solve problems only by using a deductive logic of problem solving, which consists of eliminating all factors that cannot be strictly controlled or accurately measured. What remains is a solvable problem in an isolated system with no relevance to the real world. Real problems that real entrepreneurs face are composed of the contrasting values in these chapters. Managers can't cope with these issues by using an either–or logic of exclusive options. If, at any one time (like a binary computer that is "off" or "on"), they can give allegiance only to one extreme or the other, the result is a loss of realism and integrity. Choosing between exclusive objects does not meet the requirements of living systems.

The opposites that leaders wrestle with, such as growth and decay, put tension into their world, sharpen their sensitivities, and increase their self-awareness. The problem cannot be "solved" (in the sense of being eliminated), but can be wisely transcended. Small and family businesses need stability and change, tradition and innovation, public and private interest, planning and laissez-faire, order and freedom, and growth and decay. Successful leaders get surges of energy from the fusing of these opposites.

Thus, entrepreneurs must exhibit adequacy (*adaequatio*) in order to resolve dilemmas; that is, the understanding of the knower must be adequate to the thing being known (*adaequatio rei et intellectus*, Plotinus, AD 270). Some people are incapable of appreciating a given piece of music, not because they are deaf, but because of lack of *adaequatio*. The sense of hearing receives as its input nothing more than a succession of tones – the *music* is grasped by active intellectual power. Some people possess such powers that they can grasp an entire symphony simply on the strength of reading the score; to others, it is just a noise. The former is *adequate* to the music, the latter *inadequate*.

For all of us, there exist in organizations only those patterns and dynamics for which we have sufficient *adaequatio*. Entrepreneurial leaders possess *adaequatio* for reconciling dilemmas. For example, they don't try to win an argument. Real leadership isn't about winning arguments. Human actions and opinions aren't changed by arguments –win or lose. As Sir Ross Smith said,

> A man convinced against his will
> keeps the same opinion still.

What finally creates wealth are the *relationships* between people and what they value. A product or service is a distillation of reconciled values offered to customers through relationships.

CHAPTER 22

Transcultural Competence through 21 Reconciliations

Introduction

The aim of the research on which this book is based was to discover how outstanding leaders manage knowledge so effectively. Our core finding is that today's great leaders reconcile seemingly opposing values – that's what they do, that's what makes them effective, and that's what makes them great. Senior leaders appear to know how to integrate objectives to deliver results. Successful leaders rarely give orders; rather, they create a reconciled culture of values. It is this underlying, encompassing process that is essential for real success: It delivers benefits and bottom-line business results. From extensive evidence gained both through direct data gathering and through close partnering with the client companies, we have identified a new, overarching process that we term *transcultural competence.*

In this chapter, we seek to generalize into a robust operational and practical framework what is behind the behaviors exhibited by high-performing leaders. This exercise is intended to make cultural and other value-system differences tangible, so that their consequences can be made explicit. In that way, we can all have access to a common basic model. We can all attempt to reconcile dilemmas with a chance of reaping the benefits.

This Trompenaars Hampden-Turner (TH-T) framework encompasses the three *R*'s: *R*ecognition, *R*espect, and *R*econciliation.

Recognition

The first step for leaders is to help all players *recognize* that there are cultural differences – to recognize their importance and impact.

Culture, like an onion, consists of layers that can be peeled off. We can distinguish three layers. First, the *outer* layer is what people primarily associate with culture: the visual reality of behavior, clothes, food, language, the organizational chart, the handbook for human related policies, and so on. This is the level of explicit culture. Second, the *middle* layer refers to the norms and values that an organization holds: what is considered right and wrong (norms) or good and bad (values). Third, there is the deepest, *inner* layer: the level of unquestioned, implicit culture. This layer is the result of human beings organizing to reconcile frequently occurring dilemmas. It consists of basic assumptions, as well as many series of routines and methods developed to deal with the regular problems that one faces. These methods of problem solving have become so basic that, like breathing, we no longer think about how we do them. For an outsider, the basic assumptions are very difficult to recognize. Understanding the core of the "culture onion" is the key to successfully working with other cultures and to successful alliances and cross-border collaborations.

Thus, while we instantly recognize explicit cultural differences, we might not recognize the implicit cultural differences. This explains why cultural *due diligence* is usually absent from the management agenda of pre- and postmerger acquisitions. Our research, especially evidence from practical experience, has led us to develop diagnostic instruments and validate models to reveal and measure these basic assumptions. They are grounded in the seven-dimensions model of cultural differences developed over the last 10 years and are at the core of this new leaders transcultural competence framework.

Respect

Different cultural orientations and views about "where I am coming from" are not right or wrong – they are just different. It is all too easy to be judgmental and to distrust those who give different meaning to their world from the one you give to yours. Thus, to the next step is to *respect* these differences and to accept others' right to interpret the world in the way they have under the historical conditions that made that right for them.

Because of the different views of the world and of the different meanings given to apparently the same constructs, we find the that these differences manifest themselves as dilemmas. We have two seemingly opposing views: those of contrasting cultures and those of the knower and the known – the researchers' model and the informants' model.

Reconciliation

There is growing conviction that wealth is created in organizations by reconciling values – by supplying customers ever more potent synergies of satisfaction. Our model helps to identify and define behaviors that make value-generating leadership effective. This new approach will inform leaders and managers about how to guide the people side of any organization. It has a logic that unifies differences. It is a series of judgments that makes possible effective interaction with those who had contrasting value systems. It reveals a propensity to share understanding of others' positions in the expectation of reciprocity and requires a new way of thinking that is circular as opposed to linear and sequential. Only quite recently has cybernetic thinking become acceptable to Western mind-sets.

Major Dilemmas in Need of Reconciliation

Reflecting on the principal chapters of this book, we find that there are 21 stereotypical dilemmas that our sample of leaders has reconciled. In genuine leadership, it is necessary to challenge the status quo, a process that induces dilemmas. The seven-dimensional model is a means to elicit, describe, and frame the major dilemmas organizations have to resolve when faced with the need to integrate people and systems.

The 21 dilemmas can be categorized as derivatives of each of the seven dimensions (although what derives from what is an issue in itself).

For convenience and clarity, we have grouped the leaders' dilemmas under seven heads:

1. *The Universal or the Particular.* Do people in the organization (or in collaborating organizations) tend to follow standardized rules, or do they prefer a flexible approach to unique situations?
2. *Individualism or Communitarianism.* Does the organization (or do collaborating organizations) foster individual performance and creativity, or is the focus on the larger group's achieving cohesion and consensus?
3. *Neutral or Affective.* Is the display of emotion controlled, or do you display emotions overtly?
4. *Specific or Diffuse.* What is the nature of the involvement (personal relationships) in business? Do specific propositions get defined first, out of which a more diffuse relationship may develop later, or do you have to get to know your business partner before you can get down to specifics?
5. *Achievement or Ascription.* Are status and power based on your performances, or are they determined more, for example, by which school you went to, by your age, gender, and family background, by your potential, or by the worthiness of your aspirations?
6. *Internal or External Control.* Are you stimulated by your inner drive and sense of control, or do you adapt to external events that are beyond your control?

7.　　*Sequential or Synchronic as regards Past, Present, and Future.* Do you organize time in a sequential manner, doing one task at a time, or in parallel, keeping many tasks in progress at the same time?

When you are faced with cultural differences, one initial, but effective, approach is to compare the profiles of the two parties to identify whence the major differences originate. In practice, the major origin of cultural differences between your organization and the new partner often lies predominantly in one or two cultural dimensions. By reconciling the dilemmas deriving from the differences along those dimensions, organizations can begin to reconcile their cultural orientations. *Recognition* of these differences *alone* is insufficient.

In performing our critical review of how the 21 leaders operate, we found more than 100 such dilemmas that were reconciled, but we have selected 21 of the most persistent and now summarize these according to our seven-dimensional model.[1]

Dilemmas Deriving from Universalism vs. Particularism

Universalist cultures tend to feel that general rules and codes are a strong source of moral reference. Universalists tend to follow the rules even when friends are involved and to look for "the one best way" of dealing equally and fairly with all cases. They assume that the standards they hold dear are the "right" ones, and they attempt to change the attitudes of others to match.

Particularist societies are those in which particular circumstances are much more important than the rules. Bonds of particular relationships (e.g., family or friends) are stronger than any abstract rule, and the response will differ with the circumstances and the people involved.

There are many examples of the universal–particular dilemma affecting our leaders. The dominant one is the global–local dichotomy. The question faced is, "Shall we have one *standardized* approach, or shall we try the local, *particular* approach?" There are differing views on whether we are becoming more nearly globally universal and alike or we are becoming more influenced by particular (and unfamiliar) national cultures.

The Global–Local Dilemma
The global–local dilemma may be set out in the following diagram:

1　A profile is a culture map, one wherein each party scores along each of the seven dimensions.

The Global–Local Dilemma

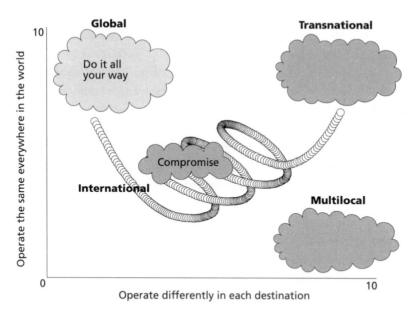

A corporation reconciling the horizontal and vertical axes must make a conceptual leap. The answer lies in *transnational specialization*, allowing each nation to specialize in what it does best and be a source of authority and leadership within the global corporation for that particular vein of excellence. The reach is truly global, but the sources of major influence are national.

International alliances need to look for a similar logic: it is the result of connecting particular learning efforts into a universal framework, and *vice versa*. It is the connection between practical lessons in a context of intelligent theories. In this dialectic, we integrate best practice, whatever its origin, and learn from the diversity of models, adopting, adapting, and combining the best. However, such a solution is not easily achieved and needs the involvement of senior leaders.

The first example we shall examine concerns the dilemma that Stan Shih of Acer Computers reconciled. He seems to have reconciled universally his own preference to be particular. In this way, he was able to build a strong brand image out of Taiwan, frequently seen as a manufacturer of cheap-quality goods.

Reconciling Universalism and Particularism: Acer's Global-Brand, Local-Touch Strategy

Stan Shih saw the need to implement more universalistic elements into Acer's strategy, such as making Acer known as a global brand name, while retaining the strong particularist elements. He therefore designed the "global-brand, local-touch" strategy. There were many difficulties to overcome. Taiwanese companies are traditionally not strong in establishing trademarks, channel structures, structured market research, and sales policies. Marketing and price setting are traditionally based on personal networks, and loyalty grows from reciprocal obligations.

Its history as a small to medium sized company and a family business made it even more difficult for Acer to establish brand names in the international market. Building a global brand image required building up that image over a long period, with dedicated staff available to answer customers' questions. For some time, Acer was forced to use creative ways to avoid putting *"Made in Taiwan"* on its products, because of the bad image. Then Acer started with its "global-brand, local-touch" strategy: the development of Acer as a global brand name with a good reputation, in combination with local assembly, local shareholders, local management, local identity, and local autonomy in marketing and distribution. Acer is now Taiwan's most famous branded product. "Global brand, local touch" is a good example of the reconciliation of particularism and universalism in business strategy.

The particularist, "local touch" part of the strategy comprises the following element:

- localization of the business structure;
- local assembly;
- local identity and local management, with local autonomy in marketing, distribution, and shareholding.

It is crucial to understand that Acer and Stan Shih have *universalized their own preference for particularism.* They have assumed that most other countries want Acer to be particular and exceptional also, following their ways of investing, assembling, marketing, and so on. One country of refugees and immigrants is appealing globally to migrant cultures, who are the creators of so much wealth. With one-third of all Silicon Valley's wealth being created by Indian and Chinese immigrants to America since 1970, Acer's strategy looks like a winner.

The second example deals with the efforts by Rahmi Koç to utilize global learning to gain local market share. His stance was directly opposite to that of companies such as Coca-Cola and McDonald's, which try increasingly to transform local learning into global products. His company, one of the largest Turkish conglomerates, has developed joint partnerships with global giants such as Ford and Fiat that have helped guarantee that Koç shares global strategies with the big boys.

What values has Rahmi Koç reconciled? And is it possible that a company that is known to be part of a closed economy can take such an uncompromising approach: "Be as close and loyal to your clients and suppliers as you can be!" (It is interesting to note that it was Koç Group's foreign operations that stimulated recovery in Turkey.)

There is much to learn from Rahmi Koç. He showed how a national champion with strong regional loyalties is able to withstand the competitive pressures of global rivals. One might have thought he would nominate a decentralized approach as the main lever for success. But look where he ended. It is not Global at the cost of Local, or *vice versa*. It is not even Global *and* Local. The main criteria for success is how to improve Local activities *through* Global learning and how to apply Locally what has been developed Globally. It is a type of thinking that we observe repeatedly among our 21 leaders, and which we call "through thinking" – this approach is quite different in sequence compared to those companies that started globally.

The Transnational Koç Created by Koç

The Koç Group is very much a home-grown champion. How could it stand up to the competitive pressures of truly global players?

From the sheer amount of donations to charity, can a company so immersed in giving *also* satisfy shareholders and customers? Rahmi Koç has avoided becoming a victim of global rivals with lesser obligations to national infrastructures. The danger was that global competitors could outclass Koç.

As a twenty-first century leader, Rahmi Koç was able to meet this competition head on and "either do something no one else does, or do it better than others." Koç Group's strength lies in traditional ties of loyalty. Some long-trusted dealers are now in their third generation of links with his corporation. Rahmi showed this could last. He identified that Japanese consumers pay 20–30 percent above world prices, in part because national companies are public beneficiaries and major contributors to learning and development. So long as Koç commanded local loyalties it would be hard to enter the Turkish market without such a respected local partner. The family could not renege on its charitable giving at this point; the only viable strategy was to utilize the loyalties won by this generosity and make it hard to enter local markets *without* the guidance and the blessing of Koç. Thus partnerships with global players would help win respect and make the group privy to global strategies. The dilemma of Global Competition vs. Local Loyalties was a tension between the leaner and meaner competitors that might tempt Turkish consumers to abandon their loyalties, leaving the Koç Group as a relic of paternalism – still giving generously but less and less able to afford these donations. The Koç Group's leadership is centered on partnering global players and in this process becoming their full equals and learning all about their thinking and strategy, their manufacturing techniques and market intelligence. The Koç Group links up with them for export ventures, so that it has grown into a genuinely global player itself, rather than just a national powerhouse.

The third major dilemma we have found in this area of rules vs. exceptions is the reconciliation wrought by Jim Morgan at Applied Materials. In a world where speed is crucial you cannot wait to get everything right the first time. Jim Morgan has designed organizational processes which accelerate learning by pouncing on mistakes and improving these fast.

Jim Morgan's Fast Learning Process through Errors

According to Jim Morgan, CEO of Applied Materials, the successful corporation of the twenty-first century "will foster a culture resilient in the face of setback, which also rewards success". This process involves reclassifying what was acceptable last month as unacceptable this month and doing better. Errors never go away, because the bar keeps rising and because you keep trying new things to see what works better. This is why Applied Materials has always been very close to first-class customers like Intel, AMD, ST, and Philips. You need their tough verdicts to improve rapidly.

Morgan has always encouraged his people to take risks, and he forgives failure, because mistakes will be inevitable in the new emerging world. It takes courage to live with your mistakes in order to transcend them and move on, learning as you go. Applied Materials, being the largest manufacturer of semiconductor-producing equipment (the machines that make the circuits), cannot have any mistakes in its machinery. Every little mistake has enormous consequences, so each must be found and eliminated.

This learning process – the error-correcting system – comes with the following dilemma. If errors are made by the score and few learn from them quickly enough, we are left with a situation in which we wallow in repeated errors. Errors are fine, but need to become an input to a possible improvement. On the other hand, Morgan knew very well that an organization full of "perfect persons" would not learn rapidly enough in a changing world. At Applied Materials, Morgan created a culture in which error-correcting systems for continuous improvement and ever-rising standards were developed. Every error needs to be an opportunity to improve, rather than the cause of shame or disgrace. People must be empowered to monitor and improve themselves, reflecting on their work and rethinking it. Beyond this tension lies the capacity to improve continuously and even to redefine "improvement."

Dilemmas Deriving from Individualism vs. Communitarianism

The conflict between what each of us wants as an individual and the interests of the groups we belong to is the second of five dimensions measuring how people relate to other people. Do we relate to others by discovering what each one of us individually wants and then trying to negotiate the differences, or do we place ahead of this some shared concept of the public and collective good? It is easy to recognize major differences on this dimension among global players.

We all go through these cycles, starting from different points and conceiving of different means or ends. The individualist culture sees the individual as the end and uses improvements to collective arrangements as the means to achieve that end. The communitarian culture sees the group as the end and uses improvements to individual capacities as a means to achieve that end. Yet, if the relationship is truly circular; the decision to label one element as an end and another as a means is arbitrary. By definition, circles never end: every end is also the means to another goal.

The effective international leader empathizes with the conviction that individualism finds its fulfillment in service to the group and that group goals are of demonstrable value to individuals only if those individuals are consulted and participate in the process of developing them. The reconciliation is not easy, but it is possible.

Reconciling Individualism and Communitarianism

Throughout our study of companies, we have found three major cases wherein individual creativity was integrated into teamwork: we define this as *co-opetition*.

First, we find the superb leadership of Christian Majgaard of LEGO. He has made communities of creative individuals by installing processes in which creative ideas were there not to be killed by the bureaucracy, but rather to be celebrated by a diverse set of team members.

The Individual vs. the Community of LEGO

At Lego, there is no problem with finding enough individuals to generate enough ideas. The challenge lies with the "business system" or community, which has to translate those ideas into the reality of viable products and services. It was not unusual for the community or system to impede the realization of good ideas, especially when those ideas came from senior people, while juniors were expected to be concerned solely with implementation. Christian Majgaard has made a vital intervention in this "force field." Ideas originate with individuals, but it is *not* a good idea to simply pass these down for subordinates to implement. The latter are inhibited in their criticism, and a consultants will need to be hired to legitimize skepticism. Instead, the originator must work *with* critics, implementers, and builders of working prototypes to help to debug the idea whenever that's necessary.

Majgaard has seen that it is unwise to give higher status to the idea than to its implementers; otherwise, defective ideas will persist, disappointing their backers. Realization is at least as important as idealization, and the two must be reconciled. You must also beware of testing ideas to the point where they are destroyed.

We can interpret this *individual vs. community* dilemma by observing with Majgaard's insight, that the membership of teams must be *diverse,* consisting of people whose values and endowments vary, yet these teams must achieve a *unity* of purpose and shared solutions. Once again, we have two polarized extremes: one at which prima donnas are created and one at which solid, viable, safe, unadventurous agreements are the result. According to Majgaard, this creates the potential for coming up with a solution that has benefited from diverse viewpoints and novel inputs, clearing the hurdles of skepticism.

The problem with highly diverse competing individuals is that they may behave like so many prima donnas, singing their own praises. The problem with unity and team spirit, above all, is that diverse and novel inputs get squeezed out. Majgaard's reconciliation is to make the superordinate goal so exciting and the process of creating new shared realities so passionate and enjoyable, that diverse members overcome their differences to realize a unity of diversities, which makes the solution far more valuable.

The second great master in this reconciliation is Richard Branson. We found it very difficult to categorize him under one cultural dimension. He seems to integrate all dilemmas through his personality. The one that shines through, however, is his tremendous ability to reconcile the personalities of "David" and "Goliath." He seems to have a great talent for creating public sympathy in favor of the *wronged individual* confronting the *collectivized assailant.* Branson surely heads a large organization, but in the eyes of public opinion, he is a man alone facing servants of power, a personality against an institution.

Richard Branson's Integration of "David" and "Goliath": The Victorious Underdog

An important repository for reconciled values is the human personality. To an extent almost unprecedented in world business, the Virgin brand *is* the personality of Richard Branson. Branson often seems to win sympathy by fighting against well-chosen opponents, thereby escaping the reputation of a bruiser or vexatious litigant. He is able to set the scene of his confrontations so as to portray himself clearly as the underdog, likely to attract public sympathy. If he wins, he wins, but, even if he loses, he wins sympathy. Although Branson seem to have reconciled many dilemmas, one of the most striking is that he comes out as a Goliath who has the approval ratings of a David!

He has taken on Coca-Cola, PepsiCo, the giant clearing banks, the pensions industry, the US gambling industry, BA's 95 percent of UK-originated airline traffic, the motor-car cartel (using Britain's right-hand drive to overprice domestic vehicles), and the closed system of movie distribution. There is public sympathy for the wronged individual confronting a collectivized assailant. In individualistic cultures like those of the United Kingdom and in North America, the individual is going to win every time. It is part of folklore that groups conspire against individuals. Branson starts from his underdog position and uses the sympathy generated to win his fights against compromised corporations. He reconciled the dilemma of the victorious antagonist with the risk of failing, of the mighty being who is the proverbial underdog, and of being part of the system while trying to beat the system. Branson, however, very often became the victorious underdog by attaining a deeply satisfying victory for the underdog against corporate power. Virgin is personalized as *the* individual who comes to the rescue of the consuming public by confounding the strength of "the oppressor."

Third, we find the very interesting reconciliation by Mestrallet, president of *Suez Lyonnaise des Eaux* (SLDE). While world wide privatization seems like a new capitalistic dream, paradoxically it was the French who were best positioned to take advantage of it because, for many French managers, the proper conduct of private enterprise has never been without a sense of public duty and social obligation to the wider community. Mestrallet, an icon of French sophistication, saw in business the opportunity to "continuously take care of the needs of your fellow man." What dilemma did he face in this humble striving? If you are *of* the community, you can be trusted to take care of it only at the risk of being chronically inefficient and underfunded. Conversely, if you are an unelected out-of-town operator, then going for profit had previously meant being insufficiently trusted.

Mestrallet: Socially Responsible Privatization

It follows that privatization, as practiced by SLDE, is less likely to lead to local communities being taken advantage of and more likely to be seen as an opportunity to care creatively. Fresh water supplies and the proper treatment of wastes have historically been responsible for doubling life expectancies in affected communities. A company dedicated to these tasks is not easy to find in *laissez-faire* economies, where self-interest is sovereign over public services. However, although smallness and localness assist the taking of social responsibility, too often the system is chronically inefficient and lacks economies of scale.

SLDE is challenged to be locally responsible *and* a large, efficient investor. Mestrallet is seeking to demonstrate that privatization not only is technically and economically superior, but also matches the concern for the local communities shown by contractors on a short leash, forever lobbying for renewal of their concessions. SLDE is targeting big cities, where its professionalism can be appreciated. It has current projects in Atlanta, Indianapolis, Gary, Milwaukee, and San Antonio, among others – with favorable comments.

Mestrallet is continuously facing the dilemma of *socially responsible privatization* vs. *regulation in the public interest.* On the one hand, we find the risk that deregulation, privatization, and large-scale economies and investments will lead to "rogue out-of-town" operation. On the other, we find that too much emphasis on community responsibility runs the risk of developing many small municipalities, close to users and responsible, but chronically inefficient and underfunded.

Mestrallet's strategy is brilliant: he is trying to have SLDE commit itself to those communities and municipalities it serves. If the tide turns against privatization, there is still a chance that SLDE could be regarded as an exception, one of the few global operators that serves its customers with honesty and dedication, thereby creating oases in a spiritual desert. This is because the private deregulated resources are used responsibly.

Dilemmas Deriving from Neutral vs. Affective (Thinking)

In relationships between people, reason and emotion both play a role. Which of these dominates will depend upon whether we are *affective* (show our emotions), in which case we probably get an emotional response in return, or we are emotionally *neutral* in our approach and display. Typically, reason and emotion are, of course, combined. In expressing ourselves, we try to find confirmation of our thoughts and feelings in the response of our audience. When our own approach is highly emotional, we are seeking a *direct*, emotional response: "I have the same feelings as you on this subject." When our own approach is highly neutral, we are seeking an *indirect* response: "Because I agree with your reasoning or proposition, I give you my support." On both occasions, approval is being sought, but different paths are being used to achieve that end. The indirect path gives us emotional support only contingent upon the success of an effort of intellect. The direct path allows our feelings about a factual proposition to show through, thereby "joining" feelings with thoughts in a different way.

The expression of opinions in an open and often passionate way by individuals with strong personalities often gels into fairly fixed opposition and sometimes into an adversarial communication style. It is frequently necessary to restate the importance of basic communications skills, such as listening.

Reconciling Affective and Neutral Cultures

Overly affective (expressive) cultures and overly neutral cultures have problems in relating each to the other. The neutral person is easily accused of being ice cold with no heart; the affective person is seen as out of control and inconsistent. When such cultures meet, the first essential for the international leader is to recognize the differences and to refrain from making any judgments based on the presence or absence of emotions.

This aspect of culture is commonly seen in the amount of emotionality people can stand across cultures. Kodak introduced an ad selling on the basis of "memories," which Americans love, but the British interpreted it as overly sentimental. It was Michael Porter who said that Germans didn't know what marketing was about. In his American conception, marketing is about showing the qualities of your products without any inhibitions. Germans might see this as bragging. It is not accepted unless you sell secondhand cars. The way in which you express positive things in Germany needs to be subtle. This subtlety perhaps escaped Porter.

What our Leaders Reconciled

We always find it difficult to reconcile reason with emotions, neutral left- with affective right-brain capacities. Looking at the essence of the innovative process, we see that many reconciliations are necessary, including the neutral check of your passion. Hear what Tom Peters said in a 1999 meeting in Atlanta: "It is cool to be emotional nowadays." In investigating, searching, and solving problems, our excitement will often point the way to what is later found to be factual and rational. Solutions have an elegance, an aesthetic that warms the heart.

We have found that our great leaders all either had passion as the context in which their reason made sense or had reason as their context in which their passion became meaningful. The first exemplar of this dichotomy that we identified is the brilliant work of Bourguignon at Club Med. His insistence that the aesthetic experience of a vacation make sense in a world of calculation rescued the company from a dark period in its history.

Bourguignon's Rational Ingredients of a Personal Dream

Club Med's prodigious growth had overstrained its traditional management structure. It had become intoxicated by its self-celebrations, week after week, and was not keeping track of costs or logistics. The company's downward spiral had begun, and now chronic underinvestment made it worse. The company was not competent in the more neutral, "hard" side of the business (travel, finance, logistics, etc.). Resorts were not profit centers, and several had lost money without anyones' realizing it. Opening was often too early in the season or not early enough. Hospitality had simply been increased, without any awareness of diminishing returns. The food and wine expenditure had escalated too far. When what one is looking for is *esprit*, ambience, and all the affective and diffuse aspects of life, leave it to Club Med – but this was also its undersponsored strength. Philippe Bourguignon was aware that he had to reconcile these neutral and affective necessities of Club Med. He helped the business refine the art of placing immaterial experiences above the bits and pieces of the material world, while ensuring that the bits and pieces paid off.

The wholeness of experience, with its *esprit* and stylishness, is vital, but, taken too far (as it was in the early 1990s), the personalized and unique vacation was driven to the point of destruction. Club Med had become a vendor of incomparable experiences, but it couldn't survive in a cost-conscious world. The opposite, more neutral approach, in which elements are standardized into a reliable, high-volume, and therefore affordable holiday would risk abandoning Club Med's founding values, however.

Because of ever-advancing living standards, the separate elements of luxury and good living are available to more and more people. What is often missing, because it is more elusive, is the integration of these elements into a diffuse and affective sense of satisfaction, a *savoir vivre*. Club Med no longer manages villages as such, but instead delivers a shared spirit, a seamless scenario of satisfactions, an *ambience* or atmosphere augmented by food and wine, as do Planet Hollywood and Hard Rock Cafes. As Pascal put it, "The heart has its own reasons, with which reason is not familiar at all."

It was immediately obvious, when we interviewed Hugo Levecke from ABN AMRO Lease Holding, that part of his success story was based on reconciling viewpoints across this neutral–affective dimension. On the one hand, the leaseholding division of the great bureaucracy of ABN AMRO, had been grown by Levecke himself into an entrepreneurial and very successful unit, independent of the more rational HQ culture. On the other, what would happen when brains met emotions? Levecke had been strategizing for nine months with unit heads, and he believed that the rational case for what he proposed had now been made and accepted in principle.

But what of the emotion? Could they bring their hearts to this far more interdependent way of doing business? Was it not skill, hard work, and results that had earned them their autonomy?

All this was a dilemma for Levecke himself. He had been part of the group. He himself had created the warm and trusting relationships. How could he turn the company around if those relationships that he developed over the years turned sour?

Hugo Levecke: How to Change an Emotional Entrepreneurial Setting into a Neutral, Rationalized one

Hugo Levecke, the president of ABN AMRO Lease Holding, needed to turn around the new division. In the past, most of the division's growth had been created by innovative entrepreneurs. With the maturing and internationalization of the business, there developed a need for more interdependence between the units. But could Levecke bring the hearts of his people to join him in this most calculated approach? He knew that there are no easy or secret tricks. Business transformation requires a personal transformation in the way we all lead; this would hurt all concerned emotionally – and that included him. He was aware that he could not turn to a linear progression, a rollout of tested techniques; rather, he faced a process of trial and error, wherein mutual support and understanding for the lessons learned would be required from all.

The major dilemma Levecke had to reconcile was the need for a rational and neutral approach in business with not losing the hearts of those people, including himself, who had grown the company through their entrepreneurial and pioneering spirit. Levecke found the source of reconciliation in monitoring the leading process of innovation and entrepreneurialism intellectually. People had to work not harder, but smarter. He focused on improving the quality of internal communication and a rapid exchange of knowledge at all levels of the organization. For this purpose, he developed a companywide scoreboard that records initiatives and results. Moreover, he introduced periodic meetings at which teams consisting of directors or of specialists reporting to them exchanged the most common experiences resulting from the initiatives being attempted by a business unit.

Teams were organized around strategic purposes and sought to nine information from one successful project to help create another. In this way, people were empowered to act so that the team could take direct responsibility for the strategies it recommended. Thus, the dilemma of taking risks while your heart was in your mouth was qualified and controlled by cool calculation that compared one bold initiative with another and drew sober conclusions. Levecke's brilliance was to create a process in which the sense of entrepreneurship survived, simply because each director now had an intelligent audience to admire and critique each initiative.

The third and last major challenge in the area of the affective–neutral dilemma is what Anders Knutsen did at Bang and Olufsen, reconciling neutral technical excellence with the emotional appeal of products. Beautiful audiovisual information had to be conveyed on instruments worthy of their content, in the same way that the instruments of an orchestra carry the spirit of the composer and express a feeling. To counterbalance the strong influence of scientifically oriented R&D, teams were sent to the United States and elsewhere to try to capture the ineffable qualities of new sounds and sights, so that these could be faithfully rendered.

Anders Knutsen: the Integration of Two Strong Traditions

B&O had two strong traditions. Knutsen knows very well that there is an aesthetic and emotional commitment to the beauty of sighs and sounds recorded and played by both employees and clients. On the other hand, there is a strongly developed tradition of engineering and technological commitment to brilliant scientific solutions. This dilemma is rich and contains many subdilemmas, the main one being the affective and neutral approaches. The client's model actually touches on three of our dimensions: the two dimensions making up the diffuse and affective experiences of particular art forms and the specific neutrality of scientific and universal solutions. They are often at odds with one another, tilting the balance of power now this way and now that.

Knutsen knew very well that neither a technical dominance nor a pure focus on a diffuse and emotional feeling for music, visual arts, and pure aesthetics would get the company out of trouble. .It is in "Idealand" that various values meet, clash, and achieve a final harmony. Each group champions its own values until these find inclusion in a larger system and in a more creative synthesis, watched over by a principle of parsimony that seeks to cut costs to the bone. The values synthesis must be spare, rich, and elegant, yet pricewise. "Idealand" was so much supported by Anders Knutsen because he saw it as a vehicle harmonizing values into viable ideas and offering them to customers.

Dilemmas Deriving from the Specific vs. Diffuse dimension

The next of our seven dimensions concerns the degree of involvement in relationships. Closely related to whether we show emotions in dealing with other people is the degree to which we engage others either in *specific* areas of life and single levels of personality or *diffusely*, in multiple areas of our lives and at several levels of personality at the same time. In specific-oriented cultures, a leader *segregates out* the task relationship with a subordinate and isolates this from other dealings. But, in some countries-every life space and every level of personality tends to leak into the others. This dilemma is also significant in small family businesses (Chapter 21), in which dilemmas arise when there is tension between family bonds and business demands.

At the global level, the dilemma shows itself clearly in the various alliances that can be observed between many of the major airlines. In our work with British Airways and American Airlines, the model helped the parties recognize and respect the different ways in which they define the relationship with their passengers. It is typically American to emphasize "core competencies" and "shareholder value." In contrast, British Airways and Cathay Pacific emphasize service, with hot breakfasts, champagne, and the like.

Thus, in this "One World" alliance, the options are as follows:

1.   Go for "serving the cattle with Coke and pretzels."
2.   Not only serve hot breakfasts, but add some massage and shoe polishing and "go bankrupt on the flight."
3.   Compromise and "serve the hot pretzel," so it becomes certain that one will lose *all* clients.

Reconciliation is the art of trying to define those specific areas to provide a more personal service and deepen the relationship. Jan Carlzon of SAS called this the "moment of truth." The future of the alliance will depend on one particular reconciliation: the competency of the employees of the airlines at consistently choosing those specific moments to deepen the relationship in the service being provided. A compromise will lead to a business disaster (and how often have we seen them in alliances of any kind).

Three Major Dilemmas of the Specific–Diffuse Orientation Resolved by Excellent Leaders

At first glance, the dilemma of *specific* vs. *diffuse* is very difficult to reconcile. However, we have seen in our research that it is one of the most rewarding. For instance, Dell's success in the computer industry has been highly dependent on this kind of integration.

Let us look first at the main dilemma Michael Dell approached and how it partly explains his major success in the industry. Because Dell was a late-comer to the computer industry, he *had* to do something entirely different, something that would differentiate him from competitors. Among many other things, he decided to bypass distributors entirely. He would sell directly to customers, thereby establishing a unique position over other computer suppliers. Speaking directly with customers, instead of using intermediaries, caused information on changing customer needs to reach the company more quickly and with greater clarity and urgency. It was possible to learn firsthand the strategic aims of major corporate customers. The model of direct selling received a welcome and powerful boost from the Internet, which was first used to sell a Dell computer in June 1996. Thus, you can get down to each customer's problems in *specific* detail, yet, at the same time, you can serve a *diffuse* array or spectrum of needs and people. Above all, specific computers swim in a sea of diffusely communicated information.

Dell's Dilemma: A Broad Spectrum of Customers vs. Deep, Personalized Customer Relationships

Michael Dell had to come to grips with the dilemma of selling either to a broad array or to a special group with whom deep relationships were developed. In fact, his newly developed Direct Selling Model had the advantage of being very broad and, at the same time, deep, personal, and customized.

Michael Dell broke with the conventional wisdom that you aim either for many customers, making your profits off volume, or for just a few clients, with complex problems and specialized needs, who need very complex high-end service (that you can charge heavily for). The first strategy is cheap, but rather superficial. The second strategy is intimate and personal, but typically niche oriented. The risks are obvious. If you go for the first strategy, distribution channels might clog very quickly, and there is no differentiation between you and your competitors. This strategy runs the risk of swamping the intermediaries. On the other hand, focusing on creating a very narrow, but deep, strategy risks creating severely limited opportunities in small niche markets.

The reconciliation that Michael Dell created was as powerful as it was simple. By direct sales via face-to-face interaction, telephone, and the Internet, he reconciled breadth with depth and complexity. The genius of direct selling via the Internet is that you reach an ever-increasing spectrum of customers *and* you can use the net to give personalized, detailed, information-rich services to those customers via premium pages for each one.

The Internet is uniquely suited to information-rich products, which can be embedded in an ongoing community of discussants and can be woven around with dialogues on details and special opportunities. You can serve the whole spectrum of net users *and* while still going deeply into specific problems.

David Komansky of Merrill Lynch is facing a major dilemma in this arena. The struggle to integrate the specific culture of Internet-based business activity with the diffuse and deep relationships that financial consultants have developed with their clients is still ongoing, but we are confident that it will lead to success. How will he do it?

Going for the Clicks that Stick
The challenge to Merrill Lynch has come in part from the unbundling of services into specific pieces. You can buy information, research, trading facilities and advice from separate sources, at combined fees possibly less than the simple fee paid to the firm's six- and seven-figure professionals. The Internet is overflowing with *data,* but this is not the same as knowledge or information. We are informed by facts relevant to our questions and concerns. We "know" only upon receiving answers to our propositions and hypotheses. The larger the Internet becomes, the more customers will need a guide to what is relevant to individual concerns.

The dilemma can be analyzed as follows: On one axis, we find low-cost specific data and transactions on the Internet. The risk here is that you create a *high-tech* solution in which your staff of brokers is bypassed by technology. On the other axis, we find the rich, meaningful, diffuse personal relationships that brokers have developed with their clients. It maintains a *high-touch* environment in which customers (over)pay for their dependence.

Komansky is working in a setting where complexity is so vast that professional relationships becomes vital to discovering meaning and negotiating the maze. Instead of relationships being eclipsed by the Internet, then, these get more and more important in interpreting the possible meanings of data flows, as what is available grows ever larger than what is relevant to each client. Hence, in this phase of the Internet, we will discover that intelligent dialogue about the bewildering complexity of financial markets is a formative influence on financial markets.

We need *high tech*, but we also need *high touch*. The more those numbers rain down upon you, the more you need to talk to someone about them. Merrill Lynch can use the Internet to give better personal service (via high tech) to its high-touch customers, while simultaneously using it to identify those high-tech customers to whom it makes good business sense to offer high touch.

A third dilemma in the area of degree of involvement has been reconciled very clearly by Kees Storm of AEGON, the large Dutch insurance company. It is a very important one; we believe that the old dilemma of shareholder value vs. stakeholder value will be wonderfully reconciled in the twenty-first century. The new forms of capitalism will be reconciled with an old form, Marxism. It will be an interesting century, in which Storm will play a pioneering role.

Kees Storm: The Synergy of Stakeholder Values

Kees Storm has frequently communicated his belief that there is nothing but foolishness in extolling shareholder value above the rights of, and duties to, stakeholders. This is because the results of all the stakeholders are interdependent, and you cannot, increase emphasis on only without damaging the whole system and precipitating a regressive spiral. Our good friend Kees did not confuse importance with priority (i.e., which value must logically come first); there is no doubt in his mind that motivating employees to satisfy customers *precedes* increasing returns and paying profits to shareholders. The reason for this precedence is that customers supply the money that shareholders later receive. If employees are, for any reason, *not* motivated, and customers *not* satisfied, then there is no money for shareholders to receive. Shareholder value tends to be specific and countable; motivating and satisfying are more diffuse. Diffuse processes can too easily be neglected or even overlooked. On one horn of the dilemma, we find specific sales and profits used to pay shareholders who reinvest. The risk here is that you will end up in "the bottom line" for stakeholders who never share. On the other horn, we find diffuse processes of motivating employees to satisfy customers. The risk here is that interests of those not physically present (shareholders) are ignored. Kees Storm has wonderfully integrated these two tensions at a higher level by joining stakeholder values with stock options for employees, who "make money and have fun." By operating his fireworks display, Kees first motivates employees to satisfy customers, thereby raising sales and profits for shareholders, who reinvest in AEGON as a result.

Dilemmas Deriving from Achieved vs. Ascribed Status

All societies give certain members higher status than others, signaling that unusual attention should be focused upon such persons and their activities. Some societies accord status to people on the basis of their achievements; others ascribe it to them by virtue of personal characteristics, age, class, gender, education, mission, or position. The first kind of status is called *achieved status*, the second *ascribed status*. Achieved status refers to *doing*, ascribed status to *being*.

Achievement-oriented cultures market products and services on the basis of performance. Performance, skill, and knowledge justify authority. These cultures will make those products into a standard only when they have proven superior in the market through competition.

Ascription-oriented cultures often ascribe status to products and services. Particularly in Asia, status is attributed to products that "naturally" evoke admiration from others – for example, highly educational technologies, or projects deemed to be of national importance because they build infrastructure. The status is generally independent of actual accomplishment.

This contrast generates dilemmas when partners have different traditions about how people move up the ladder in the organization. In achievement-oriented cultures, your position is best secured by continuous performance and by what you know. In the worst case, you are only as good as your last performance. In ascribed cultures, seniority and long-term loyalty are much more important, as well as whom you know and the noble aspects of your endeavors. This dilemma has been a fundamental issue for Stuart Beckwith, who is the founding entrepreneur and managing director of the BCIF group of companies. His organization provides a "one-stop" center for business training, consulting, and recruitment targeted mainly at small or family-run businesses. One of the main dilemmas he has reconciled, both within his own organization and for the organizations he helps, is that of the family-driven "livelihood business" *vs.* the "independent business."

Creating a Legacy through Immortality Businesses: Stuart Beckwith

Over the last 15 years, BCIF has grown itself from nothing by helping more than 9000 new businesses become established. Stuart Beckwith has been concerned with the development both of his own organization and of all those he has helped to grow from sole traders or partnerships to viable, self-sustaining businesses.

The main dilemma he was facing as a leader of BCIF and as a consultant to his clients concerned the ascribed status that is so dominant in the family business. Here, it is important to be well connected and to have the right mentors from the family coaching you. In a *livelihood business*, the family is dominant. For some family members, the activity might not even be recognized as business. There is a clear line between the family and its business. Members are judged purely on their performance and achievements. Stuart Beckwith said of this context during an interview, "Without doubt, it is the interaction between the demands of the family and the business. I have observed families breaking up through the demands of their business and businesses failing through the demands of the family. In our business, I employ some of my sons, and my wife is also a senior executive. I have always been conscious of the need to find ways to integrate these apparently competing demands." Reconciliation was found in the *immortality business* – making sure your business is a lasting legacy to your children and grandchildren.

By being conscious of the problem that many founders won't allow the next generation to get on with the business, Beckwith recognizes the importance of "planning to let go." He uses his "status" to ensure that his customers have succession plans in place and that the business will not depend on the founder's personal presence. He also recognizes the need for change: in the future, BCIF will be very different from what it is now. In an *immortality business*, the demands of the family and business and the tension between the aging founder and younger achievers are reconciled. The founder achieves "immortality" of a kind by living through his successors and leaving them to interpret what he has taught them.

A family whose business aspires to "immortality" must ask, "How can we renew ourselves?" and must give subordinates the autonomy to redefine the legacy in a new century. Pressure for change will come from changing market conditions, from family members wanting to do more or less, from those seeking to withdraw or add capital, and from major nonfamily contributors who feel that they are being shortchanged for their efforts. The "right" balance is ever shifting.

Since our original interviews with Stuart Beckwith, he has very recently broken up the evolving monolithic BCIF group into a number of components, each focusing on a number of core business competencies. By giving his children the opportunity to drive new ventures, he has further reconciled his need for survival with his family needs.

Another excellent example of reconciliation between achieved and ascribed status is the Profit-oriented vs. Non-profit status of BUPA realized by Val Gooding. Should you have a yield of 25 percent profit to shareholders *and* have to compete with Internet stocks on the AEX *or* should you make enough return to take care of the old and frail? To care about the people you serve is a precursor to success. You must ascribe status to them initially.

Val Gooding's Provident Association

There is much discussion about whether "care" should, or even can be delivered effectively by those seeking to make therefrom profits that match the rising returns that are increasingly common in the City of London. *Or* should you instead opt for the stakeholder and look at larger and longer-term goals than the next quarterly gain? For this very reason, BUPA has no shareholders, but is a *provident association*, hovering between for-profit and nonprofit status.

Val Gooding regards provident status as a strong advantage, provided that she herself can furnish the stimulus for growth and risk that would otherwise come from shareholder pull. Remarkably, she has reconciled the sense of urgency and constant striving for improvement that shareholders often have with the well-known fact that the customer is unambiguously the top priority. Because it takes high staff morale to keep customers happy, employees become the means of satisfying customers. You care for your employees up front, and they will pass this care on to customers.

The dilemma can be analyzed as follows: Most quoted companies, having impatient shareholders, cannot invest for the long term, in which current investments in upgrading equipment and call centers justify themselves 20 years from now. Shareholders want too much too quickly. On the other hand, a nonprofit, customer-oriented approach leads to an organization that is risk averse and too noble of intention to try very hard to succeed.

Val Gooding has taken BUPA from roughly the vicinity of the latter position into being a company eager to grow as fast as its success allows (with no need to pause for private enrichment), dedicated to worldwide customers, and willing to invest in their long-term welfare – and she has done that so successfully that BUPA now has difficulty finding a way to invest *all* its surpluses in long-term solutions and global expansion!

Even Richard Branson's rebel stance is a form of ascribed status: He sets out to afflict the comfortable and turns this political gesture into success with consumers.

Gordon Billage: Leading his Founding Division into New Areas of Business

Gordon Billage, as CEO of Clifford-Thames, reconciled many other dilemmas, but in the same way, he used his ascribed status as the then Managing Director to lead the business units from his HQ role. This enabled him to achieve improved business performance across the company. Not only was his title then later changed to CEO, but he was given even more ascribed status (courtesy of his local university) by being awarded an honorary degree because of his achievements!

Despite far greater emphasis on ascription or achievement in certain cultures, the two usually develop together. Those who start byascribing usually see potential in others and treat them in ways that help bring that potential to fruition. Those who start by achieving usually have importance and priority ascribed to their next project. Hence, all societies ascribe, and all achieve, after a fashion. It is once again a question of where a cycle starts. The international leader surfs the crest of this dilemma.

Dilemmas Deriving from Internal vs. External Control

The next culturally determined dimension concerns the meaning the actor assigns to the (natural) environment. In cultures in which an organic view of nature dominates, and in which the shared assumptions is that humans are subjugated to nature, individuals appear to orient their actions toward others. People become "other directed" in order to survive; their focus is on the environment rather than on themselves. This attitude is known as *external control*. Conversely, it has been determined that people who have a mechanistic view of nature, and the belief that human beings can dominate nature usually take themselves as the point of departure for determining the right action. The "inner-directedness" of much of the West is also reflected through the current fashion for strategic thinking, as if one were Alexander the Great conquering the known world.

Reconciling Internal and External Control

The major issue at stake is to connect the internally controlled culture, leading to the talent of *technology push*, with the externally controlled world of *market pull*, in order to achieve a culture of inventiveness. Take a consumer electronics company like Philips, nobody will deny its great knowledge and inventiveness in its specific technologies and the quality of its marketing. The problem the company faced was that its two major functional areas didn't seem to communicate. The success of an organization is dependent on the integration of the two areas. The push of technology needs to help you decide what markets you want to be pulled by, and the pull of the market needs to help you in knowing what technologies to push.

Leaders Reconcile the Pushes into a Pull

Again, we have found three leaders who have taken this dilemma to the core of their success. First, there is Tim Morris. He is now the founding entrepreneur and managing director of MMP Business Management, which he established some six years ago. His company provides the back office to a diverse range of organizations that want to get on with their key business. One of the main dilemmas he helps his clients reconcile is the need for control of key business processes and the need to let things go in order to be able to focus on key business.

Under- and Overcontrol and the Ability to Let Things Go while Remaining in Charge

Tim Morris believes that companies and their owners need to strike a creative balance between their need to control key business processes and the ability to let go. He said, "It continually surprised me how many small businesses don't know how much cash they have in the bank, what payments [creditors] are due in the near future, and what debtors they have. They seem to be trying to catch a flight with last month's departure screen. I couldn't sleep at night if I didn't know exactly where my business is! On the other hand, we find owner–managers who are obsessive about being in control. Just because they started the business and it has been running successfully in the past, they think it will go on forever if they continue to apply their "magic formula."

"It is a matter of avoiding the extreme. For those who are all-fatalistic and think everything depends on luck or the economy, we try to encourage them to get their business in control. We produce a daily (or sometimes weekly) snapshot of income and expenditure and exactly where they are. This gives them a greater degree of control. We do the same thing for our own business, of course. At any time, at the click of a mouse, I know exactly our cash bank balance, our creditors, and our debtors. Conversely, for those who think they are in control, with oversimplistic administrative systems, we try to show them that they are not – because in the medium term, they may be vulnerable to the external environment."

Tim Morris is also extremely insightful on two contrasting types of entrepreneurs: those who *over*control and those who *under*control. For each kind of client, he has a different treatment. The undercontrolling leader's attitude is "leave it to lesser beings." There is important and creative work, and there is support work, of less importance, done by lesser persons. Such entrepreneurs leave the control to others and disparage control *per se.*

But there is a second, contrasting tendency. Many an entrepreneur has "made it" because a set of original ideas has been mobilized within a single mind. These ideas could be ordered and sorted, with perfect control over their disposition, all resulting in breakthrough success. It is very easy for such entrepreneurs to associate any success with their own total control of key elements. As the company expands those "key elements" come to include other people, and we have the makings of the "control freak."

Morris moderates "control freakery" by constantly informing the entrepreneur of variables beyond his or her control, which *cannot* be changed or countermanded, but *can* be responded to and taken advantage of. He moderates the "leave it to lesser beings" entrepreneur by compensating for this snobbery through innovative computer-based Microsoft Office products.

Sir Mark Moody-Stuart, president of Royal Dutch/Shell Group, skillfully reconciled another dilemma in this area of inner and outer direction. It can be argued that the reconciliation of this dilemma will account for much of the success of Shell in the twenty-first century.

Mark Moody-Stuart: Beyond the Trauma of Brent Spar

The oil industry, Shell included, has long tended to look inwards. Shell's ear was not to the ground. It had a Calvinist conscience, but it was its integrity, its rationality, its judgment that was more expert than anyone else's. Criticism of the oil industry always came as a shock, even for the seasoned leader Mark Moody-Stuart. Look at what happened during the planned sinking of the Brent Spar – a massive, obsolete oil storage and loading buoy in the North Sea that Shell planned to dispose of by sinking it in a deep part of the Atlantic.

Shell saw such issues as technical, and in this regard it knew better than its critics. After all, Shell had the facts and its critics did not. These facts were typically technical, not social issues, and had the rational/empirical substance that engineers love. Of course, Shell recognized that its decisions would have social implications, but that only made it more important that they be technically sound. It was not always clear to Shell why external sociopolitical events had so many followers.

In part this came about because exploration and production are more profitable than retailing. Shell made money in inverse relation to its proximity to consumers, and this reinforced its inward-looking technological bent. Added to this was a cultural tendency for the engineers to be Dutch and the accountants Scottish, so that the profitability of upstream activities was widely known and admired. The British tended to be more commercial, trading on the back of the old empire. It was this inner-directed technological mind-set that was the root of the trouble over Brent Spar.

Although Shell had costed all the options for disposal, there were emotional arguments that also had a logic of their own.

Moody-Stuart's revealed his leadership qualities clearly when he admitted that decisions must take into consideration how other people think. And because people think and value differently, there is always a dilemma, a need to reconcile diverse logics.

On the one hand, there was support for the inner-directed technological expertise vs. the outer world of sociopolitical issues – i.e., the dilemma between Truth vs. Communicability. Organizations such as Greenpeace exploit scandals to "raise consciousness" about environmental issues and recruit members. Boarding the Spar amid crashing waves made the activists look like "cockleshell heroes," braving the elements to discover "the truth" (unfortunately false). On the other extreme there is the utterance of the underdog "thinking only of the environment," as against the might of a profit-making giant corporation.

What Moody-Stuart called for were decisions that consider *all logics*: the internal logic of inexpensive, safe disposal, *and* the concern of the Swedish minister of the environment about trying to teach schoolchildren not to throw debris into the environment we share. All major corporations take public positions, if not on purpose, then by default. Moody-Stuart's leadership created a context in which Shell could continuously learn the logic of such positioning.

A final example concerns a very intriguing reconciliation by Sergei Kiriyenko of the more inner-directed younger Russians with the traditional outer-directed older Russians.

Kiriyenko: Cutting the Apron Strings

Historically, the Russian people in general have had their fates decided by external powers. NORSI Oil was no exception. Kiriyenko knew that the old archetype of the fatalistic Russian was true and that, at present, people in Russia both yearn for and dread change. The main thing for the middle and older generations is to avoid mishap. To break a logjam, then, you might need, if not a shock, at least a threat.

The younger generation and the successful businesspeople are now motivated by success. For them, he created a positive stimulus – not a stick, but a carrot. At NORSI, therefore, Kiriyenko had to make things worse before they could get better. He had to abolish the company and the *ukase* (decree from above) upon which everyone was dependent. He had to say, in effect, "There is no company or edict coming to save you – only what you yourself create." He faced a situation in which the inner-directed younger Russians would create black markets and Mafia-type environments if they were not constrained. On the other hand, he was also working with outer-directed, predominantly older Russians. Here the risk was to be left with people that were just waiting for some new direction to save them.

He totally turned around the enterprise, by eliminating that on which everyone was trying to depend. Reconciliation was achieved by the act of abolishing the company. This forced everyone to negotiate new and better agreements through which to avoid loss, make a profit, and, in general, even survive.

Dilemmas Deriving from the Meaning of Time: Sequential vs. Synchronous as Regards Past, Present, and Future Cultures

If only because leaders need to coordinate their business activities, they require some kind of shared expectations about time. Just as different cultures have different assumptions about how people relate to one another, so they approach time differently. This orientation is about the relative importance cultures give to the *past*, *present*, and *future*. How we think of time has its consequences. Especially important is whether our view of time is *sequential*, as a series of passing events, or *synchronic*, with *past*, *present*, and *future* all *interrelated*, so that ideas about the future and memories of the past both shape present action.

Across cultures, we see two extreme ways in which people think of time. For some, the more sequential people, time is an objective measure of passing increments.

The more quickly you act and the shorter the time taken, the more effective you will be competitively. To them, we are in a race with time. Synchronic cultures, on the other hand, like to do things "just in time," so that present ideas converge in the future. The better your timing, the more effective you will be competitively. To these cultures, time is like a dance.

Toward Reconciliation

The international leader is often caught in a dilemma between the future demands of the larger organization, needing visions and missions and managing change, and the past experiences of local populations. The short termism that plagues Western and, particularly, American companies is often driven by the needs of the stock markets for annual or quarterly results and profits. The risk of a strong future orientation is the failure to learn from past mistakes.

Synchronous people can deliver in time, but they like to do it *for you, not for your clock*; and just-in-time manufacturing has proven that the best way to speed up a sequence is to synchronize it just in time.

Our Leader's Dilemmas of Time

In our research, we have found that the reconciliation of the various aspects of time is crucial. We see that keeping your traditional products that made your name in the first place can jeopardize your innovations into new products. We have found that organizing your time sequentially makes you efficient, but not very effective. Much time is lost. Long-term and short-term thinking need to be united on a higher level.

One dilemma of past and future needs of product development was exceptionally well approached by Karel Vuursteen of Heineken. He needed to integrate the traditions of the Heineken family with the future needs of the company, and he integrated the traditions of the Heineken product with the need for innovation – for example, in the area of specialty beers.

Heineken's Vuursteen: Tradition and Stability vs. Innovative Products and Markets

The Heineken tradition is big, but at the same time, the seeds of decay are in it. For over a hundred years, it has appealed to people's taste. Historically, the company's reputation has been maintained at great cost. Recently, however, many specialty beers have entered the market, jeopardizing the big established names in the trade.

In 1993, Heineken faced a problem with glass particles in some of its bottles. The rich tradition of the brand asked for a recall of hundreds of millions of bottles carrying its brand. Heineken also faced some great difficulties in the introduction of new manufacturing sites in the United States, and of Buckler's low-alcohol beer. Great misses like these have cost a lot of money, Vuursteen's approach to innovation was cautious. He had to maintain the consistency of Heineken's attraction. He had to change to remain consistent. One way of innovating in a way that's not dangerous is to clear a space for a totally new approach, which is separate from our existing success and will not endanger it.

Heineken is highly successful, but the reasons for this success are elusive. *That* customers like the brand is clear; *why* they like it is less clear. Vuursteen's dilemma is the tension between Heineken's tradition of stability and the elusive nature of its success. The risk is that it creates a "sacred brew of immaculate image." He might have decided to change nothing, for fear of damaging the sacred brew. On the other extreme, we find that Heineken's need to change and innovate could risk accidentally wrecking the company's appeal.

Instead, Vuursteen very cleverly embarked on two forms of innovation that are relatively safe. *Process innovation* searches for new and better means of creating the same result and reserving a Safe Area for Creation. *Product innovation* allows new drinks to be invented from scratch, without involving Heineken's premium product in these experiments.

Another dilemma that our leaders seem to reconcile with great talent deals with the intervals between supervisions in the sequence elapsing before synchronization. Through a very interesting approach of sponsoring empowered teams, Martin Gillo of AMD wrought a reconciliation of extremes between the need for the sponsor to be responsible and the need for the team to have time, and hence freedom, to be able to be creative.

Martin Gillo's Approach to Sponsoring the Empowered Team

Advanced Micro Devices (AMD), the large US chipmaker, made an courageous move when it decided, in 1995, to pursue CEO Jerry Sanders's vision and build a Mega-Fab (factory) for producing state-of-the art microprocessors equivalent to those of Intel® in the Dresden region of the former East Germany. From the very beginning, Martin Gillo, VP of Human Resources Europe, then in Geneva, realized that trying to import and to impose AMD's American culture on Dresden would be a mistake.

In no way can one culture produce an exact copy of another, even if it wants to – and it rarely does. Restraint was not easy; many standardized approaches, such as the work of semiautonomous teams, were so successful in the United States that there was a tendency among management to believe that those approaches also needed to be introduced in Dresden. So successful were team operations in Texas and

California, that they were defined as a nonnegotiable aspect of operations at the new Dresden Fab.

There is no doubt that teams are vital, because problems in this industry are more complex than any individual can deal with. They even grow beyond the mandate of management. You need teams to learn, through a discourse process, how the problem needs to be tackled. The risk of autonomy for the team, however, is that it might deviate from, misinterpret, or defy its sponsor's charge. In this event, the authority is seriously weakened. Alternatively, if the team is not fully trusted by the sponsor, the time between supervisions becomes too short. Letting the team alone for only days makes the autonomy low, likewise the risk and the likelihood of the teams coming up with something significant.

Gillo has done everything possible to preserve and develop "natural groups" – that is, groups that have learned and experimented together and in whose relationships much crucial information is stored. Gradually, these natural groups are growing in their reputations for discovery. This reconciliation of longer sequences and timely synchronic actions has made big differences in increasing the yields of the Fab.

Generalizability: The Authors' Dilemma!

We now seek to make general statements about leadership and that reconciliation of dilemma that go beyond our particular observations, our interviews, and our analysis of our 21 leaders. We have to consider the extent to which our sample is representative of the wider context and the spectrum of managers and leaders across the globe – and independent of any destination or home culture. Throughout, we have sought to avoid any ethnocentric approach, in which our new model works only in a single culture.

As authors, we were faced with our own dilemma! Qualitative inductive research based on semistructured interviews (like the ones with our 21 leaders) produces rich outputs that have high *validity*. However, the *reliability* may be low if we cannot transfer these findings from a small sample to a wider population.

By contrast, findings from questionnaire-based instruments can be made highly *reliable* by careful selection and structuring of the sample. However, such reliability, on its own, does not mean that the findings are *valid*. The dilemma is captured in the following diagram:

The Authors' Dilemma: Validity or Reliability?

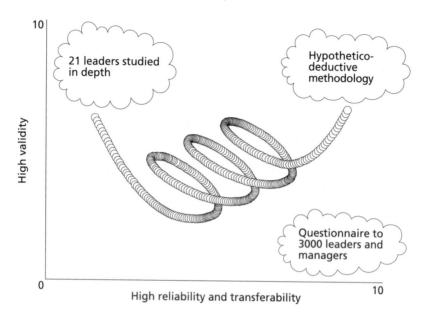

As readers will have learned from the rest of the book, we should not opt for one or the other of two contrasting approaches, rejecting the opportunity to reconcile these extremes. Doing both (interviews and questionnaires) independently is simply a compromise. We sought to practice what we preach by reconciling our own dilemma. We used the findings from initial contacts with our 21 leaders as input to the structure of our questionnaire. Conversely, we used early feedback from our questionnaires to know what questions to ask our 21 leaders.

Thus, the whole approach in this book was not to derive our model inductively from our 21 leaders. The *prima facie* case for the *dilemma reconciliation theory* had already been established and published by Hampden-Turner. We sought instead to develop an understanding of what leaders do by a hypothetico-deductive approach that reconciles the researchers' dilemma. We approached our 21 leaders with a mental model of dilemma theory already in place and sought to collect evidence to extend reconciliation theory by a synergy of these leaders with our reconciliation database.

For the questionnaire, we applied statistical tests of reliability (Cronbach alpha analysis) and were able to improve our reliability across each cultural dimension, as follows:

Dimension	Cronbach's alpha
Universalism–Particularism	0.71
Individualism–Communitarianism	0.73
Specific–Diffuse	0.63
Neutral–Affective	0.75
Achievement–Ascription	0.64
Internal–External	0.71
Time	0.74

Similarly, the internal consistency and reliability of the dilemma culture-map scales was also improved:

Reconciliation Paradigms ($n = 2980$)	Cronbach's alpha
Rejecting other values	0.71
Abandoning your own values	0.65
Reconciling opposing values	0.79
Compromising	0.68

Questionnaire Results from the 21 Leaders

We also invited our 21 leaders to complete a shortened version of our diagnostic instrument. Although this is only a small sample (maximum 21!), we observe (by using the exact tests method for small samples) that our leaders show a higher propensity for reconciliation than does our total database of general managers.

Within the limits imposed by the small sample size of the 21 leaders, the results from those who completed the shortened version of our questionnaire were totally consistent with the conclusions drawn by our authors in each of the detailed analyses given in the body of this book. Our leaders consistently opted for reconciled options when challenged with these dilemmas. In some cases, they stood up for their own values across some dimensions, but without fail, they opted for a reconciled solution for a problem domain akin to their own business or political life. The following table compares the responses of the 21 lenders with the mean of the sample of respondents with respect to the dilemmas they were presented.

Propensity to Reconcile (= Percent Selecting a Reconciliation Option)

Dimension	Our 21 Leaders	Mean from 2980 Managers
Universalism–Particularism	75	45
Individualism–Communitarianism	75	33
Specific–Diffuse	66	55
Neutral–Affective	66	25
Achievement–Ascription	80	60
Internal–External	90	30
Time	75	50

Questionnaire Results from our Database

By extending our framework to our 60,000 managers in the cross-cultural database and the 3000 leaders in the reconciliation, we were able to summarize the more significant findings.

Using the correlation between 360° feedback and responses to the dilemma posed, we find that leaders who are working internationally or have more international experience have a greater propensity to reconcile:

	Propensity to Reconcile (percent)	
Mean of all managers	35	$p = 0.05$
Leaders working internationally	73	$p = 0.05$

Leaders and managers tend to claim that their own propensity to reconcile is greater than the average in their organization:

	Propensity to Reconcile (percent)	
Average of all other managers in their own organization	38	$p = 0.05$
Leaders working internationally	52	$p = 0.05$

Leaders with a higher propensity to reconcile rate themselves higher in their own self-sufficiency and perceived effectiveness:

	Perceived Effectiveness (1 = low, 5 = high)
Self	3.7
360° feedback	2.9

Less experienced leaders, as well as those with a low propensity to reconcile, are more consistent in rejecting reconciliation and tend to retain (and work from) their own value orientation. Thus, their simultaneous score on the seven-dimensional cross-culture scale is more reliable than their score on reconciliation.

In contrast, those with a higher propensity to reconcile tend to be more concerned with reconciliation than to worry about their own cross-cultural orientation. Thus, they can start either from their own orientation, to accommodate their own view, or from the opposing value, and then return to their own in order to reconcile matters. Thus, their scale in reconciliation is more reliable than is the simultaneous assessment of their cross-cultural orientation.

By way of illustration, a Malaysian might act like a Malaysian as a junior manager, but as he or she becomes more effective globally (develops transcultural global competence), starts to travel, becomes concerned about quarterly reports, and starts to leave behind birth-counter value systems, he or she becomes more global.

There is a positive correlation between a leader's propensity to reconcile and the independent 360° assessment of his or her interpersonal effectiveness. One's propensity to reconcile also correlates with bottom-line business performance (where those data are available).

	Spearman's Coefficient of Rank Correlation	
Correlation with 360° feedback	0.71	$p = 0.05$
Correlation with business performance	0.69	$p = 0.05$

Much of the earlier data was not very discriminating. (Peer assessment tended to be bland, and there was little variety in the data, e.g., 70 percent rated the sample as a "3," and only one or two individuals were rated "4," or "5," or "2," or "1.".) Data collected more recently have greater internal variety. For this reason, it is expected that stronger correlations that are statistically more significant will be obtained. Three smaller samples, from two American clients and one Dutch organization, all show a high correlation.

Some Other Results

There is a small negative correlation between independent assessment of technical competence and propensity to reconcile. Junior leaders with a high achievement orientation and internal locus of control tend to select the compromise option rather than reconcile. Women tend to score higher on compromise than men and to have a significantly more synchronic orientation to time than men have.

The role or significance of reconciling by starting from one's own orientation or by starting from the other orientation is unclear. As might be expected, those leaders (or cultures) with an internal locus of control (e.g., Americans) tend always to reconcile by starting from their own orientation first across any other dimension. Those with an external locus of control (e.g., Japanese) tend to start from the opposite orientation and then integrate their own.

Those respondents who are in marketing or sales appear to have a higher propensity to reconcile and tend to start from the opposite (customer?) perspective first.

In conclusion, we claim that we have integrated validity and reliability. However, the final comment must go to. . . .

"Things Come Apart . . ."

I t was W. B. Yeats who wrote, in "The Second Coming,"

> Things come apart;
> The centre cannot hold . . .

Any society is haunted by the prospect of catastrophe when its diversity cannot be unified, its splits cannot be healed, its distinctions multiply beyond its bridges of mutual understanding – when all vie with all to be different and too few are willing to serve the common cause.

This may come about, even if people do not will it to be so. In the social sciences, for example, we have literally hundreds of scales and instruments to measure differences. It is deemed "scientific" to categorize, polarize, discriminate, analyze, and reduce. In comparison, the processes by which we understand, communicate, reconcile, relate, and generate larger meanings are little examined and very poorly understood.

This extraordinary bias highlights our social world selectively. We have some fairly reliable scales to identify neuroses, psychoses, behavior disorders, and even fascism (the famous F-scale). It has been proven possible to induce conformity and obedience to authority and to measure dogmatism, rigidity, anomie, and kindred afflictions. The reason these phenomena lend themselves so easily to measurement is that they are *in themselves* processes of fragmentation and disintegration. Like a smashed window, the consequence is shards, with the elements broken down for the analyst to see. Things that come apart before our eyes conform easily to scientific methods. It is much more difficult to measure wholeness, mutuality, support, understanding, reconciliation, and human development, because in these processes elements intertwine with one another in complex combinations, with simple polarities transcended. It is even harder to ascertain "the facts," because life is not a list of ingredients, but a form of organization.

This book attempts to measure integrative and reconciliatory processes, in which one difference or value encompasses and joins itself to its opposite value –

where rules, for example, are improved by the study of exceptions, where individualism is vindicated by serving one's community, where the whole reveals the processes by which its parts are organized and where inner convictions are forged by attention to outside developments.

There are alternative sequences by which values join with one another, so that different cultures celebrate their own historic paths to reconciliation. We differ widely in paths taken, but we arrive at the same clearings in the forest where the paths converge.

There is an old adage which says that what can be measured can be decreed, and what gets decreed gets done, while the immeasurable receives lip service at best and is completely ignored at worst. If, therefore, it is possible to measure values reconciliation, and if the resulting integrations are forms of wealth creation, as is argued here, then perhaps we have found an oasis in a spiritual desert. Perhaps we have learned to reassemble living processes in a world threatening to come apart.

Whether, in fact, we have achieved this integration is for our readers, and not us, to decide. But the search for paths to integrity should not be minimized in importance. We do not claim success in our endeavor; We do insist on the importance of the quest itself.

Fortunately, social "science" does not rule in corporate affairs. Common sense does. Those who experience the disintegrative forces of scientism fall back on intuition, gut feelings, and personal judgment, as did virtually all the leaders in this book. But suppose we could uncover a *logic* of intuition, of understanding, of connection and rapport? Please consider whether, in these pages, we have made a start.

We cannot reassemble the fragile shell of our humanity by force of arms or the decrees of superiors. We have to construct it ourselves, element by element. We claim only to have set out on this journey with the examples of our 21 leaders to guide us. Many more need to join us on our journey if we are to reach valuable conclusions or sufficient generality.

Accumulating and Assessing the Evidence

In this appendix, we explain some of the background to the collection and analysis of evidence obtained to support the propositions of the underlying conceptual framework on which this book is based.

Early Beginnings

Originally, the investigative work on dilemma theory was inductive. In an action-learning exploratory phase over several years, Hampden-Turner undertook many interviews with senior international leaders. The interrogations included the use of a number of challenges and options presented to leaders with seemingly opposing views and values.

Trompenaars undertook similar, as well as questionnaire-based, investigations in parallel on value dilemmas, leading to the construction of his main cross-cultural database 60,000 managers and leaders. The latter required the development of a range of instruments that were originally focused on discriminating value systems at the ecological (country-specific) level to derive models of culture and measure cultural differences. The high reliability of these instruments is well known; extensive statistical and other analytical studies using those instruments have been undertaken and published extensively. Trompenaars's database and its principal questionnaire instruments have been employed extensively in training workshops and consultancy interventions across the world. The face and content validity of the questionnaire have been constantly improved through the application qualitative and quantitative studies, including internal formalized research by university doctoral students.

Knowledge Development

After, an interpretative and inferential phase, the underlying schema of dilemma reconciliation and its relationship to leadership evolved. The schema was tested initially by the principal authors, working both separately and in collaboration, in preliminary research, consultancy, and training workshops with major global companies across the globe.

From these activities, a number of core propositions concerning the underlying behaviors that are characteristic of high-performing leaders in the global workplace were assembled. The interest was in developing a robust underlying theory to explain the global leaders (or global managers) effective performance and thereby provide a model for improving professional practice through what we have described as transcultural competence.

The central premise that evolved is that *the propensity to reconcile seemingly contradictory values is the key competence behavior required for a leader to be effective in today's digital world.*

Following this stance, an extensive deductive research operation was began to seek and verify evidence to support this claim. Extensive qualitative work (oral histories, cognitive mapping, collecting information critical incidents, and case studies) have been undertaken and are being continued by an extended research team. We also interviewed many expatriate managers in the role of ethnographic researchers. In addition, work is progressing on leveraging knowledge from the separate earlier research and quantitative studies (using the ecological database of 55,000 managers and leaders) to accumulate a new database exploiting a new multidimensional questionnaire-based instrument.

Methodological Concerns

The object of our research is to provide empirical validation for a set of theoretical postulates about the relationship between the propensity to reconcile and its relationship to effective leadership and business performance – especially across cultures and amongst diversity. The research also serves to move us away from the inductive phase to a more rigorous and disciplined hypothetico-deductive standpoint. In order to practice what we preach, we believe that (1) theory should emerge from the experience of organized teams, both practitioners and researchers, (2) professional practice is the source from which scientific inquiry gains depth and precision, and, of course, (3) the research results feed back to improve future practice.

However, research of this nature immediately places the investigator in the depths of the debate between Kant, Fichte, and Hegel, on the one hand, Compte, on the other. When ongoing case experience fails to penetrate theory, the latter becomes an ivory tower, attempting by ever loftier abstraction to cover all conceivable circumstances. The problem suffers combinatorial explosion, and fascinating local developments are lost sight of in a vast sea of generalizations.

The opposite mistake can also occur. We can lose sight of theory and cultivate small islands of "vulgar pragmatism," mounds of do's and don'ts that let you down badly in unforeseen circumstances, most especially when your foreign partner has read the same advice! As Kurt Lewin once put it, "There is nothing as practical as a good theory." And for those not getting our message, we would add, "There is nothing as theoretical as good practice."

We are not seeking an academic fundamentalism, but we aim to offer robust generalizations that are grounded in business practice ones that will stand up to the tests of rigor and criticality. Our approach, therefore, follows what Huff (2000) describes as a "mode 2" metaphor, in which research questions owe their origin to business-led problems, but avoid being epistemic and solving client's problems without informing rigorous theoretical debate.

The measurement of the constructs that groups of actors assign to their work with people in organizations is full of difficulties and pitfalls. We have to try to give qualitative variables quantitative scores, yet we cannot begin with what *we* want and with what interests us. Because the actors we study have preinterpreted the field, it has preexisting categories of meaning *for them*, which we cannot ignore. It follows that measuring social action has to rely upon the commonsense constructs in the everyday life of employees working together. We must presuppose a network of shared meanings, which is how we define an existing culture.

Moreover, the researcher inevitably contributes to those meanings, as in the well-known Hawthorne effect, where the attention of the researcher affects the results of the investigation. Persons observed are not simply "out there" like the solar system, but are in a relationship with the researchers. The researchers' methods act like grids or filters to let *some* of the contexts of this relationship permeate the "filter" and be recorded. The process is further complicated by the meaning given to the relationship with the researcher and whether it is *specific* or *diffuse*.

Even experienced researchers rediscover this effect in studying phenomena across the globe. It must be remembered that much research on how to do research has been undertaken in a single culture: Anglo-Saxon. *Thus, the knowledge of how to do research could itself be culturally specific.* Accordingly, advice on how to minimize or account for defensive responsiveness of leaders who have to challenged might work only for the culture in which the model advice was derived, conceived, and tested. We can't assume that existing knowledge and practice can be transferred and applied universally across the globe.

Sampling

In addition to the 21 principal leaders discussed in this text, we took most of our samples from multinational and international companies headquartered in many different countries. *All* samples were taken from companies with operations that faced cultural barriers of communication. Research was conducted before any lectures or presentations were given. The results were shared with the samples surveyed, and we learned much from their comments on our questions. In our sample, organizations had very similar challenges and policies. All wished to improve global communication and extend their local base with more effective policies and strategies by integrating the opposing values within their constituent marketplaces and subsidiaries.

In conclusion, the samples drawn from the variety of organizations reveal functionally equivalent sets, because nearly all these organizations were pursuing similar ends. Gender, age, education, and occupation differences are being case matched, to achieve similar distributions in each subset.

Our whole approach forsook attempting to obtain an orthogonal data set, as typified by classical market research. In that type of study, a sample is selected (targeted) with the minimum number of cases in order to obtain full coverage of each attribute (country, age, gender, etc.). This full-concept method is not appropriate to our quest because of practical difficulties. How, for example, would we find a young, female, senior Arab leader working in a Gulf country? We have adopted the approach of collecting a large data set with wide internal variety and then performing a reflective analysis that we can describe as *knowledge discovery by induction.*

Measuring Instruments

Our research tools were developed as experimental instruments with an eye toward discovering how our respondents reacted to dilemmas. The dilemma methodology imagines a conflict between two principles – for example, respect for law vs. loyalty among friends. In perhaps 95 percent of all cases, the claims of law and those of friendship coincide, but by imagining a case where these clash – for example, that the terms of a business contract have been made idiosyncratic by change in market conditions – we discover whether the respondents reject reconciliation, strive to reconcile, or simply abandon their value systems.

Final Questionnaire Design

The questionnaire, being the core instrument of the quantitative component of this comparative research, has been, and is continually being, refined. The current version is the result of accepting only those dilemmas that were clearly understood, of winnowing out those that produced anomalous results and were criticized by respondents as eliding several meanings. We finally settled on the following outline, which includes several sections containing diagnostic questions that seek to assess a number of things:

Section I: Response to Dilemmas

Multiple-choice questions were constructed, describing alternative courses of action for responding to dilemmas. The different combinations of answers that can be selected are intended to probe

- whether potential leaders maintain their own standpoint and reject reconciliation (win–lose);
- whether they tend to abandon their own values and reject reconciliation "when in Rome" (lose–win);
- whether potential leaders seek a compromise position (lose–lose);
- whether potential leaders try to reconcile seemingly opposing orientations (win–win).

The value systems underlying each dilemma that is posed owe their origin to one of the seven dimensions of Trompenaars's model of culture. Thus, the question can be used to identify simultaneously their value orientation (e.g., preferences for the rule or the exceptions, individualism or communitarianism) *and* their propensity toward reconciliation.

Whenever appropriate, respondents were also asked to indicate how they believed others in their organization might answer.

One sample question involves a dilemma based on a generic "story":

Question: The car and the pedestrian

Suppose you are riding in a car driven by a close friend, and he hits a pedestrian. You know he was going at least 70 km/hr (45 miles per hour) in an area of the city where the maximum is 50km/hr (30 miles per hour). His lawyer says that if you testify under oath that his speed was only 50km/hr, it might save your friend from serious consequences. There are no other witnesses which of the following statements best describes your response?

(a) There is a general obligation to tell the truth as a witness. I will not perjure myself before the court, nor should any real friend expect that from me.

(b) There is a general obligation to tell the truth in court, and I will do so, but I owe my friend an explanation and all the social and financial support I can organize.

(c) My friend in trouble always comes first. I am not going to desert him before a court of strangers on the basis of some abstract principle.

(d) My friend in trouble gets my support, whatever his testimony, yet I would urge him to find in our friendship the strength that allows us both to tell the truth.

(e) I will testify that my friend was going a little faster than the allowed speed and say that it was difficult to read the speedometer.

My answer: _____   How others in my organization would answer ___

As far as possible, each dilemma was posed as a story. The power of a story is to make abstract categories into concrete situations. As you do this, the possible misunderstanding of the abstract values greatly diminishes. Your friend wants more health insurance. You, the doctor and agent for the insurer, have doubts about her health. Such conflicts of loyalty are the stuff of everyday living. The meaning of the dilemma, if not its solution, is very clear to all cultures. Stories are used to *embody the abstract values* in real-life situations. Stories are where mind and body meet, where ideas encounter their consequences in action. We have chosen mostly prosaic stories from the workplace to increase the commonality of such situations. The errors of language are lessened then, when verbal categories are immediately exemplified in recognizable situations. "My legal duty to the insurance company" can be vague, but the good friend with possible health problems brings such abstractions to earth with a bang! What should you write in your report? Language categories are also *defined* (i.e., brought to an end) by their oppositions, so that the crisis in the story clarifies your choice and contrasts the values involved.

In addition, we used dilemmas based on business cases and critical incidents. In many cases these owed their origin to interviews within client companies from managers and leaders who had faced such dilemmas in the course of their work.

The next sample question is a dilemma based on a *business case*:

Question: Responding to time pressures

The design stage of your products (or services) generates the specification for the subsequent stage of product manufacture (or implementation of services). Some hold the view that design should precede manufacture or implementation, and others consider that they should inform each other and should be undertaken in parallel.

As the manager responsible for the total project, which of the following approaches would you seek to adopt? (Select first and second choices)

(a) I would run both processes in parallel and take the risk that a late design change will require some additional manufacturing (or implementation) costs to be incurred.

(b) I would commence the manufacturing set up (or implementation) only when the design has been completed and validated. Overall project completion speed requires a single minded focussed approach.

(C) Begin manufacturing (or implementation) setup as soon as I am confident that the *key* design decisions are permanent.

(d) Do as much as we can in parallel working but give early design decisions a head start and let these keep the lead.

(e) Whilst it speeds up error free projects, parallel processing makes us pay twice for mistakes or changes. I would therefore seek to trade off advantages and disadvantages of parallel working, or the 'design it right' philosophy.

My answer):___   How others in my organization would answer ___

Section II: Corporate Culture and Benchmarking

Other sections of the questionnaire seek to collect data on the following topics:

(i) The corporate culture of the organization (actual and ideal)

A sample question is as follows:

Question: You, as an expert, and your boss are making a presentation to a new client

(a) You will do most of the talking on behalf of your company, because, after all, this is the area of your expertise.

(b) Your boss does the talking, but you will always be at hand should he need you.

(c) You will decide in a discussion with your boss who will most learn and develop from the talk. The one who does will do the presentation.

(d) You expect your boss to do the talking, and you expect that you will not be asked to help, even if your boss makes an unnoticed professional mistakes.

What is the *current* situation?
Question (a) (my answer) _____   Question (b) (how others in my organization might answer) _____

What is the *ideal* situation?
Question (c) (my answer) _____   Question (d) (how others in my organization might answer) _____

Note that, in probing aspects of the corporate culture, respondents are asked to indicate both the current and the ideal situation.

(ii) Various cross-validating and triangulation measures

For example, probing the perceived effectiveness of their organization and their own self-sufficiency and analyzing of their own behaviors).

Following is an example:

Leadership Styles

Consider the stereotypical descriptions of leadership that follow. Allocate a total of 10 points among these four descriptions to describe your (and others') style(s) of leadership. (e.g., a = 4, b = 6; or c = 10; or a = 3; c = 7, etc.).

(a) He spends his time managing his function. He will take the lead in initiating new routine procedures. Although he introduces new procedures and ideas, he is the only one who knows what is going on. Your firm emerges particularly well in times of crisis. Because he solves all problems, he creates dependency. With growth, there is no one to whom he can shed tasks. There is no time for strategic thinking.

(b) He raises the level of skill in his team, but cannot let go of routine tasks. He continually refines procedures unnecessarily. Even after delegating, he still checks to maintain control. He likes to become more knowledgeable on everything.

(c) He is a master or agent of change. He develops the skills and knowledge of his team continually. He spends only one-third of his time monitoring his staff, one-third motivating the staff, and one-third building strategic thinking for tomorrow. Sometimes, day-to-day things don't get finished because the future is too important.

(d) He spends little time on actually managing, because he is either selling or working on production. He is "one of the gang." He is committed to the product(s) and customer service, but puts less energy into developing or creating a team.

Question (a) Your leadership style (total 10 points):
a_____ b_____ c_____ d_____
Question (b) The style(s) common within your organization (10 points):
a_____ b_____ c_____ d_____

In these examples, we are asking leaders and managers to assess their own adequacy for leadership. This serves as a basis for triangulation with the questions about dilemmas.

(iii) Fundamental biographical data

For example, nationality, job function, international experience.

Triangulation and 360° Independent Assessment

The overall independent (360°) assessment of leader and manager competence was also obtained for some of the respondents. Typically, this requires the manager of each respondent (or a small senior managerial team) to rank the effectiveness of each respondent on a series of Likert scales (e.g., for technical competence, for interpersonal effectiveness, and for their experience or business effectiveness in overseas assignments).

These scales also included indexes or measures of bottom-line business performance. These were subsequently used in statistical tests of correlation against the responses to the dilemma question framework.

Context and Construct Validity

We reflected on the two forms of validity:

* *content validity* – that is, whether an instrument is used in a way that reflects the concept from which it is derived;
* *construct validity* – whether a respondent's performance on the test is accounted for by the explanatory concept.

We used cluster analysis to check on content validity. Cluster analysis examines whether highly correlated items do, in fact, cluster around the concept. We used validating interviews and the "multitrait, multimethod" procedures commended by Campbell and Fiske to see if these converged upon the same meanings. We also solicited the views of interviewees about how well the items reflected life in their organizations.

Quantitative Assessments of Validity

We performed exhaustive quantitative analysis to assess the validity of alternative questions and questionnaire design in arriving at the current version of the questionnaire. These investigations were conducted at both the "world" level (the full database) and the client–organization level. Work is ongoing to parse the data at an ecological level as more cases are accumulated (i.e., for each subcell). Our aim is to draw conclusions from these scales as a basis for measuring and categorizing the propensity to reconcile and its relationship to cultural orientation.

Each component index is based on a combination of finite alternatives to each of the series of questions, so, in seeking to derive an overall index for a particular dimension of reconciliation, we generate a combinatorial (binomial) distribution rather than a normal distribution. However, because of our sample sizes, we can usually substitute the normal distribution for convenience of discussion. As a precaution, we performed our analyses on the strict binomial basis, as well as using the more convenient parametric tests, to avoid any distortion or misinterpretation. If we forcibly fit these data to a (parametric) normal distribution too early in our analysis, the summary statistics could distort our interpretation.

We should also review the degree to which any component question is contributing to the desired scale (i.e., each component of reconciliation or cultural dimension). For example, we might ask, are all the questions we are using to assess the propensity to reconcile based on dilemmas in which the underlying construct is Universalism–Particularism measuring the same thing?

Extensive use was made of reliability analysis based on Cronbach's alpha coefficient of internal reliability and consistency. Questions and combinations of questions were tested and accepted, rejected, or revised, to produce sets of questions that gave high values of alpha. For each scale, we sought to achieve an alpha value of at least 0.8.

Deriving Scales from the Responses

For the dilemma-type questions, we can extract an assessment from a single response on two separate scales. First, we can categorize answers on the basis of the respondents' cultural orientation based on the seven-dimensions model.

Thus, *irrespective of whether the respondent selects an option that involves or rejects reconciliation*, we can note which extreme cultural orientation the respondent is exhibiting. For example, the car scenario, either of the following options indicates a universalistic orientation (adherence to universal rules):

(a) There is a general obligation to tell the truth as a witness. I will not perjure myself before the court, nor should any real friend expect that from me.
(b) There is a general obligation to tell the truth in court, and I will do so, but I owe my friend an explanation and all the social and financial support I can organize.

In contrast, the following options indicate a particularistic orientation – the need to account for the particular circumstances (the relationship with the friend is more important than any abstract universal truth):

(c) My friend in trouble always comes first. I am not going to desert him before a court of strangers on the basis of some abstract principle.

(d) My friend in trouble gets my support, whatever his testimony, yet I would urge him to find in our friendship the strength that allows us both to tell the truth.

Thus, by combining responses from the dilemma-based questions that relate to each dimension, the respondents' cultural orientation can be scored.

The answers are then reexamined for the propensity to reconcile. In fact, there are further subtle differences to examine. Let us assume that a respondent answers from a cross-cultural perspective (more universalistic than particularistic). Consider the possible responses:

Answer selected	Interpretation	Reconciliation score
(a) There is a general obligation to tell the truth as a witness. I will not perjure myself before the court nor should any real friend expect this from me.	As a universalist, the respondent is rejecting reconciliation. This reflects a "do it our" way syndrome.	none
(b) There is a general obligation to tell the truth in court, and I will do so, but I owe my friend an explanation and all the social and financial support I can organize.	As a universalist, the respondent is starting from his or her own orientation, but encompassing the other extreme orientation. The respondent is trying to reconcile the differences by integration.	high (anticlockwise spiral)
(c) My friend in trouble always comes first. I am not going to desert him before a court of strangers on the basis of some abstract principle.	The respondent is unlikely to select this answer. Whoever does select it is a committed particularist, rejecting reconciliation.	none

(d) My friend in trouble gets my support, whatever his testimony, yet I would urge him to find in our friendship the strength that allows us both to tell the truth.	This answer indicates that the respondent is trying to reconcile the differences. However, in this case, the respondent is starting from the other orientation, but then accommodating his or her own orientation.	high (clockwise spiral)
(e) I will testify that my friend was going a little faster than the allowed speed and say that it was difficult to read the speedometer.	This is an attempt to avoid the dilemma – a compromise solution that fails.	none (still a lose–lose outcome)

Thus, the total spectrum of dilemma questions provides data that are combined in different combinations to:

- scores on each cross-cultural dimension (i.e., a full cross-cultural profile) and, for each dimension, scores on the propensity to
- compromise
- reject reconciliation
- seek reconciliation from *one's own cultural orientation first* and only *then* accommodate the alternative
- seek reconciliation from the *alternative cultural orientation first* and only *then* accommodate one's own

and, thereby,

- a total reconciliation score per dimension and, in sum,
- a set of total scores for reconciliation across all cultural dimensions (clockwise and anticlockwise spirals), rejection, and compromise.

These scales are then continually triangulated with scales from the other sections of the questionnaire, including classical leadership styles, 360° peer feedback, and independent actual business performance results (at the individual, team, or organizational level), as well as the independent data on bottom-line business.

The accumulation of the evidence is ongoing. Recently, with a Web site inviting online responses and interactive computer software versions of the questionnaire, the number of valid cases is increasing exponentially.

After revisions (improvements) from earlier versions of the questionnaires, based on reliability analysis, a database has been established that currently comprises nearly 3000 respondents from three continents. Respondents are also being added continually, in response both to client interests and to our desire to extend our mapping of the world.

The data has been subjected to statistical testing, including data screening, scale consistency, cross-correlation, and factor and principal-component analyses. However, because much of the data is nonparametric (in fact, categorical), appropriate, more advanced statistical processes are being applied. These include multidimensional scaling and correspondence analysis. Deductive studies continue to be performed to add to the body of evidence to support the core propositions. Inductive studies (database mining), using such products as SPSS CHAID, GoldMiner, and SPSS Diamond, were also invoked to search for hidden information.

Qualitative Interview Data

As was described in a previous section, we also accumulated much unstructured evidence from semistructured interviews. When these could be transcribed to text, we performed a number of content analyses of the text, including using Concordance Software (Oxford Concordance Program) to obtain KWIC analysis (keyword in context), word-frequency counts, linguistic analysis, (StyleWriter), NUD*IST, and similar methods. These methods provided a formal, objective approach to assist the qualitative researcher in extracting key factors and findings that complemented and reinforced the questionnaire-based research.

Results from Data Analysis

As the database continues to increase in size, there is an expectation that many of the initial findings will become more highly (statistically) significant, as the number of valid cases, and thereby the number of subcases increases.

At this stage, there is growing evidence to support the core propositions, and there are several indicators pointing to where further exploration should be undertaken. The quantitative results underpin the discussion presented in context throughout the main chapters.

Future Work and Extending the Analysis

Clearly, we wish to do more work in this whole area, to collect more data, to increase the validity of the generalizations, and to extend the findings of our research. We are currently building a neural network that is expected to give further insights into the data. For *bona fide* researchers and other interested parties, further access to our methods, tools and data analysis is available. In particular, we welcome applications from students intending to do research for a PhD to extend our work.

For further information, see www.twentyoneleaders.com.

About Trompenaars Hampden-Turner (THT) Intercultural Management Consulting

Trompenaars Hampden-Turner (THT) is a leading consulting firm focusing on such strategic intercultural management issues as post-merger integration, globalization, and corporate identity. THT aims to improve the global effectiveness of organizations by providing solutions that reconcile cultural diversity through best-practice consulting, training, and publishing in intercultural management.

The company has undertaken over 15 years of research on value systems and dilemmas as a way of analyzing cultural processes and has thereby developed the world's largest database of intercultural differences in terms of ecological, functional, organizational, and gender issues. This research has cretaed new knowledge and methodologies, including the seven dimensions of culture and methods for reconciling cultural differences and dilemmas.

The basis of the approach by our consultants at THT is the seven-dimension model, described in depth in the best-selling publication, *Riding the Waves of Culture*. This model provides a framework for discussing real business differences by reference to how people from different cultures, who cope every day with the dilemmas of operating internationally, have said they would respond to practical choices. The main benefit of using such a model is that THT consultants can establish a shared vocabulary and method for discussing and resolving cultural differences. The model is supplemented by the extensive experience of our trainers and consultants in working and managing in cross-cultural environments.

Cultural diversity expresses itself in viewpoints and values, in operational priorities, and in ways of doing things. Research and experience say that issues rooted in differences in (cultural) values of stakeholders can take on the character of basic strategic dilemmas. THT's approach to understanding and assisting an organization is to investigate these dilemmas, which cannot be resolved by deciding to go for just one of the advocated (pro)positions and forgetting about the alternative viewpoints. Stakeholders complying with an approach that is not anchored in their own orientation (or that of the group they belong to), will sooner or later develop a resistance to the course of action decided upon, will lose commitment, and will frustrate further progress. Also, going for a compromise is rarely a solution that satisfies all parties. For an effective organization, these strategic business dilemmas, therefore, need proper management and – if possible – reconciliation.

THT strongly believes that social, cross-cultural elements of strategy are crucial to the global success and integration of people, products, and services. The services of THT are therefore based on a three-tiered approach:

•   Creating awareness, at a national, corporate, or functional level, of the origins and influence of cultural differences and of culturally defined values and assumptions.
•   Creating respect for cultural differences in style and approach, thus removing one of the reasons for destructive stereotyping.
•   Reconciling cultural differences: showing people whose cultural values may make them start their reasoning from different assumptions or follow a different logic how to use the strengths of the respective values and approaches in business cooperation.

THT consultants recognize the major challenges that come from managing complexity and ambiguity in a turbulent and heterogeneous environment and in actually benefiting from the many opportunities presented by cultural variety. Recently, THT formed a strategic alliance with KPMG in the Netherlands. Through its network of consultants and its alliance with KPMG, THT can provide clients with the best resources for strategic intercultural management issues. It has recently established an office in Boston, Mass (USA) and works with representatives in the United Kingdom, Scandinavia, Indonesia, Japan, Singapore, India and Turkey.

THT's training programs are highly interactive, using case studies, simulations, anecdotes, research data, and the personal experiences of the trainers and participants to build a high level of involvement. The programs are all designed to improve the level of knowledge of the key drivers behind cultural differences and to develop respect for differences in approach to solving problems. Throughout, the focus is on the development of skills that are immediately applicable in a real business environment. Discussions of each of the dimensions of culture are tailored toward the specific needs of the group, but also encompass the basic issues of intercultural management, such as negotiating and communicating across managerial or cultural lines, building relationships, and working in teams. The different leaders described in this book provide excellent examples of such competence.

The Culture Compass Series

The Culture Compass developed by THT is used in combination with in-company workshops. The culture compass is a country-specific, interactive multimedia CD-ROM application for international managers, business travelers, expatriates, and others who regularly deal with different cultures. A multicountry module allows self-paced learning through direct feedback on the user's scores and preferences. Users can match their Intercultural Awareness Profile against the country profile of their choice. Business cases, self-tests, anecdotes, suggestions, and recommendations are all part of the basic module and differ by country per each individual's scores. Aside from such business topics as meetings, management, marketing, and negotiations, users also get insight into the important issues relating to a culture's history, social norms, and religion. The Culture Compass currently has specific feedback for 12 countries, including the United States, United Kingdom, Japan, Germany, France, The Netherlands, Korea, Taiwan, Singapore, Ireland, Israel, and China.

For more information, contact:

Trompenaars Hampden-Turner
Intercultural Management Consulting
A. J. Ernststraat 595D
1082 LD Amsterdam,
The Netherlands,
Tel: +31 20 301 6666
Fax: +31 20 301 6555
www.7d-culture.nl
e-mail: info@7d-culture.nl

Short Biographies of the Contributors

Peter Woolliams, PhD, is Clifford-Thames professor of international business at the Anglia Business School in the United Kingdom. He has worked extensively as both an academic and a practitioner management consultant throughout the world and with many leading organizations and management gurus in his specialist field of international business modeling and analysis. He has an extensive research and publication record and is frequently invited to make keynote presentations at international conferences. He is also a faculty member of Management Center Europe (Brussels) and TransNational Management Associates, New York.

He has developed strategic planning and HR software models for many of the major corporations of the world, including Ford Motor Co., IBM, Motorola, Petrofina, Schlumberger, BASF, Heineken, National Westminster, BAA, Gallagher, Applied Materials, AMD, Zedco Forex, and Swiss Reinsurance, as well as for many of the world's leading business schools. He is the author of *COMPETE: The European Competency Profiling System*, disseminated by Management Center Europe.

He has collaborated with Trompenaars for some ten years and has been responsible for the development of the Trompenaars database and its reliability and consistency, through rigorous analysis.

Maarten Nijhoff Asser is a senior manager at Trompenaars Hampden-Turner (THT), The Netherlands. He is currently developing the business for THT in the USA, and will be managing the US office in Boston, MA, due to be established by the Summer of 2001.

He has a degree in international law and intellectual property from the University of Amsterdam, the Netherlands, and an MBA in strategy, information, and technology from THESEUS International Management Institute in Sophia Antipolis, France.

In the 10 years prior to joining THT, he was first legal counsel and then publishing operations manager at Springer-Verlag, NY, USA (currently part of Bertelsmann), and, later, business operations manager of a social science publisher based in New York, USA.

He has facilitated business culture change processes for major multinationals, including General Motors, Dow Corning, Dow Chemical, Telenor, Rockwell Automation, Cable & Wireless, ABN Amro, and Swiss Re. He has experience developing and facilitating intercultural management work-sessions across the globe, particularly in Europe, India, Singapore, and the United States. He has also taught at internationally renowned business schools, most recently at Harvard Business School.

Naomi Stubbé-de Groot received her master's degree in organizational psychology at the State University of Leiden (the Netherlands) and later earned an MBA from Bradford University (UK). The child of an Indonesian mother and a Dutch father, she personally experienced a number of cultural differences. She worked for six years as a senior manager at KPMG, in the capacity of project leader on national and international assignments, after some years of experience in a variety of Dutch businesses.

Her areas of expertise include intercultural management, change management (including developing implementation strategies), organizational culture analysis and development, counseling, and management style development. She has worked as a consultant for global clients such as Merrill Lynch, Dow Chemicals, Applied Materials, Mars, KPMG, Philips, Rabobank, AKZO, and Balzers & Leybold.

During 1998–2000, she was managing director of Trompenaars Hampden-Turner.

Peter Prud'homme van Reine is a Dutch national who combines education and experience as an engineer [with an MSc degree in physics engineering from the University of Technology, Delft (the Netherlands)] and as a business anthropologist [with an MA degree in cultural and organizational anthropology from the University of Utrecht (the Netherlands)] in his present-day work in research, training, and consultancy for international management.

In his first career, from 1979 to 1993, he worked as a project manager and technology manager for Philips Electronics. His responsibilities for technology transfer to Philips factories worldwide provided him with first-hand experience of the importance of cultural differences to many management issues – differences between Europe, the United States, and Japan, and also differences within Europe. This experience led to his second career as a business anthropologist, when he joined the faculty of culture, organization and management of the Free University of Amsterdam (the Netherlands) as a lecturer and researcher in intercultural communication and organizational anthropology. He has performed extensive research in Europe, East Asia, and South Africa in subsidiaries of major Dutch, South African, Japanese, and Taiwanese companies, focusing on the dilemmas between globalization strategies and adaptation to local cultures. In July 1996, he joined Trompenaars Hampden-Turner as a senior consultant in intercultural management. He has worked as a consultant for clients such as Applied Materials, Cable & Wireless, Dow Corning, Shell, Motorola, ING, ABN Amro, Corus, and General Motors. Recently, he has been working on the cultural aspects of mergers and acquisitions.

Todd D. Jick is a managing partner of the Center for Executive Development (CED). He was a professor at the Harvard Business School for 10 years and a visiting professor of organizational behavior–human resource management at INSEAD. He has also taught at Columbia University Graduate School of Business and York University in Toronto. He earned his master's and PhD degrees in organizational behavior from Cornell University. He has a BA in social anthropology from Wesleyan University.

He has been actively involved with executive education and consulting in areas such as leadership, executive coaching, organizational change and transformation, values-based management, service management, customer–supplier partnerships, and human resources management. He has taught in Harvard's and INSEAD's executive programs and, worldwide, under the auspices of the Asian Institute of Management, Euroforum (Spain), Ambrosetti (Italy), the Australian Institute of Management, and the Jerusalem Institute of Management. His clients have included GE, Merrill Lynch, Toyota, PricewaterhouseCoopers, Pepsi, Seagram, Lucent, Citibank, and, in Europe, AXA Client Solutions, Unilever, BBV, Novartis, Cadbury-Schweppes, and Alcatel. He also was a senior consultant to GE's corporate transformation initiative called "Workout."

He has been published widely. His latest book, *The Boundaryless Organization* (with Ashkenas, Ulrich, and Kerr) won the Accord Group Executive Leadership "best business book of the year" award. His other books include *The Challenge of Organizational Change* (with Rosabeth Kanter and Barry Stein), *Managing Change*, and *Management Live!* (with Marx and Frost). He has also written more than 30 case studies on companies.

Dirk Devos is founder of the WOODSHED (www.woodshed.nl) , a home to strategic innovators. The Woodshed is a consulting practice and a (virtual) learning network focused on strategic value creation. Key practice areas include the design of unique value concepts and the creation of living-hero stories.

He helps transnational leadership teams clarify the nature of choices to be made: either–or, and–and, or through–through choices. Key applications include e-commerce, strategic branding, reinventing the business definition, creating new categories, sustainable growth strategies, and dot.com incubators (both business to business and business to consumer).

He integrates expert and process consulting. As a strategic *Dialogue* (1999, Leadership for Collective Intelligence Graduate, Dia.Logos Inc., Boston, MA) practitioner, he facilitates leadership conferences and entrepreneurial creative groups.

Dr **Park Jae Ho** is Professor of Psychology at Yeungnam University in Korea. He has worked as a consultant and trainer in the field of intercultural management, intercultural leadership development, change management and globalization with major Korean and American companies such as LG, Samsung, Hyundai, Sematech and Applied Materials. He stated to work with Trompenaars Hampden-Turner in 1995 when he was certified as a trainer for the 7D model of culture workshops. He was Visiting Professor to Harvard in 1990. Recently, he was invited as a Visiting Professor to USIU in California. Currently, he is focusing on research in the areas of "Coaching" and "Vitalization of R&D Organization via Six Sigma initiatives."

Jo Spyckerelle is director of Trompenaars Hampden-Turner. After receiving a Bachelor's degree in business administration from the Catholic University in Louvain, Belgium, he stated working for Arthur Andersen and Co. as an accountant. In 1982, he joined KPMG. He became a chartered accountant (Reviseur d'Entreprises) in 1986. He has worked for many of KPMG's national consultancy practices, including practices in Belgium, The Netherlands, the Czech Republic, and Haiti. In 1995, he became a consulting partner at KPMG's International Headquarters in Amstelveen, The Netherlands, and was involved in the implementation of a globalization program among KPMG's major national consulting practices. He joined Trompenaars Hampden-Turner in early 2000.

References

Introduction (Peter Woolliams)

Bennis, W. *On becoming a leader* (Perseus Press, 1983).
Hersey and Blanchard, (Englewood Cliffs, NJ: Prentice Hall, 1983).
R. White, P. Hodgson, and S. Crainer, *The Future of Leadership* (London: Pitman, 1996).

Chapters 1 and 2   Transcultural Competence: I and II (Fons Trompenaars and Charles Hampden-Turner)

Although dilemma theory is very much our own and has its origins in the 1970s, it is of interest that several other writers, faced with an increasingly turbulent social and business environment have come up with analogous concepts.

Especially close to our own view, yet independently arrived at, is Rushworth Kidder's idea that good clashes with good. See *How Good People Make Tough Choices* (New York: William Morrow, 1995).

Charles Handy has been pointing out that conventional reasoning does not work. See *The Age of Paradox* (Boston: MA: Harvard Business School Press, 1994), and *The Age of Unreason* (London: Business Books, 1989). Several others have looked to the "new physics" for paradoxical ideas in business leadership, see especially Margaret H. Wheatley, *Leadership and the New Science* (San Francisco: Berrett-Kohler), and Danah Zohar, *Rewiring the Corporation* (San Francisco: Berrett-Kohler, 1998).

A very close theory, again independently constructed, is explained by Barry Johnson, *Polarity Management: Identifying and Managing Unsolvable Problems* (Amherst: HRD Press, 1992). The reasons for this convergence of independent views is simply that we all face the same problem of seeming contradictions.

Chapter 3   New Vision of Capitalism: Richard Branson (Charles Hampden-Turner, Naomi Stubbe-de Groot and Fons Trompenaars)

The best and most entertaining source is Branson's own, *Losing my Virginity: The Autobiography* (London: Virgin Books, 1998). This is the origin of the two stories retold in this chapter. Attempts to capture the enigma of Branson's leadership include the following:

Mick Brown, *Richard Branson: The Authorised Biography* (London: Headline, 1998).
Des Dearlove, *The Richard Branson Way* (Oxford: Capstone, 1998).
Tim Hanson, *Virgin King* (London: Harper Collins, 1994).
Alan Mitchell, *Leadership by Richard Branson* (London: Amrop International, 1995).

For a ludicrous hatchet job, of interest chiefly to those concerned with the treatment of entrepreneurs by Britain's tabloid press, see Tom Bower's, *Branson* (London: Fourth Estate, 2000). Branson's attempt to add Virgin to Eurostar's logo is described as a "breathtaking plot" although argued openly. His motto "Have Fun" is a sinister reference to the presence at some of his office parties of – wait for it – sex. Will villainy never cease?

Chapter 4   Creating a Hyperculture: Martin Gillo (Charles Hampden-Turner)

Mihaly Csikszentmihalyi, *Flow: The Psychology of Optimal Experience* (New York: Harper, 1990).

Chapter 5   Recipe for a Turnaround: Philippe Bourguignon (Fons Trompenaars and Charles Hampden-Turner)

C. Ockrent and J.-P. Sereni, *Les Grands Patrons* (Paris: Plon, 1998).
Figaro Economie (18/10/99) "Le Club Med dévoile ses projets de l'an 2000."
Wall Street Journal (12/10/99) "Club Med's new ad campaign will push family fun."

Le Soir (22/9/99) "Philippe Bourguignon a dynamité le Club Med."
The Independent (15/9/99) "The accidental tourist."
Sud Ouest (13/7/99) "Interview avec Philippe Bourguignon: nouvelle image au Club Med."
Wall Street Journal (30/6/99) "Despite 25% jump in net, Club Med won't relax."
Les Echos (3/6/99) "En achetant Jet Tours, le Club Med entame son redéploiement."
The Financial Times (3/6/99) "Club Med buys Jet Tours amid talk of takeover bid."
Le Monde (3/6/99) "Le Club Méditerranée passe l'offensive en rachetant Jet Tours."
The New York Times (30/6/99) "Club Med gets serious, Club Med is getting a bit serious."
Chicago Tribune (25/4/99) "Club Med looks to reclaim paradise; bikinis to baby food to full family focus."
Forbes (22/3/99) "Paradise regained?"
La Croix (8/3/99) "Philippe Bourguignon, le nouvel esprit Club Med."
Wall Street Journal (20/1/99) "Europe puts Club Med back in black."
Stratégies (18/12/98) "Interview avec Philippe Bourguignon: Etre-re, est un projet d'entreprise."
The Observer (20/12/98) "Sun, sea and wishful thinking."
Le Monde (24/9/98) "Les habits neuf du Club Med."
Business Life (July/August/ 1998) "Of mice and med."
Le Monde (21/2/98) "Interview avec Philippe Bourguignon: Le Club Méditerranée mise son avenir sur la qualité de sa marque."
The Financial Times (28/1/98) "Redefining sun, sand and sangria."
The Times (15/10/97) "Club Med seeks brighter image."
L'Express (24/7/97) "Interview avec Philippe Bourguignon: réinventer Le Club Med!"
The Financial Times (24/2/97) "Club Med turns its back on idealism of the past."

Chapter 6   Recapturing the True Mission: Christian Majgaard (Dirk Devos and Charles Hampden-Turner)

No references.

Chapter 7   The Balance between Market and Product: Anders Knutsen (Fons Trompenaars and Charles Hampden-Turner)

P. Per Thygesen, *Break-Point: Anders Knutsen and Bang & Olufsen* (1996).

Chapter 8   Private Enterprise, Public Service: Gérard Mestrallet (Fons Trompenaars, Peter Prud'homme and Charles Hampden-Turner)

C. Ockrent and J.-P. Sereni, *Les Grands Patrons* (Paris: Plon, 1998).

Chapter 9   Leading One Life: Val Gooding (Charles Hampden-Turner)

Jan Carlzon, *Moments of Truth* (New York: Harper and Row, 1986).

Chapter 10   Pioneering the New Organization: Jim Morgan (Fons Trompenaars, Peter Prud'homme, Jae Ho Park and Charles Hampden-Turner)

J. C. Morgan and J. J. Morgan, *Cracking the Japanese Market* (New York: Free Press, 1991).

Chapter 11   The Internet as an Environment for Business Ecosytems: Michael Dell (Maarten Nijhoff Asser and Charles Hampden-Turner)

J. Moore, *The Death of Competition: Leadership and Strategy in the Age of Business Ecosystems* (Harper Business, 1997).
M. Porter, *Competitive Strategy: Techniques for Analyzing Industries and Competitors* (New York: Free Press, 1998).
B. Joseph Pine *et al.*, *Mass Customization: The New Frontier in Business Competition* (Boston, MA: Harvard Business School Press, 1999)
M. Dell, *Direct From Dell: Strategies that Revolutionized an Industry* (Harper Business, 1999).
See also the website: www.dell.com, and the following speeches: "NetSpeed: The Supercharged Effect of the Internet," Michael Dell's address at the Executives' Club of Chicago, October 23, 1998; "Maximum Speed: Lessons Learned from Managing Hypergrowth," Michael Dell's address to the Comerica

Economic Forum, Dallas, Texas, September 10, 1998; "Collaborating in a Connected Economy: The Power of Virtual Integration," Michael Dell's address at the World Congress of Information Technology, Vienna, Virginia, June 24, 1998; "The PC Industry: A Robust Outlook," Michael Dell's keynote address at The Society of American Business Editors and Writers Technology Conference, October 9, 1998, Austin, Texas; "The Dynamics of the Connected Economy," Michael Dell's address to Forbes CEO Conference, Atlanta, Georgia, June 25, 1999; "The Dell Advantage," Michael Dell's address to an information technology group, San Francisco, March 3, 1999; "Building the Infrastructure for 21st Century Commerce," Michael Dell's KEYNOTE ADdress at the 1999 Networld+Interop, Las Vegas, Nevada, May 12, 1999; "E-Business: Strategies in Net Time," Michael Dell's address at the National Press Club, National Press Club, Washington, DC, June 8, 2000; "Leadership in the Internet Economy," Michael Dell's keynote address at the Canadian Club of Toronto, Canadian Club of Toronto, April 7, 2000; "Building a Competitive Advantage in an Internet Economy," Michael Dell's address to the Detroit Economic Club, Detroit Economic Club, November 1, 1999.

Chapter 12 Global Brand, Local Touch: Stan Shih, Acer Computers (Peter Prud'homme)

F. Deyo, "Cultural patterning of organizational development: a comparative case study of Thai and Chinese Industrial enterprise." Human Organization, 37(1), 68-73 (1978).

M. Goldberg,, The Chinese Connection (Vancouver: University of British Columbia Press, 1985).

J. Kao, "The worldwide web of Chinese business." Harvard Business Review, March–April, 24-36 (1993).

S. G. Redding, The Spirit of Chinese Capitalism (Berlin: de Gruyter, 1993).

F. Rothstein and M. Blim, Anthropology and the New Global Factory (New York: Bergin & Garvey, 1992).

H. Serrie, Chinese Business and Management Behavior and the Hsu Attributes: a Prelimenary Enquiry. In H. Serrie (ed.), Anthropology and International Business, pp. 59-71 (Williamsburg: Department of Anthropology College of William and Mary, 1986).

H. C. Tai, "The oriental alternative: a hypothesis on East Asian culture and economy." In: The Republic of China on Taiwan Today (Taipei: Kwang Ha Publishing Company, 1989).

E. Vogel, The Four Little Dragons (Cambridge, MA: Harvard University Press, 1991).

Chapter 13 Weathering the Storm: Sergei Kiriyenko (Allard Everts and Charles Hampden-Turner)

To prepare for the interview with Mr Sergei Kiriyenko, we approached Jeffrey Deutsch (deutsch@rabidtiger.com), an expert on Russia for many years. Jeffrey kindly sent us a summary of Mr Kiriyenko's career. More detailed information on Mr Kiriyenko's earlier and recent activities came through Dr Jurn Buisman, Director of the Amsterdam office of the Russia & CIS Foreign Investment Promotion Centre of the Ministry of Economic Development and Trade of the Russian Federation.(fipc@rusnet.nl). His assistants, Dr Alexandra Boldyreva and Eugenia Lountchenkova, did additional reseach, and the latter also acted as interpreter during the interview. Finally background information was taken from various internet sources, newspapers, and magazines.

Chapter 14 Toward a New Spirit: Edgar Bronfman (Todd Jick, Charles Hampden-Turner and Fons Trompenaars)

J. C. Collins and J. I. Porras, Built to Last (Harper Business, 1997).

E. H. Schein, Organizational Culture and Leadership (Jossey-Bass Business & Management Series, 1997).

A. De Geus, The Living Company (Boston, MA: Harvard Business School Press, 1997).

R. T. Pascale, Managing on the Edge: How the Smartest Companies Use Conflict to Stay Ahead (New York: Touchstone, l990).

Chapter 15 Change within Continuity: Karel Vuursteen (Dirk Devos and Charles Hampden-Turner)

No references.

Chapter 16   The Challenge of Renewal: Hugo Levecke (Dirk Devos and Charles Hampden-Turner)

No references.

Chapter 17   Keeping Close to the Customer: David Komansky (Fons Trompenaars and Charles Hampden-Turner)

D. H. Komansky and other members of the Executive Management team on Merrill Lynch Investor Day Conference, "Leveraging Global Investments," New York, May 2, 2000.

D. H. Komansky, "Testimony on the Financial Marketplace of the Future," Senate Committee on Banking, Housing, and Urban Affairs, New York, February 29, 2000.

J. L. Steffens, *The Internet Revolution: Phase II*, Jupiter Communications Online Financial Services Forum, San Francisco, September 27, 1999.

D. H. Komansky, "Repositioning in a Rapidly Changing Industry, Merrill Lynch Banking & Financial Services Conference," New York , September 13, 1999.

D. H. Komansky, "Bulls, Bears, and Buffaloes: Merrill Lynch's Four Decades in Japan, Japan Society Annual Dinner," New York, May 26, 1999.

D. H. Komansky, "The Global Markets: Good for Some or Good for All?" The Economic Club of Detroit, May 24, 1999.

J. L. Steffens, "The Role of Online Advice," Forrester Conference, Princeton, NJ, May 24, 1999

D. H. Komansky, "America's Role in the Global Financial Marketplace," American Council of Life Insurance, Naples, FL, January 15, 1999.

W. H. Smith, Jr., "Expansion of Business into Global Markets," Richard Ivey School of Business University of Western Ontario, November 4, 1998.

J. L Steffens, "A New Investment Paradigm for the Digital Age," Financial Summit: Investing in the Future of Technology, New York, October 20, 1998.

D. H. Komansky, "A Bull Market in Human Hopes and Dreams," Goldman Sachs Financial Services Investor Conference New York, November 5, 1997.

J. L. Steffens, "Managing Wealth in the New Global Economy," Merrill Lynch Wealth Management Conference, St. Helena, CA, June 29, 1997.

D. H. Komansky "The Global/Local Paradox: Comments on the Future of the Global Financial Intermediation Club de Bourse," Paris, France, January 20, 1997

The Scotsman (4/9/97) "The Scotsman/Merrill Lynch Global Investment Challenge."

The Scotsman (8/10/97) "Investment game attracts a thundering herd."

The Scotsman (5/8/98) "Playing to win."

Chapter 18   Managing the Internationalization Process: Kees Storm (Fons Trompenaars)

K. Storm (29/6/99) "The Clear Picture," speech in Frankfurt, Germany.

Forum (17/6/99) "Interview with Kees Storm, De Kraanvogel."

K. Storm (5/3/99) "Investor Presentation," London, UK.

K. Storm (25/2/99) "Hoe Internationaal is een Internationaal Bedrijf?" speech at the Free University, Amsterdam.

K. Storm (25/2/99) Speech at the Borgen Meeting, Slochteren, The Netherlands.

The Economist (20/2/1999) "Storm across America: Aegon buying Transamerica," pp. 75-76.

K. Storm (1/2/99) "Knowledge Management: Tomorrow's Key Competitive Asset? Introductory Remarks," World Economic Forum Davos, Switzerland.

The Financial Times (11/1/1999), "Aegon plays on its local strength."

K. Storm (7/10/98) "Hoe cultuur scheppen?" CHC.ZW

K. Storm, "Zorg, Toekomst en Directeur, NCD jubileum uitgave" (1998).

Business Week (13/7/98) "Financial supermarkets? Bah."

Management Team (5/6/98) "Ik denk dat het juist is dat ik ga."

The Scotsman (26/3/98) "The dynamic duo, Aegon buying Scottish Equitable,"p. 27.

The Financial Times (6/11/97), "The Laughing Insurer."

International Money Marketing (13/12/96) "Aegon grows service with a smile."

L. Wijchers and K. Storm, *Management Bestek* (Holland Business Publications, 1997).

Chapter 19   A Corporate Dynasty: Rahmi M. Koç

No references

Chapter 20   Leading through Transformation: Mark Moody-Stuart (Jo Spyckerelle and Charles Hampden-Turner)

Shell Report 2000, internal Shell report (2000).

A. Rowell and A. Goodall, "Shell-shocked: the environmental and social costs of living with Shell in Nigeria." *Greenpeace International*, July 1994.

The Financial Times (11/8/00) "Inside track: giant that sees no evil: management energy."

The Financial Times (22/8/00) "Ban on dumping oil rigs at sea."

Chapter 21   Keeping the Family in Business or Keeping the Business in the Family: Stuart Beckwith, Tim Morris, and Gordon Billage (Peter Woolliams and Charles Hampden-Turner)

R. Donickles and E. Frohlich, "Family businesses: really different european experiences," *Stratos, Family Business Review*, 2 (1991).

S. Goldberg, "Significant points leading to effective successors in family businesses," *Family Business Annual Research Paper*, 1(1), p. 74 (1995).

M. Kets de Vries, *Family Business Human Dilemmas in the Family Firm* (London: International Business Press, 1997).

P. Leach, *Family Businesses*, 2nd edn (London: Kogan Page, 1994).

Swaffin-Smith, Woolliams, and Tomenko, *Towards a Unified Model for Small to Medium Enterprise Business Paradigms* (Earlybrave Publications, 2000).

P. Westhead, M. Cowling, and G. Story, "The manangement and performances of family businesses in the UK," a paper for the Stoy Centre for Family Businesses, Warwick Business School (1997).

Index